THE SERPENTINE THRONE

SUSAN STRADIOTTO

THE SERPENTINE THRONE

Published by
Bronzewood Books
14920 Ironwood Ct.
Eden Prairie, MN 55346

Cover Design: Enchanted Quill Press

Interior Design: Bronzewood Books

Edited by: Owl Pro Editing

Paperback ISBN-13: 978-1-949357-44-8

eBook ISBN-13: 978-1-949357-43-1

Printed in the USA

There are many people to thank in the creation of this series and Mairynne's story. The first and foremost is my son, who has had a love for dragons and most things fantasy since he figured out in the third grade that dinosaurs and dragons are different creatures. Also, a huge thanks is necessary to the writers and readers who have encouraged me to perservere in my writing. To the members of the Western Suburbs Writers Group, you've made completing a work of this magnitude possible with your feedback and encouragement. To my family, thank you for giving me the time to excersize my creativity in this way. To my readers, and especially Miss Becka Gee, thank you for following Mairynne's journey. You are all in my heart . . . always.

Dramatis Personae

Storm Sorcerers

Evangales and family

Atheryn Evangale—Tennō of Nantai; father to Karynne, Mairynne, and Yasmynne

Corwyn Dawnsgale—Nadia's consort, Solarynne's brother

Karynne "Kahry" Evangale—first daughter to Atheryn and Noralynne; Mairynne and Yasmynne's sister.

Mairynne Evangale—Lady Mairynne; third daughter to Atheryn and Noralynne

Nadialynne "Nadia" Riversgale—Noralynne's twin sister, aunt to Karynne, Mairynne, and Yasmynne

Noralynne Evangale—Kōgō of Nantai; empress; Atheryn's wife; mother to Karynne, Mairynne, and Yasmynne

Kōgō Phelyse—empress in the Second Age, second ruler of that age

Yasmynne Evangale—sister to Mairynne and Karynne; betrothed to Nestryn

First Advisors

Imrythel Sandsgale—Karynne's first advisor

Nestryn—Yasmynne's betrothed and first advisor

Clergy (raised to serve the Triad)

Arlyn Hallowgale—Priest of Otarr, the sun god/the Day-Seer

Baldwyn—Acolyte of Otarr, the sun god /the Day-Seer

Edamyn Hallowgale—Priest of Atun, the all-seeing god /the All-Seer; oldest priest

Tasmynne Hallowgale—Priestess of Selene, the moon goddess/the Night-Seer

Counselors

Azurynne Nightingale—matriarch of the Nightingale family

Lukosyn "Lukos" Thundergale—patriarch of the Thundergale family

Ohmyn Havengale—patriarch of the Havengale family

Solarynne Dawnsgale—Corwyn's sister, matriarch of the Dawnsgale family

Guards

Gaelynne

Roryn Seagale

Perryn

Tarlyn—leads the Arashi guard in Thalaj's absence

Thalaj Northerngale—Gensui of Nantai's Arashi guard

Other

Dorynne—Mairynne's attendant

Idalynne "Mother" Feathergale—nanny to Karynne, Mairynne, and Yasmynne

Jessamynne "Jessa" Feathergale—Idalynne's daughter, friend to Mairynne

Larynne—Nadia's handmaid

Makenyn the Scarred—First Emperor of Nantai

Morwyn—Makenyn's brother

Nityn—Shaman who banished the dragon from Makenyn

Sentei Summergale—healer in Arashi

Teralynne – Healer apprentice

Zafrynne Keeningale—Witch woman/spellcaster

Deities (named) & Holy Triad

Holy Triad

Atun (aka the All-Seer)—Nantai God, part of the Holy Triad the all-seeing god; father to Otarr and Selene

Otarr (aka the Day-Seer)—Nantai God, part of the Holy Triad, associated with the sun; Atun's child; the sun god

Selene (aka the Night-Seer)—Nantai Goddess, part of the Triad, associated with the moon; Atun's daughter; the moon goddess

Other Gods

Ak Ana—the sea goddess of all water holds wisdom more ancient any other element

Ebisu—the sea god who brings sailors good fortune and fish

Ryū (Dragons, Ryū dragons, dragons)

Barūdragon (Barū)—blue dragon

Guindragon (Guin)—green dragon

Kuroidragon (Kuroi)—black dragon, bonded with Makenyn at the beginning of *Call of the Storm Sorcerer*

Moyadragon (Moya)—steely gray dragon, died before the beginning of *Call of the Storm Sorcerer*

Parūdragon (Parū)—pearlescent dragon

Cloud Courtiers

Alto-Nior—navigator

Alto-Raal

Alto-Tash—Tsanseri's servant

Alto-Trea—The Swan, Filtch

Cirro-Bree

Cirro-Pith—Guard in the Navigation Deck

Cirro-Tsan—Comtesse Tsanseri; comtesse of the Masque; Lady of Masks; comtesse of Love's Court

Cirro-Vior "Viordyn"—crescent moon shape on the shoulder; used to be a childhood friend of Mairynne's

Strato-Elea—Tsanseri's servant

Strato-Kann—Guard in the Navigation Deck

Strato-Ymar—Gnoble of the caste

Fire Forgers

Din Arun—guard

Ny Boran—Chanthavy's husband

Ny Chanthavy

Phy Sovann—Captain (Issō) of the Guard

Phy Boupha—Phy Sovann's wife

Phy Piseth—Phy Sovann's son

Yuos Atith—Gnoble of the caste

Yuos Chakara—Yous Atith's brother

Frost Fighters (of the fourth caste)

Aljir Tenkara—Gnoble of the caste

Hoaris Nishikara—Called Red Bear by Kyr of the Small Folk.

Saqie Kitikara—Tenkara's second in command

Yamakar Su Almazaj—Su, for short

Sentei Besso Ken'ichi—Healer

Yamakara Jun Askari—Su's brother; only features in *Into the Evernight.*

Stone Singers

Sarangarel—Gnoble of the caste (female)

The Yisun

Baidu—yisun (male)

Chambui—yisu (female)

Jaliqai—yisu (female)

Timir—yisun (male)

Nachin—yisun (male)

Underhill Dwellers

Brimr—Gnoble of the caste

Svarta—Brimr's wife

Hjalmarr—guide

Casteless

"street rats"

Flea

Gnat

Honera

Jerek—Captain of the river barge

Sal—Inkeeper in Safaia

Wren

Sailors

Asahi—Captain of the Swell Mistress

Oshun

Tao—means "great waves"

Old Shad—Sailor who escaped syrens

Small Folk

(of Umbra and Brennmor)

Davao—Misha's eldest brother

Gyna—map maker/scribe

Isao—King of the small folk / The Small King

Kyr—Misha's partner

Misha—third son of royalty, Kyr's partner of choice

Riah—Tomei's wife

Tomei—Misha's older brother

Tsinti

nomadic people, "Nantai wanderers of the grasslands"

Baldeo

Beltrana—new baby

Buharro

Detsa

Gashparis—new baby

Janci—Yankos's son

Jorani—called Miss Firefly by Kyr of the Small Folk

Maladros

Mizo—new baby

Sinfi

Yankos—currently represents Tsinti people at parliament every seventh year, but doesn't call himself a leader (says all are equal)

Zofi—witch woman/spellcaster

Rundi Tribes

Khirundi, Mhorundi, and Zhorundi

Individuals (named) in Ise

Yohaani—leader of the Khirundi

Umu-Zimi (aka "Z")—has an eye patch; full name given by Rundi tribes is "Umu-Zimi in-jabuka ku ryōsha"

Amare—Fey Queen

Osmar—Fey Prince

Prologue

The First Emperor of Nantai

Makenyn, ascended Emperor of the Nantai people and first within the elite caste—the Storm Sorcerers—rocked back and forth on the balls of his feet, his legs bent, chest pressed tight to his knees, head down, and hands covering his ears. He wailed, "Stay out of my head and heart!"

Within the jewel city of Arashi, his mental intruder had reduced him to a cowering man alone in a black cave beneath his beloved Stormskeep. He hid in darkness, squeezing his eyes ever tighter in an effort to shutter his mind from the voice, to armor his heart from the feelings of otherness bound to his soul.

This plan you've written will bring you no peace, the voice inside rumbled as loudly as if someone other than he could hear, as deeply as thunder.

Makenyn could call the clouds and thunder to shield himself from the presence and sound were he outside, if only he had access to the elements. Instead, he chanted, "No, no, no," and curled tighter into himself. He'd chosen the cavern for its absence of windows and had had a door installed to further block out any light. The measures deprived his senses and restricted his sorcery, but that was the price he willingly paid to silence the beast within. Seclusion and darkness had worked for a time, and the Ryū dragon had slept until he grew hungry and sensed his prison. As he stirred again within, Makenyn could feel Kuroi's nerves thrumming under his own skin, trying to escape. He stood, gritted his teeth, clenched his fists, and fought the heat rising in his blood and the prickle across his skin where scales threatened to erupt.

He refused to shift.

He threw his head back and yelled, "No!" into the darkness, his voice coming back to his ears over and over again until it silenced. "I won't let it happen again. I cannot."

Makenyn, answer unto me. Why do you wish this thing? the fiend bellowed. *It will break us both.*

"Leave me, you accursed spirit!" Makenyn growled through his teeth, spittle wetting his chin.

This is not the way, minikin—

"DO NOT call me that!" The emperor's voice echoed again as the door crept inward.

"Pardon, Tennō?" a timid yet familiar voice asked, using Makenyn's honorary title even though the two were related.

"Morwyn," he breathed, panted. "Come, Brother. And close the door behind you."

Light beamed into the room, and Makenyn squinted against its burn. He paused, listening and feeling, then breathed with relief that Kuroi had retreated to someplace deeper inside . . . if only for a time.

Morwyn's feet shuffled against the floor, his steps less sure than the emperor's who'd learned every knot and bump on every stone within the room over time.

Makenyn paced, demanding, "Is the separation ritual prepared?"

"Yes, Tennō. Nityn awaits you now. I've brought material for your eyes if you'll find me here in the dark. Then I will guide you to the chamber he has readied."

Though this was the right path—the only path toward seeing himself whole once again—the emperor paused.

"Tennō Makenyn?" Morwyn asked.

"Yes, yes." He rubbed a hand over his beard, the whiskers no longer bristling under the touch as they'd grown long enough in the darkness to become soft. Aloud, but not directed at Morwyn in truth, he mused, "So, the time has come at last."

"Yes, Tennō. I have prepared everything as you wished."

Makenyn took a deep breath and closed his eyes as he exhaled slowly. Though he might perish in the casting by the shaman who'd separate him from the Ryū dragon within, he felt a certain peace—a sense of rightness in his decision. Yet two things gave him pause, tempting him to reconsider. He'd held himself in darkness for so long, only allowing the tiniest of flame on occasion to pen a decree, and his brother would be a weak ruler for the Nantai people while he recovered. Morwyn had been his mouthpiece for some number of moons. How many, the emperor couldn't count, but Morwyn remained little more than a puppet for Makenyn's decrees. No one person across Nantai could speak to the results of the impending ritual, for none before had dared attempt to sever the soul-deep bond between a person and his Ryū dragon.

I beg of you, minikin, do not go through with this ritual, Kuroi said.

Hissing, Makenyn pressed his palms to his ears as if he could block the sound. Pointless. It came from inside.

He walked to his brother, only needing the sound of his breathing to locate his position. "Give me the material. I am ready."

Morwyn made no reply, but the emperor found his fumbling hands and took the length of fabric, deftly folding it on the diagonal.

"Tennō Makenyn, if I may?"

In the darkness, the emperor could hear the slight rasp where his brother twisted and wrung his hands—the ever-present nerves and uncertainty that made him a poor fit for emperor of the Nantai people. Makenyn sucked in a sharp breath as he secured the fold about his eyes. "What is it, Brother?"

"A-are you certain of this? The green dragon—"

"Guin?" the emperor prompted, surprise riddling his mind. Why would Morwyn mention her, Kuroi's mate?

"Yes. Since you have been in isolation, the green dragon has been circling over Arashi and the keep almost daily. She is a frightful Ryū, and our people shrink and hide in their homes, fearing her wrath. Have you not heard her cries, Tennō?"

This deep within the belly of Stormskeep, insulated by the mountain and the castle's foundation, he heard none of the sounds from above. Indeed, he had longed for the normal sounds—servants bustling about or the sound of the Sundai Falls and the feel of their mists upon his face as he stood upon his terrace. Resolved, he answered, "Morwyn, that I have not heard things from above in uncountable months, that I have not been a citizen of my own empire, and that this presence inside me refuses to leave me in peace . . . those are all reasons why I have commanded Nityn to complete this ritual." Makenyn took a deep breath, his shoulders expanding and contracting. "Then the beasts can leave Stormskeep and the city of Arashi, and hopefully Nantai itself, together. You see, I am giving them what they want."

That is not how it will work, the beast grumbled.

"What do you know?" Makenyn roared.

Morwyn shuffled away at the sound.

The emperor sighed, attempting to gather himself. Of course, all his brother had heard was Makenyn's reaction. He inhaled and sighed again. "You see, Brother, I must do this thing to rid my soul of its ghosts. Now, you will take me to Nityn." He moved closer to his brother, taking hold of Morwyn's elbow and leading him to the door, the end of his dark domain.

The walk was a journey of three hundred eighty-seven paces, two dozen spiral stone steps, and another seventy-two paces to the chambers Nityn had prepared. Morwyn trembled the entire time under Makenyn's grip. As they entered, smoky smells of herbs burning in a fire and hearty smells of something brewing wafted through the air. The small sound of liquid bubbling reached Makenyn's ears, and it felt tepid and sticky inside. "Is it dark enough, Brother?" he asked, hesitant to remove the material from his eyes.

"Yes." Morwyn's arm slipped from his grip.

With eyes uncovered, he took in the room with sight and sound, musing over the connection between the two senses. Upon the far wall, a large opening lay hidden by layers of heavy material to shut out most of the light. It worked but for a bright line on either side. Makenyn averted his eyes from those points as the brightness stung, but knowing of the opening behind the drape, he listened too. So near the Sundai Falls, the sound of rushing water soothed his soul for long moments—a sight he longed to behold again, waters he wished to call upon with his own storm sorcery and stir forth a shower that would wash away the darkness and grime. The time would come. One day soon, he'd no longer be a prisoner to this evil within.

Nityn awaited behind a waist-high stone slab. A Storm Sorcerer who'd adopted shamanism and studied spellcasting in relation to ritualistic magics for years, Nityn would be the savior of all Makenyn held close, the one to separate the Ryū dragon from Makenyn's soul. Black robes hung upon Nityn's narrow shoulders, every one of his features thin and angular. Even the shape of his brows, mustache, and black beard emphasized the sharp slants of his cheekbones and jaws. He spread his arms, the robes falling like crow's wings, then lay his twig-like fingers upon the stone. "My tennō, you will disrobe and lay here upon your stomach."

A shriek sounded outside the cavern's hidden opening, and all three men jumped. Makenyn's blood and skin heated in reply, and he had to lock down his muscles to control the shift. With his eyes closed and through clenched teeth, he said, "Soon, Ryū. Soon you will be free to go with her." He refused to voice the evil spirit's name.

Inside, the grumble came again, *This is madness, minikin. This will not work as you desire. I warn you of that.*

Makenyn's eyes flew open and he looked about the chambers wildly. The others hadn't heard the gravelly voice, only his. The emperor snapped, "We must begin. Morwyn, are you ready with your oaths?" He must be certain things were in order.

"Yes, Tennō. And the High Cloud Court is due to arrive on the morrow so I may ascend and tend to matters of the realm whilst you recover." Morwyn's brows pinched together, holding his worry tight upon his forehead. As the man had been born of the same mother and father, he resembled the image Makenyn recalled of himself in the mirror, but Morwyn also seemed meeker.

The emperor said a quick prayer to the Triad that his recovery would be swift, that he'd be fit to rule in a short time. With a nod, he removed his clothes. Nityn offered him a bowl with a green-tinged liquid. Makenyn quirked a brow.

"The potion will calm you, keep you still, and lessen the pain, my tennō." Nityn's features portrayed naught of what he possibly thought in the moment.

Though he accepted the bowl, Makenyn said, "I have commissioned you well, Nityn. I trust that this is no poison?"

"Tennō, with respect due to you as emperor, I am not to receive the second half of my commission until I successfully perform this task. Furthermore, if you die in the process, my fate is likewise death. You have offered sufficient incentive to see to your health and longevity, Tennō." He bowed his head then—stiffly.

Makenyn drank, the putrid liquid poorly disguised by bee's nectar, and climbed onto the stone slab. Despite the heat and humidity that hung about, the stone felt cool. Shivers ran through his body as he lowered his feverish skin onto the rock. When he rested flat upon his stomach, he felt cooler on the front than he could recall since bonding with the Ryū, yet the skin upon his back was still ablaze. Still within the emperor's sight, Nityn meandered about the room, collecting a knife, some wicked hinged device, and bowls. He gathered coals from the fire inside an enormous stone bowl, and the knife tinkled when he placed it inside. While the blade heated, he cleared the sizable area in front of the heavy curtains—presumably where the Ryū would rest in dragon form after the ritual, the long-awaited moment when Makenyn and Kuroidragon were once again individuals.

A haze settled over Makenyn as Morwyn stepped close to his head.

"Brother," he whispered in the familiar, a catch to his voice, "I will be right here with you for the duration. In that corner there where you may see me. And until you heal, I will see to your empire."

Makenyn's eyes drifted closed, then slowly open again, and his lips felt numb. Inside, Kuroi's soul felt heavy, too, but with melancholy rather than potion. That was well enough; it would all be over soon.

Nityn chanted, incomprehensible incantations and likely an invocation of some ill deity he'd found to aide in the ritual. Though Nityn had assured Makenyn the ritual would achieve his ultimate desire, he'd wished to know little of the workings. Nityn had warned of the pain, but the emperor considered that temporary, a fair price to be alone within his mind and body once again.

"All is prepared," Nityn said, the words seeming distant and slurred. "I must create the exit along the spine. The potion will hold you still, but I fear you must endure the pain awake."

Makenyn tried to nod, but his body was indeed immobile. He marveled over the feeling. Everything seemed like a smoke dream, yet he remained aware. Nityn reached for the knife resting in the coals. The blade glowed. The shaman moved behind him, out of sight. Then nothing happened for what felt an eternity until . . .

Sharp, hot, severing pain descended at the base of his neck. Makenyn tried to scream. Nothing. The pain traced down his back. Sizzling reached his ears. His mind told him to flee. Nothing. The smell of roasting flesh filled his nose. The searing moved between his shoulders, along his spine. Nityn hissed and there was more pressure in the center of his back. Makenyn could do naught but endure. More sizzling. Stronger odors. Pain again, moving down his lower back and all the way to his tailbone. The motion stopped, his back pulsing in agony, his soul wanting to cry to the heavens, but his body frozen.

"I've completed the first step," breathed Nityn. As he took the knife back to the coals and placed the bloodied blade inside, he murmured more foreign words.

Makenyn wanted to cry, breathe heavier, anything, but the potion regulated everything. Every involuntary action continued at a fixed tempo. His back pulsed, and the sound of metal clashing and ringing filled his ears, though he thought that only inside. Nityn lifted the hinged thing and once again moved out of sight. Had he control, Makenyn would gasp in fear, shock. Yet his body wouldn't listen to his urges. At the center of his back, he felt pressure and something sliding inside, gripping at his spine. A peal sounded from the instrument and his back separated. Crackling came where ribs parted from spine, and his body rounded forward by force.

Nityn chanted.

Metal clanged.

Morwyn, in the corner's shadows, bent and retched.

And Makenyn lay utterly still, his back split from neck to tailbone, his body arching from the stone as a force beyond reckon pulled at his soul.

Nityn chanted, volume growing above the din with every exotic word.

Everything screeched, twisted, echoed, pulled, pounded, and writhed.

Until his mind could withstand the torment no more.

Part One
Call of the Storm Sorcerer

ONE

Nantai in Mourning

GENERATIONS HAVE PASSED SINCE THE Ryū Wars, the age when the great dragons and people split and became mortal foes. Yet the Nantai people, my people, remain. I have never met one of the Ryū, the dragons of old, nor have I felt the ties of companionship, but our people's lessons were ingrained. The Ryū bond represented the purest variety of evil. From before I gained knowledge of letters, my sisters and I clung to stories Father had told. Karynne, Yasmynne, and I had gathered at his feet near the throne crafted from the last dragon's skin and bone and scale, and we listened to Tennō Atheryn read from Stormskeep's annals. His voice had resonated in my blood as he'd painted the history of companionship, the most toxic of bonds between a dragon and a person.

The stories had been as exciting as they were dangerous. During the time at my father's heel, I'd been too young to understand or wield my storm sorcery with any bit of control, but my sisters would stir small gusts of wind, animating dyed sands to enact the scenes. Between Father's booming narration and the miniature scenes, I'd giggle and clap and thoroughly enjoy the show.

Over the course of the histories read, it became clear that the Ryū bond drove people to commit acts unimaginable. Father wouldn't read to us of the treachery, but he did share one story—a story that kept me awake in the dark hours for many moons, the story of the people's first emperor: Tennō Makenyn, the Scarred. After surviving the ritual that peeled away the soul-deep bond between him and the blackest dragon, Kuroidragon, he wore the scars for the remainder of his days and walked hunchbacked, limping as he went.

I closed and reopened my eyes slowly, returning to my chambers, to the now, and to myself, my shoulders laden under the weight of both the memory and the mourning robes my attendants were draping about my shoulders. The material well-positioned, Mother Feathergale scurried to the adjacent room to retrieve the lengths of fabric that would secure the garments and further restrict my ability to breathe easily. Desperate to put away the heavy garments prescribed for the sixty days and nights of mourning my father had declared in the wake of my mother's death, I asked, "How many more?" I'd asked the same question every morn as they attended to my attire.

Yet my friend and attendant answered readily, "A dozen days remain, Lady Mairynne." Jessa bobbed in deference to my impending position.

I clasped her shoulders and waited for her gaze to lift, to meet mine, then said, "Please don't treat me so. I'm the same person I was ten days ago before Tennō Atheryn Evangale went missing, and I'll be the same person tomorrow and after this period of mourning has passed."

"Yes, Lady Mairy—"

I squeezed to silence her formal objection. Looking sternly into her worried eyes, I said, "Simply Mairynne. The same Mairynne who has been at your side since we were younglings." When her tension eased, mine did the same. I gulped air, rolling my shoulders back to support the robes' weight.

Employed by my parents to care for their royal children and known to us as Mother Feathergale, Jessa's blooded mother returned to my chambers. She looked small in comparison to the swaths of belting material overflowing her grasp, but it didn't appear a burden. She used her sorcery, stirred a minor wind to carry the heavy belts, and she simply guided them toward the bed. I released my dear friend and turned to face the mirror. The royal mourning garments were extensive, so Jessa went to help. As they returned, I lifted my arms to receive the finishing touches.

To my attendants and to the Holy Triad should they be listening, I raised my chin and voice. "How are the city's people handling the loss? And the people beyond?"

Mother Feathergale revolved around me, binding my body with the blessed robes so I might feel embraced by my loved one lost. She worked proficiently and spoke with a cutting absence when she answered, "They await patiently, per tradition. And you shouldn't toil over the matter now. The Triad intends for you to focus on healing during the quiet time. Decreed by the blessed emperor and respected by all castes and the casteless alike."

In the long days while I waited idly, and more so within that moment, I felt inclined to curse the traditions, shun the robes, and escape the stony walls that bound me to the castle and citadel. I longed for action, to discover if others believed—as did I—that Father still lived. I yearned to see how the people were reacting to the loss of both their rulers. Still working to gain necessary confidence in my convictions, I spoke more quietly, with uncertainty, and voiced words that I dared not speak to anyone less trusted than Jessa and Mother Feathergale, "With all that has happened, do you not believe the rituals selfish at all?"

Mother Feathergale finished securing the ends of the obi and came to face me, her eyes blinking, then widening with bewilderment. "Why ever would it be selfish, Mairynne?"

Lowering my eyes, I smiled ruefully. Had I truly expected her to hold beliefs outside of those handed down for generations?

My aging attendant wiped her palms on her apron and opened her arms to me with a smile. I fell willingly into her embrace as she offered me what comfort she could, but in the end, she pushed me away with a solemn look, misty eyes, and slight nod. "There, you're ready for the day. Your mother would be proud. Your father too," she added.

I swallowed against the sudden burn in my throat. Her gaze left mine as she inspected the belts, making tiny adjustments while I, too, gathered myself. I would not cry. I'd done enough of that since my mother's death. For my father to have disappeared so soon after, I felt cracked, as if a fissure ran through my soul. The realm seemed to feel the same, and the recovery of a people who had lost their leaders lurked in the wings as everyone respected one of our most sacred beliefs and waited for the rites of mourning to pass. While I loathed the clothing and sense of confinement, I also dreaded the completion of the sixty days and nights and the duty that awaited once mourning had passed.

I picked up my skirts and lumbered toward the door.

"Mairynne," Mother Feathergale called, "we still need to bind your hair."

Pushing my chin higher, I said, "I think I'll leave it loose."

"But—"

I held a hand forward to halt the propriety. I would wear the clothing, but I refused the hair. Finishing my day with a headache from the constant pull was the last of my desires. Traditionally, the decision may have been blasphemous, but there were no formal ceremonies this day. Outside of going to the citadel, I wouldn't meet any of my people. My sisters and the Triad's priests could tolerate my small defiance.

The older woman clasped her hands and put on a smile. "You have always been a headstrong child. Your mother and I have always been there to encourage your determination." She curtsied. "As you will."

To my friend, I asked, "Jessa, will you walk with me?"

She lifted her own robes of mourning, although significantly less encumbering than mine, and joined me at the door. I envied her for her lack of station, but I'd little choice as to my own. These walls held me as did the propriety and custom. The robes simply ensured I couldn't breathe.

Before leaving, I turned. "Thank you, Mother Feathergale. For everything."

Despite my sense of suffocation, I'd been fortunate to have gained my majority having two motherly figures in my life—my best friend's mother and the woman who had borne my sisters and me into the world. Before her death, Noralynne Evangale had possessed strength and compassion revered by all castes of our people. Nantai's casteless and Small Folk had also loved the empress, a fondness rulers before her couldn't claim. As I turned down the hall toward the bridge, I grasped the two small tokens that hung on a chain around my neck; one stone felt constantly warm against my skin and the other constantly cold. The soldiers who found Mother had pulled the cold thing from her hand after recovering her twisted body from the border of the Evernight Marshes near the Great Sands. The warm stone I had found on my father's pillow the morning he, Tennō Atheryn Evangale, had disappeared.

WITHIN NANTAI'S JEWEL CITY of Arashi, Stormskeep Castle hugged the side of a cliff high above a great waterfall. We exited the castle proper onto a wide landing, then moved toward the bridge crossing high above Sundai Falls. Our steps carried us onward over the narrow bridge to the citadel beyond where my sisters and I would meet with priests and receive updates on the upcoming rites. Though I'd grown up in the people's central city, I had no memories at Stormskeep in which the sound of water flowing over stone did not provide ambiance. Even in the most remote corners of the castle, if I were to listen, I could have heard the wooshing and splashes. Now, as we slowly crossed the bridge over the falls, the ever-present sound soothed my nerves.

Each tentative foot forward caused the bridge to sway, and I questioned my balance. Should I fall, I could call the wind to carry me to safety, but it would incite commotion and angst over my well-being amongst any people gathered below in the daylight hours. Today, I wished for privacy, and the need to face my sisters as well as the Triad was burden enough, so I took care and held the rough rope railing as I walked shoulder-to-shoulder with Jessa. She, on the other hand, moved freely in her light-weight robes.

Again, I envied her.

"You seem distant today," Jessa said, turning to face me then quickly back to our path.

I breathed deeply and sighed. "My mind is clouded with what's needed to complete the rituals. Day forty-eight, you said?"

"Mmm, yes."

"We only have three rites remaining and then we can dispense with the sadness that hangs over our people."

"Over your people, Lady Mairynne. Afterward, do you intend to prepare for ascension?"

I stopped both walking and breathing, but my question spilled out anyway. "Why would you ask such a question so carelessly?" I said, scanning for onlookers.

She fumbled to find decorum and the right response. "My apologies, Lady Mairynne. I just figured we were alone and that the sounds of the falls would mask the question."

I had wounded her. For her to have asked only reflected my own worry; I had scolded where I should not have. "No, Jessa, it is I who should apologize. My ascension is the expectation of the people, is it not?" Truly, this was no answer, but I hoped it was enough to appease her curiosity.

It sufficed. She eased, looped an arm through mine, and offered her strength to supplement my own.

Halfway across the bridge, I stopped and turned to face the falls. Mist wafted up on the wind from the rocks, cooling my face and stirring my loose hair. To my oldest friend, I said, "If—and that is a big if—I do, I've much to prepare over the next twelve days. I'm not ready to be empress, and I fear I am not truly ready for the burden."

"Mairynne, there is reason—"

"I know the reason behind all of this." Shaking my head, I grasped her hand and eased my words for her benefit. "My parents groomed me, along with my sisters, for this very thing, but the time came far sooner than I had thought." I paused, looking down at our clasped hands. "They, my parents, that is, were taken from us before their time."

Jessa hugged me around the shoulders, her simple touch, silence, and acceptance offering more strength than she knew.

"Anyway," I said at last and a mite ruefully, "my remaining family awaits my arrival. We'd best be on our way."

Inside the citadel, we turned to the right and made for the Triad's meeting chambers behind the temple proper. At a long table, the Triad's clergy sat in chairs in a seemingly random pattern, each reading from a scroll. My sisters and their first advisors also awaited. Karynne sat at the table's head, and I wondered how early she'd arrived to secure the seat of power. To her left, Yasmynne leaned close to her betrothed, Nestryn.

Upon my father's disappearance, my sisters had wasted no time in choosing and announcing their first advisors. The thought caused my stomach to churn. Nestryn had now been elevated to Yasmynne's first advisor, yet they sat too close, too intimately for an official proceeding. Their manner had always been an open display of affection, and they paid little heed to the company present. Poised behind Karynne, the powerful, more seductive Imrythel Sandsgale rested one hand on the back of my sister's chair. She, Karynne's chosen, was almost too much to behold, ebony hair flowing, one eye covered with a black veil while the other peered back, an uncommonly piercing green. Merely looking upon her, I felt out of place in my own skin and fought the urge to fidget.

Wearing attire that mirrored my own, Karynne stood and closed the distance between us. Having our father's height, she looked down, grasped my shoulders, and folded me into a hug. "Mairynne," she said. "How are you doing this morning?"

"I do wish we didn't have to do this today," I answered. "But if we must, let us begin."

Karynne's glance flickered past me to Jessa but returned quickly, and with a smile, she nudged me toward the chair at her right. "Sister, why is your hair unbound?"

Yasmynne surfaced from her whispers and flipped a hand in their oldest sister's direction. "Oh Kahry, let her be. This is our only obligation today."

Across the table, I gave Yasmynne a thankful but questioning stare.

The elderly priest cleared his throat and rolled up his scroll. "With you all here, we may proceed."

The other clergy, each given the Hallowgale name by tradition and raised to serve the Triad, followed his lead in stowing their reading.

The much younger priestess said, "Edamyn, we should excuse the advisors." The notes in Tasmynne's voice rang high and clear as she looked meaningfully from Nestryn to Imrythel, then to my friend Jessa.

Though I had not announced a first advisor of my own, all assumed that I'd chosen my dearest friend. I had not, as I refused to accept that my father and our emperor wouldn't return. Jessa accepted her dismissal, but the others looked to my sisters, awaiting permission. Imrythel was the last to leave and made a show of pulling closed the heavy double doors.

Once alone with our holy counsel, the senior Hallowgale, Edamyn, began with the traditional opening blessing of the Triad. "May Atun, the All-Seer, guide us today."

Arlyn and Tasmynne dipped their heads acknowledging the tradition.

Arlyn offered the second invocation. "May Otarr, the Day-Seer, alight our way."

"And may the Night-Seer, Selene, give us wisdom," Tasmynne finished.

"Arlyn, do you wish to begin?" Edamyn held a shaky hand in the direction of Otarr's high priest.

"Yes, thank you." He sat straighter in his chair, folding his hands atop the table. "Otarr has shown Kōgō Noralynne Evangale the way to her next life. Time has passed enough that we may sweep the mandala sands. Emissaries from the Fire Forgers have delivered the phials. We have sorcerers at the ready to hold off any storms so we may ensure Otarr may gaze upon us. We are ready for the eighth and ninth rites to begin three days hence."

I stifled the urge to groan at the thought of two long, sweltering days under the sun overseeing the sweeping of the sands, and there would be no reprieve on the third as we handed out the phials of the ritual sands to the people. My sisters and I listened with aplomb as was our duty. Discussion continued between the Hallowgales around positioning and other technical aspects required for the ceremony, and I exchanged looks with my sisters from time to time until the insignificant details had run their course.

Tasmynne moved on. "As to the final rite, the caretakers are tending to the nymphs around the clock, keeping their ecosystem within the precise condition required to encourage the final transformation. The nymphs are preparing for their final molting cycle and are on schedule to emerge from the water and shed their skin just in time for the Rite of Release." Tasmynne relaxed back in her chair as she finished, clearly satisfied with the status of her preparations for the Nantai Rituals of Mourning.

In the swift pause that followed, Karynne leaned forward, resting her elbows on the table. "Very well," she said. "It seems all is on track to complete honoring our mother."

Just as swiftly, she turned to me and pinned me with a sharp gaze. Instinctively, I tensed, feeling my fingers digging into the wooden arm of the chair. As I scanned the others in the room, every person's focus also rested on me.

She continued, "Mairynne, are you prepared to tend to your duties once the rites are complete?"

I swallowed though my mouth felt suddenly dry. I'd foreseen this question, but that didn't make answering easier. Ultimately, I wasn't intent on abdication, only avoidance. "If you inquire about my understanding, I'm versed in the expectation that we begin preparation for my ascension."

"Expectation be damned to the hells," said Karynne. "What I wonder is if you actually plan to begin the proceedings. It is clearly what Father wanted; him having written his directive into the Stormskeep annals that you, his third daughter, shall be his successor to the throne of Stormskeep."

My shoulders tightened, my neck pinched, so I rolled my head to relieve the strain and sighed. While I adored my eldest sister, she could temper her rash demeanor with a smattering of tact. Leveling my voice as much as possible, I replied, "We have twelve sacred days remaining before I must face this decision, Kahry. Can we tend to our grief for now?"

Yasmynne reached across the table to offer me a hand. I accepted and awaited her thoughts. Her gaze flitted to our older sister, then with a gentle smile, she said, "Of course we will respect the rituals, but you should know that our people are becoming lost without a leader. Our advisors say there have been some disturbances in the streets, and we've heard rumors from the other castes."

The matter of unrest within the people concerned me more than my place on the throne; however, I needed time. "Twelve days," I responded, rigid and unmoving as I stated my will, "only then will I address the topic of inheritance."

"You must at least name your first advisor officially and make the decree in the annals," Karynne continued, seemingly searching for a way to force me to address my impending duty. "Jessa, though she is dear to you, is not an appropriate royal advisor."

Facing her, I pressed my lips into a tight line. There was little clarity in my mind as to why she believed Imrythel or Nestryn met the so-called requirements, but now wasn't the time to discuss. Pressing that issue would have only ensnared me in further conversation about a topic I wasn't ready to address. I turned to the elderly priest at my right and asked, "Is there aught to discuss regarding the rites?"

Edamyn Hallowgale replied, "No, Lady Mairynne, we have concluded our business."

I stood; the chair scraped against the floor as my momentum pushed it backward. My sisters both followed my cue. I hugged Karynne formally, then Yasmynne, who grabbed onto me and squeezed tight, showing the affection she wore in her very bones. As I broke the hug, I stated again, "Twelve days. It's not long. I value our sisterhood beyond what you will ever know, but this acceptance is mine and mine alone. I must come to it in my own time. Once I have decided, you both will be the first to know." On those words, I made for the doors.

Hot moisture gathered about my belts as I pulled one door inward enough to squeeze through and make my escape. In the foyer, I turned toward the open-air sanctuary overlooking Stormskeep Falls, desperate for some relief. In my path, Imrythel stood. My level gaze rested at the hollow in her long, graceful throat. Clenching my teeth, I lifted my chin to make eye contact.

◇◇◇◇◇◇◇◇◇◇◇◇◇◇◇◇◇◇◇◇◇◇◇◇◇◇◇◇◇◇◇

IMRYTHEL RAISED A HAND and softly ran a long finger down my face, the trail she traced burning a line from near my eye, down, and along my jawline. Against the urge to flinch away, I held myself in place and waited.

"Your sister cares deeply for you, for the Evangale legacy, and for the Nantai people," she said, her voice deeper and more seductive than a woman's voice had a right to be. "I see many questions written on your face."

Unclear as to what she suggested, I reminded myself that Tennō Atheryn's decree named me successor and trained my features into a mask of solemnity. Versed in the ways of Nantai politics, the woman before me carried a manner about her that embodied power and temptation. She used her height to exude an air of authority while her curves dripped with sensuality, and the veil she wore covering one eye cast an air of mystery about her. In choosing her first advisor, my sister Karynne clearly sought to use these skills to her advantage. As Father had instructed us all, I measured my words. "Thank you, Imrythel. In these days, I take comfort in my sisters as we, along with the rest of the Nantai people, pay due respect to my mother's memory."

"Yes." She clasped her hands behind her back, and her gaze dropped for only a moment before she continued, "Well, do remember that you must have trust in those who love you."

I donned an appeasing smile and gave credit to the truth in her words. "Well put. Now, if you'll excuse me, I'd like some time in sanctuary with my thoughts."

As I moved around her, Jessa stepped to my side.

"Lady Mairynne," Imrythel called.

I turned to see that Karynne had joined her.

Regally, they stood shoulder-to-shoulder as Imrythel added, "Karynne and I both are to champion your path to the throne; your advocates if you will." She tipped her head forward in a move so small it almost escaped me.

Yet now was no time to bend in my conviction. Giving a single nod, I passed through the grand archway leaving them to their will and my dear friend in my wake. Inside, I clasped both of Jessa's hands and asked her to wait without, as well. I wished nothing more than to be alone with my thoughts and prayers to Atun and his children, Otarr and Selene. Deeper within the citadel, each of the Holy Triad had a dedicated chapel, but I favored this sanctuary, a sheltered balcony with three altars overlooking the Sundai Falls.

For time I didn't count, I knelt at Selene's altar and called a wind to bring mist from the falls and cool me as I contemplated. At intervals, I spoke aloud to the Gods, seeking guidance. I received no answers to the questions in my mind. Atun didn't tell me why someone slayed my mother; Otarr wouldn't grant me the knowledge of where my father had gone; and Selene gave me no guidance regarding my unsettling feeling that Tennō Atheryn still lived. Fighting a burning behind my eyes, I lifted my face to the skies and cried, "Father, what would you do in my place?"

An unseen, but rich and familiar voice answered, "I know not what Tennō Atheryn would do."

"Thalaj," I breathed, wiping a tear that'd strayed down my cheek. I stood and moved in his direction.

Arashi's first guard, *Gensui* Thalaj Northerngale, stepped from the shadows, from one of the apses set into the outer wall. Exempt from wearing full robes of mourning, Stormskeep guards dressed in light leathers with a red sash from shoulder to hip, easily removed should the need arise. Weapons remained accessible.

"Your robes flatter, but I do prefer your hair unbound," Thalaj said as he approached.

"These robes are better suited to my sisters than they are to me." I moved in his direction, but before I reached him, he dropped his eyes and turned slightly away. The movement prevented the embrace I'd intended, and my shoulders felt heavy again, this time not from the robes. "Will you not give me the comfort of holding me?"

"Lady Mairynne, you know it's blasphemous." He ran a hand over his braids to the thong at the base of his skull.

Flinching at the formality, I snapped, "We have done nothing blasphemous."

"If anyone sees us in an embrace, my head would decorate the spikes at the Stormskeep gates."

"No one can persecute you for offering comfort in this time." I searched his face.

He warned me off with a look and said, "That my mother is a Storm Sorcerer is insignificant here. That she chose a Frost Fighter as my father makes me unworthy. There is the matter of contamination that is punishable only by death."

"Thalaj," I huffed. "You know that I do not hold with the caste beliefs. And you know that my mother and father supported my stance."

"And how has that worked for them?" He challenged while rubbing a gloved thumb over the hilt of his scimityne. Seconds later, he realized the splinter his words had pushed under my skin. "I'm sorry." He dropped his head and silently moved to the railing beyond the altars, leaning over toward the falls.

I joined him. As he turned to face me, I could feel his eyes, and unable to handle the silence, I pressed, "Why must such things come between people drawn to one another?" My words were more of a complaint than a question.

He answered anyway, "Mairynne, you know how to change this."

I turned to him abruptly and questioned, "Not you too?" Everyone pressed for my ascension, but I'd hoped the man who'd become a fixture in my life, as our protector, wouldn't join causes with the masses.

Thalaj looked down. "It is not my place to counsel you, but royal decrees are our only mechanism for change amidst our people. An emperor or empress must formally write them into the annals under the Hallowgales' supervision. I see little other course of action."

Though his motivations were different, he'd joined in the opinion of the majority and clearly wished for my ascension. As such, I considered the personal conversation over, nodded, and switched to business. "Have you any word of my father from your network?"

"I do not."

"And you believe he will not return?"

"That, I cannot say for certain. Though there has never been a period when Tennō Atheryn has been absent from his castle for so many unexcused days."

I reached out over the railing toward the rushing water, calling for the mist. I concentrated, allowing the power to pool in my heart, and pulled with my sorcery. A small storm gathered in my hands. Watching the mist turn into tiny thunderheads and feeling rain begin to fall onto my palms, I absently asked, "Then why do I have this overwhelming sensation that he lives?"

Thalaj sighed. "I don't know, Lady Mairynne."

Silence except for rushing water and tiny sounds of thunder cocooned us on the balcony. Calling on my magic offered a much-needed distraction and allowed an idea to bloom in the back of my mind. Stormskeep annals. The histories of our people written by rulers through the ages would surely offer guidance. I clapped my hands together, extinguishing the storm, and said, "I think . . ."

"What?" He searched my face. "What do you think?"

I glanced at him with a quirked brow and grin. "You, and everyone else, will see." Turning to the arched entry, I called the wind for assistance with my burdening robes and walked lightly and swiftly toward the foyer. Behind me, Thalaj's heels clicked upon the marble as he followed.

My sisters, their advisors, and the clergy still loitered in the foyer, likely awaiting my return. Jessa rushed toward me when I emerged; Karynne, Imrythel, and the clergy turned, but Yasmynne and Nestryn continued in their whispered conversation. I lowered my eyes, feeling a stab of jealousy over their happiness, but I refocused quickly. "Jessa," I said. "Send word to each member of Tennō Atheryn's advisory council that we will meet first thing on the morrow within the royal court."

"Of course, Lady Mairynne." Jessa curtsied, then scurried to the bridge and onward to complete the chore I'd demanded.

Yasmynne turned, alerted by my command. Karynne took a breath to speak.

Before she could utter words, I held up both hands to forestall her and said, "My sisters, Hallowgales of the Triad, and Imrythel and Nestryn as first advisors, you will all be in attendance as well at the ninth bell."

Karynne asked, "What is the meaning of the meeting?"

"You will learn with the others. Yasmynne, can you ensure that Aunt Nadialynne receives word and is present as well?"

She nodded, seeming uncertain and startled by the sudden demands which worked well to my taste.

My intent could remain a mystery for the time being. I turned to Thalaj before anyone else could utter more questions. I thought to ask for his company, but reconsidered and demanded, "You will escort me to the royal library."

Two

A Scream in the Night

THE FORTY-NINTH DAY OF MOURNING arrived with little pomp, but I didn't have grief on my mind as I took a seat in the throne room of Stormskeep. I'd spent the remainder of the day before reading the histories and searching for an obscure solution to my dilemma. Yet, fortune hadn't favored my efforts. Almost an hour before the council would arrive, I sat on a chair I'd had placed in front of the throne, not wishing to make claim by sitting on the actual Serpentine Throne. The birds sang outside the open windows in the stone walls, and Otarr watched over Stormskeep from clear blue skies. Since I would present myself as leader at the meeting with the Storm Sorcery Council, I'd allowed Mother Feathergale to bind my hair as propriety dictated. At the end of the day, I would pay with pain throughout my temples and neck.

Still, tradition reigned.

Eerie silence turned into a clamor when the meeting's attendees and the guard arrived promptly at the ninth bell. My family and their first advisors procured seats to the left of the throne, the area designated for the ruler's family, the four leaders of each large Storm Sorcerer family to the right, and the clergy at the end of the long meeting table facing the throne. As the portly Havengale patriarch moved to his chair, I discerned a cut of his gaze toward my sisters and aunt, Nadialynne in particular. Then his eyes moved to the other three advisors in flitting glances. Did he hope I wouldn't notice his manner—that he seemed insecure amid the others on this council? I cleared my throat and he gathered himself, a smile plumping his cheeks further.

Along with the Storm Sorcery Council, Thalaj brought a retinue of city guardspeople and posted them outside the throne room. He stepped to my side and asked, "Is all well, Lady Evangale?" When I nodded tightly, he brushed a hand over mine and joined his team.

I held a hand out to a waiting Edamyn Hallowgale, signaling him to call the meeting to order.

He took a few timorous steps and struck the gong with a strength his posture belied. The commotion settled, and he invoked Atun's grace. In sequence the other priests called upon Otarr and Selene. When the Invocations were done, Tasmynne bowed and took her seat. Everyone turned toward me.

I pushed myself up from my chair and held both hands wide. "My fellow Nantai leaders, I've asked you here today to make a proposal."

A rumble went up, large for a crowd of only thirteen.

I closed my eyes briefly, awaiting silence. When the questions faded, I said, "It is not my intention to declare for the Serpentine Throne at this time."

Another rumpus ensued to which I raised my hands further. Upon silence, I continued, "I do wish to hear your thoughts on this declaration. My sisters, Imrythel, Nestryn, and the Triad provided their thoughts in a private meeting yesterday at the citadel. But let us proceed in an orderly manner."

As such, my sisters sat quietly with mouths in tight lines. Nestryn reached for a goblet, and Imrythel remained hauntingly motionless, her sharp green gaze locked with mine. A chill ran up my spine, and I suppressed a shudder. To my right, I addressed the first of the Storm families, "Azurynne, please share the Nightingale concerns with the council."

The matriarch of the Nightingale family shifted in her seat. "Lady Mairynne, I mean no disrespect, but our people rely on leadership. Without an emperor or empress, thieves and murderers run rampant. From the days of Tennō Makenyn, the Storm Sorcerers have agreed that the leader keeps the laws and histories within the Stormskeep annals. Also, without a leader, there is no room for change. This is the first written law of the Nantai people."

Tipping my head to show respect, I said, "Thank you, Lady Azurynne. I do not intend to disregard the laws of Nantai, and what my forebearers have written weighs heavily on my decision. Is there aught you would add in the way of concerns from your family?"

"There is not."

I moved on. "Very well. Lukos? Will you share the concerns of the Thundergale family?"

The Thundergale patriarch stood and paced behind the families, stroking the overlong hairs extending in a point from his chin. "My Lady of Evangale, on behalf of my family, I thank you for the opportunity to address you and this council in this manner. Although it is outside of protocol during the mourning rituals."

"Yes, Lukos. I am well aware of that, but given the circumstances, I felt certain this meeting was necessary."

Lukos continued, "That is a wisdom beyond your years, Lady Mairynne."

I held up a hand and addressed the entire council, "For the remainder of this meeting, we may dispense with the titles. I am seeking debate, if you will. I do not wish to get lost in the words that often make our proceedings lengthy. We must return to the sanctity of mourning as soon as possible." I scanned the room searching for approval. Nods affirmed, and to Lukos I said, "Please, continue."

"In the markets, our family has witnessed a series of uncharacteristic thefts since Tennō Atheryn disappeared. With the help of the guards, we have arrested several pickpockets in the streets. The holding cells in the city gates are nearing full. I know we only have a few days remaining, but I urge you to accept your duty as soon as our laws allow." He returned to his seat.

Addressing the third of the four families, I looked to Ohmyn. "And the council from Havengale?"

Ohmyn, rounder than most with thinning hair, blushed a bright red as he answered, "Our concern lies with the other castes. In the haven, we have heard rumors that many of the gnobles from the lower castes are developing plans to challenge the Storm Sorcerers for the throne. The rumors say that they believe having the empress murdered and the emperor disappear shows weakness within the Evangales, as well as across the Storm Sorcerer caste."

Disturbances in the marketplace along with the concern of not fulfilling the first law were of minimal concern compared to the lower castes contriving plans against the Storm Sorcerers. "Have you followed up with the guard on these rumors, Ohmyn?"

He shook his head vigorously enough that his cheeks billowed.

"Disregard the fact that it is business and do speak with Gensui Thalaj on the matter today or tomorrow."

"Yes, Lady Mairynne. I will bring my sons who heard the gossip to the guardhouse later today." At this, he fell silent.

I raised my chin to Solarynne Dawnsgale, the final of the four family leaders sitting on my father's council. Her look struck me, as it always did, with hair the color of an apple's inner flesh and eyes so light they almost seemed clear. Such light features were uncommon among the Nantai people . . . and truly haunting.

Accepting my cue, she said, "The Dawnsgale kindred have no qualms awaiting your decision, Lady Mairynne. Patience was one of Tennō Atheryn's best qualities and may be the very ingredient that ensures the peace we've known under his reign."

"Thank you, Solarynne. Aunt Nadia," I said, addressing her in the familiar, "my mother was your twin. Do you have counsel you wish to impart?"

Ohmyn Havengale interrupted, "Lady Mairynne? If I may?"

I raised a brow toward him, shocked by his insolence.

He blushed a deeper red, but adhering to my earlier advice for candidness, he continued, "Your aunt has no place on this council."

"Master Havengale, I have called this meeting. You will see that my sisters sit here as well, and they are also not a part of this council. In the absence of my father's or my mother's wisdom, I wish to and will consult with my aunt." I turned back to Nadia, motioning for her to take the floor. "Please . . ."

"Mairynne," she started.

A stab of guilt pierced my gut as she spoke. I reached for the warm and cold tokens that hung about my neck. I'd distanced myself from my aunt after my mother's death, finding it difficult to look upon someone who was, yet who was not, the vision of Noralynne Evangale. Even her voice sounded similar in the lilt of her words.

"Nora," Nadia choked on her sister's name, swallowed, and continued, "my sister loved her children with her entire soul. But she was also a patriot of Nantai. She believed the gnobles should work together to unite the people and invite the Small Folk and the casteless into the politics of the country."

This caused an uproar from the council members. I held up my hand and waited until it had died down, then motioned to my aunt.

Nadia continued, "She gave her daughters room to grow into who they chose to be, and I believe she would stand by your instincts. I will honor what I believe would be her decision to support you in yours."

A lump grew solid in my throat, and I had no more answers than I had before. I couldn't find the words to speak for a long moment. My sisters, the Triad, and the rest present began to debate whether I should ascend to the Serpentine Throne or not, as if I were not present. Quite possibly, I wasn't. My vision blurred as I considered. When I came back to myself, I cleared my throat as loudly as I could. Some of the conversation abated, but the last I heard, predictably, was Ohmyn's gravelly voice.

"There's also a rumor that the Ryū will awaken."

"Enough!" I shouted and stood. "My mother's grave is not cold. We have no evidence that the dragons are returning. We have naught to worry about from the castes. They hold the Nantai mourning period as sacred as we do. The Small Folk have never been of concern, and my mother lost her life in her desire to unite the lands.

"I spent the afternoon and into the evening yesterday reading the histories, looking for one case that might resemble our own. It saddens me to say I've been unsuccessful so far. I had hoped to have better guidance when I asked you here to propose that we wait until we have more information on Father's disappearance. Alas, that is what I propose, that we wait and that we send a team in search of Tennō Atheryn." With less gusto, I added, "But that does not seem to be on the minds of any of our people."

Nadia offered me a smile, but the others present sat in silence until Azurynne spoke softly, "Mairynne, such a decision is unprecedented, and we have no ruler to record the decree."

Nodding once, I prompted, "Then let us take a vote. Those in favor of executing the ascension as soon as the mourning is complete?"

Karynne, Imrythel, Azurynne, Lukos, and Ohmyn raised hands without hesitation. Yasmynne and the Triad followed suit, and Nestryn, of course, mimicked Yasmynne. I felt hollow. Did they not believe there was a chance for Father? And why were they all so certain that I could handle the mantle of ruler when I, myself, held no such belief? In truth, beyond longing for my father's return, I wanted to see the world beyond Stormskeep and meet more of the people I'd rule one day. I'd been so sequestered here, in this castle, mostly apart from even the city below. Protected, my parents and caregivers had named it, but it felt like little more than a prison. I'd had so little experience with other castes. What were the Frost Fighters or Stone Singers like? I'd never met an Underhill Dweller, and I couldn't even recall the natures of the Cloud Courtiers. The casteless, the guilds within Nantai, the list went on and on. I had little but inexperience, ignorance, and naïvety to offer our people from where I'd lived within my stonewalled tower.

With a deep breath and losing hope with every second, I called for the alternative, "Those in favor of sending a search party for Tennō Atheryn?"

I raised my hand. Nadia and Solarynne did the same. The Triad and Lukos raised their hands as well for a second time in as many options. I felt my brows heavy as I turned to each of the latter one-by-one, questioning their meaning.

Lukos said, "Lady Mairynne, your question was flawed. If you mean to ask if I believe we should wait, I must lower my hand."

"That is what I intended, Lukos."

The Triad lowered their hands along with Lukos.

Defeated, I rolled my shoulders back. Eleven days remained, and I planned to spend that time with the history books searching for another solution. In the meantime, I made a choice. "Yasmynne, you will be in charge of the preparation for ascension. Do it quietly."

The most unlikely, carefree person in the room, she gasped with widening eyes when I charged her with a task so important to the Nantai people. Others exchanged surprised glances.

Good. I'd turned the tables at least a little. "As for the rest, you will now visit the citadel and swear oaths that this decision will not go beyond these walls. I still have time to change my mind. You are dismissed."

◇◇◇◇◇◇◇◇◇◇◇◇◇◇◇◇◇◇◇◇◇◇◇◇◇◇◇◇◇◇◇

REACHING FOR MY STORM sorcery worked best with my eyes closed for reasons I'd never understood. In need of the wind, I did this now and reached out with my senses, pulling the air close and envisioning the path to my quarters. The thirteen sorcerers in council, as well as all the guards posted outside, also possessed storm magic—maybe theirs functioned differently than my own—but nevertheless, the sudden gust indoors would be of little consequence. As the wind gathered, I opened my eyes and rode the gale out of the throne room and all the way to my private door where I stopped and looked up and down the corridors.

Alone. Wondrously alone.

I barred the door and planned to remain alone for the long remainder of the day. It took me the better part of an hour to disrobe and release my braids; but once they were loose, I slipped into a gloriously soft tunic and a pair of pants. My hair, crimped and wild, rejoiced with the freedom. I refused knocks at my door, even with the promise of food. My stomach roared, but I ignored its demands. If they chose, my people could reach me by window, breaking another decorum.

My space held me in safety.

Under Otarr's bright watch and for the first time in forty-nine long days, my body rested easy, even if my mind did not. Throughout the day, I tried to distract myself with the epic songs recorded by the scroll workers, but my thoughts often strayed back to the notion I'd accepted my duty to become empress. Inside, I railed against it still. When frustration and anger overtook me, I hurled a scroll across the room and cried out, "Why, Father, have you left me to accept this responsibility? Why did you not name Karynne or Yasmynne? I barely have my majority!" I sank to my knees in the center of my room, arms raised to anyone or any being who might listen. "Do I not get a chance to live first? To learn of this world?"

I received no reply.

Twilight came, but before Selene took her position in the night sky, I donned a cloak, pulled a large painting away from the wall, and slipped through the hidden door within my rooms into a network of tunnels and stairs known only to royalty and a handful of those sworn to protect the secret. I carried two candles, one lit and the other in my pocket for the return to my chambers. Eager to be outside and no longer confined, I allowed my eyes time to adjust, then padded through tight spaces, around sharp curves, and down many winding stone steps until I found the exit a small distance from where the Sundai Falls crashed into the pool below. Built high enough into the stone cliff that others wouldn't know to look, the landing consisted of little more than a foothold. I extinguished and stowed the candle and called for the wind to lower myself the final distance onto the soft ground behind a copse of trees.

Beyond the trees, a public park lined the pool at the base of Stormskeep Falls. Mourning periods left public places empty, especially in the dark hours, so I ran freely between the trees and toward the soft grasses lining the poolside, my cloak billowing in the deepening night. Before reaching the water, I fell to my knees, breathed in the night's air, and allowed Selene to look upon my face, my hood falling away. I'd fought the urge to cry all day—anxious, angry, and wanting tears. Now, I closed my eyes, gathered moisture from the falls above my head, and let it rain down upon me.

Dampening minutes later, a rich voice called my name.

"Mairynne," it whispered, a warning wrapped up in the hiss of my name.

I smiled through my tears. "Thalaj. Come. Sit with me."

"Can you release your rain shower first?"

I did, though the damp grass remained. He knelt beside me, catlike in his posture and ready to pounce at the first sign of danger.

"How did you know to find me here?" I asked.

"That information is mine alone," he answered, his voice low.

I hadn't expected more. Thalaj kept his ways close to his heart, and he had a proven ability to find his way into spaces that seemed impossible. He'd come into our lives when I'd aged enough to have a budding affection for boys. Turn after turn, he'd shown his loyalty to the Evangales in many ways I knew, and I'm certain in ways only known to my father, Tennō Atheryn. Inside of Stormskeep, we had lived peaceful lives. With three quarters of the perimeter sheltered by the mountain, the city lay within stone walls and a wide moat provided a barrier to the outside. Visits to the domains of other castes were often tenuous, and Thalaj stood at my father's side everywhere he traveled. In a time before, my sister Yasmynne had gossiped of his work to thwart a would-be Fire Forger assassin while the council of gnobles met at the High Cloud Court.

"Well enough," I said. "Did Ohmyn Havengale and his sons come to you today to discuss the rumors of caste uprising?"

"He did."

"And?"

"I have a team assigned. It's no matter for you to worry over during mourning."

"But I am to be empress before the moon goddess has completed her cycle," I spat, turning to look at him. "All of these matters are mine to worry over."

Thalaj gave me a tight smile but didn't speak. He didn't have to say a word to make his point.

After several silent moments, I relented. "You're right. You've proven yourself and your guard is more than competent to care for these matters, but we will speak of this once the mourning period has passed."

"Of course," he said.

We remained there on our knees and watching the water for some time until he said, "From the balcony, I heard your speech at the meeting this morning. Despite how afraid you must be, I believe it is the right decision."

I stared at him as heartbeats passed, trying to read beyond his stoicism. "It is what you wished. Is it not?" My words tasted sour as they passed my tongue and lips.

"It is, but not for the reasons you may believe." He bowed his head, grasping idly at the blades of grass.

"Then what are your reasons, Thalaj?" I searched his dark eyes, whether accusing or begging for answers, I couldn't be sure.

Instead of answering, Thalaj reached for me and I moved into him, resting my head on his shoulder. Being close to him never offered physical warmth, yet my very soul seemed to sigh. What his lean arms did offer were both strength and the closeness I craved, and I deplored that our culture forbade a relationship with this man solely because his blood contained two castes. If anything, shouldn't that make him superior to those of us with only one?

As we sat there in the silence of the night, a bone-shattering screech ripped across the sky, echoing from the stone castle, the citadel, and the rock faces surrounding the falls. The sound tore us apart.

Thalaj, somehow already on his feet, brandished his scimitynes, blue lightning crackling along the blades. My ears rang as I searched for the source. Water continued crashing into the pool, but despite the lingering vibration in my ears, there were no other sounds. The trees nearby remained motionless like the night.

"What evil could make such a sound?" I whispered to Thalaj.

"It's no sound I've ever heard," he replied. Sheathing his blades, he held a hand out to help me from the ground. "Maybe Selene is watching over you. Or bringing some warning. Let's go. I'll see you to your chambers." He pulled me toward the trees.

As Gensui, the head of our guard, Thalaj knew of the secret passages, so likely he knew that was how I had come to this place. I wondered briefly if he'd followed me but thought that an unlikely option since he hadn't been with me in my chambers. And he'd met with the family Havengale earlier.

When we came to the stone face, I brought the wind to lift us both to the ledge. Thalaj went first, and I severed the flow of magic as I stepped behind the stone that hid the entrance. The blackness complete, I fumbled to find the candle. Thalaj clapped, and the friction of his palms scraped in the darkness. Soon, blue lightning danced in a sphere between his hands. With a smile, he shifted his energy to one hand and held it high. The glow cast an eerie, moving light on the stairs and set shadows to dancing upon the walls. But the orb lit our way back up into the castle, and eventually to my rooms.

Once there, I opened the door, pushed the painting forward, and stepped inside. Thalaj stood in the opening, telling me without words he'd not be entering my private space. How wrong it seemed that he'd offer the fleeting contact in the park yet he wouldn't cross the sacred line into my chambers . . . much like he wouldn't cross the lines drawn by caste. For this matter, I harbored bitter disappointment, yet I understood how to enact the necessary change. The cost was steep, but without the support of the Storm Sorcery Council, it seemed a price I must pay. Tightly, I nodded and leaned on the wall at the threshold.

"Goodnight, Mairynne. I'll find what caused that noise." He dipped his head respectfully, showing deference to my station.

"Listen, Thalaj. I understand that everyone believes my father won't return." I reached for the two stones at my neck. "Something tells me otherwise."

The fall of his face told me that even he believed otherwise. "I fear that you are overly hopeful."

"That may be true." I took his free hand. "But I would like you to send word through your network. If there is a possibility that he may resume reign over Nantai, I do not want to take the throne. He and my mother were wonderful for our people." I allowed my gaze to drop to our joined hands. "And I am afraid that I will not be." I felt more fear than I wished to acknowledge—heavy fear over being contained in this castle. Stormskeep held beauty and safety because by its very nature it was a fortress. But it also served as my stockade.

"Look at me, Mairynne."

I did.

"Tennō Atheryn was a wise man. He chose his successor with confidence, and you will do his memory justice." Thalaj had missed the breadth and depth of my worry.

My throat tightened. Clearing it, I said, "I appreciate the vote of confidence. But will you do as I ask?" I pleaded.

"I have doubts that I will learn aught we do not already know, but I will do as my future empress asks." He extinguished his sphere of lightning and lifted our hands. He brushed three kisses across my knuckles—more affection than he'd normally risk— then disappeared into the darkness.

THREE

The Mandala Sands

A LIBRARIAN DROPPED A STACK OF books on the table, puffing a breath as she relieved herself of the burden. "Lady Mairynne, Lady Nadia, these are the annals from the Third Age, as you requested."

Looking up from my current read to see six new leather-bound tomes with the respective emperors' names scripted onto the spines further sucked at my optimism and determination to find a way out of taking over the Serpentine Throne. "Thank you," I said, not feeling in the least bit grateful. I sighed and slammed the current book closed, reaching for the next. "Kōgō Xenthyn has no solutions for me. Every decision she recorded seems to be in favor of increasing the ruling classes' power over the castes, the casteless, and the Small Folk. Why are our people so obsessed with all this hierarchy?" The notion disgusted me and degraded my mother's work to unite all Nantai people.

My aunt offered no reply to my obviously rhetorical and plaintive question.

With arms folded, I leaned onto the tome and appraised my aunt across the table. I might endure for many moons and seasons before I could do justice to the task. Maybe such a notion, along with grief, clouded my thoughts. "Do you think I have lost my mind? Is all this worth the effort?"

She rolled up the scroll she was reading and set it aside. The look on her face said she was preparing to provide me with an appropriate and decorous answer. "What you are doing, my dear niece, is wise. Even if you do not find what you seek, all the history you'll have learned will be of great value to you as the Nantai empress."

The leather covering of the book felt smoothly worn under my thumb as I idly traced inlaid circular designs. "Nadia?"

She inclined her head and made a small *mmm* sound.

"Did you hear anything out of the ordinary? A terrorizing squall?"

"I did." She smiled and drew her brows to a peak. "Muffled, though, within my cottage. Likely one of the mountain birds of prey coming farther south than normal. I'm sure it's nothing to worry over."

I twisted my lips and chewed the inside of my cheek. It seemed an easy and logical answer, though I couldn't recall having heard that horrid of a noise from any bird. Although, I hadn't much worldly experience either, having been so sheltered inside Stormskeep at Arashi.

Perceptively, she asked, "There is more that troubles you?" And in her regard, I could see my mother. It'd been so hard to look upon my aunt, and wrongly, I still struggled with how much she reminded me of the one I'd lost.

"I owe you an apology."

"Whyever for?" She reached across the table, placing a hand on mine.

I couldn't look her in the eye as I answered, "I pushed you away upon my mother's death."

My aunt's soft laughter drew my confused attention.

She reached for a goblet and drank. "If you owe me an apology for that, I owe myself one as well. For the first ten days of mourning, I draped a sheet over every mirror in my cottage. Looking upon my own face felt like looking at Noralynne's, and I couldn't handle the sight."

"Would you tell me about her?" I asked. "Something new to me. I just want to feel close again for a few moments."

Nadia squirmed in her chair, but at last she said, "I'll tell you a story of both your mother and your father. Much of it also involves your oldest sister. It is one that holds many emotions . . . happiness, sadness, worry, loss. It embodies who Noralynne was as a person, how strongly she believed in the people, and how much she was willing to risk, yet it warns of dangers throughout our land." She looked around the library. "As we are the only ones here, I'll trust you with this, but your sisters, especially Karynne, mustn't know what I am about to share. I only know your mother's side of the story, but I'm certain Karynne has her own version."

I agreed, hungry for the information, another story. Grasping my goblet, I filled it from the pitcher and drank deeply while she gathered her thoughts.

She began, "At the time, Karynne was the only daughter of Tennō Atheryn and Kōgō Noralynne and a prized jewel of the Nantai people. To the people, she meant that the emperor had an heir and the Serpentine Throne would no longer be at risk. To my sister and her husband, she represented only their love. Karynne learned her words early and spoke in clear though simple sentences from the very beginning. She'd learned her letters and to gather the storm's magic long before other children her age, albeit only in small doses.

"As it turns out, you all did. You, dear Mairynne, may have been the slowest to learn these basics, but you were still ahead of your peers." Nadia offered a demure smile, then continued, "Tennō Atheryn and Kōgō Noralynne took ruling the people seriously. Your father held that the people—all people, big and small—were his reason for being. He rued when conflict arose between the castes and hated that the Frost Fighters and Fire Forgers were always positioning for rank within the people. Your mother, on the other hand, turned her attention to the Small Folk. Together, they believed that since Karynne would one day rule the Nantai, she should take part in their diplomatic interactions with the people."

I clung to every word about a life so different from what I knew at Stormskeep. Father had never permitted my sisters or me beyond the bordering walls, so to learn that this may not have always been the case both startled and thrilled me.

Nadia shifted, leaning back in her chair. "When Karynne was little more than seven, Noralynne took her along as she traveled to hold an audience with King Isao of the Small Folk at Brennmor. Upon their arrival, the armies of the emperor ambushed them at the gates. The guards took Karynne into custody on the orders of King Isao himself. Fearful of Noralynne's magic, he held Karynne hostage under the threat of slitting her young throat at the first sign of storms on the horizon."

"Why would Isao do such a thing? Didn't he know my mother's intent?"

Nadia lifted a shoulder. Clearly Isao's reasoning never made it to her ears.

Dismayed, I mumbled, "And why would I have never known of this story?"

A touch ruefully, Nadia smiled. "The time that followed tested your mother and father's very beliefs on how to rule the people. It strained their relationship, and it took time to recover. Your father decreed that no one speak of the story. When you read his annals, you will see a line stating, 'The story of Noralynne, Karynne, and King Isao shall not be written and shall not be voiced, lest the teller spend the remainder of their days confined to the High Tower.' Until now, I have not shared what Noralynne confided in me. But, as you are about to ascend, I believe it is your right to know."

Taking a deep breath and trying to understand my father's motives, I motioned for her to continue.

Her eyes turned glassy as she went on, "Your mother spent more than ten days negotiating with King Isao. For the entire time, she used her storm magic to hold the clouds away from Brennmor. The Small King's ignorance as to the nature of our magic also kept him ignorant of the fact that she used her magic in this manner to protect her only daughter.

"In the end, Isao agreed to call off his guards and release the princess, and in exchange, Noralynne agreed to lessen the taxes imposed by Atheryn's father. Some considered this act by your mother treason, and in addition to Atheryn's anger, it put stress upon him from his advisors. The whole situation became the seed of disagreement between your mother and father. Although in time, Atheryn came to see she was right and wrote the decree, owning it as his own.

"That is their story though. The Small Folk guards returned Karynne to the empress in a sad state. To this day, we do not know what evil she experienced, but she'd lost enough weight that her eyes appeared sunken and bruised. Do you know of the rumors about the Small Folk?"

I tried to remember anything I'd read or heard, but I hadn't had a childhood like others where the younglings learned much of the comings and goings around Nantai through rumor on the streets. Father had sequestered me within Stormskeep. I had learned from the clergy, family, and tutors. Most play had been with my sisters. And my non-royal friends were chosen for me, much like Jessa or the occasional youngling of a caste gnoble, and we only associated under the supervision of a caretaker. With rumors being impolite in society, even younglings knew to avoid them when supervised.

I shook my head.

"I suppose not. Well, there are tales that the Small Folk who inhabit Brennmor and the city of Umbra within the Evernight Marshes feed on sorcery. If Karynne's brief time with them is any proof, mayhap the rumor is true. For the two seasons that followed, Karynne would speak to no one. I don't think she or your mother ever fully recovered. And after this, your father decreed that his children would not attend diplomatic missions until they had gained their majority and decided for themselves to attend." Nadia drained her glass.

After hearing the story, I felt heavier than I had before, but for different reasons. "My mother and father recovered from their disagreement, though? They always seemed to be so happily in love."

"Oh, yes." Her eyes lit up. "It must have been five or six years later, but they grew closer than they had been before. Within the next four years, Yasmynne and you were both born, bringing more joy to them and the realm."

"I heard my name," Yasmynne's sing-song voice broke into our conversation.

We both startled and looked up to my sister who stood beside the pile of annals.

"Delightful day, little sis. You're deep into the books, I see," she sang, wrinkling her nose. She leaned in to give our aunt a kiss on the cheek. "Aunt Nadia, how are you?"

After the pleasantries, she pulled a chair to my side. "I wanted to inform you of the plans for your ascension."

Speechless, I raised my brows, exchanging a look of sheer surprise with Nadia. This proactivity was especially unlike her.

Yasmynne continued, "I sent word to the Cloud Courtiers and received a prompt reply. The sky island will arrive the day after the last rites of mourning. Once the nymphs have gained their wings, we visit the sky island and attend the official High Cloud Court to discuss the plans."

My stomach clenched. Against my hopes that this would drag out under my sister's usual dalliance, it appeared we'd be moving rather quickly through the formalities. I'd never been to the High Cloud Court before, a place that wasn't really a place but castle grounds nestled upon a cloud in the sky. They traveled over Nantai constantly, given to the magic of the Cloud Courtiers who kept the floating grounds aloft. It enabled the castles to make lengthy journeys, retrieving gnobles from all corners of Nantai to convene in the High Cloud Court. I hadn't gained my majority the last time Father attended. Distantly, I asked, "What is it like in the Cloud Court?"

"Oh, Mairynne!" Yasmynne leaned forward, light twinkling in her eyes. "The regalia is so elegant it makes me tremble."

Naturally, the ceremonial attire and objects would be the first things to enter my sister's mind. She thought about things thinly, only reaching as far as the surface and relishing in things she could see. The tendency bothered me a little because she possessed the purest of souls beneath. I chuckled, knowing that I should be more specific when it came to such matters. "I'm wondering more about the proceedings."

"Well, remember how the meeting you requested two days ago progressed?"

Certainly it hadn't gone in the ways I'd hoped, but I answered simply, "I do."

"That is a mere sample of the ceremonial grandeur that transpires at the High Cloud Court. It should be an adventure. Nestryn and I plan to observe the proceedings of Comtesse Tsanseri's court whilst we are there." She put out her lower lip, then added, "Father wouldn't allow me into Love's Court the last time we visited the Cloud Courtiers."

Nadia and I exchanged another look. Clearly, my dear sister had ulterior motives for so aggressively pursuing the plans on my behalf.

At the far end of the library, the door flew open, commotion reverberating into the room and shattering the quiet. The librarian scurried from behind the desk and disappeared through the door. The noise intensified, furious footsteps shuffling through the stone corridor outside. I settled my gaze on Nadia, perplexed. She shook her head and pressed a hand onto the table, lifting herself from the chair. Yasmynne looked from me to my aunt in terrorized confusion too. I stood and hurried to the door.

◇◇◇◇◇◇◇◇◇◇◇◇◇◇◇◇◇◇◇◇◇◇◇◇◇◇◇◇◇◇◇◇

OUTSIDE THE LIBRARY, GUARDS were rushing past by the dozens. I reached out and grasped one at the elbow and he turned to look at me, belatedly lowering his head when he realized my station.

"What is your name?" I asked.

"Perryn, my lady," he answered, waiting for me to release my grip.

"What is happening? Why has the city guard come to Stormskeep?" I demanded.

"Lady Evangale, there has been a body discovered. If you are safe in the library, I urge you to return to your activities."

Aghast that he'd insinuate I'd turn away from such a thing, I snapped, "Nonsense, Perryn. Where is this body?"

The librarian ducked her head and slunk back into the safety of the book- and scroll-lined room.

Perryn stammered.

I gripped his arm tighter. "It is clear that we don't have all day, Perryn." Furthermore, my heart raced at the possibilities. I thanked the Holy Triad that Yasmynne and Nadia were with me rather than somewhere else. But after Mother's and Father's fates, what of Karynne? Or my first guard, Thalaj? "I asked you where. I expect an answer."

"Your chambers, Lady Evangale," his voice choked on the words.

My stomach lurched. "Do you know who? Where is Gensui Thalaj Northerngale?" I couldn't stifle the latter question.

He shook his head and fidgeted with his leather cuffs. "They didn't say, but it is good to see you standing here alive and well."

"Well, let us not stand here any longer." I fell in with the soldiers moving toward my rooms. Thankfully, the corridor was open to the elements. I reached my hand out, closed my eyes briefly, and called for the wind. The gust at our backs moved everyone along faster.

I hadn't taken time to see if Yasmynne or Nadia followed, but when we reached my doors, Mother Feathergale stood outside, her shoulders shaking as she wept, a kerchief held to her mouth and covering her cries. I pulled her to me, wrapping my arms around her shoulders and shushing her as she clung to me and sobbed.

Guards rushed in and out, so many words flying I couldn't make sense of what was happening. When my attendant had finally quieted enough, I pulled back from her.

"Mother Feathergale," I asked, looking into her red-rimmed eyes. "What has happened?"

She wailed, "Jessamynne."

A jolt startled me straight, and I peered into the room where everyone huddled. Nadia arrived at my side.

To her, I asked, "Can you see to her?"

As soon as Nadia had nodded and taken Mother Feathergale in her arms, I pushed past the guards into the room, clearing my throat and standing as tall as possible. My chambers were sizable, but at the entry and toward the attendant area of the suite, the quarters were more cramped and certainly wouldn't hold dozens of armed guards.

I took a deep breath and from my gut bellowed, "Clear a path."

The guards molded themselves to the walls on either side, bowing their heads slightly as I held my chin high and passed by. At the end of the hall, I peered into the kitchen. I balled my hands into fists at my side to keep them still as I saw Jessa's twisted body on the floor, a tray of dishware and food splattered across the floor, and her once warm eyes staring coldly into space.

Thalaj stood on the far side, and as soon as he caught sight of me, the temperature in the room dropped sharply. He swore under his breath and circled the body in my direction. "Who let her through?"

When he reached me, I clung to him—all the while keeping my eyes on Jessa and trying to make sense of the scene before me—as he pulled at my shoulders, urging me from the room.

"Mairynne," he whispered in my ear. "I'm very sorry. We'll take care of this. You need not worry—"

I pulled away, swung back with my fist, and pounded it onto his chest. "How dare you believe I wouldn't worry about this? She was my oldest friend, and she's dead. In my rooms! And we have emptied Arashi's guards to come and see to the matter? Couldn't you have handled this more discreetly?"

He looked away then as two guards appeared at the end of my soldier-lined hallway carrying a litter.

Perryn was at their backs. "The healer, Sentei Summergale is preparing space, sir," he said to Thalaj.

My first guard nodded and waved the two with the litter through. "The rest of you, return to your posts." He pulled me to the side so the litter could pass. "We'll take her to the House of Healing. Mayhap Sentei Summergale can determine what has happened."

The guards left, a murmur rising as they made their way out of my chambers and away.

My eyes prickled then, a sense of small relief settling over me . . . confidence that Thalaj and the healer would get the situation under control and provide answers. "Who did this?" I whispered.

"There is no evidence that anyone is responsible."

I clung to him and he held me gently, both of us heedless of the watching guards. I assumed the impropriety seemed appropriate given the matter at hand.

Thalaj continued, "Jessa's mother states she left her alone in your rooms where she was preparing a midday meal for you. When the elder Feathergale returned, she found her daughter as you saw her now. She ran to the guards posted at the keep's entrance who sent word to me. I have only arrived in the last few moments myself. No one has moved her until now."

The extra guards cleared out, and one of the two who had brought the litter poked his head out from the kitchen. "My lady, may we use your blanket?"

"I'll get it," a strained voice called from the door. Mother Feathergale scurried into the room, wiping the tears from under her eyes.

I went to her and grasped her arms, turning her to me. "You just found your daughter. You should take some time." Nadia had followed her inside, and I waved her over. "Mother Feathergale, you do not have to tend to me in your own time of need. We will find another."

Her lip quivered. "No, Lady Mairynne. You and your sisters are as much daughters to me as my own Jess—Jessamynne." She covered her mouth with a fist and paused. A minute or more passed, but when recovered, she continued, "And I'd worry about you the entire time. I cannot promise I'll not weep from time to time, but please, allow me this. Caring for you and your rooms is all I know."

◇◇◇◇◇◇◇◇◇◇◇◇◇◇◇◇◇◇◇◇◇◇◇◇◇◇◇◇◇◇◇◇

MY FAMILY GATHERED AT the pyre fields. The day before, intricate mandalas of brightly colored sand had covered the ground, designs meant to offer my mother up to the Gods so they would guide her safely to her next life. In the natural course of death, the bodies of emperors, empresses, and clergy would be entombed so that while their corporeal presence remained on land, their souls were freed to pass into the heavens and find their eternal homes aside Atun, Otarr, and Selene. Since Kōgō Noralynne had been murdered, the teachings of Atun dictated that she should be offered another life via a grand fire. In the ceremony following the pyre, my mother's ashes had been blended with colorful sands which the acolytes of our Holy Triad shaped into intricate sacred mandalas across the scorched land. Yesterday, when my dear friend Jessa had left this life and we transported her body to the healer in hopes he'd discover the cause of her death, the acolytes had swept my mother's sands. On this day, we gathered for the Giving of the Sands.

Jessa would receive little of this ceremony, only a simple pyre to see her to the next life. I turned from the field, closing my eyes, fighting tears, and now believing she and my mother had been far more fortunate than Father. If he had indeed met his death and hadn't received the rites of mourning through entombment or pyre, he would never meet Atun. He wouldn't walk with Otarr and Selene into his next life, and his soul would never shine in the night's sky. If I accepted his disappearance without the offering of his body through funereal rites, his soul would forever wander the land—lost.

The tragedy of my father's fate twisted my belly, and though I felt within the deepest part of me he still lived, the solution to finding him eluded me.

Today, our people, my people, would come to receive the Holy Sands so they might take home a piece of their empress. My sisters, Nadia, and I would greet each person in turn and hand them a phial. Where they would keep these sands within their homes, I did not know, but our traditions dictated that every one of her subjects had a right to own a token of remembrance of their ruler, my mother.

Along the north side of the square field, I walked the length of the platform, past thousands of tiny glass phials corked and arranged in neat rows, to meet my sisters. Though Otarr had only risen a quarter of the way into the sky, a trickle of sweat rolled down my back.

Karynne opened her arms to me as I approached and I hugged her.

She whispered in my ear, "I heard of your loss. 'Tis difficult, I'm sure, to be here today. May Selene heal your heart, Sister."

"Thank you," I said simply, then hugged Yasmynne, then Nadia.

Imrythel and Nestryn were also on the podium as my sisters' first advisors. My aunt, not believing herself royalty, had not named a first advisor. Instead, her partner, Corwyn Dawnsgale, stood at her side, offering a warm smile.

Much to Karynne's dismay, I'd arrived alone.

"After today, you must choose an advisor, Mairynne," commanded Karynne, Imrythel at her side and Nestryn at Yasmynne's.

Standing straight and holding my ground, I replied, "Today, of all days, is not the day to worry over first advisors. I have also chosen to defer selection of advisors for my council for a time. Do you wish to judge me in that matter as well?" I caught a green light, a glint from Imrythel's hard stare, and locked gazes with her one unveiled eye.

Yasmynne furrowed her brows. "I thought you would have selected Jessa."

"Jessa was a loyal friend, indeed," I replied, my throat tightening as I held eye contact with Karynne's named advisor. I swallowed and asked, "Imrythel, is there aught you wish to say?"

She smiled, and though it seemed in deference, something told me otherwise. Her head slightly tilted, she said, "It is only that the Sandsgales have not been a part of the royal council in the past. We are anxious to serve the Serpentine Throne, Lady Mairynne."

"I see"—but her words felt contrived—"and would you suggest I select someone from your family from the Great Sands near Yōtei? A Storm Sorcerer whom I have never met, mayhap?"

The bells began to ring, snipping the conversation, and any reply she might offer, short. The acolytes of the citadel, servants to Atun, Otarr, and Selene alike, opened the gates into the pyre fields. Reluctantly, I turned my attention.

People, thousands of people dressed in mourning robes, waited in the streets beyond and began to filter inside from the east. They walked the perimeter along the south, then the west, many stopping at some point and calling a tiny gust of wind into a handful of rose petals. The winds showered the petals onto the clean-swept pyre field and represented the people's gifts and well wishes to the fallen in her next life. Others knelt and dropped packages at the edges of the field—an action marking them as either casteless or of a lesser caste who had no powers to call forth and shower petals over where my mother had burned. After their offerings, each Storm Sorcerer walked the northern side and received his or her phial from one of the family before returning to the eastern gates. Tradition restricted the casteless and lower castes from standing upon the family's podium, so they accepted a phial from one of the clergy members instead.

A pause in the steady stream of people came after some time, and Imrythel took the opportunity to further her case. "Your father, Tennō Atheryn, only selected from the families at Stormskeep. I'd beg you to consider those from outside the city's walls. If not as your first advisor, at least for one to sit on your private council."

I held my tongue, not wanting to mar the sanctity of one of our most sacred rituals.

Karynne supported her advisor. "Expanding your council to include more of the Nantai people would be Mother's wish, do you not agree?"

I glared at my sister but forced a smile as the next group of people approached. Retrieving a handful of phials from the table, I distributed them. An older man, stooped and limping, came forward and accepted the last phial in my hand. He then offered me his own hand to shake. When I accepted, his skin felt paper-thin, but the strength with which he gripped perpetuated the dichotomy. And his eyes held a youth at odds with his bent posture. They were dark gray, and within his right pupil there was a white fleck, a malformation of sorts. He smiled warmly, and I felt that the heavy robes and my sweating under Otarr's gaze were a price well paid. "May Atun watch over you, kind sir," I said, attempting to bring myself back to center.

His voice hale and an octave higher than I would have imagined and somewhat forced through the nose, he replied, "Many, many thanks, Lady Mairynne Evangale. May Otarr fill your days with joy, Selene guard your soul under her silvery light, and Atun care for your path to the Serpentine Throne."

As he went, I watched him limp away for long minutes until he had passed through the gates and out of sight. My brow felt heavy, and I chewed the inside of my lip as I puzzled over the person.

"Mairynne," Karynne recalled my attention.

I swung my head around and snapped, "What would you have of me, Sister? Things are simply too difficult to make rash decisions at the moment. Would you also advise that I include a Northerngale? An Islandgale from the Vesterisles? Any of our brethren from southern Nantai?"

The others in my family looked on surreptitiously as I debated with my eldest sister and Imrythel, but they continued to tend to their duties. Corwyn, having retreated into the citadel, returned with water to quench our thirsts and stave off the heat for another hour, and the acolytes held off the people while we partook.

Imrythel refused the offer, instead responding, "If that is the will of the future empress, we would find that an equal and appropriate measure." Her words stung as if she were trying to manipulate me through deference.

I answered, "Never before has an emperor or empress demanded one of our people leave their clan to sit in an advisory council. It is why we conduct the true business of the realm at the High Cloud Court in regular cycles. What makes us important enough to make demands that would separate families for longer periods?" I sighed and more quietly said, "I am uncertain why I would begin such a tradition."

"Sister," Karynne admonished. Her defense of her first advisor rang true and steady when she continued more quietly, "Imrythel only means to include the more nomadic families."

I raised my brows to her, offended that she'd stand by someone who didn't belong to our family on such a day, heavy in the heart that she wouldn't hold more compassion for all I'd just been through. My dismay came out as an accusation toward her too. "Ah, so would you also recommend that we include a representative from the Tsinti?"

I had grown weary of the conversation, and my words were shorter than necessary, intended to stop her suggestions. I knew this wasn't her implication. The Tsinti were nomads who lived apart from the people by choice. They were us, but not. They chose to eschew our traditions in favor of roaming the lands hidden under tsym.

As my ire continued to build, I pressed my rebuttal harder. "And what of a Cloud Courtier? A Frost Fighter or Fire Forger? Maybe a Stone Singer and an Underhill Dweller? And let us not forsake the Small Folk or the casteless." Heat kindled inside as I rattled off every group of our people that came to mind until Nadia placed a hand on my arm.

She rested the other on Karynne's. "This is a conversation for another time."

Lifting my chin, I spat, "It most certainly is. We should return to our people and the Giving of the Sands." Quieter, I added with chagrin, "Thank you, Aunt Nadia."

"Mairynne," Karynne started.

I whirled on her but felt intent on bringing the conversation to an end. "My dear sister, I have duly noted your requests, but our aunt speaks true. We are spoiling this rite for us and for our people. The Rite of Release will follow in a week's time. I have until the day after when I am to host an audience at the High Cloud Court to address such matters. Today, let us honor our traditions."

My speech worked as desired and silenced the topic. From then on, we went about the rite in companionable silence, holding light and idle conversation throughout. Mother Feathergale, her eyes still swollen from her abundance of tears shed, brought a late afternoon meal for the family and the Triad called a pause so we might dine.

Later, as the sun began to set, the last of the people trickled through. Edamyn approached when all had passed to let us know that they were shutting the gates and the acolytes would begin cleaning. Over the quieter course of the later hours, I'd thought more and more of the need to find my father. I turned to my eldest sister. "Karynne, have you given thought to the party we'll send in search of Father?"

Both she and Yasmynne gaped, eyes wide and jaws working but failing to produce words. I hadn't expected otherwise, but like they both had their own agendas, I had need to pursue my own. "Karynne, I've asked Yasmynne to plan for the ascension ceremonies. Whilst I am considering my advisory council and first advisor, I'd like you to take charge of this matter and put out a call for a party who will accept such a duty and search the lands for Tennō Atheryn."

Karynne closed her mouth and hesitated, then curtsied. I did believe I'd succeeded in shocking my eldest, most poised sister into submission, if only for a time. She bowed, then turned toward the citadel to make her exit.

It was progress.

Imrythel dipped her head and joined my sister.

I turned to Nadia, who said, "You've recovered well, my niece." She chuckled as she looked after them. Then she took my arm and pulled me in the direction of the castle; Corwyn walked at her side. As we went, she asked, "I may have missed him, but did Thalaj come through today?"

Four

A Family Meal

MY ATTENTION SHOULD HAVE BEEN on Stormskeep's annals. I should have been continuing my search for a way to avoid ascension as I still felt too young, too naïve, and too broken to assume the position. Yet my eyes had grown tired of reading scripts in the library's dim light. I needed to be outside, to feel the fresh air, and to be able to call a cyclone to life if I wished, and to work out my frustration over losing my childhood friend.

True, there existed no space in Stormskeep large enough for a storm as grand as I longed to call. I settled for the open sanctuary at the citadel where the balconies curved around and offered views of Sundai Falls, the castle itself, and an expansive park a level down the mountainside.

I paced.

Fondling the tokens I kept on a chain close to my heart—one cold and one hot, one from my mother and one from my father—I walked back and forth along the railing. Worry over what seemed would be my fate whether I wished it or not gnawed at me.

Tasmynne, servant of the goddess Selene, approached. "Lady Mairynne, the acolytes have brought a tray of fruit and cheese. Is there aught that I may do for you? Something to ease your broken heart, perhaps?" Her eyes held all the benevolence of the Gods but little in the way of solution.

With a sigh, I stopped and gathered her hands in my own. "I cannot think of anything you may do to change my course. You are not at liberty to leave this place and search for Father any more than I am. Though I appreciate the sentiment."

When she departed, I leaned onto the railing overlooking the open field below. Stormskeep's guards trained. Face after soldier's face paired off in combat, each wielding a unique weapon. When my gaze traveled to the far end, I spied the very person I longed to see.

Thalaj.

No other soldier in the Arashi guard moved in the same manner, a style he'd perfected during his time with the Unseen, using weapons others had always failed to master. I watched him work dual blades against his opponent. The short, curved scimitynes reflected Otarr's light as Thalaj executed twists, slashes, and blocks, the blades seemingly an extension of the person himself. But clearly, he went easier on his opponent than his skill would allow. He made a final parry with the curved blades crossed over his head, they parted and bowed to each other, then he sheathed his curved daggers. Mayhap he felt that I watched because he turned and lifted his face to where I stood. Across long space, we connected with our eyes alone until he gave a single nod, said a few words to his sparring mate, and strode off the field.

The other soldiers continued to spar, and I moved away from the railing and back several times in my course of pacing, each time scanning those sparring to see if he'd returned to the field. Mayhap an hour had passed when a cool breeze preceded his silent arrival at my side, a whisper that let me know he approached.

I could scarcely contain the urge to ask what his network may have learned, so by way of greeting, I asked, "What news?" as I hurried toward him, wondering of both Jessa and the errand I'd sent him upon regarding Father.

He stopped, lowering his eyes and answered, "Sentei Summergale cannot find cause for your servant's death. The attendants have taken Jessamynne Feathergale's body to the common pyre fields."

My heart dove at the news of my friend. "When do they plan the pyre?"

"Tomorrow."

I nodded. "I'll be there."

"Regarding the other matter, there is hope," he said.

As if lifted then by the wind, my soul soared. With news of hope, I felt lighter in my mourning robes than I had since Father's sudden disappearance. I laid a hand on my guard's arm and smiled. My next words tumbled forward, "Wonderful to hear. Whatever knowledge you have gained will aide in the plight. Will you share the news? I've asked Karynne to gather a party to begin the search."

Thalaj's expression turned to stone.

I searched his face. "You disagree with my choice to arrange the search party?"

"You will be my empress. I am not at liberty to disagree," he answered, slipping from under my touch.

Scoffing at the propriety, I snapped, "That I will become empress—against all I desire—holds no power over your right to agree or disagree."

"That is not the common opinion, Mairynne." His temper and tone remained even, no hint of accusation entering his words, only fact.

I lost a bit of fuel as I said, "Well, it is mine."

Lips pressed tightly together, he gave a small, unconvincing nod. "I'll speak with your sister as you wish. I do have some thoughts on who might be a wise choice to go in search of Tennō Atheryn."

This course of conversation seemed sound enough as I sorely wanted to know what he'd learned from his shadowy spies. "Will you tell me the details?" As his ruler, I had the right to ask or even demand the information, yet I did so with caution, aware that he kept the secrets of the Unseen Guild close to his chest.

The ask didn't seem to offend, and he answered easily, "My sources said we should approach the Tsinti."

The mention of the notorious nomadic people, the Nantai wanderers of the grasslands, shocked me back into pacing. He watched with his classic stone-jawed stoicism as I processed all that this might mean. At length, I returned to him with arms folded across my chest. "What you say is impossible. No one finds the Tsinti. They are the ones who find the people they wish."

"Your concerns are well noted, Lady Mairynne. Even in my network, there are no known ways to find the Tsinti when they cast tsym over their caravans. Though the information still offers some slight hope." He clasped his hands behind his back, a soldier's restful position.

I clenched my teeth, released, and said, "That is not what I'd call hope." Any optimism faded fast as I looked away, my vision blurring behind angry tears. This wasn't how a leader should behave, certainly not the demeanor of an empress. I cursed the tears that presently revealed little more than my youth.

"Mairynne," Thalaj said softly and stepped close enough that I felt his cool presence again. "Come here." He wouldn't take me into his arms without my consent.

Understanding that the command reflected more invitation than demand, I went, heedless of propriety. And once in his arms, my tears flowed.

Soothingly, he said, "Crying over your father and after you lost a friend of many years does not make you weak, and yes, hope does remain."

I chuckled at that. Even though he was a guard and considered beneath my stature, he knew me better than most. I pulled away, swept my hands under my eyes, and asked, "How? How is it possible to find these hidden people?"

"There are rumors of a totem held by the Small Folk of Umbra within the Evernight Marshes. Rumor holds that this trinket has the power to allow its holder to see through a Tsinti tsym."

I gasped, recalling the story Nadia had shared of Karynne and the rumors of the Small Folk. "Do we have anyone who can navigate the marshes and withstand whatever dangers they pose? I worry about assigning someone unfamiliar with such a place to the search party."

A thought he clearly didn't wish to voice pulled his gaze from mine.

"Thalaj?" I asked, ducking to regain eye contact. "What are you considering?"

"I know of no other person who has entered and returned from the marshes, aside from me."

Pinching the bridge of my nose in suspicion of another dead end, I asked, "So, if there is no one, what do you suggest instead?"

He made no reply.

I inhaled sharply, my voice just as sharp as I pressed, "What are you suggesting, Thalaj?"

If he felt an urge to flinch away from my appalled question, I'd have never known. Instead, his words remained level. "I think you know the answer to that question."

"No," I commanded. "There must be another way. I cannot be without you to lead my guard." But there was so much more twisting around in my mind. *I cannot ask you to face this danger. And I cannot be without the hope for us,* I didn't say. Weaker then, I questioned, "I've lost so much already, and now you'd leave me too?"

A glimmer flashed in his dark, slanted eyes, but after examining my face, he reapplied his solemn mask. "I have already spoken with Tarlyn. He will assume leadership of the guard in my stead. I'd trust him with my life, and you can rest easy doing the same." He swallowed, then added, "It may also do us some good to be apart."

"For what reason would separation do us good?"

"Again, I believe you ask for answers you already know." Thalaj spoke truly, yet I disagreed.

Through gritted teeth, I said, "I want to hear you say it."

"My blood is impure, and for us to be together would contaminate you. The Nantai people are slow to change, and I fear they would not tolerate such a declaration, even from their empress. It flies in the face of the caste system. By blood, I am as much Frost Fighter of the fourth caste as I am Storm Sorcerer." He paused and sighed. "Mairynne, I feel us growing closer. I sense your desire to deepen that, but I"—he shook his head—"I just can't."

Ill within my very core, I spun from him and resumed the path I'd been pacing. To further my dismay, I did understand the reason in Thalaj's logic, or mayhap I suspected it ran deeper. And that he wouldn't share hurt even more. When I'd exhausted my immediate frustration, I sat on the kneeler at Selene's altar, face lifted toward the sky as if to ask why, and said, "Well and so," defeat resounding in the small customary acceptance.

It was as much as I could muster.

Thalaj came to me, near enough that I felt a chill but taking care not to touch. "I will update you after I speak with Lady Karynne." He turned both my hands upward and placed a kiss on each palm—a symbol of servitude to a ruler of the people. He then bowed to me and left.

I cried.

And afterward, while upon that kneeler, long hours passed in stillness—so many that night had transpired by the time I gathered my wits and stood. Anger constricted around my chest, more so than the heavy belting, and I'd come to a decision there at Selene's altar. And it was a plain one. I had to find a way to break free of all these barriers and make the things I desired happen.

I went to Nadia's cottage, still within the castle's grounds but apart from the main keep and the wings where the royal family resided. Gifted to her by my mother who wanted her twin close, it stood inside a swath of greenery and flowers. When I knocked, Corwyn answered wearing his evening's attire and a mask of concern. I breezed past him without greeting and into the sitting room where my aunt lounged.

"Nadia," I said urgently. "Tomorrow. We must figure out a way to change the course of things. Time is running out, and I won't become empress. I cannot. I am not ready. The only option is to find my father and restore his reign, but we must find something in the annals that lawfully allows for this."

Nadia stood, a sheath dress flowing around her long limbs as she came to me. She and my late mother both stood a head taller than me. My sister Karynne had their height. Yasmynne favored the women of my father's blood, and I fell somewhere in between. I wished for height as it seemed to give Karynne a confidence that I longed to possess but did not.

"Dear Mairynne, we are looking as fast as we can. Why has it become so urgent this evening?" my aunt asked.

I hung my head. "Thalaj wants to lead the party we will send in search of Father. They must travel into the Evernight."

Nadia sighed and exchanged a knowing look with Corwyn. She placed an arm around my shoulders, guiding me gently in the direction of her long sofa. We sat.

"Maybe we should go tonight," I said, urgency coursing through my blood. "We still have four ages of royal decrees to read. How are we ever going to get through all that and find a lawful solution before I must go through ascension?"

Corwyn cleared his throat. "If I may, Lady Mairynne?" He waited until I nodded for him to continue, then said, "My cousin, Solarynne supports your plight. I believe she showed as much at your council meeting. She's aged and wise and may be able to offer some advice if you would allow me to beg her help."

Though I remained uncertain how she might be able to help, the thought was still an unexpected delight. "Of course, Corwyn," I said. "I can use all the willing help available."

Nadia grabbed and squeezed my hand. "We'll find an answer tomorrow; I feel it."

I turned to my aunt. "We must. I cannot shake the feeling that Father lives, and I intend to have him returned to Arashi and Stormskeep so he may resume his rightful position upon the Serpentine Throne." I stood. "And somehow, someway, I intend to accompany Thalaj on the journey to bring him back."

◇◇◇◇◇◇◇◇◇◇◇◇◇◇◇◇◇◇◇◇◇◇◇◇◇

I'D GROWN SLEEPY AT Nadia's cottage and stayed in her guest rooms for the night. The following morning, Corwyn left us at dawn, and my aunt's housemaid Larynne prepared plates of fruit and bread and served barley tea at its side. After Nadia and I had broken our fast, Solarynne Dawnsgale arrived on the patio at Corwyn's side on a gust of wind. Her hair settled over one shoulder, the cream-colored waves unexpectedly tame. She came to me with a grin and one hand forward. I accepted, my hand open to the sky, and she laid a kiss upon my palm.

As she raised her head and ice-clear eyes found mine, she said, "I began to believe you wouldn't ask for help, young one. Imagine my delight to receive my dear brother just as Otarr arrived this morning."

"Thank you for coming, Solarynne." I'd redressed that morning with the help of Larynne, my aunt's handmaiden.

"Corwyn," she continued, "was right to suggest you seek my help. I've studied our royal histories for many years, and your father's royal council was the third on which I've served." She looked beyond me.

Nadia circled from behind our breakfast table and gave Solarynne a hug and a kiss on the cheek.

Solarynne asked, "Have you finished your morning meal?"

Nadia answered, "We have. We were visiting whilst we awaited your arrival."

"Very well. Shall we go to the royal library and begin?" The suggestion erased a decade from her age.

As we left Nadia's small garden home and entered the halls of stone, Solarynne continued, "There was an empress in the Second Age, Kōgō Phelyse. The second ruler of that age, I believe. She may be our best option to find your solution, though she was quite prolific."

At the juncture of two halls, we turned right toward the library that lay deeper within the mountain, cooler, dryer, and darker than other areas of the castle; thus to better preserve the Nantai records. We passed two young attendants who moved to the side, showing deference to our royal station. I slowed and bade them each good morning, the action drawing confused and awestruck looks between the two.

With a curtsy, the girl replied, "Good day to you, Lady Mairynne."

The boy bowed. "And may the Triad watch over you."

"And you as well." I smiled warmly to them both and continued on my path. It confounded me why people I'd spoken easily with not more than two moons before felt the sudden need for such extreme propriety. Yes, I expected the reaction. Yet it still rankled. The fact I was now heir apparent didn't change who I was in my heart.

From behind I heard, "Mairynne!"

I turned to find my sister Karynne and Imrythel moving with windswept speed toward the four of us.

"Where have you been? I went to your chambers both last night and this morning but found them empty." My sister wrapped me into her long arms. "We were worried."

Over her shoulder, Imrythel stood stoically, almost judging, watching. When released, I asked, "We?"

Karynne made a small sound but didn't answer directly.

Nadia stepped closer. "Good morning, Karynne. Mairynne, we'll get started inside." And with the few words, she, Corwyn, and Solarynne continued down the hallway and disappeared through the library's door at the end.

"Did you have reason to meet with me, Sister?" I asked.

Softly she said, "I bring some news you might find troubling. Gensui Northerngale has volunteered to lead Father's search party."

"I am aware. We spoke about it yesterday." I lifted my chin higher, working to keep my manner even-keeled.

"Ah, I see."

Clearly, my first guard hadn't been as transparent with my dear sister as he had with me about the reasonings and his intent. It gave me some solace, but not enough. "Have you gathered others? Or did he suggest others? And when do they propose to depart?"

I glanced again past my sister to the green-eyed beauty who accompanied her at seemingly all times lately. Something seemed different about Imrythel this morning, but I couldn't place it. Were the angles of her face a bit longer? Maybe she'd lost some weight. It would be understandable for one spending so much time with my sister.

Karynne answered, "The party won't leave before the conclusion of the mourning period.

I felt of different minds—relieved to have more time, devastated that a longer wait remained, and concerned whether Thalaj would find answers I needed in time. Trying to keep sincerity in my voice, I said, "Wonderful. And the others?"

"Imrythel and I will be working on finalizing those details today. May we share evening meal? I'll ask Yasmynne to join us."

Considering her request, I walked through the remainder of my day in my mind. After research here at the royal library, I needed to attend the common pyre grounds with Mother Feathergale. The last thing I wanted after that was to be in a position where I had to play politics.

I countered, "I'd like to dine with family tonight. Alone." I looked meaningfully to my sister's advisor, the black lace blocking half of any emotion she might betray through her piercing eyes. "Send word to Yasmynne, and I'll have Mother Feathergale and her new assistant prepare a table in my chambers."

An objection started within my sister's throat but died quickly. "Of course."

"I'll see you in the evening, Karynne." I turned and left my sister and her first advisor standing in the hall. Slowly, I expelled a breath along with the tension I'd held within my lungs.

Inside the library, the attendant greeted me in much the same manner as the young boy and girl in the hall and pointed me to the small room where Solarynne, Corwyn, and Nadia had already started in on a stack of annals from the Fifth Age.

Nodding into her book as she read, Solarynne looked up as I took my seat. "I believe we've found your answer."

◇◇◇◇◇◇◇◇◇◇◇◇◇◇◇◇◇◇◇◇◇◇◇◇◇◇◇◇◇◇◇◇◇

A COMMONER'S FUNERAL CARRIED far less ritual than one from the royal house. The family and close friends gathered and placed flowers around the body upon the pyre bed, then stood back. An acolyte of Atun dripped a drop of blessed water onto Jessa's lips. Selene's representative covered my friend's body with a white shroud to keep out the impure spirits, then Otarr's priest placed a knife upon her chest to drive away the evil as her soul lifted from the flame and went in search of her next life.

In the closing measure, the family and friends each lifted a torch from a nearby fire and placed it under the pyre bed. We moved away and watched in silence.

I wrapped an arm around Mother Feathergale's shoulders, and we cried silently. I prayed to the Holy Triad that Jessamynne's soul would be reborn among our people and find a happier end in her next life.

◇◇◇◇◇◇◇◇◇◇◇◇◇◇◇◇◇◇◇◇◇◇◇◇◇◇◇◇◇◇◇◇◇

PREPARATIONS FOR EVENING MEAL were well under way when Mother Feathergale and I returned to my chambers. Roasted fowl scented the air, and my mouth watered. I moved to my bed chamber and released the braids from my hair as my attendant took charge.

When I entered my main chamber, the new assistant to Mother Feathergale, a young Storm Sorcerer by the name of Dorynne, was putting the final touches on the table.

She curtsied when she caught me watching. "Lady Mairynne," she said, and her cheeks pinkened.

I smiled. "Continue with your business, Dorynne."

I wondered about the actual preparation of the food. In all my days, someone else had always prepared my meals, and it struck me now as a skill I might soon wish to have. Though I hadn't asked for the comforts royalty offered, it had been what I was born to as the daughter of the Nantai emperor and empress. I also wondered if my sisters had ever had occasion to roast a bird or bake a vegetable tart.

Mother Feathergale offered me warm glances as she worked but remained mostly silent while tending to her duty. We'd shared another sad day over her daughter and my friend, and my heart ached for her as much as it did in the absence of Jessa herself.

Mother Feathergale filled the goblets, and as she poured, I asked, "Is it difficult?"

She didn't look away from her task as she replied, "I'm sorry, dear. Is what difficult?"

"Making a meal. Cooking, I imagine."

Her brows furrowed as she regarded me. When she finished pouring the fourth and final cup, she stopped and leaned heartily onto the back of a chair with one elbow. "It's like anything else, in truth. If you've learned the ways, it's a straightforward task. Why do you worry over such menial things?"

"No reason to mention." I shook my head. "Naught but curiosity."

Quick rapping sounded on my door, and Dorynne skipped over to answer.

All three of my guests had arrived together. Before I went to welcome Nadia and my sisters, Mother Feathergale told me they'd be available in the serving room down the hall should we need anything else as we dined. She gave me a light hug and ushered Dorynne from the room.

"It smells fantastic," said Yasmynne.

Karynne came to me and dropped a light kiss on my forehead. "Yes, Mairynne, you've outdone yourself."

"The credit goes to my attendants. I merely watched as they prepared the table." I exchanged a smile with Nadia. "To have you all here tonight warms my heart. It's nice to be alone with my family. Come. Let us eat."

The earthy vegetable tarts were a delight, flaky crust melting on my tongue. Whatever ingredients went into the pastries outdid the juicy meat of the bird, but the two in combination made for a lovely flavor. I'd been hungrier than I'd known and said little as I took my fill.

When done, I turned to Yasmynne at my left. "How have you been, Sister?"

"I'm doing as well as can be expected. Nestryn has been a comfort." She nearly exploded from her seat as she added, "He plans to ask for Tsanseri's blessing whilst we're at the High Cloud Court for your ascension."

I sipped from my drink, wishing that I could be happier for my sister. "It does seem that the two of you have grown even closer since Father disappeared." I put on a smile, but as I'd never been one to mask my thoughts, my tone carried notes of all the worry and pressure I'd been facing.

Yasmynne shifted in her seat, her eyes flicking between us all.

"There's naught to worry over. In truth, I envy you and Nadia at having a partner to whom you may turn for consolation." I fidgeted with the knife at my plate's edge.

Everyone sat in silence until I changed the conversation's direction. "Anyway, since you mentioned the ascension, tell me. Are the plans nearing completion?"

"They are. We've sent invitations to the gnobles from each caste, and I received word from the Stone Singers earlier today that your crown is almost complete. I expect your first journal to arrive at the citadel from the Underhills tomorrow, just in time for the Triad to bless it before we depart for the High Cloud Court."

She had done her job well even though her motives lay elsewhere. At heart, she desired to gain an audience with Tsanseri, the Lady of Masks and the comtesse who regularly heard petitions in matters of courtly love. As for Karynne, her task had been closer to my heart's desire, and I turned to my right, giving my attention to her.

Without my asking, she began, "About Father's search party, Thalaj and I have arrived at a solid plan."

I had yet to share with my sisters that I'd only be assuming the leadership of our people on a temporary basis. Likewise, my ultimate intentions remained my own, so I hung on Karynne's every word, trying to weave together the final threads in my strategy.

She went on, "After we return from court, Thalaj will lead a team of only four to the marshes. Solarynne and Lukos have each named a junior member of their families who have agreed to make the journey, and the gensui has chosen someone from the guard, apparently a tracker he trusts implicitly."

A shadow of confusion passed over Karynne's face, but she dismissed whatever it had been with a roll of her shoulder and continued, "I'm uncertain why Thalaj believes that visiting the people of Umbra is a key to finding our father, but he insisted. As he has given our family only reasons to trust his judgment, I will defer and give him the room to guide the journey as he feels necessary."

Pressing my lips together, I nodded my satisfaction. I knew his reasons, but I knew him, too, and he likely had an ulterior reason or motivation to keep his information quiet. For my part, I had no desire to violate the trust he'd placed in me by sharing.

"Imrythel has nominated a messenger from the Sandsgale family to travel with the party so we may receive occasional word as to how the mission progresses," Karynne concluded her update.

Across the table, Nadia took the last bite of her tart, chewed, and swallowed. After a drink to wash it down, she said, "A messenger is a wonderful idea, don't you think, Mairynne?"

Our aunt seemed pleased that we were discussing the matter as a family, and though sending word through the messenger's network seemed a risk, I had little argument about the logic. It was a wise measure to ensure those who remained within Stormskeep would gain any significant information without having to wait for a traveling party to return and deliver the news. However, in truth, we didn't know what information they would find, and messengers tended to be voracious gossip mongers. Although I didn't voice concerns, my worry must have been clear in my expression.

Karynne rushed to add, "We will encode the messages. Only the search party will know the contents. A trusted messenger here at Stormskeep will decode it and deliver it to you and the royal advisory council."

She took a drink from her goblet. "Speaking of your council. Have you made your selections?" Karynne's insistence that I nominate my council and first advisor made me itch, but she was merely the loudest voice speaking of the shared expectation.

"I have," I answered easily, knowing that the council would not change as I'd be speaking only the temporary oath under the watchful eyes of Atun, Otarr, and Selene. I sighed. "It seems that everything is ready, despite that we should have been caring for our souls and mourning our mother. I suppose we have a duty to care for the Nantai in the wake of Father's disappearance as well.

"Sisters," I continued, "I thank you for spending this evening at my table. I'll let you go and attend to your own business. Tomorrow, we will release the nymphs, and the day following, we'll travel to the courts. I will ascend to the Serpentine Throne, and Yasmynne will gain a fiancé. Despite our losses, we can celebrate her betrothal."

When I stood, my sisters joined me. Yasmynne thanked me for the kind words, and we exchanged a warm, sisterly embrace.

Karynne kissed both my cheeks and smiled warmly. "You are proving to be wiser than your years, little sister."

Having put on the proper appearances for my sisters, I sighed my relief. My heart felt full in the moment of rare closeness. Maybe, given time, we'd regain some of the bonds we'd had as younglings. It would certainly go a long way to restoring a sense of normalcy, but my father's presence still called to me, and I had to answer that call first. Maybe my search would be fruitless, but at least I would be able to take comfort in the fact that I'd tried. Only then could I take the official oath and make my rule permanent.

As a group, we walked toward the door. After farewells, my sisters parted and I turned to Nadia. "Will you join me for a cordial before you leave?"

"Of course, darling."

"Thank you." I motioned to the room adjacent to the door. "One moment. I'll have Mother Feathergale heat a bottle and bring it to us on the veranda."

I stepped into the room where my attendants awaited and asked Mother Feathergale to prepare the cordials, then Nadia and I went to my small outdoor seating area where we could enjoy the sounds of falling water. A few minutes later, my newest attendant, Dorynne, appeared with two glasses of warmed fire-flower wine and placed them on the small table between our chairs.

"Thank you, Dorynne," I said.

She smiled and made her retreat.

Selene had assumed her night's watch in the skies, and with her came a chill. I lifted the glass and held it between my palms. Nadia watched me skeptically as she retrieved her own cordial. After the first sip, she let out a little *aah*. "Mairynne, why didn't you tell them you planned to take Morwyn's oath?"

"I'm not certain." I drank my warm and spicy red wine, then looked at her with a brow raised and a smirk. "Mayhap I am young, Nadia, but my father named me as his successor for a purpose. I hope you, unlike my sisters, don't believe tradition or expectation will so easily sway my mind."

She flashed a knowing smile. "As your mother always said, you have a will unlike any other."

The slightly reclined chair cradled me as I sank backward allowing the fiery wine to warm me from the inside out. Eyes closed, I enjoyed the sounds of Stormskeep and peace so easily found on this balcony overlooking the castle grounds, the residences, and markets below, and the walls that protected my people. With Nadia at my side, it felt as if some of my tension departed. I glanced over to see she had also found some ease or comfort in the quietness of twilight while sipping warmed ruby wine.

She rolled her head toward me and said, "The business with Thalaj and the search party still troubles you."

My aunt read me true. I had no desire for Thalaj to leave Stormskeep or for him to be away from me for however long the search might last, but his logic remained sound. The leader of the guard, with his time spent in the Unseen Guild, had the best and most unique qualifications over any other I could name.

As if they knew my thoughts, the tokens around my neck changed suddenly; a hot pulse flared against my chest. I reached for them. Certainly, that they'd come to me was a calling, and I felt equally sure that the sudden change was a further signal of that calling.

I would go. I had no idea how I'd convince Thalaj, and I knew the journey wouldn't be easy. Nevertheless, I would go.

Nadia spoke, pulling me from afar, "Maybe you should put away those reminders, Mairynne."

I shook my head, the twilit night coming back into focus. "The tokens trouble me, that is true, but how can I ignore them?" I searched her face, so like my mother's, for an answer she didn't have.

"You're about to accept a heavy duty, even if it's only a temporary one, to the Nantai people. Do not allow the past to distract you. You must trust that if King Atheryn lives, Thalaj will see him returned."

The ruby wine began to cool, and I finished what remained. Sitting forward, I gave her a warm smile. "It pleases me we've found a way to connect again, dear Aunt. I ask you though, is that what you would do if you were in my position? Sit by and wait."

"That isn't a choice I will ever face." She looked into her wine, finished it, and turned back to me. "So unfortunately, I cannot say."

Dorynne came from my rooms to retrieve the glasses and asked if there was anything else she could bring. As I watched her leave with empty goblets, I said, "I must choose a first advisor. My sisters once thought me naïve enough to choose Jessa."

Nadia pursed her lips, then asked, "Would it have been so bad? She was loyal and cared for you a great deal."

"Jessamyne Feathergale was my oldest and dearest friend. In the deepest part of her heart and much like her mother, she was little more than the sweetest of caregivers. She needed to grow up and find a partner to keep her safe, someone for her to nurture and give her younglings of her own to raise. She might have attended to my domestic needs for the remainder of her days and mine, but she would have never had the wisdom to offer advice on how I might best serve the Nantai people as their empress.

"And now someone has stolen the rest from her as well." I swallowed past a lump in my throat.

After some silent contemplation, Nadia suggested, "Solarynne would be a sensible selection."

"Ah, yes. She would." I answered. "For that matter, Lukos Thundergale would likely offer some prudent guidance for a young empress. However, I do not wish to unwittingly steal from my father's council. And I believe I need to add supporters of my interests. Then we have Karynne and Imrythel who suggested I choose a Sandsgale." I scoffed and looked over my shoulder.

Inside, behind where Nadia and I lounged, Dorynne and Mother Feathergale cleared the remnants of our evening's meal, the sounds of stacking dishes punctuating the ongoing notes of the Falls. I watched my aunt intently as gloaming turned to night and Selene's moon began to shine. As my mother's twin, Nadia had been around royal proceedings since my father married my mother. Her simple presence with Tennō Atheryn and Kōgō Noralynne, as well as my mother's continued work, had afforded my aunt much knowledge about the Nantai people, as well as the Small Folk. I leaned closer and scrutinized her closely. "As I have my own duty, I also have a duty to bestow upon you, dear Aunt."

Five

Into the High Cloud Court

THE SIXTIETH DAY OF MOURNING passed with my family standing on the fields that had hosted Kōgō Noralynne's funeral pyre and releasing the matured nymphs into the sky. All of Arashi gathered into the courtyard of Stormskeep, on the side closest to the fields. So many people had gathered, they had spilled out of the castle gates and filled the surrounding streets as they waited and watched. The cloud of slender nymphs rose, the nymphs fully transformed, lifting with their delicate iridescent wings to fill the sky and begin their journey into their next life. The final rite symbolized my mother's passing into her next life. Had she come to death naturally, the rite would have celebrated her life and released her into the empire beyond to take her rightful place with the Gods. Alas, with her life curtailed early, she would be reborn and walk amongst the Nantai people once again—or so was our belief.

The people drank and danced in the streets well into the dark hours, and on the morning after, we stored away our mourning clothes and looked toward happier times. For me, albeit sweet, the day also felt bitter. I'd endured enough mourning for a lifetime, but I had no time to grieve over the loss of Jessa as it was time to turn toward my other dilemma: rising to serve our people as political tradition demanded or following my heart and leaving the jewel city of Arashi behind in search of why the stones about my neck sang to me. Overnight, the High Cloud Court had moved into the sky above Stormskeep, and government affairs would dominate my immediate days ahead.

On the uppermost roof of Stormskeep Castle, alongside my father's counselors, my sisters and their first advisors, the Triad, Thalaj, and a few of his selected guardsmen, I awaited the arrival of the Cloud Courtiers to escort us into court. As the stairs coming down from the cloud formed in slow motion, I searched for Nadia and Corwyn, determined not to ascend into the courts without my first advisor at my side.

Karynne and Imrythel stood close, offering advice on how to handle myself while at the High Cloud Court.

"You should show only strength at all times," said Imrythel, an airy or haughty note to her words.

"Cloud Courtiers, illusionists that they are, will play games of deception," added Karynne.

Having been too young to attend the courts the last time my father had gone, I entered new territory that day along with having to accept the mantle of the people. I looked from my eldest sister to Yasmynne, who gave me a smile charged with excitement, then on to Thalaj. He stood to the side, stone-faced. Something about his at-ease manner told me he was anything but easy with this situation. To him, I dipped my head, acknowledging his tightly held concern, and I looked across the roof again for Nadia.

The billowing clouds met the roof's surface, and a group of eight courtiers descended two at a time, their shoulders held back and heads high, each more striking than the one before, yet all somehow alike. They, too, seemed to waft and curl and billow as they walked, and there were no features by which I could discern who might be who.

Imrythel leaned close to my ear and in her husky voice whispered, "The only way you will know a Cloud Courtier is by the emblem they wear on their shoulders. Each is unique, so as they introduce themselves, take note of their symbols."

Karynne said into my other ear, "Never forget, you are their empress, receiving your subjects. If you slip, they will take advantage."

The Cloud Courtier caste's opportunistic nature I felt well prepared to handle, but the resentment at my sister's need to constantly remind me of such things crawled beneath my skin. Her anger that Father had named me successor bled through in the sharp commands she disguised as advice. This situation weighed upon me, but as well as I knew the nature of the Cloud Courtiers, I knew Karynne's nature even better. Confronting her on that manner would do little to help, and in truth she might see it as an insult and retreat from our sisterhood all together. In this time, I couldn't afford to chase away someone who stood at my side in spite of her own umbrage.

The first two Cloud Courtiers approached, mist swirling at their feet. Their skin glimmered as if someone had dusted it with a metallic powder, their lashes reminding me of branches after a snowstorm. The first one bowed in front of me. "A glorious morn to you and yours, my lady Mairynne Evangale. I am Cirro-Vior and my companion is Alto-Raal. I remember you as a youngling, and you have grown well into the Evangale charm."

Intrigued, I regarded the courtier, taking note of the crescent moon shape on the shoulder. Much must have shown on my face, because with the flourish of a hand, the image before me changed. I looked upon the visage of a boy, one whom I remembered, a boy I'd considered a friend and who visited our castle from time to time when I'd been a child. "Viordyn?" I asked.

His hand reversed the flourish and he returned to the glittering genderless apparition who'd been there before. "The one and only, Lady Mairynne," answered Cirro-Vior. "I have grown and gained my majority as have you. Are you and your council ready to ascend?"

My chest tightened at the word; the double meaning heavy on my soul. Scanning the rooftop again and not finding my aunt, I said, "We are not. I await one more. You will forgive the delay." I motioned to the clergy, beckoning.

Tasmynne answered my call, leaning in as I asked her to send an acolyte in search of my aunt.

In delicate silence, we waited.

When Nadia finally appeared, she didn't wear clothing appropriate for court. She hadn't combed her hair, and deep purple circles shadowed her eyes. She rushed over and threw her arms around me. "Mairynne, I am so very sorry." Her voice sounded broken and quivering in my ear.

When she pulled back, I could see tears threatening to overflow. She glanced furtively at the people who surrounded her, and her throat worked, but whatever had her so worked up had also stolen her words.

Solarynne Dawnsgale stepped forward from where the counselors stood and placed a gentle hand on my aunt's back. "What is it, Nadia? Will you tell us what has happened?"

Nadia shook her head and scrubbed at her face as the tears fell. When she collected herself enough to speak, she said, "It's Corwyn. He's very ill. He's been sick all night and is resting now. I have to get back. I'm sorry, Mairynne, but I cannot attend with you today."

"Nadia, it will be fine," I said, but wondered exactly how it would.

Solarynne said, "I'll come with you to care for him."

"No." My voice cracked on the harsh word, but I'd found my command. I hadn't intended to seem cold, but I had need of my supporters. "I, too, am sorry, Nadia. You may return to your partner, but I need Solarynne at my side. Tasmynne, you will send an acolyte to fetch the physicians and tend to Corwyn until we return." I raised my voice then, looking around at the stunned faces of Storm Sorcerers and Cloud Courtiers alike. "Everyone else will continue to the High Cloud Court as planned."

"Yes, Lady Mairynne." Tasmynne motioned over a young man and set him to the errand.

Solarynne turned a hard look to me as I made these decrees, but her eyes shone with her comprehension. She would attend to the duties she'd accepted by being part of the royal council.

I gave a single nod and hugged my aunt. "Go. See to your companion, and I'll do what I can here."

When she had departed, Lukos Thundergale stepped forward. "Lady Mairynne, if you'll allow, I can act as your first advisor for the purposes of ascension."

Solarynne's eyes dodged mine. Seeing further that she felt herself not up to the task, I accepted Lukos's offer and worked to suppress my worry over Corwyn—someone who'd been a part of my life for enough years that I considered him family, an uncle. I'd be just in deferring the meetings in light of an ill family member, but my presence there wouldn't help. Responsibility for Corwyn's recovery rested with our physicians.

With a deep breath and false confidence, I turned back to the Cloud Courtiers. I didn't relish the thought of accepting these responsibilities without Nadia at my side, but duty stood before me, a duty which I didn't intend to neglect that day. I am empress, I reminded myself, receiving my subjects.

To Cirro-Vior, I said, "We are ready."

As the procession went, a pair of the Cloud Courtiers led the way up the misty stairs. Thalaj and three of his soldiers followed, and I climbed somewhere in the middle with Lukos at my side. When we crested, arriving at the large yard before the series of castles in the clouds, my interim first advisor leaned in.

"The central castle is where the we hold Royal Court. The smaller courts are there to the right, the royal quarters to the left," he said.

Though I felt grateful for his guidance, I found myself more concerned with the courtiers present for our arrival and a sense of tension that erupted around the Stormskeep guards and Thalaj. As I watched, he stood rigidly with his feet apart and staggered. His hands crept toward the handles of his scimitynes. I rested a hand on Lukos's forearm and went toward the commotion.

Karynne and Imrythel fell into step beside me.

"What has happened?" I asked.

"Lady Mairynne," said Imrythel. "It seems that one of the courtiers has put your guards on alert with some ill words referring to their captain."

"Sister," Karynne added, "it would be best if you were the one to call halt to the matter."

In agreement, I moved faster, calling the wind to speed my step. When I arrived, one of the silver-dusted beauties spread arms wide and I caught the edge of the words. "But 'tis truth that you exist outside the castes, is it not? Blood of the highest order contaminated by the fourth would traditionally be offered up to the Tsinti, is that not so?"

"Enough!" I snapped.

Silence fell again, and all eyes turned. Thalaj shot me a warning look, making his desire that I remain uninvolved clear. Though I also detected an exacerbation, suggesting what he wouldn't voice: I told you as much.

Breathing slowly to manage my nerves, I reminded myself, I am empress, receiving my subjects. To the offender, I said, "May I have your name?"

The Cloud Courtier turned to me and sank into a bow. "I am called Alto-Trea, my lady Mairynne."

Otherwise indiscernible, the emblem on the courtier's shoulder became a calling card. It showed a pattern of wispy swirls, resembling lines of the black swans that swam in the pool at the foot of Sundai Falls.

The swan, I decided, and wondered again why they all chose to look so similar. Lifting my chin, I said, "Were you familiar, Alto-Trea, with Kōgō Noralynne's work for the Nantai people, that she worked across castes and with the Small Folk alike, and that she believed all deserve an equal voice?"

I feigned a pause as if to await a reply, but before anyone could make a sound, I continued, "Before you answer, I am certain you are." I smiled, having claimed the upper hand. "As I am my mother's daughter, I shall not tolerate words, no matter how gently spoken, that slander. Is that abundantly clear?"

This time I allowed the courtier to answer.

The swan bent at the waist. "As you command, Lady Mairynne." And for all I could discern, the courtier held no emotion or reaction to my order. If animosity existed within, the swan contained it well.

In reality, amidst those gathered, every Cloud Courtier's face seemed solemn, identical. As for the faces of the Storm Sorcerers in attendance, each told a different story, but all seemed proud of the stance I'd taken. Karynne outright smiled, and Imrythel nodded once with her approval. Despite the vote of confidence, I was ready to be out of the spotlight if only for a brief time.

"Now," I started, "I understand the first of our proceedings will be this evening. I'd like to freshen up before then. Alto-Trea, as you have so eagerly welcomed my party, you will kindly show us to the royal quarters." I held the swan's icy gaze.

"Naturally, Lady Mairynne."

The courtier's manner remained poised, and I still perceived no emotion as we followed. The feeling was like nothing I'd ever experienced. It was as if I were dealing with animated dolls. Hopefully Lukos would have some wise counsel as we took repast for the afternoon. I understood now that I'd met Cloud Courtiers before, but my past experience with the person I'd known as Viordyn had failed to prepare me for this.

Inside the royal chambers, Lukos thanked Alto-Trea and closed us inside, away from the courtiers. Our rooms provided ample space for all in attendance, private apartments surrounding a common area for meals and meetings. Walls, floors, even the furniture and linens in light blues, silvers, and whites reflected light and added to the feeling of being in the clouds. I stepped to the balcony, and far below, Stormskeep drifted away as we rose into the sky. Under my feet, I hadn't noticed the movement, the Cloud Court had already departed its dock. I ran a hand over a stone wall, amazed at how cloud magic made such a solid structure lighter than air.

A throat cleared at the door and I turned to find Thalaj casually leaning to one side at the threshold.

"Join me," I said, "and close the door behind you."

"Your display back there was unnecessary."

"I disagree."

He smiled, a glint in his eyes saying that mayhap he enjoyed my disagreement by some measure.

As the soon-to-be empress, I owed no explanation. But within, a need to voice my reasons drove my agitated speech. "That was their first interaction with me as their empress. There wasn't room for leniency. What was said before I arrived?"

The spark in his eyes went dark. "That, I'll not repeat. You heard enough to get the courtier's point." He crossed over and leaned on the railing, taking in the scene below, the Stormskeep castle, falls, citadel, and city surrounded by the high wall. "It looks small from here."

"That it does. Home is a wonderous place," I said idly, resisting the urge to press him more. I had gained their meaning well enough, and hopefully my stance resonated strongly enough.

"You will be back there soon, as Kōgō Mairynne Evangale."

I looked into the distance, where the fields and forests spread across Nantai, wondering where our travels would one day take us. Feeling distant myself, I ignored the honorific and said, "For a time." Then, returning to the present and hardening my resolve, I added, "Thalaj, when I have concluded my business at court, I intend to come with you to find my father."

◇◇◇◇◇◇◇◇◇◇◇◇◇◇◇◇◇◇◇◇◇◇◇◇◇◇◇◇◇◇◇

ONCE MY FATHER'S AND now my protector, Thalaj dropped his shoulders on a sigh, his eyes shifting in an obvious search for the right response. All of his training, every instinct he'd honed to perfection, and his very foundation of being, I had just called into question with my announcement. For all his tactical agility and gallantry, he struggled when facing a proposal with which he disagreed. Mayhap the hesitation hailed from his protective nature. Maybe he felt inadequate given his intermingled bloodlines. The former, I could do little to change. The later, I would one day see handled, but not while my father lived and could still rule the Nantai people. For now, I watched. And waited for his reply. If my plight resulted in success, I'd beg for the decree from the restored emperor. Until then, I had to believe he would grant his youngest daughter's wish.

When Thalaj's reply came, it sounded as assured as if he'd known what he'd say all along. "Lady Mairynne, I am no royal advisor. I have no political knowledge, nor have I an agenda. Combat and covert endeavors are where I excel, and this is no mission for someone born to rule the Nantai people. I beg of you to trust that, if he lives, I will find Tennō Atheryn and return him safely to you at Stormskeep."

I reached for my necklace. His words struck me and, had it not been for the burning stone against my skin, I may have heeded his wisdom. "Thalaj," I said, placing my free hand on his forearm. "This has little to do with how well I trust you to return my father." I gave a single laugh freely toward the sky at how, in reality, I trusted him more than any other person. With a smile, I added, "That you will be at my side gives me the confidence to make the journey."

He pressed his lips tighter. Then quietly, he said "I can't take you to Umbra." Glancing toward the door and lowering his voice even more, he went on, "In confidence, I had planned to enter the Evernight Marshes alone. Avoiding the enchantments there requires too much concentration for me to watch over another. Especially you."

"Wha—" I began, but he'd stopped my objection before it had really begun. The fact that he'd planned to do this all on his own despite the guise of taking a team brought me up short. After a pause to gather my own thoughts, I asked, "But you will return to Stormskeep after, with the totem?"

"I will."

"And how do you propose to convince the Small Folk at Evernight's heart to part with something so prized?"

Thalaj remained silent, telling me no more about what tactics he might use, but by his silence also that he would bring back the totem at any cost. Of that, I felt assured, and I believed it with as much certainty as I had faith that my father still lived. Whatever he planned didn't leave me feeling easy, but it sufficed, allowing me to imagine the result would be worth the cost and that no one would come to harm in obtaining this relic.

The door creaked and Lukos stood in the frame, tall, slender, with hands folded in front of him. "Lady Mairynne, your attendants and your . . . sister have arrived." His lip curled and he hesitated on the word *sister* like it tasted wrong in his mouth.

The feeling seemed typical of the counselor. Yasmynne's exuberance scrubbed his cool composure like little else could manage.

"Thank you, Lukos," I said. My gaze flitted back to Thalaj. "This is not the end of our conversation."

He tipped his head forward, then stood straight and said, "My team should have searched your rooms for any dangers by now. We will help with the chests, then wait in the outer rooms if you should have need of us."

He passed Lukos, turning to slide through the tight doorway. Lukos stepped aside but remained square and kept his attention on me—a tension or possible distaste that I hadn't noticed before. With the exception of Ohmyn Havengale, my counselors each worked hard to disguise their thoughts and offer advice when needed, but as I spent more time with them, I learned and took note of what their body language said that their words did not. I had little desire to stir conflict within my own retinue here, away from our home, so I allowed the slight to pass. Lukos turned as I went inside.

My counselors gathered around a table while Dorynne, Thalaj, and his small team moved our chests of clothing on the wind to each of the chambers. Mother Feathergale was in the process of greeting my sister. Karynne stooped to return the embrace and did so eagerly, greeting the woman who had attended to all of us as children. After they parted, the small but lithe woman came to me with open arms.

"You seem a bit out of breath," I said as we hugged.

She smiled and flipped a hand dismissively. "The air's thinner. Takes more effort to gather the wind for moving around the heavies. But don't you worry; we'll get everything settled. You go about your business."

When she moved away, Yasmynne appeared in her place, placing both hands on my shoulders. "Mairynne, Nestryn and I will visit Comtesse Tsanseri's court on the morrow. She has asked that we bring witnesses to vouch for us. Will you come?" She looked nervously between her betrothed and me.

My brow felt heavy, not from my sister's request, but at the realization that the Cloud Courtier went by *Tsanseri* rather than one of the factions. Though I wasn't sure there was sufficient time on the morrow, I wanted to serve my sister's wishes. I put on a smile and answered, "Of course, Yasmynne."

To Lukos, I asked, "Tsanseri is a Cloud Courtier, true?"

"She is."

"How is it we know she is *she*?" I asked, still wondering at my next question regarding the factions.

"Comtesse Tsanseri always chooses a feminine form. She believes it better represents all the gentle things about love and affection."

"Oh, Lukos," Azurynne Nightingale admonished, "you know there is more substance to it than that."

I turned to her, brows raised and waiting to hear more about this *more*.

She continued, "Tsanseri believes herself better than the uniform ways of the Cloud Courtiers. Her given name is Cirro-Tsan, but when she began the proceedings of Love's Court, she dispensed with the faction naming, as well as with the same illusions as the rest of the courtiers."

"But do not let that fool you, Mairynne," Imrythel interjected. "People across Nantai call her Comtesse of the Masque for good reason." She arched a black brow over one glinting green eye.

Lukos cleared his throat and said, "You will know her by her seat at the center of court. I do believe it is wise for you to visit her court whilst you are here, and as we must travel to the seats of the each of the other gnobles before ascension, tomorrow is satisfactory."

Turning back to my acting first advisor, I asked, "How long will gathering the gnobles take?"

He folded his hands behind his back and paced as he answered, "Traveling by cloud is the quickest route, but it will still take a handful of days to make the circuit to the Iced Plains in the north, Kōdaina Kori, the desert's edge, and finally to the Barrows."

My hand found the stones around my neck. Hot and cold. The cold one burned this time as I spoke, "Tell me, Lukos, or anyone. Solarynne . . ."

She surfaced from her daze and turned to me, but waited.

" . . . or Azurynne, or Ohmyn, why have we not invited the Small Folk or the Tsinti to the proceedings of the realm? Should not all have a seat on the high council? And who will speak for the casteless?"

Ohmyn gasped, a shaky hand covering his mouth. Azurynne and Lukos had mirrored expressions, pressing their lips together in an attempt to measure their words.

Solarynne stood and circled the table toward me. "I am sorry, Mairynne, that I have been wearing my worry over Corwyn and offering you little counsel. In this matter, though, even your mother, Kōgō Noralynne, had trouble finding or convincing any of those peoples to join us."

Lukos found his voice again. "The Tsinti live apart from the rest of the Nantai people. We have never been able to locate them at will."

Azurynne snapped, "And the Small Folk ward their seats of power heavily. It's too dangerous to try to approach them. And they refuse meetings with us to discuss such matters." She threw a hand up in the air and asked, "Bless the Triad, when was the last time we received any of the Small Folk at Stormskeep?"

I looked at her hard. "I have noted your point, Azurynne. Albeit I cannot recall the last time a Cloud Courtier, Fire Forger, Frost Fighter, Stone Singer, or Underhill Dweller visited our keep."

She shrank under my stare.

"Karynne," I said. "Would you go to the outer rooms and ask Thalaj to return?"

When he appeared before me, my first guardsman bowed, stood, and awaited the reason for my summons.

"Gensui Thalaj," I said, "When you travel to the Small Folk of Umbra, you will deliver a message on behalf of the empress. That should be me by the time your meeting comes to pass." Swallowing the sudden lump in my throat, I asked him to extend an open invitation to the leader who held Umbra's seat.

When he agreed, I turned my attention to more immediate matters. "Now, can someone tell me how to best deal with the oddities of these courtiers?"

Ohmyn scoffed, then gave a hearty laugh. "Lady Mairynne, if you think the courtiers are your only concern, wait until you meet the other castes who will attend the High Cloud Court of Gnobles. These proceedings are, shall we say, quite colorful." He lifted a mug from the table, drinking deeply with a trail of foam drizzling down his chin.

Regarding my rotund counselor, I gnawed at the inside of my lip. At length, I gave a rueful smile, deciding to credit Ohmyn for that bit of wisdom. "Well," I said, "from my small experience today, it certainly seems that what I have learned of the Nantai peoples in theory may not have been adequate preparation."

◇◇◇◇◇◇◇◇◇◇◇◇◇◇◇◇◇◇◇◇◇◇◇◇◇

OF THOSE WHO ATTENDED court on my behalf, only Thalaj agreed to be at my side for Nestryn and Yasmynne's assignation at Love's Court. My counselors had old acquaintances they wished to see or things they wished to buy from the cloud markets. Or, in Solarynne's case, she wished to remain in solitude and offer prayer to Selene that her brother would be well. Edamyn, priest of Atun, spoke for the Triad in haughtily stating that neither Gods nor clergy attended such proceedings and excused himself, Tasmynne, and Arlyn; they would retire to Otarr's temple until the ascension ceremony itself.

Two Cloud Courtiers greeted us upon our arrival at Comtesse Tsanseri's court. They invited Nestryn alone into court and directed Yasmynne, Thalaj, and me to wait in the anteroom which turned out to be an open-air seating area with several ornately designed settees, each wide enough to seat two in close proximity. Mist floated at our feet, obscuring the floor. When the courtiers had left us alone, Yasmynne sank slowly onto the closest sofa, looking ghostly and wringing her hands.

I went to my sister, laid a hand on her shoulder, and said, "You've no need to worry. Nestryn loves you greatly, and he will show that to the Comtesse."

"But Mairynne, why wouldn't she receive us together, as a couple?" Her brows peaked as she searched my face for an answer that I could only wish to possess.

I shrugged one shoulder but found it hard to hold eye contact when I could offer little to soothe her fears. "There is little we can do but wait and see."

Thalaj waited for me to sit, then took the place at my side. His solemn look bespoke naught of his thoughts, and the three of us remained in silence for quite some time until worries began to grow in my thoughts as well. Curious about what awaited behind the silver-scrollwork doors, I whispered to Thalaj, "Have you been to this court before?"

"I have not." He shook his head slowly.

"What do you know of the Comtesse Tsanseri?" I asked.

"Very little, Lady Mairynne." He adjusted in his seat, moving one scabbard so he could face me better. "My guidance would be to remain open and calm. Observe and listen. If there is something I have learned of people over the years, it is to trust slowly. You never know where you might find an ally . . . or an adversary."

The advice embodied the man at my side, and it seemed my best course of action. I vowed to try to do the same, not only at Tsanseri's court, but for the remainder of our time in the High Cloud Courts. Time passed, and I made small talk with Yasmynne as a means to distract her while we awaited summons. After maybe an hour, the doors opened.

At last, Nestryn exited alone through the silvery door. The Cloud Courtiers standing to either side remained statuesque. Yasmynne stood as he went to her and bowed to one knee, taking her hand in his. "My love and shining light," he started. "I want you day and night."

I rolled my eyes and looked at Thalaj, trying not to laugh at the horrid attempt at poetry. A muscle jumped in my guard's jaw, and his eyes widened ever so slightly. Yasmynne, conversely, looked lovingly upon the man at her feet. Inhaling deeply, I reminded myself, open and calm, observe and listen, and I worked to keep my expression neutral.

"The Comtesse has given me her instruction and now bids that you appear before her. May I escort you, my lady Yasmynne Evangale?"

My sister grinned at me, barely containing excitement that begged for freedom, then back to Nestryn, she said, "Of course."

Nestryn added, "Comtesse Tsanseri asked that you bring the witnesses before her." He stood and turned expectantly to Thalaj and me. "Will you both join us?"

I held out a hand. "Please, lead the way."

Thalaj offered me an arm, his brow raised in question.

"Observe?" I asked, placing my hand on his forearm.

"And listen," he answered.

The courtiers at the doors pulled them wide and we followed the cheerful couple inside. Unlike the royal chambers' decor and in contrast with the whites, silvers, and airy blues that colored the rest of the High Cloud Courts, vibrant color painted the interior of Tsanseri's court—tapestries of red and gold, lively paintings, upholstery in whimsical teal or purple, and silks of yellow and orange. Much smaller than I had expected, the room smelled of incense and spice. Several artists with easels and paints took positions along the outskirts of the room, readying their supplies to capture the scene. Unattended musical instruments rested against the walls.

In the place of chairs, pillows lay in a circle, and the person who could only be Tsanseri sat on the largest at the far side, with her legs folded and hands palms up on each knee. Her auburn hair flowed in abundant waves and her skin seemed dusted with gold rather than silver. She smiled serenely, welcoming us to her court.

Two courtiers sat to her left and two to her right, all taking a similar feminine form and posed to mirror their leader. One of the four said, "Comtesse Tsanseri welcomes petitioner, Lady Yasmynne Evangale, and the man who wishes her hand to the center of our circle."

Another said, "Likewise, the witnesses, future Kōgō Mairynne Evangale and Gensui Thalaj Northerngale, honor Love's Court with their presence."

My heart flopped in my chest. I sorely desired to rebut the title, but I dared not. Not yet.

Comtess Tsanseri then spoke with a mischievous gleam in her eye and a smirk. "Please, do make yourselves comfortable, and let us enjoy this part of our day." To the courtiers who had allowed us inside, she called, "Bring the artists and musicians, and bring sparkling wine for each of our guests."

Yasmynne sat in the center of the circle on a lush pillow, Nestryn on the rug at her side. As other courtiers began to filter in and take up instruments or paint brushes, Thalaj and I each knelt on pillows to one side so we could see Tsanseri beyond my sister. A courtier appeared, offering a fluted glass filled with a glittery, bubbly wine. After I received mine, she handed the next one to Thalaj.

With alacrity, he accepted but held it before him without a taste. I tipped mine, only enough to wet my tongue, and widened my eyes. Sweet and cool, it tingled in my mouth. Not knowing its possible effects, I then chose to act as Thalaj and hold the glass without partaking.

Comtesse Tsanseri raised her hands. "Shall we begin?"

A commotion, agreement, clapping, and small cheers went up around the room. Tsanseri nodded to her left, then right. The musicians began gently playing flutes and strings. With the ambiance established, the Comtesse focused her attention on my sister. "Lady Yasmynne, what has this lowly man done to deserve your affection?"

Yasmynne held her chin high. "Comtesse, Nestryn began courting me before my mother passed." She looked in my direction with a slight smile, then returned her gaze toward the mistress of the court. "My sisters have always said that I have much need of affection, more so than anyone. Nestryn has provided that affection throughout the mourning period."

"Future Kōgō Mairynne, do you approve of this betrothal?"

Her address took me off guard, and I faltered but recovered quickly with truth. "Comtesse Tsanseri, I want naught but happiness for my sister, and I have seen that Nestryn makes her so. I will give my blessing," I answered.

"Has he brought you gifts?" she asked of my sister.

"He brings me the gift of holding me, of calming my heart and soul, of being close to me when I am in need, and of caring for me as no other can," my sister said, but her head tilted slightly.

I couldn't see her face, but I imagined it confused. Our traditions of courtship at Stormskeep involved little in the way of gifting, but everyone from the Syrensea to the neighboring nation of Yōtei had heard rumors of how Tsanseri was the true authority on love. I knew in my heart that the reason we sat in the rainbow-colored room was simply because Yasmynne craved validation.

Tsanseri said, "For a love to be fine, your suitor should bring you gifts, and many gifts at that. Has he written you poetry or letters?"

Quietly, Yasmynne said, "He has not, but—"

The Comtesse held up a hand to silence her rebuttal. "These are the foundations of fine love, my lady. How is it you seek my blessing without your betrothed having attended to these most basic of matters?"

As my sister explained their ongoing relations to her self-appointed judge and jury, I uncomfortably felt the pressure of eyes upon me. Losing track of the official conversation, I scanned the room, attempting to discern between the people who all looked the same or to see the emblem worn on their left shoulder. A violinist, rapt in her work, leaned to one side then the other as she worked the bow. A painter studied Tsanseri and dabbled on the canvas. Most were engaged in their current creations, but at length, I found the source of my discomfort. Across the room, a courtier stared harshly at me and Thalaj. She, for the courtiers had all assumed an air of femininity presumably for Tsanseri's good graces, stood angled just enough that I could see the emblem on her shoulder.

A swan.

Alto-Trea.

Almost everything about the courtier appeared differently from only a day before, but that emblem marked her. And her stare carried too much disdain to obscure the true person. I leaned toward Thalaj and said, "Remember Alto-Trea from our arrival?"

He nodded, but confusion tugged his brows together as he peered over to the new image across the court.

"It's pretty clear that the swan will be a hard-won ally," I whispered, "if not already an adversary."

By way of reply, he said, "As of yet, I would count Alto-Trea as neither ally nor adversary. It is hard to know based on a person's prejudices. Some of your counselors hold that very same prejudice." Thalaj, though he believed himself inadequate as more than a guard, once again offered an acute observation.

Rendered silent, I stared off with Alto-Trea across the room. The courtier broke eye contact first when Tsanseri clapped three times to call the room's attention.

Once silence had descended, Tsanseri made her judgment. "I have heard Nestryn's case for your hand, but this joining has not yet developed sufficiently to deserve blessing from Love's Court. For one year, one month, one week, and one day, Nestryn must practice the ways of fine love. You, Lady Yasmynne, will keep his gifts, his letters, his poems, and any art he makes in dedication to you. After this period, you will present a sampling of his finest efforts at this court." She paused for some minor sounds of approval to pass. "Then, and only then, will I be able to bless your union."

Outside, I stood with Thalaj and breathed in the unperfumed air, allowing Otarr to shine on my face for long warm moments. I remained uncertain about that in which I had just partaken, but two things seemed clearer than before. Tsanseri held a power over many of the Cloud Courtiers that I couldn't describe, one that encouraged them to disguise themselves to her liking alone. And, secondly, I needed more information about Alto-Trea.

Yasmynne and Nestryn joined us, and I turned to my sister. Putting on a jovial smile in hopes of lightening her spirits, I said, "So, it seems we will have a wedding after a year, month, week, and day?"

She returned only a thin smile. "It all just appears to be so much work, Mairynne," she said with a note of rejection.

I nudged my sister at the thought. "Nay, Nestryn has stood beside you through mourning our mother. We can all see the love he showers on you. This trial will be naught for him, and you will be increasingly happy as he gives you more and more affection with each offering Tsanseri has prescribed."

Yasmynne took Nestryn's hand in both of hers. Looking from him back to me, she said, "I suppose you speak the truth. I had just hoped that we could wed sooner."

Hugging myself about the waist, I said, "I, for one, am happy for you both. And this will give you ample time to plan for a ceremony to outshine all weddings that have gone before."

That thought brought a shining light into her eyes, and she clasped me into a tight hug. I squeezed her back, hoping that it would be long enough that I would return with Father and that he would be able to see his daughter married properly under the Triad.

Six

Ascension

The cold disturbed my sleep almost as much as the ascension ceremony scheduled to begin at midday. Arising from my bed, I went to the wardrobe and found a heavy cloak. Though I wore a long woolen gown to sleep and the blankets were heavy, the change in temperatures, certainly attributable to the current location of the High Cloud Court, chilled my fingers so much that they felt thin and ached. After I had tied the heavy cloak at my waist, I rubbed the numb end of my nose and paced the room, my chest squeezing tighter with every step. When I all but couldn't breathe, I went to the balcony and looked off into the night. We had descended, and under Selene, the land just beyond the clouds' edges appeared silver.

With slippered feet, I left my chamber, easing the door closed behind me so as to not disturb those who still slept in other areas of the royal suite. I thought the large, manicured lands around the courts would be quiet at this time and anticipated I could walk alone under the stars that guarded the night.

"Venturing out alone?" My oldest sister's voice, like a resting storm rolling in from a distance, halted me in my tracks. She strolled toward me, also wearing her heavy cloak. "I couldn't sleep. It seems you're having the same troubles."

I nodded, looking between her and the door.

She extended a hand. "Mind if I join you? You, of all people, really shouldn't be about at night on your own."

"Is there some danger I'm unaware of?"

"I wouldn't name it danger, but who knows what agendas lie among the castes. Now we have arrived at our last stop before the ceremonies, it's likely that you won't be alone even if you should leave these chambers that way."

Even though I knew ascension would commence at midday, I hadn't kept track of where we were in our journey. "Who joins us this night?"

"Gnoble Brimr, his wife, Svarta, and any other Underhill Dwellers they choose to bring to court." Karynne looked around the dark room, then back to me and smiled. "Did you have a destination? Or simply planning to wander?"

My brows felt heavy as I considered. "I only considered being outside, away from the confines of these rooms."

"Will you allow my company?"

"I will."

"Then why are we waiting?"

Having no answer, I shrugged and pulled the door open. Outside, the temperature had fallen, and I pulled the hood over my head.

Karynne hugged her cloak tighter. "'Tis cold near the Iced Plains," she said, her breath fogging the night.

Slowly, we strolled through the halls and out into the night where silver mists rolled, parting in front of us and circling in our wake. There, on an island in the clouds, little extra space did not allow for long walks out of doors; and on that quiet night, I desired the park near the River Sundai, where the waters fell from the cliffs and began the journey toward the Syrensea. It was in this silent, moon-clad moment, that I understood how much anxiety had gathered under my skin due to the absent sound of rushing water. That night, I wanted my home more than anything, but several days still remained before I'd step foot in Stormskeep once again.

To our right, a wide, trellis-covered corridor stretched to the edge of the cloud island. Under Otarr's bright eye, the markets pulsed there, merchants trading for various wares from throughout Nantai and beyond. Others had returned with everything from practical wares wrought by the Stone Singers to strands of reddish pearls from the Copper Coast to spices and minerals collected from the Great Sands Desert. Seeing their prizes, I wished for the freedom to trade rather than learning about the gnobles and how my ascension ceremony might play out.

Looking down briefly, I asked Karynne, "Where is Imrythel this evening?"

"I imagine she sleeps like everyone else."

"With the exception of the dinner in my rooms, I think this might be the first time I've seen you without her at your side since Mother's death."

"That is only in Otarr's hours. I see you little in the evenings," she accused.

We meandered on in silence for several more moments toward the courtyard where we'd first embarked onto the High Cloud Courts. My sister took her turn in breaking the silence. "Tsanseri's decision tossed our dear sister into quite the state of agitation, don't you agree?"

I laughed lightly. "Comtesse Tsanseri has a strict idea of how a courtier should treat the woman he courts."

"Aah, yes. That's similar to what Yasmynne said. Only she ranted for a good time over the matter."

"She was quite dejected afterward," I said.

Karynne rushed to add, "But I think she is becoming more and more fond of the idea with each passing moment."

"Is that not what you'd expect, Sister?" I faced to her with a questioning gaze.

She angled herself toward the light so I could see her expression fill with sheer amusement. "I find it, shall we say, an apropos happenstance that she feels forced into something she'll love, yet she can't see its value. Love seems to blind."

Those last words grated, but her expression remained open and insinuated mere observation. She took my hands in hers and went on, "Mairynne, I must apologize." Her brows furrowed and she pursed her lips.

Curious, I waited for her to continue, my eyes wide and blinking, but words escaping me. Mayhap I found myself the slightest bit bewildered that my ever-so-poised and in-command sister offered an apology so readily.

"I admit," she said with a chuckle. "I was bitter when Father wrote you into the annals as his successor. It should have been me by birthright, but that is only part of our ways. I've spent too much time worrying over that. I want . . ." She swallowed hard, struggling to get out something that had clearly weighed on her heart. "No, that's not right. I need for us to be closer again. Like we were when we were children, when we sat at Father's feet listening to the stories of the realm." She squeezed my hand, and when her eyes met mine, they glistened.

Grasping her hand tighter in return, I sighed. "Oh Kahry, despite the cold of this night, that warms my soul." I wrapped my arms around my sister, and she pulled me close. We stood there in an embrace at the edge of the only courtyard on the island, reconnecting.

"You haven't called me that in many years." When we parted, she said, "It's taken me a long while to understand the kind of sister I need to be. I only want the best for the Nantai people, and I need to help you make that happen, to be the best sister I can. Like Nadia was to Mother. I'm sorry I haven't been there for you like that before." Tears pooled in her eyes, reflecting Selene's light.

I welcomed having her back at my side. "But you're here now. That's really all that matters." So easily I forgave, because in my heart and soul, I wanted this too.

A metallic clang and thud sounded across the yard, echoing from the stone faces of the castle buildings. Karynne and I both pivoted toward the noise, and I held my breath as we tried to make out the figures moving in the distance. In my periphery, Karynne's posture eased.

"Should we go meet Gnoble Brimr?" she asked.

ONE OF THE CLOUD Courtiers caught sight of us before we arrived and met us a dozen paces out. When close enough, I could make out the crescent moon shape embroidered onto the shoulder. "Cirro-Vior, good eve to you," I said with my chin held high.

The courtier bent at the waist, one arm wrapped around the front of the waist and the other around the back. Standing, Cirro-Vior greeted us and asked, "What brings you out in the hours between?"

Glancing to Karynne and back to the courtier, I said, "We could ask the same of you."

"Lady Mairynne, the Underhill Dwellers have an intolerance for the light from Otarr. They always embark under Selene's silver light. As I have charge of receiving the High Court's guests, I am here to welcome Gnoble Brimr from the Barrows."

"If I may, Viordyn?" I began.

Almost imperceptibly, but still, the courtier bristled.

"I'm sorry." I smiled. "Cirro-Vior. Would you be so kind as to introduce us to the gnoble and his wife? Aah . . ."

"Svarta," Karynne added helpfully.

Cirro-Vior nodded. "Naturally, Lady Mairynne."

The tales of the Underhill Dwellers did these people few favors, but they also did little to depict their true image. They were a stout people who stood a head shorter than the average Storm Sorcerer but from a hunched posture rather than shortened spine. I, being shorter than most Storm Sorcerers, still needed to gaze down to greet the gnoble and his wife. Under Selene's light, their skin and hair were both so pale they seemed gray.

As the courtier called to Gnoble Brimr, the Underhill Dweller turned, and I stifled a gasp at the oddity that stared back at me. He had a wide forehead and oversized ears that each came to three subtle points. Eyes that gave off a warm yellow light regarded me. His eyebrows and mustache extended toward his sides and appeared to be something other than hair—thicker and fingerlike. I made note to inquire about that later. He loped over and extended an arm that at resting hung to his knees. His wide hand with blunt nails awaited my acceptance.

When I accepted, he folded the chunky fingers around mine, and though I'd never considered my hands dainty, they seemed wispy in comparison to his.

Brimr smiled and his mustache seemed to move of its own accord, for the person himself hadn't budged. His voice, when he spoke, was gravelly. "Lady Mairynne, I see. You have the look and feel of Kōgō Noralynne. We are pleased to know you. We have brought the journal that will be the first of your annals, as well as other papers and scrolls as gifts to the newly ascended empress and her people." He turned away briefly to yell, "Svarta! Come."

My stomach twisted into knots at the mention of Mother's name, and the icy stone resting on my chest flared. I forced my hands to remain at my sides and keep my mind with the newcomers. Mother had passed into her next life, the mourning period had passed, and I needed to tend to our realm's business.

To my continued surprise, Svarta resembled her husband in most features. The main differences between the two were in breadth, her more delicate lips beneath a mustache, and two brown bands that ran down from under her ears, down her neck, and disappeared beneath the line of her dress. Svarta had voluminous, curly white hair that hung over one shoulder, and she wore a trio of piercings in each point of her earlobes.

I held out my hand to Brimr's wife with a smile. "It is lovely to meet you, Gnoble Lady Svarta."

After she shook my hand, Brimr wrapped an arm around her waist and gruffly pulled her to him. "My wife," he said to her, "after tomorrow, this will be our new empress."

Svarta's eyes flashed, then dimmed. She reached into a pocket and brought out a compact package. Grabbing one of my hands, she placed it in my palm and folded my fingers closed, backing away with a slight smile and twitch of her mustache. She looked at Brimr and made a few clicking noises while her mustache danced.

Brimr grinned proudly and said, "It's one of the best tubers grown by my people. A delicacy. My wife believes you will be a fine empress."

"Thank you, Svarta. I appreciate your confidence," I said, though I couldn't fathom what gave her that impression upon first sight.

Karynne leaned over and whispered in my ear. "You only have a few hours left to sleep before morning."

I nodded, straightened, and said, "I am happy to have met you both, but I should return and sleep. Until tomorrow."

We went, my heart heavy at all the talk of Mother and feeling somewhat alone without Nadia here to support me. The apology from Karynne had taken me by surprise but felt sincere and difficult for her. For me, it was long overdue. I decided on that walk back to our rooms that if she could extend herself, then I should too.

"Kahry," I said as we meandered back beyond the market.

She made a small sound of assent.

I continued, "Tomorrow, the oath I will take will not be the permanent oath of ascension."

Karynne grasped my arm and pulled me to a stop, facing her. "What do you mean, Sister?"

With a look into the market alley and one down the hall before us, it appeared we were alone, so I told her about my plan. "I will open with the words of Tennō Makenyn from the first of the annals just before he underwent the separation from the Kuroidragon. His annals read, 'I shan't wholly relinquish my right to rule the people.

Before I undergo the extraction, my brother Morwyn shall take this oath and rule in my stead until I am once again able.' " After a pause, I added, "Tomorrow, I will take Morwyn's oath."

"Mairynne, what are you talking about? Do you think this will appease the Council? The Triad?"

"I don't know, Kahry, but—"

She held up a hand. "I know, you feel Father lives. You've said so enough times."

I searched her eyes for understanding, and I believed I found it. "It's also that I am not ready to be empress." I looked down. "I'm scared, Kahry." As of yet, I didn't know if I could trust my sister enough to tell her I planned to go with Thalaj. That would stir another series of questions I had no intent of answering on that night.

"Mairynne, you must inform the counselors of your intentions before we go into court tomorrow. You can't afford dissension within the Storm Sorcerers caste at High Cloud Court. If there are indeed any castes intent on unseating us as the first caste, it would open the door wider for them to step inside."

"There is no time to discuss this with the advisors, Karynne. Nadia and Solarynne already know. After ascension tomorrow, everyone will know, and I don't think our father's counselors will openly show dissent. Will you keep this between us until that time, Sister?"

She started to speak but, seemingly at a loss for words, pressed her mouth into a tight line. Maybe she only thought better of objecting as we were finally making peace. Which was the case, I couldn't say.

I didn't ask.

Rather, I inquired quietly, "Do you think it's the right thing?"

"It is not a course I would take." She looked at me long and hard. For what she searched, I was unsure. What she found, I also did not know, but she finally said with a reluctant smile, "I will keep it between us. And I do think it right. You must follow your soul's calling and be true to thine self first. Wasn't that the lesson Father always taught?"

◇◇◇◇◇◇◇◇◇◇◇◇◇◇◇◇◇◇◇◇◇◇◇◇◇◇◇

BY MIDDAY WHEN MY ascension began, the cloud island had risen into the skies once again, and I sat at the focal point within the High Cloud Court. To my left, my retinue took their seats in the pews of the first caste—my caste—the Storm Sorcerers. Lukos Thundergale, acting as my first advisor, sat in the front. Behind him, Solarynne, Azurynne, and Ohmyn populated the second row; Karynne, Imrythel, Yasmynne, and Nestryn the third. The Triad's clergy stood at the podium behind my chair; Atun's priest, Edamyn, at the center with Arlyn as Otarr's priest and Tasmynne as Selene's priestess at either of his sides. Silence hung over the court, and I watched the entourage of each caste gnoble filter into the room in ranking order—powdered and glittered Cloud Courtiers, darker complexioned Fire Forgers, small and deceptively peaceful-looking Frost Fighters, then the broad Stone Singers, and finally with dark glasses and their tentacled mustaches, the Underhill Dwellers. When each gnoble and their council had taken their respective seats from left to right in the semicircle, Edamyn called ascension to order.

His aged voice still strong, he invited the leaders, "Will each caste's gnoble state your name? Tasmynne Hallowgale of Selene will record your attendance for Nantai records."

I turned my head toward my retinue as Lukos stood and said, "I am Lukos Thundergale, acting first advisor to Lady Mairynne who is here before the Nantai people to accept the caste gifts and the treasures of the Nantai, and to take her oath."

As he sat, the foremost Cloud Courtier stood. "Lady Mairynne and Edamyn of Atun, in representation of the Cloud Courtiers, I am Gnoble Strato-Ymar." The courtier sat solemnly with a straight back and faced the next in line.

A dark-complexioned man stood. "Gnoble Yuos Atith of the Fire Forgers," he said efficiently and quickly dropped back into his seat.

A small woman in a silken cream-colored suit stood. When she spoke, her voice made music of the words. "Gnoble Lady Tenkara of the Frost Fighters."

Gruffly, the stocky but clearly feminine leader of the fifth caste said, "Gnoble Sarangarel, representing the Stone Singers." She smoothed a large necklace with many inlaid gems surrounding a blood-red ruby as she returned to her chair with a thunk.

Finally, the shorter man with long arms whom I'd met at midnight before lurched to his feet. He didn't remove the glasses shading his eyes, and his mustache twitched as he said, "Gnoble Brimr. Here from the Northerly Barrows on behalf of the Underhill Dwellers."

"Welcome Gnobles of Nantai," Edamyn said as Brimr took his seat.

In the pause between his welcome and his next words, I considered the Tsinti and the Small Folk, mourning the fact that some peoples within Nantai lacked representation that day in the High Cloud Courts.

Edamyn didn't leave much room for consideration as he introduced himself, Amar, and Tasmynne, then called for the ceremony to continue. "Today, as the Nantai people bear witness, the Storm Sorcerer heir-selected, Mairynne Evangale, third daughter of Tennō Atheryn Evangale and Kōgō Noralynne, comes before you to receive the sacred treasures and swear her oath to the people. The days that follow begin the cleansing in preparation for the Daijō-sai in which she will commune with Otarr, seeking his blessing to take her place as empress of the Nantai people. Three days later, the festivals will follow. "Gnoble Strato-Ymar of the Cloud Courtiers shall present the first treasure."

The courtier Strato-Ymar seemed to drift in his long robes, with only small bends at the knees with each step toward me at the center of this affair. I caught myself wringing my hands and forcibly willed them still in my lap. The courtier reached the place where I sat and dropped to a kneel on the large pillow before me. The shoulder marking resembled a lily that grows in the valley near Stormskeep, assuring me I hadn't met this particular person.

"Lady Mairynne," Strato-Ymar began. "Upon Atun, the all-seeing God, Selene, the lady of the moon, bestowed a mirror that enabled him to see truth in all things. Atun's mirror remains encased in the temple of the Triad at Stormskeep's citadel. This mirror"—she held toward me an open box with a circular silver object resting on a black cushion—"is a replica of Atun's mirror, enchanted that you may see truth when you look upon the glass. May you use this justly as you take the seat of the Nantai people."

My mouth and throat parched, I ran my tongue over my teeth, hoping that the words I needed to voice would sound confident. I accepted the box. "I am honored, Strato-Ymar." Lifting the small object from its bed, I opened it and looked into the glass. My reflection stared back, my eyes worried. I turned the glass so it caught the reflection of the Cloud Courtier. She, yes, she looked softer in the glass, her face full and body shaped in nice curves; and in general, I found the softer image far more attractive than her homogenous and slender illusion. Smiling knowingly at her, I put away the mirror and accepted her hands. I echoed the words of Tennō Makenyn, "Humbly, I accept this treasure and pray to Atun for guidance in its use."

The trinket seemed like something that would be of use at the High Cloud Court, but it also felt like an invasion of these peoples' privacy. It was temptation, one that could be useful but could also hurt. For reasons I didn't understand, the Cloud Courtiers willfully changed their appearances into a look I assumed they considered collectively beautiful. That I disagreed mattered little. I vowed to myself that I would keep the mirror close but refrain from using it unless it seemed necessary to a matter of ruling my people.

Idly, I thought how my father had once endured this ceremony, receiving the same gifts as I accepted now. The stone resting against my chest burned as I wondered where his mirror had gone.

"Yuos Atith of the Fire Forgers," Edamyn said. "Please bring forth the sword."

The man came forward, scabbarded sword in hand. He knelt onto both knees, head bowed, and held the sword with both hands across his thighs—one on the hilt and one on the sheath. He lifted eyes as black as coal to mine and said, "Mairynne Evangale, this sword carries no special enchantments. Yet my most talented Forgers wrought it from the purest ore vein in all of Nantai. In the same manner that Otarr, the Day-Seer, presented Atun, the All-Seer, with the heavenly Sword of Gathering Clouds, I present this to you, our empress. As Kōgō, may you see the clouds gathered for the nourishment of the Nantai people."

The lack of enchantment signified that the Storm Sorcerers, who could innately channel the clouds to water the crops, were indeed the Gods' intended ruling caste. Holding both hands forward to accept the second sacred treasure, I said, "I am honored, Yuos Atith." Once it rested in my palms, it felt light. I drew my brows together. "It seems smaller than the others." My father's sword, I recalled, stood almost to my shoulder when the tip rested on the ground. Likewise, when I had visited Otarr's sacred temple, all the retired swords had seemed larger than manageable. I slid the blade from its seat and appraised the blues and grays in the contours of the metal. This one I could hold easily at my side and would be able to swing with minor effort.

"Lady Mairynne, the Fire Forger priest crafted the blades from the blessed ore and under the watchful eyes of the Triad. Your blade is exactly as the Gods intended. I know not why it is so small." His brow furrowed in reflection of my own at his last words.

Reseating the sword and placing it on the ground next to Atun's mirror, I offered my hands to the Fire Forger. "Of course, Yuos Atith. I have faith that the blade is true. I humbly accept this treasure and pray to Atun for guidance in its usage."

When Yuos Atith had returned to his seat, Edamyn called forth Sarangarel of the Stone Singers to present the jewels. She brought forward a necklace with three gemstones. As she knelt on the pillow before me, she said, "This necklace represents the Triad itself and the gifts that Atun gave to Otarr and Selene in thanks for the mirror and the sword. The round black diamond at the center represents Atun himself. The yellow diamond on one side represents Otarr, and the silver half-moon on the other, Selene. May I, Kōgō Mairynne?" Sarangarel stood, her eyelashes fluttering as she waited for me to lean forward. When I did, she placed the necklace about my neck and turned to her people. Two of the broad men in her entourage brought forward a case and set it at my side. Without a word, Sarangarel flipped open the lid, flourishing her hands to present the jewels before sauntering back to her seat at the head of the Stone Singers.

The case full of twinkling jewels was the first of the caste gifts to their new empress. Afterward, each caste came forward in turn and offered gifts from their people. The Cloud Courtiers gave fine silks; the Fire Forgers brought fine household items of various metals; the Frost Fighters offered bottles and bottles of sweet wine; and the Underhill Dwellers offered scrolls of parchment for the royal library. As the gifts piled up around me, I worried, chewing the inside of my lip. Soon, it would be time for my oath.

When the gnobles had delivered the last packages, Edamyn's powerful voice called the group back to order. The murmurs died down and he said, "The giving of treasures and gifts is complete. It completes the first rite of Ascension. Now, Mairynne Evangale will take her oath to the people. Gnoble Brimr, bring forward the first of Kōgō Mairynne's annals."

I stood and turned as the gnoble lifted a heavy, ornately bound book and lumbered to the podium. He opened it to the first pages, opened the ink jar, and dropped in a sharpened feather. He held out his hands for me to take my position.

"Many thanks, Gnoble Brimr," Edamyn said.

As the Underhill Dwellers' gnoble returned to the rest of the Underhill Dwellers, I turned to Lukos and asked, "May I have the scroll?"

Silently, he delivered it unto my hands and returned to the seat at the head of the Storm Sorcerers. I spread it before me and carefully regarded each of the castes in attendance. At length, I said, "My people of Nantai, before I take my oath, I would read some words from the annals of Tennō Makenyn, the Scarred, first emperor of the Nantai people. As he prepared for his separation from the Kuroidragon, he wrote:

> *The shamans say that this may well take my life. They say that if I am fortunate, I will live, but I will likely be unconscious for weeks, maybe longer.*

> *They say that even when I resurface from the depths of consciousness that I will be unfit to rule for many moons.*
>
> *I shan't wholly relinquish my right to rule the people. Before I undergo the extraction, my brother Morwyn shall take this oath and rule in my stead until I am once again able.*

Lifting my eyes from the scroll, I scanned the faces in the semi-circular formation. Eyes were wide with shock, and the room didn't breathe or make a sound. They waited.

I went on, "Here, before the Storm Sorcerers, Fire Forgers, Frost Fighters, Stone Singers, and Underhill Dwellers, I, Mairynne Evangale, third daughter and decreed heir of Tennō Atheryn, swear an oath to the Nantai people, and this is my oath."

Returning to the scroll and substituting names where necessary, I read:

> *Until the return of our rightful emperor, Atheryn Evangale, I, Mairynne Evangale, shall rule the peoples of Nantai in his stead. I shall retain Tennō Atheryn's council. I shall honor the Triad and act as ruler in every way. I shall maintain annals that will be burned upon the return of our rightful ruler. Histories and laws that I record shall be nullified upon the return of Tennō Atheryn Evangale, but until that time, such histories and laws will remain in effect. Should Tennō Atheryn be unable to resume the Serpentine Throne, my annals will live on as if this oath were the enduring ruler's oath.*

Gasps went up around the room, but I continued, now speaking the traditional words of the people. Raising my voice above the din, I said:

> *Under Atun, the All-Seer, and under Otarr, the Day-Seer, I vow to honor the people of Nantai. I shall make the same vow to Selene, the Night-Seer, on this very night when she takes her place in the sky. I vow to see the people protected and fed. I give my oath to uphold the laws that have been laid within the annals before me, and I pledge to keep the traditions of the Nantai sacred. With the blessings of the Three Sacred Treasures, I accept ascension to the Serpentine Throne.*

As I spoke, the people in the room had returned to a stunned silence, and as a result, I'd leveled out my volume by the time I finished and looked up from the scroll. Thirty, maybe more, wide eyes looked upon me.

It was done.

I was Kōgō Mairynne Evangale, empress of the Nantai people, if only for a time.

Seven

Sosano & Inara

THE PLUMPEST OF MY ADVISORS waddled in a slow pace back and forth within the royal chambers, his hands shoved deep inside the pockets of his jerkin. Ohmyn Havengale, clearly more vexed than the others by the temporary nature of my oath, prattled on about how inappropriate the entire thing had been and how I should have discussed this with them beforehand. Karynne stood near a far wall, and each time I made eye contact during Ohmyn's monologue, she seemed to shrug in a manner that said she had advised as much. At my sister's side, Imrythel gave a few near imperceptible nods punctuating certain points voiced by the advisor. Her hard green stare and folded arms told me she firmly disagreed with my actions that day.

I pressed my fingers against my forehead and squeezed my eyes shut. My other advisors were also present and seated at the table in the royal common area. For a long time, not a one spoke in my favor or in my defense. I hadn't considered this moment, only the overwhelming drive inside me that told me this was the right path. Still, under such scrutiny, I held faith in the truth behind those feelings, and I waited for my advisors to work through their concerns.

Solarynne, at long last, interjected, "Ohmyn." Then she waited for him to stop and look at her.

Red-faced and eyes wide, he turned and snapped, "And now, you'll come out of your haze to join us?"

I made to stand, an objection on my tongue, but Solarynne held up a hand to forestall the chide I'd intended.

In her gaze, I could feel all the weight of a winter's storm and thanked the Triad she didn't focus her ire upon me. The temperature seemed to drop in the room as she said, "Havengale, you should be happy that your empress, Mairynne, has taken an oath that kept you as counselor. The fact that she spoke Morwyn's words leaves Tennō Atheryn's advisors in place by its very nature. Should she wish, she could write you off the council. So, I'd advise that you hold your tongue. She may be young, but she is your empress and your dissent borders on insubordination."

If possible, the red on Ohmyn's face deepened. "Does no one else object? Lukos? Azurynne?"

Lady Azurynne Nightingale shifted forward in her seat, but she portrayed little emotion as she said, "In this decision, what I believe matters little. I sit on this council to advise the ruler of the Nantai people based on our laws and what the Nightingale family holds ethical. Kōgō Mairynne's decision does not violate any values. That she has found a way to satisfy our demands but leave room for her father's return is acceptable in my eyes and the eyes of our written ways."

Ohmyn turned to his last hope for support.

Lukos shook his head. "There's wisdom in Lady Azurynne's words." After a pause, he added, "And in Lady Solarynne's."

I breathed a sigh, relieved that the majority of my council had accepted my oath, albeit reluctantly. However, my sigh had scarcely finished when the door flew open and Thalaj marched into the room.

Before he had even reached the table, he spouted, "What were you thinking, Mairynne?"

I popped out of my chair, regretting the words I would say, needed to say, before they gained voice. With my shoulders rolled back and chin lifted, I said, "Gensui Thalaj Northerngale, I have not requested your counsel in this matter. Nor have I requested your presence at my table. The royal council is no place for a guard. When we have completed our business here, I'll speak with you. Until then, you will wait in the outer room."

The few moments that followed seemed to stretch into eternity. Thalaj's face fell, then he gathered it into an impassive mask, pressed his lips tight, and pivoted to leave the room. All I could do was hope that he understood how I couldn't have such a conversation in front of my Storm Sorcerer counselors. Since I'd just barely gained the majority's support, I couldn't risk showing leniency toward the way that he'd blown into the room. I searched every face in the room, ensuring that I'd adequately retained my position. It seemed I had.

The last person I looked to was Karynne, and she offered a smile and a single nod. With that, the matter seemed well handled, and after our reconnection the night before, I felt thrilled to have her support once again.

Imrythel began, "Kōgō Mairynne, may I speak freely?" She ran a hand over the black lace covering her one eye.

Turning my gaze to her, I said, "Immediate family and their first advisors hold a place on the council. As my sister's first advisor, you are welcome to offer your thoughts on the matter." This, I offered as tradition, and custom dictated as much, though I had no desire to hear her concern.

"Very well," she started. "I will stop short of objecting to the vows you have sworn. But I fear that my people, the people of the Great Sands, may have issues with the nature of your oath. As I merely represent the Sandsgales, I feel it necessary to voice my concern."

Her words were smooth and showed the respect that Ohmyn Havengale's had not, so I motioned for her to continue.

"I would ask your leave to go to my people immediately and deliver this news in person. I believe their fear will drive continued unrest within the castes, but I'd like to confirm. If such an unrest were to escalate, it could lead to a struggle on many fronts. I think our biggest adversaries would be the Fire Forgers or the Frost Fighters, but I'd not count out the Cloud Courtiers either. Though they seem secure in their position of leading the High Cloud Court, would they pass on the opportunity to have a courtier rise to the station of emperor or empress?"

Lukos reached for a goblet and added to Imrythel's suggestions, "What she says also carries merit, Kōgō Mairynne."

Ohmyn flounced into a chair. Though tamed a bit, he added, "This unrest is what I'd warned of before. It is a danger that we should monitor heavily." Grabbing his empty goblet, he looked inside, then bellowed to the room, "Is there ale?"

From where I stood, I had line of sight to everyone in the room. I clasped my hands and said, "Imrythel, thank you for your counsel. I grant you leave. You'll return to Stormskeep to provide an update once you've delivered the news?"

"I will," she answered, tipping her head.

I continued, "None of the concerns are of consequence to the nature of my vows to the Nantai people now. I have sworn my oath, and we must now turn toward managing the people to avoid such uprisings."

"Might I make one suggestion, Kōgō Mairynne?" Imrythel asked.

"Of course."

"It might do you well to receive each of the gnobles and ask that they hold the impermanence of your vows in confidence," she said.

"That is sound advice," Lukos quickly and enthusiastically offered, "and it might go a long way in working to avoid a dethronement or attempts to usurp the Storm Sorcerers' hold on the highest caste, especially with the likes of the courtiers."

Karynne stepped forward. "I, for one, am proud of my sister. She showed a decisiveness that exists in few others. I believe she earned the throne today with her conviction and action. It will be smart to take measures to protect our station, but the result of the oath is the same. She is the Nantai empress, and she has authority to rule the people as she sees fit, and should our father not return, she will rule until her death when her successor takes her place."

Solarynne looked questioningly between Karynne and me, clearly surprised at my sister's sudden show of support. Had it not been for the midnight stroll, I would have had similar questions in my mind, but this was the Karynne I knew from before and the sister I was happy to have returned.

I spread my arms. "Counselors, you are all excused. Karynne, please stay. Imrythel, would you ask Thalaj to join us?"

◇◇◇◇◇◇◇◇◇◇◇◇◇◇◇◇◇◇◇◇◇◇◇◇◇◇◇◇◇◇

OBLIGING MY WISHES, EVERYONE departed; to which destinations, I didn't know. Nor did that concern me much. I went to my sister. "Thank you for supporting me."

"It would seem that your council is coming around. Ohmyn will be your greatest challenge. It will be a long time before he'll allow the matter to rest."

I pulled the pins that held my hair, allowing it to fall about my shoulders. "Do you know where over Nantai we are at this moment?"

"The last time I spoke with the navigators, we were traveling northwest over the Narrows toward the Copper Coast. Is there somewhere specific you're concerned about?"

"Nothing specific." My eyes drifted closed, and I breathed deeply, expanding my lungs to allow the air to refresh my body. The Narrows was a strait far to the south. I'd been attempting to keep track of the route since our arrival and found it strange that I could only vaguely sense the quick-paced travel while on the cloud island. Sometime tomorrow, we'd pass the Copper Coast and be near the Evernight Marshes.

The door opened, drawing me out of my calculations. I opened my eyes just as Imrythel entered. My sister's advisor went to her side and whispered in her ear. Thalaj, on her trail, stopped just inside the room. My first guard stood with his feet at shoulder width, hands clasped behind his back, and his look betrayed no thought or feeling. Knowing I'd taken him down before, all I had now was hope that he'd see the reason behind my words and understand, or at least trust, that my scold had been necessary.

At a side table, I refilled my goblet with a sweet sparkling wine. "I begin to wonder if this day will ever end," I said to the room, but looking at no one. "Though when Otarr retires for the evening, the Hallowgales require my presence at the Cloud Temple to begin a cleansing process only known to the Gods and the clergy who represent them. Why don't we know more about what that entails?"

Silence hovered in response to my question. At length, Imrythel answered, "Kōgō Mairynne, it is a sacred rite. Outside of the people who complete the rite, only those trained as a Hallowgale are privileged enough in the eyes of the Triad to hold that knowledge."

She'd said the obvious, what everyone had learned as younglings, but it didn't allay my exhaustion at these formalities. "Well, I'd rather not go through these rites, and I don't relish the thought of the celebrations to follow." I gazed through the windows. Many hours remained before this would all begin, and I needed a distraction. "Tell me more about the search party and the plans to find Father."

"Mairynne," started Karynne, "we've already told you the extent—"

"May I?" Imrythel interrupted, placing a hand on my sister's shoulder. When Karynne nodded, her advisor continued, "Thalaj can convey anything you wish to know about that topic. And, given the tension before, I think it would be good for the two of you to talk. I would like to prepare for my journey to the Great Sands, and I'd like to confer with Karynne before my departure."

I folded my brow in confusion. "If we are truly over the Narrows, we are many leagues from your home. Wouldn't it be easier and quicker to wait for the High Cloud Court to make the full evolution? Then you'd be able to simply descend on a gale rather than having to travel overland."

"If the route of the cloud island were due north, that would be true, Kōgō Mairynne. However, the plan is to travel north along the western coast of Nantai, then across the Iced Plains. By morning, we'll be passing over the Copper Coast, and it would be quicker to travel overland from there to my home."

"Imrythel," Karynne said, "I'd rather not attend the celebrations while you leave. Maybe I should go with you."

The two exchanged looks, some unheard conversation carried on within their shared gaze. Instead of answering directly, Imrythel said, "I think you should be here for your sister, but we can discuss it further. Should we go?"

Thalaj didn't move a muscle during this exchange.

Karynne turned to me. "Do you have further need of me today?"

"No," I answered. "You may go. Thank you again for supporting me with the counselors." Before they turned to go, I caught a green flash in Imrythel's eye as she moved her gaze between my sister and me.

Alone with Thalaj, I said, "Please, be at ease." I motioned to the wine and took a seat.

Stiffly, Thalaj remained where he stood. "You requested my presence. What might I do for you, Kōgō?"

Though I regretted my necessary harshness before, I used it once again. "You may grab a glass of wine, water if you prefer, then sit with me and have a conversation." Softer, I added, "I don't wish to command you, Thalaj. It's just the two of us now. Can't we just talk?"

He relented, poured himself a goblet from the water pitcher, and sat across the table from the chair I'd taken.

Formal expectations hovered in the air, and he would wait hours for me to break the silence.

Sighing, I began, "Before, my response to your demands emphasized our caste difference." I ran two fingers up and down the fat stem of the goblet, stroking the ridges of the pottery as I continued, "Unfortunately, in this room, with my father's counselors, I had too much at stake to allow you to question my motives too." I paused, waiting for him to answer.

His words came stiffly. "Mairynne, I meant no disrespect, but I need to know why you took such an oath. This is one of my duties to the throne"—he hesitated—"but it also comes from my concern for you."

Leaning forward, I extended a hand to him but couldn't quite reach. To my relief, he met me partway, placing his hand in mine.

"Thalaj," I said. "I welcome you to speak to me openly when we are alone. However, I can't afford to have anyone question your position in relation to their own. As Father taught me well, this is an unfortunate and necessary approach as ruler of the Nantai people. By our very nature, we position ourselves toward a higher caste, always seeking ways to gain the next level within our individual hierarchies." I ducked my head to secure eye contact. "You are not like that, and I also believe differently. But Father always said that without that order, the Nantai people would become lost."

"Then I truly don't understand why you took a temporary oath."

At that, I stalled, took a drink of the sweet wine, looked around the room, then met his dark eyes forcefully. Quietly, but with emphasis, I said, "I told you before that I intend to search for my father at your side."

"No, Mairynne. You can't go. Once you commune with Otarr and Selene, you must remain in Stormskeep to rule the people. This ensures the order so told to you by Tennō Atheryn."

"Thalaj, yes. I can. And I will." I sighed. "You can leave this part to me. In fact, I want to go to Umbra with you. I feel that the people would be more amicable to parting with their relic if I were to offer some diplomatic terms. They are, after all, Nantai people too."

Thalaj shifted in his seat, straightened his spine, and inhaled sharply, an obvious objection working its way up his throat and struggling to gain voice.

Holding up an index finger, I continued, "But I understand that this is impossible right now. Such diplomacy will have to wait."

He relaxed if only by a small measure.

I continued, "But I think you should leave the courts and begin your journey into the Evernight Marshes while I tend to these cleansing rites and preside over the celebrations to follow."

"How can I ensure your safety here while I'm gone?"

"You brought a team. I've been in no genuine danger here. Do you not trust your selected people to see me guarded?"

"I trust the people I brought beyond doubt, but—"

I interrupted, "There are too many people with eyes on me here. I will be fine. And I'd like you to return to Stormskeep as soon as possible so we can understand how we can use this token from Umbra to find the Tsinti and figure out what happened to my father. This waiting and politicking is eating me alive."

Thalaj remained quiet, but his throat worked as if he swallowed what he wanted to say.

"Tomorrow, we should be passing through the skies somewhere over the Copper Coast. That is not far from the Evernight Marshes. You should go then. Do you need help in calling a gale strong enough to lower you safely to the surface?"

"Most likely." Thalaj lowered his eyes. "As only half Storm Sorcerer, my storm magic is not as strong as yours or others, and the air is thinner up here."

I'd assumed as much and said, "You brought Roryn with you on this detail. Since you were going to take him on the journey, maybe you should take him tomorrow. I'll probably be in a bath somewhere in the temple—being useless." I huffed and reclined in my chair.

"Mairynne, that only leaves you with two guards."

I gave him a hard stare. It worked to stop his objection, but he returned it with his dark eyes.

In this silent exchange, a screech pealed through the space beneath the cloud island, shaking the very foundation of the royal chambers. Standing, I rushed to the door and out onto the balcony. As I was closer to the door, I reached the edge before my first guard, but Thalaj came quickly to my side. Beyond the railing and far below, the southernmost part of Nantai appeared as a narrow strip of land between two expansive blue seas—the Syrensea to the west and the Mannakasea to the east.

"What was that?" I asked, my pulse thudding hard in my throat. "The same we heard at the Falls?"

Thalaj shook his head gravely, pushing in front of me protectively. "I wish I had an answer," he said, his eyes growing darker than usual, seeming concerned as he turned and ushered me back inside. "But it definitely sounds like something you shouldn't face until we know more."

I pushed against him, struggling to see something over the balcony, anything that may have caused the ear-splitting noise. He wielded his lithe strength gently, but it was more than a match for me, and I soon found myself back inside and behind the glass. When he had secured the door, he turned and said, "I never discovered its source after that night by Stormskeep Falls."

Before we could further discuss, counselors from every corner of the royal chambers moved quickly, steps fueled by fear, into the room. Everyone asked after the sound at once, and though I trembled with the same fear, I had the burden of addressing my people—even my leaders. I turned and moved deeper into the room, holding both hands high. "Counselors, please . . ." I started.

Karynne placed her fingers in the corners of her mouth and whistled. When everyone looked at her, she motioned to me.

"Thank you, Sister."

She dipped her head.

"We mustn't panic. Certainly, a bird of prey is hunting this night, and the sound is different here. There is naught for us to fear inside."

Ohmyn shook his head, his cheeks blubbering. "That was no bird. There was the same sound over Stormskeep a fortnight past."

Karynne cleared her throat and calmly moved to my side. "Kōgō Mairynne speaks the truth. That sound is but a screech owl. It has been many years, but I heard it during my travels with Mother and Father."

I smiled my thanks to her, not putting much faith in the explanation but needing everyone to remain calm. "Return to your evening routines. All is well."

As directed, they shuffled back into their individual rooms, murmuring all the while.

◇◇◇◇◇◇◇◇◇◇◇◇◇◇◇◇◇◇◇◇◇◇◇◇◇◇◇◇◇◇

TASMYNNE, PRIESTESS OF SELENE, had woven my hair into uncounted braids upon completion of the cleansing rituals; and my scalp felt drawn, the corners of my eyes slanted, my brows and forehead pulled taut. The acolytes assured me the tension would ease after a few days, a matter I felt grateful for as I'd wear them for a full cycle of the moon goddess as tradition prescribed.

"When Selene's full face shines over Nantai once again, you may release these bonds," Tasmynne had said as she finished the work.

My scalp throbbed as I sat on the dais in the high court room turned celebration hall; I leaned to my left and whispered to Karynne, "Did Thalaj leave while I was at the temple?"

"He did along with his guard, Roryn. On what mission did you send them?"

I shook my head. "Nothing of importance. He should be at Stormskeep by the time we return."

My sister gazed upon me as if she wanted to question my motives further but decided to either trust my judgment or simply allow it to rest. Instead, she said with a smile, "The braids are a lovely look for you, Mairynne."

"You jest, Karynne." I laughed off her praise.

"No, I speak only in truth."

Under the dimly lit orbs floating near the ceiling, the gnobles and their retinues each wandered leisurely into the hall, gathering in small clusters and holding individual conversations. I envied their seemingly carefree vitality now that the time for formality had passed. We were there to celebrate the Nantai people ushering in a new era. Every caste wore their finest attire, and despite the veritable rainbow of colors, each set of tunics, dresses, or robes gleamed under orb-light. The very attire my people wore bespoke a lightness in the air. Yet somehow, I couldn't join my people in their frivolity.

Lifting a hand to the back of my head, I said, "If only they felt so lovely." I gave a small, sad laugh and dropped my hand. Karynne and I both looked around the room, holding a silent conversation. It seemed that everyone present had someone, and that night we drifted together as the only two who missed another half. I made another effort to extend our banter, "Imrythel departed for the Great Sands?"

Karynne nodded. On my other side and in her typical fashion, Yasmynne cuddled up to Nestryn and engaged little with others, but they seemed enthralled by the gathering of all the castes around the center stage. The scene that awaited looked like a living mountain top where a river sprang forth. Boulders and green grasses surrounded the spring. I'd never seen the legend of Sosano and Inara enacted by the Cloud Courtiers, but I marveled already at the illusions built into the set—a gently swaying tree, ever-running water, and blades of grass moving as if a wind swept through the room.

A fine meal, a feast in truth, lay before me. Although, after two nights and two days of fasting, I had communed with the Gods just before being led into the celebration hall. My appetite well sated with the sweet wine and sacred grains of the Gods, I couldn't bring myself to partake. Gnobles came forward at regular intervals to pay their respect and make conversation easily forgotten. String musicians on a balcony serenaded the guests as they finished their dinner and moved closer toward the hall's center for better views of the upcoming performance.

I sipped warmed ruby wine and observed my people for what seemed an eternity, until they stopped arriving, stopped eating, and the din of conversation almost overshadowed the music. As I sat there, fighting exhaustion, the door opened and a herald entered, motioning to the percussionist who stood on a pedestal near the door. The courtier on the percussion stand, guised to be larger than the others and dressed only in simple *ketill* pants, nodded. He lifted a mallet and struck the bell.

One . . . two . . . a dozen times, and the people encircled the stage, falling into silent anticipation. At all grand Nantai celebrations, the hosts arranged for the enactment of the most famous Nantai legend, "The Spirit Sosano, the Blooming Princess, and the Regalia of the Nantai." I had seen it a dozen or more times that I could recall, only once with a single Cloud Courtier amidst the troupe, but never with the combined talents of the illusionists.

The orbs around the room dimmed as a narrator in long black robes and a black-feathered mask moved around the stage, flourished arms toward the crowd, and sent glittering sparks to encircle the set. The sparks lifted to the heavens, revealing three people huddled on the mountain top near the head of the River Hi. An old man comforted his wife, and a woman in the prime of her beauty stood brave-faced in a simple sheath dress, wearing a string of bright, tooth-shaped jewels.

As the narrator began, I found myself leaning forward and taking note of every minor element. The scene itself familiar, the details enabled by illusionary magic painted a more original experience than I could ever recall. When the old man cried, his tears glittered like diamonds trailing slowly down his cheek. When the old woman wailed, my chair shook with her sorrow.

The black-robed narrator, double-timbred and harmonious, continued, ". . . and Sosano, Spirit of the Storm, descended from the heavens above and went to the Father. He asked the old man why he cried so, and the old man replied, 'The eight-forked serpent will soon come to devour our last daughter, Inara.' "

The old woman wailed, and I felt her pain as my own. The actors mutely portrayed their characters before the Nantai gnobles, and the crowd was as enraptured as I. The black-robed narrator danced around the mountain top, driving the legend forward:

"Sosano replied, 'If you will give me thy daughter, I will save her from the serpent, slay him, and honor your daughter for eternity.'

"And so the old man and the old woman kneeled at the spirit's feet and begged for Sosano to make it so, for their daughter to live. Thus Sosano took their daughter. With the magic of the storms, he called forth a great spinning wind that encircled Inara, and when it left, a blooming tree stood in her place beside the headwaters of the River Hi.

"Then Sosano bade the old man and woman brew eight tubs of sweet wine and place them in larger tubs of bitter-milk spirits. He instructed the man and woman to place them in a circle around the tree of the Blooming Spirit and to hide in the surrounding trees and await the arrival of the eight-headed serpent."

My hand idly drifted to cover my mouth. Where before, this had all been mythos in my mind, I then connected the story with the cleansing ritual I'd just experienced. A rite in which I ceremoniously drank from eight goblets and bathed in bitter-milk baths. A pairing with this story bloomed in my chest that hadn't existed before, and I watched and listened with every fiber of my soul while the next scene unfolded.

"When the serpent came, eight sets of eyes glowed like the red of winter's cherry, and on its back, firs and cypresses grew. But when it slithered to the headwaters of the River Hi, the sweet wine and bitter milk distracted the heads. Each head drank deeply and sank into drunken sleep.

"Whilst the serpent slept, Sosano drew his ten-span sword and chopped the serpent into pieces. When he split the serpent's belly, he found the Eight-Span Mirror of Truth and laid it at the base of the Blooming Spirit that was Inara and continued about his work.

"When he came to the tail, the blade rang and came away notched. Sosano dissected the tail to reveal a bright sword. He washed it in the River Hi and held it to the heavens. When he did this, clouds gathered above, opening with cleansing rain. The rain washed away the blood from the grasses and dissolved the serpent to fertilize the ground. Green, wet grass shone with small diamonds on each blade where Sosano had slain the serpent. And he named the blade the Sword of Gathering Clouds.

"When the serpent had gone and the rain had cleared, Sosano took the Sword of Gathering Clouds to the Blooming Spirit and turned her back into the woman, Inara. Thankful that he'd saved her from her sisters' fates, she bestowed the tooth-shaped jewels upon him. Sosano made Inara his wife in the early morning when Otarr and Selene both gazed over the land. After they had married, he presented his gifts of thanks to the Gods. To Otarr, he gave the Sword of Gathering Clouds. To Selene, the Eight-Span Mirror of Truth. And to Atun, he presented the jewels.

"And so the Nantai Treasures came to be and the Spirit of the Storm, Sosano, lived eternally at the headwaters of the River hi with his wife, Inara, the Blooming Spirit."

The scene at the center of the room fell into darkness and the orbs illuminated the awestruck audience. When the center came back into the light, the actors and set alike had vanished. Gasps went up around the room. Silently and still, I remained. I'd never known how closely the legend of Sosano and Inara was linked to the emperor's or empress's regalia and our rituals, and I felt simultaneously proud to be Nantai empress and heavy in the chest. Whether it had been the illusionary talents of the Cloud Courtiers or the reality of my ascension and cleansing, I couldn't be certain, but this enactment of the well-known legend rang so poignantly that a tear leaked from one eye as the actors returned and bowed to the audience.

The percussionist's mallet struck a shield, sending a long singular ring through the room and marking the end.

Applause erupted.

The black-robed narrator came and bowed low at my feet, the feathers of his mask brushing along my skirts. Silently then, the courtier stood and looked me in the eyes, the gray of his irises and the surrounding glittering white set into a coal-black skin within the even blacker mask setting me on edge. A chill ran from my neck to my tailbone as the narrator turned away and retreated.

I longed for Thalaj.

EIGHT

A Spellcaster in Arashi

GRAY CLOUDS HAD OVERCAST ARASHI on the day we'd embarked upon the High Cloud Court, hiding the color of our land from sight. That wasn't so when the misted island returned to Stormskeep. As we, the Storm Sorcerers, had been the first to climb those misty stairs, we would also be the first to disembark. As the island began its descent under Otarr's heat, the falls at Stormskeep appeared small in the distance. But as the cloud foundation descended further and encircled the keep's highest spire, they grew larger, pouring between lush greenery from the cliff.

It put me in mind of the Sosano reenactment.

At my side, Karynne sighed, her shoulders dropping with the long sound of relief. "It feels good to see our home again. I am certain it will feel even better to rest in my own bed this night."

The entirety of the High Cloud Court of Gnobles stood in a semicircle to bid my party farewell. In my time at the High Cloud Court, I had learned an impressive many things about the Nantai people. My people. Yet mystery and curiosity had loomed around every corner. After Yasmynne's assignation at Tsanseri's court, I hadn't seen Alto-Trea again, but Tsanseri herself had come to the royal chambers the morning after the celebrations to offer me her well wishes. She had looked humble, unlike how she'd presented herself at court, and offered me a cuff.

She instructed that I should wear it against the skin on my upper right arm at all times. "'Tis but a pretty bauble, Kōgō, but it may be of use one day," she added before kissing me on both palms, then either cheek, and finally taking her leave.

It'd been an unexpected gesture, but in the end, it reassured me to have her favor.

There on the cloud deck, I locked eyes with Tsanseri before I took the first misty step toward my castle's roof. We'd each dispensed with the familiarity, reassuming our regal personas. I touched the cuff beneath my sleeve, and she gave an almost imperceptible nod.

Down I went, anxious to be home, to see my aunt, to see how Corwyn had recovered, and to see Thalaj. He should have returned by now, and I grasped onto the notion I'd soon be off onto my own adventure in search of my father. Like many times before, the thought of Father heated the stone around my neck.

Both feet planted atop Stormskeep's high tower, I moved forward to allow the others room and scanned the roof. A sole acolyte, apprentice to the priest Arlyn of Otarr, awaited our arrival. The boy, unknown to me, watched and waited with more aplomb than I would expect of one so young. His parents had likely dedicated him to the Triad's service at birth. Arlyn gusted past me, wind shifting my skirt, and went to the acolyte. They stood close; the boy, while possessing a youth's wiry build, stood eye-to-eye with the priest. I couldn't hear their conversation, but from the quick words, there seemed urgency in his message. After a moment, Arlyn turned, a shadow across his face.

Unconscious of my steps, I joined them. "What is the trouble?"

Arlyn bowed his head. "Kōgō Mairynne, Nadialynne Riversgale requires your presence at the House of Healing."

"Still?" I demanded, looking between the priest and his apprentice. "Corwyn is still not well? Do we know what happened? Or from what he suffers?"

Arlyn shook his head and opened his mouth to speak, but it was the boy who answered first.

"Kōgō," he said, his head bowed and waiting.

It was the first time I'd met a subject beyond my household, my council, and the attendants to the High Cloud Court. I gaped at him, not wishing to accept the title for the heavenly sovereign. It took me a long moment to realize that he awaited my permission. Blinking, I shook off my surprise and said, "Please, continue."

The boy looked up, his bright eyes easily holding my gaze. He'd shown the proper respect and my royal position hadn't intimidated him, further clarifying that he'd been preparing for his position amongst our clergy for many moons. "The healers are not sharing what happened, but Lady Nadia asked me to await your return inside the spire. She bade that I fetch you to the House of Healing without delay."

"Lead the way." I held a hand forward to the acolyte, then motioned to the two guards that Thalaj had assigned for my protection.

They, along with Karynne, joined us. Instead of going to the stairs and descending through the keep, we went to the roof's edge. Arlyn called an updraft and held it steady while the other five stepped into the air. I grasped my skirt tight about my legs and joined them. As Arlyn eased the flow of magic, we floated downward until our feet touched the soft grass at the base of the castle's stone walls.

Arlyn then stumbled, leaned against the stone, and said between heavy breaths,

"Too much magic. You have enough help." He looked at each of the guards. "I'm going to retire and recover."

I reached for him. "You should have asked us to help with the magic."

Arlyn waved me off. "I'll be well, Kōgō. Please go; tend to your family. Baldwyn?"

To his senior priest, Baldwyn said, "I shall return to you in your chambers shortly." Then to us, he added, "This way." He turned for the city street and onward toward the House of Healing.

Karynne at my side, we followed. I told my sister what little information I had, which felt like significantly less than I should know. When we arrived, we continued through the clean and sparsely furnished front rooms to a door at the end of a long hall. Inside, Corwyn sat upright in the bed, pale with ashen circles beneath both eyes, and he'd lost enough weight that his shoulder and arm bones made him look more square than normal. Nadia sat at the bedside, holding his hand. She had tired shadows under her eyes, but otherwise appeared well. She kissed her consort's cheek, came around the foot of his bed, and opened her arms for a hug.

Although I imagined I lent her my strength, as we embraced, she asked, "How are you, Mairynne?"

I gave a mirthless laugh. "How am I? You've been here worrying over Corwyn's health since we left, and you're asking how I am?"

Serenely, Nadia smiled, shifting her eyes over to Karynne then back to mine. "I believe Sentei Summergale is waiting. Would you join me in speaking with the healer?"

"Of course."

Nadia turned to my sister. "Karynne, will you remain with Corwyn? If he has any major tremors, call down the hall for us."

We all looked at the frail man in the bed who, as if to demonstrate the tremors, lifted a shaky cup to his mouth and sipped. Nadia took my arm, and we left the room.

My aunt tapped on the door across the hall, cracked it open, and said, "Sentei?"

Rustling came from within, and the healer said, "Come. Do come in, Lady Nadia." His voice, though gentle, sounded as if it echoed around the bottom of a metal jug, and when the door widened, a small, balding man with a thin nose stood in the opening. Exacerbating his birdlike appearance, his eyes and mouth both gaped as he gained sight of me. He bowed. "Kōgō."

I ground my teeth and closed my eyes for a second as I grappled with accepting the new formality. Releasing a sigh and settling my gaze back onto the healer, I said, "Sentei Summergale, please be at ease."

He, well-seasoned in his profession, accepted his title far better than I accepted being formally addressed as the ruler by my people. It reinforced how ill-prepared I remained for this duty. I preferred to hear my name, or even Lady Mairynne, over Kōgō, the title for the heavenly sovereign. That my family still used my given name was a small blessing. I couldn't bear the burden of losing my identity in entirety.

The healer and Nadia shared a knowing look, and the birdlike man waved a hand toward a small table and chairs in the far corner of the room beneath the only window. "Do have a seat and let us discuss Corwyn's condition."

I went toward the offered seat, scanning the shelves that lined the long room. Someone had aligned corked bottles with various liquids, powders, and dried leaves or petals in meticulous rows. Each had a neatly scribed label, but I only recognized a few names—among them daisai, which I'd taken before to relieve the cramping around my cycle, and umeboshi which calmed a turning stomach. On the table, a book, larger than the annals I'd spent days pouring over in the royal library, sat open and scrolls littered the shelves behind where the healer had obviously been reading.

Silently, Nadia went to the window and gazed into the gardens where the healer apprentices tended to numerous herbs and flowers. I stood across the table, waiting, and Sentei scurried to the book.

"Look." The healer paused and pointed. "Do read here," he said, indicating some small script about halfway down the page.

I looked down to where he pointed and read aloud, "Primlock. Grows on the Lower Peninsula of Yōtei. If consumed will cause vomiting, diarrhea, tremors, sores in the mouth, difficulty breathing, and convulsions often resulting in death." I jerked my gaze up from the page, searching between the healer and my aunt. Nadia gave a tight-lipped nod with eyes that told me I understood correctly before I even asked the question. Heedless of that assurance, my question spilled out, "Are you stating that someone has poisoned Corwyn?"

"Yes. You have my meaning." The healer wrung his hands.

"Who would do such a thing to such a harmless man? Corwyn never so much as raises his voice." Again, I looked between Sentei Summergale and Nadia.

They exchanged another look.

"What?" I demanded.

Nadia sighed. "Have a seat, Mairynne." She took the chair across the table and the wiry healer sat as well. "I believe someone tried to poison me, not Corwyn."

I didn't want to sit; so tentatively and ready to stand again, I lowered myself to the very edge of the chair. First they'd informed me that someone who lived within my household suffered from poison derived from a plant not existing near Arashi, and to add to the matter, the poisoner had possibly intended to target another within my family. Hadn't we been through enough? What if the intended target hadn't been Nadia? I bit my lip, hard enough to feel piercing pain, but just shy of drawing blood. Forcing my voice to remain level, I asked, "How can you be so sure it's this"—I looked back at the page to recall the word—"primlock?" Beside the word was a sketch of a fluted red flower. Beneath the description of the effects, the underlined word *antidote* sat lonely on the page, nothing listed in the blank space.

"All." Sentei Summergale paused again after the single word answer, a manner in his speech I found quite odd. "Corwyn Dawnsgale has had all the symptoms listed. I've searched this book and the remainder of my library." He motioned to a tall shelf in a recess behind me I hadn't noticed. Books towered from floor to ceiling. My heart continued to fall as I turned back to him. He pointed a bony finger to the page. "This. This is the only ailment that lists every indicator. And though the book also states it often causes immediate death, those who survive display every single symptom that Corwyn has experienced."

My voice felt hollow as I asked the next logical, yet fruitless question, "Will he survive?"

Nadia sat in silence, her lip quivering and tears brimming in her eyes.

"Hope." The healer took her hand. "All we can do right now is hope he will recover. I am watching him closely and treating the symptoms, but I've never treated primlock poisoning."

"And it says immediate death is more frequent," I mused, considering how Jessa had suddenly turned up dead not so very long before Corwyn fell ill. I stood, faced the window, and ran my sweaty palms over my skirts. "Who would do this thing?" The question seemed empty, and certainly neither Nadia nor Sentei Summergale had the answer. Indeed, I hadn't expected one.

"Something." Sentei Summergale's face twisted. "There is something else. A symptom you should now about, Kōgō. In the nailbeds at the tips of Corwyn Dawnsgale's fingers, there is a discoloration. A greenish tent. Take a look when you return." The man looked down and wrung his hands. "It was the same for Jessamynne Feathergale."

I froze. Inside the healer's workshop and library, the air thickened and grew even more stale, no wind to speak of, a great contrast to the gardens just beyond the window's panes. At length, I pulled my gaze away from the fertility outside. To my aunt, I asked, "What have you done to protect yourself and Corwyn from another poisoning?"

Nadia looked down, then uncertainly back up. Running a finger along a groove in the table, she said, "Everything we consume, I prepare by my own hand, or Sentei Summergale administers."

Inconvenient, but a necessity. "Very well. We will have to figure out a way to further protect you while we try to discover the source of the poisoning. Where is Thalaj? Has he returned?"

Nadia's brows knit. "We thought he traveled with you."

"No, he left the High Cloud Court on an errand. I thought he'd have returned by now."

"Kōgō," the healer started.

I flipped a hand to indicate he should continue.

"Careful," he said. "Do take caution with whom you share this information. And do consider protecting yourself, as well as your house, until we find who is responsible."

I glared at him. The accusation—mild though it may have been—stirred ire within. "If there is one person I trust implicitly, Sentei, it is Gensui Thalaj Northerngale. I just need him to return to set the investigation into motion. In the meantime, do you have other ideas on how we can protect my family and those who attend to us?"

"A taster. A poison taster, Kōgō?"

"I couldn't condemn anyone else to such a fate. What kind of ruler would that make me? Does the primlock have any detectable smell or other property?"

"Unknown. The information I have given is all that I possess. But . . ." He scratched his beak-like nose.

"Yes? But what?" I prompted.

"Golems. There is a woman in the Bottomside district who practices the Small Folk's magic. Castings on stones and the like. She brews many of my potions, but she has some rumored skills in animation that we might find useful."

My eyes widened on an inhale. "A single-purpose golem taster for each of us. Perfect. Send someone to have her complete the task." When Sentei Summergale nodded, I turned to Nadia. "Do you have any thoughts on why someone would want to poison you?"

"I have two. It's either linked with your mother's murder—"

"Do we know if she suffered the same fate?" I interrupted.

Nadia shook her head.

"Inconclusive," said Sentei Summergale. "We can't be certain. I checked my notes for when we examined the empress's body, but I made no note of the green fingertips. It is possible I missed it."

I expelled a breath, my shoulders sagging. "That would have been too easy of an explanation, especially given the fact that Father went missing rather than turned up dead. What was your second thought, Nadia?"

She remained utterly still. "Someone may have discovered that you would name me as your first advisor."

That didn't seem possible. "We were alone in my chambers when I asked that of you, and I had told no one at the time Corwyn fell ill. Did you share with anyone else?"

She gave a slight head shake. "No one but Corwyn himself."

"Very well. The—"

The door flew open, and an apprentice healer appeared panting. When he caught sight of me, he straightened and tried to gain his breath. He addressed me formally, "Kōgō," and bowed his head, his chest still heaving with exertion.

"Go ahead," I snapped.

"Sentei, we need you to attend to another patient. He's badly battered."

"Pardon." He stood and shuffled to the door. "Excuse me, Kōgō and Lady Nadia," he mumbled as he shuffled toward the door.

Nadia and I exchanged a questioning look. I hesitated, then curious I followed Sentei Summergale, my aunt in my wake. In the front of the House of Healing, I sighted a familiar face, a guard, Roryn—Thalaj's travel companion—pulling a litter.

My hand over my mouth, I ran to the man crumpled on the litter.

SENTEI SUMMERGALE SHOUTED ORDERS to Roryn and the apprentice healers to carry Thalaj to another room and place him on a table at waist height. I refused to leave his side. I'd sent him to this fate, so they would have to work around me.

"Thalaj," I whispered over and over again close to his battered face, hoping he'd hear and it might help that I was there with him.

His only replies were grunts, moans, and a long mewl as they stretched his body long for a more thorough examination. However, he held his hands constantly in tight fists, white about the knuckles.

When Roryn had arrived, dragging him into the House of Healing, he'd barely been holding on to consciousness. During the examination, he opened his eyes only once, and when he saw me, he grabbed my hand with more strength than I would have imagined he could possibly have possessed. He placed a small object in my hand, hissed in sudden pain, and drifted into oblivion.

Though I could see with my eyes how he suffered from physical abuse rather than poison, I still needed more proof. I turned his hands to look at the coloring around his fingernails. Dirt- and blood-crusted, but no hint of green. The healers cleaned, bandaged, and examined Thalaj thoroughly, an easier task after he succumbed to his body's need for rest. With the blood scrubbed away, I examined his hand again. Only the normal olive color of his skin stared back at me. I sagged with relief.

Sentei Summergale dripped some liquid into the side of his mouth. "Sleep," the healer said. "The potion will keep him asleep as my students tend to his wounds. It appears he has been on the losing end of a combat, but no concerns similar to my other patient." He and the apprentices worked around me for some time more.

I watched Thalaj swallow reflexively. He rested and I sat by his head, watching and waiting, my fingers itching to touch his bruised eye or split lip. But I resisted the temptation and wrung my hands in my lap.

Sentei Summergale had departed, leaving us with two of his healer apprentices to finish the work.

A young woman laid a hand on my shoulder. "Kōgō?"

I looked away from the blossoming bruise on my first guard's chin. "Yes?" Sensing her hesitation and fearing the worst, I rushed to ask, "What is it?"

"You may not want to remain for this part. Setting bones makes an awful sound, one that most people never wish to hear."

By the door, Roryn blanched, turned, and left the room.

"No. I will stay." I swallowed, turning my gaze to Thalaj, then back to the woman. "The fault for his condition is mine, and I will bear witness to his recovery."

She nodded and positioned herself on the other side of the table at Thalaj's hip. She held his upper leg while another apprentice—a visibly stronger apprentice—grabbed onto his ankle and pulled, twisting slightly. The girl had spoken truth in her warning. Like the repeated sound of a whip or dozens of whips, the bone crackled and snapped as it searched for its natural position. The apprentice pulling grunted, furrowing his brow and setting his mouth in a tight line. From his apparent frustration, it seemed the bones might remain misaligned. He relented briefly, studying the shape of Thalaj's other leg, then adjusted his stance and went at it again. This time, chills raced up and down my arms as the sound of eggshells underfoot echoed around the room. At last, Thalaj's leg emitted a thunk, and the apprentice sagged over his work, sweat beading on his forehead.

He sighed as he caught my questioning stare and offered a quick nod. I eased a bit, happy that the sound was over, but also reassured that he'd gotten the bone back into place. Carefully, they wrapped the broken leg in linen, prepared a thick paste, and smeared it over the linen. This, they did several more times, then placed the casted leg on a pillow.

When their remaining bandaging and other ministrations were complete, they wheeled the table down the hall toward Corwyn's room but turned into one of the closer doors. I followed, still refusing to leave him alone. They moved Thalaj to a bed and covered him with a fresh blanket. When he was well settled, Sentei Summergale came to me and rested a hand on my arm. "Kōgō," he said and waited.

I nodded to give him leave to speak, tears brimming in my eyes and a lump in my throat preventing my words.

"He will rest for many hours now. You may return to your family. We will care for him well."

Scrubbing away the tears, I gave him a hard stare. "No. As I told your apprentice, I will remain with him."

The healer gave a semblance of a smile and said gently, "I understand," and left the room. I believed that he did understand my pain as I watched him go. Clearly, he had years of experience with this manner. Alone with my guard, I pulled up a chair and sat between Thalaj and the window. How long I remained there, I couldn't say.

Nadia came sometime later. "Mairynne," she said, sinking to her knees at my side.

My tears flowed again. They'd streaked my cheeks before, but I hadn't noticed. Now they rewet the crusty trails.

Soothingly, my aunt said, "This is not your fault."

"Nadia, I sent him into this."

Her eyes held only compassion as I looked into their depths for answers. She replied with a demanding question, "Do you think for one moment that this man went unwillingly at your behest?"

I bit my bottom lip, tears still rolling down my face. I wanted to explain it away, to say he swore to serve me as his empress and that came with certain risks. Had that not been so, he wouldn't have gone on my errand, but somewhere deep inside, the truthful answer to her question lingered.

My aunt shook her head. "No. He went because of his love for you and your father before you. He is loyal to his very end, and he will recover." She squeezed my hands. "Night is falling. You need to get some rest."

It was only in that moment that I realized how long I'd been at his side, only then that I regained some sense of time. The day had left, and twilight had descended.

"I can't," I said in a thin voice.

She pulled me to my feet and gave me a hard stare. "Solarynne is here with Corwyn. There is a bed in the room across the hall. I've slept there many nights since you departed for the High Cloud Courts. I will watch over Thalaj so you may rest a couple of hours."

An objection bubbled up my throat, but Nadia cut me off, insisting that I go. In her command, I saw everything that my mother had once been, and I relented. After a warm embrace, I relented to both my aunt's will and my exhaustion. As I crossed the room toward the door, I peered back at Thalaj.

Sleep then on my mind, I startled when Sentei Summergale stepped inside just as I reached for the handle.

"Kōgō." He waited again by the rules of decorum.

I sighed at the address, feeling a need to write this tradition out of our culture, but it was my burden to accept. I motioned for him to continue.

"Zafrynne," he said. "The spellcaster, she will be here at dawn, and we can instruct her on what we need in the way of golems."

A glance back at Nadia reinforced her resolve for me to rest. "Very well," I said. "Please wake me when she arrives."

In the bed across the hall, I prayed briefly to the moon goddess, Selene, that she watch over us from high in the night sky. I threw the covers off in one moment, then pulled them back around me in the next. An hour, maybe more, passed. Finding sleep seemed impossible as I tossed from side to side. Finally, I found comfort on my back and counted my breaths, slowing them by measures until I fell into a fitful dreamscape.

Everything from the last few months swarmed in my mind and blended into pictures that made little sense. Alto-Trea danced with my mother. Corwyn fell to his death beside a table, yet we weren't in Nadia's cottage. Rather this happened at a feast upon the cloud island, in the High Cloud Court. My father cried red tears over my mother's pyre. Tsanseri battered Thalaj until he became unrecognizable. My sisters and their first advisors mingled in the temple where I'd communed with the Gods. Nadia, Solarynne, and the rest of the council performed upon the mountain's top, and a tree grew high above me, raining down its flowers as I rested in the grass. A crackling came in the distance, growing louder and louder. A creak sounded and a thud, and I shot upright in the bed.

"Kōgō," the healer's nasally voice called, and I peeled my eyes open. The gloaming of morning cast a gray hue over the room, and the birdlike healer stood in the open door. "Zafrynne has arrived."

SCRUBBING BOTH HANDS OVER my face, I worked to gather my sleepy thoughts and banish the odd images that had littered the dream. My mind only dallied there for a moment before I pushed the covers aside and landed on my feet, and headed for the room across the hall. The healer stood aside allowing me to pass, but I sensed him at my back as I opened the door and found Nadia still sitting beside a resting Thalaj.

"Kōgō."

"Would you just speak already?" I snapped, turning to the sentei. I tired of the honorific and the waiting for my acknowledgment, longing for simple, straightforward speech. "For now, I excuse you from such formality. When this is all said and done, we may return to it."

A cloud drifted over his face—dismay at my outburst most likely—but he recovered quickly. He tipped his head forward and with a mite less assurance in his voice, he said, "Rest." He wrung his hands. "Gensui Thalaj Northerngale has rested well all night. You were right to sleep."

I inhaled, attempting to level myself. The reaction was wrong, I knew, but I was little more than a youngling myself, and my impatience was inevitable. I had to make amends, but I found it hard to let go of my frustration. Holding my breath helped, and once it had eased from my lungs, I said, "I am very sorry, Sentei." My reasons for snapping danced in my mind behind those words, but I left it at that. He had no need of explanation, and I didn't care to wash away the sentiment through further explanation.

"Well." He nodded. "I will have Teralynne watch over your guard until the three of us have spoken with Zafrynne. He won't wake until much later today, so you have plenty of time to return before then." The healer left.

Nadia stood, crossed the room to me, and silently folded me into her arms. The embrace soothed me like nothing else possibly could in the moment. "Sentei Summergale is right. Thalaj rested the night with nothing but the gentle rise and fall of his shoulders as he breathed."

"It sounds like he found the rest I searched for long and hard."

"But you slept?" She pulled back, looking me over.

"I did. Not well, but I did."

"It is something."

The healer and Teralynne, the girl who had helped him tend to Thalaj the day before, returned. She took the chair at the bedside while Nadia and I followed Sentei Summergale down the hall, past the front room and the room where they'd set Thalaj's leg the day before, around a corner to the right, and down a long corridor. The healer opened the door and a gust of warmth rushed out.

Inside a narrow and lengthy room with a kettle brewing in a stone hearth, a long table sat centered under herbs hung to dry from the ceiling. A wispy woman with heavy silver hair sat at one end of the table dressed in simple black robes, the hood resting on her curved back. The healer introduced us to Zafrynne Keeningale. She didn't stand immediately, didn't offer me the respect that the others had. She merely glanced down into her cup and then back to the three of us and said, "I'll put on more tea."

Had I not watched her gather the herbs from the plants drying above, I wouldn't have accepted the cup from her hand. But since she had, and since the sentei took a first sip, I accepted graciously and joined the gathering at the table. The healer told Zafrynne what we required in the way of golems.

She replied, "How many?"

"Ten," I answered without hesitation. I'd counted those I wished to protect yesterday upon learning of this as an option.

Her brow arched in question. "Are you certain that none of the ten are responsible for the malady already befallen the Dawnsgale?"

Glancing first at Nadia, then the healer, I allowed the suspicion to rest for a moment and asked, "How do you know it's a Dawnsgale?"

"Rumors, my young kōgō," she said, her voice sounding almost dusty, like it had dried out over decades of living in an arid climate. Maybe she'd spent too much time in a room much like this, where the fires burned constantly and smoked herbs for use in potions. She raised a brow. "Again, you are certain that none of the ten is a culprit?"

Sinking onto the bench, I tipped the cup and drank the minty warmth. It both energized and calmed me as soon as I'd swallowed the last of it, and I inspected the bottom of the cup where the herbs stuck to the glazed stoneware. "I can be certain of very little right now, Zafrynne."

She grabbed my cup and while she studied the herbal remnants, said, "It can take me several of Otarr's cycles to complete one golem. The task for this golem is simple, though, so I'd say two days for each. I will need hair from each of the people you wish to have me animate in miniature form."

Nadia cleared her throat. "Very well. The first one goes to Mairynne." She reached over and tugged a few hairs from my head.

"Ouch." I stared at my aunt, considering how strange of her to react so suddenly. Rubbing the spot where she'd plucked the hairs from my scalp, I added, "Nadia's and Corwyn's should follow. They've already fallen victim, and we need to prevent that from happening again. I'd like my sisters to each have one also. And Thalaj." As the last name fell from my lips, I tucked my chin, chagrin eating away at me for having already nearly lost him to whatever had happened at the Evernight Marshes.

"That is only six. A dozen days." Zafrynne said, seeming distant as she still examined the bottom of my cup.

I considered her earlier warning and what I knew about my sisters' first advisors. The final two I'd planned were for Mother Feathergale and Dorynne, but they posed no threat, so who would poison them? Unfortunately, I couldn't reckon what threat Nadia or Corwyn would pose either. After a moment, I resigned myself to the immediate family, Thalaj, and Corwyn. "I think that'll be enough for now." Thalaj may not even consider using the golem taster, but I felt I owed him a debt, and if he'd be recovering in Stormskeep as I had planned, he might need equal protection. I'd made the list and would leave it at that . . . for now. "Do you do this often?" I asked the woman.

"Never. Only during my training many long years ago." She took her gaze from inside my cup and stared upward, then shivered and looked back at me with a half-smile. "I only do it for you now because you are kōgō," she said, finally putting the cup down on the table with a thunk that reminded me of Thalaj's leg bone sliding back into place.

I quivered too. "I will ensure my counselors pay you well for your efforts." The words had no sooner left my mouth than I felt their emptiness echoing back to me. Zafrynne must have a reason for not performing such an enchantment since she'd learned how to do so, and the shudder she emitted led me to believe the endeavor might be dangerous. If it could harm, would gold truly compensate for her efforts?

Zafrynne reached across the table and grasped my arm at the wrist. I struggled to pull away but couldn't free myself from her grip. Her eyes fluttered closed, and she said in a distant voice, "Your travels shall twist and wind. Mayhap you have found your place, but your road has yet to reach the end. Friend and fiend, you'll encounter aplenty, but not until you plummet into the depths will you discover your soul's twin." Then, just as suddenly as she'd grasped my hand, she released it. Her eyes opened, and she smiled. "The leaves say many things, but this is all that they'll allow me to tell. I should return to begin my work."

Speechless, I watched as she stood and hobbled from the room.

Nine

A Man in Gray

KARYNNE RETURNED TO THE CASTLE around midday, stating to those of us still gathered in the House of Healing that she'd carry news of our situation to the advisory council on my behalf. I thanked her with a tight hug and returned to my guard's bedside. Late that afternoon, Thalaj groaned. I turned and leaned over him as he opened his eyes. Confusion then worry darkened his gaze as he searched my face.

"Shhh," I said. "All is well. You'll be fine, and I have the totem we'll need to find the Tsinti." The small figurine had a loop attached, and I had hung it beside the stones at my neck. I reached up and pulled the necklace from my bodice to show him. When he seemed to relax, I added, "Right now is your time to rest and recover."

He scanned his battered body and tested how it moved, issuing a grunt here and there, but he huffed loudly when he looked under the covers at his casted leg.

In the days that followed, Corwyn and Thalaj healed together, and I never left the House of Healing. On the sixth day after meeting Zafrynne, a messenger came with a package wrapped in brown paper and a rough rope securing it with a tight little knot. The healer offered me a knife to cut away the ties, and we examined the little golems. They looked so much like each of us, it was shocking. We explained the situation to Thalaj and Corwyn and how these would taste anything we wished to consume. Supposedly, they'd turn solid black if the food was of danger to our bodies or health. The spellcaster had keyed the golems to our unique person, so if something would be poisonous to one, but not the other, the golems would know.

Each came in a little box with a silver latch that we could carry securely within a pocket, though walking about with an animated miniature of myself gave me significant pause. Zafrynne had also delivered a potion of which Corwyn was to take three drops every morning as a measure to ward off his tremors. It seemed to work, and he improved more rapidly from the day he began his dosing.

I arranged for Mother Feathergale to have rooms prepared for Thalaj at the castle, and in another couple of days, we all returned to Stormskeep proper. Sentei Summergale came daily to check on Thalaj and Corwyn, but we had a plan—rest, recover, and have our food tasted by the miniature versions of ourselves. I went to Thalaj each morning, and we walked to Nadia's cottage at the beginning, middle, and ending of each day, visiting and taking our meals with Nadia and her partner. Corwyn healed quickly as the days passed. Nadia taught me to prepare food from her garden, and as such, when we ate there, we had to use our golems less than if we were to dine elsewhere. I attended to her cooking lessons eagerly under the assumption that I would have need of the skills before long.

Beyond preparing our own meals, we spent some time testing our tiny replicas. The bright orange lily flowers that Nadia tended, adding beauty to her garden, were poisonous when consumed. We brewed some of those and fed the resulting broth to the golems. They each turned a putrid gray, then blackened and fell over with a tiny choking sound. Then, like a dead plant coming back to life with a good soaking, they stood up before our eyes. Though it was a morbid game, we all laughed as the four tiny animated figurines went rigid, fell, and bloomed again. They were like new toys, and we behaved as younglings would and repeated the process several times, chuckling with amusement when their health returned.

Thalaj, ill accustomed to being so limited physically, grew increasingly frustrated with the rigid boot and restrictions imposed by Sentei Summergale. He maintained a grateful demeanor while a guest at my aunt's table, but on our walks, he repeatedly grumbled and complained. Roryn and another guard, Gaelynne, the one I'd seen him spar with in the yards, visited. It refreshed his mood slightly that he had the chance to learn about Stormskeep's protection and offer strategy and advice. When, after long weeks, he could walk without my assistance or leaning onto a cane, the healer removed the cast. Encouraging him to rest once he no longer wore the brace was near impossible, but he still attended meals on occasion at the cottage and kept his golem tucked in the breast pocket of his tunic at all times.

One evening, Thalaj had gone beyond Arashi's gates and returned with a hare. He and Corwyn worked together to skin and clean it for the pot, and Nadia and I prepared it for the evening meal. We sat down to eat, each holding a steaming bowl of the well-herbed meaty stew with root vegetables from the cottage garden. When we'd each sated our appetites, I leaned back in my chair with a goblet of sweet wine in hand.

Looking at the satisfied company, I felt comfortable enough to broach the subject. "Thalaj is gaining strength by the day. He's almost back to his full training schedule. I've spoken with Karynne about the party she's gathered to search for Father, and they should be preparing to leave the next time Selene is at her fullest in the sky." I took a drink, then added. "I will be traveling with them."

Corwyn dropped his goblet on the table and sat forward. "Mairynne, that journey is a tough fate for anyone. I fear you're not suited for it."

Sitting straighter, I said, "I am."

My near uncle persisted, "Kōgō, I mean no disrespect. But we do not know what this journey entails. Your parents sheltered you within the castle for your entire life, and you are now the Nantai empress, heaven's sovereign. The people of all the castes look to you and your council for guidance and decisiveness."

Corwyn was my subject. I could silence any objection and simply declare that this would come to pass. After all, it would. Knowing all this and that the right was mine left me with a temptation that seemed childish, so I stifled any comment. I'd felt this way since the day my father vanished. Each time I thought of him, the stone about my neck burned. Ever since the potion woman, Zafrynne, told me that the road before me stretched for lengths untold, I had never been more certain of my path. "Corwyn, you misplace your worry. The duties of the Nantai ruler are better handled by someone more mature than me." I paused, looking toward my aunt. "I've learned a great deal from Nadia during this recovery. Thalaj will be at my side along with other soldiers, so I will be safe. When I return, it will be with my father, I am certain."

He bowed his graying head. "Have you considered that Tennō Atheryn may not still live? It is so unlike him to be absent from his duties. His love for Nantai and her people was so great that he'd have sooner perished than remain away." A substantial weight sank upon Corwyn as he said these words, and it was clear that they tasted sour on his tongue.

Nadia reached across the table, took his hand, and turned to me. "All he says makes sense, Mairynne. That more than four moons have passed and your father hasn't appeared lead me to believe he will not return."

I grasped the stones about my neck. The one that rested in the center burned my palm, reassuring me in my conviction. "The thought has occurred to me many times. In truth, the counselors have voiced the same logic and reasoning to me on several occasions. Yet I still sense his life force still walking this land. I believe with everything in my soul that he lives. And this—holding court and deciding small grievances of a farmer here or a hunter there, or listening to the advice of my father's council on the matter of our next festival—is not my place. The politicsand minutia are already wearing on me."

Thalaj sat silently at my side.

I continued, "My road travels to other places. Where I don't know just yet, but on the morrow, I will go to the Triad and write the decree."

A long silence stretched between the four of us at the table.

At last, I turned to my aunt. "You have cared for me more than anyone since my mother's death and Father's disappearance. You have been wise as my first advisor and taught me what I most needed. You've shown me the same love as my mother, and you offer me only wise advice in the way of ruling the people." I took a deep breath. "I will leave the temporary leadership of the Nantai to you. You will have to visit the High Cloud Court to take the oaths in the same manner I did, but you will have the golem, Corwyn will be at your side, Solarynne will assuredly become your first advisor, and I will send a letter to Tsanseri to help you through the proceedings."

I touched the metal cuff I still wore beneath my sleeve on the upper part of my right arm. The time had arrived for us to go, and thankfully, I received no argument then and there from Thalaj.

◇◇◇◇◇◇◇◇◇◇◇◇◇◇◇◇◇◇◇◇◇◇◇◇◇◇◇◇◇

IT WAS UNLIKELY THAT I had fully convinced Nadia or Corwyn my intentions were the best for all involved. For my part, worry also gathered in my heart that the decision might be wrong, but of the options, it felt the most right. I hugged Nadia with everything I had and left her standing in the doorway with Corwyn. Thalaj walked me back to the castle itself across the lush grasses, and I looked up at Selene's countenance face as we went.

We were about halfway through the return when he looked at me, a glint in his eye. "How do you feel about a longer walk tonight?"

"Sure," I agreed suddenly, thinking that my rooms would be stifling.

I raised my skirts and followed Thalaj down the stone steps. Selene shone brightly as she approached her fullness. That it seemed so close made my heart leap, but how long did we have remaining? Four, maybe five days?

At the base of the castle's steep walls, we strolled beside the river.

Thalaj broke the silence after several minutes. "Since I've been back and you've had so many attempts on the lives of your family members, I am beginning to see the logic in you leaving."

I stopped, grabbed the crook of his arm, and turned him to face me. "Are you actually saying you want me to go?"

"No," he scoffed. "I'd much prefer it if I could take you somewhere safe and leave you there until I return."

I snorted—a horrible sound, but one showing exactly what I thought of his overprotective sentiment.

With a chuckle, he continued, "I didn't think you'd agree with the approach."

"So, stubborn though you are, you're learning," I teased, but in the deepest part of me, I welcomed his change of heart, even if it remained reluctant.

"Mairynne—"

"Wait? No Kōgō?" I needled him some more.

He raised a perfectly slanted brow and asked, "Do you wish for me to call you that?"

We shared a laugh. This man knew me almost as well as anyone, and of course I didn't relish the thought of him or anyone else calling me *Kōgō*.

We resumed walking, but his demeanor turned more serious with each step. "I think it's best if we limit the number of people who know you are going. Do you have to approach the entire Triad in order to write your decree?"

My brows drew together as I asked, "It's customary for the three Hallowgales to witness the writings of the emperor or empress. Do you have cause to suspect them in something?"

He shook his head. "Nothing specific. I'm just being conscientious. Is it possible to only have one? Is there one you are closer to than the others?"

"If I had to choose, I'd pick Tasmynne, the priestess of Selene. If you feel strongly about that, I'll only go to her tomorrow."

"I do. I think it's a wise idea."

"What about the council? And my sisters? I'll need to share with them my intentions so they can help to make the arrangements for Nadia's ascension."

"I don't think you should tell them your plans. They would know soon enough after you're gone." He hesitated, then went on, "Tell me, have you given the little people to your sisters?"

"Do you mean the golems?" I smiled. The animation of the little clay-based replica of him bothered him more than he obviously wanted to admit.

"Yes. The golems." He sneered as he spoke the word, as if it tasted sour on his tongue. "Did you give them to Karynne and Yasmynne?"

"I haven't." My brows grew heavy at this. "I'm not sure what keeps me from giving them their protection. Maybe it's that I'll have to explain the entire situation. Or, it could be that the potion woman warned me from giving out the little tasters. I don't believe that either of my sisters had a hand in Corwyn's fate, but something . . . some weird intuition . . . tells me not to." As I said this, the cold stone about my neck grew colder.

Thalaj inhaled and huffed. "I worry that your intuition may be better than you know, and I'm not certain I can fathom what that means for you, for them, or for this journey we're about to take."

"And I think I worry that something further might happen to Nadia."

He turned to me. At what point we'd stopped, I couldn't say, but we stood under the moonlight next to the rushing water, and he looked at me darkly. "If you will allow it, I will assign Roryn and Gaelynne to guard your aunt and her partner." He looked away, then back to me with a slight smile.

My heart expanded with gratitude, but something else niggled inside. "What are you not saying, Thalaj?"

"I'd need to share the situation . . . and your plans . . . with my guards to help them be better prepared."

I broke away and trod a path back and forth at the water's edge. With one hand wrapped around my waist, my free hand worried at my bottom lip as I considered the possibility of sharing this information with people I barely knew in the place of people I'd spent my entire life around. Why did I feel more comfortable with the former rather than the latter? I couldn't pinpoint it, but when I looked up at my first guard, all I said was, "Make it happen."

He nodded. "One more thing . . ."

I went back to him and looked up into his dark eyes.

He glanced up at the moon, then resumed eye contact. "Selene will show her full body in the sky on the third night hence. I will come for you that morning in the early hours before dawn. Be prepared to meet me and leave before first light."

THE PROMINENT CHARACTERISTIC OF the moon goddess's temple was the sizable quarter moon–shaped cutout in the ceiling designed for watching the goddess pass through the night skies. I found Tasmynne, priestess of Selene, there and pulled her from gathering tithes people had placed upon the goddess's altar.

"Tasmynne, I have need of you within the grand sanctuary." I latched onto her hand and pulled her forward.

"Kōgō, with due respect, what is this regarding? I have duties I must attend to before nightfall and the service this evening."

"I need you to bear witness."

Upon her hand, the moon-shaped ring gleamed . . . with the sigil of the goddess.

"Have you gathered Edamyn and Arlyn as well?"

"Your holiness"—I stopped and turned to face her nose to nose—"I won't be bringing them into this matter. While that is customary, it is not a requirement. The annals only require one Hallowgale to witness an official decree. I'd like to keep this one as quiet as possible for now. Can I trust you with this?"

Her eyes widened, and when she gave a jerky nod, I pulled her forward. I stopped outside the large open doors and looked around for others before searching the sanctuary inside. When I'd satisfied myself that no others were present, I went to the dais that held the most current of the annals. I picked up the feathered quill and dipped it into the ink. Weighing my words, I penned the date, then wrote:

> *I, Kōgō Mairynne Evangale, decree that upon my realized absence from the city of Arashi and Stormskeep Castle, my aunt and sister to the murdered Kōgō Noralynne Evangale shall ascend to the Serpentine Throne. In doing so, she shall recite Morwyn's oath, declaring that the throne shall return to its previous owner should that owner return.*

I signed the decree and handed the quill to Tasmynne.

The priestess read my words, then lifted her eyes to meet mine. "I cannot sign this, Kōgō."

"Your holy vows bind you to this duty." I pushed the quill closer.

Tasmynne took it and signed. I retrieved the black waxed candle from the altar and dripped wax next to her name. She stared at the moon ring on her right hand for a long minute until I reached forward and took her by the wrist. She didn't resist but didn't actively aid in sealing the decree either. After she'd completed the imprint, I let out a sigh just as the scuffling sound of boots alerted us to someone's approach.

We both looked up, and I closed the book as my new attendant, Dorynne, appeared in the door. She panted, but said between breaths, "Oh, good, I found you Kōgō Mairynne." She stopped and gulped, then added, "Ohmyn Havengale and Idalynne Feathergale sent me in search of you."

That seemed an odd combination, but I ignored the inclusion of the counselor Havengale as I moved toward my newest attendant, "What would put Mother Feathergale in mind to send you in such a rush for?"

Dorynne, having recovered her breath some, looked at her shoes and wrung her hands. "She just said to bring you to the council chambers quickly."

I pressed my lips into a tight line. "Tasmynne, will you find Edamyn and Arlyn and meet us there?"

The priestess curtsied. "Right away, Kōgō."

Without further conversation, I exited the sanctuary. Once outside and connected to the atmosphere, I called the wind to speed my journey. The bridge emptied on the same level of the keep as the library and my chambers. I quickly climbed the steps to the next level and hurried into the council chambers where the Serpentine Throne awaited. Inside, Ohmyn stood beside a guard who held a sword on someone in gray nondescript clothing sitting upon his knees and facing the throne.

I couldn't see his face from where I stood.

Mother Feathergale paced along the other side of the throne, and when she noticed me, she rushed forward. "Mairynne, we found him trying to enter your rooms, and he carried a phial in his hand."

A phial?

My rooms?

I looked beyond the woman I'd known all my life to the gray form on the floor and moved. I couldn't feel my legs and could no longer hear the Sundai Falls for the blood rushing in my ears. "Do you have the phial?" I asked to no one or to anyone; I didn't care which.

Mother Feathergale scurried behind me. "Havengale does."

Suspecting, or mayhap fearing, what I would see, I extended a hand. My counselor placed a corked glass phial on my open palm. When I examined the fluted red flower within, my heart turned to stone.

I passed the slender bottle back to Ohmyn made a point of not looking at anything except the Serpentine Throne—that accursed chair that represented a duty I hadn't wanted. But now it represented the ability to rain down justice on someone who had wronged my family twice over and taken my best friend's life. Mayhap this person had intended to poison me, and as such became a traitor to the throne, to my family, to the Storm Sorcerers, and to Nantai herself. When I reached the steps, I climbed slowly and at the top I turned with my chin held high and sat.

A pair of guards appeared in the doorway through which I'd just entered.

I projected my voice. "One of you, go to Sentei Summergale and bring him here to me. Ohmyn Havengale has something for him to examine. Tell him the empress believes it'll be primlock."

After they disappeared, I finally settled my gaze on the gray form cowered before me. He lifted his eyes, and within them, I took note of a white speck within his right pupil. The eyes looked youthful but peered back from within an aged face. If this man were to stand, he would stoop. In truth, his back was bent where he knelt upon the floor.

My voice sounded hollow, distant, and cold as I spoke. "You wished me well when I offered you a piece of my mother, yet you hold ill will against me for some reason I do not follow."

He remained silent, but a smile spread on his face.

"Do you have nothing to say for your actions?" Anger began to filter into my words.

"I do not," he answered, a defiant note within the once again hale voice—the sound so very at odds with the aged man.

"But you poisoned Jessamynne Feathergale?"

Silence.

"And Corwyn Dawnsgale?"

Nothing.

I leaned forward. "If you choose not to answer to these charges, I will take that as an answer of affirmation. Now. I will ask once more."

Guards trickled into the room at the back and lined the walls.

I disregarded them. "Did you poison my attendant and my aunt's consort?"

The gray-dressed man, both old and young at the same time, with the fleck in his right eye, pressed his lips together and remained mute.

Ohmyn Havengale shook his head, then stopped, his cheeks still blubbering for a second following. "Should we have him sent to the cells beneath the keep to await his death?"

No matter that he'd likely poisoned two people I loved dearly, the thought of asking someone else to slaughter him soured my stomach. "No."

I paused for long enough that those who'd entered the room began to murmur.

I raised both hands. "Let's put him in the cell within the highest spire. The cold will be upon us soon, and nature can take her course upon this traitor."

I stood and walked slowly to the door of the throne room, between the guards, and turned toward my rooms. After descending the stairs, I called a gust of wind to see me quickly to my chambers. Within, I locked the door and went to my dresser. Grabbing onto the bowl sitting on top with shaky hands, I emptied the few contents of my stomach over and over again until I felt weak but purged of having sentenced someone to a slow death.

Again, the truth rang in my ears as to how I wasn't fit to be an empress. I hadn't the stomach for such things.

TEN

Into the Gloaming

AWAKE IN THE WEE MORNING hours on the third day since I'd strolled with Thalaj and two days after I'd penned the decree and sent the man to the spire. I bustled quietly around my chambers gathering the items I'd collected surreptitiously over the last days. Though I'd laid in bed for what seemed the longest night of my life, I hadn't slept. I felt some relief that the guards had apprehended the culprit who'd poisoned Corwyn, yet my nerves still bundled in my stomach and spun anticipation throughout my mind. At the cleaning table, beside the basin, I filled a water skein from the pitcher Mother Feathergale had filled late yesterday, also at my behest. I didn't know how early she and Dorynne would arrive to prepare for the day, but after every item I packed, I went to the front of my rooms to check for their arrival, hoping that Thalaj would come before.

With my pack sealed, I stepped onto the balcony but remained close enough to the secret passageway to hear a knock. The crisp air chilled my skin, and across the sky, the full moon hung above the spires of the citadel, a yellow halo within the deep purple night. At odds with the stillness of the predawn hours, blood raced through my veins, a steady pulse beat in my ears, and I fidgeted as I waited.

I twitched at every sound and jumped when the small scratching sound startled me from inside, a noise a rodent would make as it pawed at the ground for grubs. But it wasn't an animal; it came from behind the art that hid the secret passage. I went.

When I opened the hidden door, Thalaj was holding an orb of dancing bluish lightning high to light the dark stairwell. "Get your things. It's time."

I retrieved my pack and returned. Stepping inside, I pulled the painting closed and tried to turn in the tight space.

Thalaj stopped me so he could appraise my pack, then gave a small satisfied smile, and asked, "You have the totem?"

I grasped the end of the throng hanging at my neck. It had remained there since my time at the House of Healing, a token as important as the ones that represented the souls of my parents. At my nod, he turned. I held a hand on the wall to steady myself as we descended countless stairs. Outside, under Selene's watch, I called the wind and lowered us to the grass behind a copse of trees. Thalaj scanned the area, tilted his head, and made for the city's gates. We moved precisely as planned and would meet the remainder of the party at Stormskeep's exit. Not another person stirred within the streets at the gods-forsaken early hour. Thalaj walked with purpose, in silence, but glanced over his shoulder several times to ensure I kept pace. He deftly maneuvered through the narrow cobbled streets, past the House of Healing, around homey neighborhoods, and between the shops at the market. It seemed he could make this way blindfolded. For my part, I couldn't break concentration long enough to ask questions though they stirred in my agitated mind.

When we arrived at the stables, I slowed, expecting that we'd meet the others inside and gather horses for the journey. Thalaj turned back to me, grabbed my wrist, and pulled me forward.

I resisted. "Aren't we meeting the others?" I asked.

"I sent word to the others last night to meet here at seventh bell. I plan to be well away before that hour. Pull up your hood and come on."

Beyond the stables, facing the guardhouse, I stopped. "What about the guards? Didn't you just mention that our departure would be in secret."

Thalaj rounded back on me and pulled me into the shadows. "I've staffed the night watch with only those I trust. Roryn and Gaelynne lead the shift."

I shifted my gaze uncertainly.

"What is it, Mairynne?" he asked, clearly growing short with my reluctance.

"Maybe . . ." I started.

He quirked a brow.

"Maybe this isn't the best idea," I admitted. In the depths of my soul, I knew it was my path, that I was meant to travel this road, and that this journey was what Zafrynne had spoken of when she read my fate in the herbs. So why, as I stood on the very precipice, did I fear what we faced?

Thalaj sighed. "Mairynne, your determination persuaded even me, so you're not turning back now. But time is important; your doubts will wait until we're at a safe distance."

"What if we're discovered?"

"It's early enough that no one will know immediately, and I trust my guards to keep this quiet until after someone notices your absence in the castle. It will take several hours." He pressed his lips together, then narrowed the distance between us and lowered his voice. "What you're feeling is what the Frost Fighters call the spirit of home's hearth. It's fear of facing something you don't know, but you've convinced even me of your need to go, and as the one charged with your very protection, I've the most reason for objection."

Glancing down, I said, "But what if this is exactly what Father did and never returned?"

"Do you really believe that?" He raised his brows.

I shook my head. If Father had left willingly, he would have come back to his duty and his people. The stone burned the delicate skin beneath my shift, emphasizing the rightness of my conclusion.

"Then trust me, and you'll be better by the time we enter the forest."

After another doubtful thought, I decided to put away my misgivings, pulled my hood over my head, and gave him the trust he'd earned by his service to me and my father before.

At the guardhouse, Roryn smiled widely. He and Thalaj clasped arms.

Thalaj asked, "Do you have them?"

"Aye, we do," the guard answered.

Gaelynne stepped forward with a belt holding two holstered scimitynes—weapons I knew well from having observed my first guard wield them in the training yards. Others used short or longer straight swords based on their fighting styles, and some fought with daggers or a longbow. My first guard was the only one who dared use the small curved blades as a weapon. I expected he'd strap the belt at his waist, but the three guards turned to me. I looked from face to face, unclear of their expectation.

Gaelynne guffawed after seeing my reaction. "Lift your cloak, Kōgō." The woman stood taller than both Thalaj and Roryn and wore her hair cut bluntly at her chin. I'd seen her before but never this close. Her forehead was a bit too broad for her face, but her mouth was soft. Her bold laugh made me like her immediately, and I did as she said. She strapped the belt at my waist and stepped back. "Don't take those out until someone shows you what to do with them. I'd hate to see you lose a hand or something worse."

I nodded. Of course, I would need something for protection, but it would have made more sense to give me something easier to use. Reality set in. My journey had started, and I was going alone into the world with only Thalaj. My heart patter could have been from thrill or anxiety—which, I couldn't tell. We walked past the gates that had held my entire life up until that moment as Otarr's first light painted a line across the horizon. We veered to the right, met the northern branch of the Sundai River, and followed it south.

A sense of freedom I'd imagined for months settled over me, and feelings of—not happiness, but something for which I had no accurate words lightened my steps. A truth, mayhap. But that seemed a weak explanation. At the very least, it contained purpose.

And my purpose felt right.

Mayhap it was my imagination, but on the wind, I heard my father's voice.

Truth to thine self first.

Part Two
Call of the Syrensea

ELEVEN

Beyond Arashi, Nantai

MUSCLES BURNED AND BUNCHED WITHIN my calves. A pack bounced on my shoulders. Scimityne scabbards thudded against my legs with every step, a new thing I'd accepted from the guard Gaelynne, who had helped us escape. They held weapons Thalaj had crafted specially for me and, as such, something I would treasure always. My skirts rustled over the grasses of the vale, growing heavy and damp with predawn dew. My heart and legs pumped in concert.

Away from all I'd ever known, I ran.

The moon goddess, Selene, neared the end of her watch in the westward skies, but the sun god, Otarr, had yet to brighten the mountainous horizon in the east.

Over my shoulder lay the city of Arashi, the only place I'd truly known in the passing of more than twenty summers. Since the time of Emperor Makenyn five long ages before, it'd been the Nantai's star city at the base of Mount Sundai. Held within Arashi's walls and beside the great waterfalls, Stormskeep Castle—home of the Serpentine Throne and the seat of emperors and empresses throughout the ages— watched over the city and the vale beyond.

Built around Sundai River Falls, Arashi had been where my father, Tennō Atheryn Evangale had ruled before his mysterious disappearance. The castle and city streets were where my sisters and I had played as younglings, learning the limits of our sorcery. Inside those walls, other young Storm Sorcerers and I had gathered in the citadel near the keep to learn from the Havengales—priests of our Holy Triad. Selene's priestess, Tasmynne, had told stories using painted boards to warn us of the dangers beyond Arashi's walls—the winged predators of the Rausu Mountains and the nekodai in the north. Both vicious birds and mammoth cats always thirsted for youthful blood in the tales. Younglings perished under beaks, claws, and fangs. The paintings on the storyboards had always been splattered with crimson blood, and though I'd clung to her stories, nightmares followed.

But for all the learning and despite the stories, I'd never seen the expanse of my country with my own eyes. There were so many people throughout Nantai I'd never met. Now, I ran toward them to find what I had lost—what Nantai had lost.

Father. Emperor.

Within Arashi, I had answered my duties and followed my father's decrees within the annals. Though I would have preferred otherwise, though the stones I wore around my neck called me away from the city, and though I hadn't been wise enough for such a mantle, I had ascended to sit upon the Serpentine Throne. I'd become Empress of Nantai.

Kōgō Mairynne Evangale.

I'd seen my first guard and protector healed after his encounter with the Small Folk of the Evernight Marshes—a mission he'd tended on my behalf. Then, I'd sentenced my best friend's murderer to imprisonment within Stormskeep's spires. But on this morning after decreeing that Aunt Nadialynne Riversgale, my mother's twin sister, ascend to the throne during my absence, I answered the call of the stones I kept on a necklace near my heart. Through the vale, I escaped home and duty with my protector Thalaj in search of Father. Despite my sisters', my advisers', and the clergy's beliefs, within my heart and soul, I had no doubts. Atheryn Evangale, Tennō of Nantai, lived. And the throne rightfully belonged to him.

We ran as morning's twilight came.

With my storm-fed sorcery, I called the wind when I tired. Yet, after a time, my breathing steadied into a quicker rhythm as a renewed wave of energy flowed through my body.

Gloaming lifted.

Night retreated.

Behind us, the citadel's bells began to toll, awakening Arashi for the common daylight routines. Almost to the Yubar Forest at the edge of the vale, Thalaj stretched his step. I struggled to keep pace at his side while counting the gongs in my mind . . . four, five, six. A glance behind revealed sunlight kissing the top of Mount Sundai, setting the mists of the waterfalls aglow, turning Stormskeep's spires golden, then unfolding to cover the castle and the city itself. The stone wall fortifications protecting the city within gleamed under Otarr's light as his rays stretched from them across the valley, like arms brushing the moistened grass. We left a dark trail, but the sooner we reached the woods, the sooner we could more easily cover our tracks. Only moments before Otarr's bright eyes found us, I ducked under a low-hanging branch into the tree cover. Broad leaves and shadow welcomed us into the southernmost swath of the Yubar Forest.

Along with the city and my home, I left my doubts behind. The time for my adventure had come, and with it, the time for me to let go of my imperial duties.

Between the city gates and the forest's edge, every step I'd taken had solidified my conviction. I would deliver my father back to his seat upon the Serpentine Throne. It was a new duty, one I had chosen, and a band had released from around my chest. I had to trust in my peoples' traditions and that the decree I'd written would come to pass. Eventually, I would see Arashi again, but whether I'd remain at Stormskeep then and grow into the ruler my father believed me to be remained a worry for another day. This day, I pursued my own will.

Truth to thine self first, my father's voice echoed in my mind.

"Hai, Father," I whispered in agreement and pushed my legs harder.

Ahead, Thalaj stopped under the shade of broad leaves. When I arrived at his side, he relieved me of my pack, unlatched it, and tossed me a tunic and rough-spun pants. "Change. I estimate we have an hour to get as far into the forest as possible before the warnings go up." He turned away, giving me the privacy to do as he bade.

Once I'd dressed in simpler clothing and resecured my pack, we continued deeper into the Yubar Forest, shaded from Otarr's light by the tangled canopy above. We trekked over decaying leaves, frogs croaking in the nearby wetlands along the river. While we'd left behind the roaring of the falls, the Sundai babbled gently and birds sang above. I'd been to the edge of the forest and just inside, but never this far within. Mother and Father hadn't allowed me to venture into its depths, warning that I would easily get lost or carried off by one of the wolf packs rumored to prowl the forest that stretched from the slope of the Rausu Mountains my people called home toward the Syrensea in the west. Aside from the paintings and storyboards, I'd never seen these wolves, and I'd often suspected the Hallowgales had invented the tale to keep younglings from wandering off.

The serenity under the trees allowed me to further contemplate this journey and allow my guard to do the same. I'd given him space thus far because I trusted him implicitly. But the original plan had been for him to go in search of Father with a small team of Storm Sorcerer guards. When the bells began to chime from the citadel again, quieter then as they were farther away, I skip-stepped and caught up to Thalaj, pulling him to a stop. "We're an hour into the forest. Tell me why we're going at this alone," I demanded, my words firm but lacking outrage. I had trouble putting forward a hard empress's façade when I felt a thrill to simply be free.

He slowed his pace but kept us moving. "In the Evernight, I was captured."

"I thought there was a fight, that you and Roryn—"

He shook his head. "I left Roryn in the camp while I went to retrieve the totem."

"You went in alone?" I asked, my eyes wide with surprise that he'd abandoned his only ally on the mission. "Rumor tells the Small Folk feed on our magic."

He nodded. "Aye, I entered alone. Though I am uncertain that bit about the Small Folk feeding on magic is true. I took a beating, but I'm better now." He cocked a half smile.

I shook my head. "I may never understand you, Thalaj Nightingale. You say you trust Roryn but you wouldn't work with him. Instead, you risk your life trying to what?"

He gave me a sidelong glance but refused me a believable answer. "It's simply who and *what* I am . . . how I trained." He stepped over a fallen branch and extended a hand to help me. "My methods are of little importance."

Huffing, I accepted his hand. "Had you perished in the foolish attempt, where would I be now? You are the one responsible for helping me away from Arashi."

He winced but dismissed my accusation. "Regardless of how I entered the marshes, I learned that we not only need to find the Tsinti, but we need to seek out their witch wife. To answer your question about why we left without a larger search party, I didn't believe we would have a hope of gaining entrance into a Tsinti camp if we brought a full traveling party. The Tsinti, themselves, are a private folk, only traveling under a *tsym*. We've spoken of this before. You know that they only reveal themselves to those they choose. It's why I went for the totem."

I fought an urge to reach for my necklace where the stones and the totem hung near my heart. "How will we know where to look?"

"I'm guessing a bit on that one, but they're a nomadic people. Nomads have a pattern, and I believe they will bring the silks from Yōtei in the east to the Southern Fork market in autumn."

My stomach flipped. "We're going to the Great Market?" For years, I'd begged Father to take us with them to the largest market in our lands, where everyone congregated along the southernmost fork of the Betsu River for the time between the two moons of the cooling season to share in news from every corner of Nantai and to trade.

"No. I wouldn't risk taking you into such a place."

I glared. "Why? I'll not trade the confines of Stormskeep for a travel companion who keeps me equally secluded."

The manner in which his look flitted to mine intoned many thoughts, amusement mayhap, but certainly exasperation. He chose to speak none of that. "If that had been my plan, I would have brought the travel party." He looked up at a bird calling above and whistled back. Amused, his eyes settled back on mine. "No. I plan to try to find the Tsinti in the Central Grasslands before they make their way down the Betsu."

"Oh." I slumped.

Thalaj gave a small laugh. "You're empress, Mairynne, and you have your majority now. Once we've concluded this quest, you may attend the market every year, and I will ensure your protection when you do."

We traveled in companionable silence for several minutes, then he added, "My hope is that alone, the Tsinti will welcome us into their caravan."

Otarr must have been high in the sky by the time we stopped by the river to eat. Even under the Yubar's shade, it grew hotter. I'd almost drained my waterskin, and relief struck me hard as we stopped for water. I sat on a boulder beside the babbling stream. Thalaj filled his skein, then reached for mine. As he held it in the clear, flowing waters, I lifted my hair. Holding my other hand forward, palm up, I found the center of my sorcery powers and gathered a breeze from the water surface to cool my face and neck.

Thalaj stood and plugged the cap back into place but then dropped the waterskin as a sound ripped through the sky. I shrank, sliding from my rock. My guard freed his scimitynes with a *schling* breaking the thick silence under the greenery. We both searched above for the source of the bone-chilling screech. While night had obscured the source before, trees did so then. Though after the sound, a rush of wind sent the treetops rustling and a rain of green leaves showered around us. Then . . . all went still once more. Whatever it had been had silenced the sounds of the Yubar. Frogs and birds alike paused.

I didn't breathe for long moments following, but when my guard seemed to release a bit of tension, I looked at him with wide eyes. "That thing. Whatever it is. Does it follow us? Have you heard it any time when we're not together?"

He came out of his crouch and slowly slid his weapons back into their homes. The birds chirped again, tentatively at first. Frogs joined in the chorus, resuming their rhythmic croak. The restored song seemed to signal safety had returned.

"No," Thalaj said simply.

While I'd been so certain of my journey only a couple of hours before, a part of me began to long for the protection of the castle's stone walls. "Should we—"

"No," he cut me off and turned a cold, arresting stare in my direction. "Mairynne, I have no idea what that is, but I'm not going to coddle you on this journey. We'll run into many things, and we'll face them together. If some beast truly follows us, it will eventually have to do more than screech in the sky, and we'll manage the situation when that happens. Until then, it's out of our control."

I hesitated, fingered the warm stone about my neck, and slowly reached to touch the hilt of a *scimityne* at my hip. I stiffened. A resolution formed. Beyond Arashi's walls, I was no longer Lady Mairynne, not Princess, Empress, and certainly not Kōgō. Out here, I was simply Mairynne. A world of new experiences lay before me. Certainly, we'd face new challenges and obstacles, along with all the wonder of Nantai beyond the city where I'd come of age. I could no longer reach for the comfort and safety of all I'd known.

My hand grasping the small, curved sword's hilt, I looked up into Thalaj's dark features with a new wonder. "You'll teach me to use these?"

"Not today." He smiled, obviously reading the change in me. "Not today, but very soon. I will." He gathered my discarded water bladder and handed it to me, also helping me up from my reclined position against the rock. "Before nightfall, I'd like to make it to a small grove that marks the midpoint between Arashi and the edge of the grasslands. Tomorrow, we'll press forward to seek the Tsinti on the Central Grasslands. If they accept us, we'll have their tsym to protect us from sight, and I'll begin showing you the elementary moves."

THE REMAINDER OF THE day passed as Thalaj and I hiked around trees, over fallen limbs, and southward. At our right side, the Sundai continued her path toward the Syrensea. A soft bed of decaying leaves cushioned our steps. Under our boots, sticks crackled from time to time, adding to the lullaby of the running water, rustling foliage, and chirping creatures. The light faded, green seemingly growing thicker, as the day moved toward night once again.

"If I am not mistaken, where the river bends just ahead is the clearing," said Thalaj. He looked toward the bend and up into the leafy ceiling. "Perhaps there will be enough light remaining to catch a fish for an evening meal."

When we broke through the edge of the trees, we saw a clearing reminiscent of the scene from the Cloud Courtier performance of the legend of Sosano and Inara beside the river. Small flowers nestled amid wispy grasses with the last rays of Otarr streaming down. Mist drifted into the clearing, thickening. I wondered what the delicate grasses would look like when morning's dew wept from their blades.

Thalaj dropped his pack at the trunk of a large tree and said, "Aahhh, hai. A blessed fog," seeming relieved of a worry I couldn't fathom. When I looked at him questioningly, he answered, "It will provide cover enough that a fire won't be visible from afar. Gaelynne and Roryn were to send the Arashi guards farther west, toward the North Sundai, but if any other search party has picked up our trail, the mist should help keep us out of sight."

He gathered dry sticks and fallen limbs from beneath the trees and stacked them carefully, then stood and placed his hands on his hips above his weapon belt, some hidden thoughts alive in his mind as he regarded me.

"It is disquieting when you look at me so," I said, dancing around asking directly what he thought. Thalaj had been a fixture in Stormskeep, always near and watching over our family. He had been young when he came to Arashi and dedicated himself to my father. To this day, I am uncertain he'd gained his majority at the time he joined the Arashi guard. I'd been younger still. Mayhap it had been Father's direction to watch over me, but from the beginning we shared an easy, comfortable friendship. Only in the times nearing my mother's death had a hint of something more begun to surface. This would be the first of many nights where we'd be alone together. My purpose out here had little to do with Thalaj, but I couldn't think of another person I'd prefer to have at my side. Despite that I wished for more connection, there was naught suggestive in the purse of his lips as he considered.

In an instant, he grinned boyishly. "How would you like to learn to catch a fish?"

I wrinkled my nose at first, then changed my mind and shrugged. Anywhere beyond a city, the skill might be of use. And I had no inkling of when I might return to the city. The taller grass blades tickled my palm as I crossed toward Thalaj and the forest. He squatted, retrieved a line from his pack, and grabbed a thinner, greener stick from those he'd collected and tested how it bent. When he seemed satisfied, he tilted his head toward the river and began walking. I left my pack with his beside our camp at the clearing and followed him back toward the Sundai. Upon the banks, Thalaj passed me the line and stick, then crouched again, removed his boots, and rolled his breeches to his knees. With bare feet, Thalaj stepped into the shallow waters. He hissed. The waters flowing from Mount Sundai were colder than even he—as half Frost Fighter—had expected. Dipping his hands into the shallow water, he reached deeper several times and then stood with a tiny fish writhing between his fingers. From his belt, he produced a barbed piece of metal.

I winced when he stabbed it through the baby fish, regretful for the small animal's fate. I said a quick prayer to Atun for the life given so that we might hunt for our next meal.

Thalaj took the end of the line from me and tied it around the metal. As he tied the other end of the line to the stick, he nodded to my boots. "You'll want to take those off to keep them dry."

With my legs bare too, I joined him in the water. Indeed, it was icy upon my feet and ankles, and I entered much slower than my guard.

As I reached his side, he handed me the wider end of the stick and pointed. "See the dark pool there? That's where the fish will be." He made motion as if he still held the stick. "Swing the stick and aim the line there."

I tried once, but got the barb snagged in my breeches. Laughter—a rare thing from Thalaj—surrounded us as he freed my inadvertent catch. Afterward, he demonstrated a better technique. When the line settled between us and the dark pool he'd mentioned, he handed the stick back to me.

"What now?" I asked.

He folded his arms over his chest and answered, "We wait."

In a matter of moments, the stick started jiggling in my hands.

"Oh . . . oh . . . oh, what do I do?" I stammered.

"Pull back."

I did.

It jerked and pulled.

"Good. Now just hold." He reached for the line, swiping twice before he captured it and pulled. It took several tries, but he wrestled a fish the size of his forearm out of the water. "To the shore," he barked, already moving in that direction.

I hurried over, my eyes wide and curious.

With the silvery fish lying in the grass and gaping to breathe, Thalaj pulled the barb from its mouth, removed the smaller fish, and tucked the metal back into his belt. I snarled as he reached a finger inside the fish's mouth and lifted it. "Well done, for your first time," he teased.

Near camp, the fog had thickened while we fished. Thalaj cleaned the scales from the fish and swiped his knife along the bones, pulling away chunks of white meat. The light was near gone as he handed the skewered meat to me and built a fire. The fish, smoky from the fire, near melted on my tongue. Afterward, we sat shoulder to shoulder watching the flames die down. Autumn and cooler days would soon be upon us, but that night still felt warm.

Eventually, Thalaj offered me a blanket upon which to sleep and spread out his own.

I stood and once again imitated his more experienced ways. As I finished preparing my pallet, the hairs on my arms rose and a shiver ran down my spine as a rustle in the grasses sounded.

"An empress . . ." a haunting voice, as if borne by the mist itself, began from within the fog.

I reached for my sorcery and called the wind to push the haze away, but it simply swirled. The flames flickered, threatening to extinguish our only light, so I released the gust.

The voice continued, ". . . alone in the wild with but a single guard for her protection."

The ghost in the dark fog tsked thrice. The sound echoed.

The fog pushed and retreated as if it had grown tentacles engorged with sound.

"How very odd, these times we live in," the unseen voice finished.

Thalaj brandished his scimitynes, searching for the source. "Mairynne," he hissed. "Grab your belt. Flip the buckle and pull one blade from the leather." When I had the small curved sword in hand and stared at the blade as if it were a serpent, he continued in hushed tones, "Face the honed edge away from your body and hold it in front of your chest. Like this."

My hand shook as I imitated him again.

He lowered his chin and came near enough I could feel his breath upon my cheek—cool as he clearly allowed his own source of power to surface. "Remember what I said? We'll face these things together."

I nodded.

"Now," he commanded, entirely having changed into the able captain of the empress's guard. "Stand with your back to mine. Where I turn, you turn. Keep your shoulders glued to mine and follow my lead as if this were a dance."

I bobbed my head and positioned myself.

"Show yourself!" my guard called into the mist.

A laugh, like funeral bells tolling, rang from within the dark mist, and the voice came again. "I do not wish her injury, half-breed."

My spine stiffened at the same slander I'd heard before from a voice I now also recognized. From deep within the center of my chest, I found my voice and enunciated every beat. "Alto-Trea. Do as Thalaj commands and show yourself."

The Cloud Courtier's face peeked from the mist, shoulders and hands apparent, but the lower half obscured. Though in the dark with a small glow from our campfire, Alto-Trea's visage seemed a replica of every one of the Courtier's caste I recalled from my ascension. As had been the case then, the only identification apparent was an emblem upon the shoulder.

The Swan.

It doubly confirmed the Courtier's identity.

Thalaj turned us so I faced away from Alto-Trea.

I made to move, but a wave of cold wafting from my guard stopped me. He hissed over his shoulder. "Keep tight. Others may be behind us." Then to the courtier, he said, "I would not judge you so reckless, Alto-Trea, to have come deeply into the forest at night. Alone. And for no purpose. You and others have brought a cloud island to this grove in search of something specific. Us, if I must guess. And surely you're not naïve enough to face me alone. Have the others reveal themselves as well."

Alto-Trea's voice remained even as he replied, "You seem parano—"

A shriek rang out in the distance, a sound I was growing to know all too well.

"—oid," the Courtier finished.

No longer heeding Thalaj's instruction to face away, I turned. Something that one might call a smile twitched at the corner of the courtier's perfectly illusion-drawn lips, yet it chilled my blood.

"What was that?" I demanded.

Neither voice nor demeanor changed as the Swan answered, "One day very soon, young Mairynne Evangale, you will learn."

Thalaj stepped in front of me. He stiffened his arms with his blades to either side, readying them as I'd seen him do so many times before he began a sparring match with one of the soldiers he trained. "Why not this night, Alto-Trea? It makes little sense to come to us with no purpose save to say *one day . . .*"

A flash of blue lightning at the base of each scimityne, quickly lit then extinguished, signaled Thalaj held his magic just beneath his taut posture.

"And precisely why, half-breed, would an illusionist *not* have such an agenda?"

Bristling, I gathered breath to object. But the temperature around me plummeted, stealing my reaction.

Thalaj said, "I have no favor for illusionists. I will see your true form here and now, Cloud Courtier, once your body lies at my feet."

I lay a hand on my guard's arm. He didn't look over, but also didn't pounce into an attack. Violence would gain us no purchase with one of the illusionist caste, the ones who managed the political courts. And the fog was too thick. Alto-Trea remained half obscured, and though there wasn't another soldier in Arashi as fast as Thalaj, I doubted his strike would be fast enough. Lifting my chin, I asked, "*Is* that why you've come, Alto-Trea? It seems a long journey for something so small if you've brought down an island from the skies." I flourished a hand. "As clearly you have by this fog."

Alto-Trea pulled a thumb and middle finger to a point where a beard would be—if the Swan had chosen that as a guise. For reasons I couldn't connect, that simple movement seemed like the placement of another pawn in whatever strategy game this person played.

The Swan pulled back partway into the mist. "Wise, youngling."

I bristled again but held myself in check.

The courtier continued, "But she will no longer hold me in favor if I share aught that would give you advantage. For this night, I shall bid you farewell."

The haze swallowed the Swan then slowly peeled away from the grove. It drifted over the trees and upward still. A silver outline of buildings upon the cloud flashed but disappeared as the cloud rose higher above Nantai.

Pristine silence remained.

Overhead, Selene shone brightly down upon Thalaj and me from a cloudless, starry sky.

Twelve

The Witch Wife and the Fates

AFTER THE CLOUD HAD FLOATED away over the Yubar Forest into the night, I found little rest. I daresay Thalaj felt as unsettled by the visit as me, because though he lay upon the pallet he'd spread out, periodic rustling revealed he flipped from side to side every few moments. The frogs had resumed their songs, and a night bird hooted in the dark. As the forest no longer sensed a threat, rest had seemed necessary. We tried. But after hours of pretending, I whispered, "Thalaj?"

He issued a low sound somewhere between a groan and sigh. "Hai, Mairynne?"

I sat upright on my pallet. "If you are as restless as I, mayhap we should continue."

He was beyond the fire that'd died to mostly ash, and his form blended with the dark depths of the Yubar. A pale blue orb, full of cold energy and light, sparked to life in one palm, revealing him sitting cross-legged rather than reclining. The highlights cast by his sorcery only touched parts of his face, hollowing his eyes in a ghostly visage. But the corners of his lips pulled upward into a reluctant smile. "If we are moving, at least we will make progress." He stood and offered me a hand.

We gathered our few belongings and set out again before dawn. A breeze rustling leaves, animals scurrying, and the babbling river punctuated our hike throughout the day—the only silence nature had to offer. No piercing sounds visited us, and we found no evidence of others within the southern branch of the forest. We silenced our growling stomachs on dried meat as we walked, and later in the day, Thalaj sighted and slaughtered a hare for our evening meal. As we continued until the skies darkened, he carried it at his side. My legs and feet throbbed incessantly by the time twilight arrived and we finally made camp.

The darkness would have been absolute save for the small fire that Thalaj built to cook the hare. Our meal the night before had been light in comparison to the greasy and dark meat of the hare. Afterward, my guard tended the coals and diminished the flames to embers that we could curl up next to and remain warm. Thalaj took first watch, stating that he'd wake me mid-way through the night so he could rest a little before dawn. Though the second night was cooler than the first, I slept better than I had for a single hour in the three nights before we'd departed Arashi or our first night in the woods.

When I opened my eyes, I inhaled sharply and rolled over. I'd expected Thalaj to awaken me long before dawn, but Otarr's light already filtered through the trees. Across the pit with smoking gray ash, Thalaj's form came slowly into focus. He was on his knees facing me. Still on my side, I blinked. His outline clarified, hands behind his back. Tied?

I froze. Beside him, two hulking figures stood, each with a dagger aimed at his throat. Thalaj's lips pressed tightly together; his eyes were coal black and hard. Nearly imperceptibly, he moved his head from side to side.

A warning. Do not be rash, Mairynne. Remain still. Keep your head about you, his motion said.

Mayhap I should have better heeded the signal, but by instinct, I pushed up onto one side from my pallet and twisted, assessing what danger we faced now. I desperately tried to organize my thoughts with the blood pounding in my ears. My travel pack lay just out of reach. And the scimitynes. I crept my hand toward them, hoping fruitlessly that I could grasp onto one before anyone intercepted my move. I hadn't the skill to wield the blades in my belt, but the thought of something sharp in my hand gave me the illusion of protection.

"Halt!" barked one of the men holding Thalaj at dagger point.

At the start his command gave me, I sprang from the pallet onto my feet, only to find two more assailants. I turned first to the man—burly and bearded with fiery red hairs blanketing his arms. His eyes were the brightest green I'd ever seen . . . the color of the fuzzy grass that grew on north-facing trees. Those eyes flashed with a remorseless willingness to use his brawn without a second thought. I had little hope in a battle with one so strong and ruthless, so I swiveled back to the woman just beyond the rest of my gear.

She smirked, her glance cutting down to my pack. Daring me to try.

I readied my body in a crouch as I'd seen Thalaj do when he prepared to spar. The woman raised a brow. The weapon belt between us taunted. I calculated. Could I reach them before her? Chances were slim, but what other choice did I have?

I dove.

I'd scarcely moved when a muscular forearm yanked me backward into a rock of a man. I kicked and struggled, losing grasp on the notion that we might be okay. I started to consider ways to bargain. "Who are you and what do you want from us?"

"Hush, girl," the man holding me gruffed.

The guards at Thalaj's sides conversed hurriedly in a language I didn't recognize.

The woman near my pack responded with a sly smile as she lifted the bag and draped the belt over one shoulder.

I struggled against my captor's arm. "Release me. I demand it. I am—"

"No!" Thalaj snapped. Then, in a soft and deadly dry tone, he added, "*Mairy*, stop struggling."

I looked at him, panting and confused. He'd called me by a shortened version of my name—something he'd never done. Obviously, he didn't want me to share who I was or what we were about. I took deep breaths trying to fight the fear coursing through my body. Measured exhale after inhale, again and again, I willed the tension away, first in my arms, then my legs. And as a reward, the man placed me back onto my feet on the forest floor.

The woman, lithe but stout, fingered the length of one scabbard. "Were these what you're after?"

Saying nothing, I continued to stare at her, glimpsing back toward Thalaj occasionally. When she caught me, she followed my gaze, then released the throng holding one of the blades in place. Drawing the curved short sword from its scabbard, she stepped closer, pointing the curve at my chin. "Your friend there's the smart one, eh?"

I bit down, working hard to hold my silence.

"But," she continued, "then again, if I were a betting woman, I think you're the reason the Frost Fighter's so cooperative. Should we test that theory?" She looked provocatively at Thalaj.

He growled, and I could see the muscles in his neck cording as he prepared to try and free himself.

"Quit playing, Jorani." Another man, smaller and with shaggy shoulder-length hair appeared, traipsing through the camp. Young, much younger than the others if I were to guess by the smoothness of his face and his size. He was almost pretty, except for the angry red mark painted under one eye from nose to cheekbone. He strutted like he owned this group and with a bearing that said he was much older than his appearance would suggest.

And Jorani listened.

"Bind her hands too. Who knows what kind of magic she could call if she has them free. Gather their things. Let's go. They're waiting."

"Wait, who's waiting?" I swiveled my head in search of an answer, but there was none to be found.

Our captors ignored my question.

In truth, I *had* considered using my magic but couldn't think how to use the wind or rain to stave off their attack. The smaller man was right; given time, I might find a way. With my hands bound, it wasn't impossible, but much less likely. I gritted my teeth against the pain in my shoulders as the red-haired man wrenched my arms behind my body.

The brute behind me tied my wrists, and Jorani looked at me with a grin while she poured the water remaining in my skein onto what little remained of the fire. I wanted to object, to stop her, but couldn't free myself to try. Thalaj's captors pulled him to his feet and pushed him through the trees ahead of me. I tried to catch up but Jorani held up my scimityne in front of me, warning me to stay with them. I tensed, at a loss for what to do, but with anger rolling in every muscle as they pushed me along behind the others.

We walked for an hour, maybe more, and my shoulders throbbed. My throat was dry and my stomach roared, but those things I could ignore if I could figure a way out of this situation. The morning lightened further and the trees thinned. When we reached the last tree before the grasslands, the group in front of me halted. Jorani pushed me hard and I stumbled to Thalaj's side.

Cold waves of anger rolled off his body and his nostrils flared as he stood helplessly at my side. The larger man—the one who had ensnared me—came up beside Thalaj on the other side and threw an elbow into his gut. I cried out when he doubled over with a grunt.

Slowly, he regained his strength and stood, panting.

The small man stepped in front of us. He lifted a necklace over his head, and I caught a glimpse of a totem like the one I wore. He placed it in one hand, then clapped his hands straight above his head. With his eyes closed, he pulled his steepled hands to his chest under his chin, chanting something quick but unintelligible.

The emptiness above the sea of yellow grasses shimmered and the air seemed to fold, then wave. My eyes felt dry and began to sting. The vision before me blurred into something unbelievable. I closed my eyes, allowing tears to brew behind my lids and wash away the irritation. When I opened them, blinking against the tears, my eyes painted pictures my brain couldn't begin to believe.

◇◇◇◇◇◇◇◇◇◇◇◇◇◇◇◇◇◇◇◇◇◇◇◇◇◇◇◇◇◇◇◇

WHEELED CARTS WITH ARCHED canvas roofs, large enough for several people to stand easily within, were scattered about. Dozens of them. As the tsym lifted, smells of the broad pack animals also wafted about. Yaks, they were called if I recollected from my lessons, but I'd never seen one with my own eyes. Their coats were as thick as they were broad. Each wore a harness in bright reds and white, many were attached to the wagons, and the ones that weren't wore brightly colored saddles.

What sane person would ride such a creature? I wondered.

Our abductors' dress had been simple, but the people tarrying about dressed as brightly as the yaks in loose pants that gathered at the ankle. Their bloused tunics shone in shades of red, orange, and pink. A netted belt defined each person's waist, displayed coin in varying quantities, and jingled as they moved—a sound also not heard when they remained under tsym.

The men's hair hung loose, and the women wore their hair covered with a cloth wrap. The vision reminded me of a verse the Hallowgales had forced me to recite during my youth:

Her kyrtel brystow red

With clothes upon her hed

That wey a sowe of led

Wrythen in wonder wyse

After the Sarasyns gyse

With a whym wham

Knyt with a trym tram

Vpon her brayne pan

Lyke a sintian

Capped about

Whan she goeth out

I shook off the words as Thalaj leaned toward me, his voice a strained whisper. "I'm uncertain which rumors of the Tsinti carry truth. Have caution with what you say. Don't tell them more than you must."

Before I'd gained the voice to reply, one of our guards pulled Thalaj away. I cried, "No," but in the next breath, I was also seized and dragged toward one of the canvas-covered wagons. I rounded on the woman who'd captured my arm.

Jorani.

"Let me go. Where are you taking me? Ouch!" I protested while wriggling in an attempt for freedom.

"Shut your trap." She pulled harder on my arm, and I cursed myself that I hadn't trained at all in hand-to-hand battles. Jorani wasn't any larger than me. If I had known how to fight, I might have been able to free myself, but she also still held my weapons confidently in her other hand. Still struggling, I stumbled along.

At a near wagon, she dropped my pack and my weapons but wouldn't release my arm. She climbed the wooden steps and handily pulled me up behind her. The flap closed and the sudden shade obliterated my sight. Hands landed on my arms and pulled at my clothes.

"Wait! What are you doing?" I protested, trying and failing to keep them from removing the tan rough-spun shirt I wore for travel. Flailing, I blinked rapidly wanting to convince my eyes to adjust to the lower light. Three heads wrapped in cloth bobbed around me and worked to get me naked, clucking along the way in a language foreign to my ears.

Jorani clucked back. When my eyes began to adjust, I could see her step to the corner and slather something in her hair just before she wrapped her head in the same cloth as the others. One of the women, a plumper one, knocked me off my feet and onto a cushioned bench to the side. The other two removed my boots, then held my ankles while the plump one pulled my pants and my underclothes to my ankles.

For my entire life, attendants had been present to attend to my dressing, undressing, and even bathing, so the nakedness failed to disconcert me. Their purpose though escaped me. "Why do you wish me unclothed?" I asked, pulling and pushing with my legs and hoping they'd understand the common tongue, maybe that they'd respond. At least Jorani would comprehend. But still, I received no reply. In a singular move, the two holding my ankles stepped back and the first slipped away my lower clothes. I stood quickly, bare save for Tsanseri's cuff and the necklace about my neck. The cold stone burned colder and the hot stone burned hotter, and the woman's eyes narrowed to examine what hung there. I presumed they were Tsinti and they recognized the third pendant—the totem Thalaj had recovered within the Evernight. My hand drifted toward my neck.

The women stepped back and looked at my body unabashedly. One clucked to the other, and the second agreed. With a nod, she stepped forward, grasped the necklace, and gave it a swift tug, pulling it free from my neck. I gulped and reached after the woman, but the other two seized my arms, wrestling the Comtesse's gift free as well.

"Why?" I demanded. "Please," I begged. "Leave me these things." My eyes prickled, tears barely contained. "It's all I have of my mother and father." If I had to give up the cuff, so be it, but my soul needed those stones against my skin and near my heart.

I relented my struggle; they released my arms and went out the back of the wagon. The plump woman turned. As our eyes met, I thought I read a small bit of concern in her face, but it disappeared as soon as it had appeared. Just before she stepped out of the cart with my necklace in hand, she clucked something to Jorani, who dipped her hands in whatever she'd slathered into her own hair and came to me, goop oozing between her fingers. Having been robbed of the stones, I stood quietly and accepted her ministrations. The smell of the stuff reminded me of my aunt Nadialynne's garden.

"What is that?" I asked, my voice thin and a tear rolling down my cheek. Though I cried quietly, I won the battle against the urge to sob.

"Yak's lard, brewed with wild herbs. The lard protects the hair and the *mynthe* cools your scalp while your head is bound in cloth. If you're going to travel with us, you need to look the part." Her demeanor had become easier, presumably under some instruction from the older women, but perhaps only because I stood there shivering despite the hot and dead air within the wagon.

"Travel with you?" I reached out a hand, wanting to call the wind to cool myself, but Jorani pushed it down.

"Don't, Storm Sorcerer." Some warning danced across her eyes. "You'll do much better if you're agreeable."

"I only intended to call the wind to relieve the stale air."

"It'd be best to not . . . for now."

When Jorani had wrapped my head well and tucked in the ends of the material, the women returned, each jangling as she entered. They carried clothing that matched their peoples' fashion. One handed a pile to Jorani, who changed into bright yellow pants with an orange top. To finish her ensemble, she strapped a netted belt about her and shook her hips, jingling like the others. They all laughed at fun that I couldn't quite share, but it eased my tension a bit.

The plump one came to me with a bundle and said, "Young one, clothes for you. They call me Detsa. This is my cart, and you'll travel as my guest. Sleep there." She pointed to a similar cushioned bench on the other side of the cart.

I felt a rush of relief as she spoke in the common tongue, but I remained confused as I dressed in vibrant red and pink clothes. My belt had no coin, and I somehow felt as if this symbolized that I rested at the bottom of their society. "You will forgive my lack of understanding."

The plump woman turned to my captor. "Jorani, stand outside." The others left too, and Detsa, now my host, said to me, "You don't need to worry much, but you'll wait here for a bit. We'll be on our way soon." With that, she left me alone.

I sank onto the bench, supposedly my new bed, and dropped my wrapped head into my hands. What had I gotten myself into? What trouble had *we* encountered? It seemed that we hadn't needed the totem after all, so I'd sent Thalaj into harm's way in the Evernight for naught, but that we were now seemingly prisoners of the Tsinti hadn't been part of the plan either. Although, had the wanderers not apprehended us, I now felt certain we would not have been able to see through the tsym. Having watched the little man go through the motions to reveal the Tsinti's caravan, I wouldn't have known gestures or words were necessary. Mayhap how we came to be in the company of the wandering folk would have been our only way in. Disheartened over having lost the items I'd treasured so, I remained there and trembled, wanting for Thalaj.

Of the options remaining before me, what I knew, and what I felt, I decided against Thalaj's counsel to remain silent. A different tack was obviously necessary. We had purpose here, and I needed to do something to make it happen. Then, once I had satisfied that purpose, I needed to retrieve the stones as I believed that bound within them were the very souls of my parents. Through one method or another, before we parted ways with the Tsinti, I must possess those to guide my journey.

The flap rose, emitting a ray of Otarr's golden light, and Jorani stepped inside. She brought my pack and my weapon belt. Dropping the load, she freed a scimityne and twirled it by the handle, her technique deft as she scored naught in the tight space. Jealousy stabbed at seeing her immediate skill with the weapon, the sight reaffirming my need to learn.

"They're putting the tsym back in place, and we'll be on our way," she said.

"Jorani?" I ventured.

"Mmm?" she answered.

Good, mayhap it would be easier than I'd thought. The woman seemed now amicable, pleased to be in my company even. I started, "We came in search of your people."

"Hai. This, we know."

A hint we'd walked into a snare.

I suppressed the urge to spout off the question as to how exactly she would know such information. Instead, I said, "Then you'll also know that I am Empress of the Nantai people."

"Mmhmm." She lunged and spun the blade, engaging with me but not giving the conversation her full attention.

Blades were her weapon, words mine. I continued, "I'd hoped that your people would recognize that you are also my people and treat us better than this."

Jorani stood straight and tilted her head as she regarded me. "Have we not treated you well?" she asked with the innocence of a youngling.

My brow felt heavy. "I'm not certain I could say that capturing us and separating me from my guard is treating me well."

She looked at me blankly.

I shifted on my bed, uncomfortable still but encouraged that she seemed willing to hold a conversation. "I had hoped that the Tsinti would honor me as their empress too?"

At this, Jorani laughed with a hilarity I couldn't see. She verily howled and guffawed. When she gained control of herself, she put away my scimityne and sat across the wagon, leaning forward with her elbows on her knees. "The wanderers only listen to the word of the Tsinti king, Tamás Hætyr. And even then, his law is limited. We belong to no country. We exist apart from your time, and while our caravans roam the grasslands, we encounter none of your people"—her brows shot toward the headwrap—"unless we so choose."

Lifting my chin, I demanded, "Who is this Tsinti king you speak of? I would like to meet him. Mayhap he will hear my case differently."

Jorani bellowed with more laughter, falling onto her side and grasping herself about the waist. When she had recovered enough to speak, she wiped away a mirthful tear. "A long-passed founder of our people and ways. He travels with the gods alone now, but under his decree, no person among the Tsinti shall be suffered to live within a tennō's realm. We extend that law to a kōgō's realm as well. We will forever live apart."

I had no idea how to respond to her proclamation, but it knotted in my stomach. I wanted to ask what they intended to do with us, to inquire about Thalaj, but I thought it might show weakness. Instead, I simply looked at the woman across the wagon, withholding any expression.

At length, she gave another short laugh and stood.

"Wait," I said, grabbing her arm before she left. When she turned, I asked, "Can I leave the wagon. I need to speak with your witch wife."

Jorani looked at me as if I'd just blasphemed her god. "Soon," she said in a ghostly voice. "She will join you shortly, and as soon as the witch wife reads your fates, you may walk freely among the Tsinti."

◇◇◇◇◇◇◇◇◇◇◇◇◇◇◇◇◇◇◇◇◇◇◇◇◇◇◇◇◇◇◇◇

INSIDE THE TEPID WAGON, I sat dumbfounded. Waiting. True, I could have tried to leave, to find Thalaj, but when I'd lifted the flap to peer outside, Jorani had held a dagger toward me. And though she'd left my weapons inside, I had no skill with the blades, so I awaited the arrival of the witch wife she'd promised. There were no sounds inside the cart, and the canvas muffled the milling around outside. My scalp began to tingle and cool, so I reached up to explore the headwrap by touch.

"Amazing," I mused. I no longer felt the need to call the wind and cool myself. It appeared the women of the Tsinti had shown me a kindness I hadn't expected.

"What's amazing?" an old woman's voice croaked, and a beam of Otarr's light shone into the cart. The actual woman who stepped inside didn't match the voice. When she turned to me, I saw she had no lines at the corners of her eyes or around her mouth. Her skin appeared taut like a ripe Aomori apple's and her smile glittered. She carried a kettle and two stoneware cups, and a small bag hung from a string about her wrist, her clothing a melding of bright greens and blues and purples. She cleared her throat and said, in a voice as fresh as spring, "They said you'd finally arrived. Tell me why you've come to us, young one."

I bristled at her naming me *young one*, especially given that she appeared my age or younger. The first voice I'd heard from her seemed more in line with one who would address me so, though I had to admit that I truly had no idea what a witch wife was. And so, I asked.

The woman acted as if I hadn't spoken and went to the same table where Jorani had worked. There, she poured steaming water into the two cups and handed one to me with a command, "Drink."

My look must have bespoken my skepticism, because she offered a gentle smile and added, "Don't worry, there is no poison in the cup. I'll drink with you as soon as I have set up here."

Within the warm wagon, almost the last thing I desired was a steaming drink, but I took the cup and held it between my hands. Herbs floated in the water, changing it from clear to a cloudy green color. The woman went back to the flap and pinned it open so that light streamed in. My eyes, having adjusted to the dimness within, stung, and I squinted as they readjusted.

"Drink," she said again, sipping from her own earthenware cup.

I wished for my golem, but I lifted the cup to my lips and took a small sip. My eyes popped open. I'd expected something earthy, but the flavor tasted surprisingly sweet, honeyed mayhap, but the tang didn't carry the mustiness of honey. The taste was woodsier, something I'd never experienced. I took another sip, trying to place it.

The woman pulled a pail from a corner and set it upside down between the cushioned benches, then grabbed a wide board and placed it on the tipped pail. She retrieved her cup, took a seat across the makeshift table, and pulled a stack of cards from the small pouch about her wrist. "You didn't tell me what brings you here," she reminded.

"I'm searching for my father," I said suddenly, my tongue feeling looser than it had before.

"Ah. I see."

"May I have your name?" I asked.

"Apologies. I am called Zofi by those close." Her eyes crinkled, another contrast with the smooth face, as she offered a tight smile.

"Zofi." I tasted her name, short like the given names of the Cloud Courtiers, but surely one of the second caste would not be here. They traveled by cloud, high above Nantai. I peered up to the witch wife. "You didn't answer my question either."

"No, I didn't, did I?" She handed me the stack of cards. "Shuffle these."

I accepted the cards and set my almost empty cup to the side, then shuffled.

She relaxed on the bench across from me with a sigh. "I am the one you were assigned to await. The witch wife you seek. Lay three cards face up when they are sorted to your satisfaction."

I did as she asked. The first depicted a woman sitting in the center of a radiant yellow sun. Otarr. Upon her head lay a crown of twelve stars, and her feet rested upon the moon. Selene. Her right hand held a sword, and upon her left a dragon with wings spread wide. I glanced up, unsure if I should continue. She nodded, and I flipped the second card. A skeleton stood in an empty field with hands and feet protruding in all directions, the hands each holding a sword. I flipped the third—this one, I recognized. Upon the card, the personification of Otarr poured the essence of life from one urn to another, a sword resting on the floor at Otarr's feet.

When I'd completed the task, Zofi sat forward and studied the cards.

The silence stretched out long enough that I grew uncomfortable and asked, "What do they mean?"

She remained silent for another minute, rubbing her bottom lip. Then, she reclined against a pillow. "Evangale, how much do you know of the Tsinti beliefs?"

"Very little, I must admit." This, I said with a bit of shame that I hadn't come to know more about an entire group of people who lived within my realm even though they claimed to live apart.

"These cards, young one, represent the will of the fates. There are three muses: the soul's muse, the body's muse, but the third muse has no equivalent word within the common tongue. We call it *o drom*, which literally translates to *the road*, but it means so much more to the Tsinti. To our people, *o drom* embodies one's life and very existence. It encompasses everyone you have met and everyone you will ever meet."

"Oh," I said, mesmerized.

"Your first card, The Empress—"

"What?" I slapped my hand on the makeshift table. "Even these cards think I need to be the ruler?" As she regarded me, I felt a touch embarrassed by my outburst. "My apologies," I mumbled.

"You don't believe it so?" she asked with one of the most open and innocent looks.

I shook my head, lips pressed into a firm line. "My purpose is to find Father. To restore him to the throne."

She raised a hand and nodded. "The cards don't usually mean what their names suggest. I can tell you the symbolism, but you must interpret the meaning. It may not immediately seem logical, but if it doesn't now, it will one day. The Empress signifies action." She pointed to the second card. "This card signifies transformation or change. The name of the card is Death, but once again, it doesn't necessarily mean someone will die."

I reached for the stones, a habit I'd developed since I'd donned the necklace after Father's disappearance. They provided comfort and focus, and that I came up empty-handed now made my insides churn.

Zofi went on, "The final card is Temperance. It is the card that symbolizes combining or merging of two things."

Studying the cards and trying to gather the meaning, I couldn't discern any cohesive story. Action, transformation, and joining, the symbols seemed so generic that they could mean anything. I raised my eyes to Zofi, unsure what to say.

"And what I said seems true, the message may mean little, if anything at all, to you today." She reached for my empty cup, and like the woman who had made the tiny replicas of us, she studied the herbs remaining in the bottom. Coming away apparently satisfied, she added, "However, that they are all of the swords suit means to me and my people that you come to us with pure intentions." She smiled.

My shoulders felt lighter, a pressure lifting with the knowledge that she believed my intentions pure. "But what about Thalaj?" I blurted.

Zofi cleared the tea service, placing the cups beside the kettle on the table in the corner, then tucked away her cards and stowed the improvised table. "Young Mairynne, your journey is only just beginning. There will be many adventures and many lessons for you to learn. For now, let us walk."

I leapt up from the bed, eager to be free from the wagon, to learn more about these people, and most of all, to discover what had happened to Thalaj. Strange how my perspective had shifted and twisted in the few short hours since the wanderers had taken us prisoner. With Zofi's visit, fear had subsided and curiosity shone brightly.

The witch wife talked as we walked, describing commonplace things in the life of the Tsinti—the utility of the yaks, what each wagon carried, and how to identify which wagon was which. A spoon marked the wagon that carried and prepared food, an anvil marked the metalworker, and a cube that appeared to stand out from the canvas marked the home of the reiki healer. We moved around as the caravan lurched slowly into motion.

"Under the tsym, we move slowly enough that walking about is common. Apart from dangers from the rest of the world, we rarely feel the need to hurry. You will remain with the Tsinti for some time before we part." Suddenly, she stopped and pointed.

Turning to where she pointed, I saw Thalaj tending to one of the broad beasts, anger brewing in his stance and shackles around his ankles. I lurched in his direction.

But Zofi grabbed my hand before I could go to him. "Not now. The time is not right." Warning flared in her wise eyes.

I heeded her words and remained at her side even though I twisted back to face the man I longed to free.

"Give it time," she coaxed, releasing my hand. "That one. He will always be there for you. There will come a time when you'll doubt but rest easy as he will always return."

When I spun to ask her meaning, she was gone.

Thirteen

Tsinti Swordplay

SPUTTERING, I STOOD ALONE EVEN though the colorful Tsinti went about their day all around me. Only a couple even noticed that I had joined their masses. Mayhap it had been a kindness Detsa, Jorani, and the others had done for me, but no one had taken the same measures with my escort, and that seemed out of balance. I watched him for a while before he felt my stare upon him. Tentatively, as if I'd tapped him on the shoulder, he turned and met my gaze. His mouth opened, then closed, and even across the field, I could see a muscle tick in his square jaw. He, too, had been stripped of his weapons. But moreover, someone had also stripped away his tunic and left him to brown in the sun. The dark pants he wore were his, not a colorful variety, and splotches of mud caked around his knees. A bloodied cut showed across his upper shoulder. Worry gathered in my heart. Once again, I'd led him into a battery, and I felt sick that I'd no idea how to relieve him of that pain. I tried to tell him with my eyes I was sorry, but his hardened even more. Thalaj shook his head, which I read as his warning for me not to approach, and he returned to brushing the course hair of a yak.

I stepped forward, once, twice. Despite his warning, I meant to go to him, to find someone around him and ask whomever had him bound what the meaning was. Why hadn't the Tsinti changed his clothes and treated him as the women had with me? I moved, scanning his surroundings, but at the same time, I lost track of my own.

A hard hand grasped me at my elbow and whirled me around. Jorani and I stood nose to nose, and I got a good look into her brown eyes with flecks of gold.

"What?" I demanded. "You've taken away everything that we might fight you with, and we mean neither you nor your people any harm. Why can't I speak to him?"

"Going to him will make his path with the Tsinti harder." Though it hadn't been a day, her voice had eased toward me as she gave an explanation. "Your purity had to be discovered, for him, it's his strength. Tsinti ways are not the ways of the Nantai." She looked down, then added, "He knows this too. Come."

I shot a single look backward. Thalaj nodded, and I went.

Jorani's words rang true time and time again over the next weeks as the Tsinti caravan meandered over the Central Grasslands. Their ways were not like ours. They weren't a planful or ordered people. They gathered each night around a fire with instruments that sang well into the night, rising late in the morning and meandering for several hours when the drink had worn thin. I wasn't aware of our destination, but I traveled along. After I had a chance to thoroughly evaluate my situation, I decided to heed some of Thalaj's old advice. It was before we had gone into Tsanseri's court. He'd said, "Observe and listen." When I'd followed that advice before, it had worked in my favor.

Regardless, I felt alone and deserted and guilty over having left Thalaj to tend the yak and whatever other trials the Tsinti saw fit. One afternoon, I stumbled upon a group huddled around my first guard at the center of a circle. Thalaj had a long staff that they'd given him for his own defense, but members of the caravan, including the ones who'd abducted us in the Yubar, took turns assaulting him with blades. I flinched and gasped, a high noise that pulled his gaze in my direction, but that, I only did once. Owed to my diversion, Thalaj suffered a new blow, sending him to his knees with a heavy groan. Thereafter, I learned to hold my tongue so as to not interrupt his concentration. Instead, I hugged myself as if I could physically hold my anxiety within my own body.

When stubs of his staff littered the ground and the remaining piece only extended by a hand's breadth from his grasp, the Tsinti discarded their weapons and moved in on him with hands and feet. If anyone could take the abuse, it was Thalaj, but it battered my heart to watch. When they parted, he lay on the grass. I started toward him, but was halted again by Jorani. She motioned to two young men from the healer's tent who came and took him to the cart with the painted block appearing to extrude from the canvas. I didn't see him for days after, and when I tried to approach the healer's cart—something I'd learned the Tsinti called the reiki cart—the boys who had carried him inside turned me away.

I asked everyone I met for more information about the witch wife of the Tsinti, but each and every person with whom I inquired blatantly ignored the question. Day by day, my mood sank further and further into a blackness I'd never fathomed. With no idea of what sway the witch wife had upon my journey, no knowledge of where they'd stowed my necklace or my arm brace, and no access to my only confidant, my hope waned.

On a late afternoon, under Otarr's hot gaze, I reached for my storm sorcery and tried to cool the camp, but all that answered my call was a soft and still hot breeze. After the attempt, I felt immediately exhausted and sagged with further disappointment. Even deprived of everything else, I never imagined my magic would also forsake me.

I lost count of the days, but I'd left in spring and the hot season was still upon us. I didn't see Zofi again, which puzzled me considering the relatively small caravan. Sleep came easier in my new bed, and in the days that followed, Detsa shooed me around her home cart in a way that had me in mind of a hen clucking after her chicks. She rarely spoke in the common tongue, and I began to gather bits and pieces of the language. I learned they called the tongue of the travelers *Romani*. I remained lost, but I also began to reluctantly acclimate to the Tsinti way of life. With all other options removed, I decided to throw myself into becoming closer to them. Maybe if they saw me as one of their own rather than an outsider traveling along, they'd be more willing to invite me into conversations or answer my questions.

And so I asked Detsa to teach me to weave and learned eagerly under her foreign instruction with several other young women who practiced the talents required to create the colorful patterns within their harnesses, baskets, rugs, and tapestries. The language became clearer with the continued interaction, reinforced by the back and forth between Detsa and her other students. At times she wouldn't reply to me unless I asked her questions in Romani. On a day when my mother hen had to tend to driving her yak, I grabbed my weapon belt and went to find Jorani.

As I walked through the caravan, I garnered a few strange or wary looks, but no one approached or made to stop me in my path. I found Jorani sparring with the short man who wore the red mark beneath his right eye, the leader of the party that had captured us at the edge of the Yubar Forest. She still wore the wrap around her head but dressed in plain clothing, tighter around her legs, allowing for easier movement and avoidance of slashing blades. When they took a break, I approached.

"Jorani?"

She turned to me, smile widening as she looked at my weapons. Before she'd even made eye contact, she said, "I wondered when you'd gather courage enough to ask."

◇◇◇◇◇◇◇◇◇◇◇◇◇◇◇◇◇◇◇◇◇◇◇◇◇◇◇◇◇◇◇◇

JORANI WELCOMED ME TO the group and introduced Baldeo and Yankos, the former being the larger Tsinti who'd elbowed Thalaj upon our arrival, and the latter the leader with the red mark beneath his eye. "Come, djecmas," she said.

The word brought me up short, and when inquiring about its meaning, I added the Romani word for sorcerer to my growing vocabulary. "*Djecmas*," I repeated. "How do you say *storm*?"

"Ha!" Yankos scoffed. "Romani doesn't work that way. *Djecmas* is your people. It's all that's needed." He pointed to the weapon belt I carried. "Now, are you going to pull those things or didn't you want to learn?"

The trio watched me. Yankos leaned upon a hefty sword he'd been using to spar with Jorani, and Baldeo stood with his feet wide and arms folded across his broad chest. Jorani tucked both her daggers back into her belt and quirked a brow. I reached for the hilt of one of the scimitynes and pulled. It wouldn't free, so I tried the other. My face heated when I couldn't figure how to pull either of my own weapons from their scabbards.

A look, one that well excluded me from the silent conversation, passed between the Tsinti scouts, then Baldeo barked a laugh. "I'll get the toys." And with that, he trotted away.

Jorani sighed as if her task would be more daunting than she'd believed. "Put 'em down and come here," she said.

I marched over, eager to learn how to wield my weapon.

When I once again stood nose to nose with her, she asked, "Have you learned to dance?"

Biting the inside of my lip, I shook my head. I'd seen people dance. In truth, dancing seemed a particular talent in some of the castes. The Fire Forgers had stolen the stage at my ascension celebration after the enactment of *Sosano and the Blooming Princess*, and they'd pulled others onto the dance floor well into the night, but it wasn't proper for a lady of my stature. Amidst my people, dancing was an activity for the laboring class of Storm Sorcerers and for many of the castes beneath the Cloud Courtiers. The art entertained lords, ladies, emperors, empresses, princes, and princesses alike, and those who partook seemed to glow with an energy I'd always envied. But the breaks in rank within our culture were customs I didn't feel right sharing in present company.

"All right," she said. "Well, that comes first. Fighting isn't much more than a dance in which you trade moves with your opponent. Except for the fact that you may be aiming to kill your partner in the fighting dance."

Baldeo trotted back with four swords, wooden at both blade and hilt. They appeared too small for his usage, and his reference to *the toys* became clear. Indignation stung in my chest, but I had naught to do but stifle it.

Jorani made a pained face while shaking her head. To Baldeo, she said, "Put those over there for now and come stand here." As she made this command, she snapped her fingers and pointed to the ground before me. "We have to start from the kids' lessons with this one."

The big man groaned, earning a laugh from Yankos that he answered with a sneer and a scowl. Although reluctant, he did as Jorani instructed, grumbling, "I hate the dance part. Don't they dance where she's from?"

I tucked my head, cheeks blazing. "Not really." It was small relief that the burlier man didn't seem to recognize the reasons I'd never learned to dance. Jorani and Yankos both held their thoughts behind impassive masks, so if they gleaned the truth, I didn't know.

Jorani explained the mirroring moves necessary to develop the proper stances. When Baldeo stepped back with his left foot, I was to step forward with my right. When he placed his right foot forward, I was to lunge back onto my left. "But keep your weight centered," she said as she grasped my shoulders and straightened my torso. "Like so, and keep an eye upon his waist."

The lessons went on and on. Side moves followed, then moves at various angles. My first session consisted only of footwork. And by the time Jorani and Baldeo had showed me all the steps, a small crowd had gathered about us. One of the onlookers began a steady beat on a drum. I looked questioningly at Jorani.

She gave a nod. "Now you do it with a rhythm," she said by way of answering my unspoken question.

And so we danced. Jorani and Yankos picked up the wooden swords, and when I misstepped, they scolded, tapping me on the calf, thigh, or shoulder that had strayed from the pattern.

"Enough," Yankos called after a good while, holding out a hand to halt the drummer.

"Thank the fates!" Baldeo said and sloughed away.

"Not so fast," Yankos grabbed his arm with one hand and passed him the toy swords with the other. Then he turned to me. "Now, with someone smaller."

By that time, beads of sweat trickled down my neck and back, yet surprisingly, the herbal balm in my hair did wonders to keep my body cool enough that I could focus on sparring. The correcting blows increased immediately, but soon I understood the purpose of the change in partner, and I started to glean the nuances they'd been hinting at for what seemed hours. If I watched at the hip, he hinted his intended direction before he actually moved.

When the skies grew a dusty gray from the fading light, Jorani called a halt to the activities and flipped her hands toward the assembled people to send them about their business. They clapped and cheered before they left to retrieve their pails, the makeshift chairs they'd use at the night's circle, and their musical instruments. Soon every Tsinti in camp would head to the evening's fire for the nightly festivities.

There I remained, watching them disperse with legs shaking from exhaustion and a grin forming on my face. For the first time in more days than I could count, I felt as if I belonged to something apart from myself. Jorani clapped me on the shoulder. "Nice start." I hadn't heard my name on another's lips since I'd met Zofi on our first day with the Tsinti.

Our, I reminded myself. *Thalaj.* And my lightening heart stopped in midflight.

As the days went on, I wove with the girls in the morning, walked along or rode in Detsa's cart with the caravan at midday, and practiced the dance with the Tsinti scouts in the late afternoon. It became a simple routine, and I saw my body change. Where there had been soft curves before, I felt hardened ridges and the muscles in my legs became roped. But all the while, I rarely crossed paths with the man who'd led me out of Stormskeep, the one I'd trusted as my protector, and when I did, he simply pressed his mouth tighter and turned away. At least I'd seen with my own eyes that he'd healed. I wished—no I longed—to know what labors they wrought upon him, but I heeded his signals and let it be.

There was little indication to my untrained senses in which direction we traveled. One day, it seemed we went north with Otarr to my right in the morning hours, but the next, I would judge we had turned south. The heat persisted. My sorcery that I'd relied upon my entire life to call winds and rains from the skies above remained muted for reasons I couldn't understand. I assumed it had much to do with the tsym, but if I tried to call the rain, the air simply grew thicker, more moist. My new, and hopefully temporary, life seemed pure confusion; the only reliable things I had were working a loom and learning to dance with weapons, so that is what I focused on.

We arrived at the river after many days spent dancing and wood-sparring with Jorani, then Baldeo. The scouts discussed my progress and agreed that I was ready to face their leader, and presumably the more skilled fighter. It would be a final test to allow me to train with real blades. They would judge to see if my clumsiness had left and determine if they felt I had gained enough control to harm neither myself nor my opponent. Yankos and I faced off within the circle of Tsinti, each of us wielding two wooden short swords. The dance began.

Somewhere outside my sight, the drumbeat sounded, and I placed my feet to the rhythm the drummer pounded. Yankos did the same. We crouched and circled. He flipped one toy sword, then the other as we revolved around one another, a lascivious smile growing on his face and stretching the red mark unnaturally. I concentrated on his hip, his shoulder, waiting for him to reverse or begin to attack. He did the same.

"Will you charge, little one?" he taunted.

"I stand taller than you by near a hand, *little* one," I retorted.

"But you are thinner. I outweigh you by a stone."

"I have longer reach." I felt a grin break across my face.

He grinned back, a vicious smile, and I saw within his eyes and a jagged line of his teeth that he'd won battles upon battles to become the scout leader he was. But I breathed, twirled one of my own toy swords, and reversed the dance. We encircled one another in the other direction for many beats. Then, his hip twitched, warning of his attack. He lunged and I parried.

"Good," he praised, then sprang forth with the opposite sword.

I blocked again.

The dance resumed.

"What do you want from this, little one?" Yankos asked.

I drew my brows, failing to understand the relevance of his question, but the answer seemed obvious. "To learn to wield my own weapons," I answered.

"Ah, but there must be something more," he pressed, eyes narrowing.

If there was, I couldn't think of it in the moment. It took all my concentration to place my feet as I'd learned, to watch his tells as I'd been taught, and to plan my next move.

Yankos leapt at me again, a three-blow attack I'd encountered before. I raised my weapons to meet each strike, and after, he retreated on the balls of his feet.

Pleased with my defense, I spat, "Thalaj!" through gritted teeth. "I want my guard freed as I am." I leapt forward, returning the same three blows.

My opponent waved off my swords as if they were feathers and laughed, an insulting and infuriating crow. "Now we're getting somewhere. But there's more still. Tell me," he said, then hissed, "*Little* one."

My muscles coiled and ice-cold rage filled my thoughts over all I'd sacrificed—

so much—so many things frozen in my mind's eye. But I inhaled through my nose, pushed the air away through my mouth, and then repeated the calming breath. In the heat of that moment, the time wasn't right to release all my burdens. I pictured a field, clear of all Tsinti. The only people existing in Nantai or beyond were me and my foe. I locked my arms and attacked with singular purpose.

Yankos parried and blocked, sending each jab and hack away from his body. After, he gave a satisfied smile and nod just before we locked into the quick-time dance and traded strike after strike, slash after slash, and stab after stab. There wasn't time for more words; my breath quickened. I spun, stabbing backward, but found myself within his grip, his sword in front of me, poised at the river of my life's blood. Thankfully, his test wasn't complete with that move, else I would have failed and suffered the implied slit of my throat. But he shoved me away, following with strikes like lightning, blow upon thunderous blow, until one landed in my gut and I fell backward, air whooshing from my lungs. Instinctively, I reached for the wind, tried to gather storm clouds, but all the effort did was drain my strength.

I collapsed onto my back. I gasped for breath as Yankos, the small but hardened Tsinti scout, closed in again. Raising his toy sword high and jumping in a move that would strengthen his blow tenfold, he came down upon me. Somehow, I pulled the swords in front of me, rolled, and sent his attack into the dirt.

Time slowed. I coughed and hacked and rounded around the pain in my gut. Thankfully, no further siege came. I heard whimpers, and only later realized they came from my own throat. And as I gained my breath, I heard a splash and felt a splatter upon my face.

I sucked in a gloriously refreshing wave of air, rolled, and stood. The pain beneath my ribs still throbbed but receded slowly. My fingers ached with the tight grip on the swords as I lifted my head and opened my eyes. Beyond a smiling Yankos, a large urn lay emptying water onto the ground; and behind that, Thalaj stood, fists clenched, and pure iced fury reigned within in his eyes.

◇◇◇◇◇◇◇◇◇◇◇◇◇◇◇◇◇◇◇◇◇◇◇◇◇◇◇◇◇◇◇◇◇◇◇

HIS HAIR HUNG LOOSE from its typical knot, a frame of scraggled waves around his high cheekbones. His skin had burnished in the sun's rays, and while he'd always been lean, it seemed to stretch tighter over his arms. The depth within his almond-shaped eyes sent a chill over me. I'd watched Thalaj train his soldiers for years, and toughened though he was by the Tsinti labors, my first guard was undoubtedly preparing his body to fight.

As I scrambled for my feet, he lunged toward Yankos. The scout nodded to the other scouts, and they moved to seize him just as another Tsinti burst through the circle and clubbed Thalaj across the back. Thalaj coughed but kept moving forward. Jorani and Baldeo grasped his arms just before he reached Yankos.

Furiously fighting against the hands that held him just out of reach, Thalaj kept writhing toward my opponent and growled, "How dare you hit a lady?" Nevermind that he'd so often sparred with the female guard Gaelynne, I was a different matter altogether—his *empress*.

Thalaj lunged again, and Jorani had to brace herself with both legs to hold him in place.

Yankos flipped a wooden sword in the air, catching it by the hilt and looked at his would-be attacker with a raised brow. "Your *lady*, as you will, asked to learn to fight. I am merely obliging her wishes."

Thalaj pulled. This time, Jorani's grip slipped and he swung the free hand toward Yankos.

Yankos ducked and came up laughing, still confident either that Baldeo wouldn't lose the beast he held or that he could easily handle Thalaj.

I wasn't so sure.

"Stop!" I cried.

The crowd circling the scene cheered and heckled. "Let 'im go," one yelled. "Fight, fight, fight," several others chanted. The commotion continued until Yankos held up both hands and walked slowly about the circle looking at the crowd. He finished his revolution standing in front of me once again.

"This *little one* here. She has learned to fight. She bears the soul of the warrior. Would you deny her such an honor, *soldier*?" He looked at Thalaj, then back at me. "And you, *Empress of all of Nantai*, believe this prisoner should walk freely among the wandering folk?"

I lifted my chin, the pain in my midsection forgotten. "I do." The two words seemed inept as if I were telling a wolf to hold a hare close to his bosom. But they hit stronger than I would have imagined.

Yankos said, "What good do you believe he may do for the Tsinti?"

"If you believe I possess a warrior's soul, test him. All I know about determination, control, and bravery, I have learned through watching this man." I swallowed once I'd freed the words, worried that I'd just sent him into more harm.

The scout leader looked at Thalaj from head to toe, and as he did, Thalaj's nostrils flared in response. Silently, I tried to tell my guard to allow this, that I was okay, and that this was the right—and maybe the only—way.

"Very well," Yankos said at last. "Maladros?"

I'd forgotten about anyone but Yankos and Thalaj, but the man with the club stepped forward, answering to his name. And now that I studied him, I recognized him as one of Yankos's companions when they'd taken us from the edge of the Yubar Forest south of Arashi.

To Maladros, Yankos continued, "You'll have to find yourself a new plaything. Get me his weapons and let us test his worth." He turned to face me, holding his hand, palm up, to Jorani. "I will use yours."

Jorani placed my belt with the scimitynes still sheathed into his waiting hand.

I gathered all my training and poise so that I could stifle the gasp that gathered in my chest. I'd never seen Thalaj battle another warrior where both used the scimitynes.

In fact, it surprised me that Yankos would choose to wield a weapon not his own. Surely he could not have known the movements of the curved blades as intimately as Thalaj. All I'd learned over the recent weeks in combination with having watched Thalaj train for years upon years informed me that the dance with scimitynes wasn't the same as with straight blades. Instead of push, pull, stab, the moves would roll, whirl, and slash. Even a slash with a straight blade differed from slashing with a curved. This knowledge I had in my head, like something read in a book, though I certainly could not have executed the differences between the two with my own body. Though Yankos had praised my growing skill, I remained an amateur, new to the craft.

As two unknown wanderers brought the weapons forward, I stepped to the side, hugging myself to bind the worry within my body and not allow it to distract the battle.

The men circled each other, but there was no playful banter like Yankos offered when sparring with me, and Thalaj had never been one to speak during a match. There wasn't much foreplay in their dance, either, before Thalaj loosed his whirling attack, a combination of a left slash, then a right, the two quick pivots in opposite directions, each with a deadly slash. Yankos met the blows and returned them. The action seemed to roll as blades clanged and sang against one another over and over and over. Soon, they were both bloodied about the torso, but neither seemed to notice. I held my hands over my mouth, attempting to assure my silence. When four curved blades locked between them and they both sneered between the metal at each other, I finally couldn't hold it any longer.

"Enough!" I snapped.

They stopped, and the drums died along with the chanting.

When the silence was complete, I said, "You have no call to kill one another."

Relenting, they released the entangled blades and both faced me, panting. A movement caught my eye and I turned. Zofi stood at my side wearing a wide, satisfied smile.

FOURTEEN

Here Goes the Road

ABOUT HER HEAD, SHE WORE a wrap woven of bright gold and fiery red. Zofi raised her chin high toward Otarr in the sky and called to the onlookers, "The leader of Nantai is right. This is done. Wanderers, let us take repast and prepare for the naming this evening. We are to welcome our children into our caravan tonight under the watchful eyes of the fates. Go now and prepare."

Thalaj came to my side unhindered as the exhilaration dissipated and the crowd filtered away, rivulets of blood running down his bare torso.

Zofi took my hand in one of her own and patted it with the other. Peering at my first guard, she said, "Go see the reiki master to tend to those cuts, then to Detsa for some clothing appropriate for the evening's fire." With the offering of a small smile and a nod, she turned and left us there.

Yankos sheathed my scimitynes and handed the belt to me. Then, the scouts went as well, leaving Thalaj and me alone. It seemed he'd proven his strength at long last and now enjoyed the same privileges as me. Though he still held his weapons, I dropped the belt, threw my arms around his neck, and squeezed, heedless of the blood.

He grunted, then sighed and pulled back from the embrace. "Are you truly well, Mairynne?"

I nodded vigorously, afraid to try to speak with how my throat had tightened. His voice sounded rough to my ears, very much a reflection of the wear upon his body and the long hours working under Otarr's light. I took him to the cart marked with the extruding block, refusing to leave him while the healer cleaned and bandaged the cuts. Fortunately, all were mere scratches and, though they had painted his chest and back in crimson blood and might leave scars, they would heal easily enough. Afterward, we went to my home cart, Detsa's, and Thalaj dressed in a burnt-orange tunic and a new pair of green bloused pants with red, orange, and yellow vertical stripes. Detsa placed a bright yellow sash around his waist, and he secured his weapon belt on top of it. The worry upon his brow lifted, if only by a bit, at having that security sitting about his hips once more.

"Do I look thoroughly like one of the wandering folk?" He held out both hands and raised a brow.

I smiled. "Mayhap we both wear the clothes well." My attire seemed more vibrant than his, and for the first time since we'd joined the caravan, the attire seemed a bit more formal, silken skirts embroidered with tiny flowers at the hem. They swished and flourished over the ballooned pants as I moved. My netted wrap still hung free of the coin that the Tsinti wore and jingled as they danced around the fires in the night. The shirt Detsa gave me for the evening was fitted and showed part of my midsection, which I hugged and fidgeted to try and hide when Thalaj set his eyes upon me.

Tended and dressed, Thalaj and I walked to the banks of the river. The reunion had been mostly in silence, but without other details to occupy the space, the air felt thicker between us. Uncertain where to begin, I asked him, "Do you know where we are?"

Simply, he said, "No." Then after space for a few thoughts, he added, "I lost track, but that may have been the point of laboring me so."

"Why wouldn't you allow me to try and help?"

"Think on it, Mairynne. What have you learned about these people?" he asked.

My brows furrowed, his lack of answer frustrating. Observe and listen, he'd instructed me before. I reached for all the things I'd experienced, sifting through them to consider if what I'd learned would answer my question. I talked, working my thoughts aloud. "I've learned to weave with the women, and in doing so, I've picked up a great deal of their language. *Romani*, they call it."

He scoffed. "That is more kindness than the men would spare."

I continued, "Lately, I've had dreams where everyone speaks the Tsinti tongue. It's weird."

"That's a valuable skill, and one that I've never been able to master. Mayhap we will complement each other. You can master the language and leave the fighting to me." He looked at me sideways, accusing.

"What? No!" I snapped. "Why?"

He didn't offer an answer, only a stern look.

I went on, "I've come a long way, and I'm proud of the progress I've made. You said yourself that you'd teach me to use the scimitynes. Outfitting me with the blades was your idea after all."

"Hai, yes. An action I've quickly come to regret." He swept a hand over his hair, now tied back into his preferred knot. "Seeing you on the ground today, curled into a ball was more than I could bear."

"Then you'll have to teach me to fight well." I nudged him with my elbow.

We shared a small laugh at the gesture, then he sighed. "I will. Reluctantly, I will. If for no other reason than to keep you from such a fate again."

Strolling, we eventually ran into Yankos and Bandeo sitting on a jut of grass near the river. Yankos had a fiddle, Baldeo a drum. Yankos picked quietly, and Baldeo answered with taps to the drum's skin. It seemed a conversation through their respective instruments.

"Join us," Baldeo called.

Yankos moved over so the four of us could sit in a circle.

The mood, even between Yankos and Thalaj, remained lighthearted. After a few minutes, Thalaj said, "I wouldn't have made you out to be a fiddle player."

Baldeo answered on behalf of his friend, "Well, his mother named him after the Tsinti who cheated the devil, and she swore she wouldn't have a son named Yankos who couldn't play the fiddle."

I leaned forward. "Who is this Tsinti? Will you tell us about your namesake?" I said, intrigued to learn more of their lore and history.

"Really." Yankos rolled his eyes. "It's not that interesting, and it's a bit of a long story."

"How long do we have before the fire?" I asked.

Baldeo clapped Yankos on the shoulder. "Long enough," he said and began the story.

Yankos played a wandering tune on the fiddle as a quiet backdrop while Baldeo told the story of *The Wanderer and the Devil.*

When Baldeo had completed the story and Yankos struck a final note on his fiddle, I shifted focus to the scout with the angry red mark under his right eye.

He smirked and chuckled. "There you have my story . . . the wanderer Yankos who bested the devil."

I smiled. "So we do. Mayhap you can play the csárdás for us now?" I lifted my netted over-skirt. "Though I have no coin to offer for your performance," I teased.

"It's time!" A young boy came running down the hill calling to the Tsinti scattered along the water's edge. "It's time! The fire's ablaze. It's time!"

◇◇◇◇◇◇◇◇◇◇◇◇◇◇◇◇◇◇◇◇◇◇◇◇◇◇◇◇◇◇◇◇◇◇

WE CLIMBED THE HILL, four abreast, toward the smoke rising into the sky. The dancing flames came into view as we neared the top.

Yankos, in a mood lighter than I'd believed he possessed, said to Thalaj, "Now that you've learned the story of my name, that we've battled, and that I've seen your strength, we must call ourselves friends."

From the other side of my first guard, I sensed reluctance in his returned silence.

At the side of the fire, Yankos stopped and held up his arm in an L-shaped gesture I'd seen amidst the other Tsinti men. Thalaj looked at me, but I offered no counsel. The decision to accept the friendship Yankos offered was his, and his alone. I waited with the hope that he would.

When Thalaj lifted his arm in a mirrored form and clasped hands with Yankos, I breathed again, and like Baldeo, Yankos, and Thalaj, a smile grew upon my face. With a few shared chuckles over the battle, it seemed that we'd entered a new understanding with the Tsinti. And I, for one, felt more complete for the connection.

Yankos said, "Now, I must find my wife. We have a little one being named tonight." He nodded to Baldeo, who joined him as they left, the stature of the two men at odds with each other. They stopped at a group gathering with more fiddles and drums, handing over their instruments. Then, before they left the musicians, Yankos swooshed his arm to them as if he were the conductor, and so the music of the night began. It was then, in that moment many moons into my time with the Tsinti and only after having spent weeks sparring with his so-called scouts, that I realized Yankos was the leader of the caravan.

Gaping, I felt Thalaj's eyes upon me, watching me watch them. When I returned his gaze, he said, "You've come to enjoy these people, my _kōgō_."

Balking at the term I'd hoped had remained in Arashi, I didn't reply immediately. Instead, I considered for several long moments while more men and women, called forth by the music, joined the gathering around the fire. "I suppose I have," I said, and it seemed true that the simple routines and customs of the wandering folk had wormed their way into a corner of my heart. "I don't know when it happened, but it seems you're right."

"Come. Come, come," Detsa interrupted. "You belong to my wagon; you'll sit with me for the ceremony." She shooed us to where she had three makeshift chairs, pails turned upside down, facing the fire, then shoved a plate of cured meats and cheeses into each of our hands.

Across the fire, a woman approached, wearing a heavy patchwork cloak. By the stance, I would have guessed her to be Zofi, but she appeared more advanced in years. A stick in one hand, she lifted her hands and face to the sky, the wide sleeves fell back around her elbows, and the hood fell away. In a clear voice louder than the music, she said, "Tsinti people, we come before the goddesses of fate this eve to welcome our newborns into this world." When she said these words, I no longer wondered. Indeed, Zofi, the witch wife I'd met on my first day in the caravan, led this ceremony. She went to four points around the fire, drawing a circle at each. "With this wand of hazelwood, I draw their life circles. Parents, come place your child within the circle."

Zofi retreated to the side as parents stepped forth. The mother and father who caught my eye were Yankos and his wife. His gaze met mine across the fire, and he grinned. The children looked anywhere from born under the current moon to maybe nine moons past. The parents spread blankets under their naked children and placed a large bowl behind the circle.

The woman returned with a stack of small earthenware plates and positioned three between each babe and the fire. Upon the plates, she placed bread, repeating an offering to each of the fates—the same muses she had named when she'd had me turn the cards. The soul, the mind, and *o drom* I recalled meant the road.

Meat and cheeses untouched, I sat forward, watching the proceedings before me. One-by-one, Zofi went to the babes and slathered them in something from the large bowls behind their circles. When she'd finished, and only one of the babes had cried, she lifted her hands again and said to the stars in the night sky, "Only one shows the sign of coming sickness. Bring his navel cord." The mother brought forth a jar with a withered snake-like thing inside. Zofi took the jar. "Father, gather coals from the fire," she commanded.

The babe's father did as the witch wife bade, placing the burning coals inside the jar with the wasted thing. The crowd around remained silent as this ritual went forward, so silent that I could hear the sizzle of liquids remaining within the cord. My stomach turned, and I thanked the Triad that I sat far enough away not to smell the burning flesh. Zofi waved it over the babe, speaking in Romani to the fates to banish the child's sickness. I understood most of the speech and felt proud of what I'd learned. When the chanting ceased, Detsa handed Thalaj a vial, then passed one to me. I looked at her with curiosity.

"For anointing the clan's new babes," she said as if I'd asked the most basic of questions.

The fathers gathered the babes and walked the circle greeting each of the Tsinti families and presenting his new son or daughter. The Tsinti each tipped a vial and dabbed something from their index finger onto the child. Yankos reached us first, and he gave a broad smile. "I would like you to meet Janci." He held a baby boy, dripping with fat in a blanket toward us.

I repeated the routine with the vial that the others had done and said, "I hadn't realized you were the leader of this clan."

Yankos shrugged. "We are a community. I speak for my people at parliament every seventh year, but we don't name ourselves leader."

"Yet the Tsinti defer to you."

"They simply show respect. Were I to do deeds unbecoming of a leader, they would choose another. There are no laws binding me to the position. There is no lineage. Had Janci here cried, Zofi would have burned his navel cord above his head also. We exempt no one from our traditions and hold no one above the others. We are one as a people. Wanderers. That is all. Now, you'll excuse me." Yankos smiled and left us then, speaking with other families as he traveled around the circle.

Three more proud fathers introduced their babes to us for anointment, and we graciously smeared droplets of oil upon the brows of Gashparis, Beltrana, and Mizo.

After the ceremony, the music started again and the parents cleaned the pallets where their babes had been offered. As they gathered their things, Zofi came to us with a smoking pipe in hand, still wearing her patchwork coat and a ban of gold atop her head. She sat beside me on Detsa's downturned bucket and nodded toward Yankos. "He makes me proud. He may be rough, but he is strong and just. A good Tsinti leader." She took a puff from the pipe and offered it first to Thalaj.

He politely declined, so Zofi passed the pipe to me. I took a long drag and let it pass my throat too soon, suffering a fit of coughing as the price. My eyes watered, my throat itched and burned with fire. She laughed, retrieved the pipe, and grasped my hand. I recovered as we sat with music in the air, watching the flames and the people dance, and made no conversation. At length, things began to blur and the whirling people seemed to spin around me. They wore the faces of everyone I'd known in my life—Karynne and Yasmynne, my mother and father, the Triad priests, Jessamyne, Nadia, Corwyn, Imrythel, Tsanseri and Alto-Trea, Viordyn turned Cirro-Vior, and many, many more. I blinked hard to try to clear my vision, but soon, the fire and people and Zofi herself were all gone. I stood alone atop the highest tower in Stormskeep. *What devilry is this?* I wondered. A nightmare, certainly, but I felt awake. Lightning gathered in the sky, and when I held out my hands, it struck. After the flash had lit the sky, I spread silvery leather wings from my own back and thunder crashed, shaking the ground and castle beneath me. I closed my eyes, startled at the power, and when I reopened them, I sat on the bucket by the fire between Thalaj and Zofi.

Zofi squeezed my hand just as I started to speak, halting my words.

"Shhh," she said. "The smoke dream is a message for you alone. The message I bring to you tonight is one of parting."

She handed me a wooden box that I hadn't seen in her hand when she'd approached. Without more ado, she stood and left.

◇◇◇◇◇◇◇◇◇◇◇◇◇◇◇◇◇◇◇◇◇◇◇◇◇◇◇◇◇◇◇◇◇◇◇

AFTER THE FESTIVITIES HAD calmed, I crept into the wagon to sleep for the night. Thalaj remained outside, and I couldn't be certain if he slept there or sat awake beside the dying fire under Selene's watch. But when I emerged from the canvas-covered cart, he was waiting and tending our packs before the journey.

Detsa emerged from the wagon behind me and bade us farewell, wrapping me in a quick hug and turning away without eye contact. She muttered, "Safe and long travels, young one." She grasped onto Thalaj's forearm and added, "Care for her well." Then, she gathered some spun yarn and away she waddled.

Being back in my travel clothes felt bland. The simple brown pants, cream-colored tunic, and browned leather belt and boots were comfortable and would enable us to blend in with other travelers in villages along our way, but I would miss the liveliness of the Tsinti attire. Thalaj helped me into my pack and asked, "Are you ready?"

I nodded. "It seems strange to me that after all this time and after they went to such lengths to keep us apart, they are simply sending us away. Easily and with no restrictions I can see."

We walked through the gathered wagons and around the fire that'd reduced to smoldering ash overnight, meeting Yankos, Baldeo, and Jorani at the edge of the caravan. They slowly walked with us toward the river for a time, until gruff Baldeo broke the silence.

"I'll miss dancing with you, *little one.*" His words mimicked Yankos's when we'd sparred, but in them, there was a fondness I wouldn't have expected.

I rested my hand upon his arm, over the downy red hairs and freckles, and stared into his moss-like green eyes for long moments. Whether I'd meet this man again, I had no way to know. And while he'd seemed formidable in the southern reaches of the Yubar Forest, I sensed the loyalty within his soul for the people he claimed as his own. Feeling solidarity with that impression, I could find no words of farewell. So I squeezed his arm with affection, smiled, and lowered my gaze.

When he had gone, I asked the two remaining, "Won't you need to drop the tsym for us to leave?"

Yankos said, "No. Simply walk far enough away, and when you turn back, you'll not see the caravan anymore."

Jorani grasped my shoulders. "I would set out with you on this journey, but Zofi tells me your road will take you across the watery plains. That's no place for a Tsinti. Here." She placed a stoppered vial in my hand.

I looked at her curiously.

She pointed to my head, where my hair remained wrapped in the bans. "Before you meet others, you'll want to wash the fats from your hair and leave it loose. We only wear the bans within the caravan. *Kai zaſo drom*, Mairynne." She hugged me fiercely and left us there alone with Yankos.

The three of us made it to the Betsu River's banks before Yankos stopped and prepared to take his leave of us. "Do you have everything?"

"I do." As I said the words, I felt the hard metal cuff embrace my upper arm, sitting just above a bulging muscle that hadn't been so prominent before, and the cold and hot stones along with the totem against my breast. Those were the important things.

"Very well." He grasped my wrist, turning my palm upward. He laid his other hand across mine, transferring something unseen, and folded my fingers. "If you should come back to us, you will need this. You witnessed the movements when I released the tsym before. Do that, and speak the words, '*kai zaſo drom.*' "

"Here goes the road," I translated with a small smile—both the words of farewell and the words to release the tsym. I looked at the totem in my palm with new eyes, a long green and black stone with a face carved at one end. When I returned my gaze to Yankos's, tears blurred my vision. "But how will I know where to find you?"

"You've lived among us for long enough that you'll hear a fiddle on the wind. Otherwise, simply call for us once you're upon the plains." He squeezed my hand and released me. To Thalaj, he raised his arm into the L-shape and waited for my guard's acceptance. When Thalaj locked hands with the Tsinti leader, Yankos gave him the words of parting, adding at the end, "Train her well. Don't be overkind. And, after many a roaming year, mayhap we shall meet again."

Thalaj and I followed the river Betsu as Zofi had instructed toward Kōkai, the City by the Sea. Her words echoed back to me on that walk: "Through a small forest, but always to the left, and your path will be true." When Otarr was high, we reached a copse of trees and stopped to eat. I looked back, but instead of a caravan of covered wagons atop a hill, all my eyes would see was an empty field. I reached for the stones around my neck, comforted to have them back. More of Zofi's advice from the night before sang again in my mind:

> *You chose rightly when you took leave of your people. Your mother and father walk with you now. Times will come when you'll choose again and again, but one day, you will be ready for that which you most fear. For now, your heart speaks the truth; your father still lives. Though it is uncertain how long he can remain in stasis. You'll travel over the Syrensea to the island nation of Ise, and inland still until you find people called the Abatwa. Your journey will be long and winding. Face this day's challenges today and leave the rest for the morrow.*

As I had slowly come to realize that Yankos was the leader of the Tsinti clan, the clarity of Zofi's role struck me hard there by the fire. "You are the magic woman I needed, yet I met you upon my first day," I'd said, a flat statement rather than a question once she'd spoken her words of wisdom. And now, there by the Betsu, Thalaj and I had begun the journey anew, leaving behind another people who'd found a place in my heart and soul.

Still chewing the last bite of salted meat, Thalaj stood and went to the brook to fill our skeins. He turned, and as he handed me mine, he asked, "Are we ready?" My first guard had renewed purpose now that we had direction, and he walked faithfully at my side, just as Zofi said before.

There beside the Betsu, I thanked the Triad for my time with the Tsinti and for Thalaj. I then turned to him, leaving the caravan behind me with parting sadness but a heart filled with wonder over what was to come. I nodded and said, "Here goes *our* road."

FIFTEEN

Safaia - The Trader's Town

THE BETSU RIVER OUR GUIDE, we traveled south and west at her side. Thalaj caught fish in the small pools and shaved meat from their bones, and I gathered some of the rigid stalks that grew along the riverbed and shaved them clean so that we might use them to spit the meat over a small fire. Seasoned with herbs from a pouch Detsa sent along, it made for fine yet tiresome meals. For the first day, we walked almost ceaselessly; but in the days that followed, we traveled in the mornings, rested during the hot part of the day, and Thalaj worked to teach me the dance with the scimitynes in the evenings. We met no others until we came to a spot where the river cut into a ravine, the rocks on either side rising a dozen feet from where the water flowed. Here, our path also forked. We took the upper trail, climbing over shallow roots toward a small trading village that overlooked the gorge.

"Safaia," Thalaj said as we approached.

"You've been here before?"

"I've passed through. The innkeeper is as sour as an old sow, but the rooms are always clean and comfortable. Maybe we can catch a boat downriver if anyone's coming this far inland for trade. It'd save us a fortnight in walking." He appraised me as he said this, then added with a smirk, "And ease you into living on a boat before we hit the open seas." I'd discussed Zofi's foretelling with Thalaj, and he took several opportunities to tease my anxiety after the matter. I nudged him with a shoulder then, and we both laughed.

Safaia was little more than a cluster of several common buildings, an open area with makeshift tables to all sides, and a large stable. The buildings encircled a pedestal holding an unnaturally blue-black stone the size of a person's head. Presumably the village's namesake, the surface gleamed and appeared smoother than river rock worn down over time. We stopped under the sign reading "Safaia Inn" in burned and uneven script. Thalaj went inside first. As the door opened, it triggered a jingle and another when it closed at our backs.

The room had a couple of windows to let in the daylight and all the accoutrements to welcome the inn's guests—a small desk and chair, a closed ledger on the desktop, an ink bottle and quill beside the ledger, and a door behind the desk. Otherwise, the space was free of either decoration or clutter. The opposing door swung open, no bell to announce the woman who entered—large in both breadth and height, smoking a cob pipe. Considering the effects of Zofi's pipe, I wondered at once about the contents, but this smoke had a sweeter odor than what we'd smoked by the Tsinti fire.

When she looked up, she squinted, pulled her pipe from between yellowed teeth, and said, "Ah, Thalaj Northerngale." She held out a broad hand with knobby knuckles.

Accepting the shake, he asked, "How are you, Sal?"

"Ah, ye know. Taking care of this town keeps me young." She groaned—not very young-like—and sat behind the desk. "Who's ye lady?"

"Mairy," he introduced me by the same shortened version he'd used with the Tsinti scouts. Though, as it had turned out, the Tsinti witch woman had known me from the first moment and likely had been responsible for sending Yankos and his three scouts into the Yubar to locate us.

I shot Thalaj a sideways glance, but only long enough to see him give a single nod and look that suggested I go along. I offered my hand, imitating the way the innkeeper, Sal, had. "Mairy Summergale," I said. If I needed an alternate name, I decided that a last name would complete the image.

Sal stood halfway and shook my hand, then plopped back into her chair with a sigh. "I'm afraid ye've come too late. There've been so many travelers on the road lately that my rooms are all taken hours before supper's bell."

My shoulders sank, but the matter appeared to bother Thalaj very little. "Are there any boats coming up the Betsu in the next day or two?" he asked.

"Not in two, but three," she answered. "I've got a load of supplies being delivered. Expect him just after midday."

As it turned out, Sal also managed passenger bookings for the cargo barges departing Safaia upon the Betsu toward the City by the Sea. We were the first in line for that, so she flipped to the back and scrawled our names in the ledger, using the same rough script as above the inn's door. "For both, the cap'n'll charge ye a copper mon. For tonight, head over to the tavern, grab a bite to eat, and ask around there to see if anyone has a bed nearby for ye to rest. If not, Mac's letting folk sleep in the bar for an iron mon each, if ye're desperate for shelter. Come back tomorrow, and I'll have a room for ye."

In the tavern, Mac handed us a couple mugs of ale and plates of stew. We took an empty table in the back corner, Thalaj sitting in the chair with the best view of all the patrons and the door. I pulled out the small wooden box that Zofi had returned, opened it, and placed a droplet of the stew next to the little replica of myself.

Thalaj chuckled. "It's doubtful a barkeep would poison his patrons, but it's nice to have those back. Who knows where we'll find ourselves in another month's time?" Seeing that my little taster had no problems with the stew, he lifted the wooden spoon and slurped. "It's good. Try it," he said, the words garbled from sucking air. He fanned his mouth to ease the heat, swallowed, and shoved in a second bite.

I waited for mine to cool, then tasted tentatively. The spiced, meaty stew felt wonderful on the tongue after the fish and water vegetables that had sustained us for the last few days, but it didn't wash away the desires I harbored for a bed and bath. Thalaj hurried through his meal and went around the room to ask several of the patrons if they lived nearby or had a room we could let for the night.

My hopes fell again as he returned to our table, shaking his head.

"Every extra room for an hour's walk is full." Thalaj waved a hand at the table. "So, we sleep here, or we can go back to the river and make camp."

With a wistful sigh, I said, "Had you asked me two seasons prior, it never would have crossed my mind to long for sleep in a covered wagon under the cover of a Tsinti tsym. It'd be nice not to have to worry about a wild animal wandering into our camp or"—I looked around the room at the worn and ratty crowd—"having to deal with whatever night noises will arise from a group like this. Neither of us sleeps well when we have to stand watch against unannounced intruders." A tang of guilt soured the back of my throat over having slept so hard the night Yankos's party arrived.

I hadn't intended my words to seem an accusation, but Thalaj's cheeks flushed with color and he apologized, his fingers tightening on the spoon. "I know I failed you that night in the Yubar. I have vowed my protection to you, but it seems I've already failed you twice. Mayhap I was wrong to have left without a larger party."

Resting a hand over his, I added softly, "The time with the Tsinti turned out fine for me. You're the one who suffered."

He pulled away, his stoic nature settling back into place. "I'd hoped we could both get a full night's rest without a watch too." He shook his head. "Let's go back to the river. Maybe if we trek into the ravine, we'll find a little shelter against the rocks before it's fully dark out."

In the night's sky, the moon goddess, Selene, had waned to a sliver and shed little light. Twilight had already come and gone by the time we paid for our meals and left the tavern.

As we crept back down the hill and into the thin forest, I stopped with a sharp inhale when I heard a twig snap behind me and off to the side. Thalaj spun, freeing one of his scimitynes and scanning the area. I searched too, but nothing around us moved. Several long beats passed before Thalaj satisfied himself that it must have been a small rodent more scared of us than we of him. We moved on. Leaves rustled under foot as we crept down the trail, and the night's song of insects, river creatures, and the lower tones of the nocturnal birds echoed through the trees. It'd been our serenade for several nights, so naught apart from the ordinary that night. We wound down a footpath to the spot where the Betsu cut between rock faces and followed the other fork along the shoreline into the crevice.

At about a hundred paces, Thalaj held up his hand in a fist. "A cave."

In three steps, I caught up to him and peered inside—complete darkness beyond the entrance. Thalaj placed a finger over his mouth in a quieting gesture, drew one of his blades, then opened his hand with the palm up. An orb of soft light formed and cast a bluish glow inside the cave, revealing naught but rock and a small pool to one side. He led and I followed, placing my feet with care on the slippery stone floor.

"It may fill when the river overflows her banks, but I believe we'll be safe here for the night," Thalaj said as he turned back toward me and the cave's entrance, but then . . . his almond-shaped eyes stretched wide just before a clatter echoed within the cramped space.

I jumped.

Slipped.

Thalaj steadied me with a hand at the elbow.

The clamor reminded me of the heavy gates around Stormskeep—the ones we'd opened during my mother's funeral rite of the Giving of the Sands. But the sound behind me had been one of gates closing.

My heart pounding within my chest and crawling toward my throat, I didn't turn immediately; instead I clung to Thalaj and uttered a prayer of safety to the Triad. My guard closed his eyes and a muscle ticked in his jaw as he, too, apparently realized we'd walked into a trap. I glanced back. Indeed, and seeming impossible, a heavy metal door blocked our exit. When I spun back to Thalaj, my hand over my mouth, the cave extended into darkness well beyond the wall I'd perceived before. Two smaller people, standing no taller than Thalaj's chest height and wearing hats crafted from fox hides, pointed spears at my first guard.

The Small Folk.

I hugged myself around the waist as my stomach twisted. Sucking in breath and holding, I attempted to trap my sorcery inside. What if they'd come to feed upon our magic? *No, Mairynne,* I tried to calm my thoughts. Thalaj had discredited those tales after he'd gone into the Evernight and returned with his intact.

"Easy there," one said, and from the pitch, it was a woman. Or maybe a girl?

"Drop the blade," the other said in a gruffer voice, though still several notes higher than seemed possible.

Thalaj turned slowly, lowering the scimityne he'd drawn to the floor as he moved. The little people danced on the balls of their small booted feet as if they were ready to strike, the girl giggling maniacally. From deeper within the cave, a heavy foot fell clumsily into a puddle with a *thunk, splash.*

"What have we here?" a voice boomed just before an orb, similar to the one Thalaj held, went aglow.

Thalaj squinted, jutting his head a little forward. "Hoaris?" he asked, his recognition and delight obvious.

"Thalaj?! It's about time you made it this way." A few more splashes. The man dressed in furs came weaving and bounding into the sphere of our light, extinguishing his own, and seized Thalaj into his arms.

"Aawww, Hoaris," Thalaj said, disgust dripping from his voice, and pushed away from the man. "When was the last time you bathed? You smell like a drunken dead animal."

The little ones swung their spears, looking between the two men with as much confusion as I felt.

"Come on in, my man," bellowed Hoaris. "Bring your lady. Misha, Kyr, put away your tiny sticks."

Hoaris, with an arm around Thalaj, pulled him deeper into the cave. The two little ones cackled between each other. They seemed to speak in the common tongue, but their words were too fast for me to comprehend. At length, the female one—I wasn't certain if it was Misha or Kyr—said, "Get on," and pointed the small spear after the two men.

I hesitated, but the other said, "You heard her. The tips are poisoned, and we won't hesitate to use them."

"Misha," Hoaris boomed, then slurred his words together, "bring-'er-in, an'-be-nice."

Misha tucked his chin and mumbled. I furrowed my brows—so odd, brooding even, for a boy-sized man. I failed to understand Misha's words, but they clearly showed his frustration. Soon, he tilted his head toward the corridor with a resigned sigh and started walking.

Kyr, at my side, shooed me onward. "Move along, lovely. Move along."

◇◇◇◇◇◇◇◇◇◇◇◇◇◇◇◇◇◇◇◇◇◇◇◇◇◇◇◇

AS WE BURROWED DEEPER within the cave under Safaia, I had to stretch and speed my step so I wouldn't fall too far behind the longer-legged men. The Small Folk took three steps to my one but had no problem keeping pace, each planting their spears like a walking stick as they moved. They were a curious thing, sized like a youngling but having already reached adulthood. I kept cutting curious glances toward Misha, then Kyr. For all the time my mother had spent with the Small Folk in her attempts to unite the people, I had never had the occasion to meet any one of them. They struck me as peculiar and inexplicably quick in every action. On we walked and the darkness slowly ebbed. A soft amber glow shone on the walls, hinting at more ahead.

Eventually, we reached a wider area, and the light's source became clear. On the outer walls, stones lit from within illuminated a dining area. Aside from the table with four stools, a long counter stretched along a rough stone wall adjacent to a small hearth. Coals glowed beneath a dark iron crock. The smell of roasting meat also enveloped my senses as we entered, but my stomach protested the thought of eating after the hearty stew we'd had at the tavern. Misha went to the hearth, propping his spear against the stone wall, and checked the meat spit over the heat, then stirred the contents of the pot.

Thalaj and Hoaris chatted like old friends, but I was too rapt with the activities of the Small Folk and didn't follow the conversation. Kyr, at some point, stowed her spear and went to the counter and chopped leafy herbs. She made a long chatter, and within it, I thought I made out the words, *"Near done?"* Misha chattered back, then they both moved in a hurried blur.

I blinked repeatedly, willing my vision to keep up. Before I could calculate the rest of their movements, the cooked animal was on a platter in the center of the table with five full bowls awaiting our attention.

Tradition in Nantai held that refusal of offered food portrayed insolence, so I felt grateful when Thalaj spoke up on our behalf.

"You'll forgive us. We had stew at the tavern, and after days of living on light fish and grasses, it's not a good idea to eat more right now," he said.

"Ah, not to worry," Hoaris bellowed and reached across the table, grabbing Thalaj's bowl and dumping it into his own. "I'm half-starved, though," he added in contrast to the size he carried. Mayhap being that large simply required more in the way of sustenance than I could fathom.

The stools were large enough for people our size, but there were only four. Being half my size, Misha and Kyr shared one. I took the last stool and sat uncertainly with the group. Hoaris looked fondly at my bowl until I pushed it toward him. Happily, he scooped it up as well. The confusion on my face and the many questions behind it fighting for my attention must have been quite obvious, because Thalaj gave me a small, reassuring smile and nod that all would be well.

Through a mouthful of the hare's meat, Hoaris said, "You can be at ease here." Then he pulled another bite from the leg and chewed with open mouth.

Thalaj laughed. "I've known Hoaris for as long as I can remember."

"Longer than that, pup," Hoaris barked as he finished off his portion of meat and wiped his hands on his pant legs. He seemed a bit loose with too much ale. The combination left little wonder as to the cause of his smell.

"So, where ya headed?" Hoaris asked, jutting his chin in my direction, a trail of animal fat dripping into his beard.

I bit my lip, wondering what he knew of me.

"It's all right, Mairynne," my guard said. "Hoaris is the one who directed us to find the Tsinti. He knows what we're about." Then Thalaj backhanded his friend and rolled his eyes. "Clean the rabbit from your chin and quit acting like an old sot."

The admonishment seemed more jovial than I often witnessed from my first guard, and I wondered how well acquainted the two had been before. I stifled a small, amused smile as Misha and Kyr chattered, stealing Hoaris's half-witted attention. He stared at them with one eye squinted, and when their conversation died, he turned back to me.

"Evangale," he started, suddenly sober and leaning both elbows onto the table toward me. "We've been waiting for you here under Safaia. Misha says you have the look of your mother, that he remembers Noralynne coming to his home when he was a youngling. He says she showed great kindness to his people." Hoaris chewed loudly, washed down another bite, and slurred, "They, like I, only wanna help."

It struck me that he didn't call me by title, either my ascended title or simply lady. My thoughts went back to Stormskeep briefly, and I wondered if Nadia had ascended to the throne in my stead. Had the gnobles of each caste spread word of her ascension throughout Nantai? Maybe I was no longer kōgō, which in truth offered more relief than concern. But I wondered . . . did that leave me titleless? If so, I didn't know whether to mourn or sing. I wrung my hands in my lap, still unsure how much of my plight to share in present company.

Each person watched me intently.

At length, I decided to offer as little as I could and remain honest. "We're headed to Kōkai. Thalaj bought us passage on a riverboat three days from now." As Thalaj seemed to trust this man, and I trusted my guard, I concluded that it would be all right to share this simple bit. Yet, for some reason, my stomach still twisted as the words passed my lips. I clutched my hands over it to hide the rumble.

"Are you sure you aren't hungry?" Hoaris said, looking down at the awful sound's source and back to my eyes.

"Quite the opposite," I answered, feeling flushed and queasy as if I were about to revisit the stewed supper I'd eaten before. Taking a deep breath, my stomach settled a bit and I shifted the focus. "Are you a Cloud Courtier?" I asked Hoaris.

He barked a laugh. "Hardly. Do I look so pretty to your eyes?" He wagged his brows suggestively.

I drew mine together, tilting my head. "But the illusion at the entrance . . ."

"Thanks to Misha and Kyr. They bewitched the stones. Same with the glowing rocks." Hoaris waved to the amber all around the room.

My head spun as I looked around, and I began heating from the inside. I swiped at my forehead and tried to refocus.

Hoaris continued, "Not sure if you've heard, but there's something amiss at Stormskeep."

"What?" I asked and inhaled slowly, trying again to calm my churning gut, and blew the air slowly through my mouth.

The burly man took another long gulp of ale, wiped the froth from his beard, and said, "They've closed it up tight. No word about what's happening inside, but there was a great storm over it a moon back."

Suddenly, the heat inside me exploded, sweat broke out all over, and I felt a chill run through my body at the same time. I wanted to know more of what had happened at my home, but my stomach had an entirely different desire. "Is there . . ." I started but sealed my lips, unable to finish. A metallic tang in the back of my mouth started, then flooded. Giving a small headshake and clasping a hand over my mouth, I stood, looking for somewhere away from the kitchen, swayed, and stumbled toward the cave where we'd entered. Before I made it from the room, I fell to my hands and knees and emptied my dinner onto the floor.

My vision blinked in and out, and I heaved again, the rich stew burning as it exploded from my throat until the purging halted long enough for me to gain breath. Vaguely, I heard the Small Folk chattering as I gagged a third time, and when nothing more would come, I lost myself to blackness.

Sixteen

A Mother's Battle

PRATTLE. SOMEWHERE IN THE DARKNESS, and seeming to come near then fade away again, high-pitched prattle extracted me from sickly sleep. My spine, knees, hips, everything ached, though my back remained chilled. A shiver crept through my body, becoming a full shudder. Amber light glowed against rock walls and ceiling as I peeled open dry eyes and groaned. The weight of a blanket held me down, but the bed beneath was curiously frigid.

When I glimpsed movement and the chattering neared again, I pulled myself upright. The natter hailed from Kyr and Misha who bustled around the cave and tended to traveling packs against the wall. I ran a hand over the bed where I'd slept, the smooth, cool rock at odds with the sticky and warm air within the cavern. When Kyr sighted me upright, she scurried over.

"How do you feel, lovely?" she said, placing a hand on my arm and clearly slowing her speech for my benefit.

Her small fingers tingled against my skin, but she nodded. Kyr, concern still shining in her eyes, hopped onto the bed at my side and reached for my cheek. I pulled back but then relaxed, concluding I had nothing to fear from her touch if she'd done naught but tend to me while I slept. Her smile reinforced that she only meant well.

Somewhere in my addled mind, I imagined I should respond, but I couldn't yet put together the words. I pushed back the blanket, examining the simple shift I wore.

"You gave us quite the alarm," Kyr said, hopping down. "How's your pot?"

I stared blankly at the small woman, only understanding what she meant after her eyes shifted suggestively down toward my stomach then back as she stood there with hands on her hips.

"Oh, yeah . . ." I ran a hand through my hair, recalling the purging feeling in the cavern kitchen. Looking around then for the room where I'd toppled and retched, I absently added, "I think it's settled. Where are we?"

"We're just in the back cave. The main area is through there." She pointed and moved over to add some more items to the packs.

Misha returned, saying something to Kyr but stopped when he saw me sitting upright. "Good, you're awake," he said at what I judged a normal pace of speaking and passed a small package to Kyr.

"Where is Thalaj?" I asked.

"Above. In Safaia," said Misha. "With Hoaris."

Hoaris. The conversation just before I'd lost control of my stomach came back to me. He'd mentioned something about Stormskeep, that there'd been a great storm, and that they'd sealed the gates. Furrowing my brow, I tried to sort out the cloudy memories, but I couldn't recall if there was more to the tale. Likewise, I wondered about the sickness. Had Thalaj gotten sick as well? It couldn't have been a poison as the tiny version of myself accepted the stew without reaction.

Kyr fished into a pack—mine, I judged by the scimityne weapon belt at its side. "There," she said, satisfied, and brought clothes over to my bed. "They went to talk to Sal about passage on that riverboat."

Absently, I said, "But we have already secured our passage."

I received no answer. Kyr spread my pants out flat on the stone and began folding the garment with meticulous care, and Misha disappeared through the door. Thoughts piling in my mind, I absently ran my hands over the cool bed again. Another curiosity, I thought, looking at the smooth stone.

Seeing me puzzling over that and much, much more, Kyr said, "We spelled the stone to help break your heat. Seems like it worked. The red in your cheeks has faded." She shot me that reassuring smile once again as she finished folding my tunic and placed it in a neat little square on top of the rough-spun breeches. She stood straight with her hands on her hips, then pointed. "Just around that corner there, there's a hot spring pool. Some soap and sponges on the ledge. Get cleaned up."

My eyes popped wide. A spring-fed pool? A warm bath? Not a bucket and sponge beside Detsa's wagon or a cold dip in the Betsu River, but a full pool with warm water in which I could soak away the aches of travel and the stench of vomit? I wanted to hug the small woman, but I couldn't push past my stunned silence.

She grasped my hand to urge me from the bed. I accepted willingly, relishing such tenderness in her touch. It reminded me of when I'd been a youngling and the way Mother led me patiently toward Selene's sanctuary when I wanted naught more than to kick a ball around with the other younglings in Arashi's streets. I never wanted to go, but now, the memory of how my small hand felt in my mother's offered comfort. Strange how Kyr's little hand comforted me now in the same way.

"Once you're ready, lovely, we'll head up to meet the others in Safaia. We need a few supplies for the road."

"What?" I asked, slowly coming out of the memories and meeting a new realization. The men had gone above to secure passage for Hoaris and the Small Folk. They intended to join us on the journey to find my father. I shook my head. "No. This is something I must do. I can't ask you to come with us or put your lives in danger."

"So says the sick," she squeaked accusingly and raised a brow.

Beneath the thicket of sable-colored hair, Kyr's eyes were wide set, her most prominent feature. Her small challenging expression made her nose and mouth seem more pointed and smaller, but this glimpse darted quickly away as she busied herself again. She retrieved my clothes and placed them in my waiting arms, then made a shooing motion toward the bath. I watched her shuffle across the cavern to the door where she stopped and looked back.

"You speak nonsense, lovely. The plans were all worked out while you slept, so never you worry." She touched her tiny nose with a finger, pointed at me, and left.

Still slow to react, I sucked in air to further object, but she had gone. My aching joints protested with every step, but I could feel the steam from the room beyond. The warm waters called. Blessedly, once I'd settled into the pool, the heat soothed the lingering twinge of pain from travel and the ache of sickness.

When I was cleaned and back in my travel clothes, I moved more freely. The three of us left the cave to hike back to the small trading town. As we climbed the path, I said to both the Small Folk, "I don't understand why you're intent on leaving your home and traveling with us."

"Well," Misha answered, placing his walking stick and stepping carefully over a large stone in the path, "It's not truly our home, just where we've been staying for the time. We owe Hoaris a great deal, so we go where he does."

I pushed a branch out of the way. "But do you know what we're about? For whom we search?"

Misha shrugged.

"It's really not important to us," said Kyr. "We left home with plans to travel. We tried to join the Tsinti and become wanderers in the true form, but even those who live apart wouldn't take in Small Folk."

My heart ached over that, and I speculated how Misha would endure tending the oxen within a Tsinti caravan to prove his strength. I also wondered if this implied shunning had been an issue my mother had sensed as keenly within these folk. Had the desolation laced within those few words in some small way driven her work?

"Where is your home?" I asked at length, failing to understand why they'd want to live apart as the Tsinti did. "And why don't you wish to live with your own people?"

Misha kicked away a small branch, further clearing our path. "Our people have strict traditions, by which we were unable to abide." His words tossed quickly like throwing stars, he scurried ahead, clearly avoiding the impending dive into his history.

Kyr lingered with me. Looking after him and softening her voice, she said, "We were both born in Brennmor. Sons are rare within our people. Couples who produce one can usually produce more, and they automatically become leaders within our people."

I nodded toward Misha, "So he is of royal blood?" These words I said with a kinship that seemed haunting. If as a leader he left his family, we had some shared experience.

"You could say that," she said, a knowing and rueful smile pulling at her mouth. "But he didn't flee any royal duties. His problem was with the ordering. The first son is promised to the protectors until the time he assumes his father's position. The second is pledged to cultivating the fields and raising the animals. The third is sworn to the women's houses as soon as he gains his sexual majority to breed. The first and second sons may take a wife at will, but the third may only take a wife after he has fulfilled his commitment. So at fourteen, Misha would have been committed to work as nothing more than a stud for three decades or until he produced a son with one of the women."

Misha returned from scouting ahead and added, "Or if I *had* put a son in a woman's belly, I would have been forced to take her as my wife. Our people would have expected us to *work* to produce more. I'd have been no more than a stud." Bitterness cut through his every word.

I gasped, appalled. "That's—"

"Slavery? Rape?" With a heavy shake of his head, Misha held his walking stick forward, closing his eyes as if he didn't want to hear how horrible I thought the practice. "I don't need sympathy," he snapped, clearly warding off sentiments he'd heard before. "It doesn't matter. When I told Papa that I wouldn't, he said it brought shame on his family. He named me *wanderer*. To the Small Folk, that is anathema. I was no longer his son and was unwelcome in his home. That's been many years, and I am happy to *wander* now with my love here." He opened his arm. "If we have children, it will be of our own choosing."

Kyr went to his side and wrapped herself about him, offering him the support of her touch. As they exchanged a warm look, I felt as if I'd intruded and thought of Thalaj. *He'll be there for you time and time again,* Zofi had said, yet my people considered him ill-worthy of my attention as he'd been born of mixed caste. I cleared my throat and looked away.

Misha, shifting his attention from Kyr, said, "Anyway, the market is in full swing. We should go. Hoaris is surely waiting at Sal's. The man's insufferable around her."

As we walked up the final measure of the path, I began to wonder how the traders in Safaia would accept the small ones, especially if the Tsinti hadn't even welcomed them, so I asked.

Kyr responded, "In small trading villages like this, there's an unwritten tradition. Anyone with goods to bring to market or mon to spend is welcome. There's mixed folk—the casted and the casteless alike. So we're not noticed as much."

"But we didn't bring goods for trade," I said.

"Mon works just as well, and you never know who has that," said Misha with a smirk and jingling a bag at his belt.

We wandered our way through the loose crowd, people milling about a handful of tables with various wares, toward the Safaia Inn. Inside, Hoaris leaned on Sal's desk. Sparks leapt between the two as she smiled sweetly and he responded by moving even closer. Again, I felt like I was intruding on a moment until I felt a hand on my shoulder. Turning, I met Thalaj's worried gaze and gave him a smile. "I'm well. Better," I said.

He nodded, his lips tight.

Misha went over to Hoaris and Sal, distracting the burly man from his flirtations by pushing at his shoulder with the staff. "Do we have a deal?"

"Oh." He stood, straightening his tunic. "Ah, yeah. So, *Mairy*"—clearly, my guard had instructed him well—"there're only two rooms on the barge heading south. You all right bunking up with Thalaj? The littles can sleep in mine."

I flitted a nervous glance toward my first guard, more concerned how he felt about the proposition than any worry I held. But he only shrugged, so I nodded our agreement.

"Right, then, we're all set for tomorrow," Hoaris barked.

"Tomorrow?" I asked.

With a nod, Hoaris said, "Yea—"

"SHRIEEEEEEK," a spine-tingling sound went up outside the inn. Familiar now. Roars, screams, and pattering feet as the crowd scampered about.

Thalaj's hands went to his scimityne hilts, but he didn't free the blades. The inn doors flew open and people flowed inside, panic written on their faces. I grabbed one woman's arm, asking, "What is it?"

"A . . . a . . . d-drr-dragon," she stammered and scrambled further into the room.

Thalaj and I shared a knowing look, one that acknowledged all the implications. This sound was the one we'd heard before at the Falls, while we were at the High Cloud Court, and as we left Stormskeep. A dragon—one of the elder race, Ryū—the creature I'd learned about in my father's stories read from Stormskeep's annals. A dragon, the same beast that Tennō Makenyn had torn from himself, souls ripped apart, brutally leaving the first emperor of our people handicapped and scarred. But if one still lived in Nantai, had it formed another Ryū bond? And if so, who claimed companionship?

"Stay here," Thalaj commanded as he moved through the crowd toward the door.

Silence had fallen outside, and I wanted to know what was happening, see for myself the creature that'd made such a hair-raising noise. My heel twitched, bouncing my leg and through my body with nervous energy, and I disobeyed. Behind my guard, I struggled to get a view of this being we thought banished from Nantai.

Thalaj gained the door and pushed outside. I followed. A noise, *thwap-thwap-thwap,* echoed. Dust swirled. My guard freed his weapons and stood ready to pounce.

Arriving at his side, I gazed up. With wings spread wide, the long-bodied beast blocked out Otarr's light and descended upon Safaia. When it came close to the ground, it seemed only slightly larger than the largest of the people scattering about, and the midnight-blue scales gleamed where they caught the rays of the sun. The wind gusting from the flaps lifted my hair. I held my breath, pressing my lips tight, as two clawed feet alighted on the ground next to the large blue stone—the town's namesake at the market center.

◇◇◇◇◇◇◇◇◇◇◇◇◇◇◇◇◇◇◇◇◇◇◇◇◇◇◇◇◇◇◇◇

FOR A SELECT FEW, curiosity outweighed the terror of seeing a roaring mythical creature descending upon the town. Some held swords or spears in defensive positions against the perceived threat. Some tried to act with bravery and close in. Others backed away slowly, seemingly too enraptured to look elsewhere, or perhaps they worried someone would attack from behind.

But the dragon made no immediate moves to attack.

Sal, a woman who I'd assumed feared very little, spoke with terror vibrating in her voice from the inn's deck behind me, "It's after the stone. Stop him."

The dragon roared, dual rows of sharp teeth and fangs bared in our direction. Heated breath near scalded my face.

Sal gasped, then weaker, she said, "That stone's supposed to protect the town, not attract a danger we thought long dead."

Also behind where Thalaj and I stood, heavy foot falls approached—a prelude to Hoaris's gruff voice. "Sal, go back inside. Try to calm the people." The sound of a sword sang free of its scabbard, and Hoaris stepped heavily to my side opposite Thalaj.

Scimitynes hung in scabbards at my side, but instead of reaching for the blades, I spread my arms wide, swallowed, and called upon the storm. Winds began to collect, adding to the gusts the dragon's wings stirred. The gale I controlled encircled us, the blue dragon, and the stone. All I would need to do is send in more energy and tighten the circle, and a cyclone would rip the creature into the sky. Though there was the risk I'd sweep people upward along with the creature. If I could separate them, I could call the lightning to remove the danger from this town permanently. Thunder rumbled low in the sky as clouds billowed overhead, and an electric charge pulsated in the air as I charged the atmosphere with my sorcery, preparing for the lightning. In my periphery, even the brave people around began to back away from the gathering storm, swiping the hair from their eyes.

I'd pulled the wind across the Betsu and sent moisture upward into the clouds. As the squall built above, raindrops pelted heavily onto the dusty ground. With more energy, I could rain hail down upon the beast, but I held it back for the moment . . . for reasons I didn't understand. I felt a pang in my stomach as it growled, and my body felt weak. Would I have enough strength after sickness?

The dragon lowered its head, intent on me, and I clenched my jaw, dropping my brows.

"Mairynne, stop," Thalaj commanded, no longer pretending with my disguised name. Concern rang in his voice, and he sounded distant as if he struggled to reach me.

I responded, curious why he'd ask me to back away. Easing the ferocity of the storm, I called back the lightning and rain, allowed the winds to move wider and softer toward the edges of town, but I held the rumbling clouds close. With my feet planted in a wide stance, my arms spread, and the power flowing through my fingers, I held the tempest close and ready to strike, but even in the wind, a cold sweat broke out on my forehead and I breathed heavier.

"Mairynne," Thalaj said again, this time with almost a growl.

The dragon snaked its long head toward him.

I pulled the winds closer and yelled, "No!" I tightened my grip on the storm. I wouldn't let this beast hurt him. He'd been through enough after the Evernight and at the hands of the Tsinti, and I wasn't about to put him through more. I ground my teeth, determined to pour every bit of my energy into this if necessary.

The blue beast moved to keep Thalaj in one eye's sight while the other diamond-like iris narrowed to a slit toward me. The one glittering eye implored with me.

Thalaj yelled again, echoed by Hoaris. The blue Ryū before me growled and swished its snake-like tail toward the burly man. With agility I wouldn't have anticipated, Hoaris feinted in one direction, then leapt over the attack. Thalaj tried to move between the dragon and me, but something about the eye contact made me release the storm with one hand and hold it up, turn it on my guard, and halt his advance.

"Wait," I said, panting and staring deep into the crystalline eye. It watered, a turquoise pool forming on the lower lid and leaking onto the dragon's snout. I recalled a legend I'd once heard about how tears from the Ryū held all the emotion a dragon felt when they wept and could drive a person mad with pain, fear, or the joy they held if a person consumed the liquid. But even without tasting them, I felt a heavy loss, pleading, and a vast emptiness. "Stop. It's sad," I tilted my head as I watched. "She . . ." Yes, it was a she, I decided. I knew so. Beyond any possible doubt. With a stronger voice and more conviction, I added, "She wants something. She's missing something. Yearning."

Thunder rolled through the clouds above as they thinned. And though I'd released my power completely, a dark cloud still hung in the distance.

The dragon's gem-like eyes leaked another pearlized drop, and my fear evaporated. My thoughts of saving the town, of saving Thalaj, seemed inconsequential. She, this dragon, was the victim here, not us. Not this town. I dropped my hands, no longer wanting to speak with sorcery. The remaining clouds, save the one in the east, floated away as my shoulders sagged. Otarr shone, illuminating the dragon's scales as she turned in my direction—a gesture, I knew, of the purest gratitude.

Then, in a single lithe move, she pounced, ripped the blue stone from its mount, and slithered onto the dying winds, toward the lonely cloud in the distance. Her screech as she flew away from the now stoneless trading town chilled my spine far less than it had before. In the place of Safaia's namesake, their protective talisman, a pile of crumpled rocks rested in a mound. And something upon the cloud in the east glinted like a mirror catching the light.

Thalaj put away his weapons and reached for me.

I fell weakly into his arms then, panting. "I need food and more rest." I gladly accepted what strength he offered. After the retching and the expending of all my magic energy, there wasn't much left within to manage walking on my own.

Hoaris sheathed his sword and walked over. "That was something," he bellowed. Overly excited, he went on a bit about seeing something out of legend. Then he turned to me. "You've quite the power there."

I smiled at him weakly, feeling that it took all the remaining power I had to simply remain upon my feet.

Hoaris nodded. To Thalaj, he said, "Take her back. There's some bread on the table and leftover vegetables over the coals." With a gruff whisper, he added, "You should be able to walk straight through the wall illusion. Just pretend it's not there." He clapped Thalaj on the shoulder as he passed, climbed the steps, and went back into the inn.

◇◇◇◇◇◇◇◇◇◇◇◇◇◇◇◇◇◇◇◇◇◇◇◇◇◇◇◇◇◇◇◇

WITH THE BLUE BEAST gone, most of the traders pretended to go back to their business, surreptitiously cutting glances in my direction as Thalaj supported me back toward the trail to the Betsu. A couple, seeming braver than the others, hesitatingly stepped forward, but Thalaj waved them away. When one particularly large man approached at a quick trot, we slowed, and I felt a rumble in Thalaj's chest as he raised one of his blades.

I placed a hand at his heart and said, "Don't you believe we should answer some of their questions too?"

"They aren't my concern. You are." He pulled me along, ignoring the man.

Holding on, for I hadn't the strength to fight, I walked with him. Although I couldn't let the topic lie. "They are our people, Thalaj." To this, I felt more than saw him release a long sigh.

He lowered his voice, hissing, "Would you stop acting like a ruler, Mairynne? Out here, you must consider yourself first in order to survive. Here, most people don't know that's what you are. If we're going to get through this safely, it's not the wisest thing to announce it to the masses."

Father's words echoed in my ear, *Truth to thine self first.*

What did those words mean in this case where the duty I'd learned as a youngling opposed the purpose I'd chosen?

His caution mingled with my confusion and brought my intent to a halt. "I don't understand your meaning, Thalaj." I struggled to maintain my breath as we continued onto the path, then downward toward the cave. "Do you believe there are ill feelings toward the royal family? Or toward Storm Sorcerers in general?"

"Mairynne," he said on a plaintive breath. "Let us get you back to the caves so you can rest before we board the riverboat tomorrow.”

“I need no coddling,” I snapped, but the sentiment held little heat. “True, I am weak, but I'll not have you dismiss my questions.”

Thalaj sighed. “It is possible. I merely mean to exercise caution and protect my charge. These people will go about their lives, spreading rumors throughout the trading posts. The next time you hear this story, a bard will likely be singing the tale. We will be away on the morrow, so please, rest for me today.”

“On the morrow?” I asked, recalling Hoaris had said as much. And Thalaj echoed it now. Confused once again, I pressed, “Did I lose a whole day to the sickness?”

“Aye, you did.”

Another lingering question resurfaced then. “Were you ill too?”

“No.” He eased me over a root that blocked the path.

“Then what was the cause?”

Thalaj laughed with little humor. “Hard to know. I’m no healer.”

It seemed as if I needed to speak to maintain my upright position. If I stopped, I feared I might fall into slumber at the side of the Betsu. “But clearly it wasn’t poison. The figurine didn’t show signs, and you ate the same stew.”

“No, not poison. It’s most likely just a normal twist of the stomach people suffer from time to time. At least your skin is cool to the touch again. Kyr took good care of you.” He lifted a corner of his mouth.

“Were you surprised by her ministrations?”

“A bit. Watch your step.” He went first over the large boulder that stood in the path into the ravine and held his hand back so that I could steady myself.

We walked the rest of the way in silence, me watching my every step along the rocky path and babbling unimportant observations, Thalaj measuring my balance the entire time. At the mouth of our cave, I glanced downriver to where the water suddenly widened—a curious thing really, that so much water flowed from so little trickling over the rocks. It appeared small in the distance, but upon the shore beyond the ravine, a docked barge awaited, ropes running from the end toward the trees to keep it from floating away.

“Is that the boat we’re to take on the morrow?” I asked.

“It is,” Thalaj said and ducked into the mouth of the cavern.

The metal doors didn’t slam shut again, and it felt strange to pass through what seemed to my eyes to be solid stone. In fact, I had to close my fooled eyes in order to convince my brain to go. But once past the two large spelled rocks that created the illusion, I opened them to the amber light cast throughout the caves by the other bewitched stones.

At the table, Thalaj saw me to my seat, emphasizing that he would get the food, and went to the hearth. In his hands when he returned was a bowl and two large chunks of bread. He handed one to me along with the bowl, then took a large bite of the other.

Spoon in hand, I stirred the hot vegetable soup and leaned forward to let the steam rise to my nose. The smell alone made me feel as if I had enough energy to skip resting, but I knew what the storm's magic extracted from a sorcerer. I'd need the sleep before I would feel fully myself again. I sipped the hot liquid and swallowed cautiously, judging my stomach's reaction. When satisfied that the soup would stay in place, I reached for the bread and asked Thalaj, "Did you learn what's happened at Arashi? Why the Stormskeep gates are sealed?"

He shook his head, swallowed, and said, "We'd have to return to figure that out. Is that what you want?"

Chewing the sour bread, I dropped my spoon and reached for the stones about my neck. Hot and cold both flared in my palm. "No," was all I could utter, but I worried about my sisters, about Nadia and Corwyn. "No," I said, more assuredly. "Whatever may come to the keep, my path is forward. Nadia, Karynne, Yasmynne . . . they'll all have to manage it without me now." I hoped that my decree hadn't caused the unrest, but there was little I could do about it from afar.

Father's words echoed again. Yes, away from Arashi and Stormskeep was my true path—of that I held absolute certainty.

Thalaj watched me work through these concerns in silence, slowly tearing pieces from the bread, chewing, and swallowing rhythmically. If he had thoughts on the matter, he didn't share, and when I held my silence, he put down the crust and said, "All right. Now, can you tell me what happened back there in Safaia with that dragon?"

I shook my head. "I wish I could, but I haven't a clue."

He pursed his lips and ran a thumb over the table's rough wood. "Well and so. Why did you call the storm?"

Dropping my eyes to my soup, I murmured, "It's what I could do to protect you." Though the words spoke only of fact, I expected his ire.

He didn't disappoint, his fist crumpling the crust just before it sailed into the coals. He stood and paced the kitchen. "I can protect myself, Mairynne. But I cannot protect you from harm you'd bring upon yourself." His voice was deeper than normal and, if it wasn't loud, it sounded hard like the walls of the cavern in which we sat. A chill filled the cavern, his sorcery flaring cold with his temper.

In the rational part of my mind, I never questioned his ability to protect himself, but I'd already put him through so much. It sickened me that he hadn't been able to prevent the beating he'd taken when he'd gone upon my errand in the Evernight. For all his prowess, he wasn't invincible. Patiently, I dipped the bread into the soup and took another bite, watching him. I'd let his anger run out before speaking again. After several trips back and forth before the hearth, he sat.

He searched my face and said, "Protecting *you* is why I am here. Yet I am helpless if you overuse your own magic until . . ." He groaned, sliding a hand through his dark hair. "Could you consider being a bit less willful?"

Willful. I frowned. The word my mother and Mother Feathergale had used for me as a youngling.

I finished the soup, and some energy flowed through me again, or at least my thoughts seemed to clear. Thalaj remained quiet, and the silence grew uncomfortable. The echo of Thalaj's phrasing opened a wound, scrubbed it around in the dirt, and made it as raw as it had ever been. My gaze met his, then darted away again, but finally I relented. "I'll try." I answered with little confidence. "That is as much as I can promise."

He nodded, seeming to accept this little bit.

I went to stand but hesitated. Though I felt better, I still needed the rest to return my strength before tomorrow, but I had one other bit of curiosity rumbling around in my mind. "Thalaj?"

"Hai?"

"What do you know of dragon lore?"

SEVENTEEN

The City by the Sea

OUR CABIN ON THE BARGE was so small that Thalaj and I could barely walk around one another, and if we put our packs on the floor, we couldn't open the door. We decided to stow them on the bunk until it was time to sleep, and how we'd position ourselves for sleep in the tiny space remained a question. We'd just turned to go above deck when the barge lurched away from the shoreline and I stumbled.

Thalaj reached out to stabilize me, finding some unfathomable mirth in my loss of balance. "Did I not warn you that you being on a ship would make you feel different all over? You'll grow accustomed to the movement."

"And when have you had time to gain your legs at sea?"

He smirked and waggled a brow. "No time recently, but my training with weapons keeps my balance tuned better than most."

Before we left our packs, I tucked my coin purse out of sight. Thalaj did the same. Hoaris and the Small Folk had traded well at the market yesterday, and we divided the proceeds of both mon and goods by weight according to what we could each carry. Before leaving Stormskeep, I'd never dealt with irons, coppers, bronze pieces, or the mon strings I'd seen upon the traders' belts within the trading town. All I had ever needed was to instruct the council or the priests, and everything coin could buy would appear without need for my consideration. It felt passing strange to be carrying around the heavy pouch of mon coins.

Outside the berth, we took care to pull the door tight so it didn't swing when unattended. With the latches well worn, it took some thought to avoid having it hit someone walking down the skinny hall. We climbed four rickety steps, pushing the hatch open above and emerging onto the deck.

When that morning had arrived, I'd slept well and was up before the others within the cavern. My energy had persisted even after we boarded the small trading barge. As we emerged in the blazing sun above, the fresh air lightened my step even more. Captain Jerek barked orders to the four men rowing the boat away from the shore and moved about collecting the ropes that had tied off the barge to the trees. He stopped when he sighted us and came over wearing a half-cocked smile and clearly chewing on something in the side of his mouth.

"How long will we have to sail until we reach the City by the Sea," I asked.

Jerek looked up to the sky; birds flew downriver overhead. "Two nights journey to Kōkai," he said, tossing a coiled rope into a bin and standing tall with hands on his hips. Sizing me up, he said, "Unless you want to call the wind to push us along a little faster."

The suggestion stirred temptation.

However, I hadn't a chance to answer when Thalaj stepped from behind and wedged himself between me and Captain Jerek. I rested a hand on his arm, silently asking him not to try to protect me in this situation. The captain may have been ignorant to the fact that I'd exhausted my storm magic in Safaia's square the day before, and his request seemed only to serve the interest of time.

Jerek read Thalaj's manner too and held up his hands as if to surrender. "No ill intent, but you put on quite the show yesterday with that dragon. A bit of the storm's magic, eh? Too bad you let it go. The scales would've fetched a high price in the city downriver."

Heat suffused my face as I learned how wrong I'd been. A blend of chagrin and relief boiled within—a confused tangle. I'd sympathized with the sad blue dragon despite all the lore told me they were dangerous, the enemy. Then there was guilt over whatever I'd deprived the traders of; but intermingled with that truth, I felt a weird, angry sensation, mayhap offended that he reduced such a magnificent creature to only the value of mon her scales would bring. Did they not realize she felt things as keenly as we did? Could they not see that in her eyes? Why did people seem to only consider what would line their pockets? Yet, of course, I'd never been concerned with prices of things before. A symptom of living in the keep, of being raised a royal, of never wanting for anything, mayhap. I couldn't know, but it seemed that this sailor and trader only cared to make his way in the world.

The notion added substance to my being and the duty I might one day hold as true ruler of the Nantai people. I couldn't argue with his basic need to earn his living. Only deep inside, there burned a desire that begged to crawl up my throat and lash out at him. Whatever his motives, slaying a dragon for its scales and the mon he'd make was not honorable, not when she was only trying to protect her unhatched youngling.

I turned away before I said something that might anger the captain of the ship and lose us the ride down the Betsu. Swallowing, I gathered my wits and said over my shoulder to Jerek, "I cannot explain how I know, but the blue dragon meant no harm to the people of Safaia."

"Well, little lady, I'm not so sure about that. According to all the bard's tales, they have a white-hot hatred for the Nantai people. It was more likely the lightning you called that scared her away." Jerek leaned over and spat off the side of the barge. "Anyway, you're welcome on most parts of the boat. Stay out of the rowing pits though."

Hoaris, Misha, and Kyr surfaced from below just as he returned to work.

Jerek gave Hoaris a distasteful glare. "And keep those Small Folk out of sight when we pass through towns or by other ships." He chewed on whatever he held in his mouth, then added, "And out from under my feet."

I startled at the slight and opened my mouth to retort when the boat's nose distracted me, pointing toward the other shore. Absently, and to no one in particular, I asked, "Don't we need to go that way?" I gestured. "Downriver."

The captain pivoted back around to me, grabbed my arm, and pointed to the middle of the river. "See that dark patch there? With the ripples."

I nodded. It looked black against the rest of the dark-green-tinged river.

"That's where we're headed. Water's deep there and flows the fastest." On that abrupt note, he left us.

Hoaris and Thalaj both chuckled at my astonished look while Misha and Kyr cackled to one another. We went to the railing, and I looked down into greenish water, shocked that I could still see the stones on the riverbed. "Should make for an interesting ride," I mused to Thalaj.

The next days followed quietly. Hoaris played dice with some of the crew, earned a few irons and coppers here and there, and taught me the game in the dark hours under an orb of light within the darkness.

The first night, when it came time to sleep and Hoaris and the little people had retired to their cabin, Thalaj and I faced off awkwardly within our small space. Even though we'd been traveling alone together for some time, something hummed in the air between us. We met toe-to-toe, arms fidgeting and neither of us knowing where to turn or stand to relieve the strange charge. I giggled like I hadn't since I was a young girl, and eventually, I stilled within the dark and silence, allowing my eyes to adjust. I wanted him to touch me, but Thalaj simply smiled, reached around me, and grabbed the pack from the bed. He curled up on the floor in front of the door, using the pack as his pillow, and pulled a rough blanket under his chin. With a longing sigh, I crawled into the bunk and went to sleep.

The next night, the routine seemed easier, and on the second morning, we awoke to bustling, clanking, and shouting above deck. I turned to the cabin wall so that Thalaj could dress, then he stepped outside to give me privacy to do the same. Clothed, I went above deck and saw stretched before the small barge a sprawling white stone city, green veins running through the marbled rocks used to construct the walls and buildings rising up from the river. The mouth of the Betsu yawned into the Syrensea before us. Flags flew from the towers along the wall, and a towering keep overlooked the city. From the river, Kōkai glistened under Otarr's gaze, and I wondered how its white stones would appear under Selene's silvery glow. Mayhap we'd remain long enough to see that sight or sail away at night upon one of the large ships with the many-colored sails along the dock in the far distance.

Since the incident Aunt Nadia had explained, when Karynne had been held captive by the Small Folk King, Father had restricted us from traveling. There and then on the deck of that small and creaking barge, my chest burned with desire to see this city. I felt a passion for the newness of this sight—one I hadn't known existed within—and I reached again for the stones at my neck. They didn't flare this time in my grasp, so this city likely held little to do with my path. But something entirely different within me screamed to explore all the streets here, to meet the people, and to see and do and experience all this city had to offer, as well as much, much more. On a sharp inhale, I scolded myself for the frivolity. Purpose had driven me here, and seasons had already passed while we roamed under the Tsinti tsym. This was but the beginning of my real journey, and I had duties to uphold . . . to find my father and restore Tennō Atheryn Evangale to his rightful place on the Serpentine Throne. On that reflection, the stone heated against my palm, reinforcing the rightness of my mission.

Decided. Once I had fulfilled my duty, and only then, would I return to discover more of this new curiosity brewing within my heart.

◇◇◇◇◇◇◇◇◇◇◇◇◇◇◇◇◇◇◇◇◇◇◇◇◇◇◇◇◇◇◇

JEREK AND HIS FOUR oarsmen bustled about the deck above; the captain's muffled orders sharply different from how they'd been in the days before. Below, while I dressed, the footsteps beat out a chaotic rhythm on the deck boards. Thalaj had me braid my hair before I went above deck, commenting how we were fortunate the treasures hadn't yet minted my first year's mons or distributed them into the world before we left on this journey. As such, Hoaris and Thalaj claimed reasonable confidence that the average person wouldn't recognize me, and in truth, they worried more about the renowned emperor's guard who wielded curved double blades in each hand. For that, Thalaj stowed his scimitynes and only visibly carried a set of straight daggers strapped to either hip. Standing between Hoaris and Thalaj, I marveled as the green-veined walls grew by small measures over the course of our approach.

When the barge felt somewhat stable against the smaller docks still inside the mouth of the Betsu and some ways from the larger ships and bustling port into the city, the crew helped us step onto a set of planks. Underfoot, they seemed only a bit more stable than the barge's deck. The Small Folk hopped over the gap, each with a two-footed leap, and I had to stretch to make the expanse safely. Hoaris held my hand, helping me across as Thalaj moved over to where Jerek tied off the boat.

The captain stood and accepted a small pouch with the mons that served as the final payment for our passage.

As he handed it over, Thalaj asked, "Any idea which of the long ships we might gain passage upon?"

Jerek spat into the water, a repulsive action to which I averted my eyes toward the water below the pier. Between the river's calm waters and the wavy sea seemed to be a collecting spot for leaves, sticks, some discarded papers, and other debris. Jerek's brown foamy phlegm drifted into the refuse, and I lifted a lip in disgust. I had little fondness for the man who commanded the barge, but he'd navigated a true and timely course to the City by the Sea. After all, we'd arrived even ahead of his projection.

The captain wiped his mouth in the elbow of his already browned sleeve—clearly not the first time he'd done so—and asked in turn, "Where are you headed?"

"Across the Syrensea, to Ise," Thalaj answered on our behalf.

Jerek tucked the tail of his shirt into his breeches, considering with the motion. "You might have some trouble with that, but if anyone will provide that passage, they'll be over there." He pointed to the long dock teeming with larger ships.

The five of us gazed in the direction he pointed and listened intently to his continued instruction. "You'll see the flags that tell where each ship is destined. Blue means they're going north, toward the Iced Plains. There'll probably be a few of those this time of year making the last voyage before the ice gets too thick to pass." Jerek chewed a bit, then went on, "Yellow means south, along the Copper Coast. Green, they're heading to Lu Galen on the Vesterisles. But you might have the best luck if you can find someone flying a white flag."

Hoaris folded his arms over his chest and grunted for Jerek to continue.

"Those are the ships for hire. They go where they can for the money, but finding one to cross the Syrensea . . . well, that'll be quite the feat." Jerek wove between us and went back to securing his boat. When done, he grabbed a pack, tossed in the purse, and slung it over his shoulder. "Thank ya much for th' fare. Take care now." He tipped his head in the direction of the city, and his men joined him.

My party, increased by three after our time at Safaia, stood there on the dock watching them find footing atop the shifting pebbles as they ambled away. When they were nearly out of voice's reach, the captain turned back and shouted with hand cupped at his mouth, "And you might want to hide the Small Folk while you're askin' around."

We walked to the shore. Even after only two days aboard the riverboat, it felt odd to be on solid ground once again, the rocks slipping from under my boot soles as we strode toward the long dock.

Several steps led upward to the pier, and waves crashed around the stones beneath supporting the weight. One plankway jutted into the city and the other led to the large boats docked out beyond where the waves crashed into the shore. I went for the wooden steps but stopped when I realized Misha and Kyr hadn't followed. Rather, they'd pulled Hoaris to the side.

Misha placed a couple of clear stones in his hand. "Shake these together when we're ready to leave the city. We won't be of any help to you up there. More harm likely."

"Same for within the city," Kyr jumped in.

I called down, "Where will you go?"

Kyr grinned up at me, shielding the light of Otarr from her eyes with a raised hand. "Never you worry, lovely. We have the ways of the Small Folk, so we'll be around."

Hoaris put the stones in his pocket and shook Misha's child-sized hand. When the burly man came to join Thalaj and me at the stairs, I climbed. I peered back to find the little ones were nowhere in sight. Hoaris clapped a hand on my shoulder with a chuckle. "Like she said, *Never you worry, lovely*. Come along this way; they'll be fine."

The imitation of Kyr from his bearded mouth was passing strange, and as I'd grown closer to him over the dice games, I backhanded his arm lightly to scold him for poking fun. We shared a laugh, but humor faded as we turned toward the task at hand.

Passage across the Syrensea.

Thalaj stopped and faced us. "Let's take a look at all along the way, then we can decide which ones to approach." His voice seemed wary but, as was his usual demeanor, he set his mind wholly to the chore.

Sighting only a couple of white flags, I feared our chances for success were slim.

Jerek had predicted accurately; the majority of the ships flew yellow flags, signaling their southward destinations, but a couple would sail north for the Iced Plains or west to the Vesterisles and the city Lu Galen. I counted only three flying white flags by the time we'd reached the far end of the docks.

Thalaj crossed his arms over his chest. "It may be best if we learn the cost for trips north and south before approaching one of the for-hire ships."

Hoaris gave an agreeing nod. "It'll be a good baseline to begin our bargaining."

Again, being the least experienced with such matters, I couldn't follow their logic. I moved closer. "We do not know how far the journey across the Syrensea is. How do we compare such things?"

Thalaj remained silent, scanning the representatives standing on the docks, but Hoaris made a throaty sound and answered, "We don't know anything. The best we can do is guess and see if someone will take the offer. There's little reason to trading and bartering as it mostly hinges on what one person finds valuable."

My first guard tilted his head toward a ship heading north. "I'll speak with him. The two of you go to the yellow flag there." He nodded to the other side of the dock.

I stood beside Hoaris in silence as he opened the conversation. "How are the seas?" he asked looking over the waters to the west.

"They can start getting rough this time of year, but not so much to the south. Are you destined for the Copper Coast?" He looked past us to where Thalaj spoke with another, a ship flying a blue flag.

Hoaris shifted to block his view. "We're looking to leave the city but have no set destination in mind. How many can you carry on your ship there?"

The man looked to the sky, seeming to calculate. "We have room for seven more. It'll be a copper plus two iron mon each if you're heading our way."

Without any point of reference for if the pricing was just, I held my tongue and willed my expression serene.

Hoaris pursed his lips and stroked a hand over his beard. "Seems fair. I'll talk with my mate over there and get back to you. Many thanks."

The man called after as we turned, "You'd best hurry with deciding. We'll be full up before the morn."

Returning to Thalaj, we shared the cost of each option among the three of us. Those amounts in mind, we approached the closest ship flying a white flag. A grungy man stepped forward. His hair appeared not to have seen a comb in years, and he made Jerek's habit of chewing and spitting seem clean, but the boat behind him looked pristine.

Thalaj nodded toward the long black hull. "She's pretty."

"Aye, she's a beaut," answered the scroungy man.

They didn't exchange names, but Thalaj went straight to talking business. I assumed that if we struck a deal, we'd learn his name then. Hoaris and I hung back while the business ensued, but stood close enough to hear the exchange.

"You're her captain?" Thalaj asked.

The man cocked his head sideways with a squint. "That I am."

"What's your charge?"

" 'At'll depend on where ye're headed."

"Where do you sail?"

"Been all over. Where's your fancy?"

I liked the man less and less with every word, every question he answered with his own question. He moved closer to Thalaj, seemingly emphasizing a more shady intent. His voice to me slithered like a snake as he darted his tongue between his lips at each pause. Thalaj moved into a wider stance with one foot forward, a position I'd grown familiar with after training with both him and Yankos's Tsinti scouts. He could pounce and slit this man across the throat before anyone could blink, yet I recognized it not as an aggressive move, but as a defense against whatever danger he sensed.

"We're looking to travel beyond the Vesterisles." My first guard kept the description vague, reinforcing an uncertainty I had growing in the pit of my stomach about this dealing.

The man rubbed his stubbled chin. "Into the Syrensea?"

Thalaj nodded.

"Whaddye offerin'?" With everything he said, his tongue seemed to slip more into a crusty and clipped kind of speech.

"Well," started Thalaj, "it seems that those sailing north are charging a bronze mon per head." He turned toward us. "What did you say they were charging to go south?"

"Half that to the Copper Coast," Hoaris answered.

Thalaj folded his arms and turned back to the man. "I'm thinking we'd be somewhere in between."

I held utterly still, surprised by the low value of the offer and knowing that the journey across the Syrensea would extend well beyond the known destinations along the Nantai coast. The grungy man busted out in hoarse laughter, spittle flying from his lips. He blubbered on for several long minutes, slapping his leg and wiping tears, whether real or pretended, from under his eyes. "Have ye any idea what it takes to sail into the Syrensea?"

Thalaj, I knew, did not possess this insight. But he held his ground and kept silent as if expecting that the man would assume he understood.

"I'd risk me ship and every soul aboard. Not many a ship return from that venture." The man walked back to his stool, bow-legged, sat down, and pulled out a knife with which he proceeded to clean the grime from under a thumbnail. I fought the urge to raise a lip in disgust.

"Ye see," he said distantly, "ye have two problems."

"And what are those?" Thalaj remained utterly still, cool waves wafting from him.

"First, I had to let me crew go on account of no business. So ye'd have to staff me boat here."

I had no idea what the pay for a sailor was, but it couldn't have been within the reach of the coin we had in our small purses.

Stoic as ever, Thalaj simply said, "And the second?"

"Ye'll have to stock the ship for the trip." He looked up, flicking a chunk into the sea. "For the whole crew, there and back."

I couldn't hold back any longer. "That's robbery. Certainly you'd profit from the travels in other ways. We'd do better to buy your ship directly."

"I'll not be sellin'." The grubby man crossed his legs, making himself more comfortable. "If ye can't agree to my price, check the others then. I'll match any price ye find."

Thalaj raised a brow at the promise. "Well, sir, we thank you for your time, and mayhap we'll return with an offer." He turned away, then looked over his shoulder, "That is if we feel you'll have reason and consider it."

He called after us, but Thalaj whispered to me, "Don't look back. Let him wonder."

Several paces away, we stopped to further discuss.

"We surely don't have that kind of mon." I whispered, not truly comprehending what it'd cost to fully stock a ship. "How are we supposed to gain passage if they're going to ask us to foot the entire cost."

Hoaris guffawed. "She's new to this travel thing, eh?"

"Mairynne," Thalaj said, "They always start high, which is the reason I started so low. We need more room to negotiate. Let's talk to the others."

The second white-flagged boat had its own crew, and I liked the nature of the woman who stood at the plank bargaining for passengers. She bantered just as confidently as the men who lined the docks, and she worked the crowd even better with an ample amount of cleavage showing. "Come aboard the *Seaduction*," she hawked. "Your destination can be ours too."

When we approached her asking about sailing into the Syrensea, she shook her head vigorously and shooed us away, claiming the journey too unpredictable. After the second miss, we went to the third. I looked back over my shoulder to the grungy man who watched us surreptitiously as we went, still imagining him every bit the serpent lying in wait. And despite the fear we may remain without transport, I resolved not to travel with the scoundrel.

At the third boat, a man stood beside a table under a white flag. Far less boisterous than the woman working the crowd at the *Seaduction*, he tinkered with a gadget. A shipwright, perhaps. In comparison to the man at the first ship, he presented a cleaner appearance, save for the grease around his fingernails. He seemed reasonable and offered a shy smile as they approached. But he had to take the request on board to ask the captain before he could make an offer. Unfortunately, his offer was roughly the same as the slimy sailor's.

After exhausting the options, Thalaj stood for a long moment looking at people milling about the dock, the other passenger long ships, and the fishing boats on an adjacent dock before he spoke again. "We should venture into the city. Maybe we'll get a better idea of our possibilities there. At least we can inquire about sailors for hire and what it'd cost to stock a ship."

Seeming like our best option, we ambled across the plank, following a long line of people in one direction while passing fisherpeople and other sailors returning to their ships. Some went down the stairs and trekked up the rocky coast toward the dock that supported the barge we'd arrived on and where Jerek's and three other riverboats waited. Inside the narrow stone streets, we passed several shops. My stomach rumbled at the smell wafting over from an eatery on my right. Several tables with patrons littered the walk before the building in which someone grilled meat. But the odor of dead fish assaulted me from the left and replaced any signs of hunger. I turned toward the offensive smell to see a wiry man rushing out from behind a wet and bloody table. He had a silver and yellow fish by the tail, blood dripping onto the stones. He scurried across the street to the eatery that had smelled so wonderfully before. We pressed on.

I followed for another hundred paces or so, stretching my stride again in an attempt to maintain pace with the men. With their longer strides, they'd distanced themselves from me by ten paces. The crowd was loose enough that I could easily catch up with a few skip-steps, but lingering seemed of little harm. One merchant drew my attention. He haggled with an older man over a copper kettle and the merchant's table displayed a dozen other pieces forged from the metal . . . bowls, bracelets, and knobs. My focus fell little upon what he sold but more the clothing the man wore. Bloused pants, sandals, and a loose shirt with a vest—not terribly colorful, nonetheless fashioned in the Tsinti style. For a time, I lost myself, forgot that I strolled through cobbled streets in Kōkai, and felt the grasses of the Central Grasslands beneath my feet. During the mornings before the oxen moved, several men in Yankos's caravan had worked the golden orange metal over small fires. The work with copper hadn't seemed important then, but I smiled as another piece of the wandering folk clarified in my understanding. Under tsym, the Tsinti had never bartered with mon though they readily displayed it on their overskirts. I veered toward the merchant when a voice, so gentle I almost missed it, said from the shadows, "You'd do well to visit the gnoble in residence at the city's keep."

EIGHTEEN

The Casteless

HALTING, I TURNED MY HEAD, my brow furrowing. A cloak hid the owner of the voice, but there were no others around to whom she might have spoken. In my periphery, Thalaj spun, hand on his hilt, apparently having heard the meek suggestion as well. Perhaps his training with the Unseen allowed him to discern the quiet tone, or mayhap he'd taken note of her as he passed. The woman—no, a waif-like girl even under the cloak—stood against a wall. She pushed back the hood to reveal her smudged face. When the hood fell to her shoulders, I noted her hair hung in a messy braid, and wide, clear eyes regarded me as if she felt apprehensive about approaching us. Moving closer, I took more inventory of her appearance. Threadbare clothes. Small, dirty hands. A hole in the toe of her boot.

She seemed too young to be able to have worn the same boots long enough to wear a hole through the toe, and the space behind the hole was dark. Her feet didn't reach the end. Clearly she'd come by the boots after most of their life had been exhausted by another with much larger feet. She said no more as I moved into the shadows to meet her. Thalaj joined me, some of the gusto leaving his posture as he took in the nonthreatening sight. Hoaris trailed him but stayed closer to the street.

"Did you mention there's a gnoble present in the city?" I asked.

The girl gave a few tiny, jerking nods and wrung her hands.

"Who?" Thalaj snapped.

She flinched.

I held out both hands in an attempt to calm her. "May I have the name and caste?"

She backed away. Her voice mousy, she answered, "The Stone Lady, Sarangarel."

Thalaj and I shared a silent exchange.

I wasn't sure, first of how this girl would have known to approach us, and second how the Stone Singer gnoble would be able to help with our needs to sail across the Syrensea. But the small girl lifted her face with certainty and captured my full attention. Sarangarel would at least recognize Thalaj and me from the ascension ceremonies at the High Cloud Court. It followed to reason that she'd be willing to help the person she'd seen through ascension and called Kōgō in the days that followed.

Strangely, the girl's eyes shifted all about even though she seemed confident in having called to me and offering information. I gave her a smile in hopes I could reassure her further, let her know that we meant her no harm.

"May I have your name?" I asked, keeping my movements slow and my voice soft.

Thalaj placed a hand on my arm, a protective signal to be cautious. When he stepped closer, the girl backed away again, pulling further into a shadowy alley between buildings.

"Truly, we don't wish to hurt you. I'm Mairy." I rested a hand over my chest, over the ever-heating and -cooling stones, and a haunting thought came to mind. Sarangarel. The Stone Lady. What if Stone Singers had been responsible for the stones that hung about my neck? Mayhap Thalaj's paranoia wasn't so misplaced after all. With her retreating, I had little time to worry over such puzzles, so I stowed the thought for later.

My first guard, also recognizing that he scared the girl more than I, tucked in behind me and whispered, "I'll stand with Hoaris. Find out if she can take us there." His voice quieted so only I could hear, cool breath at my ear, as he added, "And if she pulls a weapon, hold up a hand."

When he left, the girl relaxed a bit, the drawn features on her face smoothing and making her look five years younger. I smiled at her again. "What do others call you?"

"Honera," she whispered, her eyes dropping and then returning to mine.

"Honera," I repeated. "Thank you for signaling to us. How do you think Lady Sarangarel may help?"

"I-I can't be sure." She shook her head, but I waited patiently for her to continue— something I'd seen my father do on occasion when he tried to gain information from my sisters or me. Inevitably, one of us had felt the need to speak under the pressure of his gaze. The silence worked and she went on, "Along with her people, they're always looking for business."

I pursed my lips. How odd that a young girl would worry about such things. "Business? Of what sort?"

"They bring in lots of stone and gems from the rock fields to the east. They're always sending someone down to bargain with the ships, sometimes taking short jaunts out to sea. A moon back, they sent a crew of miners from the fields over to the Vesterisles. I just thought . . ." Honera twisted her fingers in front of her.

I pursed my lips and narrowed my eyes on the girl. Indeed, she'd been watching us since we'd dealt with the ships on the pier.

She fidgeted. "I-I'm sorry. Mayhap you search for something else."

"No, you did well. Thank you. But how did you know to choose us?" I asked.

The girl glanced behind her and shook her head when she focused back on me. "You have the lost look."

I could say the same of her. "*Honera* you said is your name?"

A nod.

"Well, I've never been to the City by the Sea. Can you guide us to the keep where Lady Sarangarel is in residence?"

Honera looked past me at Thalaj and Hoaris, then turned and looked down the alley behind her, but she still appeared uncertain.

I glanced back questioningly at Thalaj. His answering look urged me on. To the girl, I asked, "Will you allow my friend speak with us? He is my protector and seeing that you intend me no harm, he has no cause to hurt you either."

Again, she flinched, still twisting her fingers. Her eyes were wide, but she nodded yes. Thalaj approached when I waved him over. He moved cautiously behind me and said, "I have two mons for you. One now and one after you show us where to find the gnoble."

Honera pressed her lips together and extended her fist. At full arm's length, she unfurled her fingers. Everything about her stance said, *Well and so, but do not come closer.* Heavy black lines shone from under her broken nails, and grime painted every crease of her revealed palm. Thalaj passed me an iron mon which I placed lightly into her cupped hand. The dirt-stained fingers snatched it away, and she turned quickly, calling, "This way!" as she trotted down the small space between buildings.

I lost track of the twists and turns, hoped that Thalaj or Hoaris would have a better sense of our way back to the docks, but I stayed on her heels. Suddenly at the center of a long alleyway with stone walls rising on either side, Honera stopped and pressed her back against a wall. "Up there." She pointed. "Street rats aren't welcome. The Stone Singer guards push us away with their rock hammers. We try not to be seen around them."

When Thalaj stepped forward, clearly intending to head to the end and take a look, Honera stood boldly in front of him, hand extended. "I did my part," she demanded, not at all the timid thing she'd appeared before.

My first guard looked down at her. "So you did, young lady." He placed the second coin in her palm.

She scampered back down the road but took a left where the cobbled streets formed a T instead of the right that would have retraced our path.

With only a small flit of his gaze to the scampering girl, Thalaj said to Hoaris, "You stay here with Mairynne. I'll take a look." He climbed the remaining paces to the top of the hill and turned the corner. After only a few seconds, he returned. "The gates to the house itself are well guarded. The guards refused my entry on the premise I had no appointment with the Stone Lady."

Lifting my chin, I said, "Did you ask in the name of the empress?" I despised that I found need to use my position, but speaking with Sarangarel felt necessary. In truth, Thalaj, though his father had been Frost Fighter and his mother Storm Sorcerer, outranked anyone within the Stone Singer caste. Yet I had enough trouble using my own position, and knowing how my guard viewed his station of mixed blood, I resisted mention. Focusing on mine instead, I added, "As kōgō, I hold higher caste rank than anyone here. It seems they'd be willing to show me directly to Lady Sarangarel upon my command."

Thalaj rubbed his chin. "Neither you nor I possess knowledge of aught that may have passed in Stormskeep. You disrobed yourself of the title when we set out on this journey. And in this case, it could very well pay to our advantage to assume the worst."

Hoaris grunted. "Doesn't hurt to just ask. Let me try." He started for the keep.

I smirked to my guard, cocking a brow.

Snatching him by the sleeve, Thalaj said, "Do you really think the Stone Singer guards will accept a Frost Fighter into their fortress?"

"We're not at constant war with them like the Fire Forgers and that tyrant of a leader, Atith."

Their gazes locked, each challenging the other, until without grace, Hoaris shrugged. "Guess we'll see; I'm going in. But in case it doesn't work, we might need to find a way to get a message delivered."

Thalaj rubbed the back of his neck. "I'll get the girl back. She won't take a message herself, but street rats know the city and will do just about anything for mon. As should be apparent by her quick change in attitude. Had she been quicker of hand, she might have slipped our purses."

The men nodded to one another, a plan and backup plan in play. Hoaris left in the direction of the guards.

To me, Thalaj said, "You wait here. I'll only be a few minutes."

As he went and I remained in the alley alone, my senses went on high alert. I strained to listen for their steps. Hoaris's fell heavily, but Thalaj made no sound. I backed up toward the wall, rested my hands against the rough stone, and tried to meld with my surroundings. My success in this endeavor felt meager. Any passerby would have recognized my awkward presence. Fortunately, none passed.

A few minutes trickled away, and my leg began to twitch; my breathing grew shallow. Worry seized me as I looked from one end of the alley to the other, but still, no one appeared. After another several long moments, a rustle came from the direction Thalaj had traveled. I stopped breathing. No voice reached my ears, but by the sound, people struggled nearby. I dropped a hand under my travel cloak to the hilt of a scimityne, feeling more confident with the blades after the season we'd spent with the Tsinti. I held my other hand outward, palm up and ready to gather the storm within.

THE ENERGY I DREW fizzled as Thalaj came into view dragging a kicking and thrashing Honera down the alley. For reasons I couldn't reconcile, she didn't scream or cry out. Mayhap that was the way of the casteless in Kōkai. Would a cry for help bring the opposite? A glance over my shoulder told me we were still alone, and I sighed, relieved it was only him.

Clear exasperation on his face twisted his mouth, and I stifled a chuckle at seeing him so.

The girl made herself as heavy as possible while wriggling to get free and prying at his fingers. Then, she started grumbling. "I did what you asked. Let me go." Though still hushed, her tone grew panicked the nearer she drew. "You have no right! We're getting too close. They'll shred me!"

When he reached me, Thalaj huffed, grabbed her under both arms, and placed her on her feet facing me. In her fit, she didn't see me and continued to flail.

Reaching past her clawing hands, I grasped onto her upper arms. "Honera," I snapped.

She stopped, opening her eyes frenetically and looking around like trapped prey.

"Honera," I insisted, dodging to catch her shifting gaze. When her eyes finally rested on mine, I added, "We're not asking you to go in there. Settle yourself."

The girl turned her head one way then the other, searching for what I couldn't tell. Had my anxiety over being alone in the streets seemed stifling, hers spoke of certain fear for her safety. I wondered if she feared more than the Stone Singer guards.

"Look," Honera snapped, "I had a job to do and they're waiting on me."

"Who?" I asked.

She jerked her head around again.

I held tighter onto her grungy sleeves, shaking her once. "Who, Honera? Who is waiting on you?"

That silenced her. She definitely feared someone—or perhaps protected them. When I lifted my gaze to connect with Thalaj, the look he wore stated he clearly believed the same.

Breathing measured breaths, I urged her again. "As I said before, we mean you no harm."

"Then why is your brute holding me like this?" She shrugged, trying to pull herself from our shared hold.

I tightened my grip, considering how this version of the casteless girl behaved far bolder than she should. Tougher, too. She was too young to be so hard. What could have possibly brought her to this way of life? Not for the first time, I wondered about her parents and where she lived. Was she orphaned? And it rang strangely to my ears to hear her refer to Thalaj as a brute. I'd never seen him as anything other than safety, but now that I looked at his hard-lined jaw and broad shoulders, I had to admit she had a point. To anyone he didn't swear protection, he certainly would appear deadly.

Heavy footsteps from the end of the alley halted my words before I could reply. Hoaris trotted downhill over the cobblestones, pack bounding on his back, and he held his scabbard so that it wouldn't interfere with his run.

Honera tensed in my grasp; Thalaj tightened his hold. The big man wore his thoughts in the way he carried his head, shoulders, and brow, and I could read him without words. He'd had no luck with the guards.

I turned back to Honera who'd begun to writhe again. "Shhh. We need your help again, please."

"I'd no permission to *help* you before," she sneered.

Thalaj repositioned her so he had her about the waist within one arm. She kicked.

Hoaris stepped forward, addressing the girl freely now. "Why? Who said you couldn't help us?"

The girl pressed her lips together as if to hold back the words by force, but her resistance seemed to wane as the three of us pressed her.

I glanced around, hopeful others wouldn't witness the three of us holding tight to a smaller person while she thrashed for her freedom. Yet we needed her cooperation. Time to try one more time. "If my friend lets you go, can we talk? Will you stay and hear us out?"

Her nervous look cut between the three of us, then she jerked a nod.

I sighed and motioned for Thalaj to release her. She stood closest to the wall with the three of us surrounding her—still a threatening formation. She wouldn't make it very far if she tried to bolt between us. By the Triad's grace, she didn't. She straightened her shirt and turned her head, cracking her neck.

I started again, "We need to get inside to meet with Lady Sarangarel."

"To be sure; that's what I told you before," Honera said, folding her arms and jutting a hip.

I fought to keep reason in my tone. "The problem is that they aren't willing to simply allow us inside at our request."

"How is this my worry?"

Through gritted teeth, I continued, "We need someone to carry a message inside."

Honera held up her hands and shook her head vigorously. "Uh-uh. No. I told you before; they'll shred me."

But behind the action, in her eyes, there was something more. Mirroring her motion, I held up my hands too. "We're willing to pay if you have another idea of how we can either get her a message or get inside unnoticed." I raised my brows, waiting hopefully to see if she'd accept the bait of more mon.

Slowly, more softly, she said, "You got the wrong girl for that," and turned her eyes toward the gutter.

"But you have another idea?" I coaxed.

Reluctantly, she groaned, rolled her eyes, and held out her hand expectantly. "Filtch is going to hang me."

<hr>

AGAIN, WE WOUND THROUGH the narrow streets, heading in a direction that seemed dingier, less populated, and with more crumbling buildings. The doors often hung in shambles, some fastened by chains with heavy locks, others were just splintered wood that looked like they might fall apart if you pushed on them. I looked toward the roofs occasionally, at many of the stone walls collapsing from ill-repair. We moved at an easy pace through the streets. I walked beside Honera with little conversation, but she held us back at every corner and peered up and down the crossing passage before moving forward. The action seemed curious as I would have expected more threat from one of the buildings falling down upon us than from the open street. But she lived here and now offered her cooperation, so I followed her lead.

Several turns later, she pushed through one of the decrepit doors—one missing a chain. Honera went first, I followed, then Hoaris, and Thalaj pulled up the rear, keeping an eye over his shoulder at all times. She led us down a long hall, up two sets of stairs, and down another corridor before she turned into a room at the end, the precariously hung door open and awaiting our entry. Before going inside, I looked to my companions for guidance.

Thalaj shrugged one shoulder and touched the door. It issued a creak with little movement. "Can't be a trap. This door wouldn't hold a youngling, even before the babe learned to walk."

Inside, we climbed a set of worn stairs, followed down another hall, and crossed another threshold to our left. The only furnishing was a large square table with four benches, every surface scratched, pocked, and scarred as if someone had marked the wood with a knife. The walls had cracked and fallen in places, leaving piles of rubble in the corners, and the only light came from a small paneless window.

I held out my arms expectantly. "Where's this Filtch person?"

"Oh, he's not here." In a repeat of her stance in the alley, Honera jutted a hip, arms folded over her chest.

Cold anger rolled off Thalaj as he let out a huff and folded his arms as well. "Then why are *we* here?"

"My friends will be here soon. Getting in with Filtch takes a bit of work."

Her words only barely foreshadowed footsteps approaching from down the hall. Thalaj's hands drifted to the hilts of his daggers and Hoaris's to his sword as two boys, thin and dirty like our little guide but at the threshold of manhood, strode into the room. Assaying little threat, Thalaj and Hoaris eased their stances. The boys appeared more alarmed than Honera and shifted wary glances around the room.

Honera skipped over. The taller of the two grasped her arm and pulled her into the corner to talk. I watched her hand over the iron mons we'd given her and wondered if this was Filtch. Even though I strained my ears, I couldn't hear more than whispers. Clearly having agreed to something, the taller boy called over the shorter one and then . . . they both left.

I lurched forward. "Where are they going?"

"Oh." Honera shrugged and sat at the table, seeming far less feeble than she'd been in the alley. "Just downstairs. They'll be back in a quick."

"And who are *they*?" I took a seat on another of the benches.

"We call 'em Gnat and Flea." She drew her brows together. "Not sure what their real names are." And that didn't seem to bother her as she crossed to the table, took a seat, and traced the engravings with her dirt-encrusted thumbnail.

Indeed, only a few moments passed before the footsteps came again down the hall, slower this time. When the boys appeared, the taller one handed Honera a plate of steaming food. It looked and smelled like some variety of stewed meat, and my stomach growled.

"Thanks," she said and took a bite of the bread from the plate. With a full mouth, she introduced us.

Flea, the shorter one, tossed an apple to each of us. It wasn't as hearty as the girl's meal, but it was whole, and the peel seemed intact.

Gnat said, "We didn't think you'd eat cooked food from us. You look smarter than that."

I thought of the golems in my pack, but we only had the two. Hoaris would still be at risk. Regardless, they didn't know of our little animated friends, so the assumption seemed sound.

Gnat walked to the window. "The fruit's from the tree there." He pointed.

Thalaj went to look, nodded, then wiped the peel on his shirt. He took a healthy bite, the crunch filling the silence. I grinned and did the same, sweeping away a trail of sugary juice that ran down my chin. It was a tiny pleasure, but I chewed and got lost in the sweet moment.

The tall boy leaned against the window, arms folded and shoulder slumped to one side. "Filtch will only see the girl, and not until sunset."

"Not an option." Thalaj gave no time for Gnat to continue or for anyone else to reply, and his words were finite.

I'd seen him exert that command before, but then didn't seem the time. "Thalaj," I said softly.

He raised his dark eyes to me. "No, Mairy. I'm not leaving your side. Remember what I told you in the cave at Safaia? My sworn duty."

Gnat stood, arms spread. "Then, I believe we're at an impasse."

Standing, I went to Thalaj and placed both hands on his arm. "Do you have a better idea?"

Thalaj simmered but remained silent. He looked warningly at the boys and at Honera, who chewed her food eagerly while we discussed. Hoaris stood to the side and ate his apple while he watched and waited for the next move.

I turned to the trio. "Can we have a few minutes alone?"

"Certainly," Gnat said, and they left, shuffling heels across the dusty floor.

Honera stood with her plate and followed, still chewing.

When only the three of us remained, Thalaj spun to me. "Mairynne, there is no way I can leave you to go into some stranger's domain alone. You know that. You know it would break my vow to your family in the worst way."

I tucked my chin. His accusation rang true. What I asked was a violation of his pledge, but this seemed to warrant it. I couldn't remain passive here when I could possibly gain us another step in Father's direction. For reasons I couldn't name, I didn't see the same danger as he. Mayhap my guard's intuition stemmed from his training or his intent to pose the danger himself. Possibly I remained the naïve little princess who'd never ventured from her father's home, but I had it in my mind that all would be well. The stones about my neck remained even in temperature, not offering indication one way or the other. When I looked back up, I said as much, pulling back my cloak to reveal my scimitynes and adding, ". . . and between Yankos, Jorani, Baldeo, and you, I have been well trained in how to use these."

Thalaj eyed me skeptically. "You're only beginning to learn how to use those."

Hoaris bellowed a laugh from the other side of the room, distracting us both from our debate. As we turned, I could only imagine the twin questioning looks he saw. With another guffaw, he said, "You two bicker like my gram and pop. She'll probably be fine, Thal. It's just another of the casteless."

My cheeks felt hot at the comparison to an old married pair, but his reassurance pleased me nonetheless.

"None of the casteless have been much of a threat." Hoaris took a final huge bite of the apple and chewed. "Skinny street rats and not much more. Send her in with a few mon, and she'll be back before you know it."

I turned back to my guard. "Well and so, and I've rested enough on the barge and haven't used the elementals in days. If needed, I can call upon the storm. All it would take is a single burst of lightning and I can be free." That wasn't something I could do often, and the act drained my energy like no other usage of the magic inherent to my people. But I could call it if I were short on options and had access to the skies. With the state of the windows in these buildings, I didn't see that as an issue either.

Thalaj pursed his lips. Then he rubbed his normally smooth chin, but because he hadn't shaved in days, the motion issued a rasping sound. His eyes shifted and he worked his lips a little more as thoughts ran behind his eyes. Then, he relented. He went to the door and motioned to the three casteless who'd likely eavesdropped the entire time.

With everyone inside again, Thalaj said, "Well and so. She'll go with you at sundown. I'll return to the market in the meantime. Hoaris, can we have a word outside before I take leave?"

My jaw gaped. Though I'd all but demanded I go, I hadn't expected him to leave me there to wait for Otarr to retire for the day. I also didn't hear what passed between the men in murmur outside the door, but I trusted Thalaj. Zofi's counsel echoed: *He will always be there for you. There will come a time when you'll doubt but rest easy as he will always return.* I reminded myself of that and gave him the space to seek whatever he needed at the market. With the boys and Honera, I took a seat, awkward silence hanging heavy within the room.

Hoaris returned with a wide grin and heavy step, and flounced onto the bench across the table. He pulled out a small purse and looked questioningly at the three younglings. "Dice?"

None of the three knew how to play, so Hoaris explained the simplistic rules to Gnat, Flea, and Honera the same way he'd explained it to me on the barge. I listened to him, ineptly craving an answer to what had transpired between him and Thalaj in the hall. But alas, I had resolved myself to trust my guard.

We played for hours, using the seeds from the apples we'd eaten as pretend mon. Hoaris, of course, won time and time again. After each victory, he'd redistribute the seeds and we'd start anew. By late afternoon, Gnat was getting pretty good. He bested Hoaris twice before light footsteps in the hall approached, and Hoaris swept the dice into his pouch.

A woman appeared in the doorway dressed in simple gray, but her attire was clean. Distaste wriggled upon her lips as she peered around the room and its dilapidated condition. She looked down a long nose at the five of us sitting around the table. Hoaris stood, but she walked straight past him and stared at Honera. "He'll deal with *you* tomorrow." Then to me, she held out a heavy cloth blindfold and said, "Filtch awaits your company. My *lady*."

Nineteen

Filtch, Patron of the Casteless

HONERA SHRANK UNDER THE WOMAN'S haughty words and anger flared inside me at the way she looked at and talked to the girl. It mattered little in my view how low Honera was in terms of caste or class, she remained a person. Though I owned the most authority in Nantai, I hadn't considered approaching anyone of the casteless in such a superior manner.

"What gives you authority to treat others so?" The words flew from my lips before I'd considered their weight, before I remembered that I wasn't the empress here. Despite that, I felt justified in the question and pushed my chin higher as I stood from my seat. "And who are you?"

She'd seemed larger while I sat—possibly from the air of supremacy she held about her—but standing, I looked down to meet her eyes, ignoring the swath of material in her hand.

She didn't answer my questions but looked coolly at Gnat. "Since you didn't return with word otherwise, I thought she'd agreed to Filtch's conditions." Her hand holding the blindfold dropped to her side.

"What conditions?" I asked. "The only condition shared was that I go alone, without Hoaris or Thalaj."

The woman's glare shifted to me. "You brought a petition to us. If you wish to speak with Filtch, you will come with me now, alone *and* blindfolded."

Hoaris pounded a heavy fist on the table, the dice rattling. The bench scraped the floor, and the temperature in the room dropped suddenly as the mountainous man stood. "No one spoke of blindfolds. That implies prisoner."

The clamor didn't seem to influence the woman. She simply looked up at Hoaris as if she had grown tired of the conversation. "You'll understand that our master wishes to retain his anonymity. We have not bound her and only expect she follow without sight. These are the terms, Filtch's offer of his service, if you will. If they aren't to your liking, we can close the deal now and I can be about more important business." She lifted a brow.

I tapped my foot through a pause where all eyes in the room turned in my direction. Seeing little alternative, I leaned across the table toward Hoaris. "You went to the guards. Do you think there's another way to reach Sarangarel? Do you think there's another way to secure our passage with the mons we have?"

The manner in which he dropped his eyes told me he had naught but doubts regarding our odds.

"Filtch can help you, I am certain," the woman interrupted, any inflection absent from her voice. "Although, I haven't all night to await your decision."

I reached for the stones under my tunic, pressing them against my chest to see if they offered any guidance, any flare of cold or hot, something to make accepting the risk more palatable. Once again, they remained at an even temperature. My shoulders sagged. Apparently, the spell cast upon them only reassured me when I questioned my path, reasserting in the conviction that I must find my father. Precisely *how* I went about the task, they would leave to my discretion. Zofi had warned that time was of import to Father, that he could only persist in "stasis" for so long.

Stasis. Another concept beyond my understanding. Yet in that moment within the rundown room, Father's uncertain time and future drove my answer.

"Very well." I sighed.

Victory danced in her icy-blue eyes. "You can leave your pack here with your friend." She pulled the cloth through her hands and reached to tie it around my head.

I pushed my traveling bag toward Hoaris, grateful she hadn't asked me to divest myself of my weapons or the purse I carried on my belt.

I'd never seen him aught but jovial, but now he shot me a wary look. "I-I'm not so sure about this. Th—" He pressed his lips together, then restarted. "Your protector will see that my throat yawns if anything happens to you."

The woman said, "Rest assured, we mean her no harm. This is only for our protection. She will return before dawn."

"Give me a moment," I said to the woman. Rounding the end of the table, I rested a hand on his arm. "Unless you have another idea, I must."

Even through his beard, a muscle jumped visibly in his jawline. He gave a small nod. "If you're not back at first light, we'll tear the city apart," he said to me, his eyes fixated on the woman. "And I'll have your name before you may take her."

Again, she jutted her chin higher. "You may call me Wren."

"That's it? Wren?" Hoaris boomed.

I pulled at his arm. "It's enough.

After he had settled, I said to Wren, "Shall we?" I turned my back, vulnerable and hoping that her words rang true, that she and her master intended only aid and information, as she secured the black material in place.

Night had been falling before. The room had been in shadows.

Now, it was black.

Wren took my arm at the elbow and guided me away. We walked slowly and with little conversation aside from small instructions on where to place my feet. Through the door and hall, down the stairs and the lower hall, then we stepped outside. The air on my face felt fresher, more alive, and I took note of the difference. Several counted turns later, we entered another building, the air once again stale. Throughout this all, Wren made no remark beyond *step up, step down, right, left, . . .* Inside, we climbed six runs of stairs. I breathed hard by the time we stopped, and I listened for her to do the same. Nothing. Had she called upon some assistance from the elements to aid her journey? There'd been no wind, cold, or heat. Mayhap she'd simply trained her body to climb so quickly. The pressure on my arm hinted at her reach toward something ahead, and a door creaked. We moved forward again, the enlivened air hitting my forehead, nose, and chin once again; outside then. On a roof, I imagined.

At another twenty paces, Wren said, "Climb again," and we scaled another run of twelve stairs. She pulled me along, not seeming to go in any particular direction, and after much wandering, she stopped and reached again. This time, no door creaked, but then she urged me forward another dozen steps and drew to a halt, at last releasing my arm. Someone—*Wren?*—worried at the knot and the blindfold fell away.

The room in which I stood wasn't much larger than the decrepit room where we had spent the day playing dice with the casteless—Gnat, Flea, and Honera. It was clean and boasted decorations, a clear display of affluence. A carved wooden desk, three chairs with scrolled backs and arms, and a cushioned seating area furnished the space. There were many shelves lining the side walls, and each supported clusters of candles or a candelabra to provide light. Behind the lit and flickering tapered candles, mirrors reflected each flame's amber glow to make the room seem brighter still. At a hearth, a figure stood gazing upon the fire. I drew my brows to a peak as I, too, peered at the fire. It glowed and danced like any other, but it didn't put off smoke. There was no chimney, and the stone around it didn't show signs of char. Yet the flames flickered. And for all the fire within the gray stone room, the temperature remained cool.

Wren crossed to the figure by the fire—Filtch, I presumed—bowed her head, then left us. I followed her path, taking note of the intricately carved double doors she closed behind her. So at odds with every other building we'd passed earlier in the day. I faced the stranger—long, thin, and plain in appearance, Filtch wore clothing fitted to his form, clothes like none I'd seen before, light in color with no material sagging or flowing as was customary among the Nantai people. He wore his hair trimmed close to his head, also unlike our customs. When he turned, I took in his smooth, too-faultless complexion. Eyes, brows, nose, mouth, and chin, all balanced in a way that suggested a portrait rather than a person.

In a voice equally as flawless, he said, "Evangale, the youngest *once*-empress of the

Nantai people, it is truly my pleasure to meet you again."

THERE I STOOD. IN a room seemingly having no place in the City by the Sea, I gaped at the pristine person before me, ageless to my eyes as if he'd been sculpted rather than born. Confusion danced through my mind. He should only recognize me if he had spent time in Arashi at Stormskeep. And then only if he'd seen me in an occasion of less formality or growing up when I was freer to dress casually and wear my hair free as I desired. Even as I'd approached my majority, my mother, Kōgō Noralynne, as part of her royal duties, and Mother Feathergale had been grooming me to look the part of an empress. When Father had written me into the annals as his heir, their ministrations had only intensified.

But this young man before me would know nothing of those times. "How is it—Filtch, is it?" I waited for him to nod his assent, then continued, "that you know me, but I don't believe we've met before this moment."

Filtch moved to the desk, took a seat, and flourished an arm across the tabletop toward a chair.

I hesitated, but in the end, I'd gone blindfolded with Wren to see this man who offered a sliver of hope in getting a message into Lady Sarangarel's grasp. One of my hands covered the small pouch at my belt, and the other felt for the hilt of a scimityne. Reassured by the presence of the weapons, I sat on the edge of a chair and rolled my shoulders back to lengthen my spine. "Will you honor me with an answer to my questions as well?"

Filtch reclined in his chair, folding his fingers together under his chin. "I understand that this is difficult for you, but it matters little to me that you don't recognize me from your past experience. Although, if you search, you might find a way to discover my true identity.

"Regardless, that is of little importance. We're here to see what I might do for you, is that true?" He smirked.

He'd posed the important question, but the other niggled under my skin. I couldn't place him. Regardless, I shifted in the chair to move the weapons so I could settle back for the conversation in the same manner he clearly had. "I understand that you might be able to get a message delivered for me."

"I have many messengers. To whom do you need to send this message?" He sat utterly motionless, his eyes boring into me as he spoke.

Honera had known our plight, suggested it even, so I hesitated. Wasn't he the patron of the casteless? Slowly, I answered. "The Gnoble Lady Sarangarel."

He spread graceful fingers to either side. "And what possible favor could you have to beg of one *four* castes below your own?"

Again, Filtch stilled, but I sensed disdain in the sharp edge in his words. I narrowed my eyes, trying to infer his intent. The casteless, the *rats* as Honera had pointed out, would care little of the upper caste machinations. So why was it that a leader within the casteless of Kōkai would worry about me stooping beneath my ranks? His worry hinted that he had more involvement with caste politics, that he was someone more than what he appeared.

I cleared my throat. "You'll forgive me, but since you know my position within Nantai society, you'll also be informed the topic of caste is one I'd only discuss with advisers and those sitting upon the Gnoble Council."

Again, he gave a small and superior smile. "And, Lady Mairynne, you will also forgive my impropriety, but I believe you are the one in need here." He folded his hands once more, as if to close that part of the discussion and iterate my obvious position in this conversation.

Clearly, there were no others present or begging his help.

We stood at an impasse, each unwilling to meet on middle ground. This matter wouldn't succumb to negotiation or haggling. Given the comfort of the office where we presently sat, he wasn't a street rat in need of mon. Were that so, I would offer my purse. Though he possessed the information I required, Filtch clearly would offer nothing more while I refused him such discussion. Yet I found myself unwilling to put our plight at a further disadvantage by divulging more than truly necessary. In faith alone, I'd risked leaving my companions and going with Wren, and it seemed a possible mistake.

I placed my hands on the chair's arms and pushed to my feet. "Well, I must thank you for the time, but it appears another solution will be necessary. Can you ask Wren to return and see me back to my friends?"

Filtch closed his eyes and took several measured breaths. At length, he stood too. "Wait." He stepped away from the chair and closer to the cool fire in the hearth.

Mayhap he possessed a version of the Frost Fighters' sorcery, for I still couldn't believe the fire before me.

He held his hands clasped in front of him and turned in a slow circle. When his back faced me, his head lolled forward and his body shimmered, grew transparent like mist. It reformed as he completed his revolution. Completing a full rotation, he raised a neither feminine nor masculine face to meet my watching gaze.

I hissed air in through my teeth, eyes wide, and my hand covered my mouth as the emblem stared at me. Upon the shoulder . . . a swan.

The Swan.

"I believe this is the face and attire you will recognize," said the Cloud Courtier, Alto-Trea, and reversed the slow circle, reassuming the clean and simple visage of Filtch.

Throat tight, silenced, and insides heaving, I sank back into the chair. Filtch took his seat too as I searched for words. So much had been amiss about the path to this room and about the room itself. It had seemed too nice to exist within such a rundown area of Kōkai. We hadn't traveled far enough to reach another district. That meant—

"We are within a cloud castle," I said, all hope having fled.

Mists in the darkness within the Yubar . . .

The cloud that had lingered over Safaia . . .

Filtch, a person who'd followed us from Arashi, issued a single nod, his fingers steepled at his chin.

I turned to the door, my heart pounding furiously in my ears, then looked back at Alto-Trea—no, Filtch, or—

By the sacred Triad, I didn't know what to think. One thing I held certain: Thalaj wouldn't rest if they failed to return me safely. The room about me wasn't the airy version of the castle at the High Cloud Court. Even in the amber glow of the flame, it held a heavy grayness, like a storm cloud ready to empty over the earth.

"We are still within the city. You have naught to fear." Filtch's tone was one that seemed wont to calm my anxiety or maybe belittle my worry, but just as easily as he'd tried to allay my fear, he added, "Yet."

"What interest do you have in the casteless of this city?" My skin prickled, outrage balling inside my stomach. Though I feared for myself, I still worried over the people. "Why do you so disguise yourself? Do they know you're a Courtier?" A hundred other questions boiled in my mind, but those were the only ones that would surface in the maelstrom as I attempted to trace the Cloud Courtier's motives.

"Ahh, young Evangale, you begin to piece things together. I have shared my true identity with you, and I trust that you'll keep that information between us. Will you now share your reasons for seeking the assistance of Sarangarel?"

I noted the absence of her gnoble title but gritted my teeth. Another small, albeit carefully played slight prodded at my patience. However, my need to know if he could—or *would*—help gained urgency. "I seek to charter passage across the Syrensea."

"Oh, truly?" Filtch tilted his head, interest the first apparent emotion I could recall written upon his face since having entered this room.

"Truly."

"And what is your destination?"

"How is that of import to my request of you? I merely need you to help with delivering a missive to the *Lady*." I measured my voice, carefully emphasizing the title.

"Well stated . . . *Lady Mairynne*."

I lifted a brow. "I believe the address you're searching for would be *Kōgō*."

He smiled. "Might I offer some fire-flower wine?"

My mouth flooded at the mention of the cordial I hadn't tasted since my departure from Stormskeep, but I hadn't brought my taster. The golem remained in my pack with Hoaris. Steeling myself for more courtly banter, I smiled as sweetly as possible. "That would be pleasing. But would you mind terribly if I asked you to drink from my glass before I partake?" *He* would do equally as well as my little animated self.

Filtch contemplated for a long moment, certainly rolling around my accusation in his mind. Then he stood and went to the door. When he returned, he had two of the bubbling glasses in hand. He sipped from each and handed me one. "This is a rare pleasure that you don't experience when traveling afoot, I presume." He sighed. "I cannot fathom the unpleasantries of sleeping upon the ground. I lost you for a time after the night we last spoke, but having a sky island helps in navigating Nantai, you see." He sipped again.

I took a drink; the bubbles danced on my tongue, and I longed for the keep where I'd grown to my majority, where my family remained, where I knew every turn, and where I felt safe. Indeed, my body ached from the travel and a part of me yearned for the comforts lost.

Home.

But as I swallowed, the stones flared around my neck. One hot, the other cold. Despite the wine's simple pleasure and the reminder of what I'd sacrificed, my path ahead would veer away from my lands and my people, "*. . . over the Syrensea to the island nation of Ise, and inland still,*" Zofi had foretold.

"Thank you for the wine, Filtch." I placed my almost empty glass on his desk. "You are being a most wonderful host. However, I wonder if we might return to my purpose? My friends await."

"Ah, speaking of your friends, to where has your loyal first guard disappeared?"

"To tell you the truth, I do not know." And for the time I was glad that Thalaj had only spoken to Hoaris. "I believe he went to the markets, but he didn't share his purpose or destination."

"Do you know when he will return."

It cut that I hadn't that knowledge either. I lifted my chin. "Our understanding of this little arrangement was that I'd be back before dawn, so I'd assume he will return to the building before Selene has finished her night's journey." I paused, again feeling that the trajectory of the conversation meandered. "So, you will understand my need to conclude our business in a prompt manner."

"I do understand, Lady."

Again, the ill-address rankled, but I measured my breathing and held my tongue. Kōgō had never been a status I'd wanted but somehow, as this disguised courtier kept using a lesser title, anger stirred from the depths of my soul.

Filtch drained his wine. "You inquired before why I had interest in the casteless, Lady Mairynne. I do have a certain fondness for simplicity." He seemed far away as he spoke, but then shook off wherever his mind had wandered. "I must say, though, it is not only the casteless within the City by the Sea that I take interest in."

"I fail to follow." I blinked several times, feeling something had fallen into my eye and clouded my vision.

"Are you aware that there is a large purse, strings upon strings of bronze mon, offered for your return to Stormskeep?"

"Why would it surprise me that my aunt and sisters would offer a prize to have me returned safely?" I answered without hesitation.

Filtch folded his fingers and reclined again. "You misunderstand my meaning."

Again, I tried to relax into the chair, a solid attempt to maintain control. "Then I presume you will enlighten me?"

"There is a price for both you *and* Thalaj Northerngale."

This news was a bit unexpected, but as Thalaj had been our father's protector before mine, it wouldn't be an entirely absurd notion. "You've still told me nothing that would be cause for alarm."

"As I said, I take interest in the casteless within multiple cities. Arashi is one, and the messenger network is a particular interest of mine."

I tensed. Hoaris had mentioned that someone had ordered the Stormskeep gates sealed. Naturally, they would put out word beyond the walls if they were offering a reward for my return. But his words suggested that he had connections inside.

Filtch went on, "There is a new empress sitting on the Serpentine Throne."

I'd decreed that Nadia would take my place in the interim. "This is as I expected. I couldn't leave without appointing another to the duty."

He spread his hands, then refolded his fingers. A smokeless flame flickered in his eyes. "Once again, you misread my intentions."

"Then would you state it plainly?" I snapped, losing my careful control within, but I maintained my poised posture.

Filtch tsked. "We have had quite the uncommon number of ascension ceremonies in recent times. It gives my people in the clouds quite the purpose, you see. We thrive upon our courtly duties, so we are more than happy to accommodate."

Frustratingly, he dallied. I sat there as calm as possible while a current ran through my blood and my muscles twitched in anticipation of flying into action. I toyed with the hem on my cloak, rubbing the rough stitches with my thumb as the only outlet for my growing frustration.

A grin split Filtch's face. "Shortly after you disappeared, your aunt, Nadialynne Riversgale, completed the rituals. Our production of 'The Spirit Sosano, the Blooming Princess, and the Regalia of the Nantai,' I must admit, was one of our finest. But I do believe the one following your sister's ascension will be written about in songs."

"What?" Standing abruptly, I launched toward the table, leaned closer to Filtch on both arms, and spewed forth shocked question after shocked question. "My sister's ascension? How is that possible? Nadia would have never decreed such a thing. Which sister? Certainly not Yasmynne! So . . ."

"Hai." Filtch sat forward, holding my gaze evenly. "Your logic is true. Kōgō Karynne Evangale is the sitting empress of Nantai. So you see, it would not have been appropriate for me to call you *Kōgō*."

Karynne, my loving but strong-willed sister—the very sister who'd proclaimed to me before my ceremony that she was past her jealousy over our father having named me heir—had somehow figured a way to take the Serpentine Throne for her own.

I paced the small room in an arc, giving action at last to my coiled muscles. Filtch couldn't have had a hand in the situation, but how? Who? . . . and why? I grasped at the stones around my neck. Even through the material of my tunic, they flared hot and icy-cold. My parents expressed anger to me in the only way possible . . . from wherever their souls had traveled.

I hadn't a clue what action I should undertake next. Should I go home? The stones returned to normal within my hand. Should I continue on my current venture? Heat flared in my palm. I'd never been so certain of my father's presence near my heart, and despite the gut-wrenching spectrum of possible treachery, I knew beyond doubt . . . I must stay my course and follow the stones.

Throughout my pacing and puzzling, Filtch sat behind his desk with calm satisfaction, and I despised him for that. I wanted to lash out, to scream until my frustration had run its course, but that seemed a youngling's reaction. If anything, I needed to maintain a level of maturity and control. I stopped my pacing in front of the door. Turning to him, resolved, I said firmly, "I need to get that missive to Stone Lady Sarangarel. Can you help me or not? If you cannot, I will be on my way."

I yawned.

"Oh, but Lady, you've overlooked something."

Shaking my head, I demanded, "And what, pray tell, is that?" I held my hands in fists at my sides, resisting the urge to call the storm, but there were no windows. I had no connection to the skies or water. And then . . .

My arms grew heavy; my legs weakened.

"You've assumed that I *will* help you. Having such ability and exercising it are two entirely different prospects. Offering assistance to you and your guard would mean treason on my part." He lay a hand over his chest. "The notion of imprisonment within a spire at Stormskeep . . . well . . ." He shivered. "You see, that is not a fate I'm willing to endure."

The room darkened. I pressed my eyes wider open, fighting. "What have you given me?"

He flipped his hand, gracefully but dismissing my worry. "It was but a mild sedative."

"But . . . you drank . . . from my glass?" I stammered slowly.

"Hai. So I did. The elixir is one I take on an almost nightly basis. I have trouble sleeping otherwise, you see. Honestly, I envy your intolerance." Filtch stood. "I'll have to drink another to find sleep tonight, I believe. Mayhap even a third." He walked around the desk.

The room spun as I tried to focus on him. Vaguely, I heard the door opening behind me as my knees gave way. The lights dimmed. Filtch caught me before I sank to the ground, and before I slept, I heard him say, "Find her a room for the night. We'll leave with the thinning morning fog."

Twenty

The Escape

THE BED IN WHICH I awoke felt almost like my own with ample cushion, plump pillows, and a heavy blanket. I stretched as if that were true, but as soon as clear and conscious thought settled upon me, I sprung upright. Darkness hung thickly within the room, and though my eyes were wide, I couldn't see. Reaching for the wind, water, or charge in the air, I felt none, no connection to the sky. No windows, I concluded. My captor understood my sorcery's limitations well enough—as a Cloud Courtier would. I patted my chest, arms, and legs, breathing relief that I still wore my own tunic and pants. But my cloak, weapons, belt, purse, and boots were all no longer about my body. I squinted, blinked rapidly as if to clear a blur, but the blackness remained. I turned my head slowly this way and that to search out any sliver of light, but there was none. My chest constricted, and I sucked in a breath, holding it and hoping the tightness would relent.

Think, Mairynne. Think.

Filtch—what an appropriate moniker for the Swan. Alto-Trea's reappearance and the conversation before I'd fallen to the elixir thundered through my mind. Each remembrance sizzled inside me as if each new fissure in my soul shot lightning through my core. Unfortunate, how it failed to produce a strike that might be used to free me from whatever prison in which I'd awoken. Feeling so torn and confused, I often would have summoned the rain, but when I had no connection to the skies or elements, I couldn't release the storm's magic..

My throat felt dry and my palms wet.

How had Karynne shifted the mantle of leadership from Nadia to herself? How had she convinced our sweet aunt? Or *had* she convinced her? Had Karynne forcibly usurped the Serpentine Throne and thereby . . . the price placed upon my head had little to do with her sisterly love? If she'd intended something aught, worse perhaps, I'd sorely misjudged her intent. If she'd sponsored an ill fate upon our aunt, what harm did she intend for me? Sealing the keep's gates was an action only taken in treacherous times, but Nantai wasn't at war. What danger could possibly exist for the residents of Stormskeep? Regardless, it seemed my sister or my aunt—or perhaps both—had betrayed my wishes.

I reached for my necklace, happy to find the stones in place. Then I touched the cuff on my upper arm beneath my sleeve. Still there. So they'd relieved me of my weapons and other accessories, but they hadn't searched me fully. Tsanseri had mentioned I may have need of the trinket one day, but what could that have meant? If she were here, would she act against Alto-Trea—one who'd participated in her audience within Love's Court when Yasmynne made her petition?

Huffing, I dropped my hand to my lap, regretful over not heeding my protector's warnings. Pushing the covers back, I swung my feet over the edge of the bed. The floor, cold and smooth even through my stockings, felt like the ones in the High Cloud Court. Standing, I kept a hand on the bed and stretched the other blindly before me. I took shuffling steps until I came to a wall. Feeling my way, I did the same along the wall. Strange that no furniture obscured my path. When I reached the corner, I turned. At three more paces, my thigh bumped the corner of a table. I explored. My frantic, trembling hands ran over the surface and below—no drawers, only a simple table—but on top, I found things. A belt. A purse. Rough-spun wool, folded neatly. *My* things? I fumbled to open the purse's clasp and feel inside. Coins, a few stones from the Stone Singers' gift at my ascension, and the mirror. I'd forgotten about the tiny circular mirror that should allow me to see things in their true form. How helpful that would have been upon my arrival . . . and something I should have used with Honera and the other casteless. I closed my eyes, rueful that such a thing had slipped my mind. Yet that particular object confirmed these were indeed my belongings.

Beside the table under darkness still, I donned the belt, purse, and my cloak, then I continued my slow journey-by-feel up and down the wall. On the floor beside the table, I kicked something and reached for it—my boots. The absence of sight also erased balance, so I sat to prevent toppling over, slipped my feet inside, and laced them. The only missing items were my weapons and scabbards. I groaned. What would Thalaj say when he discovered that I had lost the weapons he'd had crafted especially for me?

Keep searching, Mairynne. You don't know that you've lost them yet, I reminded myself.

I made it down the third wall, encountering no other furniture, and on the fourth, presumably on the opposite of the bed where I'd begun, I found the door. I tried the latch; it wouldn't give. I beat on the door, called out for help, pounded until my fist ached, then I pressed my ear close and listened.

Nothing.

For long, empty moments . . . only silence.

With my back against the wall beside the door, I sank to the floor, at a loss for what to do next other than wait. My last recollection within Filtch's office hadn't been more than two hours after dark. Without light or access to the skies and awakening from a drugged slumber, I couldn't guess if morning had arrived. I assumed Alto-Trea had tucked me into a room upon his sky island. The time was of more worry.

"Find her a room for the night. We'll leave with the thinning morning fog," Filtch had said as the elixir pulled me under.

Did that mean—?

I strained my ears and listened hard, tried to hear or feel the soft hum I recalled from my time at the High Cloud Court. Again—nothing. For all I knew, we could have departed from the City by the Sea and arrived somewhere else while I slept. Everything had turned into a youngling's game of guessing.

Aloud, I whispered, "Oh, Thalaj, I am so sorry I wouldn't listen." My head fell back to rest on the wall. Had I listened, I wondered if we would both be in my current predicament. Mayhap, but at least we'd be together.

After several long minutes there against the wall, I heard a series of small clicks, fumbled my way to standing, and held my arms wide, ready to call for my powers. If the door opened to a space where I could connect with the sky or a source of moisture, at least, I could call upon the storm's power and defend myself against whomever was there. I held my hand forward, ready.

The door swung inward; the soft light was bright enough that it pierced my eyes, yet night still kept the city in shadow. I squinted as my eyes adjusted, but no one stood in the opened door. Cautiously, I went forward, peering out to one side, then the other. The exit revealed an open space and the sprawling city beyond wisps of dark clouds. The room had blocked sound, but waves still crashed in the distance. I turned my head left, straining to hear more. A soft keening—akin to the sounds the blue dragon had made over Safaia.

I looked to my right for someone. Anyone. The skies remained dark from horizon to horizon. Selene still hung low above but would soon turn her watch over to Otarr and the light, but I had no way to know how much night remained. Beyond the few city lanterns still aglow, there was a vast darkness. The Syrensea. I reached toward the darkness to test my theory and could feel the moisture from the huge body of water gathering to answer my beckoning. I held tightly to the power as I searched for something or someone.

Who had opened the door?

I turned to the left where a hallway led into the castle. The keening came again— so much pain within the sound. It riveted my feet in place as my heart pulled in two different directions.

Where had the woman, Wren, brought me? How would I return to Hoaris and Thalaj? If I went toward the city, would I find cloud steps down? Who had opened the door?

Why did the dragon mourn? Did the Cloud Courtier hold her captive as he held me? Did she yearn for her freedom the same as I, or something more? Alone and out of imminent danger, I ruled out calling a storm as it would certainly set my captor on alert. I desperately wanted to find my scimitynes, if only for the security of having a weapon in my palm. But overall, that seemed less important than getting back to Thalaj and Hoaris.

Father's voice replayed in my mind, *Truth to thine self first.*

Zofi's then about Father, *It is uncertain how long he can remain in stasis.*

And hers about Thalaj, *He will always be there for you. There will come a time when you'll doubt but rest easy as he will always return.*

My heart broke for the dragon, but I needed to answer Father's call. Braced in the doorway, I looked both ways several more times, judging, trying to decide. How long did I have before first light? Attempting to help the dragon again wouldn't further my cause. I'd aided her once, but certainly she was stronger than Filtch and could care for herself this time. "I'm sorry," I whispered to her, my eyes burning. Unable to endanger myself further, I stepped through the door, the cool air raising the hairs on my arms, and started toward the city.

A croon sounded again from behind and halted my flight. I pivoted and jogged the other way—toward the sound.

"No!" a distant voice cried. Muffled. Familiar.

A jolt surged up my spine, halting me at the corner. I pressed my back to the wall and looked back toward the room where I'd been held captive. *Kyr?* I would have sworn that voice belonged to the Small Folk woman, but I saw nothing. My heart pounded in my throat, and I fought to control my breathing. Just my imagination, or mayhap Filtch's elixir caused more than sleep. I closed my eyes and inhaled. *Ten.* Exhaled. *Nine.* I opened my eyes; inhaled. *Eight.* By the time I reached five, I'd gained control and listened again for the dragon's sounds.

I might have missed it if I hadn't been concentrating, but the dragon's voice was still there, a soft and constant rumble punctuated occasionally with a higher-pitched whine. Then she emitted a louder wail that sounded hoarse as if she'd exhausted herself from the efforts. Then, it faded again to the low grumbling. I stayed close to the wall and peered around the corner, right then left.

I shrank into a low crouch when I caught sight of two people stood not more than fifty paces away engaged in hushed conversation. Both were dressed in attire of the people who dwelled in the Great Sands region that stretched from the eastern border of Nantai across the northern half of Yōtei. I'd only seen the clothes in illustration— loose pants that fit tight at the ankles, knee-length robes with long billowy sleeves, an ample scarf about the neck, and another draped over the head and affixed with a dark band around the crown. I could only see one of their faces, a young man whose olive skin, inky black hair, and lighter eyes reminded me of someone. At the distance, I couldn't tell his exact eye color, only that they weren't the dark browns that normally accompanied such deeper-colored features. I watched, trying to place the familiarity, until he moved into a position where the other person obscured my view.

My eyes stretched wide when beyond the two, a blue scaled tail stretched out. Another crooning sound pierced the night at the same time I placed the young man's resemblance—Imrythel. A hand seized my arm and pulled me around. I gasped, lost balance, and landed on my backside. Something I couldn't see pressed hard over my mouth. A hand?

My eyes roamed but found nothing. No one. In my ear, I felt a hot breath and heard muffled words. "Back to the room, lovely."

Kyr? I sucked in air through my nose and lifted my hand to call the wind.

Another force batted it down. And a second muffled voice commanded. "The room. Now." Then the force urged me upward. The force on my mouth gone, and another touch pulled me forward by the wrist.

"Misha?" I hissed.

"Hush," he answered.

I started, "Why can't—"

"Shhh." The invisible hands pushed me back into the dark room.

Sounds rustled toward the bed.

I swiveled my head until the Small Folk man appeared standing beside the rumpled bed.

"Wh-What are you doing here?" I stammered. "Where's Kyr? Why couldn't I see? How did you . . ."

But I lost my words as Kyr materialized beside her mate, lifting her hand away from a stone on the bed. My mouth worked wordlessly, disbelievingly. Misha dug in a small pouch and whispered a few seemingly foreign words as he placed another stone in my palm. They both picked up the ones they'd placed on the bed. Their forms shimmered, dimmed for a second, but they didn't vanish.

Misha said, "Okay, now we're ready."

I felt no different as I gaped at the tiny, nearly clear but dull stone.

"Invisibility spell," Kyr said and shooed her hands toward me. "You're hidden too." She widened her eyes and put a finger over her lips in a shh motion, then added, "They'll dull sounds some, but not completely. Now, on with you, lovely."

"Hold on." At the door, I hesitated, curious about how the stones and spell worked and still itching to go toward the castle to help the dragon and find what I'd lost. "My scimitynes. They took them." If these stones allowed me to travel unseen throughout the castle, I desperately wanted to go in search of them. Returning both myself and my gifted weapons would be the best avoidance of Thalaj's impending scorn.

"No, no! This way." Kyr urged me along behind Misha.

He halted at the next corner with his hand holding us back as he searched the open space. As I crouched behind him, he pointed across the open space and slightly to the left. "That's the way back."

I grabbed his shoulder. "How long do we have until dawn? With these, we can go back, help the dragon, and get my weapons before we leave."

Misha gave me a sideways glance, impatient and warning.

Kyr grunted. "Nope. Not an option. We're to get you off this cloud." She nodded at Misha who turned and darted toward the escape. Kyr prodded me into a jog behind her mate. "Thalaj will take care of the rest."

"What?" I barked, stopping in the open. Thalaj was here? On the sky island? Taking care of . . . what?

Misha turned and scurried back to me. Exacerbated, he grabbed my wrist, and pulled. His words came harshly if hushed still. "We're getting you off this sky island, weapons or no. And that dragon is strong enough to care for herself."

But I'd forgotten the dragon when learning Thalaj had come too. Where was he now? I tried to resist but felt torn between my own safety and my first guard's. "If Thalaj is here, we should help and leave together. What if he gets hurt?" What I left unsaid broke me almost as much as the thought of his pain. My scimitynes were gifts from him and I didn't believe I could bear their loss.

Misha barked again, "He has a stone too." Then he grumbled, "Not that people can see that man moving in the night."

Kyr added, "You worry overmuch, lovely. He'll meet us back where you left Hoaris. Now we're under orders. We must move."

I went, driven by a niggling feeling that I should trust my companions as the last time I hadn't, I'd walked right into Alto-Trea's trap. We scurried across the remaining yard. My heart wrenched when another keening echoed from behind through the predawn skies. Misha turned back, grasped my hand, and pulled me along. With quick steps, we trotted down clouded stairs, our destination the roof of one of the crumbling buildings. There, I stopped and looked up. Watching us without movement, Filtch stood. His eyes settled directly upon me, apparently seeing through the spelled stones and holding my gaze. Still, even as I'd made an escape and his scheme would no longer unfold like he desired, he portrayed no emotion.

Something about the Cloud Courtier disguised as patron of the casteless held my attention while I asked Misha, "How did you know where to find me?"

"Thalaj came to us and we returned before you left. We followed you, then waited."

"Did you go inside the office while I spoke with Filtch?"

"No, lovely. We didn't get the chance to slip into the room," answered Kyr.

"So we waited outside," Misha added.

"Why didn't you save me earlier while I was asleep in the bedroom?" My voice sounded distant even to my own ears and my eyes remained on the Cloud Courtier.

"We had to wait for you to wake up. We're not strong enough to carry you so far," Kyr whispered.

I tilted my head to Filtch. He mirrored my action, and I felt my brow grow heavy. "Misha, you know he sees us?"

"Impossible." Misha stood beside me and looked up. "But if he does, we're away now, and we need to get further."

I raised a hand. Filtch did the same. The young man from the Great Sands I'd seen before stepped up to his side and followed his gaze. But his look was entirely blank, unseeing, and confused. Filtch smiled, grabbed the man's arm, and turned him away. They retreated from the misty edge. Gone.

The hidden blue dragon wailed again—the sound sadder than any I could fathom. Misha and Kyr both flinched. I tensed, my eyes prickling. Hers would be another soul that rested heavily upon my heart. Mayhap another day we could save her too.

Misha shook his head. "I don't know how he could see us, but that's even more reason to move."

"No." If he could see us, he could see Thalaj. "I can't leave Thalaj."

Kyr pulled on my cloak. "Trust your protector. He has sufficient training with the Unseen. He knows how to escape these situations."

"She's right, and Thalaj said as much," urged Misha.

I finally peeled my eyes away from the edge where Filtch had been and looked at the small man. Most of me wanted to pull back, run up the cloud stairs, and protect my first guard from any further harm on my behalf. Another part wanted to rescue the dragon from whatever her fate. Something seemed off about the people from the Great Sands and why they were present at a Cloud Castle on the coast of the Syrensea. But the other part of me—wiser part, I suspected—knew the Small Folk were right.

"Trust him," Misha implored.

With a final glance back, I decided.

And fled.

◇◇◇◇◇◇◇◇◇◇◇◇◇◇◇◇◇◇◇◇◇◇◇◇◇

ONCE AGAIN WITHIN THE run-down room where I'd spent the majority of the prior day, we found Hoaris leaning up against the wall, head thrown back, and mouth hanging wide open. A soft, rhythmic snore rumbled from his throat. The casteless— Gnat, Flea, and Honera—were no longer present, and it surprised me that Hoaris would sleep without a watch. I placed my invisibility stone on the table, and with that out of my hands, Misha and Kyr vanished. They uttered some quick words, and once done, they both stood visibly at the table as they dropped the stones into their pouches.

I thought how strange their magic was, not tied to a source within but to words and objects. They simply said some phrases in their strange language and things happened—unexpected things. For my magic to work, I needed a connection to the sky or a water source, and it always built from inside and resulted in wind or rain unless I pushed harder. With enough energy, I could gather the thunder and lightning, but those expressions of my sorcery were only possible because I manipulated the winds in the atmosphere to build energy. The other castes had similar focused magic—the Cloud Courtiers relied on a force inherent to Nantai earth to float their castles and change appearances, for example—but the Small Folk could learn certain ways with words and cause all sorts of things to happen. I wondered if others could learn their ways but put the thought aside and went to Hoaris to wake the burly man.

As I leaned down, Kyr hissed, "I wouldn't—"

But before her words sank in, Hoaris grabbed my wrist with lightning speed and had me pinned in a sitting position against the wall, his broad hand holding my throat. With a small squeeze, he could sever my airway. I latched one hand onto his forearm. A rush surged through my body and my heart pounded like wilderbeasts stampeding across the plains. With my other hand, I reached for the storm's power. A gust came rushing through the window, howling around the room, and recognition registered upon Hoaris's face. He released me and sagged at my side.

Kyr giggled. "Red Bear doesn't wake happily, lovely."

Hoaris scrubbed his hands over his face, rasping over his beard. "Did you . . ." He cleared his sleep deadened throat. "Did Filtch agree to send our message?"

"No," I said.

He looked at the Small Folk, confusion clearly drawing his brows to a peak. "So, what do we do now?"

Misha said, "We wait for your cold friend."

Thalaj.

I still worried but also wondered about Honera and the boys. "Where are the casteless?"

"Couple of dice games after you went, they left too." Hoaris lumbered to his feet, scrubbing sleep from the corners of his eyes. "Where is Thalaj anyway?"

At his question, a heavy clunk on the table echoed around the room. Thalaj stood, becoming visible as he left a spelled stone visible on the table. "I'm here."

I sucked in a breath, my hand covering my mouth. He appeared as he had before, carrying naught but his own weapons, but the angles on his face seemed chiseled in ice. By force, I had to hold myself in place to keep from leaping up, soaring toward him, and throwing my arms about him in a hug. Even if he hadn't reclaimed my scimitynes as I'd hoped, he'd returned safely before Alto-Trea's cloud castle departed. For that alone, I said thanks to the Holy Triad. Outside, morning was just beginning to break and Otarr would soon assume his watch over the day. If the Cloud Courtier's orders held true, the castle would be misting away like a morning fog. Standing, I approached him slowly, heeding the warning in his posture and still fighting the desire to rush to him. He stared at me, his dark eyes cold and his anger chilling the space between us. Frost Fighters controlled heat in the air, dispelling it at will as Thalaj often did when he was angry.

"I'm so sorry I wouldn't listen," I said. Clasping and wringing my fingers, I hoped his angst would ease now that we were all safely away. I refused to break eye contact as he glared at me, feeling I deserved his admonishment. So I waited.

He squeezed his eyes closed and took an audible breath. As he exhaled, the air fogged. My face felt cold and the hairs on my arms rose, but as soon as the cold had arrived, it receded. When he opened his eyes, he'd regained control. I touched his arm, growing more hopeful when he didn't recoil.

Hoaris leaned heavily on the other end of the table. "So . . . this Filtch person didn't agree to deliver the message. Whadda we do now? How do we get the message to Sarangarel?"

Kyr chattered, "Who's Sarangarel?"

I sighed. "She's the gnoble of the Stone Singer caste residing in the city's keep at the moment. We had hoped she would sponsor a ship to sail across the Syrensea."

I crossed to the window, regretting to some extent that we'd followed Honera and hadn't made progress on understanding what it'd cost to hire a crew for ourselves. The one sailor had warned of his departure on the morn; had we missed an opportunity through our dalliance? Would a white-flagged ship still remain at the docks by the time we returned?

Misha folded his arms over his chest and issued a harrumph, pulling me from my musings.

"You people and your castes," he said.

Raising both brows, I stared at him wordlessly. The statement seemed odd after the story he'd told me of his exile. The small people had rankings too, so how was it that ours seemed so strange?

Chatter passed between Misha and Kyr, too fast for me to follow. Just as I was considering using the invisibility spelled stones myself, Misha said, "I'll go in. Where is this gnoble?"

"Wait." I looked intently at each of my friends' faces, dreading the need to deliver the news I'd learned from Filtch. "I'm not sure she'll accept us now."

Thalaj quirked a brow. "What do you mean? Gaining an audience was the challenge. She'd certainly listen to a request from an Evangale."

I held a fist to my mouth, trapping the words that thought to spew forth, and considered how much I should share regarding my conversation with the Swan. I crossed the room and took a seat. At length, I said, "I fear I may have lost any influence I once possessed."

A chair scraped across the floor, and Thalaj dropped into the seat beside me. "At the risk of repeating myself, Mairynne, what do you mean?"

I took a deep breath and told them everything. That Karynne had ascended to the Serpentine Throne. That she'd offered a reward to have me and Thalaj returned to Stormskeep. That I didn't know how it all had happened. And that it would be risky now to trust any one of the gnobles at this point. My hand locked around my necklace stones, heat suffusing my palm. "But one thing is certain . . . we need to get out of Nantai, find my father, and then return to set things right in Stormskeep."

As I'd narrated the information from the night before, Hoaris, Misha, and Kyr had also taken seats, and we sat in silence for a long while after I finished.

Awkwardly, Misha asked, "Why don't we hunt down that Cloud Courtier and make him ferry us across the sea? He seemed fond of you as we left."

Shaking my head, I said, "That Cloud Courtier is as dangerous as they come, I believe. Filtch is an illusion, and I still don't know fully what he has to do with the casteless. His real name is Alto-Trea, and I wouldn't trust him with the simplest task, let alone something so important."

Thalaj agreed. "All that matters little, though. Their magic is connected to Nantai. Their sky islands wouldn't travel past the Vesterisles."

Hoaris stood and held out a hand to Misha. "Give me one of those invisibility rocks. I'll go in and find this Sarangarel."

My first guard placed a hand on the big man's arm, urging him back into his chair. "Hoaris, can you watch while I sleep for a couple of hours?"

"I should go now," he objected. "Catch her before the day gets too far in."

Thalaj shook his head. "If I can get a couple of hours of sleep, we can all go together. We'll find her while she's alone. She'll listen to us together"—his face hardened—"whether by her own will or by force, she'll listen."

TWENTY-ONE

The Stone Lady

INVISIBLE BY THE SPELL ON the stones and unable to speak lest we give ourselves away, the five of us snuck through the stone halls in search of the Stone Lady, Sarangarel, occasionally ducking to one side as a group of Stone Singer servants passed. The house was abuzz with daily activity, and if I were to guess, these people had the keenest sense of hearing of all the castes and the casteless. Though seemingly so graceless in their stout statures, their ears twitched at the slightest sound. When others were around, we carefully matched our steps to theirs lest we draw attention to our invisible intrusion.

After some time, we arrived at a room from where more Singers came and went than the others. Standing in a nearby corner, we watched and waited to discern the patterns of the servants. When a last group filtered out, Kyr scurried forth and held the door while we slid inside. The rooms to my measure were almost a replica of my own at Stormskeep, and I felt a momentary pang, a longing for home. But as I looked around at the things, the differences became starker than the similarities. The Stone craftsmen had inlaid gemstones upon everything—a mirror trimmed in shimmering green, a nearby sofa with burnt-umber stones on the woodwork, the utensils on the table decorated with white stones on the handles. The glittering stones gave the room an ostentatious feel similar to the necklace Sarangarel had presented at my ascension.

The rooms were quiet, and the five of us stood in silence for several moments trading questioning glances until the soft flap of a page turning alerted us to the space behind the curtains. Someone was reading on the veranda behind the material gently swaying in the breeze. I, being the closest to the door, went through and found Lady Sarangarel reclined in a chair and indeed reading a book.

The vision before me stole my breath. No longer in regalia fit for ascension pomp, the curves I'd judged before as stocky and stout now appeared plump and inviting. Her hair, customarily woven in tight braids before, now hung in a heavy dark-brown curtain over one shoulder in flowing waves. Her slanted eyes caressed the words on the page, and I wondered how they might caress a person.

Heat suffused my cheeks as Thalaj stepped to my side, nudging me to behind her.

As we'd decided before, he would present himself to her alone and beg her help in their situation. We held no certainty our plan would work, but it seemed worth a try. Mayhap I allowed him this action out of guilt over my previous poor decision or possibly wisdom lay in deferring to his greater experience.

Thalaj placed the stone upon the railing, whispered the words, and lifted his hand. The air shimmered around him as the spell lifted and he became visible to more than just our party. I twisted my lips, musing that he could speak the spell while I still needed assistance from the Small Folk. Something I'd need to revisit.

Sarangarel didn't move, didn't so much as lift her head from the words upon the pages of her book, and her voice was even as she spoke. "Have you orders for my death, Shadow?"

Thalaj gave a wry smile, one that said many things but nothing at all, one that would tell you things true and imagined; but having not peered up from her book, Sarangarel could not have seen this smile. I, on the other hand, watched as he stalked in front of her like the predatory nekodai of the Iced Plains. Grace and power coiled within every one of his muscles. He prowled. Death walking the veranda in the daylight and preparing himself for a civilized conversation.

Sarangarel moved her hand to the table at her side, lifting a steaming cup to her lips. She sipped but still said naught. Had I been the one faced with such an intruder, I don't believe I would have been as calm as this gnoble. Either she had made peace with whatever fate and Thalaj had in store for her, or she knew something we did not. I looked toward the door, but seeing no other threat, turned back to the scene.

Thalaj tempered his smile and said, "Quite the contrary, Lady Sarangarel. I have come to ask your help."

The thought might have startled someone less poised than the Stone Lady, but from my point of view, she didn't move so much as her little finger. Things between the two seemed tensely cordial, but Thalaj's posture said anything but.

"Thalaj Northerngale, First Guard to Kōgō Mairynne Evangale," she said, my name a bit louder than the rest. Folding the book and placing it onto the table, she added, "The rumors of your stealth are true, but I must inquire about this stone you use." Her head tilted slightly, suggesting she appraised the stone as she finished.

"This?" Thalaj reached for the stone. "It's merely a rock." Having dispelled the magic when he placed it on the railing, he tossed the thing to her.

Sarangarel raised her hand slowly as if she had all the time under Otarr's watchful gaze, and even so slow, she plucked the stone from midflight. "Then I must inquire after how it sings of invisibility."

"That is beyond my knowledge," Thalaj said simply with a small shrug. It wasn't a lie. Though he could use the words to activate and deactivate the spell, I didn't believe he had the casting knowledge to bespell stones. At least it was a talent I'd never witnessed.

Misha and Kyr were smiling beside me, but they stifled their chatter for the time being in favor of maintaining the silence. Hoaris stood stock-still, hand on his hilt, and ready for whatever might come next, but he betrayed no reaction to the conversation before us.

Lady Sarangarel twirled the plain white stone in front of her face, examining something I couldn't discern. "This is no natural song," she mused. "The veins remain quiet." And with that, she tossed it back.

Thalaj's movement, unlike hers, was quick. His hand blurred as he snatched the stone from the air.

She tilted her head slightly. "I'll leave you your secret for now. But I do find it strange that you, of all the people in Nantai, would be here begging a favor given the fact that there is a price posted for you that would make it well worth my while to detain you. But I am no foolish woman. Please"—she flourished a hand—"be on with it."

Thalaj tipped his head forward respectfully. "Lady Sarangarel, we would ask for you to arrange passage for our party of five upon a ship across the Syrensea."

The gnoble of the Stone Singers barked a throaty laugh. "I have two questions for you, Shadow. First, why is it you assume this is within my powers? Secondly, what would be in this bargain for me or my people?"

The way they used titles and names seemed a dance. They traded them as if they would either honor or slight the other. I couldn't distinguish the intentions. *Shadow* would seem, in my mind and the gnoble's tone, to be an insult, but the title meant prestige to those of the Unseen. Would Sarangarel possess such knowledge? By the grace of the Triad, though, she hadn't referred to his blended heritage, both Storm Sorcerer and Frost Fighter. Perhaps there was a tinge of respect laced into her words, but it confounded me.

I rubbed the bespelled stone still resting in my hand and hiding me from sight. A quick toss would reveal my presence and allow me to join the banter, but a watchful Hoaris read my intent and shook his head slowly. He was right. Prudence bade that I should trust and wait for Thalaj's cue as to when I could safely join the conversation.

My first guard rubbed a hand over his stubbled jawline. "I am unable to make an offer we can pay in the present hour, but I do speak on behalf of the Evangales."

Sarangarel stood, issuing another humorless laugh. "*The* Evangale *herself* placed the reward upon your return to Stormskeep. Why am I to believe that you would be able to offer more?" She sauntered toward Thalaj, swaying a hip suggestively toward him. I felt a stab through my chest, and my mouth went bone-dry. She ran a finger, nails lacquered blood red, down his chest. Her eyes followed.

I made to move, but Hoaris held up a forestalling hand.

Thalaj glanced over her head to where I stood. He couldn't see my reaction without being under the cloak of invisibility, and for that small wonder, I felt immense relief. Jealousy was an unbecoming mask upon any who wore it.

Sarangarel lifted her gaze back to his. "And, were I to detain you, mightn't the youngest Evangale come in search of her most favored guard?"

I took one step. Hoaris gave me a look, his lips in a tight line, eyes wide and hard with warning. On a slow inhale, I worked to hold myself in place, releasing the air bit by bit.

Thalaj smiled, but I saw naught but calculation in his dark eyes. "There isn't need for you to wait." He lifted a hand in my general direction. His eyes followed but looked to my side ever so slightly. Naturally, as eye contact with the invisible was nigh impossible.

Unless the person in question was Alto-Trea.

I shook away that thought. Another time.

The Stone Singer turned. Shorter than me, as I could tell by the top of her head not quite reaching Thalaj's shoulder. Indeed, she was lovely. She wore her dark curls as a waist-length cloak, and her plentiful curves—shadowlike under the simple shift and so unlike my own—begged for a caress. Swallowing and thoroughly confused, I stood straighter and reminded myself that despite whatever my sister had done that I was still the rightful heir to the Serpentine Throne by Tennō Atheryn Evangale's decree. That was if, and a doubtful if, my father *had* perished.

With the thoughts of Father, the stone resting beneath my tunic flared, reassuring me further.

Hoaris held out a hand for my stone. I can only imagine the vision Sarangarel beheld as I shimmered into view. Each time I'd seen someone revealed, I'd also seen the stone they'd dropped. Handing my stone to someone who remained unseen, it must have appeared that I stepped from thin air. I pushed my chin a little higher, the thought giving me more confidence. And there upon the balcony in the open air, I spread my other hand and called the wind.

A soft breeze lifted my hair and stirred Sarangarel's hair-made cloak. Behind her, Thalaj gave a small smile as our eyes met. Then he said, "It is our understanding that your caste always welcomes new opportunities for trade and the possibility of discovering gemstones currently unavailable in Nantai."

"And so," I added, the imagined bonds upon my voice finally releasing, "given your relative wealth, we hoped that you would sponsor a ship on our behalf. Once we've completed our travels and I return to Stormskeep, I will ensure that the treasurers send thrice the bounty upon our souls."

"Indeed, that is quite the offer, young *kōgō*."

I looked at her curiously, still confounded by the usage of the titles, and even more so by this one. Across all castes, that was the most sacred title for the empress of the people, and she had just given it to me. Yet my sister had ascended to the Serpentine Throne. Did that mean Sarangarel supported my plight rather than Karynne's? Did that mean she knew more than she let on? Did that mean she would help? Instead of asking these questions directly, I waited to see how she would play her turn.

She began to pace, though to call it pacing would give it urgency. No, she began walking, swinging her hips with every step, back and forth along the edge of the veranda, and in silence.

I waited.

Observe and listen.

And Thalaj waited as well.

At length, she started calculations aloud. She named off the crew members necessary to man a ship, each with a number attached. How she kept the figures within her head I couldn't fathom, but I had never been one for numbers.

"How long do you believe this journey will take?" she asked.

I had no answer.

Thalaj, clearly unable to guess at a duration either, said, "As long as it must."

"And to where did you say you wished to sail?"

I took a breath to speak, but my guard held up a hand. "We didn't. Only across the Syrensea."

Sarangarel sighed. "You must forgive me, but without these details, I fail to see how this voyage is worth my time and investment."

Urgency built and fueled my angst over the possibility of losing the opportunity. I started, "Lady Saranga—" but she silenced me with a small, dismissive wave.

"Kōgō and her Shadow," Sarangarel mused, tapping a lacquer-tipped finger against her lips. She walked the terrace for several more long moments in silence. Clearly more variables and the sky's gods only knew what other thoughts raced through her mind, but she reserved those reflections.

I went to stand beside Thalaj. Cold poured off of him in waves, a sure sign that he worked with all his might to maintain solid control. Though he managed them well enough, politics and negotiations were not his favored activities. I understood. And like him, I felt better, more at ease, with a blade in each hand and performing the dances of death. I'd only begun to learn, but he'd honed them for so many years, they existed in all his movements. This I knew now as his student. But there on Lady Sarangarel's veranda was not a place for such things, and then was not the time. He understood that as well as I. After our conversations with the deck hands on the docks, after my encounter with Filtch, and with the measly mon within our purses, the Stone Lady seemed our last hope for gaining this passage. All we needed now was for her to decide in our favor.

Sarangarel shook her head. "My people have a saying. Mayhap you're familiar with it?" She stopped, facing us and awaiting our answer.

Thalaj and I exchanged a clueless look.

"Well. It goes like so . . . 'The world's heart gem holds the steepest value, albeit a single stone and one nigh impossible to obtain. Shallow stones will provide.' "

The last of this I'd heard from her lips before. She'd said as much upon the sky island that boasted the High Cloud Court during one of the many ascension ceremonies I'd endured. Court. Having the first part of the saying, I understood better, and it made sense to the nature of the Stone Singers. They were a solid people, and though the gems they traded were of great value to their patrons in Nantai and beyond, they only dug deep enough to provide for their people.

Her eyes were rueful, couldn't quite make contact with either my own or Thalaj's. But then she changed in an instant. "But I am well provided for and have more than necessary. My people have done well under Tennō Atheryn Evangale, then under Kōgō Mairynne Evangale." She looked at me then. "Although the short time you ruled may not warrant entries in the history books. There are signs that the newest leader of the Nantai people has less pure intentions in her heart."

Karynne.

The thought sliced into me, a painful knife searing me in two. I despised that my eldest sister sowed discord among my people. I'd worried at one time when she'd been so eager to guide my decisions, but during my ascension I'd believed those issues resolved. How naïve I had been. Thalaj moved closer; had he sensed my pain? Nadia, my mother's twin sister, had been the one person I had felt most confident would hold to my father's ideals and to mine. Regretfully, it seemed she no longer held such power.

Someday, somehow, I had to rectify the situation in Stormskeep as well . . . *after* I found Father.

The stones flared.

"Your sentiment is much welcome, Sarangarel," I said in gratitude.

Sarangarel lifted her chin. "There is naught for you to welcome. I believe our people need you as *kōgō*. I believe your father showed wisdom in his choice of heir. I do not know how your sister came into her ascension or what happened to Nadialynne Riversgale." Her eyes darkened. "I do hope your sweet aunt is well," she added with a mournful glance.

I took a step closer. "Does this mean you will help us?"

She pursed her lips. "I will, but as you well know, bargains with the Stone Singers are ne'er inexpensive." Her eyes shifted between me and Thalaj.

"Then name your price, Lady Sarangarel," Thalaj snapped.

Chills ran over my arms. I could hear ice in his voice. His tolerance for such politics ran thin, and I breathed a sigh of relief that we hadn't allowed him to come into this meeting alone. In truth, he should have dealt with Filtch while I managed the Stone Lady. I glanced over to the space where Hoaris and the Small Folk had been standing—still stood, I hoped. I considered the Tsinti and our time with them, the people in Safaia and Kōkai, even the sailor Jerek; all people in Nantai deserved better.

Whatever her conditions, I would honor them.

"I have three requirements," she said, her eyes flashing deviously. She stepped to the railing where Thalaj had deposited his stone. "First, you will share with me the secret of your unnatural stone."

Thalaj shifted, moving slightly in front of me. "That is easy enough," he said, "but we will have your remaining demands before we decide."

"Of course, I will send a party of my people on the journey with you. They shall be allowed to pursue errands on my behalf." Sarangarel looked past my guard, holding and embracing my eyes with her own. "And finally, I will have Mairynne for the evening—for the late meal *and* to warm my bed this night."

Twenty-Two

The Yisun

BRIGHT OTARR DIMMED AND MADE his way toward sleep for the evening, and I stood within the Stone Lady's suite, unable to divine where the night would take us. Offering her the secret of the spelled stones and agreeing to take her people with us upon the journey had been the easy part of the deal. For the rest . . . the negotiation took the better part of the day.

As soon as she'd made her demand, the heat had dissipated from the veranda. Shards of ice had flashed blue in my guard's eyes, and I'd believed only violence would resolve the situation. As stunned as I had been by Sarangarel's demand, I had stammered to object. But Thalaj's outcry had overshadowed my own. And despite invisibility, Hoaris's blade had sung free of its scabbard, calling Sarangarel's attention to the seemingly empty space near the door. I had reached for my first guard, seized his arm just before he started for the Stone Lady.

"There is little cause for attack. It's merely a decision to be made," I whispered. "*My* decision." Earlier, she had been so unwilling to even consider our plight for any reasons beyond her own wealth. That she asked so little else as payment made her offer near impossible to refuse.

When he'd turned to me, his face had been a whitish shade of green. His dark eyes had implored with me. "Mairynne, no. You cannot."

Afterward, my attention had been focused for hours upon trying to convince him that this would be okay. I'd stopped short of issuing a command. After much debate, and once provided with comfortable accommodations just across the hall from Sarangarel's rooms, he had relented. But he'd carried a bitterness with him that made my heart ache.

Within the first quiet moments while Sarangarel went to speak with a servant about our meal, I had a long overdue opportunity to sort out my own feelings about the arrangement. My mind. My heart. My body. They were all at odds with one another like three siblings vying desperately to have a parent's sole attention for herself—even if only for a time. That scenario, I knew well; but to have that same battle raging within myself was a matter unto itself. Though my mind spun with all of my first guard's logical arguments—that I was selling my body, that we would figure out another way, that I was too young yet to understand the implications—my heart ached for the words he hadn't said. Throughout this confusion, my body tingled with anticipation. I had noticed her voluptuous beauty early in our meeting, and I had felt a pang of jealousy that she'd swayed her curves in Thalaj's direction. Whether the jealousy had been over him or her, I couldn't be certain.

And for all of the desire building, Thalaj was right. Indeed, I was inexperienced when it came to this—beyond the years where other girls had explored such things, young nevertheless.

But as the princess and the decreed heir, I hadn't the liberties of most. Once, I'd listened dreamily as Jessamyne Feathergale had spoken of her first kiss. We'd giggled over her description of the awkward wetness, but I'd imagined it as my own experience with the young man by the name of Northerngale who'd recently joined the guard that protected the royal family.

Thalaj.

I sighed.

Upon that thought, Sarangarel appeared with two fluted glasses, a deep amber liquid within. She'd changed clothes, now wearing a strapless shift the color of the deep red stones that decorated her neck and wrists. The dress shimmered as it caught Otarr's dying light. She handed me a glass and placed her own on a table upon which I assumed we'd dine. From a small cabinet, she retrieved more gemstones, each roughly the size of her fist. As she placed them upon the table, she closed her eyes briefly. When she lifted her hand, they began to glow.

She smiled, more beautiful than she'd been in the daylight, and lifted her own glass to me in a toast. "The wine will ease you, my kōgō." To my ears, her voice sounded at once a soft and warm caress around the title I hadn't wanted before. There and then, I found her use of it more inviting than threatening. Despite the knowledge that she'd purchased me for the night, I craved what she offered—whatever that was.

I wondered briefly how this would impact my ties with Thalaj, but I put that thought out of my mind. Though I would have welcomed more, our relationship hadn't been one of intimacy. He'd countered that notion by repeatedly citing the impurity of his bloodlines. Another idea I cared little about. But this evening, he had no place within Sarangarel's rooms. Dinner went on, light conversation ensued, and I took my second glass of wine; my soul eased while Selene climbed into the sky above Kōkai.

The meal complete, Sarangarel took my hand and led me into her bedchamber. I stopped at the door, pulling my hand from hers. What terror she read written across my face, I couldn't say. Yet her only reaction was a small smile. Circling the room, she touched several stones, singing them to life and casting the room in a soft amber light.

When she returned to me, she offered a soft shift. "Here, you'll be more comfortable for the evening in this rather than those travel clothes. I'll be back shortly." And she left me alone in the most private of her rooms.

Examining the material of the shift she had offered, it glittered, and I looked closer. The seamstress had woven a thousand or more tiny white gems into the fabric. I marveled at the softness given that stones decorated it. As I placed my own clothes on a chair nearby, the bronze cuff a garnish on top, words from earlier rang through my mind: "*. . . purchased . . . a whore . . .*" The Nantai people didn't frown upon the profession. In truth, in Tsanseri's court, the Courtiers and those who visited celebrated it. The only people who would ever know of this assignation were those within my small party, and beyond that knowledge, only Sarangarel and I would know what transpired within these rooms. With eyes closed, I took a deep, cleansing breath and let it out on an audible sigh.

"Mairynne"—Sarangarel's voice hugged my name as it had my title—"you need not worry or fear. I will not force you into any act against your wishes." When she finished, her voice was near, behind me.

She'd read my worries well, but where there was trepidation, there was also desire. I turned with a smile and reached nervously for her. "May Atun, Otarr, and Selene help me," I said, looking deep into her eyes and moving my body closer to hers. "Lady Sarangarel, my body has an appetite I've never truly known. Show me if you will, not because I am offering myself as payment, but because you have the same desire as I. If this is anything less than that, I ask that we not dive further into this intimacy."

She licked her lips. "It is naught but desire, my *kōgō*." She cupped my cheek and our lips met.

So much tenderness.

Anything but awkward, she tasted sweet and rich like the wine. For many hours into that night, we explored one another, sought pleasure, laughed, and within each other's arms, we erased another line between our castes.

◇◇

I AWOKE TO A new and colorful world, my body and soul having experienced delights I hadn't imagined possible. My muscles felt strained in new and unexpected places. Within the drapery around Lady Sarangarel's bed, cocooned in fluffy blankets and plump pillows, she kissed me awake from my neck up to my lips. A smile spread across my face when I looked up into her eyes.

She returned the smile and thanked me for an amazing evening, but then regret settled over her brow. "While I'd relish spending another day here with you, I have duties. We should make the arrangements for your ship."

"Wait." I reached for her, ducked my head for a moment in shyness, and then lifted my gaze again. "I must thank you too for last night." My voice wavered, but it was all the grace I could muster.

She squeezed my hand and pulled me from the bed. We both stood naked and glorious in Otarr's morning light.

"Would you bathe before we deal with your jealous young man?" Her smile seemed downright devious.

"He . . . he's not *mine*," I stammered, blinking in disbelief.

She flashed a knowing smile and said, "More yours than you know," as she reached for a bathing cloth from a tall set of drawers. "Despite the privilege you have granted me for a night, I won't have you beyond. You'll have him and he'll have you for much longer."

The words reminded me of those the Zofi had said when we'd first encountered Thalaj working within his bonds. "*That one,*" the Tsinti witch wife had said, "*he will always be there for you. There will come a time when you'll doubt but rest easy as he will always return.*" I hoped they held true.

I bathed for the first time since the caverns beneath the trading town, Safaia, luxuriating in the sweetly scented waters. The feeling of cleanliness gave me a sudden flush of embarrassment over the intimacy with Sarangarel and having not washed before, but she hadn't protested. I emerged into Sarangarel's empty main room with hair wet and wearing the freshest of my travel clothes. It felt as if I were a new person. Despite the pleasure of the night before and the new appetites awoken within me, my journey called.

I grasped the stones at my neck. "Father," I said on a sigh.

Heat flared to life in my palm, but it seemed slower to warm this time. Somewhere he awaited, and time grew critical. I'd reset my determination and stepped toward the door, intent on finding my travel companions. We'd dallied here in the City by the Sea for far too long.

Sarangarel reappeared as I reached the door and exited her rooms first. Across the hall, she knocked and waited. It was Misha who answered and welcomed us inside. He and the Stone Lady bantered for a bit while I searched the rooms, finding only Kyr and Hoaris, both wide-eyed and brows raised with apparent worry, or mayhap warning. Where was Thalaj? Did I dare ask?

But the conversation between Sarangarel and Misha persisted, filling the room. At length, Sarangarel asked, "Now that I've returned her, will you teach me how to place the spell upon your stones?"

Misha's laugh rang like chimes in the wind. "I cannot teach you such a spell. Your mouth isn't formed properly to make the words."

She stiffened. "But this is part of the bargain."

Kyr jumped in. "The bargain was"—she raised both brows, widening her eyes—" '*you will share with me the secret of your unnatural stone.*' The secret is that there is a spell cast upon the rock by the Small Folk. There is a word, *mekoilieu,* that you speak to activate and deactivate the spell. That word is pronounceable in your tongue, and therefore you may use the spells already cast upon the stone. You made no demands that we teach you how to create the spell." Kyr shrugged and gave me a wink.

I mouthed the word, committing it to memory, "Mekoilieu."

The Small Folk, if I had ever met any linguists, were the sheer embodiment. They'd caught me once or twice in the technicalities of my words and the nuances of language. Sarangarel looked at me as if she wanted to ask how I tolerated such insolence. All I could do was shrug in the same manner Kyr had done. But I didn't wink, because I knew too well her frustration.

Sarangarel lifted her chin, the paths in her mind working again. "Well and so. Does it have to be a particular stone, or will any gem work?"

Misha took a seat. "The only requirement is that it be of a solid color. Mottling within the rock won't hold that spell."

The Stone Lady went to another chest and pulled a handful of bright gems— greens, oranges, yellows, in various sizes but all small enough to tuck safely into one's pocket without being seen—and dumped them upon the table. Misha picked through them, found the three largest, and said, "Three. I will offer three. The spell wears on me, you see."

"And what of her?" Sarangarel pointed to Kyr.

They chattered, pitch too high and fast for my understanding, but at last, Kyr shook her head. "Our women aren't the spellcasters."

Misha added, "Things could go too awry. It's too much risk for her to try. I have offered more than you bargained for yesterday upon your balcony." He sat back from the stones, folding his arms over his chest, and allowed his dangling foot to swing some ways above the floor.

Sarangarel agreed, but within the set of her jaw, she betrayed that it displeased her to have her expectations lowered so.

"Find your young guard," she said to me, caressing my arm and grasping onto my hand. "I will retrieve the Singers who will accompany you over the Syrensea and return shortly." She rushed from the room, her hips swaying faster.

Hoaris barked a laugh. "You got her well, little one."

Misha gathered the small stones she'd left on the table—all except the three largest he'd set aside—and tucked them in his pouch.

I shot him a questioning stare.

He lifted a shoulder. "She left it up to us how exactly we shared that information. She should be more precise in her demands."

Hoaris roared again as Misha turned toward the three stones and began whispering over them.

"Where is Thalaj?" I asked, at last having the opportunity to satisfy my curiosity.

Hoaris turned solemn and pointed toward a door.

Kyr eyed me. "Careful, lovely."

Heedless of the warning in the big man's posture or upon the little woman's face, I went for the door. Inside, the moisture from my breath created clouds, and I rubbed my arms to create my own heat. He had drawn the curtains against Otarr's watchfulness. As the door behind me closed, the only light was a small slit in the heavy drapes. There wasn't enough to see the room given I'd entered from a brighter area. If it was a mirror layout of Sarangarel's, a bed lay to my left. I turned in that direction, but his word came from my other side.

"Here." Quiet and hoarse and gruff, a tone I had never heard in Thalaj's voice before.

I swallowed, thankful for the cover of darkness to hide the unspoken words I'm sure shone upon my face. "All is well. We should be able to set sail at first light. Lady Sarangarel has sent word to the docks and went to collect the party that will travel with us upon the ship."

"All. Is. Well?" he rasped. "More apt to say all is done." A surge of cold rolled from the direction of his voice.

I didn't know how to answer the short and bitter words, so I stood awkwardly wringing my hands until he spoke again.

"Leave me. I will come momentarily."

I went, the doorknob like ice under my touch. Time. Would time ease his cold rage? I'd give him that for now, but once we were on our way, I'd have to force conversation.

In the common area, I wondered if what Sarangarel had said was true. Could he possibly still be *my* young man, or had that changed after my choice last night? I remained torn, confused. He'd always told me that *we* couldn't be because of his blended blood. Was he angered because I'd chosen someone of an even lower caste or because he wanted something for us? He couldn't believe that I'd remain virginal for the entirety of my days, so it must have been that I'd chosen someone beneath me . . . and beneath even his station. The thought that he held so much stock in this hells-imposed caste hierarchy saddened me even more than that he'd rejected me under the claim of his unworthiness.

I dropped into the chair beside Kyr. She grabbed my wrist and squeezed, and when I looked up, she offered me deep sympathy in her eyes and a rueful smile.

Misha had finished spelling the stones and rested with his head against the back of the chair and his eyes closed.

Hoaris came over and placed a strong hand upon my shoulder. "Give him space, and he'll return."

The door slammed and heavy booted feet traipsed inside—three Stone Singer men and two women stood to the side while Sarangarel walked between them, head held high and a bejeweled headdress closely resembling a crown resting upon a nest of sable-brown curls. She'd put away her soft and sheer robes for the regalia that bespoke gnobleship among her people. Her gait wasn't one of grace as she entered, but one of sturdiness and strength. Beyond doubt, I knew that she had earned her place among the Stone Stingers with that very prowess.

As I stood and rounded the table, she cut her eyes to me for only a split second, then held a hand toward the closest in an official manner. "These men will accompany you."

The two females boasted tight curls and plentiful breasts, but elsewise might have been men themselves for all I could tell under the heavy armor. Both men and women were broad at the shoulders. For the men, conversely, their chests lacked the soft round cleavage I'd so pleasantly experienced with Sarangarel the night before. Noting that she mentioned only men, I wondered if she intended the five of them to accompany my party or only the three males.

Sarangarel continued, "They are *yisun*." And she introduced them each in turn—Yisun Timur, Yisu Jaliqai, Yisun Nachin, Yisun Baidu, and Yisu Chambui.

I'd listened carefully, but with the foreign nature of the names and her natural inflection, even the first one mentioned escaped my mind.

The man, clearly reading my failure to retain the information, stepped forward with a cocked grin and a fist over his chest. "Timur. Yisun leader." Head bowed, he dropped to a knee briefly, then stood and returned to ranks.

I felt a cool draft from the side. Thalaj, hearing the commotion, must have decided to join us. A sigh lightened the weight in my shoulders, a grateful feeling that the breeze no longer resembled winter's gale.

The remaining Stone Singers made the same introductions as Timur, and I inferred that the first part—yisun, yisu for the women—was a title or shared name. A unit maybe. I'd ask later, but for the moment, I focused on their unique names. Timur, Jaliqai, Nachin, Baidu, Chambui; I worked to commit them to memory.

After we'd exchanged introductions, Sarangarel came to me and offered me a warm embrace. When we parted, she glanced at the door where I knew Thalaj stood, from where I still felt a cool breeze wafting around the room. Her eyes returned to mine, and she said quietly, "Thank you again, Kōgō. We'll certainly meet again." Then louder so the rest of the room could hear, "You must pardon me now. We have made all the arrangements with a ship called the *Swell Mistress*. You have the freedom to wander the house. Our servants will see to your meals here in this suite. You may rest in the rooms here this evening. Timur and the other yisun will return for you an hour before Selene passes the skies to Otarr. They will escort you to the docks where Captain Asahi will be ready for departure. I wish you well on your voyage." She kissed my cheek and left, followed by her yisun.

Alone with my small party, silence hung, a deadly chill in the room. I turned to meet dark and hard eyes and pleaded with my own gaze for him to thaw, if only a bit. Instead, he looked at no one other than me, then dropped his eyes to the floor. Without a word, Thalaj followed in the trail of Sarangarel and the yisun.

Twenty-Three

An Unexpected Gift

EARLY MORN—MORE THE SLEEPING HOUR than when people greeted the day in earnest—we awoke and departed from the keep at Kōkai. For the remainder of the day, into the eve, and during the night before we took our leave, I never encountered the Stone Lady again to bid her farewell. Though Sarangarel held a piece of my heart, the road, the sea, and Father called to me. And alas, farewells were too final. A smile lifted the corners of my lips as I looked over my shoulder at the white stone walls. One day, mayhap we would meet again.

On this night, the clouds hid Selene's face within the skies. Heavy and woolen, a gray cloak covered Kōkai, though there was no storm, no energy crackling, no thunder rolling or lightning biting through the darkness. It misted. I lifted my face toward the skies and tiny droplets prickled my nose, cheeks. The veil covering the City by the Sea, Nantai, and at least part of the Syrensea cried upon us.

Thalaj walked ahead. For my part, a distance between us had grown I wouldn't have wished. Yet I could not change my decision to remain with Lady Sarangarel two nights before. And had I the magic of reversing time, I wouldn't choose differently. The only hope I had for him now was for time to heal the burden.

A door within my life's house had closed, another ending felt keenly as we approached the docks. Did the feeling lie in parting from Nantai? Or mayhap it was my soul ripping away from who and what I'd always known, away from all I considered my own. Certainly away from Thalaj. I peered back at the white-walled city, bidding her farewell. Time, distance, and the unknown awaited. The waves beyond the dock rolled gently, calling me onward. The last to go, I lowered my head and boarded the ship—a swell mistress indeed.

Captain Asahi shouted orders all around, sailors bustled about on his command, and my travel companions went below deck to settle into their cabins. The sailors loosened the ropes, freeing the vessel from the dock, and pushed away. The ship floated, directionless.

For all the commotion about me, I felt alone. We'd made it one step closer to finding Father, and the stones upon my breast verily vibrated their approval. Hot and cold surged against my skin.

Alas, I turned my back, making for the underbelly to settle into my cabin as well.

A screech pierced the night.

Whirling, I sucked in a breath. My body trembled.

The blue dragon snaked toward the *Swell Mistress* from the skies above. Sailors clamored away. In her claws, something dangled. As she arrived, she encircled the ship, slithering through the air above the deck. Her motion caused a gust. My hair whipped like a banner in the night. On her third pass, she swooped down and dropped the package not a dozen paces from where I stood speechless.

She splashed into the water and raised her head above, fixating me with her diamond-like eye. Mayhap I imagined as much, but I believe she nodded just before she arose into the sky and disappeared into the blanket over Nantai.

I took one step . . . two . . .

The showers came heavier. My cloak clung damply to me as the water soaked through. My feet slipped on the wet deck as I rushed over. Pain sparked in my knees when I landed on the deck with a thud. Wet and reaching, I grappled at the straps.

Tears fell.

I grasped my weapon belt . . . the scimitynes Thalaj had bestowed upon me before we left Arashi. I clutched the scabbards to my chest . . . the very ones I'd believed lost forever to Alto-Trea upon his cloudy island.

Restored.

Part Three
Call of the Ryū Dragon

TWENTY-FOUR

A Different Tack

HEAVY RAIN POUNDED THE DECKS of the *Swell Mistress*. Alone amidst the scurrying sailors, I stood once again with my weapon belt in hand and turned to watch our departure from Kōkai, more commonly called the City by the Sea, on the western coast of Nantai. The clouds overhead drifted northward, the downpour cleared, and my tears dried along with it. Otarr, the god who watches Nantai by day, broke over the horizon. The ship's nose pointed westward, and I moved to the back railing. The white-walled City by the Sea shrank as Otarr climbed into the skies. As we sailed west, away from my country, the blue dragon had returned my weapons—scimitynes given to me by my protector, Thalaj. And even though he had still not spoken to me after my assignation with Sarangarel, having the blades within my grasp brought hope.

Despite being estranged, I would offer Thalaj his space and maintain that nugget of hope within my heart.

Misty wind pelted my face, lifted my hair and made it dance like a flag in the wind.

Captain Asahi took a space beside me, filled it with overwhelming height and lanky limbs. In my periphery, he swiped a cloth over his face, then secured his hat, the wide brim sheltering his eyes from the bright morning light. He leaned over and rested both elbows on the rail, which diminished him to roughly eye level. He trained his gaze to follow my own. "The Bright City we call her from the sea. A beauty, eh?"

"Hai." I gave him a weak smile. "It is."

Though hope shimmered within my heart because of the blue dragon's gesture, there were many things troubling me still. That morn, I sailed away from the only land

I'd ever known and loved, and I had left Nantai in turmoil at the hands of my sister. Thalaj had distanced himself from me, still present in body but absent otherwise. And I toiled over Father, although the last should be a happier thought as we were yet another step closer.

"We normally don't move away from shore quite this fast." Asahi rocked back onto his heels, pulling me from my thoughts. Then he leaned forward again.

I turned to him, pursing my brows in wonder as to what he meant.

He chewed on a stick, brown and long, and shrugged. "That is to say, if you maintain this gale, we'll overshoot the Vesterisles by a league. I need to gather the remainder of my crew from Lu Galen, or *you* will be forced to man the sails."

Whatever he insinuated fell short of my understanding. The look on my face must have said as much.

He went on, "I'd ask you to keep your winds to a minimum so I can keep control of this wench." He patted the boat railing thrice, winked, and left me there alone.

Pinching my eyes tight, I inhaled, collecting as much breath into myself as possible before releasing it. Of course. I'd called upon the wind without so much as a conscious thought. That he'd approached me about it meant the sailors must have been fighting against the force. I focused, brought the unconscious thoughts to the forefront of my mind, and released my hold on the magic. The wind eased. Mist no longer fell upon my cheeks, which glowed hot as I looked around. Watchful eyes averted here and there.

Facing the sunrise again, I decided I couldn't care or worry how others read my angst. How they judged me mattered little.

Before long, I felt another presence at my side—no, two. I stood between the two voluptuous yisu women. Unfortunately, they looked so much alike, I struggled to place which name belonged to which.

"The journey we face is long," the one on my right said.

I knew as much and fretted that it had begun at odds with the one person I trusted most in the world. With these two strangers, I hesitated to share the depth of my concern.

The woman on my right added, "You needn't worry overmuch." She sighed dismissively. "It's hard for men to brood for long."

"You're too blunt, Jaliqai," the other snapped. "I must apologize, my kōgō."

It eased me a bit that Jaliqai had been so forward. I chuckled. "Well and so, Chambui. I have enough confusion in my life. I appreciate Jaliqai's direct words. We'll all be better friends if you feel you may be forthright with me. And please, do not refer to me as kōgō."

"See, Chambui, she's who I said," Jaliqai said with an air of superiority.

To me, Chambui said, "Yisu Jaliqai may speak truth. Your shadowy friend will ease upon this ship because he has nowhere to run or hide from you." She glared at her friend. "But it could have been put to you with more delicacy and respect."

Jaliqai rushed to add, "I see the stubborn upon him, but the way he watches you and waits, he will come around probably sooner than seems logical."

"Thank you, Jaliqai," I said. "I do prefer the raw honesty," I added to them both. But I felt the need to direct things away from my worry. That Thalaj would come around was all I could hope for, but discussing it wouldn't bring his acceptance about any sooner. I'd caused the conflict by the time I had spent with Sarangarel, but I would never trade that experience, and what passed between us was private—something I'd never share with my guard and protector in word or deed. It had opened new possibilities to me and bloomed curiosity. In its own right, it held a beauty I couldn't have fathomed, nor could I explain it in words. However, it did make me wonder at the nature of relations and relationships between the Stone Singers in a more general sense. Looking between the two women beside me, I decided I'd ask when the time felt right and turned my attention to learning more about these people. My people still. "Yisu? Will you tell me about this title?"

With one last look, I turned my back on Nantai and the City by the Sea, and as we strode around the deck, Jaliqai started, "*Yisun* is an ancient term. In Nantai, it means *nine*."

"*The* nine," Chambui interjected. "The number nine is very lucky to our people."

"But there are only five of you," I objected.

Jaliqai chuckled. "There are nine, but the others remained with Gnoble Sarangarel for reasons threefold. The others have littles right now, and that is a rare gift they wouldn't leave unless it were a matter of life and death. Secondly, our peoples' leader never lets us all go on a mission together. There must always be someone to train others should we not return."

Silence fell for several minutes until I asked, "You mentioned a third?"

"Communication," Chambui said shortly.

I halted in my tracks, sucking in a sharp breath. "Communication? Across the Syrensea? How is that possible?"

Chambui clasped my hand in hers. "Kōgō Evangale, our Lady Sarangarel has said that we may trust you. Our men are skeptical." She looked down at our joined hands.

Jaliqai looked around as if wanting to make certain no one listened in on our conversation. "We are putting a lot of trust in you by sharing this secret. We ask that you keep it in confidence."

I nodded. "Of course."

Chambui squeezed my hand. "Even from your shadow."

My shadow. The label seemed fitting, yet aside from the Sarangarel and her Stone Singers, no one had called him that before. "Understood." I swallowed. "And . . . I will."

Jaliqai produced a blood-red stone, opaque as the night, from a pouch she wore around her waist. She held it in cupped hands so that only I could see, then tucked it back into her purse as quickly as possible. "It's the rarest gem we know. And our people have had them since before the first age. Stone Singers call it *yarikhgüi yarikh*, which literally translates to 'speak no speak,' but in Nantai, we simply say 'talking stone.' To our knowledge, there are only nine. One each in the custody of a yisun."

The other yisu urged us along. "Enough of that. Just so you know, we can use them if needed." Chambui grinned. "So let's talk of lighter things. The journey is long."

I learned a little about the lives of the Stone Singers that morning, that their lifespans were almost double that of the rest of the castes of Nantai. They weren't certain why, but their teachings said it had something to do with their connection to Mother Earth herself. The way they spoke of it, it seemed almost as if they worshipped her rather than the Triad, but I left that questioning for another day.

About their relationships, Chambui said, "It is almost impossible for us to mate with a singular person for so long. Everyone changes over time, so we dispelled the notion of monogamy long, long ago. The only time we settle is in the time we breed and raise littles. That is often enough for people to grow, change, and ready themselves for the next stage in their lives. Maybe it is another breeding cycle or maybe something different altogether."

The concept confounded me but seemed logical as they presented the notion. Given the Stone Singers' longevity, I inquired about Sarangarel's age. She'd looked older than me, but only by a matter of seasons, not decades. They both flinched, but in the end, Jaliqai said straightly, "She's just entered her second age."

My jaw hung. "You mean she's passed four hundred seasons?" That alone was longer than any Storm Sorcerer could hope to live.

The women both smiled and raised their brows in mirror images.

Jaliqai added, "Our bodies don't age until our last twenty or so seasons; the decline is quick. By the time we show our age, we are typically nearing our third age."

"Though," Chambui said, "there are those among us who have lived into a third age without showing the signs."

I strolled, in awe by the manner in which they revealed the knowledge of their people. They seemed to know more of the other castes, Storm Sorcerers included, than we knew of them, and I internally cursed our method of learning and bonding as a nation . . . heavy books penned by the first caste and handed down by decree from ruler to ruler. Each emperor or empress held so little knowledge about the world beyond Arashi and the High Cloud Courts. I wondered what facts they'd omitted from the histories with intent throughout the ages. It'd also been the Triad's duty to bless each and every book before it found its way into the library at Stormskeep. Had they had a hand in censoring information as well?

Certainly, the Storm Sorcerers believed it was a means of sharing knowledge—I had to believe that much of my caste and kin—but could they not have listened and observed first?

That I had never learned these basic details of a people I also called my own due to this inadequate practice angered me. If I were to ever repeat my ascension, I would decree changes to this tradition, that we would welcome those from other castes into our city to maintain histories of all our folk. Or mayhap we would allow them to pen their own and share them across the land. Perhaps by my decree, we could erase the notion of castes entirely. I sighed at the thought, doubtful that such a day would come. Yet one could hope.

I vowed then and there that when I restored my father to the throne, I would request these things of him before I took my leave. The small taste I'd had of other ways of life had whetted my appetite. I wanted to travel to the farthest corners of the world, meet as many people as possible, and learn their ways. The thought of sitting on a cold throne soured my stomach. Something had bored its way into my skin and bones, and I felt that seedling sprouting into an overwhelming desire to experience whatever this journey to find Father held and much, much more.

Over the next days, I came to know Yisu Chambui and Yisu Jaliqai better, and I had several occasions to witness the freedom of which they had spoken that first morning upon the *Swell Mistress*. The days were long in the hot season, and throughout every day and night, it seemed that Thalaj would avoid me as long as possible. I tried to take comfort in the things about him others had witnessed—that he would return to me time and time again, that jealousy angered him, that he watched from afar and tried to balance his ire with us still being there together . . . yet he still seemed reluctant.

One night, it remained light as we just finished the day's last meal. My party save Thalaj gathered around the large table above deck, Hoaris with his cup and dice.

Yisun Baidu dumped a large pile of gems upon the table that we'd use as currency for the betting. There were colors aplenty, and we each gathered the color of our choice. Mine were a deep amethyst, so dark purple they barely caught the light within their facets. Others were red, blue, orange, green, and almost any other color one could imagine. Baidu put away the leftovers and we diced for an hour or more, laughing as we passed stones to the right when we rolled a four, to the left when we rolled a five, and put it in the pot when we rolled a six. Everyone would blow on the dice for luck and hope to roll low numbers. When someone won the pot, they seized the pile of rainbow-colored stones in the center of the table.

On we played. The game remained friendly, and when someone ran out of stones, the others would return their color and we'd begin another game.

Just as Otarr sank in the sky, Captain Asahi arrived with a wooden cask under one arm and a lantern in the other.

Misha issued a peal of high-pitched laughter while he and Kyr dug into their purses. "Put that out." The small woman waved a hand at the lantern. "Things can get dangerous over dice. I'd hate to burn the ship."

Kyr placed four stones on the long table and set them to glow with a quick word. The captain gave a satisfied nod and extinguished the lantern in favor of the safer lights. He grabbed some metal cups and filled each from his cask, passing them around as he did. When I sipped, it burned a streak down my throat and a fiery shiver erupted from my stomach shaking my entire body.

"Whoa," I breathed as if trying to expel the fire from my throat.

Asahi dropped a hand on my back. "Take another. It gets better." He walked around the table. "May I join ya?"

A series of rumbles and cheers went up, and I tasted again. He was right; the warmth in my throat was nice the second time around, and even nicer with every drink following.

The dicing and drinking went on well into the night. At one point, I lamented for my trusted protector, but I tried hard to keep those thoughts at bay.

Selene was a sliver that night in the sky, and the stars were brighter than I'd ever seen. They swam in the darkness above as the ship rocked gently on the sea's waves beneath me. The combination was dizzying.

"They are pretty, lovely," Kyr said, pushing one of the lighted stones closer. "But you'll wanna keep level. Keep your eyes on this. That's good. You'll feel better that way."

We played some more. Laughter rang through the night and roared around the deck. It was the wildest night and time I could recall until people calmed and drifted toward sleep. While Jaliqai had retired with Timur the prior evening, she presently cuddled at the end of the table with another of the yisun, Nachin. The same was true with Chambui. She'd spent last evening with Nachin, but showed favor for Baidu.

This went on for a while, and I glanced at Timur. It appeared he'd be the lone man out that evening.

Seeing my glance, he gave a crooked smile and a half-laugh. "No worries about me. That one"—he nodded toward Jaliqai—"wore me out last night. I'll be in for a good sleep after this drink." He polished off the last of it and stood, holding onto the rail and still weaving as he made his way to the center of the ship where he could climb down to the private cabins.

I bit the inside of my lip, worrying if I'd be able to make that journey on my own. I watched after him and tried to plan my steps for some time. The laughter died out, and others retired for the night.

"Do you need some help there, Mairy?" Hoaris boomed.

I stared at the man's beard, red though I knew it was, it seemed dark gray in the night. *Fascinating,* I thought. Then, a pale hand from nowhere rested on his shoulder and a soft familiar voice said, "I have this, old friend."

Hoaris stood and left by way of the railing.

I looked up. He slipped out of the night's shadow, and I held his almond-shaped eyes with my own gaze as he sat across the table.

My eyes prickled as I breathed, "Thalaj?"

Twenty-Five

A Syren Song

MUCH LATER IN MY DARK cabin, I tried to find sleep. When the boat lurched, my stomach did the same. I didn't know what time it was, but I fumbled my way out of bed and onto my knees, flipping the bucket over just in time to catch the spew of burning liquor from my excess during the dice game. My core muscles clenched time and time again to rid my body of the poison I'd consumed. It may not have been poison in truth, but it felt so in the moment. When I'd emptied all that seemed possible, I sagged beside the bucket and leaned my head against the wall.

Above, heavy thuds, banging, scrapes, and squealing noises assaulted my ears and felt as if they ripped my head in two. I groaned. "Never. Never again," I said aloud.

"Never what?"

I cracked an eye open. The light in the door also hurt, but Thalaj stood there. Foggy memories returned. He'd helped me back to my cabin the night before. Had he gone then? No. I remembered him sitting beside me. On the—I looked at the bucket beside me and gagged again.

That must have been it. By the end, I had no more of the burning liquid coming as my gut muscles continued to spasm.

Thalaj passed me a cool cloth and draped another about my neck. I sat back against the wall again just as he turned for the door.

"Wait," I called. "What's happening? Where—" I had trouble uttering more.

"Lu Galen, but only long enough to unload and reload." His footsteps resumed, and the squeal of the door behind him ripped into my skull anew.

I pressed the cool cloth to my face. It felt good . . . relatively. But I'd wanted to see this place, to meet the people. Still a part of Nantai, they were *my people* too. I stumbled to my feet, noticing that I still wore the same clothes as I had the night before. Too much pain to care.

Above deck, there was commotion everywhere. Sweat coated my forehead and neck, and I felt at the same time cold and hot as I watched the yisun carry crates off the ship and others loading new crates onto the ship—the source of the awful sounds. At least it echoed less above deck. I went to the far rail and took a seat on an empty bench away from the commotion. I sat, keeping the wet cloth still around my neck, although it had grown warm against the heat of my body. Shakily, I patted my face with the other. I'd lost all contents within my stomach, so how did I still feel that bad?

From my seat, I glanced out over the tiny town, really no more than a scattering of thatched roofs upon glistening sand with a few palm trees shading doorways here and there. From the number of people loading onto the ship, I wondered if any would remain in this westernmost town on the Vesterisles. Lu Galen was much less than I'd expected, but still, I wanted to explore. Sighing, I resigned myself. In my current state, I wasn't fit to meet anyone.

I squinted out over the railing to where the sea glittered. The flashes burned in the back of my eyes, but I couldn't look away from the clear waters and waves crashing against the boat. Below, a school of silvery fish reflected Otarr's light. But I could only look down for a moment before my muscles clenched for a third time. When I heaved over the side, there was little except yellow stomach fluid, but the small fish teemed after it. I closed my eyes, took several deep breaths, and sagged against the rail.

"By the skies . . ." I cursed, wiping my mouth.

The yisu were the first to come check on me, but only briefly. They had duties to attend to on behalf of Gnoble Sarangarel before the *Swell Mistress* could depart the Vesterisles. Chambui looked concerned, but Jaliqai giggled, saying, "We've all been there, young kōgō." And then they left, joining their men. I heard Chambui telling Timur I'd be okay once I'd worn off the drunk.

I murmured, "I told you not to call me that," and clutched my stomach again. *And never again will I drink from that damned cask!*

Hoaris checked on me too, but he seemed nervous and had little to say. I grasped his forearm and squeezed. He offered little support, only patted my hand and went ashore to help the yisun. Indeed, he could think more clearly than I. He'd make six, and the even number would be better to carry the crates.

Closing my eyes, I drifted momentarily, but came to quickly when a thud sounded upon the bench next to me. I looked up to see Asahi, chewing on one of his brown sticks.

"Canna hold your rum, eh? Well"—he looked out over the water, toward the west where we'd be sailing soon—"it doesn't agree with everyone. We're loading some wine and ale. You should be better with those."

I squeezed both my lips and eyes shut. Neither of those options sounded any more appealing than the rum.

He barked, "Tie that off over there," to one of the new men who'd boarded the ship.

"You got your crew, I see," I said.

"They're getting everything ready and giving the *Mistress* a good once-over." Asahi put a foot up on the bench and leaned onto his knee. "We'll be pulling out as soon as the yisun and your man Hoaris are back."

Sadness tugged at my heart over being too liquor sick to meet the people of the Vesterisles. Mayhap I would upon our return from Ise.

Gazing around the ship with half-lidded eyes, I searched for my guard. "Have you seen Thalaj?"

"Not of late." The captain sighed, turning to leave. "I'ma certain he's lurking in shadow though."

That Thalaj had cared for me last night gave me a glimmer of hope, but he'd gone absent again. He'd even remained at my side into later hours—how long or late, I couldn't say thanks to my drunkenness—but . . . *hope*. I closed my eyes, my memory returning in snippets. He'd brushed off my attempts at conversation, said it wasn't good to try given my condition. And, to my chagrin, he'd also brushed off my weak attempt at flirtation.

Covering my eyes with a hand, I uttered, "Oh by the Triad. Never. Ever. Again."

"Never what?" Misha's pitched voice interrupted my wallowing, and it occurred to me that I hadn't seen the Small Folk working alongside the others.

"Nothing. Just. Nothing." I breathed in through my nose and out through my mouth, slowly. "I just feel horrible."

I rubbed my temples. Each boot on the deck and crate dropped thundered painfully behind my eyes. Across the deck and amidst the sailors loading the ship, the yisun and Hoaris returned. They each carried armloads down the stairs toward the cabins, but their burdens were much lighter—a jug here, a bag there. What was inside each, I didn't ask, I couldn't tell, nor did I care much in the moment.

Kyr hopped onto the bench beside me and offered me a small stoneware cup. I looked inside; a small black pebble sat at the bottom of fizzing liquid. "Go ahead, lovely, drink up. If you can keep it down, it'll soothe your head and gullet."

It tickled my mouth, throat, and nose, but had little taste. I clasped a hand over my mouth, hoping that through force I could keep it inside. As I fought the nausea, Kyr took the empty cup and left me alone with Misha. We sat in silence, companionably. Eventually, the drink began to work. Cramps subsided in my midsection and the fierce pounding in my head turned to a dull ache. And though my fingers still trembled with weakness as my body worked against the rum, I felt like a new person. The peace and quiet between Misha and me eased my soul as much as Kyr's drink had eased my stomach.

Around us, the newcomers worked the ropes and sails and levels below—below even the sleeping deck—oars poked out and splashed in the water. New crew members and mayhap some of the old pushed us away from the dock and the very western edge of Nantai. In concert, they pointed the *Swell Mistress*'s nose west, and soon the sails snapped and billowed, catching the wind above. A pair of gruff-looking men in pants that ballooned above their knee-high boots and had wide, colorful bands at the waist spanning to their mid-chest areas passed Misha and me; each carried a rope over their shoulder, their upper torsos bare save for a small vest, chests hairless, and their skin kissed by Otarr. They paid us little heed.

One said, "We're away again, Tao!" Delight radiated through his body such that he nearly bounced with enthusiasm as he stored his rope in a bin at the end of the bench where we sat.

The other youthful sailor, Tao, piled his rope in the same manner and gave the first a devious grin. Running a hand through his hair, he smiled, seeming happy to be heading back to sea; but he wasn't quite as electrified by it. He looked over the rippling blue-green waters, took a deep breath, and ran his hands around his belt, stopping with one on either hip. "Aye, Oshun. The sea . . . she calls. Think we'll find a syren this time?"

◇◇◇◇◇◇◇◇◇◇◇◇◇◇◇◇◇◇◇◇◇◇◇◇◇◇◇◇◇◇◇◇

FROM THE TIME WE departed from the docks at Lu Galen, my stomach continued to fight the rise and fall of the ship. It became more relentless as we moved away from the land and the only sight upon the horizon was blue waters. The concoction Kyr had brewed helped, but it only lasted for a time. As the days passed, I could only eat after drinking another small fizzy drink. And even then, I only took a few spoonfuls of the tasteless porridge the sailors served on the ship. After four or five bites, I tended to turn away the over-cooked grains.

I blamed the rum for several days, but I began to wonder if the incessant urge to vomit arose from the sea herself.

In my cabin, I slept for longer and longer hours, wishing for the swell to abate. After uncountable days, I simply chose to remain in my cabin throughout the day. When I awoke, I turned to the other side and willed myself back to sleep. Misha and Kyr took turns bringing me the drink and a bowl, waking me, and ensuring I consumed something. When they came together, they chattered, but I didn't try to understand. Perhaps sailing wasn't a feat I'd survive.

On the day when I awoke feeling as if the *Swell Mistress* had docked, a thrill ran through my body and I leaped from bed. Immediately, my head spun. I sank back onto my bed, and the revolutions slowed, then stopped. Too long sick, and too little food.

I washed. The cloth and cool water against my face felt wonderful, like washing away dust that'd collected over years of neglect. True, though I'd lost count; surely I'd only been like this for a number of days. Yet a good scrubbing always felt the best when I'd exhausted myself or suffered from an illness's. After parting from the Tsinti and finding Hoaris and the Small Folk, I'd fallen to an unknown ailment. The baths afterward, in the caverns beneath Safaia, had been veritably heavenly. Washing my face now was a close second.

Dressed and with my hair tied up, I left my cabin, ready to be part of the group once again. My knees, elbows, and back ached from weakness that had gathered in my joints, and the muscles in my arms and legs protested as I latched onto the steep stairs to climb onto the deck. When Otarr's light hit my face, I closed my eyes and took a deep, salt-tinged breath. When I looked around, my spirits that had been lightening with each passing moment suddenly felt as if a storm cloud had appeared within the crisp blue skies.

I searched solemn face after solemn face, and each one watched me with a mixture of concern and something more. Fret? Worry? Over me? No, it was concern, but also an air of stagnancy. Jaliqai rushed over and grasped my arm beneath the elbow, urging me toward a seat.

I pulled away gently with a word of assurance. "Truly, I will be well," I assured her.

Amidst the faces, I found Thalaj's dark almond-shaped gaze. I thought we connected in that moment, but he turned at a movement to the side. And then, he and Captain Asahi exchanged a silent and tense conversation of their own. There was a warning upon my first guard's brow, and the captain gave a small nod as he crossed the deck and met me where I stood.

I worked my throat—still dry. "Wh-what has happened?"

Chambui joined Jaliqai at my side. "The sailors worry over the calm seas. They say it's a bad omen."

One of the bare-chested men, Tao if I recalled correctly, spoke up. "Means danger. Beware of glass waters, they silence even Ebisu." He seemed to be the more sage of the two.

A murmur ran through the others—wary agreement.

Seeing my confusion, Tao added, "Ebisu is the sea god who brings sailors good fortune and fish."

Oshun, the other bare-chested sailor, chimed in, "True words. Sailors never find fish in still waters." He widened his eyes and waggled his brows. "They fear something unknown."

Asahi leaned closer then, and Thalaj took a step forward. The captain cut his eyes sideways and waved as if attempting to offer reassurance, but despite my guard's warning, Asahi persisted. "How are you, Mairy?" His voice sounded more kind than I'd heard to date.

I searched the faces of each person in my traveling party, the gathered sailor's grim expressions, and looked into Captain Asahi's deep sea-colored eyes. "I was happy moments ago, felt like I might recover and enjoy my food for a change. I wondered if we'd reached land. No"—I swallowed, shaking my head—"I had hoped we had reached land."

Yet the water beyond the rails stretched to the horizon and, indeed, appeared as solid as mirrored glass.

I added, "But I guess that hope was in vain."

He pulled one of the brown sticks from his pocket and placed it in the side of his mouth. Starting to chew, he said, "Well, it looks like you'll have a bit to recover. Maybe this is Ak Ana taking pity upon you. The goddess of all water holds wisdom more ancient than any other element. We'll see if the current returns now that you're settled." With one last glance at Thalaj, he ducked past me to climb below deck.

Kyr smiled, a gleam in her eyes, and waved me over. "Over here, lovely. Let's get you some eats. Breakfast is still up." The way she dished it up, it appeared she'd taken over the cooking for the entire ship and relished in every minute of her work. It reminded me of how she'd bustled around the caverns when we'd first met.

Other eyes followed me as I went, but the thought of food sounded too good to pass. My stomach agreed with a roar as I sat to eat.

Apparently, this was enough to put the rest of my party and the crew at ease because they returned to their various activities. Some of the crew sat with Hoaris at one end of the long table where I ate, and they played at the simple game of dice. Tao and Oshun sat at the other end sharpening long knives on flat stones. Seeing an opportunity to put their efforts to good use, Kyr went below deck and brought up the knives from the kitchen and dumped them on the table beside the men without a word. Oshun, the more excitable of the two, harrumphed, but when Kyr swatted him on the back of his head, he smiled, grabbed the nearest knife, and went to work.

Kyr collected my bowl after I'd cleaned as much from the bottom as possible and drew her face close to mine. "The dark under your eyes looks a bit better. Stay up here today. The sun'll do you well."

As she went below deck, I studied the men sharpening the knives. My stare must have caused their senses to prickle because they both looked up at me a couple of times, curious.

"Tao," I chewed on the name, drawing his attention. "It means great waves, yes?"

Oshun laughed and tossed a fist across the table, nudging his friend. "After the great waves he's mastered aboard many a ship."

Tao took the goading in stride and swept a long, curved blade over the stone again. It sang through the air. A break to the otherwise silent deck. Oshun started his work again, and together, their swipes of the blades made a steady rhythm . . . *zhing, zhing, zhing.*

"What did you mean by what you said back at Lu Galen?" I asked Tao.

He looked at me, clearly without understanding my meaning.

"The syren. 'Maybe we'll meet a syren,' you said."

Tao cocked a smile but it was Oshun who answered, "That's the legend of the Syrensea. Aren't you familiar?"

I tried to recall if I'd ever heard such a legend, but nothing came to my mind. Lips pursed, I squinted and shook my head. "Can't say that I have."

Oshun finished honing one blade and ran a thumb over the edge. Satisfied, he grabbed another and started anew. "Maybe it's a tale only mothers tell their sons who wish to wander the seas." He reached across the table, swatting at Tao. "But those like us wouldn't listen, eh?"

I smiled. "We have our own stories like that where I am from. Mammoth cats in the north we call *nekolai* and the winged predator birds of the Rausu Mountains." I lowered my gaze, recalling Tasmynne's storyboards. "But I'm unfamiliar with stories of the sea." Rumors of ships never returning from trips across the Syrensea had made their way up the rivers, across the plains, and into the mountains. Even in Stormskeep, that much was well known. It stood to reason that seafarers would also spin warning tales. "So, syrens are the rumored reasons ships have gone and never returned?" I asked.

Tao turned and spat—something I'd seen several of the crewmen do. Then, he said, "Syrens are said to visit sailors at sea. Winged tempters or temptresses, depending on your like, you see. They take the desirable form."

"And . . ."—Oshun leaned onto the table, pointing one of the blades in my direction—"they sing sweetly to you like the birds of your homeland. Their songs lure you, no matter how strong your will." His eyes danced, brows waggling suggestively at the thought of such tempting danger.

His more somber friend shrugged one shoulder. "Some men reportedly have walked right off the decks of ships to follow their call, leaving their ships to eventually find their way to a rocky shore or sandy bottom with no more breath in their chests."

"But there's a better part of the tales," continued Oshun. "The calm part of the sea is where the syrens lurk. They wait for us in the skies and only come forth when we're stranded with nowhere to go and little food remaining. It's why most of our men quiver with fear." He pointed around the ship deck with the end of a knife. "And 'tis why Asahi has a bug in his bonnet."

I hadn't sensed that much, but it certainly explained the reason Thalaj shot him warning stares.

"Some of us, though . . ." Tao looked suggestively and admonishingly at Oshun. ". . . are intrigued by the thought of meeting one and living to tell."

"Aw, Tao, Old Shad did, why can't we?" Oshun pouted.

Tao rolled his eyes and persevered at his work. "Old Shad was a windbag. You can't believe a thing that withered old man said."

"But his ships were the only ones ever to return from the Syrensea. Who are we to say otherwise?"

Tao raised a brow and spat again. I swallowed hard a few times to control an assault of nausea. Thankfully, the crew scrubbed the deck every afternoon, and when the great swells came, the saltwater washed it away as well.

I stood to go. The sailor legends were fun enough, but certainly we could do more to sway our fate. I needed to know how much longer we had until we reached Ise. The stones at my neck buzzed a little with the thought. Maybe it would be wise to begin using the oars below deck. Something, anything, to get the *Swell Mistress* moving once more. Also, there was tension between my first guard and Captain Asahi. Something had passed between them and I wanted to know.

And . . . I tired of the distance Thalaj had been keeping between us. Now that my gut wasn't swimming as bad, it was time for us to have a nice little chat.

TWENTY-SIX

Shadow of Night

I HAD SEARCHED THE ENTIRETY OF the Swell Mistress twice, stopping to talk to people within my party or on the crew, but Thalaj lived up to his moniker, Shadow. It seemed an appropriate title for him as someone always near but not always in sight. After some time, I could no longer ignore the necessity building, and I went below deck to relieve myself. I halted with a hand upon the door pull, hearing sounds in the hall.

Footsteps, then a voice I'd known since early youth boomed, "Absolutely not." Thalaj's tone held the finality he used with his soldiers in Arashi.

"She may be our only hope," Captain Asahi pleaded.

There were no more footsteps, and I imagined Thalaj turning on the captain with cold rage pouring off of him. "She has been sick for days. She won't have the energy to call upon the storms yet."

Finally, I understood the reason for their argument. Having sworn to protect my family under my father, Tennō Atheryn Evangale, Thalaj protected me now, blindly and at any cost. Despite the danger Asahi feared, and despite that the captain saw my abilities as a way to save all the souls aboard the *Swell Mistress*, Thalaj persisted. I pulled the door open, my eyes locking harshly with my first guard's. But he stared me down, conviction apparent within every single fiber of his body.

I moved slowly, placing every step carefully. I lifted my chin higher and infused as much of my regal training as possible. I made my words a demand. "What seems to be the problem." No question. I expected an answer.

Thalaj knew as much and tipped his head forward. "You should rest. Recover your strength, Kōgō."

I tried not to flinch at the formal address. Doing so would undermine my purpose. It was the first time he'd used that word in a long while. I supposed by my action I commanded such deference. However, after having said so few words to me since I'd spent the night with Sarangarel, his use of it pierced and stung. In that one word, he communicated so much. That he did his duty. Nothing more. Nothing less.

I rolled my shoulders back, feeling the exhaustion Thalaj had warned of pulling at my muscles even as I spoke. "If you wish to discuss my welfare and what I might do to aide in this journey, I should be party to the conversation."

Captain Asahi, casteless but the commander of this vessel, nodded once, also in deference. Small though I may have been, I had learned well how to use the resources at my disposal. Having Thalaj's regard was a tool within my belt, and I would use it as such. If Asahi made a move to thwart me in any way, he'd have a scimityne at his throat before any of us could blink.

Asahi's gaze shifted between the two of us, and I read the same knowledge in his eyes. With a smug and satisfied look at Thalaj, the captain said, "Aye, you most definitely should."

Within his words, the hidden message sounded almost as loudly, *She echoes my argument.*

How long had he argued as much with my first guard? To the implication of the words and exchange, I answered, "There is little need to dispute with the captain, Thalaj. I wish to help in whatever way I can."

"You haven't the strength presently," my guard objected. Though I didn't want to admit it, he spoke the truth and I turned to look at the captain. "How long do we have until sailing is critical?"

"We have rations for ten days' delay, but fresh water for only six. That is the more dangerous prospect, but we have weak ale enough for another two if we trade off between ale and water."

"Well and so. It seems we can come to an agreement after all. I have a handful of days to recover."

The captain dropped his gaze ever so slightly.

"What are you not saying, Captain Asahi?" I asked.

"We cannot always predict our delays, and we don't have many who have traveled to Ise and returned to tell the stories. If we are to use our reserves now, we can afford no further interruptions."

"In that case, how long are you comfortable waiting?" I pressed.

He looked down. "Not more than two more days."

I clenched my jaw, seeing the logic in his assessment of the situation. Unfortunately, Thalaj had also accurately assessed my abilities. "Will you give me some time to discuss this with my first guard?"

He agreed, and I demanded Thalaj see me within my rooms after I visited the latrine. I turned on my heel and left.

I thanked the Triad for the calm seas and the reprieve during which I could eat and restore myself. I wasn't anxious to re-enter the roiling seas, but I *was* eager to set foot upon Ise, the place where I felt certain I would find Father. Furthermore, I had grown overly weary of the prolonged silence between Thalaj and me, and I intended to address all matters shortly.

Inside my cabin, Thalaj walked the space twice then stopped, standing at attention and awaiting my order.

"Thalaj . . ." I started toward him.

He took a small step back, and the room grew cold.

"Why?" I asked.

"Kōgō—"

"No," I barked, stepping forward, inserting myself into his space despite the cold he exuded. "You will not use that title as a weapon or defense against me. You know my feelings about that position and that you've never used it before when we were alone. Do not insult me now by using it."

"Mairynne," he said, a hint more gently, "you've been sick for too long to use your magic. You haven't eaten more than a few spoonfuls a day, and then only after Kyr treats you with the fizz. And after all this, you believe that you can call a gale strong enough to sail us from these dead seas?" As he spoke, the volume increased.

"I am beginning to gain strength," I countered.

"Not enough." He lowered his gaze.

"The captain has given me two more days in which I can recuperate."

"And you don't believe that it is still a risk to try such things? What if—"

"No. I've been using this magic all my life. There is no reason I cannot do so now, or when I feel a bit stronger. Anyway, you are one to speak." I waved my hands in the air toward the upper deck. "You would put everyone aboard this ship at risk just to allow me to rest? That seems too extreme. You'd risk losing not only me, but yourself and everyone else on board to some sea syren." I spat the last at him.

He raised a questioning brow but then tipped his head forward, deferring to me yet again.

"Thalaj." I took another step toward him.

He had nowhere left to retreat. Instead, he tensed, folded his arms across his chest as a barrier. And in his silence, I read two things—one, he had in fact not considered the others, and secondly, he needed to maintain a distance between us.

I paid his warning no heed and went to him, placing my hand upon his forearm. "Thalaj," I repeated. "I think it is time we talked. Do you not agree?"

I said another thanks to the Triad that he didn't move away or try to push past me to avoid the contact. Under peaked brows, his eyes softened, rounded, and searched my face. What thoughts or feelings traveled behind those eyes, I couldn't say, but I had little doubt that they ran as deep as the still waters outside and all around the *Swell Mistress*.

"Mairynne, as I have said before . . ." He swallowed, haltingly as if the words stuck within his throat and resisted passing between his lips. "It's for the best if I remain true to my duties and honor the vows I made to your father. I'm here as your first guard, to see you safely through this journey. That is all."

What he didn't say stung more than what he did—that he couldn't be intimate with me, that I couldn't be a lover to him, that there should be no more between us, and that the castes that separated us were too great to overcome. But I didn't understand how he still believed caste mattered to me, or to us. And if my time with Sarangarel had hurt him, it should have at least demonstrated my ill regard for the constructed hierarchies within our society.

Yet, I wouldn't speak of my private and precious time with Sarangarel to Thalaj. It belonged to only us. However, I had learned a great deal from her in that solitary night, and I didn't hesitate to use it there in my cabin in that moment. I placed my other hand upon his arm and pushed my hip toward him.

My words were the same words I had said to Thalaj before. "Caste is a false division between people, and I see none between us now." I urged his arms down from where he held them crossed and defensive over his chest. Placing one hand on his heart, I added, "We started to grow closer before, and we have been through so much."

I lifted my face to his, so close I could feel his cool breath against my lips. He held them tightly together, equally as rigid as his entire body. My body flushed despite the chill in the air, and it seemed to grow warmer as I stood there, offering myself to him. I pressed closer, my weakness forgotten. He didn't pull away which only encouraged the connection I sought—the one I'd wanted since I was a youngling barely old enough for my first crush.

As our lips touched, I kissed gently, tilting my head to the right, then to the left, urging him to respond. Through half-lidded eyes, I watched his face. His lips pressed tighter; a muscle ticked in his jaw. And when he finally relented, I heard a sharp inhale through his nose just before his lips crushed my own. The kiss he returned carried desperate fervor. He felt cold and hot against my mouth as our tongues danced. He tasted of frozen lemon cream, then of hot smoky spices. His arms grasped me as if he were holding on to his last breath before sinking into the Syrensea itself.

And then, it was done. He pushed me aside, gasping. "This can't. *We* can't. Mairynne. I want, but no. It's just not . . ." So many thoughts again warred behind his eyes, but his words wouldn't, couldn't explain. He shook his head and left my cabin.

Time. He needed more time.

I smiled, running my fingers over my tingling lips.

◇◇◇◇◇◇◇◇◇◇◇◇◇◇◇◇◇◇◇◇◇◇◇◇◇◇◇◇◇

OVER THE NEXT TWO days, I gained strength with each meal and rest I took.

And hope grew in my heart. Thalaj and Kyr often ushered me away from socializing with the crew or the yisun and encouraged me to nap between each meal. Unnecessary though I believed their ministrations, I slept each time and even harder at night. Once, I suspected Kyr had laced my porridge with something to help me into slumber. I couldn't complain. Those were probably some of the easiest days I'd passed since leaving Stormskeep.

What I learned in my conversations with the ship's men was often of little interest, but fun and often heartwarming—many had wives and some had younglings living near Lu Galen. But what intrigued me more was that in place of cities or towns, the Vesterisle people lived in small settlements scattered across the islands, each consisting of only family.

I tried to imagine growing up with only my sisters for conversation and only meeting others my own age at infrequent gatherings. It wasn't so hard to fathom the solitude. I'd often felt the same within the castle inside Arashi. Although there, I had the secret passages and I could sneak out and mingle with others in the streets of the city, working to blend in and dream of a life with less formality. I'd often envied the ones who welcomed me into their regular afternoon games of crook and cane. When those memories stirred, I grinned fondly. But when my thoughts turned to my sister Karynne, my stomach soured.

As for Thalaj and me, that kiss in my cabin had started something. It was hardly a romance, but a reconnecting of sorts. I kept myself restrained, thinking I would be happy to see us return to the relationship we'd had before the City by the Sea. Truly, any kind of relationship would have been better than the tense and silent avoidance of the matter. Strained is the best word I possessed to describe how our situation had been. I tried hard in those calm days and so did he. Hoaris, Kyr, and Misha watched us from afar, the Small Folk sometimes chattering at the pace I couldn't comprehend. It bothered me little that they observed and talked about our efforts.

At the close of the second day, I found Captain Asahi and told him that I'd be ready on the morrow to call the winds and fill his sails. Pleased, he invited me to dine in his cabin that evening. Thalaj, passing by, heard this, and his attention turned sharply to our conversation.

I demurred. "Thank you, Captain. That is quite generous of you, but I think I'll pass this evening."

We did talk and strolled the deck for some time before he left me that evening. In our conversation, he dismissed any notion of syrens, stating how sailors had too much time on their hands and simply invented the fanciful tales. "If they've told one story, they've told a hundred, a thousand, or more," the captain commented with a wistfulness in his eye. "Mind you, syrens are the oldest of the seafaring stories, but to my knowledge, they're purely mythical."

At this, I held my tongue. It didn't escape me that I was also in search of a race that seemed equally as mysterious and quite possibly a figment of others' imaginations. But when I went to the railing and watched Selene's reflection upon the mirror-like waters, I grasped the stones about my neck.

"Wait for me, Father," I pleaded.

Heat suffused my palm, and once again, I knew the truth in my mission. Father lived, and I would find him. I felt desperate to do just that. Somewhere, somehow, I would return him to our home and to the Serpentine Throne as its rightful owner.

Home.

That seemed a long way behind me now.

"Are you worried?" Thalaj's quiet voice broke my contemplation in the night.

A small smile spread at hearing his voice. He worried, even if I did not.

He came to the railing beside me and placed a hand over mine. "I must apologize to you for how I've acted. I've only done what I believed right. Never had I intended to cause you heartache."

His words took me aback, but as we'd eased into a routine, I ventured, "Does this mean you're ready to speak of us?" I turned my hand over in his, interlacing our fingers.

A cloud passed over his eyes. "There is no us, Mairynne. *Us* cannot exist, and it's not a matter of caste, but a matter of position and my personal beliefs." His words seemed rushed, like if he didn't get them out, they would fester and never sing freely into the night.

"I miss your meaning." The smile fell from my lips.

Thankfully, he didn't let go of my hand. "Your heart . . ." He stood there silently for a long moment, then said plaintively, "Three hells, Mairynne, your very soul is a free spirit." Then, he rushed again, "I, as proscribed by the lessons I learned in the Order, have bound myself to you, and I do curse the Triad and myself for that on occasion. Had I known the feelings I would develop or the temptation I would endure, I would have made other choices long ago."

Fear struck a chord deep inside my heart. Could he be preparing to leave? To forsake his duty? "What is it you're saying?"

"Beyond my oath, there are other factors. As I said, your soul is free and searching. I would never change that, but my father always told me . . ." He laughed humorlessly. "Well, he said that when I had the right partner before me, she would give herself completely. All and everything, she would give to me, and I would do the same in return." He tried to slide his hand from mine.

I gripped tighter. "And what you're telling me now is that it comes back to your mother's all-consuming love for your father?" An angry storm brewed inside, gathering and lashing out. I tried to bite my tongue and swallow it, but my will for that was absent and my words came in a torrent. "The same love that drew her apart from her family and had her and you and your father too, living on the outside, away from any caste. Beyond the Storm Sorcerers, yet also not quite fitting in with the Frost Fighters. You, different still as a result of their whole dedication to one another?"

"Hai." He didn't try to explain further. His simple answer sufficed.

He'd spoken truth: my heart and soul hadn't yet settled, and I wondered, sometimes doubted, if they ever would. I felt this even through my single-minded desire to find Father, and I suspected that once we restored my father's mantle, I still wouldn't rest easy within Arashi. I would likely never be a polite little princess. What Thalaj said to me in that small word was that he wouldn't forswear his promises, yet he also wouldn't have part of me without the whole.

"And, you'll deny yourself and me the joy of what I am able and willing to give?" I demanded.

He bowed his head. "I am sorry, but yes."

The space behind my eyes and nose felt tight, a storm in its own right gathered there. I didn't know when or whether I would be able to give him what he needed. I didn't know myself well enough then to say if ever was even a possibility.

Somewhere during that horrid conversation, my hand had released his without intent. I stood, facing the water and trying not to sob.

Thalaj grasped my hand again and turned me to face him. He held both of mine then. "Mairynne, I have loved you for many years, and I wouldn't change these things about you ever. But you must know I also cannot change these things about myself. So though I desire you—gods damn me, how I desire you—it would be best for us to remain as we are. I will be your protector as I always have, and I will work not to be jealous when you take another lover. That is what I can promise to you."

I opened my mouth to speak, to say I would take no others, but he silenced me with a kiss so gentle and wishful and mournful that my soul cried. It said, *I'm staying, but for now, I'm saying goodbye to us.* His lips begged, *Please understand.*

When he pulled away, he said, "Hai, you will take another. There is no need to deny that or feel ashamed. You must take another, and another still. I have had lovers of my own. It is a part of finding yourself."

This pulled at my heart, but reason held. I had no right to any feeling of jealousy over his past dalliances.

He went on, for I couldn't hope to speak. "You do not understand your own needs until you have learned through experience. I recognize these things now, as will you one day."

"But what about"—my voice caught—"about you?" I sniffed, pulled a hand from his grasp, and wiped a tear from beneath my eye. As the floods started, I felt like I had an empty space where my heart had been.

"Tomorrow, we will be as we have always been. That is good enough." He turned, dropped my other hand, and disappeared into the shadow of night.

* * *

THE NEXT MORNING, I called the winds, opening myself and all the hurt I'd felt when Thalaj had spoken so candidly of our situation and differences. Thunderheads built high before the first gusts reached the ship. Lightning danced between the clouds, then struck the water in several long purple lights. Standing there on the bow of the Swell Mistress, I emptied my heart, soul, and very being into that storm, and the winds answered. My hair whipped about my face. Tears fell but blended with the saltwater mist the winds had gathered from the surface. Frothy white foam capped the waves as they rolled toward us. Around me, the crew rushed to control the snapping sails. Asahi shouted commands to orchestrate the crew and control the ship within the squall.

And in that maelstrom, the winds blew so hard they created a swell and carried us to Ise on a single gale.

Twenty-Seven

Bring the Storm

WITH THE PORT IN SIGHT, a light touch landed on my shoulder.

"That is well, young sorceress. Thank you," Captain Asahi said. "My sailors can steer the *Mistress* in from here."

I relaxed, eased my hold on the magic, and breathed in the freshness upon the air owed to the storm. The winds dwindled to a gentle breeze, and I stared at our destination—Ise. How I knew as much, I couldn't say. A long pier jutted into the green and blue ocean from a white beach. A few small structures dotted the shore in sparse intervals. Unlike Kōkai, Nantai's City by the Sea, the pier and dockside ahead didn't appear to be part of any city. Zofi of the Tsinti had mentioned a place by the name of Seleucid. While the land may be Ise, it certainly wasn't a settlement worthy of a name. Beyond the white beach lay a line of trees, verdant and thick. Peeking over treetops from deeper inland, a few rooftops hinted at more. Strange, but mayhap the foliage obscured the city.

When the ship's sails deflated, a small natural breeze and the sound of waves crashing against the hull were all that remained. The air thickened and my skin grew sticky. Members of the crew batted down the sails while others relayed directions to the oarsmen below.

I, no, we had focused on this moment for what seemed an eternity. Now that it was within reach, new challenges opened before us. Zofi's words, *. . . over the Syrensea to the island nation of Ise, and inland from there*, replayed in my memory.

I hadn't considered *how* we were to travel inland upon our arrival. The greenery seemed too thick to navigate easily. Shortly beyond the building tops, the elevation climbed into mountains covered in thick trees without so much as a visible trail through the forest's depths.

The *Swell Mistress* drew closer, but nothing upon the shore moved. Where were the people? I'd assumed the citizens of Ise and Seleucid would meet us on the docks. And I'd wondered if they would speak a common tongue. It seemed unlikely. And if we were to travel inland from here, would Captain Asahi hold the *Swell Mistress* here, awaiting our return? That also seemed doubtful without the opportunity to restock his ship.

Then, what of the yisun? What mission had Sarangarel set upon them? Too many questions and too few answers.

I sank onto a bench nearby, heavy with worry.

Thalaj appeared, more concern than necessary upon his face. "Are you well? Did you use too much energy?"

I shook my head. "No. I am well enough."

But he had known me long and could read me better than others. "Then what ails you?" He looked me over even as he asked, presumably searching for signs I'd pushed my abilities too far or of the sickness returning.

Searching his face, I found no answers to my worries. "Have you considered what we're to do now? The stones are quiet." I rested a hand over the stone pendants resting on my chest.

"From what the Tsinti seer said, we need to find the Abatwa." This, he said as if my memory were failing.

Could he not think deeper through the matter? When I found my voice, the questions gushed forth. "Do you know what that is? Or *who* they are? Do you understand for what we search or how we are to travel there?" I jutted my chin toward the shore. "Do we have any understanding of the dangers that may await us there? What if the people who have crossed the Syrensea actually arrived here in Ise? What if it isn't the sea that's treacherous at all?"

For all my first guard's training and travels while with the Unseen Guild, those assignments had never extended beyond the borders of Nantai. Nor had Thalaj crossed the Syrensea. Yet I must give him credit that he bore my ranting questions with unparalleled ease, listening without rebuttal as was often my mother's manner and something I sorely missed.

The thought of Mother quieted, nearly choked me, and my eyes flitted away from his steady gaze, stinging. Once I settled, I took a deep breath and finished voicing my current worry with more aplomb. "It is entirely possible that the people of Ise will see us dead before they will help us in our search."

He wiped a stray tear from my cheek. "Am I to be your voice of reason and hope now?" The question challenged me more than the words alone.

I clasped my hands together at my back, trying hard not to fidget. It would have been so nice to have his ease, to remain so utterly calm in the face of so many possibilities, to not concern myself over these things. But his manner had also distracted me from my own worry. Issuing a small chuckle, I answered, "If you could, it would be immensely helpful."

Thalaj furrowed his brow, then asked, "Do you recall Zofi's warning words about our journey?"

Breathing seemed laborious with the thickness of the air, but I sighed. "Not all of them at the moment."

"She never warned about specific encounters. Her words only foretold a need for patience. 'Face each challenge as it comes,' " he echoed, " 'not before.' "

While those hadn't been her exact words, they held the same meaning. Once again, Thalaj had proved himself the calm eye in the center of my raging storm. He faced the land as the boat pulled alongside the dock. "You trusted the Tsinti more than I when we were there. Mayhap trusting in her words now would also be prudent. True?"

◇◇◇◇◇◇◇◇◇◇◇◇◇◇◇◇◇◇◇◇◇◇◇◇◇◇◇◇◇◇◇◇◇◇◇◇◇◇

ONCE THE SAILORS HAD secured the Swell Mistress, I went first from the boat. My steps were sure-footed on the long, rickety dock, but I wobbled on sea-weakened knees after reaching solid ground. My feet sank. White sand, like sugar, poured into my shoes, making me wish I'd chosen my boots over slippers, but what stopped me cold was the singing from the stones about my neck. Rather than temperature, high voices lifted as if in praise to Atun, Otarr, and Selene. Or whichever gods the people of Ise might worship, I considered in afterthought. I scanned the dock back toward the boat, curious if anyone else had heard their clear voices on the air. Asahi's crew and my travel companions continued about their tasks.

When I wrapped my fingers around the stones, they quieted, as if soothed by my touch. And the worry that's twisted my guts receded. I finally had some much-needed reassurance that I'd followed their path truly. Here, somewhere on this new piece of earth, my father lived. There only remained the simple matter of locating him. My gaze drifted from the line of thick foliage in the distance down to the now quiet stones in my palm, but they looked like nothing more than simple pebbles. Though their natures had changed, it seemed any assistance they could offer still had limitations. This journey began to feel like an exaggerated version of the youngling guessing game, *Thunder or Lightning*. I squinted up to the blue skies, wondering if Father's mysterious captor cheered for me as I neared the hidden treasure.

Expelling a long breath, I dropped the pendants. Little help though they may be, I'd accept what they offered.

The trees at the edge of the white sands remained silent save for a small sway in the breeze from the Syrensea.

I listened.

Silence.

No sounds like those in the Yubar Forest.

It was so quiet. *Too* quiet.

Thump. CRASH! The ground shook, or so I would forever swear. Fine sand sprinkled against my pants with a *thwap*. My heart raced in a tizzy. I leaped sideways, glaring at the evil crate that'd landed at my feet. Tao and Oshun laughed and went back down the creaking pier toward the *Swell Mistress*.

Asahi bantered with them in passing, then ate up the rest of the pier with his long strides and skipped the stairs, stepping directly into the sand. His boots sank to nearly the ankle but didn't allow for the sand to seep in like my slippers. I'd removed the annoying things and stood barefoot in the soft white grains. They were warm on top, but cooler underneath where Otarr's light couldn't penetrate.

The captain carried his hat and chewed his stick—spiced wood, I'd learned as we'd strolled the deck and talked about his desire for me to call the winds. When he arrived at my side on the beach, he lifted the hat, not putting it on his head but holding it high to shade his view as he squinted toward the tree line. "What's your plan now, young empress?" he asked from the unoccupied side of his mouth.

"We're certain this is Ise?" I asked, more so to make conversation or even stall than out of true curiosity.

"As certain as the maps we have in Nantai can tell," Asahi answered.

"The buildings within the jungle. Do you think that's Seleucid?"

He pressed his lips and shook his head. "Can't be certain on that. The maps we have only show the mass of land."

"Then I guess my plan really comes down to one option. Find people. Ask questions. Hope we're close." *Find my father.* Though I left that thought unsaid, the stones vibrated against my chest.

In silence, we stood there for several long minutes. Two sailors I hadn't made acquaintance with brought another crate from the ship and dropped it at our feet. The yisun disembarked, each carrying a long-handled axe with a large metal head, red stones inlaid in the metal, and a deadly curved blade. Those each served as both a walking stick and weapon but made the short and stout team of five appear overly menacing.

I looked askance at Asahi and asked, "What of you? Will you stay here and await our return?"

He chuckled and fixed his triple-pointed hat onto his head, moving it from back to front to secure it in place. When he seemed satisfied, he folded his arms over his chest and faced me. Taller than me by more than a head, he blocked the brightest of the sun's light. "Little lady, you've got to be my most favored cargo ever . . ." He trailed off as something toward the boat stole his attention.

I followed his gaze to Thalaj who was making his way toward shore followed by the remainder of my party. "But there's a *but*?" I cut my gaze back and up to the captain. His eyes were the color of the sea beneath the dock, and they glinted. But there was a hint of regret behind that light.

"Aye, there's a *but*." He inhaled, sighed loudly. "A sailor's life is hard, filled with stocking just the right amount of rations to care for the ship's passengers and restocking at each dock. Then, there's the constant search for work. Never free, you see."

He danced around the topic, but I understood his implication. "Will you return for us? Or are we left to find our own passage back to Nantai?"

Asahi plucked the stick from his mouth and twisted his lips to one side, considering. "How long do you think you'll remain?"

"I wish I had an answer . . . As long as it takes, I suppose. I don't have much direction from here." Even as I said it, the edge of that thought stabbed deep within my gut. I paused a moment to collect myself and added with a shrug, "All the information I have is that I need to find something or perhaps *someone* called the Abatwa."

His sea-green eyes went blank, hinting he understood as little about that as I. He gnawed on the stick and shrugged. "Well, I will search for work that doesn't carry us far. Sarangarel didn't command as much, but she asked. Not sure how well you know her, but she's a hard woman to refuse."

My face heated. I knew that well enough.

"In the meantime," he started, "I'll leave a small crew here to guard the *Mistress*, and the rest of us will accompany you into"—he waved a hand at the trees and the nestled buildings within—"whatever lies beyond that thicket there."

"As will we." Chambui hopped down from the pier and planted her axe in the sand.

Jaliqai and the yisun joined her.

My travel party followed. Thalaj stepped to my side, and a cool breeze lifted my hair. I wondered if it was a simple sea breeze or some barely controlled emotion rolling off my protector. I squelched the thought and tried not to wonder about his state as he'd made his position on the matter of *us* rather clear.

"Chambui." I grinned, looping my arm through her elbow opposite the axe. "I'll be happy to have the yisun travel with us. The party growing beyond what I'd expected."

Timur, leader of the yisun, answered in her stead, "We have orders from the Stone Lady to bring back something of worth." Regretful though he looked, he took a firm position. "We will not be able to be at your side for long."

He shot Chambui a warning. Her cheeks darkened as she dipped her head.

Timur, naturally in charge of the group by both appointment and manner, continued, "We will go with you into a city. When we part ways, we should make plans to regroup for the return journey." He placed a reassuring hand on Chambui's shoulder as he walked past her, moving several steps closer to the tree line.

We'd spent too long for my taste gathering upon the sands, and my nerves twitched with our stagnancy. I turned quickly, made eye contact with Thalaj and Hoaris, then Kyr. When I came to Misha, a thought took root, and I pulled him aside to whisper my inquiry. If they could enable us to travel unseen and unheard, it would give us some small advantage as we trekked into the unknown.

Misha folded his arms, eyes shifting around the gathered people as if making hundreds of calculations. Pursing his lips to one side he shook his head. "It's too much. If we'd considered it on board while we sat upon the quiet seas, I might have had enough time. But if you wish to go today, we only have mine and Kyr's."

"You gave the others to Sarangarel?"

He shrugged. "It was the quickest option."

Thalaj approached. "Is there something amiss?"

"No. I just wondered if we might go into the forest with stones of invisibility like we did when we went to see Lady Sarangarel." Intent on breezing straight past my guard, I began walking. After several plodding steps forward, I wanted to curse the futility along with my injured pride.

As a testament to his loyalty, Thalaj tipped his head forward and handed over my weapon belt as I approached, the scimitynes tucked neatly into their scabbards. The weight felt nice, offered security.

I halted and fastened the buckle around my waist. "Will we begin training again soon?"

"*I* never stopped." He smirked, turned away, and joined Timur in observing the foliage at the end of the sand.

I clenched my teeth and hinted, "Shall we venture inside the woods?"

Tao and Oshun went to the crates.

"Can we not return for the crates?" I protested. "They'll slow our progress."

Oshun looked at me sideways. "Whadda we face in there, eh? Do you know what we'll need? Think your blades there are enough if we get lost? Or worse? Hrmmm?"

He challenged me with a brow cocked while Tao lifted the lid and retrieved packs, passing one to each person. After examining the contents—some dried meat, water, a small rope, a knife that folded on a hinge, and a small roll of cloth—I gave him an apologetic smile. "Well received, Oshun. Thank you both."

Tao barked a laugh and elbowed Oshun as he passed another pack. "Don't thank him too much. His ego's already oversized."

The pack had one long strap. Mimicking the sailors, I fastened it across my body so that the pack rested on the back of one shoulder. Weapons at my sides and both hands free, I set my body toward the trees and took my first laborious steps through the sand and deeper into the unknown island nation of Ise.

THE BUSHES WERE THICK with broad leaves and slowed our movement. Though we'd seen the building tops, it seemed we'd hacked and crawled for hours before we found any signs of civilization. Hoaris, who'd been leading the party, held up a fist for us to halt, his blade still positioned in front of him. Everyone froze mid-step and listened. Singing. Faint, but clearly voices lifted in song for some purpose, and they serenaded to us from the left.

Hoaris turned, making eye contact with me, then Thalaj, and held a finger over his lips. He nodded toward the sound—his message clear that we should follow silently. As we neared the singing, two distinct sets of voices sounded above the others. The song seemed a call and response, but still in an unrecognizable tongue. The first group called, an odd recurring click punctuating the words, and the second group responded. The lyrics sounded similar, but the clicking and a few flourishes of other tones came only from the first group.

The chanting reached a crescendo as we neared, the undergrowth thinned, and we were able to walk between the broad-leafed bushes at an easier rate. After a hundred paces, a large stone building tapering toward a peak entered our view. We crept nearer, inch-by-inch, until Hoaris gestured to take cover.

Thalaj pushed me toward the base of a tree. We ducked behind a leaf broad enough to shield us both, and he guarded me bodily from whatever threat might be waiting. I didn't see where the rest of our party crouched, but I guessed they'd scattered, maybe paired off under their own bushes. Five yisun, six sailors, and the five in my own party didn't make for an easy group to hide.

I moved aside the bush's younger growth to gain better sight of the song's source. Engrossed in the scene, I allowed my jaw to hang and took in every strange and wonderful vision I could. The singers in stature seemed much like any people I'd known. They all stood with bare feet within a packed sandy opening before the peaked stone building, two rows of people lined an aisle leading to wide stone stairs. Their simple pants gathered just below the knee, and everyone's hair was as white as a fresh dusting of snow and rested close to their scalps. Many wore circlets upon their heads. None were clad above the waist, but they each displayed more golden metal than existed in all of Arashi. Some wore elaborate golden chains or stacks of tighter golden bands about their necks, and every one of the people gathered boasted golden bands around their upper arms, wrists, and ankles. From my vantage point, their hands appeared equally as decorated, but I couldn't be certain from the angle. Smaller details were difficult to discern at such a distance.

Forgetting about my traveling party and my plight, I ogled the strangeness before us. At the end of the aisle, two people stood facing one another. Both were naked except for even more ornate chains around their bodies at every place possible—neck, waist, thighs, calves, wrists, and more. Another stood between them clad in a robe that made the body seem featureless from shoulder to ground. The mask the central figure wore over the eyes appeared part tree itself, growing branches and reaching toward the sky. The robed person clearly must have been a priest or priestess presiding over the ceremony. People lining one side sang, clicked, sang some more. The other side answered but without the clicks. The priest handed a deep-red-colored bowl to one of the naked subjects who drank from it. The other mirrored the process but with a bowl the yellow of Otarr.

When they'd finished, the priest made a loud announcement, and the subjects turned toward the stone stairs. Before my eyes, the couple transformed. I blinked and rubbed my eyes to be certain of what I had seen. The one who'd drunk from the yellow bowl grew genitals I'd call male while the other's body rounded and softened, the areolas darkened, and the face plumped.

To my right, something fell, thudded to the ground. From the weight, it could have only been one of the yisun's axes. Silence followed in which neither I nor Thalaj breathed. Then, a violent wail ensued from above—a roaring cacophony, barking so loud and haunting that my spine trembled, and I cowered with a terrified moan. Tears ran from my eyes. I covered my ears, shaking and curling into a fetal position in a weak attempt to protect my head and body from whatever noise accosted me. I couldn't say if the others fell into similarly weakened positions as I was too concerned with blocking out the bone-wrenching howl.

Seasons may have passed, or mayhap only minutes, as the ear-piercing keened on and on. My ears continued to ring, and my bones continued to shake long after the noise had faded. And when I finally gained purchase to unfurl and breathe easier, I stared at three green stone arrows at the end of long spears.

Twenty-Eight

Captivity

TOGETHER, WE STOOD IN AN ample space exchanging dumbfounded looks as our eyes adjusted to the dimness within the tent's leather walls. The enclosure was spacious, tall, and a small fire burned in the center. A hole at the apex between posts sucked smoke upward. Only ten plus myself encircled the fire, whereas thirteen of us had crawled into the jungle.

Absently, I reached to my side and I grasped onto Thalaj. "Misha? Kyr?"

"Their stones," he whispered, always at my side . . .

My shadow.

His presence along with the Small Folk's invisibility-spelled stones kindled my hope.

The capture had been chaos, and I'd never found the source of the crippling sound. Our captors had judged the danger of each member within our party truly. More spears had pointed at those who were clearly the bigger threat. Thalaj had faced a dozen if he faced one. One of the spearmen had deftly stripped me of my pack and belt and forced me to move. I had stumbled along, leery of the arrowhead. They had barked and clicked at us in their own tongue and herded us to the tent.

Each time someone had reached for a weapon, our captors had stopped us with a blow. Oshun's arm bled now from his attempts. With none of the white-haired people inside now, we slowly began taking inventory and trading stories. Our worst losses were the weapons, but they'd confiscated everything we had carried. My hand drifted upward, covered the place between my breasts where my pendants still rested, and I breathed a sigh of relief for that small blessing.

Asahi started pacing the perimeter of the tent, examining the posts and the stretch of the leather as I'd seen him do with the sails aboard the *Swell Mistress*. At the back, he found a space just loose enough for someone to slide through. Lifting it, he started to crawl under. I held my breath—mayhap we all did—as he fell to his stomach and began to shimmy his way under. Mere seconds passed before his wiggling reversed.

"By the Deep Demon!" He stood, sputtering and grasping at a cut on his hand.

Collectively, our shoulders and faces fell with his failure.

"What's out there?" Hoaris boomed.

"Hoaris!" Thalaj hissed.

"What? It's not like they're speaking our tongue." He went to Asahi and examined the cut. "Not deep. Gimme that cloth around your neck."

Asahi pulled it over his head with his free hand.

While Hoaris bandaged the wound, he asked again, "What'd you see?"

The captain hissed, squinting as the makeshift bandage tightened on his hand. "The tent's encircled. Not a gap wider than my shoulders between any of the guards."

Jaliqai said to Chambui, "Maybe we can seduce them away."

Chambui raised both brows. "Did you see that ritual? I'm not sure they'd see romance the same way."

"It might be worth a go." Jaliqai pursed her lips. "It might even be fun if we could get our hands on whatever they drank from those bowls."

Timur cleared his throat, silencing Jaliqai's banter, but the two continued whispering to one another.

Others took up in the same manner, each voicing an idea, then working through the possibilities of success. Unwilling to sit and accept their fate, the yisun and sailors alike traded many ideas. The volume inched up and up as they systematically and categorically dismissed one suggestion after another.

I moved closer to Thalaj—the calm center of my inner storm—as I watched with an ever-sinking feeling growing in my heart. Cool waves wafted from him, settling, reassuring, and offering relief from the overheated air. If I could be grateful for anything in the moment, it was that he welcomed my nearness, angling his body slightly toward me.

Small, but an acceptance nonetheless.

The stones between my breast rested in silence. Ideas stormed through my mind as well, but I kept them bottled inside. I reached for my power and connection to the elements, testing my magic, but sorcery has limitations. Unlike in the open halls of Stormskeep, there wasn't enough air to gather a sufficient gale. The most I would be able to manage within the confined space was to gently stir the already thick air. I cursed myself for not calling a storm when we were first assaulted.

Perhaps our Small Folk friends would find a way to free us like they'd freed me in

Kōkai, but that seemed a bleak possibility as well. Invisibility only went so far. Misha and Kyr wouldn't be able to hide the motion of opening of the tent. Nor would they be able to sneak us out in such a mass. When they'd saved me before, I had been alone, without guard. Filtch, no, *Alto-Trea* had been overly confident we were safe within his home on the sky island. If he'd assigned guards to watch over me or taken the cloud to the skies before the Small Folk had arrived, he would have been successful in his intent. If guards surrounded the tent as Asahi claimed, the Small Folk wouldn't have such an opportunity.

Any hopes for escape seemed bleak.

Likewise, without the ability to communicate with these people, our situation seemed grim . . . at best. The arguments within the tent went on, turning into a singular sound rather than individual voices and growing louder. Louder.

Until . . .

The flaps whooshed inward and the din hushed at once. Two guards, cotton-like white hair on both, stood in the triangular opening. One spoke some harsh words, syllables separated definitely. "*Un-do.*" Pause. "*Em-boo-ka.*"

Clear ignorance masked everyone's face within the tent. Muted glances passed between the yisun, the sailors, and my party.

The first guard, for I had no better way to describe or distinguish between the two, rattled off something else. I drew my brows together, trying to discern anything. The tone and inflection weren't quite as emphatic and the syllables flowed together, but it still rang with an odd combination of *B*, *M*, *ooh* sounds and strange stops.

I swallowed and stepped forward, but a cool hand seized my wrist. Turning to my first guard, I attempted to reassure him with a quiet look. He relented, but the cold upon my back marked his nearness as I stepped closer to the two guards.

So alike in all features, neither moved. They had the advantage and knew it well. I held each of their gazes for a long moment. If I'd considered the homogeny of the Cloud Courtiers drastic, it was naught in comparison to these people. The only difference I could name was that the one on my right had slightly more slanted eyes.

I gave a small smile, hoping to reassure them we intended them no ill will. "Many greetings to you."

As if one individual turning to look at their image in a mirror, they faced one another, clear incomprehension upon their faces similar to my party's confusion seconds before. The second one answered, stating something I failed to comprehend. Then with widened eyes and a sharp inhale, the guard turned and went outside. Two returned. Three now conversed at length before they stopped and looked at me expectantly.

If they'd asked a question, I couldn't say. I greeted the newcomer in the same way. This generated a string of new dialog between the three.

After more banter, I lifted my chin and said with all the authoritative force I'd learned growing up at my father's side, "I need to find the Abatwa."

The new one understood something of what I'd said. "Ab-at-wa," he repeated—I couldn't bring myself to refer to any of them as an *it*, so I chose *he*. Then he dove into another monologue directed at his companion guards. I caught *Abatwa* repeated and another similar word, *um-ut-wa*? As he spoke, he became more unique, somehow distinguished from the others, though I couldn't say how. It confused my eyes and made my head hurt. What was this magic or the nature of these people that they changed so? When he had finished his words to the other guards, he rattled off something to me, shook his head, then hurried from the tent.

The two guards barked some more words and held up their weapons in a clear warning. The tent flapped closed behind them and we found ourselves alone again in the spacious tent with small fingers of smoke rising to the flue from the embers.

"We have to do something!" Yisun Baidu burst out and launched into a lumbering pace.

"What are we to do, Baidu?" Jaliqai stepped in front of him, placing both hands on his chest. "They took all our weapons."

Hoaris grumbled, thick arms folded over his chest. "Hells, they even took the wee knife I had shoved in my boot."

Baidu continued, "Who are these people anyway? And why do they all look alike?"

Jaliqai curved her body into his. "Bai, you are a fierce one, but your anger does us no good yet."

Even as she spoke, he looked around the tent frantically, his eyes seeming to glow with an electric blue I'd seen in many a night's storm. They settled as he relented to her ministrations.

Yisun Nachin took a seat near the fire.

Yisu Chambui joined him, crouching on her heels before sitting flat. "Doesn't seem we have much option but to wait."

The sailors stood as close to the walls of the tent as they could without hunching. Uncharacteristically, Oshun remained silent. Asahi and Tao also said nothing, only watched and waited with wary eyes. Each person within the tent tried in their own way to come to grips with the situation. I paced slowly, Thalaj at my side. Even in this, his only motive to protect his charge. He made no motions to try and escape, said nothing that hinted at a need to flee. Indeed, he'd donned his armor of duty. When I asked after his thoughts, as stoically as ever his words were as I had predicted.

"You are my only concern here, Mairynne."

I placed a hand on his chest, leaning close to his shoulder and stealing comfort I didn't believe he wished to give. But he endured it.

After some time, another set of identical twins, no, tri . . . quintuplets entered the tent. Each carried a load. They talked to us as they handed out a roll and a folded blanket to each. Arms emptied, they'd completed their duties and departed.

Hoaris threw the items to the ground and clenched his fists several times at his sides, breathing in and out through his nose. His face above his beard turned bright red. "We're just to relax here?! Sleep? What about relieving ourselves? Should we dig a hole in the corner?" He threw out a hand to indicate a corner, then stopped short. "Hells, there is no corner. It's going to stink to the heavens!"

In mere minutes, the guard who had recognized the word *Abatwa* returned carrying two stools crafted from tree stumps. He placed them beside the fire and coaxed me to sit. Placing a hand over his bare chest, he spoke very slowly, willing me with his eyes to understand. The words sounded as "nay-twa yo-ha-a-ni."

Then faster, "Nay-twa yohaani."

And faster still, "Naytwa yohaani," and it occurred to me that he was introducing himself.

"Yohaani?" I repeated.

He nodded with the vigor of a delighted youngling. "EE-GO, eego. Naytwa Yohaani!" He nodded, pointing to himself, "Di Yohaani!"

I wondered about his age but put that aside with an eagerness to be able to communicate with these people. I pointed to myself. "Nay-two . . . Mairynne."

"Nay-*twaaa*," he emphasized.

"Naytwa," I echoed with a smile. "Naytwa Mairynne."

"Eego, eego."

Hoaris rushed over. "Ask him about a toilet."

I looked up, exasperatedly squinting at the burly man. "I only know one word."

Thalaj pulled him away.

Annoying though his request had been, I said to Yohaani, "My friend needs a toilet."

This request struck Yohaani dumb. I held up one finger and stood, deciding to play the youngling theater game. I mimicked unbuckling my belt, unfastening my pants, and sitting down. He continued to look at me strangely, so I grunted and lowered my brow as if straining, then stood and pretended to fasten my breeches. Yohaani's eyes went wide with understanding.

"Ku-nee-ya," he enunciated, nodding.

I repeated.

He nodded and held up one finger in a universal signal to wait. He ducked outside and returned with three guards. And after speaking with him, I could clearly distinguish Yohaani from the others. As he spoke to the three, I studied them. How was it possible that he'd changed physically simply because I had spoken with him? I wondered if my companions had witnessed as much.

Chambui stood, clearly intent on going with Hoaris, but the guards waved her off. Yohaani held up one finger again. One at a time, it appeared. Singularly, the guards escorted the members of my group to take their relief. When Jaliqai went, she attempted to nestle into her escort, overtly flirtatious, but they pushed her away and held their spears to keep her equally triangulated between the three. She pursed her lips at the thwarted effort, but something about the look in her eyes and the set of her shoulders said that she relished the challenge they'd just laid before her.

When it was my turn, they showed me to a tiny stone room and pulled a curtain across the door. A burning torch provided light, and a fall of water ran from halfway up the wall and flowed into a hole in the floor. Odd though it seemed, I did what was necessary and returned to the tent. I scanned the area as we walked between the toilet and the tent. Other twin-like tribespeople milled around, cutting me glances as they attended to their business. Apparently, the ceremony had completed or our interruption had curtailed it, because life seemed as normal to them as ever, though I heard a group speaking some ways away, the clicks punctuating their speech.

Odd, Yohaani must be part of one clan, and the clickers part of another. They must have been in the midst of making some alignment through marriage or coupling. If I ever learned enough of the language, I'd have to inquire more about the ritual.

◇◇◇◇◇◇◇◇◇◇◇◇◇◇◇◇◇◇◇◇◇◇◇◇◇

THE REMAINDER OF OUR first day in captivity passed quietly, and at night, we took turns sitting watch while the others slept. With eleven of us, we each missed only a short amount of sleep during the dark hours owed to the duty. Yet if the others were as worried as I, we all gained little precious rest that first night. The following day, the white-haired people pushed the remainder of Asahi's crew into our tent at spearpoint. None had weapons or any belongings to mention when they stumbled inside. Some time after their arrival, more of the locals returned with bedrolls for the newcomers. I sighed at the numbers. The second night would present us with much tighter sleeping quarters. Asahi explained to his sailors what we'd learned since our capture, but their presence for me was an ill omen. The only remaining allies we had in this foreign place were Misha and Kyr.

Days passed, marked by infrequent trips to the toilet, the delivery of firewood and kindling, and the fading or growing of light at the apex of our tent.

Though they kept us sequestered, the white-haired people brought food and water, and Yohaani stopped in almost daily to teach me a new word. We settled into a tiresome routine. The men who'd initially railed against our imprisonment calmed, and Jaliqai gave up her attempts to seduce her way out of captivity. Hoaris had a set of dice in his pocket they hadn't confiscated, and although we had nothing to bet, we all took part in the game. I daresay we enjoyed the game. When the guards heard laughing, they peeked inside curiously but generally left us to the game. Jaliqai refocused her ministrations on the yisun, sailors, and once on Hoaris, whose skin turned the color of a ripe ringo fruit growing on the trees in Nadia's gardens.

One evening when a couple of guards entered, Chambui lay curled up against Timur's chest. The guards chattered and yelled at them until they separated their pallets.

I looked forward to the daily interaction with Yohaani; my vocabulary increased some, yet it still remained insufficient for communication. Sentences made no logical sense. I felt like a baby repeating words to her parents, but it sufficed to care for our basic needs. I tried to share some of my words with the others, but Yohaani scoffed at their attempts at his language. He didn't even bother to correct their intonation like he did with me.

Several days into our stay, the guards gathered us all and escorted us again at spearpoint to a stream. Boulders dammed the flow creating a small pool of clear water that trickled over the edge in a constant tiny waterfall. Yohaani walked along with us and, at the stream, he handed me a bag with small balls inside. As I looked, a clean floral scent wafted out.

"Soap?" I asked.

"EE-YO-ZA," he said, pointing to the bag. Then he turned away, leaving us there in a large group with the guards.

"Ee-yo-za," I repeated softly.

A bath.

Closing my eyes, I grinned.

But my relief faded quickly. I opened my eyes when I felt something, another material, brush against my arm. A guard handed me a pair of pants and another empty bag. My mind reeled as he did the same with the others. An empty bag? Perhaps for our dirty clothes. Mayhap they intended to launder them on our behalf? But more confounding, why had they scolded Timur and Chambui's affection, yet allowed, or even wanted, us to bathe together in the small pool?

Desperate for a good scrubbing, I shrugged and passed out the balls of soap from Yohaani. *Eeyoza.*

Our men wouldn't have the mass mingling of sexes during our baths, more out of respect than shame. One by one, they turned away, waiting for the two yisu and me to take our turns in the water.

As we stripped our clothes, the guards exchanged confused looks. When we moved into the water, one pointed, lowered his voice, and said something to the other.

Coming of age, I'd always bathed in heated tubs and vastly preferred a freshly hot bath to one that'd cooled too long. Here in Ise, after the constant heat within the tent, I didn't even flinch when the cool water bit my skin. Tired and dirty, I ignored the guards' whispers and washed until my skin felt raw from the scrubbing. Then I scrubbed my hair until it felt squeaky between my fingers. Afterward, Chambui, Jaliqai, and I dressed in the pants provided and sat topless on a large boulder nearby while the men went toward the pool.

The guards' bantering by the pool became louder—more pointing and whispers. Finally, one of them barked, "KU-NU-MA!"

An order.

The group fell silent.

A leader among them?

I added the word, *ku-nu-ma*, to my meager collection. If it worked to silence the guards, mayhap I'd find use for it.

WHEN WE HAD COMPLETED our baths, they escorted us back to our tent and took the bags of our clothing. Clad in only the simple pants of the tribespeople from waist to just below the knees, we waited. Chambui and Jaliqai seemed perfectly comfortable, but I fought an urge to shield my breasts. I had the sense that Thalaj thought it wrong as well as the temperature in the tent remained much cooler than it had before despite the constant warmth from the fire.

The night creatures gathered outside, their songs chirping into the darkling sky, and I curled onto my pallet with a thin blanket. Mayhap I couldn't see her face with my eyes, but I imagined how Selene watched over this remote land. I prayed, imagining her silver light upon me as I whispered, "Goddess Selene, Night-Seer, please hold my father a while longer. If it be your will, help us find our freedom from these people. Watch over Thalaj, Hoaris, the yisun, and the sailors. I beg you to guide my journey further into this strange land. And please, will my sister's heart to open to me upon my return." I sucked in a breath at the last. I'd stifled thoughts of Karynne for a long time, and the memory surfacing in prayer hit me hard. Tears welled in my eyes, a knot formed in my throat, and I fought the weeping that followed.

Grateful for the darkness, I wiped away tears and swallowed several times.

The flap flew open, a breeze wafted across my bare chest, and someone leaned half inside. A man, clearly not one of the tribe, stood within the triangular opening and scanned our faces. Clad in leather boots, simple pants, a tunic, and a leather vest, he wore a patch over one eye and stood with legs wide, holding the leather back with one hand.

He pushed a torch into the tent's darkness with his free hand and took a deep breath.

"Heya!" he said. "Where's Mairynne?"

Twenty-Nine

Demons of the Sea

SNIFFLING, I SCRUBBED THE REMAINING tears from my eyes, flung the thin blanket away, and clumsily scrambled to my feet. "Th-that's me." I straightened to my full height, chin up and smoothing down my simple pants.

He looked me up and down in the dim light, turned, and spat outside the tent. "Just a minute." And as soon as he had appeared, he disappeared, the leather swinging slightly before it settled.

The others in the tent gained their feet as well, everyone appearing as wary of the newcomer as I. Whoever he was, he'd come for me, asked for me by name, and the guards had allowed him to pass. His hair wasn't white, and he looked distinguished like an older man. With a quick thanks to Selene, I leaped at the lifeline. I'd made it halfway to the exit, chasing him, when the flap opened again. I halted. Something flew at my face, and I threw my hands up to catch it.

A shirt.

"Put it on and join me out here," the leather-clad man said. "Don't worry. The Rundi guards will allow you to come to me."

The flap closed again. I examined the shirt—nothing special, simple spun, cream colored, and too large—but I put it on and went to the door, more tentatively this time. A hand in the dark landed on my arm, cold against my skin. The grip pulled and spun me into Thalaj's chest. My heart pattered with irregularity as I looked up into his almond eyes.

That kiss we shared was all I could think.

But he looked at me with a warning and demand. "What are you doing?"

"I'm going out there to see what he wants."

"The hells you are."

I shivered in his arms. "Thalaj. He must be here to help. Why else?"

"You cannot go out there without me. I need to see you in order to be able to protect you." He gripped me tighter about the upper arms, my now clothed chest to his bare chest. Had he done this seconds before, we would have been skin to skin. His nostrils flared and my legs weakened.

Yet the free streak my mother had always named in me also came alive. I pushed against him. "And how exactly do you propose to protect me if there are a dozen guards out there with spears pointed in your direction?"

"I . . ."

Breathing deeply, I said, "I didn't expect you to have an answer. They've had a hundred or more times to kill one of us. Or all. You're overreacting."

He seethed, cold wafting from him.

I moved my hand to cover his heart.

At length, he sighed. "Do not go farther than earshot from the tent." He released me and went to stand next to the entrance. Crossing his arms over his bare chest just below tattooed red scimitynes with interlocked blades, he nodded his readiness.

I ducked and walked out into the night. The evening air upon my cheeks made me long to free my sorcery. I allowed it to flow through me, tingling in the ends of my fingers, but only long enough to lift the ends of my hair. The feeling of magic coursing through my veins was exquisite. Yet I severed the flow, wary of how the guards to my right and left would react.

The man in the vest sat on one stump; another awaited me. A line of three torches anchored behind him silhouetted his form in the night. He bent over something, whittling with a knife that seemed too large for the delicate job. His patched eye faced me, so it surprised me when he acknowledged my presence with a single word and a wave of his knife. "Sit."

He folded the small figure into a cloth and put both it and the knife on the ground at his feet before he studied me with one amber eye, so light brown it seemed to glow in the flickering torchlight. Up close, his skin appeared too browned to match his light hair. Lines spidered out from his good eye, as well as from beneath the patch, and there were several creases upon his forehead.

So many questions . . .

I settled for inquiring after his name; he had mine after all.

"They call me Umu-Zimi." He flourished a hand toward the guards.

"And why have you come for me?"

"Yohaani sent for me. Said there were people from the east here."

"And why did he send for you? For what purpose?"

"He said you were seeking the Abatwa. Thought I might be able to help."

I thought on his name. "Are you one of them?"

He bellowed a laugh. "The Triad save me—no."

Squinting, I asked in slow, measured words, "So, you're . . . Nantai? You pray by Atun, Otarr, and Selene. The same gods my people serve."

"You think I learned your tongue here?" He laughed as if that were the most absurd notion. "Have any one of these people uttered one word in your language? Even Yohaani?"

I cut a glance over to the guards of the tribespeople. They were the only ones about in the darkness. Yohaani, though he had supposedly summoned this man, was nowhere in sight. I considered the implication in Umu-Zimi's outburst of laughter. Yohaani had tried to teach me his language, but he hadn't so much as attempted mine, outside of my name. I said, "You may not have learned here, but it is quite possible that you spent time in our lands but are not of the Nantai people." I raised my chin, attempting to gain some semblance of the diplomatic nature I'd seen within my mother and father and I only played at imitating. "Or you might hail from one of our bordering nations. Yōtei or Baiu, perhaps? Or Engaru, just beyond the Great Sands?"

He chewed and spat on the ground, rubbing a black mess into the sand between us.

My stomach turned at the sight, but I held my composure.

"I am Nantai. One of your *people*, if you will. Casteless, I believe one such as you would label me. I hail from a small town near the Copper Coast, and I sailed across the Syrensea many long years ago in search of something better than the half-life of that class. You see, Mairynne—a Storm Sorcerer's name if I've ever heard the like—the life of a thief or a servant simply wasn't in my blood."

I stopped everything—breathing, blinking, trying to hold my composure. I simply halted at the anguish in those words. I'd never viewed our caste system as bad, per se. I'd thought many of the rules silly or unnecessary. I'd disagreed with some of the traditions. But at its core, I never understood the separate castes to be *wrong* before. The farther I went from home, the more I learned about how contrived and how belittling it truly was. And there I had sat, on top of it all. Kōgō Mairynne Evangale.

Neither the queasiness at the sight of whatever he'd spat nor the seasickness upon the *Swell Mistress* compared to the nausea over coming to realize who and what I was. This man, rough around the edges as he was, had a gentle quality about him, a humble nature, a common mortal feeling of wanting to control his own life and destiny. What was so wrong about that? In my heart of hearts, I knew the answer—*nothing*.

I looked down, into my lap where my hands now toyed with the hem of the shirt he'd offered.

"That doesn't matter anymore though," Umu-Zimi said.

Obviously, it mattered so little to him that he accepted a name the people of Ise had given him. Umu-Zimi was clearly a name from their strange language. I chose not to ask after his given name.

"Well and so," he began, "if you so wish, I can help you find the Abatwa, but only you. The rest of your friends will need to leave these lands. Those are the terms the Rundi leaders have set forth."

"What? No." I answered, then furrowed my brow. "The *Rundi* leaders? These people?" I waved to the guards around the tent.

He nodded. "Possibly you don't understand the offer. The two Rundi tribes gathered here have offered that you may leave with me and the others may leave by ship. Or, *you* may also leave by ship with your party. Otherwise, they plan a series of sacrifices." He said this with no sign of aberration, as if it were an everyday thing.

"Sacrifices?" I echoed, appalled. "Sacrifices of what nature?"

Umu-Zimi laughed, a sound that only went to show how naïve he thought me. "Isn't that obvious, my dear? You. And your people." He looked over toward the tent.

I blinked in disbelief. Maybe it was a commonplace practice here. Maybe that's what had happened with this man's travel companions or others who'd crossed the Syrensea. Regardless, I couldn't allow that fate for Thalaj or Hoaris. Or any of the people I'd come to know upon our trip across the Syrensea. "I cannot separate myself from my party. Or at least a few of them."

He nodded, spat again, and bent to retrieve his carving and knife. "Very well, then. I shall tell Yohaani that you've chosen to leave with your group. They'll send you away with the ship on the morning tide two days hence."

As he stood, I reached for him, grasping onto a leathery arm. "No." The stones buzzed between my breasts. I had to follow. Leaving now could be a death sentence for my father. I stood, rising almost to his height. "You must work harder on them, these Rundi. I beg you to try and persuade them to allow you to take three. The rest may return to the *Swell Mistress* and sail from this place without us."

He turned. Looking sideways at me, he chewed and said, "I can't promise success." Then he called to the guards in their tongue, and two of them urged me back inside at the green tips of their spears.

I curled onto my pallet, pulled the cover up to my chin, and cried. I mourned the discord that my people felt, I shed tears over my mother, and I wept for the possible impending loss of my father. I also cried for the possibility that by my decision, I stranded three of us here upon Ise with no means of return to Nantai, Arashi, or Stormskeep.

Maybe I'd been wrong to even try. Maybe I should have stayed upon my throne and maintained my ignorance.

Deep within, Thalaj's words replayed, *We'll run into many things, and we'll face them together.* And, as if my thoughts called him closer, he crouched beside me. "Are you okay?"

"There's still hope." I sniffled. "Though slight. Did you hear?"

He nodded and rubbed my arm through the sheet that covered me. Damn him to walk the hells. I wished for him to lay beside me, wrap his strong arms around me, and hold me safely until I fell asleep. But I couldn't ask for those things. He'd made our positions clear, but for once, couldn't he have put aside his overwhelming sense of propriety just to give me what I so desperately needed?

"You're an idiot, Thalaj Northerngale," Chambui said, approaching from my other side.

She lifted my cover and urged me to make room. I did, and she slid in beside me and wrapped us both tight under the cover. Her embrace was strong too, and I accepted the compassion willingly. Thalaj left us then, sufficiently scolded, but without the cold anger he so often exuded. At some point, I cried myself to sleep within her arms.

With sticky, swollen eyes, I screamed myself awake.

Chambui sat up with me, concern written in her eyes.

"A dream," I said between pants and hugged my knees to my chest. A horrible, jumbled dream . . . a screech through the night, my mother's body twisted, then my father's twisted in death as well, the blue dragon we'd met in the trading town, and a little story Father had once told and I'd forgotten ringing in my ears of one who might be worthy. The flashing visions embodied everything I feared. And then it was over, and I was awake and ripped back into reality.

"Why?" I wailed. "Why am I putting myself through this? Maybe Karynne had it right. We should just let these people send us back on the tide and stop trying so hard to find what's obviously go—"

Chambui grabbed my shoulders and shook. "You're a mess. Stop this." She no longer consoled me but snapped me back to my current predicament. When I looked at her, stopped by her grasp, she continued, "The Stone Lady doesn't choose her mates or whom she protects lightly. That she sent five of us with you tells that she saw a strength in you that you'd best live up to."

I bowed my head, fighting the tears that threatened again.

Chambui lifted my chin. Cutting her eyes to Thalaj, she said softly, "He's stubborn, but you bend his will. Don't give up on him. And don't give up on why you're here."

It took some time, but I collected myself. The day passed as several had before. The guards came again to take us to the pool to bathe. This time, they returned our clothes, cleaned. As the two yisu and I were dressing, Umu-Zimi appeared alongside Yohaani.

Anger boiled in my blood, and I called a wind without thought to help me in my rush toward the two men. I didn't hide the burst of anger as I greeted Yohaani shortly, "Ga kāya nāza." Then I turned to Umu-Zimi and demanded, "You *will* take at least three of us. Preferably four. You may return the others to the *Swell Mistress*, but at least three of us will face whatever challenges we must to find the Abatwa."

⬦⬦⬦⬦⬦⬦⬦⬦⬦⬦⬦⬦⬦⬦⬦⬦⬦⬦⬦⬦⬦⬦⬦⬦⬦

YOHAANI RANTED AT ME in his own tongue, then to Umu-Zimi. A handful of our guards moved in until the man with the eye patch spoke up. He calmed the Rundi people in their own tongue and clearly said something that convinced them to give him some time alone with me. We sat on a rock ledge near the pool, in eyesight but out of hearing range. When I looked across the pool at Chambui, she nodded reassuringly, then turned away to grant our men their privacy. I did the same by turning expectantly toward Umu-Zimi.

He exhaled on a long sigh and grabbed a green blade from the long grasses on the backside of the rock wall. As he spoke, he folded the blade this way and that. "The Rundi tribespeople are not pleased with your arrival. They believe it an ill omen from their gods." He gazed out over the water. "They have refused your request. You must sail, or you alone may go with me deeper into Ise."

"Why are they so angry with us? We've been naught but compliant since our arrival."

"Your arrival alone was ill will enough in their eyes. They believe the Syrensea itself is evil. They pray to their gods to protect them against the sea demon. Your very arrival over the sea says to them that you were borne of that demon."

I narrowed my eyes at him. "But that is not the extent of it, am I right?"

"Nay, it is not. You interrupted their most sacred ceremony."

Failing to understand, I countered, "It looked like a wedding. How is that their most sacred ceremony? Weddings happen all the time."

He shook his head. "Not for the Rundi tribes."

"I don't follow."

"The Rundi tribes are by nature a peaceful group; although their gods teach that outsiders of any kind are evil, but especially those coughed up by the sea demon."

I started to interject as he'd already said as much, but he held up a hand.

I relented and he went on, "They are also not very fertile. Do you see children running around the area when you're led through to the waste room?"

"No." I'd noticed as much early on and had also found this intriguing.

"The ceremony wasn't a wedding so much as a rite of fertility. The tribes have experienced far more deaths than births over the last hundred seasons or so." He laughed. "They would likely hang me up for their mother god if they knew I told you all of this. But they don't understand our tongue. They refuse to learn it, thinking it the language of the sea demon.

"Regardless, the two tribes you saw at the ceremony were the Zhorundi and the Khirundi. The Zhorundi click when they speak, so you can likely deduce the ones who have you captive are the Khirundi. Yohaani is their leader. It takes several moons to prepare for the fertility ceremony itself. They make a pilgrimage into the mountains to search for a rare flower that only blooms for a day when the snow thins. They make an extract from the flower that causes their bodies to change and become ready for reproduction. You interrupted their chance for a child that would further unite these two tribes, and their next opportunity will only arrive after they can retrieve more of the snow flowers."

My stomach felt hollow in the silence that followed Umu-Zimi's explanation. I now comprehended the gravity. Not only did they believe some devil beneath the seas had sent us, they also believed that this devil intended their extinction by restricting their ability to produce children. We remained in silence for several long moments while I considered how worrisome that knowledge might be, how utterly disheartened it must seem for their people to not have a next generation to carry on their hopes and dreams.

"Would it help my case if they knew that I was merely searching for my own family?" I asked.

The man shook his head. "I don't think so."

"Can you teach me how to apologize?" I asked, hoping that an apology would go some distance in helping my case.

Umu-Zimi clenched his jaw. I saw little hope in his one bright eye, but he answered. "To say *I'm sorry*, you would say *m-por-ay*."

I repeated the word, the first sound quiet and a breathy emphasis on the second.

"But," he warned, "saying the word isn't enough to the Rundi. Apologies are also elaborate and sacred. They require a cleansing of the soul in order to be accepted. You'd have a chance since you've started to learn their tongue, but they won't allow your other people to remain while you make the attempt.

"In fact, your aptitude for learning their words is the only reason they didn't sacrifice you one by one to Dea, their goddess of fertility, as recompense for the children you stole from their wombs."

I flinched.

"Hai, that is harsh, but that is also the nature of these people."

Curiosity stirred . . . Why had they accepted him? After a moment of silence, I asked, "How did you end up here and gain this knowledge? How did you learn to speak their language so proficiently?"

He reached up and removed his patch to reveal a sunken and scarred hollow where his eye once was. The smile that spread on his face appeared purely savage and his teeth seemed sharper than normal, and I took his meaning . . . One must dig deep and be willing to make whatever sacrifice necessary to come into the Rundi tribes' good graces after bringing so much evil.

In that moment, I also decided that Umu-Zimi would be an excellent choice to guide me into the wilderness of Ise, another unknown front, to find another unknown people. Since these tribes viewed us so poorly, I wondered if the Abatwa held such beliefs about our origins as well. Would they have other reasons to wish ill will upon us? I just couldn't reconcile parting with Thalaj, or with Hoaris and the Small Folk. I chewed my lip, thinking.

A stick cracked nearby. Then another. Umu-Zimi stood in one lithe motion, crouched and ready to combat whatever had stirred in the brush nearby. I looked up, hopeful that no further howling, barking, or bone-rattling sounds would accost us.

Blessedly, none came. I held my breath.

Could it be Misha and Kyr?

Stillness. Nothing.

We settled back into our conversational positions, but the feeling of being watched didn't leave. I looked out to where Thalaj and Hoaris bathed alongside the sailors, and I hardened myself as I made a decision. I only hoped it was the *right* decision.

In a low voice, I finally said, "Give me tonight with my people, and tomorrow, I want to watch them go. At dawn, we can send the *Swell Mistress* away, and I will go with you to find the Abatwa. Alone."

And so, at Otarr's first light, I stood shoulder to shoulder with the old man in leather upon the shore and we watched. The Rundi people stayed within the trees; apparently they viewed the beach as the wastes of the sea demon and didn't wish to step foot onto the sand. Thalaj looked at me just before he climbed onto the dock. Maybe it was my imagination, but the temperature around me seemed to drop. Then, I spread my hands slightly in front of me and called to the winds. They stirred the sand into a white whirlwind that swept over my party as they trod down the dock and boarded the *Swell Mistress*.

And then, when none remained upon the pier, I released my sorcery. The sandstorm dissipated. The *Mistress* drifted and oars pulled her seaward. Salt returning unto the sea.

Thirty

...And Inland Still

HUMILITY—A MASK I WORE INTENTLY as we packed for travel inland. I often looked toward the beach, allowing worry to show upon my face, hugging myself about the waist, or chewing at my nails. I did what Umu-Zimi instructed listlessly, lacking the energy that I felt when Thalaj had been at my side. Sometime during our preparation, I learned that we had not made it to Seleucid which lay on the western coast of Ise at the mouth of a river by the same name. In fact, the largest river on the island divided two nations, Ise to the south and Tamatori to the north. We'd landed in the central part of Ise on the eastern coast at a pier built by people from Seleucid for the infrequent occasions when they came to trade with the Rundi tribes.

Trade, I also learned, was a choreographed ordeal. The Seleucid people would travel in boats a mere third of the size of the *Swell Mistress* and leave their goods just inside the line of trees. They'd set off a cannon when they returned to their ship and wait. Two days following, the traders would return to the trees. By then, the Rundi tribes had exchanged their goods for handcrafted or carved items that fetched a nice price with the wealthier people in the only city upon the island.

The Zhorundi had taken their leave of the area well before Umu-Zimi had come to save me. The tribes being nomadic and roaming up and down the eastern coast of Ise, the Khirundi were also preparing to leave their temple to allow the next tribe, the Mhorundi, their time to commune with the gods. The Khirundi would travel north. Our destination was west, where we would cross the mountains and make our way through thick forests until we met up with the Seleucid River, then north from there.

Parting was nothing to speak of. Yohaani barely grunted as he passed, but I sensed a relief in him that hadn't been there before. Umu-Zimi hefted his pack, said, "Let's go," and trod past me without a backward glance.

We walked.

And walked . . . and walked.

At times, my guide hacked at our path, clearing growth preventing our travel. About midday, he handed me some salted, dried meat and a bladder of water to wash it down. We ate on our feet.

And we walked.

At times, we climbed.

And then, we walked some more.

We didn't talk. Everything around us remained silent except for some birds and insects chirping about their days.

When Umu-Zimi decided it was time to make camp, he dropped his pack and said to me, "You're stronger than I believed. I was shocked when you sent your people away so easily."

I said naught, still filled with worry . . . and if I dared, hope.

In the twilight, my guide instructed me to be still and quiet as he hovered near a thicket. After several minutes, he pounced into the brush. The leaves shook and then he popped up holding a wriggling hare. I winced when he snapped its neck. It went limp in his grasp, but who was I to complain. The meat would nourish us for the night and likely into the following day.

As darkness fell, he lit a fire and spit the animal over it to cook. I couldn't see Selene or the night sky for the verdant cover above. Our clearing was small, and the night cooled quickly. As he curled up beside the fire, he said, "There's nothing here to worry over. We can both sleep." He'd no sooner closed his eyes than he began softly snoring. I wrapped myself tight in a blanket, suspecting there would be little of the fire left by morning and I'd be shivering in a ball beside nothing more than smoking ash.

Contrary to that belief, I awoke sweating beside roaring flames, the dawn not fully upon the land. I sat, flinging away my covers and searching my surroundings. Across the fire, Umu-Zimi's pallet lay in a messy heap with his pack untouched beside it. My heart sprang into a gallop and I stood drawing my scimitynes. Praise be that the Yohaani had seen me as little enough danger to return those to me upon our departure. There I crouched with the blades held in the defensive just as Thalaj had taught me. Should I call out? What if that awakened whatever had taken my guide? *Think, Mairynne. Think.* I counted my breaths, stretching the exhales out as long as I possibly could in order to calm my racing heartbeat.

Nothing stared back from the brush for a long time.

I kept my eyes stretched wide, hoping to find something or someone in the dark green-gray.

No sounds.

Then, a rustle.

I tensed.

Prepared my body for the fiercest strike I could recall from my lessons with Thalaj and the Tsinti, Yankos, Baldeo, and Jorani.

When at last my eyes saw the source of the movement, I breathed heavily. Relieved.

Umu-Zimi came out of the brush. "Thanks for tending the fire," he said, looking at me askance. His eyes questioned why I'd gone on guard, but he didn't voice the words.

So I didn't reply, but I put my blades away.

"It's nice to wake up warm for a change," he said.

"You're welcome," a chirpy, quick voice called from the dimness beyond the fire's light.

"Misha!" I cried and launched toward him. In a few quick steps, I swept him into my arms like he was a lost youngling.

"Me . . . Mairy . . . oh my, Mairynne!" He slapped my shoulder and protested. "Put me down." Then, he laughed and so did I.

I did as he demanded, though with the Small Folks' flittery voices, it was difficult to view it as a demand. "Where's Kyr?" I asked.

With a chirp, her voice came from the brush too. "Here, lovely."

After giving her a quick hug, I turned back to the fire.

Our positions had switched. Umu-Zimi had gone on high alert, grabbing a burning log from the fire to hold high as a makeshift torch. In the other hand, he gripped his curved knife. "Who are these younglings?"

"NOT younglings," Misha snipped, fiery energy crackling in the air.

I stopped the small man as he made to lunge for Umu-Zimi, answering the question asked. "Certainly, being from Nantai, you are familiar with the Small Folk. This is Misha and his partner, Kyr. They traveled with us upon the *Swell Mistress*."

"But they weren't in the prisoner tent with the rest of you." His stance didn't ease at all, and as we moved closer to the fire, he made certain to keep the flames between us. "This isn't all right. I'm going to have to find one of the tribes and inform their elders. They watch for trespassers. You've been given the freedom to move about the Rundi lands with me, but they have not."

"Why does it matter?" I asked. "There's no one here but us."

"They have eyes and ears everywhere." He scanned the area with one wide eye. Settled, he added, "We'll go in search of Yohaani. They shouldn't be more than a day's trek if we angle toward the north." He bent and began packing up his gear.

I started to rebut his decision, but my words fell short and my breath hitched as Thalaj appeared from nothingness—a shadow—behind Umu-Zimi. My first guard held a weapon in one hand and slipped a stone, clearly spelled, into his pocket. He lifted the scimityne into Umu-Zimi's sight just below his chin. "No. We will not be finding Yohaani," he said, voice as cold as the ice crusting Kōdaina Kori, the great lake surrounded by the Iced Plains of Nantai.

Carefully, Umu-Zimi turned to look at Thalaj. Either he visibly shivered or the cold rage that rolled from my guard fogged the air. I smiled.

"Sit." Thalaj motioned to the ground where his blankets still covered the ground beside the fire.

Umu-Zimi obeyed.

"How goes it, Mairynne?" Hoaris stepped out of the brush with a thud, gnawing on some unknown fruit.

My guide gasped. "Are they all following? How did you—"

Thalaj moved the blade closer to his throat, and Umu-Zimi swallowed his words, looking wearily at the group who now surrounded him.

I gave Hoaris a hug and turned back to the one-eyed man. His eye shifted, wide and dreadful, but conscious of Thalaj's deadly blade, he sat stock-still with his hands raised beside either shoulder. My first guard took the torch and placed it back into the fire and likewise relieved Umu-Zimi of his knife.

"This should be it," I said. "The rest truly boarded the *Swell Mistress* and sailed." I bit the inside of my lip, my eyes dropping for a moment in regret.

Hoaris smirked. "Almost . . ."

I folded my brow as I peered up at him, then turned to look at Thalaj with the same question. As I did, Chambui appeared from thin air, seated beside Umu-Zimi and lifting her hand from a spelled stone.

My hand flew over my mouth, and I inhaled sharply. Hoaris barked laughter. The Small Folk giggled and chattered. Umu-Zimi jumped and scrambled away as much as Thalaj would allow. I caught the corner of my protector's mouth twitching as if he wanted to smile, yet he trained his face back to the stern mask.

I eased my hand away, weight lifted from my shoulders, happy tears flooded my eyes, and a smile spread across my lips.

◇◇◇◇◇◇◇◇◇◇◇◇◇◇◇◇◇◇◇◇◇◇

"UMU-ZIMI," THALAJ MUSED. " 'Tis not Nantai. What does it mean?"

After we'd explained the spelled stones, the weathered man began to ease into having all of us there. Thalaj pulled his scimityne away from Umu-Zimi's throat but kept it unsheathed. My guide lifted a stick from near the fire. While trying to settle into a nonchalant routine of whittling, his eyes still shifted to each of us as he spoke. "It means *spirit* in the Rundi language. It's short for *Umu-Zimi in-jabuka ku ryōsha*. In full, it means *spirit from beyond who comes to make good*."

"How did you acquire this name?" Thalaj pressed.

He looked at my guard with his one good eye. "I spent more time in the prisoner tent at Yohaani's camp than you, and I gave my right eye to make amends to the Khirundi and gain my freedom to walk across their lands. I've paid my dues. You"—he pointed with his whittling knife to each of us around the fire—"have not."

"What's your given name?" The manner in which Thalaj asked this seemed unalarming, but if I heard the tone correctly, he intended it to be a demand rather than a question.

Umu-Zimi remained quiet for a long while, making long knife strokes that removed bark. Then, almost a murmur, he said, "I left that in Nantai, and I'm not planning to return any time soon." His volume rose as he continued, "And I'll not guide you through these lands in betrayal to the Rundi tribes. I can't afford to lose my other eye."

This exchange between Thalaj and Umu-Zimi went on. My guard remained patient as he questioned Umu-Zimi about his time here in Ise and the one-eyed man gave him information somewhat willingly, as if there was nothing really to hide. It appeared that the only thing he feared was betraying the Rundi.

Hoaris, Misha, and Kyr hovered some distance from the fire. Chambui sat still, waiting and watching, and I took a seat beside the yisu of the Stone Singers, happily surprised that she'd chosen to join my company rather than returning with the other four. She took my hand as I sat and simply held it.

For my part, I watched Thalaj work on the man. He'd press him a little about the journey to find the Abatwa, then he'd back off to a more welcome topic. The exchange rekindled so many memories from Stormskeep. The way he talked with the other guards and how he remained utterly patient with each of them during their training. He'd won them over little by little, never forcing them to acquiesce to his leadership, but in time each had developed a loyalty to him that I hadn't otherwise seen surpassed. He'd been in a delicate situation then, because in truth, society considered most of the people he led a superior caste. Many had come to his ranks believing his Storm Sorcerer blood tainted by his Frost Fighter father's. As the soldiers' confidence in his abilities grew, so did their natural tendencies to follow him and defer to him in almost every decision. He used the same tactics on Umu-Zimi, and I could see it beginning to work. It was something that had always been a part of him, yet I had never put it into words until that moment around the fire deep within a jungle on the other side of the world from home.

Home.

I longed for Stormskeep and the ever present Sundai Falls, but I felt happy then and there, where we were, holding Chambui's hand and watching Thalaj work his own subtle magic. Something simply felt good with close friends at my side and him, my solid center, there with me.

Chambui shook my hand and chided softly, "You wear your love for that man too much upon your face."

"I don't . . ." I started, but thought better of it and straightened my face.

Thalaj began to press again. "You've heard of the Order?"

Umu-Zimi folded his brow. Clearly, it rung familiar, but he couldn't place it as he'd been so far removed from Nantai. In Thalaj's long conversation, he'd revealed that he'd lived in Ise longer than I'd taken breath. He gave up trying to puzzle it out and shook his head.

"Well," Thalaj continued, "we came upon you unnoticed."

"This much is true," said Umu-Zimi.

"I spent most of my youth in training to move quietly and unnoticed through life. Hoaris too. Let me just say that I've earned the nickname *Shadow* because I've a knack for being beside someone before they are aware. There should be no problem with us outing you to the Rundi."

I tucked my chin, unwilling to mention the spelled stones that helped his endeavors here.

Misha, apparently not seeing a point to hiding the information, chirped in, "The only thing better is our stones. We can walk invisible through this land, as you've just witnessed."

Thalaj smiled. "And we shall use those for most of our travels." He turned to the guide. "But I assume that we will be traveling some distance yet. It is inconvenient to remain unseen entirely. Will you give us a day's journey as a test?"

The one-eyed man stood, dusting his hands on his pants, and took a long couple of breaths. "All right, we'll try," he said at last. "We'd best be going then."

Hoaris barked, "Hey! Umu . . . *whatever* is a mouthful. Can I call you Z?"

Umu-Zimi gave Thalaj a look askance as if to beg that he keep his friend quiet, then nodded once, grabbed his pack, and began clearing a path through the jungle once again. From that point forward, we all called him Z.

◇◇◇◇◇◇◇◇◇◇◇◇◇◇◇◇◇◇◇◇◇◇◇◇◇◇◇◇◇◇◇

KYR HANDED ME A stone too, with a wink and a nudge. I tucked it away, recalling but not using the word to activate its magic, mekoilieu.

As we began to move, the others activated the spells, and to anyone watching, it would have looked like only my guide and I trekked along the path. Thalaj, though invisible, walked just behind me, the coolness of his essence always present. The time ticked by in silence outside of Z's knife slashes and constant forward movement.

When the light started to dim, my guide turned and said, "We camp here."

Thalaj, visible then, stepped to my side. "And now you see that this is possible?"

Tight-lipped, Z nodded.

At camp, my friends released the spells on their stones, but we spoke in hushed voices around the small fire Z had built. We hunted for game and ate. Then, with more than only two of us, we appointed shifts to stand watch overnight; by morn, there had been no threats seen or heard.

We continued on the next day much as we had the first. At times, we climbed. Others, we had to steady our steps to not slide down a rocky hill. I didn't have much opportunity to speak with Thalaj, but when he didn't use the invisibility spells, we exchanged small smiles now and then. Despite my aching back and blisters forming, it felt good, like something might be starting anew.

On the third day, we made it to a river.

Z announced, "It's the Seleucid. Another day that way"—he pointed—"and we may find what you seek."

"May?" I asked.

He took a few steps along the water's edge. "Hai, may. That is if they wish to be found."

My stomach grew hollow and I grasped at the stones, worried. They vibrated mildly against my chest. "I . . . I don't follow."

Z laughed. "The will of the Fey folk is terribly unpredictable." He dropped his pack against a tree and went across the rocky shore to the water. There he began to strip his clothes, clearly intent on washing the days' worth of hiking away.

In the moment, I cared little about propriety. I wanted two things—to know what by the name of the Triad he meant by *Fey* people and to ease my aching feet and body within those waters. I followed, stripping my clothes at a large rock near the water and sinking into one of the still pools. Dipping my head under, I surfaced with a sigh of relief and wiped the water from my eyes. It was cool but not the same cold as the river that flowed through Arashi.

As the others came into the water too, I swam nearer to Z and peppered him with more questions about the Abatwa. All he would say was that they appeared in different forms, but in their natural form they were small.

"However," he cautioned, "don't ever say anything that would lead them to believe that you think they are small. They're sensitive about that."

There on the banks, we finished bathing and built a fire. We boiled some water to refill our water bladders, snacked on some dried meat, then packed up and continued north by east up the Seleucid. Others went invisible, but Thalaj strode at my side. Here, I could see Otarr in the sky where the trees parted for the waters. I said a prayer again, this time that we find these Fey folk, then my father, and that I could remain focused on that until I had delivered him back to the Serpentine Throne in Stormskeep.

As the day waned and I was beginning to expect Z to stop for the night, Hoaris cursed loudly from fifty or so paces behind us. When I rounded, he appeared, the spelled stone rolling from his hand. He swatted at something around him. A dark cloud?

"Stop!" Z said and ran toward the scene. He dropped his pack along the way, waving his hands in the air. "Don't hit them."

Thalaj and I exchanged a look and followed.

Hoaris dropped to his knees, seeming to succumb to the swarm of insects around him.

Z crouched on one knee beside him reverently. "Fey prince, with your immensity, I saw you from the mountain top way over there." He gestured to a distant peak. "We have come to seek the help of the Abatwa queen. Will you show us to her?"

Thirty-One

A Fey Prince

Storm sorcery had always been a staple in my life. Other caste abilities also didn't seem beyond reason. More recently, I'd learned of the Small Folks' spells on stones, but I'd never seen the likes of how this Fey prince shifted from the size of my small finger to a full-sized man before my eyes. I stumbled backward as I looked closer at the insect swarm. Tiny people flew through the air, mounted upon the backs of winged ant-like creatures. The dark cloud began to settle, and these tiny people dismounted and moved about their prince's feet. Meanwhile, the prince stood stoically, a red band around his head, bare-chested, a cloth around his loins, fringed bands around each calf. A quiver rested upon his back and a bow in one hand. His nostrils flared as he appraised Z bowed in supplication before him.

My heart raced, but whether from fear or hope, I couldn't be certain. Though this man stood rigid with a stern face, we'd finally found the people Zofi of the Tsinti had prophesied. He might raise his bow and shoot any one of us, or his small army might suddenly become full sized and do the same. I stood stock-still, hoping that they would hear my plea and help me in finding Father, and I desperately hoped that this wouldn't be another unfortunate event in my search. I hadn't considered the notion until the moment when I faced the Abatwa prince, but I grew weary, thinking I couldn't handle another obscure clue in this scavenger hunt. I didn't believe I had it within myself to go and face or seek out another mysterious race.

"Who begs to see our queen?" The prince carried an ethereal quality, and his words, spoken in Nantai, were as crystal clear and regally accented as any Storm Sorcerer's or, better still, as any Cloud Courtier's.

I tripped forward, and shuddered, "I . . . I do." In contrast to the poised man before me, I likely appeared casteless, someone groveling to my superiors. A fire lit in my cheeks. It seemed I had all the eloquence and grace of a young girl who hadn't yet obtained her curves. *Where did all your grooming go, Mairynne?* I asked myself bitterly.

Focusing on the rocks near the river and my breathing to clear my head, I inched my spine straighter and lifted my chin. My gaze locked with his. The color of his eyes unlike any I'd ever seen, they swirled with gold, hints of red glowed in the irises, and then they settled into a more solid amber. They were bigger than any of the Nantai people's and bigger than the Rundi tribes' as well. Their otherworldliness gave me the sense they read every thought, feeling, or word written on my soul. Despite my discomfiture, I gathered myself. "I do. Mairynne Evangale, empress of the Nantai people, daughter of Tennō Atheryn and Kōgō Noralynne Evangale. And you are?"

Silence stood between us, and a small spark glittered in his expression. Recognition, perhaps? He didn't answer. Instead, he scanned across the tiny army at his feet. Apparently finding the one for whom he searched, he barked a name and tilted his head. Another man, shorter than the Abatwa prince but similar in otherworldly features, dress, and weaponry materialized at his side. The shimmer in the air once again made me blink my eyes hard to reconcile the shift. I'd missed the small army's movement to make room for him.

They leaned their heads closer together. Maybe Z could understand the words they whispered, but neither I nor my party could, so it baffled me that they bothered with the hushed conversation.

Their exchange complete, the prince turned to us, "I will take your plea to Queen Amare." He scanned the shore and the tree line behind us. "The Seleucid bends nicely here. Make camp and await my return. You may build a fire. You will remain unseen as long as you do not stray beyond the bend or too far into the forest. My army will keep a perimeter while you recover from your long walk."

Z tipped his head forward. "Prince, we will need to hunt for food."

The prince inclined his head. "My army shall provide for your needs. You may go just inside the forest to tend to private matters but do heed the warning signs. If you stray too far or deep, you'll forfeit the possibility of an audience."

The air beside me grew cold, forewarning Thalaj's voice and movement. "You cannot hold—"

Z's arm flew out to block his progression and he scowled at him in warning. "He can, young Frost Fighter," Z snapped. To the prince, he bowed and with an air of false grandiosity added, "Thank you for the offer of your vast army's protection. We will await your return."

Tension chilled the air around me, and I called upon the wind, pulling a misty breeze across the water and onto shore. "Prince, I too would like to thank you for begging an audience with your queen. When can we expect an answer?"

Glittering sands swirled in his irises, the pupils elongating. "I cannot give an answer on behalf of Her Greatness."

I went to speak again, but the air around the prince folded like iridescent heat rising from hot sand, and neither he nor his guard stood large before us. The army swarmed and flew away upon the breeze, but his voice drifted back, an echo in the air, "Remain and be patient."

When I turned to the bend in the Seleucid, a camp awaited that hadn't been present before. Four tents stood proudly welcoming us, and after some exchanged wide-eyed glances, Hoaris shrugged and clomped over the rocks to inspect. Three of the tents had two bedrolls spread out, and the fourth and smaller one would only support one occupant.

I stood from peering into the last tent. "Chambui and I can share. And the little ones can take one for themselves."

Hoaris clapped Thalaj on the shoulder. "Guess that leaves us in the last one, brother." He ducked inside the nearest tent, and a groan sounded hinting that he'd stretched out and was perfectly happy to for some relaxation.

The air near Thalaj still carried a chill. He took three steps to the tent's entry and dropped his pack, then turned toward the river without a word. When he made it to the water, he crouched and splashed his face. I relieved my burden as well and started after him.

Chambui placed a hand on my arm, halting me as I turned. "Be easy with him. He's only trying to protect you."

I gave her a jerky nod and went to the water's edge, rocks crackling under my boots. "You've been cold," I said as I arrived at his side.

As if my words were a command, the temperature dropped further. He grunted a humorless chuckle. "More waiting." With a shift of balance, he sat backward on the rocks with his arms resting on his knees and gazed across the river.

I kicked at the pebbles at a loss for what to say. I sought to reconnect with Thalaj, go back to the way we'd been before that passionate kiss on the *Swell Mistress*. And by the Triad, I desperately wanted to connect with him in that passionate embrace again too, but he'd made it clear that was off limits. I hoped instead to erase the doubt I'd had since that moment, the worry that we'd never be the same. That my protector harbored an ideal that I couldn't live up to burned a hole in my heart. Yet, I couldn't change myself at the core to become what he needed. I had no regrets about Sarangarel, and I couldn't promise it wouldn't happen again. At length, I sat beside him, close enough that we almost touched.

"What might we do instead?" My voice quivered as I asked.

He grabbed a rock and skipped it across the water. "From what I can tell, not much. We're at the mercy of these . . ." He flourished his hand in the air but didn't finish the sentence.

He didn't need to finish. He meant the Abatwa prince and his tiny army.

"You've worked your way out of tighter situations," I said.

Thalaj looked back at the group. "Never with seven people. If it was only me, or you and I were alone, it might be possible. But I have also never witnessed anyone shift as that prince did. I'm unfamiliar with whatever magic they possess, and it renders all my training fairly impotent."

"Ahhh . . ." That explained his current cold shoulder. For his adult life or more, his training with the Unseen had provided him comfort and given him self-assurance. He'd long practiced the arts and sciences of people, battle, and covert missions. He used that in his protection of my family and of Arashi. This *waiting*, as he'd put it, cut to his very core. Again, I had no words to quell his frustrations, so I remained in silence beside him.

At our backs, the others were making camp. I could hear the high-pitched voices of Misha and Kyr bantering with one another but couldn't comprehend. Their domestic bickering, despite our situation, brought a smile to my face. Mother had been right in her desires to connect our people, to invite the Small Folk inside, and to eliminate the castes. There was naught but their size and some customs that really made them different from us. The thought of her didn't send the stones about my neck into song, which gave me a pang at the bottom of my chest. I hoped beyond any wish or desire I'd ever experienced that their silence signaled that I'd finally found the place where I needed to be, that they were only quiet because they were, at long last, satisfied.

I allowed my eyes to drift shut and pulled in several long, soul-cleansing breaths. I sensed the water and the wind around me. Though my sorcery itched for freedom beneath my skin, I fought the urge to pull it forward and let it rain upon us. At length, I opened my eyes and gazed back to the tents. Hoaris had begun to teach Z how to throw dice. And between my protector and me, I needed to lighten the subject, to ease Thalaj's brooding. I tentatively leaned my head onto his shoulder, half expecting him to shrug me off. Instead the air warmed a bit.

"Why don't we find a distraction?" I suggested.

Thalaj made a sound in his throat that urged me on.

"You know everything about my upbringing. Will you tell me more about yours?"

Under my head, he stiffened.

I lifted my head and looked into his dark eyes. "Too much?"

His hard gaze softened as he shook his head. "No, just unexpected."

Just then, Hoaris bellowed a laugh. We both looked, then turned back to one another and chuckled softly. At least it'd broken the tension, and Thalaj's demeanor turned thoughtful, like he reached deep within himself for a story that would satisfy my question.

◇◇◇◇◇◇◇◇◇◇◇◇◇◇◇◇◇◇◇◇◇◇◇◇◇◇◇◇◇◇◇◇

THALAJ BREATHED IN AND out loudly through his nose, then smiled. Having found something, he started, "Hoaris was always big. Growing up, I never thought he'd noticed me. I'd always been under his radar, lesser in his eyes like I was in everyone else's given my mixed blood. I'd go out of my way to try to be invisible."

"Shadow-like?" I interrupted.

"I suppose you could say that." He chuckled. "I even begged Ma to teach me my letters and numbers so I wouldn't have to mingle with other younglings. But she insisted I take lessons. There wasn't a schoolhouse for Storm Sorcerers near the village, not that they would have accepted someone with lower caste blood. So, when I finally went to school, I spent most of my time avoiding the main group of Frost Fighters. The funny thing is, no matter how dangerous they thought they were, they always scattered when Hoaris came into view. He didn't have to say a word, they just tucked their chins and scattered." He shifted, folding his legs beneath him.

I leaned my head back onto his shoulder. It seemed right, like we fit that way. "So, I presume this story ends in how you and Hoaris came to be friends."

"Mmhmm. You know the Frost Fighters control temperature."

Curled into his shoulder, I nodded.

"Well, I'd taken my fair share of beatings. I always tried to wear long sleeves and keep them from punching my face when they decided it was time, so I hid the evidence of my beatings well enough from Ma and Da. I'd become an expert in tending to my own frostbite. When everyone else, including the boys who preyed on me for fun, started to grow, I remained a wiry kid—very little muscle to conceal the knots in my legs and arms. Hoaris got big early and just kept growing. Some said he'd never stop. I didn't start the change to man until after my sixteenth year. You'd think being smaller would make it easier to hide in the crowd, but it was like I had a beacon on my head."

He paused long enough for me to jump in. "But you have storm sorcery too, why didn't you just call the lightning down upon them?"

"Young. Dumb. Scared. You name it. Neither Da nor Ma thought to teach me any use for my magic. The leader's name was Kitakara Su Almazaj—Su, they called him simply." Thalaj issued a noise that said a great deal about how little he thought of this Su person. "His name literally means *ill-temper*. I guess his sport of beating up on the smallest youngling should be expected with a name like that. It was on the night of Selene's festival, in the fall before the time when we welcome the lengthening of the dark hours. I'd gone with Da and Ma to the festival, but while they danced around one of the many fires at the center of town, I stood as far from the activity as I could. Turned out to be my undoing.

"Su and his gang nabbed me from behind and took me to the outskirts of the village. They tied me to a fence post, dropped the temp all around me, and beat me bloody. My eyes swelled shut, I was shivering and spitting blood when everything just went quiet. Then I heard a series of grunts and outcries from the gang, so I tried desperately to open my eyes. Barely getting one cracked, I saw most of the gang running away except for Su who shook from the rapid impact of Hoaris's fists."

At some point in his story, I'd lifted my head and turned to look at Thalaj with, I'm certain, a look of horror on my face. The inside of my lip was raw from where I'd been chewing on it as he talked. "What happened after that?"

"It goes without saying that Su and his gang never bothered me again. But that's how Hoaris and I came to be friends."

I shook my head. "No, there's a lot more to the story of your friendship."

He smirked at me. "Hai, but story time is done. Should we spar? It's been a while." He stood and offered me a hand.

Thankful that I'd drawn him out of his brooding, I accepted. We gathered the scimitynes and spent the next few hours working to improve my pitiful technique. I worked until my muscles shook, but I still failed to master the grace of my teacher's movements with the blades.

At dusk, several small animals and some root vegetables appeared near the fire. The animals were something I'd never seen before, but Z called it an aardwolf and moved on to cleaning the carcasses. The meal tasted heavenly, a rich red meat and tangy vegetables, much better than we'd had since we left the City by the Sea and Sarangarel's keep. While we ate, a cat the enormous size I imagined a nekodai from the northern reaches of Nantai wandered by but didn't take notice of us or the camp. He simply went to the water, drank, and pranced back into the woods on oversized black paws. It seemed passing strange that such a predator would take so little notice, especially with the smaller animals we'd just roasted over the fire. By the time we'd had our fill, Selene was beginning her journey through the night sky.

Chambui said, "We should set a watch schedule."

Z stirred the fire and added some wood. "No reason."

"There's plenty of reason," she retorted. "What if those ant-like men come back and slit our throats in our sleep?"

Hoaris howled with laughter. For my life, I couldn't understand what seemed so funny. Mayhap the big man just considered the whole scenario funny.

When he'd almost recovered, he haltingly said, "Z's right." He took a drink. "They got me when I was cloaked with your rock thing."

"You make my point," said Z. "You saw how that jungle cat didn't even notice us or the food we had cooking. We're hidden by their magic right now. You'll never see them coming, but mind you . . ." He pointed the end of a knife at Hoaris. "Don't ever compare them to ants where they can hear you."

"Still," Chambui insisted, "I think it'd be better to see it coming than to bleed out in our sleep."

"Very good," I jumped in. "I'll take first watch." Whether because I believed my father within my reach or I'd felt a reconnection with Thalaj over the course of the late day, energy buzzed through my veins. Though darkness fell, the night grew colder, and the only light was the fire, I was reluctant to go to bed.

The first watch came and went without event. Thalaj was curled up by the fire, having refused to take to the tent either. I woke him when I finally tired and went to bed.

When morning arrived, everyone reported the same uneventful watch.

Days passed.

We slid into a similar routine to the first day, less Thalaj's willingness to regale me with stories of his childhood.

Food appeared at dawn and dusk, and with the bountiful amount, I certainly put on some weight that I'd shed since leaving Nantai.

But the routine also grew wearisome. I went to Z and asked, "How long will these little people keep us waiting? How long are we just supposed to abide by the prince's wishes? It seems that they're not planning to return for us. While we sit here and grow fat around a campfire in the middle of oblivion, while my father may very well be taking his last breath?"

Z gave me an absolutely blank look when he replied, "Have you met many fey creatures, Mairynne?"

I looked at him with drawn brows. What in all of Nantai could he possibly mean by that?

He nodded. "I thought not. Time is their toy. A game to them, I believe. If there's something I've learned here in the wilds of Ise, it's patience. Even the Rundi run on their own schedules—dictated solely by their gods and travel patterns. That they don't venture from Ise toward your home is a blessing to those who live in Nantai. If they found their way to those lands, the Storm Sorcerers would no longer be the most legendary magic users in the land. Your caste system would crumble, and those who subscribed to it would likely perish in the overtaking."

At my side, Chambui planted her staff. "Then tell us, Z. What is it you've seen of them? We should make ourselves ready."

Thirty-Two

The Prince Returns

NO ONE STOOD WATCH THAT night. Nothing had happened over—what had it been? Eight, nine nights? I'd once again fallen asleep with a full stomach to the sounds of crackling fire and wildlife singing night songs, and Chambui's soft snores inside our tent. But when I awoke, the Abatwa prince had returned alone but in full and glowing glory.

Utterly still, he crouched blocking the only exit. I wouldn't have been able to make out his form were it not for how the air shimmered around him—quite literally he radiated his own light. Before I could make a sound, he placed a finger across his lips in a shushing motion and hardened his gaze with warning. I had no concept of time, but through the flap, the darkness hadn't lifted. Sitting, I glanced over. My rustling must have broken through Chambui's sleep. She stirred, but the prince lifted a hand and her rhythmic snores resumed.

"How did you—"

"Shh," he answered.

The tent being so small and the Fey prince the only source of light, the sands in his eyes clearly stirred once again as he turned his gaze toward me. "Queen Amare has agreed to meet you."

My heart thudded in my chest so hard that I thought it would wake the camp. Father waited, needed me as a soft buzz against my chest confirmed. My hand drifted to the stones. Finally! It was the first time they'd responded to a thought in a long time. This must be it, what I'd journeyed all this way to find. I stood.

"Sit, young Nantai ruler." His voice was as smooth as well-tanned hide, and in a conversational tone—as if I might be the only one who could hear.

I tested my theory, and he made no effort to silence my words this time. "We should be on our way. Time is important. I need to wake the others."

"We aren't going now. And there is truly no need to wake anyone." His eyes settled, growing as hard as glass as he spoke.

Shaking my head, I glared at him in confusion. "Why?"

The prince came and sat on my bedroll where I'd left space. Instinctively, I recoiled to the far end. He laughed, a menacing sound scraping over my skin and causing tiny hairs to stand at attention. With him so close for the first time, I processed his bulk, the swell of his bicep and the width of his bare chest. His skin glimmered, and the contrast of something so light with such an imposing presence struck me hard. Wisdom having abandoned my mind, I reached forward, drawn to him and curious whether the apparition before me was real. Maybe this—him being here—was all a dream. I focused in, seeing nothing but my hand and his arm nearest me.

"I wouldn't," he warned, breaking whatever trance had settled over me.

Thankful for the distraction, I straightened my back in an attempt to seem larger. "Why shouldn't I wake my friends? If your queen has offered an audience, I don't see why we're wasting time." I didn't look back at him as I spoke, weary of the magnetism I'd felt seconds before.

"You must decide."

That pulled my gaze back to his.

"You may only bring one with you into the Abatwa realm. In all honesty, you *must* bring one. And unfortunately, I cannot offer assurance that you'll remain united once there. Furthermore, I cannot guarantee when you'll return or even that you'll return. Maybe only one will return. Whatever happens in Fey is beyond my control."

My stomach churned. I pulled my knees into my chest, hugging them tight and dropping my head—anything to quell the sudden nausea. Thoughts sparked to life, one after another in rapid succession. What if I didn't return? What if this was a trap? What if two of us went and never returned? Should it be Thalaj and me? If we never make it back, how will anyone else know our fate? The string of questions went on and on.

"I can read your confusion. Whatever you're questioning is all valid. I will give you a day to decide and return in the fey hour."

"And that is?" I snapped without looking up.

"Now . . . just before the bright lady is at her peak in the night sky." He smiled.

Were those fangs?

I took a breath to speak and lifted my head, but the prince had vanished between blinks, the glimmer around him fading in his wake. Sudden exhaustion overwhelmed me, dragging me down to my bed and into a dreamless sleep.

◇◇◇◇◇◇◇◇◇◇◇◇◇◇◇◇◇◇◇◇◇◇◇◇

I NEXT AWOKE TO Chambui shaking my shoulder. "Mairynne. Mairynne. Thalaj asked me to check on you. It's almost midday."

"What?" I scrambled out of the bed, remembering the prince's visit and worried that I'd wasted so much time in making my decision. Then I stopped, pushed a hand through my tangled hair. What if that had only been a dream? I searched Chambui's face but there would be no recognition from her. She'd gone back to sleep with whatever magic he'd used on her. Or had that been my imagination too?

Chambui dropped her brows and lifted a hand to feel my cheeks. "You're flushed. Are you all right?"

"Hai. I mean, no. I feel fine, but . . . Where's Thalaj?" I went outside, squinting against Otarr's light. Chambui was right, I felt hot, so I pulled a breeze across the river and into my face. As it lifted my hair, I raised a hand to shield the light and searched the area for my guard. Misha, Kyr, and Z were around the fire, and Hoaris was near the water practicing fighting motions with two daggers. But I didn't see Thalaj. That imaginary belt about my chest began to constrict. Chambui mentioned he'd sent her to check on me, so where had he gone?

When he appeared from between the trees, the tightness in my chest loosened and I started in his direction. I hurried in the beginning, but my steps slowed as more uncertainty grew. My instinct was to tell him openly and have him be part of my decision, but with each step, I changed my mind. If the prince's warning had been true, mayhap I should take someone I cared less about. Thalaj certainly wouldn't let me go alone if he knew that I was traveling to another *realm* with this Abatwa prince warrior. But then again, I'd burned one bridge between us when I spent the night with Sarangarel. Would my leaving without him be too much for him to even remain at my side after I returned? I couldn't decide in the few seconds it took to cross the camp, so when I reached him, I asked, "Should we practice my scimityne skills again today?"

His brow furrowed. "You just woke. Have you eaten? You look pale." His confusion clear, he looked me up and down.

Apparently, the flush from when I'd come out of the deep sleep had subsided when I'd called the breeze. "I'm all right. Refreshed in truth." And I found that I was. Since the time when the Syrensea had stilled and my seasickness had subsided, I don't believe I'd slept as soundly as I had after the prince's visit. Whatever he had done to send me into the repast had been good for me—physically at least.

Thalaj turned me by the shoulders, and we walked back toward the fire. "Eat something. I've promised Hoaris he could have a go at me right now. If I'm standing after that, we'll work on your form."

He pointed to the remnants of the morning meal, roasted meat upon a spit, but before joining Hoaris, he turned back. "You might want to do something about . . ." He offered an uncommon teasing smile as he pointed to his head.

I reached up and ran my fingers through the tangled mess I'd neglected upon waking.

After tending to morning necessities and braiding my hair, I ate—*hyrax* and beans this time, according to Z. The bird's white meat had little flavor other than the smoke from the fire over which it'd roasted. At least the Abatwa provided variety. As I chewed, I watched the match near the water. Thalaj, with his curved blades, and Hoaris, with straight daggers, performed an intricate dance. Frost Fighters learned fighting in a specific style apparent in their movements even though they didn't use the available water and their sorcery to create any weapons from ice. They were both masters in sparring technique whereas I was a fledgling. Together, they had also honed their skills in their time training as shadows within the Order. Although, Thalaj had taken to the shadow part more than his friend.

I had little doubt that they could each also use long and heavy blades, but they always opted for the lighter weapons. *It lessens the burden when traveling*, Thalaj had once told me. Hoaris held the daggers with the blades facing downward, and his blocks and slashes all seemed to be backhanded. Both men, shirtless under Otarr's midday heat, gleamed with sweat as they whirled and spun and each traded turns pinning the other. I winced when Hoaris landed on his back on the rocks, imagining how that must feel on bare skin. Good-naturedly, Thalaj extended a hand to help him up once the big man called, "Yield."

Though he'd filled out and no longer had a youngling boy's knots for knees and elbows, Thalaj was still lithe and wiry in comparison to Hoaris. To see Hoaris, the thought of him as a lumbering fighter sprang to mind, but that wasn't an accurate image. He had almost as much grace in his moves as Thalaj—almost. He won the next bout, backing Thalaj into the water and knocking him off his feet with a low leg sweep. Everyone at the fire, myself included, laughed heartily as Thalaj stood wiping the water from his face. The two men laughed as well, and started toward us.

Hoaris looked at me. "Your turn, sweets. I got him all mad for ya." He clasped a hand on Thalaj's shoulder and gave me a wink. "He's all yours," he added, tossed his daggers on the ground and grabbed another spitted bird.

I stood on wobbly knees. I couldn't hope to match their bout, so I hoped he'd go easy. My weapon belt lay at the entrance to the tent, so I left the fire to retrieve my scimitynes, then I joined my protector and shadow upon the banks of the Seleucid River. With a shaky voice, I said, "I hope he wore you out a bit."

Ever the mentor to his soldiers, he answered, "This is about your form. I'm not trying to *win* with you."

"Maybe you should," I mumbled.

"What was that?"

"Nothing." I took my stance, grateful he let the comment slide.

"Lower, more weight in your thighs," he commanded.

I obeyed, and my thighs burned.

"We'll work on defense." He spun and rained down a blow with both scimitynes.

This was a move I knew well, and I parried gracefully, rolling away from his attack.

"Good," he praised, then whirled and came at me with a backslash.

I turned, deflecting his blade. These starting moves were routine, easy for me to predict and only warming me up. But when he made the third turn for an upper cut, my blade glanced off his and I stumbled, landing on the rocks beneath our feet.

I grunted. "Ow!"

Thalaj tilted his head, looking at me with confusion. Rightly so, as I'd grown exceedingly competent in this routine.

Standing, I said, "My foot must have slipped on the rocks. I learned on grasses after all."

He probably didn't believe my weak excuse for a second, but we started again from the beginning. When I faltered on the same move, Thalaj sheathed his scimitynes and offered me a hand. "You're off. What's on your mind?"

My shoulders sagged. I should have known I wouldn't be able to use fighting to cover up the fact that the conversation—or dream if that's what it had been—weighed so heavily on my mind. I couldn't get by with not telling him, so now I had to figure out a way to convince him not to come. I put away my weapons and tilted my head, asking him to join me. Strolling to a tree away from the group, I sat. He waited a beat then followed, giving me the space and time to prepare my words. But I knew well enough that he wouldn't let it die.

Both of us settled in a patch of grass, I sighed and blurted it out. "The prince came to me last night."

Thalaj's nostrils flared and his eyes rounded from their normal almond shape. He cursed. "Someone should have been watching. We've gotten too comfortable." He fidgeted, a sure sign he wanted to stand and pace and rid his muscles of the anger that'd begun to coil and ripple inside. His jaw muscles ticked and the cords in his arms twitched under his bronzed skin.

I placed a hand on his arm, and it worked to keep him seated. Although, he continued to seethe.

"Why didn't you come find me?" he asked.

My eyes flitted away, then I met his gaze evenly. "It was over so quickly, there was no time. And . . ."

"And . . . What?" he ground out through clenched teeth.

"I'm not certain it was real." I dropped my hand into the grass, played with the thick, rubbery blades. My gaze followed as my face flushed.

That eased his tension, but his words were still a bit edgy when he commanded, "Tell me, Mairynne."

I did, finishing with a shrug and, "I guess we'll see in the *Fey hour*—whatever that means."

He nodded tightly. "Chambui can sleep in the tent with Hoaris tonight. I think they've been itching to—" He cleared his throat as he looked toward the two of them sitting alone and close at the fire.

Misha and Kyr had gone to the river on the far side of camp to bathe, and I couldn't see Z either. Indeed, the burly Frost Fighter and the yisu of the Stone Singers seemed to have found something in common. I smiled, happy for them both, yet still lonely in my own right.

Thalaj continued, "I'll stay in your tent tonight."

I pressed my lips together tightly.

"What?" he asked.

"I don't think you should be the one to go with me. I think I should take Z." I didn't look at him as I said this, certain that it would further anger him.

"That's laughable."

I moved closer to him, reaching for him and imploring with him to see reason. "Listen to me, Thalaj. The way the prince made it sound, it's highly likely that one or both of us won't come back. I'll need you to handle things if I'm unable to return." I dropped my gaze again, so sad to be saying the rest of what was on my mind. "Aside from what I need and the Nantai people will need, you've been through so much for me, I can't ask this of you too. You deserve to go home and resume some form of a normal life. Take back up your position in the guard at Arashi or somewhere else— mayhap more peaceful—and find that woman your father told you you'd want. The one who can be your everything." My eyes stung and I stopped talking, more words prevented by the lump in my throat.

He reached out a hand and lifted my chin. "You don't seem to understand my position. I've sworn my life and everything I am to *The Evangale*—the rightful ruler of the Nantai people. Romance isn't a part of that. Duty and service until my dying day is." He wiped away the tear that leaked from my eye then released me. "Besides, remember what I said the other day?"

I shook my head and rubbed the remainder of the unshed tears away.

"If it is me alone or you and I alone, I am certain I can get us out of any situation." He stood. "I'll talk to Hoaris. If all this is true, and we are not here when they wake in the morning, you're right. Someone needs to be able to take word back to the people of Nantai. I'll tell him to take Chambui to his tent tonight and to wait for us for Selene cycled fully through her phases, but then he can return to Nantai with word that we're likely dead. I know your sister usurped the Serpentine Throne, but I hope she'd give you the rites of mourning nonetheless. We'll wait for the prince together in your tent tonight." He walked away without giving me the opportunity to say another word.

I watched him stride away. He'd forgotten that without my body, the rites couldn't pass. Yet that worry seemed mild in comparison to what we faced this eve. I put my face into my hands and cried. If it came down to my choice, I didn't know if I possessed the strength or wisdom to choose between Thalaj and Father—the man I loved or the man the Nantai people needed as their emperor. I'd traveled into the unknown to find my father. Duty and principle dictated I should choose him when the time came.

You must, Mairynne, I counseled myself. *When the time comes, you must choose the emperor over Thalaj . . . or yourself.*

Tennō Atheryn had been a great ruler. He would be again, and the fact that I battled with myself now so selfishly proved how I could never live up to his honor. All that had transpired in Stormskeep since we left remained a mystery, but I had a niggling feeling that I also needed someone with a better claim to the Serpentine Throne than Karynne or me to settle our lands—someone our people would follow instinctively.

That wasn't me.

◇◇◇◇◇◇◇◇◇◇◇◇◇◇◇◇◇◇◇◇◇◇◇◇◇◇◇◇◇◇◇◇◇◇◇

THALAJ AND I SAT in my tent well into the night. One of us rested while the other kept watch, yet I don't think either of us really slept. The fire crackling outside died down, nature started its song, and we heard Hoaris and Chambui laughing, then creating their own personal joy from within the adjacent tent for a long while. I daresay the sounds charged the air within our tent.

Eventually, everything grew silent and we still waited. There wasn't much in the way of conversation. Thalaj had been more stubborn than I despite the fear and confusion I felt, and I was happy to have him by my side regardless of the possible consequences.

A small buzzing sound announced the prince's arrival just before he transformed into full size. I blinked against the shimmering air, sensing he chose a bigger form each time we met.

He looked at me, looked at Thalaj, then said, "You've decided. Follow me."

Thalaj already had his scimitynes strapped at his waist. When I reached for my weapon belt, the prince placed a hand over mine.

"I wouldn't," he said. "You may never see them again."

The temperature in the tent dropped, and Thalaj's nostrils flared. I left my weapons where they lay, and my soul shivered for anyone who wished to take my protector's scimitynes from him.

The prince lit the path we followed into the woods for what seemed hours. Twice, Thalaj made to speak but the prince silenced him. The entire trek passed without a word until we arrived at a small pool with a waterfall flowing into blue-green waters. It glowed in the night.

"You may enter from that boulder." The prince pointed.

Thalaj folded my hand into his, squeezed, and urged me onto the rock at his side. "Hold your breath," he whispered.

We jumped.

THIRTY-THREE

Queen Amare's Purpose

IN THE NEXT INSTANT, THALAJ and I were walking in a forest with lavender leaves raining onto a bed of soft vibrant green grass. The air felt cool against my skin, far more comfortable than at our camp beside the Seleucid and a bit reminiscent of the way the air in Arashi felt near the Sundai Falls. It made me long for home but also tore at my soul and stirred the worry over what I would return to find. I looked at Thalaj, then down at myself, searching for any signs of the water we'd just taken a feet-first plunge into. Nothing. We were both dry as dust. The prince was no longer at our sides; possibly he'd remained behind to deal with our sudden disappearance, or perhaps he wasn't allowed here—wherever here was. I should have asked more questions, but his appearance at night and my sleep-clouded mind had thrown me off. Following him, jumping into the pool—Fey realm as he'd called it the night before— was foolish. I squeezed Thalaj's hand, thankful that he stood at my side.

A comfort I certainly wouldn't find in Z's touch.

A gentle tinkling, chimes on the soft breeze called to me. To us. We both turned toward the delicate sound and without agreement or a moment to question, we walked toward it, magically drawn to it. It had to be magic as it felt like when I called the wind. Moving was easier, I felt lighter, floated. We drifted for a long time but finally arrived at the foot of wide steps that climbed maybe a dozen high onto a platform before a pure white building. Yet the building had no roof, only the canopy of soft lavender and white light beyond.

No sign of Otarr.

No hint of Selene.

The pastel leaves continued to fall around us as we lifted a foot onto the steps, but none cluttered the floor. Everything glowed or glistened. With one foot up, the presence of Abatwa warriors became clear to me—around us, behind us, following us, but not halting our progress. It seemed as if they were apparitions. I squeezed Thalaj's solid hand to reassure myself some of this was real. At the top of the steps and across a long white floor, a woman stood alone, golden hair cascading over one shoulder and beyond her waistline, hands clasped before her, and dressed in a delicate blue gown scooping across her chest.

Come, be welcome in my home, my castle, and my realm.

I heard the voice in my head, but the chimera before us made no move. Even her lips appeared stonelike. Turning to Thalaj, I read the same confusion upon his brow.

Do not fear, young Evangale. Come, the musical voice repeated. It had the same quality as the chimes on the wind. Perhaps it *was* the source of the soft ringing that had drawn us to this place.

We went.

The warriors followed, not a one making an aggressive move, only trailing in our wake.

Her face held such beauty that I struggled to catch my breath. Her skin glowed brighter than the prince's had in my tent the night before, and her hair glistened and moved as if it floated on water. Her faint smile rendered me further speechless, and my gaze fixated on her silvery blue eyes.

She broke the connection and turned extending a hand to one of her warriors, then she did the same to one on the other side. Two men, similar to the prince, grabbed Thalaj's arms. It happened so fast, yet felt so slow. I tried to call the wind—nothing. I tried to reach for my scimitynes—missing. Where had they gone? Thalaj reached for his weapons too, and likewise found nothing. Confusion splayed on his face as he struggled against the men, the Abatwa, the *Fey* who dragged him away kicking, thrashing. His mouth opened, but no sounds emerged.

I lifted one hand to him. *Lift your foot, Mairynne,* I told myself. *Follow him!*

But I had no strength or control to do so. My soles wouldn't budge from their place on the glowing floor.

He will be well, little one. Come with me. Let us converse. The woman held out a hand, and though I heard her voice, I still hadn't seen her lips so much as twitch.

Returning my gaze to her, I couldn't find words either, but I poured all my worry and doubt into searching her face for an answer, three heavens and hells, many answers. Why was I floating along in some meek dreamlike state? Why had she taken Thalaj? But I recalled the prince's warning on that. Why could I hear her but not see her speak? Why, just why? And where was my father? Did she—they—have him? Who was this woman? Where had my sorcery and my weapons gone? Where had my protector's gone?

Her face softened, and she came to me, extending a hand. The cord knotted around my neck unfastened. The stones lifted and floated away from me.

Grab them, Mairynne! I scolded myself. What was I doing standing there without the least bit of will to move? Finally, I convinced my muscles to work and I stumbled forward trying to catch the necklace, my last lifeline to my mother and father. To my sides, warriors moved closer.

The silvery-eyed woman held up the other hand, the one not awaiting my necklace. The warriors stopped. At last, the woman spoke clearly, visibly so that I not only heard it in my head, but could connect her lips' movement with the words. "Young Evangale . . ."

I halted again.

My necklace landed softly in her palm.

Fingering the stones, and the Tsinti totem I kept there too, she continued, "You came here freely, and I welcome you. However, I have welcomed you for the sake of *purpose*. There is *purpose* that lies between you and me alone."

Haltingly, I found my voice. "Wha—who are you?"

Music laced her words as she said, "My name is Amare. I am queen to all the fey creatures."

"What? What *purpose*, then, do you have in welcoming *me*?" I watched her fondle the stones and slide the cord of my necklace through her fingers. Then she stretched both hands and her fingers wide, and the necklace vanished. I gasped, feeling a searing pain in the very center of my soul. My entire reason for this journey had rested with those two stones, and they were now just gone.

Queen Amare offered a purely vicious smile, at odds with the beauty of her voice. "You have many questions. I have many answers. However, I shan't guarantee that you will enjoy what you must hear, young Evangale." The crystalline sands in her ice-blue eyes whirled around the irises, and in them I read a deep wickedness.

Louder, I asked again, "What is your *purpose*?" I stiffened my spine as I spoke.

"Ah, there's the spirit we've seen in you afore."

I blinked, and she appeared at my side, a shining arm laced through my own. She waved the other, dismissing the Abatwa gathered in our midst.

"Child, I mean you no harm. This way." She led me to one side of the large room, between columns.

The walls were lit much like the floor, and it struck me how light here came from everywhere. Everything simply glowed without the hand of Otarr upon it. It'd been night when we leaped into the pool, but it was neither day nor night here. It was only light, not blinding, but comforting light. And then, in that wall, images formed. Images I recognized. A vision flashed of my sisters and me sitting at my father's feet for story time, of Tasmynne reading from the storyboards, of my sister Karynne curled into a ball next to a stone wall. She couldn't have been past her twelfth season. The images continued— my ascension ceremony, the mourning rites for my mother, Jessamyne's limp body, me holding council in the High Cloud Courts before my ascension. They all jumbled together, but they were all visions of my life.

I snapped my head to look at Queen Amare. "What is this? What do you show me here? And I'll ask again, what do you want with me?"

"Not only you, my darling. This way."

We walked past one column and paused at another white wall. The clouded vision before me formed, showing a man, face down, his back rounded off of a stone slab, howling in pain. Black wings erupted from his spine. I recoiled. He bellowed and writhed while a cloaked figure stood near with a book open and chanting. The image faded.

"Your Tennō Makenyn," the queen said.

Blinking several times in disbelief, I tried to reconcile the stories Father had told with those images. The words couldn't match the horror in the mirage upon the walls.

We continued on. The image on the next misty wall was that of a black dragon curled on a lit floor—here, somewhere in this place—his head down and pools under its chin growing with each glistening tear. My heart shattered, a searing pain pounding in my chest.

Beyond the next column, the wall displayed a desert landscape. A woman with long hair, blacker than night, standing with one hand lifted toward a majestic emerald-green dragon standing on hind legs with wings lifted and head bent to her touch. I looked closer. A veil covered one of her eyes. I inhaled, my hand lifting to my throat. "Imrythel?" I breathed. The image evaporated, and I turned to Queen Amare, calmer then. "I don't understand why you're showing me all of this."

"The Ryū bond, young Evangale."

I folded my brow and pinched my lips—uncertain of her meaning.

She sighed musically—strange that someone could issue chiming notes on a mere sigh. I still found myself in awe over this woman. Then she beamed a smile revealing perfect white teeth between her soft pink lips. No, not a woman. The Abatwa. Umutwa? The Fey queen. Queen over all fey creatures.

She said, "But all of this is aside from our *purpose*. I wish for peace once again between the most precious of my creatures and your people—the Nantai."

I felt weightless, as if I were falling. Yet we weren't moving. In this place of light, everything around me darkened and reddened. Anger flared to life in my gut and clouded my vision with a haze that made the light of this place burn. I backed away, knowledge solidifying within.

"You," I spat, and then my words came, flooded. "You arranged all of this? You killed my mother and left that stone in her palm? You left the other stone in my father's room? You took him? What have you done with him? All of this you did as recompense for the evil Tennō Makenyn relieved us of? You've been planning this for four ages? More? What gives you the right to toy with our lives from your little remote island?" I balled and released my fists. Had I use of my sorcery, I would call thunder and lightning down upon this *Fey queen*, ruin her. I'd find Thalaj and return to my home. I paced as I ran out of fuel for my words—no, I wasn't running out of fuel. My words had jumbled so tightly in my throat, none others could find their way free.

"It is reasonable for you to assume such things"—Queen Amare's tone eased some of my fire—"but rest assured that I had no hand in your mother's death. That may be attributed to bitterness and age-old heartache."

I whirled on her. "But my father?" I paused while she glanced down, but before she could speak, I added, "And why did you wait so long to make an attempt at whatever your plan is now? The Ryū war is four ages gone."

She scanned around the large room, then settled her haunting eyes back on me. "Time is of little consequence to the Fey. Makenyn's betrayal was but yesterday to us, young one."

Clenching my fists and my jaw, I seethed. "I. Am. No. Youngling."

"In our lives, you are but a blip in time. You will remain a youngling in Fey eyes until long after your death. In your realm, the realm of people, life is fleeting. We endure. Our children live three of your lives before gaining their majority. Now, you will calm yourself." She raised a hand, then lowered it.

I did calm. Against my will, my body eased, a peaceful feeling washing over me as her hand descended. Tension flowing out of every muscle became almost visible as it left my body.

"Thank you for that." She inhaled and breathed a sigh of relief as if the anger and confusion had left her rather than me. "As I said, it was not I, and it was not my people who were responsible for your mother. As for your father . . . Tennō Atheryn Evangale is here. We are the ones responsible for his rescue. I had my people save him from the same fate as Kōgō Noralynne at the hands of Imrythel."

That was twice Karynne's adviser had entered this picture. I glanced at the now still white wall, then faced Amare again, narrowing my eyes. There should have been shock, surprise, something, but I only felt numb. I echoed my earlier question, "Imrythel?" Even my voice sounded distant.

Amare's eyes softened. "Do you recall the dragon you met in Safaia?"

I nodded, feeling like I viewed this exchange from outside my own body. How did she know of our meeting?

"Her name is Barū. Or Barūdragon. She is young and has not been to our realm yet. That she bred so young is a tragedy in itself, but I believe we owe that to Imrythel and her companion Guin." The queen shook her head, frowning. "Barū has no companion, and her life will be cut short if she doesn't enter Fey before she matures."

Amare sighed, shifting out of her sadness and resuming her regal stature. "Mortal lands, Nantai, Yōtei, Ise, and others, are protected from my people. We may only inhabit the mortal realm for long periods through a bond to a mortal. The dragons are also fey creatures, and the only people they have been able to bond with are the Nantai. Perhaps that has something to do with the native talents you each possess. Regardless, the Ryū loved your people for ages before the betrayal Makenyn thrust upon them, and then he chased them from a place they called home. They mourned. Many of them mourn to this day." Amare turned and started walking. "This way."

She led the way between two other columns into another endless white room.

Inside, coiled in the center of a backlit floor was the black dragon I'd seen in the vision on the wall, the glimmering pool still acting as his pillow.

She flourished a hand. "This is the Kuroidragon—we call him Kuroi for short. He is the former companion of Tennō Makenyn . . . until the emperor betrayed their union."

This vision in the wall had been heart-shattering before. Face to face with the beast, I still felt naught but dazed and disconnected with my own emotions.

The queen continued, "The powerful fey beasts have grown sad. When the life of a bonded Nantai ended, the dragons didn't die but carried a piece of their person's soul within as they returned to Fey. Eventually, a dragon would find another person he or she felt worthy of companionship and return to your lands. Since the Ryū bond has been banished among your people, many have died true deaths of broken hearts. You see, dragonkind needs you. *You* are my purpose."

Amare raised her hand, and all the rage I'd felt before, all the hurt I had felt when seeing the pool of tears beneath the dragon in the vision, all the instincts I'd felt when I'd seen the motherly blue dragon at Safaia, all the connection and division from Thalaj, everything came crashing down on me. Whatever hold she'd placed on my heart and soul, it lifted. And the gravity of all else crushed my soul. Hope at the possibility of seeing Father again shone as the only pinprick of light within my heart. Yet perhaps losing Thalaj or having to decide between him and my father terrified me and split my soul in two halves. The result to all this confusion—I stood frozen. In place. Jaws locked. Eyes wide. Totally stunned. Still and silent.

Then, in my mind alone, because I had stopped seeing aught but a blur before me, Queen Amare's voice rang, "You, Mairynne Evangale, hold the power to change all of this."

Thirty-Four

Prince Osmar

For the third time, I stood at the foot of the bright steps ascending into Queen Amare's palace—or I assumed it was a palace even though I'd seen no furnishings, nothing but light. This time, I folded my arms, put out a hip, and pursed my lips in frustration. I'd walked in a straight line away from the palace twice now and ended up in the same position. Wandering. Circling. But how? The first time I had simply walked. The second I'd marched with purpose away from the palace, thinking I had to get away from the peculiarity and find Thalaj.

I'd turned my fear into action and run . . . from the evil beast that rested inside the palace, from the confusion over why I felt such drastic depression on his behalf, and from the absurdity Amare had insinuated.

But twice, my paths had returned to this place. If every straight line led back to where I began, I couldn't fathom in my limited imagination what necessitated the chimes that'd drawn us here before. But my father was here? While Queen Amare had confirmed that, I still doubted. She had Thalaj too, and I had done that to him. I had to free him and then I had to free Father too. I tried to recall what the Tsinti woman Zofi had said. Stasis. What could that have possibly meant?

As I stood there with my hands on my hips, puzzling over my next move, the prince appeared. He wore robes rather than the warrior's garb he'd worn when he came to me at the camp. I daresay they suited him better—less visible skin and rippling muscle. Mayhap, in truth, they suited me better, allowing me to focus on him rather than his body.

"How do you find Her Greatness's realm?" he asked.

"Confusing," I answered in blatant honesty.

He gave a small, knowing smile, and the sands in his golden eyes swirled again.

"I don't believe I've learned your name still," I stated more than asked. "And 'tis our fourth meeting."

"I don't believe I have given it," he also stated.

"Must I ask?"

He lifted a brow. "You must always be willing to ask for that which you want, young empress." Where Amare's voice had rung with high notes, his sang a low melody that made my mouth feel dry, my tongue swollen.

I twisted my lips into a grimace but then asked, "May I have your name?"

He rewarded my question with a dazzling grin. "Osmar." Then he descended the steps toward me and held out a hand. "Shall we?" He indicated a path to my left.

Strolling at his side, I felt tiny, my head not reaching his shoulder.

"You said you're confused," Osmar began.

"I am. I've walked away twice only to end up facing the steps once again."

Still strolling with his hands clasped at his back, he laughed. "You try to impose concepts from the realm of people here in the realm of Fey. It won't work."

I lifted my hands, shrugging and wondering what under Otarr he could possibly mean by that.

Without my prompting, he continued, "Direction. There is no such concept here. Where you end up is a matter of intent. As you walked, where were your thoughts?"

I considered, understanding dawning. "On my father and Thalaj."

He glanced at me and nodded. "You see, your thoughts bring you back again and again. There is *purpose* here in the Fey realm, and that's the core of our being."

Queen Amare had mentioned purpose several times, and now Prince Osmar had surfaced it again. The word began to resonate deeper meaning. "I don't believe I follow. And if my thoughts were on Thalaj, why didn't I find him during my wandering?"

His eyes darkened, the sands inside stopped moving, and they were as hard as amber when he looked at me. "You are new to our lands. You don't know the rules well enough yet."

I read an explanation about Thalaj left intentionally unsaid, trapped in that amber stare. But my mind latched onto one word. The *yet* he left at the end of that sentence rankled. "I don't plan to stay long enough to know it well."

He quirked that brow again and the sands in his irises stirred again. "Did you miss the part where I said the concepts of physical things are not the same in Fey? Time is also relative."

I huffed and my hands flitted in the air. "W-what?!" Suddenly, I worried about my party back at the camp and how long they'd have to wait. Then what of my father? Of Stormskeep? Though she'd taken the throne, certainly Karynne would be just in ruling once she gained experience. She'd learned the same lessons as I as a youngling. But what would my people believe if I returned too far in the future and with Father. They'd consider me a necromancer or worse. We'd both burn in the courtyard before the Keep. "Will we age? I-I'm repeating myself, but I don't understand."

"Your age while here follows Fey rules. That could seem like a long time in the realm of people, but sometimes, it could also seem like no time at all. And then there is the possibility that it may seem reversed."

I harrumphed. "It seems like these *Fey rules*"—I tilted my head as I echoed his words—"aren't rules at all."

He only offered a tight smile in response.

I grunted, furrowing my brow. "So, I've stumbled into a place where I could theoretically live forever?"

He nodded like the Hallowgales when a youngling only began to voice correct answers to their inquiries. "That is true by your realm's rules. Yet here, it would feel no different to you than the way time passes in your own lands."

Shaking my head, I said, "You're not helping me understand."

Hands still behind his back, he continued upon a trail that seemed to have no end. "Well, it isn't important that you do. You're here for a purpose. Yours is to find Atheryn Evangale. Ours is to save dragonkind, and you."

A shudder ran up my spine.

He continued, "Will you accept that you are the one who can fulfill both our purposes?"

I had no answer, so I said as much, then added my reasoning. "Though Father believed in me enough to decree me as his successor, I never felt the position right. Somewhere deep inside, I felt the need to meet other people, to travel the lands, to roam, to . . . fly." My brow grew heavy. Why that word? And why would I share all this with Prince Osmar? I stopped, turned, and looked up at him with my mouth wide. "What are you people doing to me? Why am I so off? Placid when meeting a gods-forsaken dragon, then sad. Then, we come out here amidst purple-leaved trees and I tell you my whole backstory and deepest feelings without a second thought. This is just wrong."

Osmar chuckled. "Think on it. Might this all be *purpose*? What gave you comfort when you fled Arashi?" He moved closer.

My breath hitched at the memory. *Purpose.*

"*Purpose?*" I breathed.

Again for reasons beyond my mind's capacity, I didn't stop his progress toward me. No, instead I lifted a hand and placed it on his chest. In my peripheral vision, there were no longer lavender trees and green grasses. Inexplicably, we stood in a room with daylit walls and a large bed against the far wall. I looked around, then heard my own hollow voice. "How did we get here?" I'd been awake for a long time by then; so long I couldn't remember. Day no longer seemed a pattern of reality here. Neither did night, but exhaustion washed through me like never before. I didn't want to sleep. My mind wanted to figure this place out. My heart wanted Father and Thalaj. But my body wanted . . .

Prince Osmar.

Thirty-Five

A Companion

ROUTINES—ODD THINGS, AND ONLY PATTERNS I recognized when they were absent. After Osmar put me to bed, thankfully not acting on my embarrassing advance, and inside my pre-sleep state, I'd made my decision that I'd do what they asked. Before, I'd been absolutely certain I would have done anything to get my father back, and I couldn't stray from that mantra now no matter what I faced. Toilet facilities appeared at my urge and disappeared after I'd washed, and I stood alone in a room that seemed made of endless light, the bed where I'd rested gone.

I fidgeted, smoothing my clothes, running fingers through my hair to remove any sleep-knotted tangles. My eyes searched for where to go or what to do next. Before there was enough time to work my nervous energy into a frenzy, Prince Osmar approached with Queen Amare, her hand resting in the crook of his elbow.

"I'm pleased with your decision, young Nantai empress."

"How do you—" I started, but stopped as soon as I realized, or recalled, that answers in the Fey realm were vague at best. "Hai, I have decided that I'll do what's necessary to bring Tennō Atheryn Evangale back to my people." With that decision, I'd also decided that I had to trust in Thalaj. His training and abilities might not have prepared him to free himself from this place should they force me to leave him here, but it was a decision he had made when I shared all the knowledge Prince Osmar had imparted. He had skills enough to survive. And if the need be, I would see Father returned to our people and reinstated upon the Serpentine Throne, then I'd return to the Abatwa and to the Fey realm to bring Thalaj home too.

Prince Osmar looked at his queen with love and adoration, and my heart cracked at the opportunity I might have missed before I'd fallen into bed and slept. Although, my body's want for the Fey prince may never have had the chance of being reciprocated. I banished the thought. Love would be a better prize, and mayhap I'd just decided to leave that behind as well.

Thalaj.

The prince turned to me, "Very well, let us go."

He and Queen Amare led the way.

"Wait," I barked. Maybe this effort would be fruitless, but I had to try something before I just relinquished Thalaj to a fate of the Fey's making or to his own creativity in finding an escape. I pushed my chin forward. "Bring back my protector and I'll do whatever you require of me to meet your *purpose* and my own. When this is all said and done, the three of us will leave your realm with all *purposes* fulfilled."

The queen turned back to me with a rueful smile. "You seek guarantees and absolutes, child. Our realm also requires give and take—an exchange if you will. I have no answer for you in regards to your warrior friend." She walked away.

I rooted my feet to the glowing floor, thinking to make a demand, but Osmar urged me forward with soft words and a hand at the curve in my back. "Her Greatness didn't precisely refuse your request. You have hope."

As soon as he came close, my body responded again. What Sarangarel had awoken within me wouldn't rest. I yearned again . . . wanted to know what lovemaking would be like with a man. With this man—Osmar. But he was Fey, and I couldn't fathom what price that coupling might extract from my soul. I dropped my gaze, bowed my head, and moved after the queen.

We walked, or more truthful, I followed the Fey royalty. They seemed to glide along with their feet falling silently, while I plodded. Next to them, I felt like a beast lacking grace. My footsteps were the only sound interrupting the serenity of this place. The forest appeared as it had been before I slept. Lavender leaves rained and air flowed, but I couldn't quite call it a wind or a breeze. I chewed the inside of my lip. Weather, I wondered, was that a concept here? Or was it like time and direction? The whole place, the entirety of this realm seemed to be an unchanging dream.

"Stasis?" I mumbled. Zofi of the Tsinti had used that word, and it now made sense. My father was in stasis, and I then understood—to the extent I could comprehend— what that meant. This realm embodied stasis. The space between my world, the realm of people, and between walking with the Triad. I stopped walking, inhaled sharply. Then I shook my head. No, the thought was illogical. Our dead either went to Atun's lands or wandered ours for eternity—apart from our people but not joining our dead. This felt different, but if I was wrong, had Thalaj and I followed the instructions of a goddess of death?

A screech tore through the sky, or what would be the sky. I gasped. Above, overhead, a dragon approached. The same sound as the blue dragon—Barū, Amare had named the beast we'd met in Safaia. Instinct told me to crouch, to try to find cover, but I resisted. I turned. We now stood in a clearing amidst the lavender trees, white overhead. Amare positioned herself to my left, Osmar to my right, both gazing upward with looks almost reverent. I traced a line from their eyes to the skies.

A shadow resolved through misty light into an enormous dragon, wings spread wide holding it in the air.

I stepped backward but Amare lifted and lowered a hand, brushing a calm over me.

The dragon descended for what seemed an eternity while I watched with my mouth agape. When it landed upon the green grasses, wind whooshed past me and tested my balance. The details of the white dragon came into clear view. A majestic beast with crystal-like scales stood on powerful hindquarters, then folded its wings as it lowered its upper bodyweight onto the smaller forearms, four sets of massive claws digging into the greenery where it stood. The long spiny tail curled about to rest near a front leg, and the dragon's neck snaked, turning its head with squared jaw and snout, in our direction. Spiraling horns protruded a person's full height from behind intense, diamond-like eyes.

I started to feel light-headed and gasped for air. The dragon's warm breath heated the air around us. I blinked several times in rapid succession. *This* dragon stood thrice the size of Barū. The head moved slightly toward Queen Amare and lowered as the dragon closed its eyes—a clear signal of deference to the ruler of the realm. In my peripheral vision, Amare nodded back.

Then, the dragon turned to me.

Amare raised her hand, lifting whatever spell she'd laid upon me.

Ideas rushed into my head, and knowledge settled over me. More assured about this than I'd been about anything before, I knew her at once. My soul called to hers.

I belonged to this dragon. And *she* was also mine.

◇◇◇◇◇◇◇◇◇◇◇◇◇◇◇◇◇◇◇◇◇◇◇◇◇◇◇◇◇◇◇◇◇

"IT IS AS I thought." Queen Amare's words carried her apparent joy and relief. "Mairynne, meet Parūdragon, one of the eldest Ryū."

"Parū," I corrected, unsure how I knew this, but it seemed right. The dragon's name was Parū. Parūdragon merely described her as a great pearlescent dragon.

"Parū," the queen echoed, a knowing and satisfied smile upon her lips. She clapped her hands together. "I see the first part of the Ryū bond has already formed."

Pulled from stupefaction, I snapped my head toward her, my mouth hanging at the mention of the *evil* notion she suggested. All I'd learned as a youngling forbade companionship. But at the same time, I felt connected to Parū. My brows dropped heavily and my eyes burned as I wrestled with what she suggested. Nothing about the dragon's presence felt evil. Quite the opposite indeed.

"Yes, young Nantai, this is our *purpose*. For you to have your father back, we require you and Parū to accept the bond of companionship." She peered at me as if she weren't suggesting I go against everything I'd learned as a child, against every writing from the time of Tennō Makenyn and the Ryū Wars, against even my father's teachings.

"I can't." Even to my own ears, my voice sounded hollow. I broke away and marched behind them, the royal Fey. My stomach lurched into my throat, and I thought I might be sick at any moment. Cold sweat broke out across my brow and my back. I pivoted and paced and stopped and started again. They—all three of them—allowed me space to work through my stupefaction. She'd just asked me to take the very devil into myself in exchange for the one person I'd spent months now seeking, believing he was alive. Somewhere here, in the realm of Fey, my father still lived. With my acceptance, Amare might have returned him with no further strings, but he would surely reject me in kind. There wasn't a win in the deal. Our *purposes* collided, gnashed against one another. My legs froze underneath me when a smoky feminine voice—neither Amare's nor Osmar's—spoke to me.

What is your fear, Mairynne?

The voice could only belong to . . . Ever so slowly, I looked toward Parū, questioning both if the voice belonged to her and if my mind had devolved into a hallucination.

Yes, the voice is mine. While the dragon's giant jaws didn't move, the sound reverberated in my ears and mind.

At Parū's side, gently stroking a ridge of scales behind one diamond eye, Amare gave a single nod, solemn but affirming the dragon's words. Osmar did the same. Unable to answer or reconcile all that I saw, felt, and heard, I dropped my head into my hands, physically trying to contain the thoughts racing through my mind. I crouched into a ball. Maybe if I became smaller that would help to put some boundary to the noise. Remembered images of story time with Father flooded back—all those stories about how the Ryū Wars began, about the division of needs between the people and the dragons, about how Tennō Makenyn saved our people and set an example for everyone that we were in control of our own destiny, that we didn't need the power of the dragons to be strong, so much, so much, so . . . very . . . much. Tears stung, brimmed, fell onto the grass. I would give anything to see Father back in Arashi. But my father would never forgive my acceptance of this price. He would rather pass from existence than see me turn to such evil. I envisioned him turning me away, banishing me from Stormskeep. Could I pay the price of his love?

Why do you believe this of your father, minikin? Parū asked.

I looked up at her, tears streaking my face and my throat so tight I couldn't give voice to my thoughts. But she could read them all.

Your father, Tennō Atheryn, do you not believe him the greatest emperor in the history of the Nantai people?

I did. A nod was all I could offer in reply.

And you know his strength surpassed that of his predecessors?

Again, yes. A small nod. But everything I'd learned as a child told my mind that dragons were evil. The enemy.

Parū lowered her head and moved it forward between Amare and Osmar to where I crouched. She turned so that one diamond-like eye regarded me. She blinked twice, or maybe only once. The strangeness of the sight stopped my breath as a vertical lid closed, a horizontal lid closed over that and opened, then the vertical lid reopened. I inhaled as my eyes widened.

Do you feel that I am evil? she pressed.

So much kindness in those words.

I found my voice. "No." The suddenness of the word surprised me as did the truth. If she were evil, she could have destroyed me right then and there in the opening within the fey forest that rained lavender leaves. I cleared my throat and said more softly, "No, I don't." And at the realization, I felt chagrin for thinking such a thing in the presence of the majestic beast.

You are correct. I can be a beast, but never with the person I'd choose to forge a bond with.

I felt confusion drawing my brows together as I turned to her questioningly.

She laughed, a sound that rumbled like thunder, reminding me of how much I missed my connection to the storm. I stood, eased from the sudden internal tornado of thoughts spinning out of control. At the same time, I had so many other questions.

I started with the easiest. "How am I hearing you?"

Let us say for now that it is because I am a fey creature. I believe you will understand this before long. For the moment, let us return to the topic of your father, Tennō Atheryn.

"Hai." I pursed my lips, considering. Then I rolled my shoulders back. "I would like to see my father before . . ." I sensed myself, my soul, slipping toward agreement, but I wanted to talk with him before I stepped over a ledge into something I couldn't reverse. I wanted to feel the love between us, father and daughter, one more time in case he couldn't forgive me.

You are Atheryn's most precious creation, Mairynne. It may shock him to learn what you've done, but love will heal that divide. Love as pure as his is for his blood will endure regardless of your decision. Love has the capacity to change one's own beliefs. Love is the only fuel for acceptance and forgiveness.

"You believe you know my father's heart?" I challenged.

Amare and Osmar looked on in silence, her hand resting in the crook of his arm as they both allowed me to connect in this way with Parū. They almost faded into the background, but they remained larger than life and I could still sense their presence.

I do, little one. As I now know yours. Parū double-blinked again.

I pursed my lips. We would see about how well she knew my heart. In an instant, despite that this might cause Father to turn from me and that Thalaj likely wouldn't return to my side, my decision about this—about companionship—billowed up inside.

And not seconds after I had become aware of my own choice, Amare sighed her relief. "This union will heal what has troubled your people and our kind. We believed you'd be strong enough, and I am pleased to have that confirmed." She, alongside Osmar, came to me.

Parū pulled back to allow them access.

"Wha—" I began, wondering at how she'd already read my decision. Then I shook my head. They'd read my thoughts so many times thus far.

Osmar grinned and reached for my hand. "Mairynne, thoughts are reality in the

Fey realm. Have you not seen enough evidence of that?"

Direction nonexistent.

A simple thought takes you where you need to go.

Imagining the need for toileting facilities bringing them forth.

But I needed Thalaj. I needed my father. Why couldn't I will them to my side? "I fail to follow. Again. I can need for a bed or toilet and it appears, but the real things—people—I want, I cannot? And why can you hear my thoughts, but I can only know your intentions once you voice them?"

Osmar squeezed my hand; a jolt sizzling up my arm. "You are an honored guest here in the Fey realm. We are fey creatures. If we wished, we could speak to you in the same manner as Parū. I believe Amare did upon your arrival. However, we find that this is more comfortable for you."

I opened my mouth to speak. Nothing came out.

The prince continued, "Once the bond is forged, this will change for you. You'll understand even better, but you will also find that this is only possible in Fey—aside from your companionship bond. It will fade when you return to the mortal realm. We will give you time with Parū." Osmar stopped and inclined his head toward the dragon. "You are most welcome, old one." Then he returned his golden gaze to me. "I will return for you later." He kissed my hand on the back and in the palm, then extended an arm to Amare.

Thirty-Six

Acts of Bonding

QUEEN AMARE AND PRINCE OSMAR left us alone in the clearing.

Parū asked, *Will you trust me, Mairynne?*

I peered at the grasses about my feet, unable to grant her that yet. There were too many reasons to *not* trust anyone. Alto-Trea, Imrythel, Karynne, the list grew longer and longer as time passed.

Well and true enough, she said in my mind, her voice a deep and soothing rumble, *you have been on a journey most will never travel, and we owe you for finding the strength to answer the Fey calling despite those who urged you otherwise. I will promise you this. All I ask of you now is to sit in the grass and close your eyes. No person or fey creature will touch you in the meanwhile, and no harm will find you. I wish to show you more of what it will mean to become my companion, but you may remain safely in this clearing while I do.* She lifted her great head, her snout pointing skyward. *You have already decided to accept the offer, I beg you to trust me in this small thing.*

Wringing my hands, I considered. After several louder than normal heartbeats, I lowered myself to the ground. Parū's pleasure over my acceptance washed through me, and I closed my eyes. The moment of deeper connection seemed as easy as calling upon the winds. It felt as if I breathed for the first time after surfacing from below the water. My lungs expanded, burning with heated air.

Prepare yourself, young one.

My legs tightened with the sensation of muscles coiling to leap into the air, yet the ground remained beneath me. *Her* legs. Behind my closed eyelids, the clearing appeared once more, only this time, each outline of every leaf to the very tops of the lavender trees appeared crystal clear. The dark limbs beyond no longer hid within. The sight extended so much farther than what my mortal eyes could manage. I inhaled as my chest opened, and my arms lifted as if to call the storm. Yet my body only answered to the wide pull of Parū's wings stretching and readying for flight. When she sprang upward, my arms lowered gently until my hands rested in the soft grasses.

My breathing arrested as I felt the gust of wind upon my face—*her* face.

Relax, Mairynne. Breathe, she thought back to me.

The grove where I sat became smaller in my vision, a view from above. Within the grove, I saw myself from above. My heartbeat matched the beat of her wings, heavy in my ears and upon the air above. A sea of light purple stretched as far as even her dragonsight could see and at the edges, it blurred with the white. Another nature of the Fey realm, I presumed.

Ready? Parū rumbled.

Yes, I was, but she needed no reply. She coiled in the air, a new inexplicable sensation to me, twisting, weightless, and free. And then she moved. The edge of the lavender-white blur changed—purpose, Parū's. Green trees passed beneath us, and the feeling of wind upon my face continued. The green gave way eventually to blue, a great sea.

Breathe, she reminded.

Fascinated, it seemed I lost connection to my own body while flying with her. *The Syrensea?* I thought.

No, Parū answered, *I still fly within Fey. We call it the Eternal Sea.*

She dove into the blue depths, reminding me to breathe yet again. It felt as if I stood under the waters of Sundai Falls, and then the wetness blew from me as she took to the sky once again. And then she returned to where she began in less time than it'd taken her to reach the Eternal Sea.

Purpose.

When she rested in the clearing near me, I opened my eyes and settled back into myself, alone. I stepped toward her, tentative at first.

Parū purred, her welcome and acceptance flooding through me as if it were my own. Eyes wide, I reached my hand forward, closing the distance. When my palm connected with her snout, the scales felt cool and slightly damp from her dive into the water. Her eyes closed, first one lid then the other, and a rumble rolled from within her throat. Consequences aside, we would soon be one.

"Mairynne? Elder One?" a smooth voice interrupted.

Parū issued a low grunt, acknowledging Prince Osmar.

I answered with a short, "Hai?" not wanting to remove my hand from the dragon's scales.

"I apologize for the intrusion," Osmar said, "but I've come to prepare Mairynne."

BATHED, HAIR COIFFED, AND dressed in the gauzy Fey robes, I stood in a barren room with Prince Osmar and Queen Amare once again.

"Will I be able to see Father before we . . . I accept this bond?" I intertwined and twisted my fingers together painfully, a feeble reminder to myself I'd still be here afterward. The *what if* questions fought for daylight. If I looked different after the Ryū bond, would Father accept me? Or, if I felt different, would I be so willing to deliver him back to Arashi where he belonged?

Unsympathetic, Amare shook her head. "I'm afraid not."

I pressed my lips into a tight line. Then with more gusto, I demanded, "You must let me speak with Thalaj before this accursed bonding ritual you have planned happens."

Osmar's broad chest expanded slowly as he watched Amare. Did I read fear in his regard for the Fey queen?

The queen's eyes never wavered, but the irises swirled, reversed, and stirred in a different direction. Her voice sounded resigned, but firm. "There is naught you may command that we—as Fey—must do, young one. I admire your convictions. Things will be complete soon." She trailed a hand down Osmar's arm. "Care for her," Amare said gently, turned, and left, fading into the white as she walked away.

The prince sauntered toward me until he stood close enough I shared in the heat radiating from his skin. His clean and woodsy smell overwhelmed my senses as I tilted my head upward. What had she intended by those words, *Care for her*?

Mayhap I should have stepped backward, recoiled, or at a minimum been leery of the closeness, but I had quite the contrary urge. His full lips tilted into a smile—the personification of the desire I'd sensed before, igniting and coursing through my veins. His eyes dropped and brushed over my lips, neck, shoulders before meeting my gaze once more.

"Since you've been in the Fey realm, Mairynne, we have sensed yearning within you." He stood closely, but also didn't make immediate movements. The sensation exaggerated every natural bodily reaction—our breathing brought our bodies closer toward one another, and the exhalations pulled us apart. The air felt hot, or perhaps that sensation originated from within.

We? I thought belatedly.

He amended, "*I* have felt it. Do you feel it as well? Can you name it?" His voice stirred a thirst within my heart.

No, not my heart. This was merely my body's urge and curiosity. Natural, as Thalaj had told me before when he had armored his own heart. *"Hai,"* he'd said, *"you will take another. There is no need to deny that or feel ashamed. You must take another, and another still. I have had lovers of my own. It is a part of finding yourself."* In those words, he'd offered acceptance for whatever action I chose here and now. He'd granted me a freedom he couldn't have anticipated. I closed my eyes, Thalaj's face swimming behind the lids.

Osmar placed a hand on my waist and turned my back to his front. "Do not feel regret," he whispered into my hair.

A bed upon a platform the same as I'd slept in the night before now lay before us. My heart pounded for several beats, then eased as I forced my protector from my mind with a final thought of gratitude for all he had offered. There would be another time with us. I would see to that. For now, I yielded to my body's need.

My breath quickened as Osmar's hand caressed my shoulder, and I gasped when he dropped his head and fluttered kisses at the crook of my neck. I sighed and stretched, granting him more access. My insides turned to liquid, weakening more and more with every touch. His strong arm wrapped around me, first dragging me against him, and then he lifted me into his arms.

A small giggle escaped my lips as I wrapped my arms around his broad shoulders, but the humor quickly returned to heat as he kissed me. The prince laid me on the bed and stretched his long body beside mine. He trailed his lips up my neck, under my ear, and across my jaw, then pulled back to peer at me with his molten eyes. "Release your doubts," he breathed. "This is an act of beauty, and an experience you'll not have with complete privacy again once you are bonded. Companionship is eternal."

His words sounded as if they were borne from my very soul . . . a feeling of never being alone with my own thoughts and actions ever again. I licked my lips, wanting, and ran a hand over his shoulder. He pushed his into the hair at the base of my neck and held my head as he kissed me—so gentle. Then his lips grew stronger upon mine, demanding my response. Willingly, I deepened the kiss, opening my mouth to him. Our tongues danced for long moments until I felt urgency growing. Osmar ran a hand down my side, into the curve of my waist, and over the swell of my hip. He pulled my body flush to his. Our hips moved, drawing closer together, then retreating from one another in a steady rhythm.

Then, suddenly, he pulled away.

I groaned, protesting his absence, but fervor quickly replaced my grumbling as he undressed me first, then himself. He covered my body with his perfectly bronzed and sculpted form. I reached for Prince Osmar of the Abatwa, a fey creature, with abandon. We kissed, deep, shallow, then deep again. A prelude. His weight settled on top of me. My heart pounded against his in anticipation. My body had called, his replied. This was naught about exploring a heart's need for love. But it did offer me broader knowledge about myself and where I might fit within this world. For these moments, I wanted to be selfish, forget all the heartache, and simply escape. If there was meaning in our union, *that* was it.

When he broke through my barrier at last, Prince Osmar stilled and swallowed my sharp cry. Every muscle within stiffened against the pain, held it. It reminded me of life itself and that *I* still thrived.

Ease yourself, Osmar said into my mind, unrelenting in his kiss.

Then, like a tide pulling away from the shore, the cramping ebbed.

Desire quickened again.

Together, we answered.

◇◇◇◇◇◇◇◇◇◇◇◇◇◇◇◇◇◇◇◇◇◇◇◇◇◇◇◇◇◇◇◇

I AWOKE ALONE. A table with a single chair and a meal spread upon a white cloth awaited.

My stomach growled.

Searching for Osmar, I ran a hand through my tangled hair, a mess from the night—no, from the activity before I'd slept. My face flushed at the thought.

After pushing the covers away and standing, I went to the morning meal. Only, I couldn't call it morning, because things in Fey were ever light. Furthermore, I hadn't an inkling as to how long I'd been awake before I had slept a second time. All I could conceive when I'd fallen fast into sleep was languor, satiation, and heavy eyelids. Despite my body's natural cadences, time—day, night, morning—remained a people's concept I couldn't divest myself of easily.

The simple routine of breaking my fast wouldn't have seemed strange except that I hadn't eaten the entire time I'd been in the Fey realm. In truth, the thought of food never occurred to me. Perhaps it had only been a matter of hours since Thalaj and I'd leaped into the pool and the following morning hadn't even dawned in the mortal realm.

Thalaj.

I pushed the food away and rubbed the bridge of my nose; my eyes squeezed tightly shut.

My body felt different, stretched and seasoned in new ways. My time with Osmar had been beautifully tragic. It had filled physical needs and carved other emotional caverns that might always remain empty, but I couldn't allow myself the time to wallow given what I faced.

"Did you sleep well?" Osmar asked.

I opened my eyes and smiled up at the Fey prince.

"Are you ready?" he asked, offering a hand to help me up from the seat.

Without another thought over the food, I placed my hand in his. A jolt associated with remembered pleasure ran between us, but we didn't linger over the moment. Though the experience had been beautiful, it meant naught but need fulfilled. Now, the time had arrived to address the purpose for which I'd entered into the Fey realm. Osmar had returned to take me to Parū.

This time, we didn't meander from my rooms or through the soft purple forest, the bedroom merely fell away and we stood in the room where I'd first met Queen Amare. Parū waited as did the black dragon, Kuroi, but he kept a distance and coiled about himself. Tears still washed obsidian eyes even though he'd lifted his massive head to observe the coming affair. Many of the Abatwa were present, standing in a wide circle. Osmar released my hand and took his place beside Queen Amare.

I locked eyes with the elder white dragon, swallowed the clot in my throat, and moved to my own position at Parū's side.

I am as nervous as you. It burns, if I recall correctly. But the pain is easily forgotten. Are you ready? the white dragon asked.

"I am," I whispered, remembering the searing pain I'd felt with Osmar. A pain that had preceded unimaginable pleasure. I desperately wanted this price to be as rewarding. Furthermore, I was ready to have Father at my side, to leave this place, and to be on with all the business that needed my attention after Parū and I forged the Ryū bond. Nantai needed saving now, but I would find a way to rescue Thalaj too, if it was the last thing I did.

You are a spry one, minikin. Amare chose well. The pride in Parū's words felt palpable.

I hoped it wasn't misplaced.

Queen Amare glided forward, a silver chalice held between her graceful fingers. She passed it to me. I drank. Then she touched her cheek to mine, her gratitude clear though she said naught. She grasped my shoulders and faced me toward Parū before she retreated to Osmar's side. When she turned to us again, the chalice had vanished. Nerves sizzled along my skin, itched to be on with this thing, until I drifted into a waking dreamlike state. The Fey realm itself seemed like a dream, but in this trance, I felt sleep-heavy too.

Through the haze, the Abatwa surrounding us began to play music or mayhap it was simple voice they offered as they undulated about us. The chiming notes sounded around Parū and me and drums joined into the chorus—or was that my heart? Parū's? Ours? Whichever, the beats filled my head, body, and soul. Thudding vibrated the ground where I stood. The pounding grew heavier and heavier and heavier until I longed to cover my ears and cower under the tremors. But I couldn't move.

And though my feet seemed firmly rooted in place, the movement of the Fey around us gave the dizzying sensation of falling aimlessly. My eyes and Parū's remained locked together, only allowing for us to see whatever transpired around us in blurred periphery. It seemed as if I traveled through a portal, through time, through . . . something other, and I wondered how I would come out on the other side. I worried how Father would see me, what Hoaris and Misha and Kyr would say, if Thalaj would ever have the chance to know what I'd chosen to become. Sadness ripped at my heart as I began to burn, searing heat rising within and without. Remotely, I felt a scream building in my chest but it wouldn't come, couldn't escape the chaos pressing downward and inward upon me. At last, I squeezed my eyes shut. I levitated—not of my own doing and not by my storm sorcery—but the weightless feeling swept me upward. It swept *us*, Parū and me, up. This I knew though I didn't see with my eyelids pinched.

Where the vision had been dizzying before, true swirling started. My stomach lurched. My head pounded. Heat. So hot. Floating. Rising higher . . . higher. Revolution after revolution.

An all-consuming force pulled me toward the vortex, a draw stronger than a cyclone's power. Clothes ripped away from my body. My arms cracked, legs broke, joints separated. They reformed new and stronger. My back bent, contorted. Fire inside—so much fire. I couldn't breathe or speak, couldn't control myself, couldn't find my center where my sorcery lived, wanted to cry out for Father, to scream for Thalaj, to hold my mother. I splintered into a million sparks, until . . .

I floated in darkness.

Death?

Parū groaned.

No, not death.

No. 'Tis life, minikin, Parū said, her voice strained.

Everything stilled, and I breathed. *We* breathed. Together.

My eyes remained closed, and Amare seemed far away when her words drifted into my ears, "The bond is complete." Her soft hands brushed reverently over my bare shoulders, cool to the touch like Thalaj's had always been. "Dazzling beauty." Awe laced the voice as it thinned and trailed away in the dewy air. And when she spoke next, her words were a harsh command. "Now, return to Nantai and recover your people."

For an instant, I maintained awareness of the Fey realm and all the concepts Amare and Osmar had tried failingly to explain. But it misted away with Amare's last order. I still burned inside and upon my skin's surface, but the chaos had gone. The air against my naked skin prickled, and the sound of flowing water reached my ears. I opened my eyes, alone, to meet the dawn upon the banks of the Seleucid River.

Thirty-Seven

Like a Mother's Embrace

EVERY PEBBLE BENEATH MY FEET pressed into my bare soles. So much more awareness, more than I'd had before. Each drop from the morning mist over the river tickled my exposed skin, sizzling as it made contact and evaporated. The skies above shifted from a deep blue-black to gray lined with orange and yellow as Otarr stretched and awoke brightly to greet the day.

Pulsating within, I felt my sorcery had returned, though it seemed weaker than before and mayhap the power within stemmed from something other. Fey? The dragon? Without movement, I called the wind. Aware of tiny things external and within, I let the morning come, my hair floating on the light misted breeze. I'd been the one to finally soothe Parū's deep need. Ages of yearning for a companion, finally answered. Her consciousness floated, lazed contently inside my skin. The bond likewise eased a place in my soul that had been empty, yet it couldn't mend the void left by Thalaj's absence.

Two more spaces of emptiness had existed before my trip into the Fey realm. One, my mother's which wouldn't be filled until I passed through the Nantai burial rites myself. My father, however, lay at my side swaddled like a child, but resting peacefully. The Abatwa had lifted his stasis and ejected us both from the Fey realm, but he would need time to regain his strength. I hadn't witnessed where they'd held Father, but the awareness had come through my bond with Parū, knowledge that wouldn't have been there before yet was.

Hidden deep within me, the parūdragon held no form in the morning mist. Yet her presence felt all-consuming, simultaneously new and old. I had learned her grace and strength when I'd connected with her when she had flown over the lavender treetops. I felt her magic being coiled within my own bones and muscles and burning upon my skin. All seemed right, yet the cost had been high. I had chosen a course I must complete. Though I'd found success thus far, I'd also failed.

Thalaj.

Trust in me, he had said before we entered the Fey realm. That little bit would be the hope I would carry to Nantai and one day back to the banks of the Seleucid River so that I might find him again.

Chirping started behind me; a voice grew nearer. Kyr rushed up. "Mairynne, that you, lovely?" When she reached me, she circled Father and me, wearily scanning my body up and down, then she stopped in front of me with hands on her hips. "Why are ye standing here naked?" She bent down to the bundle on the ground, gasping when she flipped the blanket back to reveal my father's face.

I couldn't move, couldn't break my stillness, wasn't ready.

"Oh me. Oh . . . Oh!" She scurried away, chattering loudly as she went. Words my mortal ears hadn't been able to understand, but through new senses—Parū's fey senses—I understood every word she spoke as she called for Misha to come and help. "Bring a blanket! She'll catch a malady," Kyr finished as her boots crackled over the rocky camp.

Footsteps, heavier than Kyr's, crackled the rocks behind me, and a deep throat-clearing sound rumbled. Hoaris had come too. Soft cloth settled on my shoulders. I inhaled sharply at the immediate burn that startled me out of meditation. I faced Hoaris's bare chest and lifted my eyes to his. Nothing about him had changed, and the familiarity felt good. His hazel eyes were strong, but worry and questions splayed across his face. The joviality I'd known in him since the caves beneath Safaia erased. I tried to offer a reassuring smile to let him know that all was well, but it wasn't. The questions then began in earnest, and slowly, I connected each set of words with the speaker.

"Where've ye been?"—Kyr.

"How'd ye get back?"—Misha.

"Where're your clothes?"—Kyr.

"Where'd ye find Tennō Atheryn?"—Misha.

"Where's Thalaj?"—Hoaris.

Thalaj's oldest friend looked around as if my protector and his near brother would appear at any moment with his scimitynes brandished and ready to fight. When he failed to find him, Hoaris turned back to me.

My eyes brimmed with tears. As the questions had flown, I had held my tongue—our tongue. Had other bonded Nantai felt such confusion over simple identity? Afraid to speak? Now, when tears were on the verge of falling, all I could do was shake my head. With the motion, the water leaked down my face.

Hoaris pulled me into a strong embrace but immediately pushed me away again. "You're burning hot," he barked.

Kyr came closer, pulling on the shroud at my shoulders and reaching up to feel my face.

I turned away. "I'm okay. It's okay. I'm . . . just happy to be back." My words were unconvincing even to me, but thankfully no one argued. "Thalaj is not returning with us."

Those words hung heavily in the air. Not one of my three travel companions said a word, but I could read shock in their gaping mouths.

I let them believe whatever their imaginations concocted. The slim knowledge of what had happened was mine alone. Instead of further addressing the matter, I said, "Hoaris, can you carry Father to a tent? He'll rest for a good time before we can leave."

"You got it." He stopped, more questions in his eyes. He thankfully kept them to himself. "Ye-yeah. He can have Z's tent. The wanderer has taken to sleeping by the fire. Since the ant people left, there is no longer a magic perimeter protecting the camp."

That meant . . .

My brows furrowed as I regarded him. "Truly? You've been free to go?" I asked.

Minikin, Amare, and Osmar only wanted you. They dropped the barrier when you entered the Fey realm, Parū said lazily, unseen.

I jumped, looking around. It was the first time I'd heard Parū since returning, but that was impossible. *Oh, by the Triad, how am I going to handle this?* I thought.

You'll grow accustomed to our connection. I'm still here, only inside.

"What's wrong, Mairynne?" Hoaris reached for me.

I'll deal with you later, I thought to Parū. I couldn't share. I didn't comprehend it myself. Certainly, if they knew I was hearing voices, they'd believe I belonged in the mountain camp where the haunted Nantai people lived. "Sorry. Nothing. Just felt a tickle." To change the subject, I ask, "Where is Z?"

Misha spoke up, his high voice another soothing sound. "He's hunting. The food stopped appearing about the time you and Th . . ."—he hung his head—"you disappeared."

I bent and lifted his chin. "Do not hesitate to speak his name. Thalaj. I need him to be with us in spirit. And you can be assured you will see him again."

The small man searched my eyes, nodded, and said, "You're not the same." His brow furrowed. "Your eyes are—"

I stood, averting my gaze. "I am the same. Still the person who set out to find her father. Still the person who traveled across the Syrensea and into Ise with you." I swallowed and finished, "It's still me." It must be.

Hoaris shook his head. "Your voice is different too. Deeper."

Averting my eyes, I changed the subject again. "What about Chambui?"

Misha and Kyr chuckled and regarded Hoaris.

The big man shuffled uncomfortably. "She rests. Long night."

That brought a smile to my face. At least they'd found peace in one another. "Let's get Father into a tent."

"And you into some clothes," Kyr admonished.

Misha and Kyr went ahead, and I walked beside Hoaris as he carried my father. I'd never fathomed that Father would seem small, but in Hoaris's arms, he seemed but a youngling. Maybe I'd experienced enough that he would no longer seem larger than life like he once had.

You're bigger—a dragon inside, Parū reminded me.

I sealed my lips, thinking, *Not now.* "How long have we been gone, Hoaris?"

"We've seen Selene six times."

My time in the Fey realm had only felt like a couple of days. I couldn't help trying to work out the math.

But Parū reminded me, *Time isn't the same concept here and there.*

"Thank you," I said to Hoaris.

He pursed his lips, not understanding my intent.

"For waiting," I added. "We'll need to wait several more days before we can travel. It will allow Father to gain some strength."

"Where did you go?" he whispered.

I opened my mouth to speak, but Parū forestalled my words . . . *Be careful with what you tell.*

"It's not important. What matters is that we recover and go home."

◇◇

CLOTHES, ONCE I'D DRESSED, felt worse than the blanket. Itchy, confining, and hot. I ate some stew that Kyr had set over the fire the night before, and we passed small talk well into the day. Otarr neared his apex in the skies when Chambui emerged from the tent she and Hoaris now shared every night. She questioned me with keen interest and a constant suspicious glare. I maintained my silence about where I had gone and what had happened, choosing to focus on the more important result of my time in the Fey.

Father.

I'd done what I had set out to do—retrieve the emperor and the one person who would best serve the interests of the Nantai people. Yet we still faced a long voyage back to our lands and plenty of uncertainty about what we'd face when we arrived in Arashi. I knew naught of what had happened with Nadia but grasped onto hope despite my fears. And what of my sweet middle sister, Yasmynne? But the confrontation I dreaded most was with Karynne, and the matter of her first adviser, Imrythel, bonded companion of the green dragon—Guin.

Everyone took turns checking in on or tending to Father, but he didn't stir. After a good deal of quiet conversation, tending the fire, and simply waiting, I yawned and retired to my tent for a supposed nap.

In privacy, I removed my tunic, wincing as the scratchy material raked over my skin. It felt as if I'd spent too many hours under Otarr's light and he'd kissed each of my shoulders with his radiance. I sighed relief when the cool air brushed over my shoulders. "Does this burning get easier?" I asked in a hushed voice. Speaking to Parū still seemed unnatural, and I naturally gravitated toward vocalizing my words.

It does, minikin. Parū stretched.

Yes, the sensation passed strange, like I spread my arms as wide as they would go and they continued on for miles of their own accord. However, my body didn't move with the sensation. I looked down at one shoulder, then the other. Tiny white scales glistened on my skin. I gasped. "Could my friends see that?"

Only if they looked closely enough. Doubtful with the mortal eye.

"Why do you seem so . . . Don't you wish to fly? Be free? Explore? Maybe just move a bit?" The last of my words trailed off.

She chuckled sleepily. *Later. Dragons need plenty of rest. Our natural resting rhythms run much longer than the night of a mortal. And the bond drained my energy.*

"I expected—well, I don't know what I expected, but not this inactivity."

Why don't you rest there on your pallet? We'll fly later. Tonight, when the others sleep. She yawned.

Answering the sensation, I did too. My voice sounded sleepy, but having the thought of flight put out there so, a nervous twinge ran up my spine. "We can't leave them," I hissed.

Do not worry. We'll be back before your friends wake to meet your sun god.

"But I cannot sleep every day and be awake all night."

Minikin. Notice how I rested until you called for my attention?

I nodded, not that she could see, but presumably she could feel.

You can do the same after we shift forms. You will understand better after our first flight.

◇◇◇◇◇◇◇◇◇◇◇◇◇◇◇◇◇◇◇◇◇◇◇◇◇◇◇

RESTLESSLY, I TRIED TO nap, but the effort grew hopeless. I dressed and went outside. Allowing my thoughts to drift to Parū, it became clear that she slept deep within. Z didn't return that day, and Father didn't wake. I sat at his side for much of the day's remainder. He appeared frail, with lines about his eyes that I didn't recall and white at his temples. Had he been showing such signs of age before? I wondered if I had been so remiss in my observations, if I had been distant enough from him to not know that he'd drifted into his later years. I touched the coarse white hairs. Or had this been a result of his time in the Fey realm, in stasis? That didn't seem right either as all the Fey people I'd met had a youth about them, almost as if the realm made that so.

I took his hand, rubbing my fingers lightly over spots that I also hadn't recalled marring his olive-toned skin. A pinch formed behind the bridge of my nose and tears welled in my eyes. I let them fall. "I wish you could have been there for the rest of Mother's funeral rites," I said. "Releasing the nymphs was one of the most spectacular sights I've ever seen." I paused for many long moments, swallowing and trying to clear a constant lump in my throat. Tennō Atheryn Evangale rested so peacefully, his chest rising and falling at even intervals. I questioned if he could hear the things I said, but I told him anyway. They eased my soul if not his. "Your entire council all but demanded that I ascend. I didn't understand my hesitation at the time any more than they did. I worried about you walking the endless plains for an eternity, but I think it was more than that. I believe your life force still pulsating in this world drew me away. Ha! Maybe that's what Amare infused into those stones. They were the ones who called me here."

But there was more I didn't voice. Purpose. The dragon, the Fey, the bond, they had all lured me too, but I wouldn't share that with Father. Not yet, at least. I told him about my eventual ascension and how I'd left a decree that Nadialynne should ascend temporarily in my place while I quested to find him. I reserved the part about Karynne's treason though. If he were to regain his strength, he didn't need that worry upon his shoulders yet.

At length, I placed his hand back over his chest and went from the tent. I didn't know if he'd heard anything or even sensed my presence.

Parū stirred inside. *You did well enough, minikin.*

She'd fully attached her soul to mine; the affectionate name told me as much, and I smiled. Though it felt strange again to be addressing someone inside, I thought to her, *I fear how he will see me when he learns of you.*

◇◇◇◇◇◇◇◇◇◇◇◇◇◇◇◇◇◇◇◇◇◇◇◇◇◇◇◇◇◇◇◇◇◇◇◇

LONG AFTER THE CAMP slept, I awoke in the fey hour and relieved Hoaris of the watch. Parū began to stir, energy building, but I wanted her to wait. When I heard his steady snores begin from the tent, I gave her leave to do what she would.

Go to the river, she instructed. When I arrived at waterside, she added, *Remove your clothes so we do not rip them.*

I did. While my skin had burned before when I'd dressed, it began to heat even more. Hotter and hotter it burned, until I felt every part of my body fracturing again—both like and unlike the bonding. Though it hurt less, and when it was all done, I stood tall, looking at the treetops. Glancing right and left, white leathery wings spread wide, catching silver from Selene's light.

Ready, minikin?

"Hai," I thought I said, but maybe I only thought.

Whatever the case, Parū heard and the powerful muscles bunched, she—I—crouched. Wings pumped and we leaped into the air. Her body, my body, no—*our* heavy body passed through the air as our wings pushed further and further into the sky. We soared above the trees, through wispy clouds, up and down the river.

This felt different than before when I had remained safely upon the ground in the small clearing. Then, I'd only felt *her* sensations, seen through *her* eyes how she interpreted the world. This time, I was free, soaking in the wind upon Parū's skin and snout, gazing over the land through Parū's diamond eyes, but seeing with my own vision too. *We* gulped huge amounts of air into her vast lungs. Her heart pounded steadily like a massive drum, working to feed her entire body. I felt the release of her muscles when she simply soared upon the wind. We climbed and circled and dove toward the ground. We tilted and glided and rode the high winds until frost formed on Parū's scales. And I understood the heat I'd felt for the better part of the day. If I had breath, this would have stolen it, but the breath in our body belonged to Parū. I was merely along for the ride.

Parū turned toward the sea, and from the height we soared, a vast blackness spread before us with the silvery line Selene cast over the waters.

You may rest now, minikin.

And suddenly, I knew what she'd meant before—how we were one yet separate. My soul sighed a relief there in the night's sky. I imagined myself curling up in Parū's belly, warm and protected and lulled. Worries of the day gone, I was no more than a youngling being rocked to sleep in her mother's arms.

THIRTY-EIGHT

Reunion

"MAIRYNNE, TIME TO WAKE." KYR shook my shoulder. "Tennō Atheryn is awake! Come. Come."

"Father? He's up?" I pushed the hair from my eyes and sat. Belatedly, I remembered my nakedness and pulled the blanket about my breasts.

Kyr nodded vigorously and scurried over to grab my clothes. "Here ye go, lovely. Get dressed and come out. Hoaris has him by the fire."

I donned the clothes with a bit less of the burning sensation, allowed myself a moment to recall the feeling of the dragon flight last night, and composed myself to face my father. Parū would remain my secret for the time being.

Outside, Father sat on a stump near the fire. He put down a bowl just as I emerged from the tent and smiled.

I rushed over, shouting *Father!*, crouched, and pulled him into a tight hug. I'd expected the brawny man who I'd known all my life, but the man in my embrace felt withered. My stomach lurched, my eyes burned, and tears fell suddenly. I shook with them for long moments as I held him tighter than anything I'd ever grasped onto.

He allowed my sobs for some time, and when they slowed, he pushed me to arm's length and searched my face. He seemed hale enough though the muscle had fallen from his bones. The question remained if he'd be strong enough to travel by foot through the jungles.

"Mairynne," he said on a sigh. "What troubles you so?"

I shook my head, looked down and back into his tired eyes. "It's just been such a long journey, and we're only half done."

Father said nothing, but I could see confusion in his eyes. Hoaris lugged over a stump for me.

"What do you remember," I asked, taking a seat but keeping my hand on his arm to reassure myself that he was real.

His throat worked, his eyes roamed, and at last he said, "The last thing I recall is preparing the pyre for . . ." He propped his elbows on both knees and let his head fall into his hands. His thin shoulders then shook with his own grief. Mother's—his wife's—death had to have seemed as real to him as if it were a day or two prior.

My heart split into more pieces for him, adding new cracks to the ones caused by my recent loss of Thalaj. It was then, in that moment and far too late, that I knew my error with my guard. I should have been willing to wholly give myself to him. Love should have allowed me that, but I had been young and foolish. I was still young, but the events of the recent past had made me slightly less foolish. I understood what I could not have before and that it was only me who stood in the way. I only wished it wasn't so late in coming.

Almost as soon as the grief and heartbreak settled over me, my chest started heating. Anger flashed white-hot in my vision, then eased. I refocused on Father, blinking.

Hoaris, standing behind him, opened his mouth as if to comment but then shut it without a word. What evidence of my ire—or my dragon—had he seen then?

"Excuse me," I said, the words strained and halting. I stood and paced. *Why am I so angry?*

Parū responded, *The bond. Dragons are angry creatures by nature. I work hard to control my temper, and you'll have some odd sparks for a while.*

I took long breaths in and even longer breaths out as I walked to the nearby forest. *I can't do this to him. I can't handle his grief and pain. It'll break him when I have to tell him the sacrifices I had to make to get him back.*

Minikin. Yes, you can. You are an entirely different person now and not only because of the bond. You've loved, made love, lost. You're strong and he is weak, and you must share your strength with him now. Do not let this come between you.

A stick cracked behind me and I whirled on the sound. Chambui held up her hands as if to surrender. Tension dropped from my shoulders and I sighed, welcoming her.

"May I?" she asked.

I spread my arms and answered, "Sure."

She quirked a brow at me, drawing closer. "You're different somehow. Can you tell me what happened while you were away?"

I glared at her, saw white again, then shook my head. "I shouldn't."

"Your eyes just flashed with a strange light. What's changed?" Yisu Chambui said with all the calm in the world, like it was something she might see every day. She'd always been a steady companion on our trip, always given me nice insights on Thalaj, and just been there steadily while I worked through my troubles. Her calm had always soothed me, and it was no different now.

I squinted at her, contemplating. A tree had fallen near where we stood, so I tilted my head in invitation toward it. We sat, straddling the log and facing one another. She waited.

At length, I inhaled through my nose and blew it steadily through pursed lips. "I need to trust that you won't share."

She raised her brows. "Kōgō, you have my assurance."

"Don't call me that. I'm not technically the empress, and now that Father has returned, the title will go back to him once we've made it back to Stormskeep and he sits on the Dra—" I couldn't finish. ". . . upon the throne. He may have to ascend again, but the castes will support his case."

The yisu only nodded.

I gave her a small smile. "I'm happy that you and Hoaris found one another. Jealous," I admitted with a smile, "but happy."

"That seems beside the point, Mairynne." Chambui reached across the gap and placed a hand on my arm, but she immediately recoiled—shock, unusual though apparent, on her face.

I sighed and told her. Everything. All that'd transpired since Prince Osmar came into my tent. I spoke of the bargain I'd made with the Fey queen and how it'd cost me dearly. Unabashedly, I shared how I'd lain with Osmar in the end and how the act had taught me something of myself. I needed someone—a friend I could confide in—and Chambui seemed more level about all things than most.

Good summary, Parū praised me when I had finished.

Chambui didn't appear surprised or anything more than who she'd been all along, one who took everything in stride. She pursed her lips, then took a deep breath and said, "Are you aware that the Stone Singers also pride themselves for having the best of the Nantai seers?"

I barked laughter. "Seers are a myth."

She shook her head with slow deliberation and a solemn look on her face. "It's something I shouldn't share with a Storm Sorcerer, especially given that you're an *Evangale*. But here's one of the most well-known prophesies among the Singers . . ."

> *One soul divided*
>
> *One endured*
>
> *One soul lamented*
>
> *One devised*
>
> *Two souls united*

One defeated

I studied her when she went silent. The words made no logical sense.

She huffed and ticked off the lines on her fingers. "One soul divided—Tennō Makenyn. I don't know what the next three lines mean, but it seems pretty clear that 'Two souls united' might refer to you and your dragon." She folded her arms over her chest, clearly proud of her deduction.

"It sounds like a fortune teller's words," I dismissed. "They could mean anything."

"Hrmm. Well and so. We can hold our separate beliefs, but I'll warn you not to make too light of it."

"Very well," I said, "but I have your assurance that this will remain quiet for now, yes?"

"Of course."

I laid a hand on her arm. "You don't know how grateful I am to have you to listen and not judge. Should we go back and see how soon we can get moving? I'm ready to be on the trail home."

Chambui cocked a half-grin. "Home has a nice ring."

In unison, we stood. With each step, sticks crackled beneath our feet. Then a memory returned. "Chambui?" I started.

"Mmm?" she replied.

"Do you still have one of those stones? What did you call them—the talking ones?"

The yisu sighed and sadness drew her lips into a frown. "The *yarikhgüi yarikh*. Along with our axes, our captors never returned those."

Recalling how Jaliqai said there were only nine, I realized another loss. "I'm so sorry everyone has lost so much on my account."

Chambui grasped onto my hand and squeezed. "We chose this, and I would choose it again." She pulled me into a reassuring hug, and my soul sighed with relief.

We returned to the camp circle where the others had gathered around the fire. Seeing me, Father placed his hands on his knees and tried to stand. He stumbled. I rushed over and caught him, holding him up and exchanging a look with Hoaris. Questions danced behind his eyes. Father was frail but still a large man—much larger than I would have or should be able to support. I staggered intentionally. "Hoaris, help me?" I groaned like every last muscle strained under his weight—though, it did not. When Hoaris slid under his other arm, I pulled away, gulping deep breaths.

This wasn't good. Father would need time to build strength, something we didn't have in abundance. "Help him walk," I commanded Hoaris. "We need him to build strength so that he can handle the trek out of this jungle."

IT POURED RAIN THAT night. While the others slept, I had given my body over to my dragon again. Soaring through the dark with rain pelting down upon Parū's back, lightning struck, and I felt my sorcery stir within, but couldn't bring it forth.

'*Not in this form,*' Parū said.

Of course. Not in the Fey realm, so likewise not when I took a fey form, I thought sardonically.

Laughter growled in Parū's chest. *We can share the power that fuels our individual magic, but I cannot use storm sorcery any more than you can fly or breathe fire, minikin.*

I supposed what the great pearlescent dragon said held logic, but it saddened me in the moment. I extended myself into Parū's senses with a thought, feeling the wind in her face and the rivulets running from her back. The storm didn't matter as the water slid off her scales and wings. Seeing the dragon flight through her eyes was the most amazing thing I'd ever experienced, and in a storm, it held even more magic for me—one with natural mastery over the gales. After only once through a mental connection and a second time inside, I was coming to love this almost as much as the storm. Flying, unlike calling the wind to float, was powerful, active, exhilarating.

It's the best thing about having wings, she said.

It's the only purpose for having wings, I scoffed at the thought.

Parū's laughter rumbled deep in her chest again.

Mentally, I sighed. *This is fun, but I should probably rest while you're out.*

Yes, you should, minikin. But before you do, can you bring forth memory of the time upon the boat that brought you to Ise? It will help me find this ship.

I thought back, recalling the stroll I'd taken around the *Swell Mistress*'s deck with Captain Asahi, the spindles upon the deck railing, the dark colored wood, and the powerful sails billowing in the wind above.

The images sufficed to give Parū context of the ship for which she searched.

Perfect. Now sleep.

I did. Sleeping inside the dragon was a strange affair; complete awareness of the outside world left me as I drifted in warmth and the rocking motion.

A MOUTH CRUSHED MINE. Thalaj? I gasped between punishing kisses. His spicy taste and cold desire lingered just beyond my reach. Then, I saw Osmar's hands against my stomach, dark upon my olive skin. His hands slid up my sides, and we traded wet, needful kisses just before he sank inside me, stretching and filling me. There was no pain this time, only pleasure, deep and roiling. I closed my eyes and lost myself in the sensations. Faster and faster, we moved together. Harder and with more fury, he thrust into me and my hips lifted to meet his. A heavy urge gathered in my stomach. My muscles clenched and pulsated where his body penetrated mine. As the waves began crashing over me, I opened my eyes and locked intense stares with Thalaj. I fell over the edge freely, willingly, wantingly until . . .

◇◇◇◇◇◇◇◇◇◇◇◇◇◇◇◇◇◇◇◇◇◇◇◇◇◇◇◇◇

I AWOKE WITH A start. My legs, no, *our* legs shook, and Parū growled, *What was that?*

We were no longer in flight, and I flushed with chagrin over the dream.

Never you mind. I know what it was. Parū shook, water flying from her wings.

I said a little thanks that I was inside and no one could witness my embarrassment, though certainly, she felt my mortification as her own. *I believed we were apart,* I thought at Parū.

Mating is different, she said.

I wasn't mating! The force with which the objection erupted certainly would have been a shout were I in my mortal form.

Parū grumbled sardonically. *The result was the same. Anyway, that's a matter to discover later. Your* Swell Mistress *is there.*

I looked through the dragon eyes. The landscape stretched and curved unnaturally, but her vision gave a wider and brighter view than my own eyes would have been capable of. In a shimmer, our bodies shifted, shrank, and we traded primary consciousness. I came to the forefront, naked and standing upon a beach. Waves crashed upon the shore, and indeed, the *Swell Mistress* sat at the seaward end of a long wooden dock. Without clothes and without a second thought, I walked the length of the pier and boarded the ship. Parū stayed alert inside, watching every move I made and observing if people stirred. Barefoot, I made little sound. Having spent many days at sea on this boat, I knew my way to the captain's quarters by heart and followed that path. When I arrived, I tested the handle—unlocked. I slid inside.

Asahi, in only his breeches, hugged a pillow and snored. I looked down at my absence of clothing. Though I had no shame, it was probably best that he at least wore pants. I had no desire for this man in that manner. I went close to the head of his bed, glanced out the porthole briefly, then leaned down and sang his name sweetly.

"Aaa-saaaa-hi."

He turned over, adjusting his codpiece as he did.

Louder, I barked, "ASAHI!"

◇◇◇◇◇◇◇◇◇◇◇◇◇◇◇◇◇◇◇◇◇◇◇◇◇◇◇◇◇

PARŪ AND I RETURNED from Asahi's ship that night knowing the route between the Seleucid River and the eastern coast.

Within the camp, we never again saw Osmar or his ant-mounted army, and we left the tents to whatever might have them when we departed two days later. We walked by day and slept around a fire at night. Z, seeing that I knew the route, made his farewells and left us on the second day of the hike. I wondered, as I watched him fade into the undergrowth, how he managed in the wild lands of Ise without other mortal companionship.

Our trek progressed slowly, and I constantly worried over Father to the point where he'd gotten short with me on several occasions. Fortunately, once freed from Fey, his storm sorcery had returned and he could use the wind as a crutch when his body's strength failed him. I tempered my words and gave him the space he seemed to need.

When the brush became too thick to pass, Hoaris and I used my scimitynes as Z had used his heavy curved knife to clear a path. They were lighter than the wanderer's knife but aided in our progress. With each swing, it left a new slash upon my heart in memory of my protector, my companion, and the man I would long for until I saw to his return. The days and nights passed. Parū only flew and hunted every third or fourth night, and she returned quickly so we didn't stir suspicion. We had one close encounter with a Rundi tribe, but Hoaris, Misha, and Kyr steered us far enough around so that we wouldn't end up captive again. Although, should that fate have befallen us, I had a new weapon at my disposal with Parū. Selene made another full cycle—fully diminishing then growing to her full girth—before we made it back to the coast where the *Swell Mistress* rested at the small dock.

As we cleared the trees onto the sandy beach, I turned to look back. A memory lingered of Amare and Osmar's favored word, *purpose*. I had purpose for the moment to recover my home and set things to peace with the Nantai people, but when I had completed that purpose, a new one awaited.

"Thalaj," I whispered. "When this is done, Parū and I will return for you." I touched my fingers to my lips, recalling the feel of his crushing them aboard the *Swell Mistress* and again in my dream. "I swear this to you." And, when I had him at my side once more, I would offer him the whole of me. Everything and anything he needed or desired.

The remainder of the crew and the yisun already aboard the *Mistress*, Asahi met us on the sand. "Mairynne, so nice to meet you again." He raised a brow and lowered his voice. "And clothed this time."

I narrowed my eyes, choosing to ignore the captain's flirtatious remark and make introductions. "Captain Asahi, this is my father, Tennō Atheryn Evangale of the Storm Sorcerers."

Asahi appraised him skeptically. Upon my father's thinning and straggling hair and slightly hunched shoulders, I could imagine what the captain judged, but he would be wrong. The way Father's storm gray eyes held the captain's shone with his inner strength. I waited for an eternity, expecting one of them to break the tense silence.

Asahi found his voice first—a sign of weakness that he clearly couldn't comprehend. "Well and good. Upon the *Mistress*, there are no emperors or empresses. Ak Ana's or Ebisu's wills are all that might out-rule my command. As long as that's clear, let us sail." He turned on a heel and climbed the dock.

Hoaris, Chambui, Misha, and Kyr stood to the side showing due deference to the royal family. Hoaris issued a barely audible grunt. My father and I held one another's eyes for a moment until I grew angry over how weak my father seemed in the moment. He should have been the one to demand respect, but he awaited me to do his bidding as if he'd forgotten all the lessons about leadership he had imparted unto me. A protective instinct stirred in my gut—a feeling I hadn't expected—and without looking toward the sea, I called a gale so strong it brought a wave crashing over both the dock and Captain Asahi. I swirled the wind about me so that it lifted and carried me in the direction of the captain. I controlled the power, lessening the force to allow the winds to lower me to the dock before Asahi. He stood still, dripping with his mouth agape and hands spread wide. As I lit upon the rickety boards, his jaw worked wordlessly.

I glared at the man. Heat in my chest, but calm lacing my words, I said, "If I recall, I am the only reason you and your crew did not perish at sea. Where was your sea goddess, Ak Ana, then?" I paused, but he offered no answer. Giving a knowing nod, I added, "Maybe you should call *me* your sea goddess. My father may seem weak now, but if my powers are fierce, my father's are tenfold when he is in full health. Your little ship will bear us back to Nantai, because it is both your duty *and* your desire to serve your emperor. And you will give my father the ceremonial deference where it is due."

Asahi's jaw worked, but he found no words.

I rolled my shoulders backward. "Or the next time I come to you in the night, I will lure you into the sea like the *syrens* of the tales your sailors spin."

From deep inside, Parū smirked. *See how you've grown, minikin. A new and fierce person. And I am proud that you are mine.*

Thirty-Nine

The High Seas, Once Again

PARŪ SOARED OVER BLACK WATERS. Night over the Syrensea held an eerie quiet for which I had nothing to compare. Even over water, there were no water sounds like the ones that'd comforted me during my youngling years at Stormskeep. The only sound remained silence for leagues and leagues. Through my dragon's eyes, I gazed amazingly far into the distance with only half of Selene's full light, and on occasion in the black waters below, some beast would crest or a school of fish would dart beneath the surface.

Suddenly, though I rested small within her, drowsing toward sleep, I felt her chest expand and air rush deep into her lungs, filling more space than I would have imagined possible, saturating our long body deep into the gut. Verily, our serpentine dragon form grew and grew as the wind rushed into me, her, us. Strange how her form now seemed one of my own.

Then, Parū tilted, tucked her wings, and dove, the cool and damp night whipping against her snout as she lengthened her tail and pointed directly for the water. She closed her eyes, and I too was blind, just before—

SPLASH!

The cold water made my soul shiver, and Parū pushed air through her nostrils at a slow and constant pace. In the blues and grays beneath the surface, she only opened the outer sets of her double eyelids, the others remaining shut and protecting her eyes from the sting of the salted water. Bubbles trailed behind us where she expelled breath. She darted after green and yellow fish, gulping a dozen or more before she broke free of the water and sailed back into the sky. Water drizzled from her scales and cascaded off her wings, finally sounding like the splashing of the Sundai Falls beside Stormskeep.

I felt breathless though I had no need for air in the place I resided. My companion's power permeated my being and I felt her stomach stretch and work on the meal she'd swallowed. I'd been growing fond of companionship, understanding more and more aspects of it by the day. Alert after the exhilaration of the plunge into the cold waters, my mind worked. Questions whirled within like couples across a dance floor.

How can you eat so much yet I am still able to shift back to my own small body before morning's light?

I eat only what I can digest before the change, Parū answered in her typical growl, a tone that brushed softly over my mind and calmed me more than I'd have expected a season past.

You just consumed an entire school of fish, I objected.

Parū bellowed her laughter. *Like all processes of the body, my stomach works in concert with my size. If you think on these things, you'll find you already have the answers.*

Mayhap I *could* access her knowledge, but I hadn't that experience yet. Nor did I have the patience. Her answers led me to more questions. *Have you hunted other beasts already while we've been joined?*

Yes, minikin.

Why haven't I known this?

I will show you.

Memories came flooding back to my dragon, shared with me. An animal for which I had no name, just larger than one of the Small Folk, hung limply between her claws with blood dripping from its mouth as she landed on one foot. In a rare clearing in Ise, Parū curled protectively around her prey. The space in her mouth at the back of her tongue watered in anticipation of the treat. As she looked over the carcass, I saw the large and powerful back legs and smaller forearms. She breathed fire upon the creature, then inhaled—her way of testing to see if her meal had been cooked enough. The smell of burned hair and seared flesh reached her nostrils, and Parū swept her long tongue out to either side of her mouth to lick up saliva that trickled from her jaws. She bit into one of the back legs. Bones crunched as she chewed and separated the muscle in her mouth. With her head tilted toward the sky, she swallowed the greasy meat and discarded the snapped bones. And when she had satiated her hunger, she stayed there in the clearing and relished in her belly's fullness.

Had I been wholly myself, I might have gagged. As my human form only existed in spirit for the moment, I felt my own resistance to the images intermingled with her satisfaction and satiation after the meal she'd enjoyed.

Parū chuckled again, if I could call the deep rumble a chuckle. *Yes, minikin, your reaction is why I hunt while you sleep.*

◇◇◇◇◇◇◇◇◇◇◇◇◇◇◇◇◇◇◇◇◇◇◇◇◇◇◇◇

THOUGH I'D BEEN HAPPY to see the remainder of the yisun, as well as Tao and Oshun, when we boarded the Swell Mistress, I kept to myself for the first few days at sea. Admittedly, I checked on my father more than he wished. And when above decks, I'd tarried about speculating as to when he'd regain enough strength to discuss what Amare had shown me in her white walls. Likewise, I worried how I'd ever speak plainly to him of the Abatwa, given he remembered naught of the experience after his abduction. That must have been the meaning of the word Zofi had used—stasis, a great pause in one's existence. 'Twas almost how I felt upon the Swell Mistress as we traveled slowly eastward.

Since my command upon the pier, Asahi had kept mostly to himself and to his crew. Even without Thalaj here acting as my protector, he seemed to fear me rather than desire time with me. Rightly so after I'd appeared to him in the night like a syren the sailors fancied.

I fought exhaustion as well. My dragon didn't need to fly every night, but since we'd been at sea, she had. We'd searched for land to gauge the time remaining before we were upon Nantai's soil once more. The extended flight with no place for Parū to land or rest only added to the drain on our shared being. I slept in my cabin for many hours even as Otarr crossed the sky. Some days clouds billowed and others, they veiled the light.

A day arrived with no clouds in the bright blue sky. Otarr heated the air over the sea to an almost uncomfortable point. The stillness above reminded me of the dead seas when we'd traveled into the west, yet the *Mistress* gently rocked upon the Syrensea's waves and wind gathered in her sails. Our journey continued. Hoaris and Chambui, Misha and Kyr, and the remainder of the yisun—Timur, Nachin, Baidu, and Jaliqai—sat at the long table throwing dice when I emerged from one of my longer naps. I yawned and stretched, then joined them, hurdling the bench to take a seat between Baidu and Jaliqai.

Hoaris rolled, then slammed a fist on the table after seeing the numbers. He dropped several more coins into the pot, then slung an arm around Chambui. I tucked my chin and hid a smile at their sweet togetherness—something I found myself wanting now that I'd experienced both coupling and loss. Happiness for them warred with how part of my heart remained in Ise—*in Fey.*

Do not worry so much, minikin, Parū reminded me. *We will find him again. I will help when I have fulfilled my duty in Nantai.*

I stopped breathing, tried to maintain control and not speak aloud to the dragon inside. *What duty?* Searching the knowledge I possessed with her now as my companion, I couldn't find her memory of the matter.

The time for you to know some things has not arrived, minikin. I am sorry.

Chambui cut her eyes toward me, drawing me back to present company. She rolled the dice. "Look-see there!" she said with a lean toward Hoaris. "One-two-three-four-five-and-six." She swept the pot into a neat little pile in front of her. She stacked the coins and turned to Hoaris, then kissed him hard, commandingly taking what she believed hers.

When they broke apart, she squealed and Hoaris grinned with a glint of mischief in his eyes. He looked at me and said, "She's a little tease, but I'm a bit taken with her."

"As I can well see," I replied.

Jaliqai nudged me. "You're not sick this trip at all."

Having no response, I grabbed a mug of ale and drank deeply. Across the table, Chambui and I stared at each other, silently and communally speculating that it might be due to the changes I'd endured in Ise.

My bond with Parū.

Cannot be assured, Parū spoke up from inside, *but as much could be true.*

If so, I'm grateful, I thought back to her, remembering the way my stomach had roiled with every wave the last time we'd sailed across the Syrensea. Parū shuddered inside at my memories of repeatedly heaving into a bucket beside my small bed.

It is a wonder you survived, she said.

I tucked my chin and hid a tight smile from the party about the table.

The dice rolled time and time again. Everyone threw mugs of ale back and refilled on occasion. And I settled into the normalcy of the situation upon the *Swell Mistress,* laughing when one or another allowed frustration to seep through over a poor roll. I jumped at a loud thump.

Boots behind me halted, and for a split second, I held my breath. Could it be Thalaj? Mayhap I hoped, but hope died almost before it took root. My companions on the other side of the table stood with their heads bowed in deference. I turned to Father. He was still some distance away and holding himself up on a makeshift cane. I leaped from where I sat to help him, but he forestalled me with an extended arm and warning look.

No words emerged, but his message, *I'll do this myself, Daughter,* was evident.

Right, I thought. I must afford him his independence and dignity. *He'll recover,* I assured myself.

The boat's rocking might aide him now, Parū said.

With her words, I wondered if the sickness of the sea plagued him as it had done me or if he simply remained weak. I held onto the wooden bench to prevent myself from reaching out to steady him as he neared the table. An aching moan escaped his throat as he lifted one leg then the other over the bench.

"May I get you food, Father?" The action might at least appease my need to ease his discomfort.

He grunted again and gave a nod, his brow still furrowed.

He simply needs his strength, I reminded myself, turning and standing to greet him.

Father's voice sounded gravelly from disuse when he spoke. "One would think I'd be wide awake after spending so long in . . . What did you call it, Mairynne?"

I kissed him on the cheek, smiled, and answered, "Stasis, Father." Then I went below deck to retrieve a bowl from the galley. When I returned, I sat across the table from him and watched him eat. That he could hold down food told me he didn't suffer from the same sickness I had endured. While he ate, I chewed the inside of my lip, wondering if it were time to begin a conversation about what we were to face in Nantai.

Rapt in my own thoughts and how Father fared, I hadn't noticed the awkwardness of the others who surrounded us.

Jaliqai, in her bubbly voice, broke the silence. "Yisu Chambui, let us show you what we've brought for Lady Sarangarel from Ise." She tilted her head in the direction of the hold and looked meaningful at the rest of the yisun. Her efforts, though well-intended, didn't quite dissolve the tension. Regardless, it was a kind effort, and it served to draw the others away.

Misha's eyes gleamed. He grabbed Kyr's hand and said, "Can we see too?" Judging by his keen look, he clearly wondered if there were any stones within what they'd found he could use for the Small Folks' spells.

Slowly everyone trickled away, and I remained alone with Father.

He looked up at me when he'd finished the last of the stew. "How long did you say I've been away?"

I twisted my lips, calculating, but having spent several moons amidst the Tsinti, time upon the sea, uncounted time with the Rundi tribes, and then some unmeasurable time in the Fey realm, I quickly gave up on that and simply said, "It's been a long, long time. Long enough for the remainder of the funeral rites to pass and for us to travel for many turns of Selene to find you. Seasons have passed in truth." I absently traced a groove in the wood of the table with a thumb. After a few more thick moments, I slapped my hand down where I'd been fidgeting and looked dead into my father's eyes. "I believe we face something even worse upon our return to Arashi, and quite honestly . . . I am terrified."

My declaration hung heavily in the air, and I stared deep into my father's thunderstorm-gray eyes. They were vacant, but something behind them, somewhere in there, was the father and emperor I'd known. He fought with himself to regain control and make sense of all that had happened. It was only a matter of convincing him of who he'd once been. We *all* needed to recover who we were—as a family, as Evangales, and as the rulers of Nantai. My eyes fell to the table. One problem remained. I had no idea how to force that need into reality.

The best hopes I had were memories. I held out a hand and called the wind, bringing the mist from over the sea into my open palm. I held one finger above my open palm and stirred until a miniature waterspout danced and swirled. "Remember when you told us stories and animated them in your hands like this? Or when"—I swallowed—"Karynne would bring the characters in the tales to life with the wind and sands? Remember how I clapped with glee over that small thing?"

He searched my face, clearly wondering where my questions had started. He sighed as if he no longer had patience to handle youngling games. Yet his words were soft, patient. "Mairynne, that is what any Storm Sorcerer father does. It is common among our families, and younglings learn to control their sorcery through those small reenactments."

I dropped the water onto the table with a tiny splash. Hot anger flared in my chest—entirely unnecessary, and certainly owed to the still stabilizing companion's bond. But, by the Triad, I had grown tired of waiting for him to return to himself in his own time. Seething, holding my eyes closed, I clenched my jaw to restrain the anger.

Patience, minikin, Parū rumbled.

I gave a singular laugh. *Strange how my conscience had turned into a dragon's voice.*

You will learn to temper this tendency. It will take time, but you are strong enough. Simply breathe now. In. Out. Good.

When I had gained a modicum of control, I looked to this shell of a man before me. I wanted to shake him, to yell, "Where has the emperor of Nantai gone?" And in my ire, I wondered, *Why hadn't Amare given him a dragon and made him strong again?*

He wasn't right for the dragons or companionship.

What do you mean? He's better than I. Far more worthy. He knows deep down how to lead the castes and the casteless. He only forgot.

Do you recall, minikin, how Amare and I knew your mind in the Fey realm? Osmar too? Parū asked, her voice inside sleepy. I'd clearly woken her with my sudden anger.

I do, but—

We knew his mind too. And Amare doesn't give a dragon away. We are creatures unto ourselves, free of rule, individuals with hopes and dreams. Do not think us less than you. We go to people with a purpose, much like the reasons you harbored when you fled from Arashi. We choose our companions for ourselves.

Then why didn't you choose him?

He would have resisted, and as weak as he already was, the bonding would have slain him. This was a better way. You were strong enough to contain a Ryū's soul.

So, though I desire as much, I should not tell him of you?

Not yet, minikin. She yawned and faded away from my awareness once again.

"What troubles your mind, Daughter?" Father asked.

I refocused on him for long moments, before I uttered, "May the Triad damn me, I wish Thalaj were here." I slapped my hand on the table and averted my gaze. Swinging a leg over the bench, I faced sideways and allowed my head to loll forward. Upon the words being freed, the sting of tears welled up. I couldn't fight them this time and watched as wet droplets hit the bench.

In my periphery, Father stood and circled the table. Then the bench moved as he sat behind me. Gently, he wrapped an arm around my shoulders. I entered willingly into his embrace and curled into the crook at his shoulder that I'd loved so much in youth. Though I no longer fit the way I once had, he held me while I cried out my frustration and loss—at least for the moment. When I had finished, I pulled back and scrubbed my hands over my face.

Father placed a hand on my chin and lifted my face to his. Between sniffles, I glimpsed the person he had once been. A flash. Protective instincts stirred in his fatherly appraisal. His posture straightened ever so slightly, strength he clearly willed into his stature now for me, his daughter. His eyes cleared and his jaw set tighter. "I know what it is to suffer having a morsel of your heart torn from your chest, Daughter. Do not lose yourself to despair as well."

His touch warmed even my heated skin, and if he felt the heat, he either failed to notice or didn't care. He merely held my questioning gaze and reminded me without words that Tennō Atheryn Evangale, the father I'd once known, still thrived within the withered man before me. Had I known my apparent weakness was all that'd been necessary, I would have shown it long before. Words percolated in my mind as the winds shifted and changed around us. With the spark of his Evangale lightning returning, the time seemed right. How much I could say before breaking him again was the delicate line I treaded before speaking.

"Do you remember Imrythel?" I ventured.

He furrowed his brow. "Karynne's friend?" A nod as he placed her eased the line between his brows, and he almost smiled. "Ah, yes. The one who wore the veil. I often wondered what she hid beneath that black lace."

What she hid physically, I didn't know. Yet I felt certain it had to do with her companion. I couldn't immediately push the words from my lips. The images of her with the green dragon in Amare's white walls haunted me. The extent of her treachery remained a mystery, but within my very being, I understood that they had been companions the entire time. I suspected her hand was the force behind Karynne's actions after my departure. Parū didn't stir inside, so I tucked that nugget away to discuss with her later, to learn all that she knew of the green dragon. Instead of spilling all my suspicions, I backtracked.

"She's from the Great Sands," I said.

"We don't have many people who live there." Father's eyebrows peaked as he mulled over the information.

"I believe there are more than we might know." I cleared my throat. "As we dealt with Mother's mourning rites, the advisers on your small council, my sisters, everyone it seemed pressured me to ascend to the Serpentine Throne, and Imrythel seized every opportunity to try to place a Sandsgale upon my private council."

"Would that have been an absurd notion? Noralynne always wanted more participation from others throughout the land, and the Sandsgales *are* Storm Sorcerers."

I shook my head, stung at the mention of Mother's name. It wouldn't have been out of line, save the knowledge I now possessed. "Mayhap it would have been of no consequence. Yet in the shadow of whatever has transpired since I left Stormskeep, I believe otherwise." Images of Alto-Trea as Filtch, then The Swan, then Filtch again spun in my mind. Sarangarel's words also echoed in my mind: *There are signs that the newest leader of the Nantai people has less pure intentions in her heart.*

Father removed his arm from my shoulders and moved away. He reclined backward, resting his elbows on the table at my side. "There is much you do not say, Mairynne. You must bring me current on all you know."

My lips twitched, wanting to smile at the fact that he seemed to be addressing business—an emperor's business—but I stifled the urge. In a rush, I said, "Karynne ascended to the throne after I left."

Father scratched at his graying beard. "Mairynne, had it not been for you—the most free-spirited and feisty yet the most level thinker of my three daughters—I would have decreed Karynne ascend to the throne upon my death. It seems like the logical course of action without you present. I must say . . ." His brow furrowed. "Your concern seems misplaced."

I tucked my chin and my voice grew hoarse and strangled when I gave him my reason. "I ascended using Morwyn's oath. Are you familiar?"

Father shook his head.

"It is an oath that would allow me to return the mantle to its rightful owner once he . . . once *you* returned. Before leaving Arashi, I decreed that Aunt Nadialynne should use the same oath and guard the position until our return. It would have allowed us to revert the ownership of the throne to me, then you."

Silence dropped over us, deafening. Even the crew remained utterly silent in word and motion. I ventured a look up to see understanding dawning on Tennō Atheryn Evangale's face.

"I am unfamiliar with such an oath," he started slowly, "but you believe . . . Are you suggesting that . . ."

I waited for him, hopeful that he put the implications together without me having to say the words.

"You think Karynne seized the throne by force?"

Yes, he understood. I sighed my relief, nodded, but I also looked for other answers from Father. "Why didn't you simply name Karynne as your successor? She is your eldest, and that would have been the natural course of action. And she wanted it desperately. I didn't." I looked down again. "I still don't."

Parū scoffed inside.

Father said, "Those, Daughter, are precisely the reasons I chose you. You respect and fear the station. Karynne . . ." His throat worked. "Though I love my first daughter dearly, she covets the power."

My gaze shot up to him. My skin felt on fire, and I saw white as I spat, "But granting her that may have prevented this whole ordeal."

He recoiled, and I tempered my rage, certain that signs of my companionship had flashed or perhaps still shone, within my eyes. "Mayhap if you had just given it to *her*, Mother would still live. Thalaj may still be protecting us all at Stormskeep." And there it was; my frustration with his reasoning had finally surfaced. I turned away, retreating from him. My voice hardened as I gave him my new purpose, "Once I have returned you to Arashi and restored your position upon the throne, I do not intend to remain in the city of the Storm Sorcerers. I fully intend to return to Ise to find Thalaj."

Launching from the bench, I walked to the railing. I plunged my fingers into my hair and pulled it to one side so the dark waves settled over my shoulder. I dug my fingers into the tight muscles in my neck as I gazed out over the Syrensea. "When I found you, I'd hoped that all would be right. I believed with my entire soul *you* would have the answers like you always did. I still believe you're the answer to keeping the gnobles in their places and the casteless from rioting within the streets. But I had hoped, well, it seems I had hoped too much."

He stood also and came to me. Covering my hand upon the railing with his own, he waited for me to look at him before he said, "I'm touched that you think so highly of me, Mairynne, but I am only mortal. I live and love and mourn like you. Like anyone else. And . . . I will one day die like any other."

I kept my eyes upon the waters around the *Swell Mistress*, not trusting myself to look at him.

"I've lost everything," he said simply, sadly.

"You?" I scoffed. I couldn't reconcile his words with how I burned inside. "I've lost everything and more. I lost my mother, my father, our empire"—my voice cracked—"and now Thalaj."

Father squeezed my hand, and I finally peered over. His eyes sparked, an old, familiar light dancing inside, a strength my soul needed more than my waking mind would acknowledge. His jaw remained as strong as it had always been, a muscle ticking in his cheek beneath the beard.

The emperor, Tennō Atheryn Evangale, nodded hard and stated, "Well then, it is time we take it all back." These words he pronounced as decisively as if he'd sat on the Serpentine Throne only that morning. "You take back yourself. I take back myself. And together, we move forward into the next age of our existence. I'll never be the emperor or the father I once was. I've lost too much. But you and I, we'll do what we must for the people who need us, and when it's all said and done, we'll have a ruler, likely an empress, upon the Serpentine Throne we can be proud of."

A thud sounded behind us.

We both jumped, and in unison, we turned to Yisun Timur. He stood there with both hands on the table, something inside each of his fists. When he released them, two sparkling white gems glinted back at us, faceted many times over and catching every ray of Otarr's light. "Lady Sarangarel sent the yisun to help and protect you, Mairynne Evangale as Kōgō of the Nantai people. Whatever you need, our emperor father and our *empress* daughter, the yisun and the Stone Singers will be at your sides."

The other yisun stepped to his sides. Hoaris stood behind Chambui with his hands upon her shoulders. The Small Folk, Misha and Kyr, circled the yisun and stood at Timur's side, smiling up at Father and me.

"Thank you, Timur." My voice creaked like the rickety old wood of the *Mistress's* decks.

Kyr came to me, offering her hand. "It's no less than what your shadow would have us do, lovely."

Behind everyone, Hoaris winked and gave me one final, determined nod.

Part Four
Call of the Scorched Empire

FORTY

Kōkai—The City by the Sea

CAPTAIN ASAHI AIMED THE SWELL Mistress true, her bow pointed toward the now vacant docks in Kōkai, the City by the Sea. My fingers gripped the railing so tightly, the wood might have splintered under my grip. While she had been a city bustling with commerce when we'd embarked upon this journey, only smoldering ruins lay sprawled before me now.

Upon the *Swell Mistress*, I moved around the bow, away from the others who stood gaping at the land.

What could cause this destruction? I mused, fearing any answer my dragon companion, Parū, might offer.

Her words came to me in a sad rumble, in part a musing answer, *The breath of the Ryū. I'm sorry, minikin, but I cannot imagine a natural fire could cause such broad desolation.*

It acknowledged the worst of my fears. Heavy stones twisted and churned in my gut, and my temperature climbed with every moment we drew nearer to the shore. The planks atop the pier's rocks had been burned as well, leaving only the naked rocks. Asahi would have little leverage to tie off the *Swell Mistress*. The crew rowed below deck, and other sailors carried orders from the captain back and forth.

Behind me, and as if to answer my thoughts, the sailor Oshun rushed toward another. "Tao," he called, a might breathless. "Asahi's orders. Steer the *Mistress* into the shallows there. We'll drop anchor."

They both disappeared, presumably to command the crew working to land the *Mistress* safely.

I inhaled deeply; the smoke billowing from the buildings still some distance away burned my nostrils. Around the docks, ships that'd once been tethered were now naught but floating driftwood, charred on the ends. No sailors or merchants moved about the once-bustling seaside markets. I'd remembered this place, this sparkling City by the Sea so fondly, in part because of the touch the Stone Lady Sarangarel had offered, lovingly and tenderly, juxtaposed with her persona as the leader of an otherwise hard people. Was she still here? Had she perished along with the once glittering white marble that'd been scorched so deeply? I wondered if even the Stone Singers with their magics for bringing brilliancy forth within stone could return the luster.

White flared at the edges of my vision, but I blinked back the urge to give myself over to the anger. *The green dragon?* I asked.

Hard to be certain, but Guin carries a wrath inside her that may make her capable of such a feat.

But for what purpose would she burn one of Nantai's largest cities? No sooner had the thought crossed my mind than a new fear sprung to life. *Karynne? Could she have commanded such a thing?* I hoped and prayed my sister hadn't lowered herself to such treachery, but I recalled Sarangarel's words: *"There are signs that the newest leader of the Nantai people has less pure intentions in her heart."*

My body started to shake.

Minikin, do not let yourself fall to your anger and fear. Use it to understand and change, Parū rumbled.

"Mairynne," Oshun said.

Turning to him, I blinked several times in rapid succession to see him clearly.

"Can you move there?" He pointed. "I need to move past you to drop the front anchors."

Obliging, I turned from the sight. I flexed and released my hands at my sides. The night before, when Parū had flown and we'd seen the line of land in the distance, so much hope and relief had flooded my soul. I'd slept wonderfully once we returned to the *Mistress*, dreaming of how peaceful Nantai had been. Cold and empty and abandoned seemed more appropriate descriptors for this place now—a place where I'd anticipated feeling the magic of my people coursing through my veins once more.

Once they'd lowered the anchors, I went to stand near Father and the others. Yisu Chambui reached for me, pain written upon her face. She clearly offered comfort and needed it in return, but I stiffened, unable to find the gentler emotion. I felt naught but raw confusion and enmity. The white-hot haze across my vision wouldn't allow me space to mourn yet, but I bit down, my jaws clenching under the knowledge that she only wanted to share in the sadness we both felt. She only desired connection with someone she viewed as her leader. With the destruction before us, surely she and the rest of the yisun believed they'd lost a good number of their own people. Mayhap even the gnoble of the Stone Singer caste—Sarangarel. But I'd cared for her as well. And the people of the Stone Singers, as well as the casteless who'd lived in Kōkai, were mine too. Certain about the source of this ruin, I focused my animosity toward Imrythel and taking back my homeland.

I hadn't the time to mourn the loss of my people within the city walls. I reached forward, touching her shoulder lightly, but Hoaris enfolded her in his arms from behind, giving what I could not.

For long moments, I couldn't tear my eyes from the city. A solitary mangy mutt with ribs visible even from a distance sniffed around a pile of broken rubble, likely searching for any rotting morsel remaining—a sad glimmer of hope that some may have survived. When I'd committed the sight to memory, I turned to Father, searching his stormy eyes for answers born of his long years serving as emperor of the Nantai people. But wisdom failed him in our moment of silent conversation.

When Asahi came bounding onto the forward deck, I grasped his arm. "Do you have plans?"

"I did before . . ." He waved one hand at the shoreline and put a stick of spiced wood in the corner of his mouth. "I'll send in the dingy. The first trip will take a team of my men to the shore to assess the situation. Once deemed safe, I'll allow passengers."

At my side, I balled a fist. "I will go in the first boat."

The captain quirked a brow. "This trip and our safe return across the Syrensea may be attributable to you, Kōgō Mairynne, but I would be remiss now if I threw away Nantai's most precious cargo." His eyes drifted past me to my father and he nodded. As he went back to work, he added, "If you must defy my orders, we can lift anchor. I'll sail to Lu Galen, and you may find another ship and another captain to bring you back here."

I closed my eyes and took several cleansing breaths, reaching deep inside for the sorcery. It coursed through my veins, not as powerful as it had been before I left Nantai, but it was there, tingling through my limbs.

I will help you, minikin, Parū said.

Spinning back to face the shore, Father stood before me, regret and an apology apparent upon his brow. "Magic weakens with more time spent away from our home lands. But if you insist on using your ability, I will do what I can to help." He leaned closer and lowered his voice. "With you on land, Asahi wouldn't dare leave port."

I jerked with small hesitation, then knowing that it'd work with Father's and Parū's help, I threw my arms around him. Smaller, frailer, his frame had strengthened some but still felt slight; I eased my grip about his shoulders. For only him, I whispered, "Thank you, Father . . . and Tennō Atheryn."

Poised at the center of the forward deck with my hands held wide, I nodded to Father and called for my magic. Wind snapped the sails, and the boat lurched forward but was held in place by the anchors. It lifted my hair, and as I felt Father's magic join the mix, my body felt lighter. My bare feet lost contact with the deck, and I lifted on the gale. Inside, Parū focused a steady stream of fey magic from her being into mine, and it boosted my own ability. I inhaled deeply and with a long, forceful exhale, I thrust my sorcery into the wind and glided forward, over the pointed bow of the *Swell Mistress* and toward the coast. When I reached the water's edge, I relaxed and floated downward on the ebbing breeze until my toes touched the wet pebbles. I sighed, loosening my hold on the storm's power, and the air fell still.

At long last, my feet rested upon Nantai's shores. The stench of burned flesh aside, I was home.

◇◇◇◇◇◇◇◇◇◇◇◇◇◇◇◇◇◇◇◇◇◇◇◇◇◇◇◇◇◇

INSIDE ME, PARŪ RELEASED a chain of grumbles, a language I couldn't understand but clearly recognized as a string of obscenities. Mayhap it was that I felt the same, wanting to see justice served for the burned rubble and ruins left before me. Even the dog had scurried away, leaving only blackened rocks and desecrated buildings.

I speculated before, but I am now certain, minikin. One of the Ryū wrought this destruction upon your city with dragon's breath alone.

The sense of desolation in Parū's words felt raw, echoing the ache in my chest. My home had splintered further after my departure. Aloud with no other souls to hear, I answered my dragon, "We will make this right. If it takes the remainder of my lifetime, we will see the being responsible pay for this."

Behind me, my party cheered. Shouts and pleas for us to wait peppered me from afar, but I couldn't. I had to see the extent of what lay before me. Turning, I raised a hand. The first dingy traveled toward me as fast as the sailors could row, but my party . . . my trusted companions . . . awaited upon the *Swell Mistress*. I would return for them, but for now, I wouldn't wait for Asahi's plan to pass.

I walked slowly through the streets, still absorbing an influx of Nantai's magic. Strange that I hadn't felt it fading but the return intoxicated my mind. I measured my progress, committing every piece of ruin to memory. Filing it away so I could write of it one day in the annals and so I could tell this story one day to children at my feet. And if for some reason I failed to return to Ise, the tales of my journey would keep Thalaj alive, if only in verse. My feet carried me along the same path the casteless city rat Honera had led Hoaris, Thalaj, and me many moons ago toward Lady Sarangarel's stone-walled castle. The streets were different now, no vendors tarrying around their street carts or hawking at potential buyers, only death and destruction lined these streets.

Half-walls still stood in the alley leading up to the castle where we'd stopped, but the castle itself was naught but a pile of scorched rock. Had there been Singers inside, they now rested in a stone grave. I closed my eyes and lifted a hand to my cheek, remembering Sarangarel's soft touch. My fingertips trembled across my lips—as gently as her kisses. Then down my neck, and over my shoulder, my hand absently traced their path. I recalled her hands upon my hips, calloused skin moving so gently over me, then driving me to pleasures I hadn't known possible. She'd been a first in the way of love-making, and I'd forever be indebted to her for the kindness she'd shown.

I wept for her and the people she'd loved and served within this keep.

Deep inside, I had understood the bargain we'd struck—my innocence for her aid in gaining passage upon the *Swell Mistress*. Standing here now, knowing all that had passed, the loss of such a strong woman hardened me more. Even having the dreadful knowledge of the Rundi tribes, the Fey realm, and that I'd lose the man I truly desired as a partner in this life, I would remake those choices today.

A rodent skittered along the cobbles nearby, announced only by its high-pitched peals, but it sufficed to ground me in the present once again.

Parū, I reached for her consciousness inside me.

Groggily, she answered, *Yes, minikin?*

I wish to fly—soar over this rubble and see it all for myself.

Have patience. Your father may not take well to the sight of a great white dragon circling a burning city. She paused, waiting, but I had no reply. *Under the cover of night will be a better choice. I will bring you here once darkness has fallen so that you may look upon the ruins in the company of your goddess, Selene.*

Her caution rang true. I'd taken care thus far to allow Father his time to heal, but the time I shared my secret with him grew near. He deserved to hear of the bond from my own lips, lest he learn another way or in a manner I could scarce control. My leg twitched, begging for movement, and though I held little certainty as to where I traveled, I walked through the charred streets, wound around the fallen roofs littering the streets, and turned several times until at last I stood before a familiar building, the once light façade blackened. The door hadn't been any strong obstacle before, but only a few charred boards now hung by one hinge, splintered and blocking the passage at a graceless angle. The buildings surrounding were naught but debris, but this one that'd been decrepit when I'd visited before stood almost hale.

The door fell from the weak pin holding it in suspension with the slightest touch, and I dodged to let it clatter to the ground. The final splintering sound echoed from the stones, and dust and ash billowed from where it landed. My feet were unclad and now soot-blackened, and I stepped carefully inside. Surprised at the strength of the stairs inside, I climbed, lives lost in this city haunting my every step. How many Stone Singers had perished? How many casteless?

Had Imrythel acted alone, or had the blue Ryū been part of this?

Parū perked up at my last meandering thought. *The blue Ryū?*

"Yes," I whispered as if she walked at my side, remembering the first time I'd sighted a dragon. "I once helped her retrieve her egg from a town named *Safaia* after the large stone that rested at the town's center square. A boulder they'd believed . . . immovable." I pictured the scene, the storm I'd called, and then the Ryū's small nod of thanks just before she took flight with her egg nestled within her claws.

If we do not find her with the green dragon, we must search her out after, Parū grumbled, sadness lacing her words. *We thought she'd perished since she didn't return with the others of my kind after the Great War. Barūdragon.* She paused after sharing the dragon's name, shielding any other thoughts from me for the moment. But then she added, *A Ryūling has ne'er hatched outside of Fey, and she will go mad protecting her babe.*

Words and emotion balled in my throat, stung behind my eyes over the depth of sadness she intoned. "I'm sorry," I breathed. I hadn't an inkling what havoc a Ryū's madness might cause, but it felt like something I never wished to learn. Resolving to her cause, I started, "We will see to her once . . ." The promise hung in the air as I arrived at the door leading to the room where I'd waited before, where *we*—Thalaj, Hoaris, and I—had waited for Filtch. Then this room had been barren; now, it was littered with what seemed discarded furniture, some of the wooden edges blistered at the corners. It appeared as if someone had collected these items and positioned them as a blockade.

A small scraping reached my ears. More rodents? Then . . . an irrepressible sob. Then . . . quiet again, as if the sobber had thrown a hand over a mouth to stifle more unwieldy and alerting sounds. But I honed in on the sound and moved forward. My feet silently landing on the floor, I slid through the small path between the furniture, working my way toward the corner and searching to find the source of the convulsive lament. As I rounded a large shelf, a small form huddled into the corner—a child by the size.

I narrowed the distance, cooing, "Shhh, little one. All will be well."

When the head moved and turned to me, my eyes widened, and I gasped. The last time I'd looked into that face, there'd been smudges on her cheeks. Now, there were lines under her clear eyes where tears had carved away the soot and ash. Her clothing that'd been threadbare, but serviceable, now hung from her in tatters, and her boots barely clung to her ankles, the toes cut away to allow her bare digits to hang over the front of the soles.

Not once did I consider it evil that this little girl had once betrayed me to Filtch—Alto-Trea in disguise. She'd only been fighting to survive and survive she did. In the face of a dragon breathing fire upon the city, she'd somehow lived. With a tear straying from my eye, a small droplet of hope at seeing her strength, I crouched beside her, her name a prayer upon my lips. "Honera?"

Forty-One

Many Goodbyes

HONERA HAD BEEN AN IMAGE of small strength, scrappy and defiant when I'd met her last. Now, within my arms, her frail shoulders trembled like a tree weathering a storm.

"I, I . . ." She sniffled and clung to me. "Before . . . I didn't mean . . ."

"Shhh." I cradled her head into the crook of my shoulder. "You were afraid. I can see as much, but you have nothing to fear with me." I pulled her away and looked into her clear eyes. "Will you come with me now?" I didn't wish to take her freedom, and there was little in the way of security I could offer for the remainder of our journey. In truth, I feared we headed into more danger than safety. "Have you lost Flea and Gnat?"

She nodded into my shoulder.

I looked up toward the ceiling. "You are welcome to join me and my friends, Honera. I cannot promise your safety." I pushed her back by the shoulders. "But you are strong to have survived, and I believe the Triad must see a purpose for you yet."

Worry shone in her shifting eyes.

Hardening my gaze, I said, "We'll offer what protection we can, but you'll have to help out where you can."

In small jerks, she nodded again.

"Can you speak?" I asked.

The girl tucked her lips between her teeth and bit down. Then she took a raspy breath and croaked, "Yes."

My Ryū shifted inside, disapproval hot in her mind, but I cared little. *You do not know the struggles of my people in current times or the struggles of the casteless within Nantai.* Honera, and any other who answered my call, was my charge, and mine alone. Upon her death, my mother had bequeathed the care of the casteless and the Small Folk to me—a truth I was slowly coming to understand through my travels and the people I'd met. Taking in Honera, caring for her, making her welcome at my side was as much my duty as a calling within my heart and soul.

"Whatever has happened here in Kōkai, I have a duty to see it set right. If you join me, will you aid me in this and remain loyal? No more betrayals to the likes of Filtch?" I pressed.

Honera didn't find more words, but she nodded her acceptance eagerly.

I cannot believe this is a wise move, minikin, Parū insisted. *We fly into danger, and you're accepting a youngling into your care. 'Tis too much.*

Then you'll help me keep an eye on her until we both believe she deserves our trust, I thought to my dragon as we retraced my path, descending to the shore at the water's edge. When we rounded the final set of obliterated buildings, I stopped, taking in the scene of my party and the sailors moving about on shore. They had gathered upon the rocky beach and buzzed about with disjointed purposes. The yisun and Hoaris had pulled a fisherman's barge to shore and inspected it for seaworthiness. Some sailors stacked crates they'd borne ashore from the *Swell Mistress* and tended to the small dingy. Asahi oversaw the work, and the Small Folk, Misha and Kyr, sat atop one crate inspecting the contents of a purse. I'd stopped to appraise the team I'd come to adore. Several looked up, taking notice of our presence.

Chambui backhanded Hoaris. "I told you she'd be back on her own. He was ready to rush into the city to find you."

Others twitched in my direction but Hoaris leaped off the barge, splashed through the water, and ran up the slope with the enthusiasm of someone who'd been lost. When he reached me, he enfolded me within a bear's hug, lifted my feet from the stone, and swung me in a wide circle. Honera laughed at our side, and I too giggled with abandon for a second before the depth of the impending journey reached my mind once again.

The time had come.

As he lowered my feet back to the ground, I patted his shoulder. "Gather everyone, Hoaris," I commanded, solemnly and with regret over the decisions we now faced. I left the large Frost Fighter to his task.

In my periphery, Hoaris, as easy-spirited as ever, tousled Honera's hair and greeted her with big-brotherly affection. A small squeal of her laughter ensured me I'd made the right choice in accepting the casteless girl.

Parū still watched suspiciously from inside me, but so be it. We didn't have to be of one mind in all things.

Misha and Kyr stood, starting toward me, but I waved them off, intent on speaking with Asahi. Carefully, I padded over the rocks under my feet and heated by Otarr's light toward the water's edge where Asahi supervised his men. The pebbles, bathed by the waves of the Syrensea, grew progressively cooler under my soles until I once again felt the chill of the sea washing around my ankles.

Asahi stood slumped with his arms folded over his chest and his attention focused solely on the men unloading the cargo onto the shore.

"Captain," I called as I arrived at his side.

He turned and straightened to his full height, a head taller than me, but waited for me to speak.

"I understand you wish to return to the Vesterisles and Lu Galen."

"Lady Mairynne," he tucked his chin briefly, then refocused on me. "This desire is no slight to you or your father. I have fulfilled my end of this bargain, and I now have stories to tell of venturing across the Syrensea. I'll have enough fame as it is. Like I told Hoaris there, I have no further need for adventure."

My brows dropped and I squinted at him. "You will not fight the force that burned this city?" I felt on the verge of disbelief, yet I understood the inner need to find peace.

"With due respect, the battle is not mine to fight. To be sure, I'm an islander and a sailor. There is no battle save conquering the sea that is mine to fight."

I held my hands on either hip, nodding, accepting his stance. "I understand your position. Truly, I do. But I'd like to ask your sailors if they'd rally to my cause after traveling with us for so long."

Asahi held out a hand and lifted his brows as he spat on the rocks at his feet. "Do as you wish. I need but a handful to see the *Swell Mistress* back to Lu Galen. But may I ask, where do you plan to sail? And what will you do for a ship?"

I dug my teeth into my lower lip and glanced over to the yisun who'd left their tinkering with the barge to join Hoaris, Father, and the Small Folk. I considered how much support we'd need upon our return to Arashi, and I contemplated the various possibilities where I might gain this support. Hoaris would need to go to his kindred upon the northeastern shores of Kōdaina Kori, and the quickest way save by cloud was by boat, north along the Nantai shores. Had I known how to call a Cloud Courtier or one who might aid me in my need, I would have. Alas, it seemed travel by sea remained the more solid choice. I shifted my weight, rolling my shoulders back as I proceeded with my intended proposition. "About that, Captain Asahi, if I were to allow a team to accompany you back to Lu Galen, what intention do you have for the *Mistress* once you retire to become a minstrel of the Vesterisles?"

◇◇

I FOUGHT THE TEARS as I prepared to exchange not goodbyes, but sentiments of until our paths cross again. The yisun and Hoaris would accompany Asahi and the sailors upon the Swell Mistress back to the islands west of Nantai proper before heading north along the coast toward the Iced Plains of Nantai. Once there, Hoaris would cross the Northerly Barrows and the great frozen lake, Kōdaina Kori, to find his kin. There, he'd work to engage his brethren Frost Fighters and hopefully bring them to support my cause.

As the sailors brought supplies from the *Swell Mistress* ashore, we loaded crates onto the barge. Chambui and I dropped our shared load in one corner, and Hoaris placed the one he carried on top, then turned to me. "Thalaj will have my skull for letting you wander the land alone."

I placed a hand on his chest. "I am not alone. I will have Misha and Kyr, Father, and Honera."

He scowled. "But you do not have a protector. No warrior or person skilled with blades travels with you now."

Chambui tucked one hand in the crook of his elbow and lay the other on his shoulder. She looked up at him with pure adoration and tolerance, then turned her gaze meaningfully to me as she said, "Thalaj himself trained Mairynne with those blades she wears, and I believe she holds more strength and wisdom within her than any of us know."

My dragon veritably chuckled inside. *I like this one. She's smart and has kind words.*

I dipped my chin and fought the urge to smile at how Parū preened. When I had gathered myself, I said to Hoaris, "This is the only way. I will need help from your kindred when it comes time to confront my sister. You are the only one who can manage that."

"But let us send one of the yisun to accompany you," he persisted.

"Hoaris, you worry over much." Chambui squeezed his arm. "Once she's in Safaia, mayhap she can find a swordsman to travel inland toward Brennmor with them."

We exchanged another knowing look. With the Small Folk, Father, and Honera, I would travel overland to meet with King Isao of Brennmor. Even as we made the plans, the memory of the Small King's treatment of Karynne worried at my consciousness. But that remained a matter to deal with in the future.

As for what I planned for Safaia, I believed it unlikely that I'd invite another—a stranger—to travel at my side. I wanted to keep my journey quiet, only sharing my Ryū bond with those I felt certain I could trust. "I will see who we may find. In the meantime, Tao and Oshun seem proficient enough with their fat-bladed swords. They can likely chop through a man's neck as easily as they cut away ropes."

"She has a point there." Oshun stepped to my side, the muscles in his bare upper arm bunching as he hefted the short sword. It wasn't much longer than a scimityne but built for force rather than finesse. "With its weight, a solid blow will cut through a tree the size of my arm."

Tao stuck his head into the cabin. "We're ready when you are, Mairynne."

The two sailors agreed to travel with me and navigate up the Betsu River toward Safaia.

They had never traveled the river, but I recalled the way and they could better judge the waters. There weren't many turns; a right at the Betsu's fork seemed the only decision until we reached the small trade town. But to be certain our path remained clear, Parū and I would fly over once night had fallen. I fretted about the slow pace, but I couldn't leave those for whom I cared so deeply now—my father first and foremost. As I watched him joining into the effort to shore up the barge, I considered when and how I'd tell him of the bond I'd made. Parū even encouraged the conversation now, disliking the need to hide in daylight hours.

Yet I couldn't predict how he would receive the news. I feared the worst.

WHEN BRIGHT OTARR LOWERED over the sea, the seven of us remaining stood on the shore waving to the Swell Mistress as she sailed into the sunset. By morning, Asahi would be home. Well and so, I thought and turned to the others in my smaller party. "Should we search for shelter within the city for the night?"

Honera shook her head with wide eyes.

Kyr wrapped an arm around her shoulders. "I think we may do better in the barge."

Misha didn't wait for anyone but set off in that direction.

Oshun cocked a half-smile. "I'm more than happy to sleep on the water."

Tao nodded solemnly. Father and I brought up the rear as we crossed over and climbed aboard.

The cabin consisted of a single, large and open space, and we spread blankets in various recesses between our supplies. I lay awake, waiting for soft snores and even breathing from all, then crept above deck. I stepped as lightly as possible from the barge onto the shore where I gave Parū control and she shifted into the great pearlescent Ryū.

Satisfying my needs first, Parū flew over the City by the Sea. After we'd both recorded the obliteration in our shared memory, she stroked broad wings, snaked in midair, and soared northeastward in a line with the Betsu River until we saw the small town of Safaia. A scorched circle marked the center where the blue dragon's egg had been. As we both had traced our route and all seemed in order, I curled my soul up inside her and slept, giving her reign to hunt.

"Mmm, Mairynne," Parū said, her voice rumbling with after-meal satisfaction. Many hours had passed, and she'd woken me just before landing on the shore near the barge. The wind felt cool under her wings as she soared to a stop. With her claws upon the rocks, we moved, shifting with each step back into my human form. Naked, I stopped at a tree branch protruding over the water to retrieve my clothes and dress.

When I climbed back onto the barge, the wood groaned beneath my feet and I caught a glimmer of movement on the far end of the deck. My father's white hair caught Selene's dying light as he turned from where he had stared out over the Syrensea.

My heart beat faster than dragon wings and harder still. What had he seen? We had tried to be so quiet upon our return. I prayed to the Triad he hadn't witnessed the great pearlescent dragon landing or the transformation.

He yawned, lines pulling at the corners of his eyes. He appeared a little lost.

"Where have you been Mairynne? I woke to find your pallet empty."

Sensing no signs of fear within him, I ventured, "I couldn't sleep. I went to see more of Kōkai." It was the best I could do without spilling the entire truth and also without uttering a bold-faced lie.

"I know the feeling. Come sit beside an old man." He sat on a wooden ledge and patted the seat beside him.

I went, wondering if now was the time to share my secret. I searched for words within myself but none seemed adequate. My throat felt sick and dry.

And before I could start, he spoke, "This city looks like the descriptions from stories of the Ryū Wars. And the destruction I've seen today with my own eyes reminds me of a painting hung in our citadel. Do you remember the one?"

"I do," I said weakly, stifling the deep-seated desire to speak with the father I missed so much. He'd chosen the Wars to describe the desolation. Clearly, he still believed in that cause.

You presume, minikin.

He is the one who told me the stories, Parū, I thought indignantly.

Part of me felt scorned by his mere mention of the Ryū Wars and the belief he would rebel against my companion. I couldn't risk losing him after just having found him. *Another time,* I thought to her. With a huff she curled up in the corner of our consciousness, small, remote, and catlike.

My father continued, "It is such a stark reminder . . . heartbreaking even . . . of the destruction and ruin the Ryū are capable of. I had believed it only a part of our ancient history, and now it seems we face it again."

I remained silent, a new fear building inside. If he learned of my bond now, would he believe it was my dragon that had caused such desolation? I wanted to weep over how he clearly believed such horrendous things of the Ryū. I had escaped a prison of royalty within Arashi and landed in another, this one of the mind and a secret. How did I convince someone so established in his beliefs?

Parū warned, *Holding this secret will haunt you, minikin.*

I know, I acknowledged, *but I need time. He needs time.*

As we sat there in companionable silence, Selene retired, leaving the sky godless and dark. Long moments passed without word. The emptiness stretched thickly around us. I grew tired because of my alertness late into the night. Yet, as always, the sky turned gray and began to lighten with Otarr's awakening.

Sound started from within the cabin below. Father reached for me, welcoming me into his arms. I hugged him back for all I was worth until he pulled away.

His brows creased with concern, "You are so warm, Daughter, are you well?"

"I will be well enough, Father. One day soon." Of that assertion, I felt certain. Although, feeling *well* wouldn't come until we'd taken Stormskeep back from Imrythel, until I had my father's blessing upon my companionship with Parū, and only after I had Thalaj at my side once more.

FORTY-TWO

The Tradesman Taurusyn

THROUGH BONDED EYES, THE SCENERY up the Betsu River appeared differently, not necessarily brighter, but more alive. Every leaf on every tree hanging over the water, every curve of the shoreline, every boulder around which the water flowed seemed to have an aura. I saw things in a new light, both physically and emotionally—so changed as a result of my Ryū bond. It felt as if everything burned with an inner life and I had been blind to it before. Sailing against the current took more time and labor on the parts of Tao and Oshun than when Captain Jerek had followed the currents from Safaia toward the Syrensea.

We leveraged the wind for the return, my father and I taking turns in calling it forth, but Tao and Oshun often had to muscle us around obstacles barring our path with the long stick. For my part, patience remained the focus, and I spent many hours on deck, simply focusing on my breath. Parū slept inside me for days, giving me the space to remain still and try to bring forth an inner peace. Yet I remained aware of her presence at all times. It sang in the very life force that flowed through my veins, and when others shivered against the cooling nights, I relished in the reprieve. Thoughts of the heavy robes necessary for the mourning rites I'd experienced on behalf of my mother kindled an unfathomable fire within my bonded soul. I could scarcely imagine the heat and sweat, and I hoped not to have to endure the ritual again in the coming seasons.

The simple state of being back in Nantai afforded Father a more expedient recovery and mild rejuvenation. He'd likely never return to the image I remembered—a mental picture of strength and power that reached idyllic proportions—but there were glimmers of his fortitude and resolve in the small motions. He grew ever confident in the placement of his steps, and his small touches became more and more frequent.

As he stepped from the ship onto the rocky shores just outside Safaia, his spine even seemed straighter.

Regardless, I offered him my hand. "Father, it heartens me to see you gaining your stature once more."

"It is enlivening to have Nantai's magic flowing through me once more." His thunderstorm-gray eyes held a peaceful sadness that said more than words as to how he felt. Keenly, I knew his sadness. Though my understanding of his partnership with my mother had been only from a daughterly perspective, I felt the loss of Thalaj might at least touch on his pain.

Off the barge, I asked Misha, "Will you go to the caves?"

"We still have supplies there, so I think yes." He accepted Kyr into his arm as we waited for the sailors to toss over the packs we'd wear upon our backs as we traveled beyond Safaia and inland to find the Small Folk. "When you're ready, come find us," he added.

"Father and I will climb the hill to the town. If Sal doesn't have a bed for us, we'll join you in the cavern." I bent, locking arms with Misha.

Kyr grabbed both my hands and searched my face with worry-filled eyes. "You've always been a mite reckless, lovely. Please care for yourself while we're apart." The little woman exuded her quiet and caring nature as she always had.

I dropped to my knees, took her in my arms, and squeezed tightly. "I promise, I'll be all right, and you will see me again on the morrow at the very latest."

When I released her, Honera stepped off the barge, quietly fidgeting as she joined the group. She stood at a height with the Small Folk, and it was odd to look upon them side-by-side—an exquisite contrast between the youth in Honera's now cleaned face and the wisdom held within the few deep lines radiating from both Misha's and Kyr's eyes. The child now wore one of Kyr's dresses but said nothing as she wrung her hands.

I placed a hand on her arm. "Do you wish to go with Father and me or remain with Misha and Kyr?"

Worry danced in her eyes, and they darted to Kyr.

"Go." I tilted my head up the river and shot her an encouraging smile. "Trust that they will take good care of you. They did the same for me once."

For a moment, Father and I watched the three of them hiking along the Betsu until Tao and Oshun came to an unusual stillness at my side.

"Everything's secure," Oshun said with finality, tucking a key into his pocket. "Or as secure as it will be."

"Into town?" Tao asked.

The remaining supplies were meager at best, so there wasn't much concern over robbery, and we each had a pack that contained our small, more important belongings. Though our attire showed signs of travel and seafaring, the change of clothes was nice to have in our packs. However, all I truly worried over were the handful of spelled stones Misha had given me. Bedraggled from our adventure, we had little to offer in trade, so our situation remained tenuous at best. I hoped Sal would remember that I'd saved the town and willingly assist. Mayhap others would also rally to my cause, though I feared announcing the quest to the world prematurely.

Father pulled up the hood on his tattered cloak as we neared the edge of town. We hiked into Safaia, passing the scorched town's center before entering the Safaia Inn. The bell above my head sounded, and Sal looked up from her position crouched over an open book. Her face had been close to the page and she now relaxed the squint she'd been wearing in favor of open surprise. A pot of ink with a quill protruding sat to the side, seemingly unused. Sal rounded from behind the counter, waddling over with arms wide.

The gap between her teeth appeared a bit more pronounced as she said, "Mairynne!"

Within her pillowy hug, I smiled into her soft shoulder. "Sal," I said as I pulled away and turned. "This is my father"—I lowered my voice—"Atheryn."

Mayhap it was that Hoaris had once held fondness for this woman, or perhaps another reason rang true in my inner self. She held power and knowledge simply by serving the traveling peoples in this central trading town, and I sensed I might one day be grateful to have her support. But beyond that, I couldn't put specifics to the feeling that Sal genuinely had my best interests at heart and I desired to allow her inside.

Father kept his head lowered, turning slightly sideways.

"Oh me!" With a delighted gasp, she wiped her hands on her apron and then bowed her head with proscribed deference. "Tennō Atheryn. My inn is yours."

Looking around, I saw no one but the innkeep. Nevertheless, I moved closer to her, shushing the portly woman. "We don't wish to make our presence known to the travelers in town. Our intent is to only pass through as other merchants would."

Understanding lit upon her with a tiny, swift inhale and rounded lips. "Oh, right and true." But it only took her a beat to turn to business, and she shooed us toward another door. "Why don't you go into the back room and help yourself to some stew. It's been boiling since late last night over the fire, so the lamb should be nice and tender."

"There is no one back there?" I asked, pressing my need to remain somewhat anonymous.

When she had allayed my worry, I nodded for Father to proceed. "I'll be behind you shortly."

Father moved through the door. Tao and Oshun followed, naturally falling into their place as unassigned, untrained, and self-appointed guards. I watched after them, a slight smile creeping across my lips over how simply Tennō Atheryn Evangale's presence evoked a sense of loyalty. It helped to explain the reasons I felt myself ill-prepared for the mantle of Nantai empress.

Sal turned to me, wringing her hands in her apron. "Where's your scimityne master?" She waggled her brows and added, "And Hoaris?"

Coal seared my throat, and I grunted to speak, my words surfacing coarsely. "They have other duties to attend to at present. From you, now, I need a tradesman. We need overland transport and supplies."

"Yea, yea, I'll see to the need." She scurried over to a side table behind the desk and returned with a large stoneware carafe. "Here's some ale. Mugs are in the cupboard near the fire in back." She looked me over, a gaze speaking of my bedraggled appearance, painting a picture as if I'd spent a long, hot summer trekking across the Great Sands with little food, water, and only the clothes on my back. Her assessment would be true if only she'd known it had been a watery desert with salt instead of sand scenting the air.

I had little need to share the extent of my travels, so I accepted the ale. "We have little to pay, but once we've secured transport, a clothing merchant might be in order as well."

Sal tipped her head forward, satisfied, then made for the front door. I joined Father and the sailors, coughing on the woody smoke clouding the air in the back room.

Tao had already opened the door leading out behind Safaia Inn and stood nearby, attempting in vain to wave the thick cloud from the room. "By Ak Ana, how does she breathe in this thicket?"

Smiling, I retrieved stoneware from the cupboard and poured the ale while Oshun dished up bowlfuls of the stew. He and Tao remained near the door, gulping ale while Father and I took opposing seats at a small table. Clearly this tiny room had only been intended to serve the proprietors, and the inn's dining remained elsewhere in the building. Or mayhap she sent her patrons over to the tavern like she'd done with Thalaj and me before.

I lifted the spoon and blew. The stew had a rich, herby flavor on my tongue, and the chunks of lamb and rooted vegetables were indeed tender to chew. My stomach attacked the hearty meal with delight at first, but would only accept a few bites at a time. Father's reaction appeared similar. Having survived on small portions of grain and dried meat over the course of the return trip, the richness of the meal slowed us.

Smoke gradually cleared from the room, but soon, a shadow moved over the light from the opening, and with a heavy stomp, it came to a halt. Alerted to intrusion, Tao and Oshun moved to block the path. A person nearing the size of Hoaris and wrapped in an animal's hide stepped through, chewing on something in one side of his mouth. "I'm here at Sal's behest," he barked to the sailors who looked to me for permission.

I waved him through, and he swiped the mug from Oshun's hand as he lumbered past him into the room. As he sat, he banged a heavy hand on the table; the bowls and mugs jumped, ale sloshing over Father's cup brim. I reached instinctively for my own. The man tipped Oshun's mug and drained the contents, then reached for the carafe for a refill. He sized us up as much as I did him. Father, conversely, only offered his profile and continued with his meal. Despite the abundance of wiry hair, this tradesman was light-complexioned with one squinting eye and one side of his mouth in a perpetual snarl, yet he seemed satisfied with whatever he saw in us—Father especially.

Turning my body square to his, I pressed my shoulders back and sat to my full height. "Good sir—"

"Taurusyn," he bellowed, eyes fixated on my father.

If Father betrayed any signs of recognition at the name, he hid it well in lifting his mug, sipping, and leaving foam clinging to the white hairs on his upper lip.

"Taurusyn," I repeated slowly, rolling out the last of his clearly Storm Sorcerer name. "Of which family?"

He grunted and swung his head back and forth. "Not important anymore." He seemed older, but not as advanced in years as Father.

As I prepared my plea, I mused over what connection he could possibly have to my family. "We have little to offer you in trade."

"Never you mind that. If the Nantai emperor might be restored to the throne, the merchants across Nantai will rejoice and come to your aid. What have you need of?" Taurusyn asked.

His immediate willingness heartened me, and I answered, "Horses." The Tsinti caravan flashed in memory. "Mayhap a cart and horses. And another pair of scimitynes if those could be found. If not, some small blades will suffice."

Father returned to his stew, forcibly not making a connection with the tradesman though the other couldn't tear his attention from the *Nantai emperor.* The connection or bond or possibly simple desire to return to the peace under Tennō Atheryn's rule radiated from the man. I couldn't be sure, but he clearly had no recognition of me. Although, he couldn't be slighted for that if he hadn't resided within Arashi's walls in recent history. I hadn't held the throne long enough to even have mon minted in my likeness. And before my escape from the keep, I'd never traveled or visited the people—all things my father had planned for me once I gained my majority. Yet, the timing of his disappearance and my arrival at adulthood had collided and set me upon this journey.

So many plans . . . so much goodness annulled by the tragic fates of my parents.

Taurusyn pursed his lips, still chewing on a prize hidden in his cheek. After mulling this over for a moment, he spoke. "I haven't those things at the ready. I'll need days, maybe three."

It wasn't the answer I'd hoped, but more information lay here with this man. It scratched like a feral cat at a window, deepening my curiosity more and more. For that, I relented. "We have the time."

"I'm uncertain of that, young one," he barked, slamming his hand down on the table once again and moving to stand. What he intended by those words festered. Instead, he said, "If you remain here, I'll return in two days with word."

Remain.

My heart sank, gut hollowed as if punched, but the tradesman strode through the door before I could find words. "I'll be right back," I said to Father, leaped up from the table, and rushed after him.

Outside, I trotted to catch up, placing a hand on his arm to regain his attention. The town appeared quieter than the time Thalaj and I had been here before, fewer people milling about the center.

When he turned, puzzlement dappled his brow. "What more, young one?"

"What do you mean by we may not have the time?"

He chewed again, brows heavy with speculation, then asked, "Who are you to Atheryn?"

"I—that is of little consequence," I answered. "Let us simply say that you and I wish for the same outcome—his reinstatement upon the Serpentine Throne. But you'll forgive me. Atheryn and I have been absent from Nantai for a time."

He stiffened. "I'll have your name at least."

Pulling my bottom lip inward, I sank my teeth into the skin. Of certainty, he'd recognize Mairynne, but to be traveling with the person he knew as Tennō Atheryn Evangale, I needed a Storm Sorcerer's name. And surely he'd recognize any close to the royal family. But one came to mind. "Gaelynne, apprentice to the leader of the guard at Stormskeep, Thalaj." To my own ears, my words sounded hale, though it hurt to utter his name so casually.

Taurusyn looked around and into the sky before pulling me into the shadows. "Where do you return from, girl?"

How much could I share? I considered for heartbeats. If he supported our quest, a portion of truth should serve. "Fa—Tennō Atheryn, Tao, Oshun, and I traveled upriver from the now scorched City by the Sea."

Knowledge darkened his gaze, made his head seem heavy on his shoulders. "That is a fate we all fear since Kōgō Karynne ascended to the Dragonscale Throne. The tragic truth written in the annals at Stormskeep about the return of the Ryū has come to pass."

I inhaled sharply at these words.

"Aye, young one. I once lived in Arashi, and I know the annals well enough."

That meant he had been close to the advisers or the royal family. How much could I ask without betraying my true identity?

He stood straighter, removing his hands from my shoulders and scratching his significant beard. "The empress has levied taxes across the land so steep they have plummeted any wealth or prosperity. Then there's the dragon."

I bit my tongue to keep silent.

Taurusyn continued, "Even the bards' tales of horror do not compare to that green dragon's wrath, and every person across Nantai now lives in fear of such ruin."

My sister's name upon his lips in such a harsh tone turned my stomach, and drawing my hand from his arm, I trembled with worry over the reason he'd looked to the sky before speaking. His point had been clear at least to me, and I feared how exposure of my own Ryū bond—of Parū herself—might be judged.

Dare I ask after the blue Ryū?

My dragon stirred. *I do not recommend so, minikin. Let them make the first mention of Barūdragon.* The intoned doubt within her voice heightened my own disquiet.

Taurusyn latched onto my shoulders and bent to look me in the eye, his one eye still narrowed. "Return to Tennō Atheryn. Remain at his side and keep him hidden within the walls of Safaia Inn. I will do what I may and bring you word."

My steps were heavy, yet I felt disconnected from my body's movement as I returned to Father. Though I'd known the source of the destruction before, my entire body seemed laden with all the toil of having the worst confirmed through one of the Nantai people, a Storm Sorcerer at that. I'd wanted to ask so much more of Taurusyn, but his recount and unwitting foretelling had stolen other questions from my lips.

Forty-Three

First Call to Action

HAVING SO MANY MISGIVINGS, I'D been reluctant to give Parū control and allow her to fly, but she'd rested for so many days, her need to hunt had become overwhelming within. After we shifted, I tucked my consciousness into the corner, curled around myself, and rested as much as possible. In the early morning, she landed beside the Betsu, woke me, and gave me control once more.

Shifting back to my Storm Sorcerer form, I entered the cave where Misha, Kyr, and Honera awaited. The darkness near complete, my eyes couldn't focus, but Parū lent me her Ryū vision so that I might navigate obstacles. The auras within every earthly object radiated an outline visible in her fey-gifted sight.

"Who treads there?" Misha's alerted voice called, softly from deeper within the cave.

"It's me, Misha."

A soft, warm light from one of their spelled stones illuminated the depths. "One moment," he called. "Hold your place, and I'll be right there. You won't be able to pass the barrier while it's active."

I did as he bade, knowing that he'd likely laid that and many other traps to ensure their safety.

"Can you bring a blanket?" I called back. I'd left my clothing nearer Safaia. Looking down at my nakedness, I added, "Maybe two. Then we can talk beneath the stars." I retreated to the bank of the Betsu and waited upon a boulder with my toes cooling in the water.

Shuffling alerted me to Misha's return before he spoke.

"Why're ye naked?" he asked, approaching with a blanket proffered and his eyes averted.

Smiling, I accepted the blanket, wrapping it around my body beneath my arms. "I'm covered now. Come, sit with me." I patted a boulder on which he'd sit a little higher than me.

He clamored up, spread the blanket, and sat, facing the river and following my gaze up to the sky. Selene rested over the trees and the stars twinkled in the clear night.

I inhaled the night air deeply into my lungs. "Misha?"

"Yes, Mairynne?" To his credit, he hadn't asked why I'd come to him in the night, and he hadn't pressured me further about my lack of clothes.

"Do you fear returning to Brennmor?" It'd once been his home, and one he left as a result of bitterness between his father and him. He'd rebelled against his people's traditions, and I felt a certain kindred spirit with that after all I'd chosen and endured.

He mulled over private thoughts for a moment, then answered, "I am too old to fear such things. It will be uncomfortable, but I will be well enough."

"Your father. Do you worry over his judgment upon your return?"

Misha picked up a pebble and tossed it into the water. "That judgment is long past. Do I hope he will change and accept my choices? Of course. Do I lose any sleep over it at night? Never." He raised a brow at me.

"Mayhap one day I will be as mature about my worries over Father's acceptance as you," I mused.

He looked at me then with his brows drawn in confusion. "Your father has nothing but adoration for you. Anyone can see that."

I ran a hand over the cool rock at my side. "Many people hold secrets, Misha."

He turned to me. "What troubles you, Mairynne?"

I shifted to look at the small-statured man on the boulder at my side, measuring his fiber stronger than many. My burden, the bond I'd only shared with Chambui so far, begged to be lifted, so I chose. He listened without judgment or reaction as I recounted my time in the Fey realm, of Amare, of how I'd given the last of my separate self to Prince Osmar." I didn't blush then, simply owned the decision as I owned what I'd shared with Sarangarel. But then I told him of my true worries.

"I accepted a bond while I was away, Misha. A Ryū bond to an ancient pearlescent dragon named Parū."

"And you worry over this because . . . ?" he pressed.

"Because of our teachings. How the Nantai hold so much animosity toward the dragons. How am I to tell Father that I sacrificed myself and accepted a soul-deep bond to free him from that place?" I turned my face to the skies, seeing no other way than to bear the brunt of Father's disapproval.

Misha chuckled beside me. "And you fear your father will think less of you for making such a sacrifice?"

"I do."

He simply nodded.

After a long pause, I continued to unburden my soul. "Worse than that . . . I not only had to accept the bond, I also had to leave Thalaj. I made the choice, and I have no way of knowing if it was right. Mayhap I should have simply gone with what everyone said before I began searching for Father."

Misha pressed his lips together, then asked, "Would you do it again?"

I peered at him purely confused.

"It's a simple question. Would you make all the decisions you've made so far again?"

"Yes. In an instant," I spouted without thought.

"Then you have your answer, true?" In the predawn twilight, Misha surprised me once again when he rested a small hand upon my arm, awe widening his eyes as he said, "I would very much like to see. All of you, in full form. I want to look upon Parū."

I retreated, gazing over my shoulder to where Otarr would light the land within minutes. "It is dangerous in the light. Another time." I turned back to him, taking in his awe-filled eyes, questions heavy in my own. "You don't wish to run? To persecute me?"

"Not at all. Quite the contrary. Mairynne, my people have prophets too. I've prayed the foretelling would come to pass, and I am here with you, my kōgō."

◇◇◇◇◇◇◇◇◇◇◇◇◇◇◇◇◇◇◇◇◇◇◇◇◇◇◇◇◇◇◇◇◇◇◇

AT DAWN TWO DAYS later, pounding on the wood-slatted door launched me from one of the small beds. The rickety old thing scarcely protected Father and me from any potential intruders, and the knock sounded louder than Atun's thunder rattling the boards. "Father," I hissed, wanting him conscious and at the ready. As I threw on my new yet still somewhat worn overcoat, I retrieved a scimityne from my belt and gathered what energy I could, given my limited connection to the skies above. It answered, coiling within my core, although I rued that I'd never learned how to channel my magic through the weapon as I'd seen Thalaj do on occasion.

The door rattled again. I jerked, spun. Wood creaked under the force of each blow, and the small metal latch clanged. Father ran a hand over his gray hair, calmly tamping it back into place. He'd always been easy to wake, immediately alert, and as calm as still waters. Now, his simple relaxed posture encouraged some tension to ebb from my shoulders. The confusion of sleep lifted. Had the visitor intended us ill will, that poor excuse for a door would have provided little restraint.

I breathed, air gushing from my lungs. "One moment." I bent, slid on my boots, leaving the laces untied, and crossed to the door.

Dim light filtered in from the window, but the hallway beyond remained dark in the early hour, affording me no sight of who awaited our attention. Even armed with the belief the intruder meant us no harm, I stood at arm's length as I pulled the door open, my small curved sword poised and ready to strike.

Taurusyn filled the frame, slightly hunched and holding one hand on either side of the opening. "As Otarr rises, Gaelynne," he greeted.

My brow felt heavy as I peered back at him, confused. But ah, yes, I'd given him that as a false name.

Shortly, the brawny man turned to business. "I was only able to obtain a horse and a mule. Trade is hard in these times, but Sal and I have gathered enough provisions that you'll not want for food or water before Brennmor, assuming you take a direct route. The mule can carry your packs. And here . . ." He held out a weapons belt. "I found these in the junk at the back of the old barn. They're rusty, but they'll do in a pinch if you've the training. There's wired wool and oil in the pouch for cleaning. If you work them, their luster might yet return."

Stunned that he'd found a set of weapons from the northern castes, I accepted the offer. I still had mine, but I'd lost them before. A spare set might come in handy. I recalled Thalaj's mention that the Frost Fighters designed the weapons small so training could begin as a youngling, and I'd brought Honera into this ordeal. Mayhap in our downtime during travel, I could show her some of the moves I'd learned from my protector. I stepped back when Taurusyn leaned his burly head to the side and through the door.

He peered past me. "Tennō Atheryn, good to see you better rested."

His words rang true. With each day Father remained on this land and gathered his strength again, he appeared healthier than the one before. Yet, my father didn't answer the greeting with any more than a nod and fleeting glance. Again, I wondered at the connection between the two.

I tucked the scimitynes and belt under my arm and dismissed the tradesman. "Thank you, Taurusyn. We will gather our packs and meet you downstairs for morning meal." Closing the door in his wake, I sat next to Father on the small bed. "Tell me how you know him?" I begged.

Slowly, sadly, Father shook his head. He placed a hand on my knee and said, "Many stories and many lessons I have shared with you over the seasons. Some though aren't meant for a daughter's ears. Suffice it to say, Taurusyn is a good person and we are fortunate to have his support."

I agreed. "If he is willing, would you have him join our party?" Without Hoaris, without Thalaj, he seemed added protection if for his size alone.

Clouds passed over my father's eyes, but he gave a brisk nod.

During our stay at Safaia Inn, Sal had lent us her kitchen for our private dining, and by the time we arrived, the sailors, the Small Folk, and Honera had broken their fasts on boiled grains around the table. The back door stood open, the two animals Taurusyn had mentioned visible beyond. I motioned for Father to sit with the others as I stepped into Otarr's early light. Taurusyn busied himself strapping supplies to the mule.

"We call her Speck." He patted her rump, calming the twitchy nerves she displayed as I approached.

Mayhap I read more into his words, but they seemed spoken with a hint of love and regret. Who was *we*? Was this an animal from his own stock he'd offered for our journey? I reached for her, but her skin trembled under my touch. *Of course*, I thought, backing away, *she must sense the predator within.*

Taurusyn tilted his head toward a small pile. "Blades. Nothing so fancy as scimitynes, but your party may choose from what is there."

"Well received. You have done well for the emperor," I said. "You may take the barge at the river as payment. Sell it or use it for what you will."

A look crossed his eyes, gratitude and something else familiar.

After a pause and with little preamble or grace, I added, "Would you consider joining us?"

Taurusyn coughed, spat on the ground, and bellowed a laugh. "No. I'm afraid I cannot. You see, I'm settled in the woods nearby and I won't leave my wife and daughter." A haze passed over his face. "But I will see how I may help from afar."

I twisted my lips sideways, considering. "Well and so, then. I thank you for outfitting us, but I'd ask one more thing."

"Mmm?" He lifted a brow.

"It is clear you know the emperor, but I'd have you tell me how," I finished.

He didn't look at me when he answered, "The story is more his to tell than mine." He trailed his fingers through Speck's mane in several long strokes, then smiled as if reminiscing. "Let us say . . . I was an ill fit for the clergy in Arashi. Yet for my sins, the emperor didn't judge me—*or my family*—as harshly as was his right. Your priest of Atun, Edamyn, wished for my head along with my family's. Tennō Atheryn is responsible for saving my life, my wife's, and giving my youngling daughter a future. I am, and will be, forever in his debt."

The only treason the Hallowgales would seek to persecute was . . . marrying outside one's caste. Blood contamination. As I remembered, my eyes flew wide, and I went to his side. "Taurusyn! You're a Thundergale. Younger brother to Lukos?" Long before, there had been rumors throughout Arashi about the Thundergale who'd dedicated himself as a Hallowgale—acolyte of Atun, the All-Seer. Then, he'd taken a casteless as his wife in secrecy. The act had forsworn him from service to the Triad. Though in the lessons I'd learned as a youngling, it'd been the emperor following Makenyn who'd written the decrees regarding caste mingling. Taurusyn's marriage had remained concealed while he climbed almost to the third and final rank of the acolytes before Edamyn discovered his contamination.

His eyes went wide too, worried.

I shook my head and rushed to reassure him. "All is well. Lukos acted as my first adviser when I ascended at the High Cloud Courts. Lukos was one of the wiser counselors my father kept on his small council." My gaze flitted downward, then back to his. "And I do not hold to the beliefs around contamination."

Taurusyn turned and peered at me sideways.

Belatedly, I stammered, "I-I'm so sorry. I forgot I disguised myself from you. My true name is Mairynne Evangale, youngest daughter to Atheryn. I didn't know if I could trust you before, but I no longer have that worry."

The man appeared a bit detached as he mused over what I'd just laid at his feet. His brows bunched and eased several times before he finally asked, "Do you mean to say you're the youngling empress who abdicated the throne?"

My heart stopped. Had I trusted him in err? My mouth ran before I had a chance to control the words. "I didn't abdicate." My vision flashed white at the edges, though I should have expected this spinning of my story. Filtch, the Cloud Courtier who'd lured me into a trap in Kōkai before we sailed west on the *Swell Mistress* had indicated as much. Faced with the accusation now, I couldn't allow such untruth to fester. "No, I carefully planned for both my exit *and* my return—with Father. Had events transpired as I decreed, I don't imagine I'd be having this conversation with you now, kind sir."

Taurusyn looked over a shoulder to the door, then back to me thoughtfully. "Having seen you with the emperor, I see why you left," he added, eyes wide with wonder. He also scanned the area, then leaned closer. "Are you aware Kōgō Karynne has issued a heavy price upon your head? Dead or living. You must take care with your words."

I swallowed. "I know. But you see my evidence, and you have cause to support my father's cause." I held a hand toward the kitchen's back door. "Where's the empress's evidence I abdicated? In what about her cause do you put your faith?"

Taurusyn scratched his beard. "You have fair points, young Evangale."

"And you said you'd do all you could to help the rightful emperor?" I pressed.

"Aye, I did," he drawled.

"Well and true. I have no plan as of this moment, but I intend to confront my sister and take back the throne. If there is aught you may do to help from afar, may we send word for you here in Safaia? By way of Sal?"

The big man with meaty hands reached down and grasped me about the wrist. He turned my palm to the sky and laid a bristly kiss within. "As I said before, anything to help the rightful emperor."

"Many, many thanks, Taurusyn Thundergale." While he crouched before me, I placed both hands on his shoulders and peered into his eyes. "And if you know of merchants wishing to travel in support of our cause, it would be good for them to gather in Arashi beyond Stormskeep and await a call to action."

FORTY-FOUR

The Lessons We Learn

THE PATH WE TRAVELED, EAST from Safaia, seemed to stretch into eternity with our lumbering pace. Misha and Kyr, Father, and Honera took turns walking and riding, more often offering the mount to those with shorter strides than to Father. Attempts at calling the wind to aid in our journey required more energy than either Father or I wished to exert, the extra people, large beasts, and supplies proving too great a burden. Before our departure, Taurusyn had also armed us with a compass and map to keep our aim true for Trailhead, a trading post marking the routes of the merchants. Once we arrived at the trader's outpost due east of Brennmor, the trodden path would lead us to Sendatsu North Post, Midway Post, then to Appi Post from which we were to follow the Appi River's path toward the Gulf of Yōtei into Brennmor. According to Taurusyn, the trading outposts weren't in use this time of year, so the most we'd see to mark them would be worn ground and scorched earth where merchants had made camps before, and if we were lucky, a wooden sign marking the outpost may still stand.

The pilgrimage felt desperate and I grew wary, wondering about the retinue I may have commanded had I simply maintained my position as kōgō. And while I had ample time for regrets—over leaving my people and over leaving Thalaj—I pushed them away when I glanced over at Father. I dared not voice such concerns to him, taking care to keep my party's spirits high. I daresay, the situation took its toll on us all. After the first day, silence and disquiet followed us with every step. Tao and Oshun, ever the sea-hardened sailors, minded and rationed the water, uncertain whether it would last until we reached the Sendatsu River where we could refill the skeins.

On the first night, we camped upon the grasslands within a shallow valley between the rolling hills, and for the openness, we dared not build a fire. The second day's progress moved as slowly as the first's, and Otarr's light shone hot enough upon us that we covered our skin as much as possible to protect from burning rays. After Otarr's apex on the third day, my mouth had dried from the rationing of water and I began to desperately want for a spring. The Triad answered my prayers when a small copse of trees came into view on the horizon. Our steps lightened as we moved toward the greenery, and we reached the canopy just before the Day-Seer rested for the night. Inside, there was indeed a small pool, little more than the spring for which I'd asked, yet it bubbled from and returned to a source hidden within Nantai's earth.

Our thirsts quenched, it also provided enough water that Father and I could stir a light misty fog with our sorcery. It cooled the night as my party made camp, lighting a small fire. Misha and Kyr placed an iron pot we'd also brought from Safaia in the center of the fire and filled it with grains, morsels of smoked meat, and water so that we'd have a hot meal after two days and nights of tough dried meats and crusty bread. While the stew simmered, we took turns ducking behind a tree and changing into fresher clothing. As the mist coolly met my skin, I breathed a long sigh of relief, wishing I could dip my naked flesh into the pool. Instead, I reached deeper into my inner being and loosed more magic so that droplets swirled around my body, dappling me with dew as rivulets ran down my chest and back.

When I joined my party afterward, I felt renewed.

We dined, cleaned, boiled water, refilled the skeins, and the others curled around the dying embers for the night.

"Misha?" I stepped to where the Small Folk had rolled out their blankets, Honera close by. "Will you take first watch with me?"

A thrill flashed in his eyes, and I rested a hand on his shoulder with a small smile, staying the promise for a little longer. If there was time once the others slept, Parū and I would give him the sight he'd requested days before. Inside my body, she yearned to fly. I felt her anxiety as if it were my own, trembling through the fibers of my muscles, but the risk of exposure had been too great in the open grasslands.

Misha and I strolled around the perimeter of the copse, still having little to say that hadn't already been voiced. I hadn't counted the steps or measured our progress, merely watched Selene climb into the sky, but my heart quickened. Heat infused my body and Parū's essence became a maelstrom inside when I felt what she sensed. The air shifted. A chill preceded a flapping sound, something beating against the night. Then a deafening warning lacerated the night—thunder, only in the highest pitched, most bone-freezing and blood-icing tone.

I surged, hustling to move Misha beneath the trees and to safety.

Parū's being swirled inside me, railing against the bounds of my body, bidding me, clamoring to give her flight. Under the trees, I sank to a knee and hardened my resolve.

No, I thought to her. *We are not ready to meet this challenge.*

You may not be ready, but I am, she growled.

Before this companionship, the way fear fueled my heart into a stampede had been terrifying enough. Now, the movement of her inside me took everything I had to contain. I called upon my magic, attempting to contain the storm inside. Voices from within the copse stirred, murmuring.

"Go to Kyr," I commanded, working hard to keep my voice quiet. "Gather everyone around the horse and mule."

"But, Mairynne—"

"No, Misha." I pressed my lips together, blew hot breath out through my nose, and removed my hands from the small person so that I might curl them into fists.

"Your eyes . . ." His were wide as he looked at me in awe.

I closed them. "Just gather the others and find as much shelter as you may. Keep them quiet."

Free me, minikin! Parū howled inside. *That is the sound of a Ryū ready to stake claim. We must protect, fight.*

Clenching every muscle in my body, I thought to her, *We cannot.*

I couldn't. For Father, for fear of the lives of everyone here, for myself and those I cherished, I held my ground. *We cannot fly into battle now, Parū. It will give us away.*

The peal cried out once again in the night, and a shadow crossed Selene's light—wings spanned from a long, shadowed body. The sound moved away. The Ryū in flight hadn't spotted us, merely seemed to be hunting as we'd done so many times since our bond. Parū continued to storm and thrash inside.

"Please," I finally begged aloud, voice straining, "Just. Wait!"

◇◇◇◇◇◇◇◇◇◇◇◇◇◇◇◇◇◇◇◇◇◇◇◇◇◇◇◇◇◇◇

"TO WHOM DO YOU beg, daughter?" my father's even voice sounded from behind.

I breathed deeply, keeping my back to him, knowing my eyes shone unnaturally, wanting desperately to not have to share this now. "Father, please go stay with the others."

"I will not." Strength and determination resonated in his voice. "Mairynne, you must talk to me."

With my senses heightened, each step he took toward me crunched the grasses loudly in my ears.

"Daughter, look at me." Not only his fatherly demeanor had returned, but also his imperial mien.

My heart thumped in my chest, and I kept every muscle clenched tight against the dragon's will to transform. I closed my eyes, hot tears squeezing from between the lids and trailing down my cheek. "I cannot."

"Misha said to give you these."

The sound of stones rolling in his hand called to me, calmed me, or maybe merely distracted me from the turmoil. When I turned, his eyes fixated on two glimmering blue stones in his palm.

Wings beat the air above. We both jerked and investigated Selene's skies, but the source of the sound remained invisible against the darkness even to my dragon-enhanced vision. And blessedly, there were no more immediate cries.

"Take them, Mairynne. Use them." These words, he said with knowledge beyond what I believed he possessed.

I searched his face for answers, waited for him to admonish me or retreat, but he held his ground and maintained eye contact with me though certainly he witnessed the otherness within.

"What are they?" I asked, reaching a hand forward. When I accepted the stones, they felt cool within my palms and also cooled the Ryū rage hammering throughout my body, soothing and lulling Parū though the effect maddened her too. Angrily, she pulled away from my consciousness like a petulant child. The sensation befuddled me. Whereas before, my Ryū had been the voice of reason, when faced with another Ryū, she couldn't contain the flare of her instinct or the need to rush into the fray. The imminent battle reflected in my soul, but the reaction remained mine to manage. The spelled stones in my palms helped, and from a distance, Parū's words replayed in my mind. *You were strong enough to contain a Ryū's soul.* This must have been the meaning behind those wise words . . . that I possessed the will to contain this power.

Another screech sounded but far away now, distracting us both from the current conversation. While the sound still echoed across the open skies, the fading signaled the Ryū had moved beyond, and Father called me to sit with him beneath a nearby branch.

"I've known, Daughter," he said without preamble, voice strangled. Father's throat worked for a moment before he continued, "I wanted you to come to me and share this with me without prompting. Stasis in the Fey realm didn't block consciousness entirely. I laid there motionless, frozen in time and space, and listened to the machinations of Amare and Osmar and so many other fey creatures. It seemed a dream at the time, and when I woke with you and the others in the camp, I questioned my own mind."

I searched his face for long moments, but only a breath of a question surfaced. "Truly?"

Father nodded. "I witnessed conversations with the black dragon who came reluctantly when Amare bade, but carried an air of sadness within his scales and trailed rivers of dragon tears. It was the strangest thing to watch all this while sleeping.

"I both rejoiced and mourned when you came to find me. For though I remained in a dream state, I understood your fate long before you arrived on the island nation of Ise and wended inward to find the entrance into the Fey realm."

The insides of my throat felt sickly thick, yet unlike the coughing illness, it remained dry. "And you're not fearful? You don't fret that I will wreak destruction like we witnessed in the City by the Sea? You know that was neither me nor my dragon?" I took a deep breath, my eyes stinging. "You do not wish me ill because I have accepted a bond that flies in the face of all you taught us at your heel?"

"My dear Mairynne." He reached up and ran an aged knuckle across my cheek, catching one of the tears. "The accounts recorded in the annals are not *my* teachings.

They are merely the histories of our people as seen through their leader at the time. Did you read mine?"

"Of course, but—"

"And did you find any words against the Ryū or the bonds we once formed with the dragonkind?"

Confusion drew my brows together. "No . . ."

Father smiled then. "The writings in the annals are limited in perspective. Had I more time with you before . . ." He couldn't seem to speak of mother's demise or his abduction by the Fey. He pressed his lips tighter for a minute, then continued, "Well, I would have encouraged you to assess the stories for yourself, evaluate where one of our emperors or empresses disagreed with another, asked you which tales seemed lucid and which appeared nonsensical. I'd have had you form your own opinion about the topics that make a difference in the lives of the Nantai people."

"Like you did with Taurusyn?" I ventured.

Father's eyes smiled sadly, and he nodded.

Another silence spread between us filled by the nocturnal sounds of small critters. I desperately wanted him to continue; as he made no move to return to the camp, I held my tongue and waited—something I'd seen him do when others had spoken to him.

Rewarding my patience, he began again, "As younglings, we gather information. At our majority, we develop the capacity to analyze that information and form new and knowledgeable conclusions. This ability to discern translates to true power, but with it comes benevolence. These lessons come only from experience." He cleared his throat and stood. "Something you've gained an abundance of during your time away from Stormskeep."

Contemplatively, my father placed his hands on his hips and looked up into the quiet night, breathing deeply. When he offered a hand, I accepted and stood, feeling settled in a new way, as if I were an entirely different person than who I'd been only moments before. He appraised me, pride filling his gaze, and deep within my being, I understood how much I needed this man, his strength, his wisdom, and his always present ability to calm my soul. Whether he returned to the throne or not, and despite the cost I carried upon my soul, the unease I'd felt when all believed him dead had abated. For that at least, I could rejoice.

I hugged him tightly and whispered, "I've missed you."

Within the trees, our party stirred, the horse whinnied.

Father wrapped an arm around my shoulders. "Let us return to our people, rest, and face together whatever the morrow will bring."

◇◇◇◇◇◇◇◇◇◇◇◇◇◇◇◇◇◇◇◇◇◇◇◇◇◇◇◇◇◇◇◇◇◇◇◇◇

MORNING BROKE, AND PARŪ still avoided my attempts at conversation. Strange how she could hide from me from within my own mind, but I still felt the effect of her presence in my heated skin and blood. So, along with the others, I loaded our packs onto Speck and prepared to resume our journey. After the alarm the night before, sleep had been a tenuous thing. Regardless, we pressed on. I studied the map and compass, asking Tao and Oshun for guidance as well. With their experience at sea, certainly they were better suited to the task than me.

I pointed to the parchment, tracing a line from Safaia right across the page. "We've been traveling due east. If we continue and veer slightly north, we should be able to cross the narrow waters of the Sendatsu, then intercept the trail at Midway Post."

Oshun grunted. "Yeah, you've a good point."

"If the terrain follows steady as it has been for the past days," said Tao, nodding, "I'd say it should be a better route."

"A quicker one at a minimum." I dropped a finger to trace the trade routes. "It'd cut off a number of curves and two trading posts along the way."

Tao stroked his wiry beard. "So we're decided? A few degrees north?"

"I'm game to cross the sea of grass like we would a watery plain." Oshun nodded.

I rolled the map and handed it over to Tao, then I slipped the compass from around my neck and offered it to Oshun. They both accepted their new mantles with a small tip of their heads, and their eagerness boosted my spirit. And so, the sailors steered our party across the grasslands as they'd have sailed the *Swell Mistress*, and I do believe they felt more themselves for having the task.

FORTY-FIVE

Trust Them, Minikin

ON THE SECOND MORNING FOLLOWING our night in the copse of trees, we arrived at another narrow stream winding its way into a forest. After some study of the map and consideration, Tao judged it the Appi River.

"Toward the Gulf of Yōtei," I echoed Taurusyn's instruction.

Tao cocked a brow, a gleam in his eye. "And all waters flow toward the sea."

We followed the river's current throughout the day, and the trees thickened along the banks. At times the footpath narrowed so severely we had to pass in single file along the water's edge. Onward we traveled, until we came upon a clearing late in the daylight hours. A hut and an open-air circular building, both with thatched roofs, were the only structures. There were no people but plenty of spaces for merchant tents and a scorched ring at the center where there'd most likely been a fire. A trail led away to the west. We searched the camp, and eventually, Kyr called out that she'd found a sign.

"It's Appi Post," she cried, relief and eagerness to reach the Small Folk's city loud in her voice.

Along with the others, I trotted over to observe the weather-worn sign near the trail.

Misha took Kyr into his arms. "Yes, love, Brennmor is not far now." Though he clearly wished to support his partner's anticipation, his tone also sounded as if he'd seen a ghost. Different from Kyr, his visions of homecoming appeared fraught with turmoil. I had asked before, but he'd claimed comfort with his choices. Seeing and hearing his reaction here, I wondered if somewhere deep inside he did worry over his father's rejection . . . or that his people might shun him entirely?

Hoping to turn his attention to practical matters, I asked, "Should we camp here for the night or are the gates of the city within reach?"

Misha raised his dark eyes to meet mine and blinked away his concerns. "We'd do better to remain here until morn. The city is within reach when the day is fresh, but I fear the darkness will hinder our travels if we continue."

Once we'd hobbled the steeds and relieved them of their burdens, we built a fire and gathered. Our days and nights had been eerily quiet since the near miss with the dragon. After several fretful conversations, everyone had settled back into a companionable travel routine. Father had been a sound voice of reason amidst our party when worries started to build, but he'd also looked to me to allay their fears in a more decisive manner.

"Mairynne," he'd counseled as we rode, "the people who travel with us have come to place faith in you as a leader. Before we arrive, and before they have unplanned opportunity to witness your bond, you should reveal the Ryū to them as well." He'd paused for several thoughtful moments before adding, "And as she now is a part of my beloved daughter, I'd very much like to meet her."

Throughout the remainder of our day's travel and as we made camp, I considered his imparted wisdom. When we sat to eat the evening meal, I made my decision. I chewed slowly and waited until all had finished before setting the story in irrevocable motion. "Before we arrive in Brennmor, I have something to share."

It didn't take much to captivate my companions' attention, and those who couldn't see me directly shifted into new positions to hear what I had to say. Honera came to my side and curled near me, reminding me of how my sisters and I had listened to Father's stories, or how younglings moved into a clump around Selene's priestess, Tasmynne, when she retrieved the storyboards. It brought a small smile to my lips and shifted something in my heart. Mayhap I would reunite with my sisters again in the near future and revisit some of my own youth. For that, I could only pray to the goddess when her face shone later. But mayhap there was more of my mother in the feeling.

Measuring where to begin, I searched my memories of the tales Father had imparted and started with a question. "Who here knows the story of Tennō Makenyn?"

The casteless girl at my side gasped, her voice innocently thrilled and terrified as she asked, "You mean the hunchbacked emperor who vanquished the Ryū?"

Her wonder reminded me of a time when Father's stories of the emperor who ushered in the First Age had seemed too fantastic to contain truth, grand adventures that held little possibility of happening. I'd once believed Makenyn a hero for our people, someone who freed us from evil. Now, secure in my companionship with Parū, I knew him a flawed person at the core, a villain in his own right . . . someone who had stolen a precious thing between the Ryū and the Nantai. I ran a hand over her hair.

"Yes," I said, looking to my father who offered an encouraging nod. And here I sat, taking over his position as storyteller—a position I'd never aspired to own. Awareness of how we'd grown twisted inside and begged for attention I couldn't give in the moment. "He is the one, young one. He paid many alchemists, physicians, and holy priests to search for a way to extract his bonded Ryū before he found the shaman Nityn. Makenyn failed to understand or believe the blessing companionship could be. In his actions, Makenyn violated a phenomenon the Nantai people, as well as the Fey people from a world beyond, once held sacred. Something the dragons view as a gift and a choice."

To Misha and Kyr specifically, I said, "When I left you there on the shores of the Seleucid River in Ise, I journeyed into the Fey realm. 'Tis where I accepted Parū's offer of companionship. Yet, I also met Makenyn's Ryū, Kuroidragon, and even in the Fifth Age, he still mourns his loss."

Oshun slapped his knee, dust billowing from his pants, and threw back his head in laughter. When he had recovered, he said, "You tell stories better than any sailor I've known."

I focused on him, allowing dragon heat to suffuse my body and white to flash across my vision. Then I smiled. "Mayhap, Oshun. Only *I* speak truths."

His typically slanted eyes went round, and Tao laughed at his friend.

Oshun stammered, "You're serious."

"Perhaps when you return to the seas, you will have new and better stories to tell, my sailor friend."

I fell silent, but my companions leaned close, waiting for me to continue. So I told them more of my introduction to the Fey realm and its creatures, saving the gift Osmar had given for my own memories. I shared how the prince came to me in the tent, how Thalaj and I leaped into a glowing pool within the trees, how I met the Fey queen, Amare, and what I could recall beyond the pain of bonding with Parū. When I'd finished, Misha and my father looked upon me with a pride echoed by Parū's feelings within my chest. Her temper had faded and she returned to me. The closeness of family and companion stirred a sense of warmth inside, and I felt grateful for the orange glow of the fire to mask the heat filling my cheeks.

"May we meet her now?" Misha asked.

After the haunting Ryū call before, they will be afraid, minikin, Parū warned.

Yes, they will. I dropped my gaze to the ground before me.

You must reassure them before we shift.

I cleared my throat. "Yes, Misha. But before, be aware that looking upon a Ryū is more terrifying than that screech that split the night or the feeling of heavy wings beating the air. Parū is unable to voice words aloud in our tongue, but rest assured she means us . . . *you* . . . no harm. Quite the opposite in truth." I twisted my fingers in my lap. "Likewise, I will not be able to speak to you from within either, but I'll see everything."

Father—no, *Tennō Atheryn Evangale*—raised his chin. "Daughter, you have traveled with these people for many days, seasons even. True?"

He paused for me to acknowledge, then continued, "Had you or your dragon wished us ill, there has been opportunity aplenty for that to manifest."

I held my lips in a tight line. Did I dare to allow that sprouting hope to blossom into a full bloom? Mayhap his words held truth. At the same time, I considered how long Imrythel had remained in Arashi and I hadn't known of her companion—Guin, the green dragon.

Others' voices went up in agreement, and I stood, turning to leave, to undress and save the few clothes I possessed. "Give us a while, and she will return."

Parū circled in the sky, happy to be free of my human form and stretch her body, flap her wings, and soar into the cooler and thinner air high above the land. She darted upwards, spinning, making loops, and feeling the power flowing into the length of her tail and the ends of her clawed feet. Happy for her to experience such simple delight, I retreated but still observed. When she landed by the water, the others turned to greet her. Through her keen sight, I could see the terror they tried to hide and I worried for us.

Trust me, minikin. And trust them. They've come to adore you. Why else would they have traveled so far at your behest?

I had little choice, but I wouldn't have backed away now either. The time when I should have allowed them to meet Parū had come and gone, and all I could do now was instill the same faith in others that they'd given me thus far.

Very well, my Ryū, I thought to her.

She approached the fireside, lowering her head submissively and waited for our friends to gain enough courage to come closer. Tao and Oshun encircled Parū while Misha and Kyr were the first ones to approach. Kyr held onto Misha as her eyes darted over Parū with wonderment. She blinked as she placed one palm upon the ridge behind Parū's right eye, and a smile spread within my soul to witness their reverence as they both laid small hands upon Parū's pearlescent scales.

Near Parū's horn, Misha leaned in and whispered, "Magnificent, Mairynne and Parū."

Honera stepped in front of the Ryū's snout, her clear eyes wide as she reached one small hand forward. Through Parū, I felt a breeze radiate from her hand and gasped within. Magic. Sorcery even. I railed, *Parū, let me out, I need . . .* I wanted to wrap her in my arms, wanted to speak with her about what she felt, wanted to show her so much more, but my soul was trapped. She, this casteless girl, had just shown the ability to call the wind. The abilities of Storm Sorcerers.

Patience, minikin. It will still be there tomorrow. It is likely my fey magic calling to hers. Perhaps she doesn't even realize it's happening, but the concept you've learned of casteless is wrong. There is no such thing as a casteless Nantai person in regards to possessing magic. There are those who have dormant ability, but sorcery is inherent to your people in this land.

What? I thought to her. *How have I not known this until now?*

She rumbled slightly, naught more than a purr, but enough to silence my questioning.

Tao and Oshun returned, having completed their inspection. Oshun's mouth worked silently.

Tao breathed, "Amazing," but that was the only word spoken by the sailors.

I longed to ask what they thought. And then, I couldn't leave alone the thought of everyone having a sorcerer's ability. *What of the sailors, Parū? Do they have magic too?*

'Tis possible, yet magic is weaker on the Vesterisles.

When the others had settled, Father came forward. He ran a hand over Parū's snout, traced the ridge behind her eye, and patted her horn twice. "All is well. I am pleased to meet you, Parūdragon, in the waking form. Take care of my daughter," he bade.

Parū blinked twice. *Always,* she said, though only I could hear.

Father smiled. "Now fly, hunt. We'll be well here, safely awaiting your return."

He stepped back, and through Parū's eyes, I saw proud tears pooling in his eyes.

Parū took to the skies.

Forty-Six

Brothers and Sisters

WHEN WE RETURNED IN THE wee hours, Parū relinquished control and we shifted back to my human form, the cool night kissing my fevered skin. I dressed and fastened my weapon belt about my waist but remained barefoot—a state I'd grown to favor even more since making the bond of companionship and even more since we'd arrived upon Nantai soil. It connected me to the earth, the land, my home. As she'd hunted, Parū had saved two large prairie hares for our morning meal around the fire. I grinned when I saw the freshly dead carcasses, saying an internal thanks to my Ryū for her consideration. I'd asked her once before about her ability to hunt something so small relative to her size, and she'd merely harrumphed and snorted her offense.

My party had spread their bedrolls around the fire, which had diminished to red embers as Selene had crept toward the western skies and Otarr had stirred in the east. The bedrolls were full save one. The roll next to Kyr lay flattened. Somewhere, Misha stood guard. Mayhap things had been so quiet that he'd wandered down to the Appi's banks.

I began walking in search of the small man. Several yards away from camp, my steps halted and ears pricked at a soft rustling noise like rodents burrowing beneath the brush. Odd, I hadn't sensed animals in the area before—mayhap a new ability I'd been learning since the Ryū bond. Parū and I had been away for the majority of the dark hours, and it held reason that animals might have been drawn to the scent of Kyr's hearty salted pork and water-grass root stew prepared in the open the night before. I tilted my nose to the sky; yes, to a beast's nose, the smell lingered.

In predawn grayness, Star, the horse we'd named for the white four-pointed marking between her eyes, whinnied, and Speck brayed, drawing my attention to the shelter where we'd tied up the steeds and stowed our packs for the night. I narrowed my eyes and caught the movement—a small booted foot barely visible and brown versus Misha's fawn-colored boots. My hand slid down to unfasten the tie holding my right scimityne in place, then carefully slid it from the scabbard. I crept closer, reaching a hand forward and placing it on Star's brown neck. Her dark eye twitched with fear toward me, and I clicked my tongue softly, a soothing sound I'd developed to calm her over the course of the days we had trekked through the Plains. She expelled a breath through her blubbering snout, covering any sound I'd made, and I moved around her. At the packs, a person, one of the Small Folk, dug so intently within our bags, he likely wouldn't have heard had I stomped up behind him with Parū's full weight.

I reached forward and grappled him at the collar, pulling him back and away from the ground with very little effort. His clothing hung from his frame as if it'd once been much tighter. Shocked and frightened eyes searched frantically from within a mud-covered face, and his hair hung limply in unwashed clumps around his face. I leveled the curve of my sword at his throat, and braced my body so that his thrashing in my grip didn't swing me off-balance.

"Who are you?" I demanded.

His mouth worked, wordless and breathless, like a fish gasping for the water. Then his wide eyes cut to the right and he gasped. "Riah, no!"

I followed where he'd looked to find another of the Small Folk also disguised by filth such that I couldn't place the normal features of the person. "I'll offer but one more chance," I started, then hardened my voice more. "Your name?"

It wasn't the person I held above the ground kicking at thin air who spoke; it was the other . . . the one he'd called Riah . . . and by the manner similar to Kyr's, I assumed her his mate. Hands held out as if to calm me, she spoke haltingly and with broken words that favored an accent that I'd only heard on the rare occasion from Misha and Kyr. "No. Please. No harm to 'im. We mean ye none." She pointed a shaky and dirty finger, indicating her companion. "Tomei." Then slowly pulled her hand back and lay it on her chest. "Riah."

I dropped Tomei. He scrambled over to Riah and they groped at one another, clearly feeling to reassure themselves that the other remained whole while looking upward at me with terror. They chattered a few words quickly and quietly to one another. I didn't try to make them out as they seemed mostly fearful, domestic, and mutually protective. Although, to credit their sense of worth, they didn't shrink away.

Another high-pitched voice I'd become well acquainted with during my travels pitched to my right. "Tomei?"

I turned my head slightly, keeping the pair of scavengers within sight, yet I sought to understand the notes within Misha's single-worded question. Breathy recognition, a small squeal of shock, and deep familiarity all rang within the two tiny syllables. "Misha, you know these people?"

He ignored my question as wide eyed, his gaze shifted. "Riah?" he asked, similar notes resonating.

"Misha," I demanded.

He blinked. "Sorry. Yes, my kōgō, I do."

His emphasis on the honorific wasn't lost on me, nor was it lost on Tomei or Riah by their jerky reactions.

Riah spat on the ground. "Brother by marriage, clearly you've assumed the denounced status bestowed upon you by Isao. You wear it like a well-fit glove." Her words erupted as an unbroken and hale accusation, the frailty of what I'd inferred before—vanished.

Gut-shot, I now looked upon a portion of the family Misha and Kyr had spoken of, and they appeared worse for having remained in the city of Brennmor. Possibilities and questions danced in the air, just out of reach, held off by the harsh moments of reunion. Neither Misha nor Kyr had ever mentioned a sister in Misha's line, so I wondered whether Tomei was Misha's eldest or second brother? I watched for Misha's response.

His shoulders pressed backward, spine growing straighter, and his entire frame hardened. "You speak with ignorance, Riah. But then, you were always one to offer scorn prematurely."

Riah's nostrils flared but Tomei squeezed her around the shoulders, silencing her.

To Misha, Tomei said in a more appeasing tone, "You look well, Brother. You wear your travel, but your health seems far superior to the fortune the residents of Brennmor have experienced." While his mate's words had a bite, his merely contained sadness.

Misha's shoulders rose and fell with a slow, deep breath as he scanned the duo from head to toe. "I wish I could say the same for you, Brother." Hesitation paused his welcome.

I could only imagine how the image disconcerted him. Though I worried over Karynne's actions, I didn't relish the thought of my sisters dirty and starved. If that came to pass, I hoped I'd handle it with as much grace as Misha.

Eventually, he motioned to the hares I still carried and said, "It appears Mairynne has brought fresh meat for breakfast. Please join us and share with me the fate of Brennmor's people."

◇◇◇◇◇◇◇◇◇◇◇◇◇◇◇◇◇◇◇◇◇◇◇◇◇◇◇◇◇◇◇

GREASE FROM DARK MEAT squirted as Tomei sank his teeth into the roasted hare's leg, other juices trapped within running down his fingers and over his wrist. Heedless, he bit into it again without regard for the mess and before he'd properly chewed the first bite . . . the behavior of someone ravenous beyond the normal day's hunger. Riah looked on with jealous, wide eyes as she awaited her own portion.

Misha reached forward, stilling his brother. "You'll make yourself ill. Here." He handed him a mug of steeped herbs from the kettle Kyr had boiling over the embers. "Let what you've eaten settle and sip this. It'll calm your gullet."

Taking the remaining half of the leg from Tomei, he handed it to Riah. Her hands trembled as she looked longingly at the meat, licking her lips in anticipation.

"Slowly," Misha cautioned—wise advice, I believed.

The others in my party took breakfasts with the manner of one who'd only fasted for twelve hours but longed for the delicious treat of fresh meat. After so long on salted and smoked boar with only a few vegetables, the meat melted on the tongue. My travel companions allowed their meals to cool before ripping hunks and savoring the taste with a few groans. For my part, I took a small piece simply for the taste, but I left the larger portions for the others. Mayhap my mental connection to Parū sated my hunger after the hunt under Selene's light, or perhaps the arrival of Tomei and Riah had chased away my appetite. No matter the reason, I leaned closer and asked about the journey into the Small Folk's city, Brennmor.

Tomei's eyes darted around the circle like I'd disturbed a treasure he'd been protecting. "Why do you ask?"

Riah moved closer to his side, eschewing the same essence of fright.

"It is our destination," I answered slowly. "We seek the assistance of the Small King." I kept the need for their support close to my breast, but I didn't fail to notice when Tomei and Riah flinched in unison.

Misha interjected, "If you are this far from Brennmor, Tomei, something's happened to your home."

" 'Twas once your home too," Tomei said almost too quietly to be audible.

Kyr slid her hand into Misha's as by way of reply, and he nodded and pressed forward in the conversation. "Will you tell us what has transpired?"

Tomei swung his gaze around the circle, beginning with Tao and Oshun, then my father and me, and finally settling back upon Misha. "I will. But first, answer me this. What have you seen or heard of the other cities in southern Nantai?"

Misha inhaled, preparing his answer, but I cut him off. "We've avoided cities for the majority of our journey, traversing the Plains from Safaia and meeting with no others along the way. Safaia seemed hale, if less populous than the last time I'd visited, and there were rumors of ill fate across the land, but we witnessed nothing." I shot Misha a warning stare, willing him to remain silent as I finished. An inexplicable sense of dread tempered how much information I wished to impart. We'd offered a starving person food, and thus, I thought it best to hear their stories first.

Tomei's eyes grew too large for his head, but his voice shrank to a whisper. "The dragons have returned."

Everyone in my party held utterly still, watching the small man. I assumed, or mayhap I hoped, they felt wary over his implied distaste.

Misha shifted in his seat. "The prophecies have foretold such a day. It should be promising news, so why do you believe that so dire?"

"The prophecies are lies! Our soothsayers have been slain for their falsehoods," Riah snapped, but quieted, looking upon Tomei with apology as he patted the back of her hand.

He swallowed and cleared his throat. Though his words sounded thick with accent, he now spoke with more alacrity than he'd possessed when I caught him rustling through our packs. "Our beloved Brennmor is no more. Our crops have been burned by Ryū breath. Our people have taken to the forests lining the Appi, sheltering under trees but not daring to build any structure for fear of being discovered by the evil *beasts*."

I winced at the epithet, as did Parū.

Tomei continued without notice, "We've sent three convoys northeastward toward the Evernight, to seek help from our brethren in Umbra. None have returned." Without the slightest hint of humor, he barked a laugh. "Our people have farmed the land for so long that we've forsaken hunting and gathering. You'd believe the skills would be similar, but you'd believe wrong. We've turned to scavenging, but even at that, we are no experts . . . as you can well see.

"Our daughter's daughter died of the wasting, her mother's milk having dried from lack of nourishment. And all the while, the Ryū watch from above and prey upon our people like rodents. It is all we can do to keep our father, King Isao, hidden from sight. So many of our spells are used in cloaking the tent we've erected to protect him. With as many as we have lost and as scattered and weakened by hunger as we are, there is little magic left in us to help with sustenance."

My heart ached for these people, but the reality of the Ryū terrorizing turned and soured my stomach.

Parū spoke softly from within, *This scars me in the very center of all that I am, minikin. Of all that we are as a race. The Ryū have never behaved so . . . with such malice. But he said dragons. More than one?*

Puzzled, I thought back to her, *Do you believe it the blue mother Ryū? Barū, you said was her name?* Then another speculation struck, sending ice through my blood. *Do you think it possible that Barū has bonded with another of the Nantai?* I recalled the story Aunt Nadia had imparted about my sister Karynne and the Small Folk—it'd been King Isao who'd had her captured. The possibility wedged into another crevice within my heart.

Parū had no answer and merely suggested with some measure of impatience, *Why not inquire deeper with the hungry little people?*

Heeding her word, I began, "Tomei, have you seen these dragons with your own eyes?"

"Only shadows in the sky or upon the moon. They often come at night, so we receive little sleep."

"But you've confirmed there is more than one?"

For an instant, confusion flashed across his eyes, unspoken thoughts whirring within. But he answered with clarity, "I'm confident there are two, at minimum."

Father spoke softly, "And have you divined their purpose?"

Riah scoffed, but Tomei kept her silent under his touch.

He spoke as if he were an emissary, the voice of Brennmor. "The beasts have not come close enough that we may hold conversation with them if that is what you ask.

What we know is that they arrived shortly after a retinue of Storm Sorcerers from Arashi visited demanding an increase in our taxes that far exceeded what the city and farmers of the land could afford. Two nights after our refusal and the soldiers' departure, the Ryū returned to burn our city and crops to the ground."

I pursed my lips and nodded. "Will you take us to speak with your king?"

Both Tomei and Misha started to object, to which I held up a hand. "We only wish to help. We seek the same peaceful ends as you."

Misha leaned into his brother and whispered. From my position some distance away, I couldn't hear the words, but I had other things on my mind. I waited for an answer.

At length, Tomei nodded uncertainly, and I turned to my father. "May I have a word?"

Father nodded and stood.

"We'll return shortly," I said as we stepped away from the fire and morning meal.

When out of hearing distance, Father prompted me from my troubled musings.

I sighed, lifting my face to Otarr's light through the trees. Nadia had woven the tale in a manner that reminded me of how troubling that time had been for both my parents, so I worked to gather courage to confront him. Direct, I decided, was my best approach. "Father, I am loath to accuse my sister, but there was a time and incident—something about the Small King in Brennmor and Mother . . ." My words left me then; tightness curled within my throat.

Without doubt, people carry the scars of life's events upon their souls. Those we've loved and lost take a small piece of us when they leave. Upon the island of Ise in the Fey realm, Thalaj still held a larger piece of me than I wished to acknowledge. Merely speaking of my lost mother quartered me even further as I felt certain was the case with Father.

However, there are also events in one's life that may not involve loss, yet they hammer and mold the soul into ugly divots or protrusions. Father's regard for me in that moment appeared as a twisted, sorely damaged sculpture. "That event was a true failing of both my fatherly duties and my imperial mantle. Karynne suffered. That much was clear, but to what extent remains known only to her and the Small Folk who had assailed her."

My upper lip twitched, wanting to snarl bitterly. "At the hands of King Isao," I said. This Small King had done naught to win my favor by his banishment of my now dear friend, Misha. And if he'd sent my sister into a state where she'd go to such lengths to exact her revenge, I didn't know if I could overlook my own ire long enough to hold any kind of civil discussion with Isao.

Father clasped my hands in his. "That is possible. But your mother convinced me that he only protected the people he viewed as his own. Karynne was his tool for negotiation, and that she'd never speak of the event left me without recourse if I wished the favor of my people. I cannot speak to any malicious intent from the Small King." He sighed deeply. "I may offer you what small amount of wisdom I own—to rule justly is to listen to *all,* without prejudice."

I chewed the inside of my lip. If Karynne had caused this treachery, I must also deal with her, without any sisterly prejudice. "Do you think it possible that Karynne's trauma warped her will enough to seek revenge of this magnitude against an entire race within our people?"

Father's sad, storm-filled eyes answered—a tragic affirmation—by filling and pouring over onto his cheeks and into his beard.

Turning away, I covered my face with both hands. The same horror burned my eyes too, and hot tears clouded my sight.

FORTY-SEVEN

Parlay

OUR PARTY SEPARATED; I FOLLOWED Misha and Tomei down the Appi River toward where the Small Folk supposedly hid the Small King, Isao. The sailors held the camp at Appi Post with Father, Kyr, Honera, and the horses. For some insurance, I insisted that Riah remain behind as well. Kyr had little taste for Tomei's mate, so I felt certain she would keep Riah well mannered. Furthermore, it also provided reason for Tomei to remain true to his word—assuming he'd been truthful thus far and held pure intentions regarding introducing me to Isao.

While I felt confident Parū could manage the dragon alone—or at least they'd be well matched—I needed support if I was to enter Arashi with the intention of invading Stormskeep. Certainly Karynne had gathered her own council and supporters, so I assumed we faced more than Guin herself. I hoped now for the aid of the Small Folk, and for that, I needed more knowledge. How many of them remained? What resources did they have with possible value? Given the state in which Tomei and Riah had presented themselves, it seemed the Small Folk of Brennmor might be more hindrance than help, but I reserved hope.

As we walked, Tomei seemed lighter of heart. "If you are honest and wish to return peace to our lands, that would involve eliminating the dragons."

I seethed over that statement alone but allowed him to finish.

"Should you possess ways to accomplish that, I'm certain Father will offer what assistance he can. After the attacks, he's been desperate to find a way to save our people. Yet without reason to believe we'd survive, he fears sending anyone else across the Plains toward our kin at Umbra."

I held my tongue, stepping around another branch at shoulder height.

Apparently needing to fill the quiet, Tomei continued musingly, "Our prophesies said that when the dragons returned, they would bring peace and happiness to the land. I never thought I would live to witness a second Ryū War set upon Nantai."

At that, I could no longer remain quiet. I tried to level my voice as I said, "If there is aught we can do to avoid such a fate, remain certain we will." I wouldn't share that I'd forged a Ryū bond of my own. They hadn't earned my trust, and it seemed the information might do more harm than good.

Wise, minikin. You do not know what awaits us in the Small Folk camp either, said Parū.

True, I thought to her. *And with the Small Folk magic I've seen from Misha, I fear what revealing ourselves would mean.*

Father had also cautioned against me going alone, but we'd taken Misha. As we said farewells for a time, I assured him that I could simply give control to Parū should the need arise. That choice, I'd reserve. I didn't wish for my dragon to be accused of burning cities to the ground. Nay, it would be a final option, but having it strengthened my will.

I couldn't easily welcome Tomei and Riah into my party as they'd taken to acting as thieves against us, nor could I easily receive Small King Isao with confidence after the burden he'd laid upon Karynne's soul. Compounding the dilemma, the ease with which he'd discarded Misha, his own blooded son, from his home and city clearly showed the Small King didn't hold the same set of values as me.

My mother had wanted the Small Folk united with the rest of the Nantai people so badly that she'd spent a good portion of her last years working toward those ends. I desired naught but to honor her memory, but after so much ill-favor around King Isao, I struggled to share her mindset. It remained a mystery to me how she had continued in that quest after what he'd done to Karynne. Mayhap Isao and Mother had more in common than I'd ever learn.

You're jumping to conclusions, minikin, Parū warned, reading my inner musings.

The Small Folk are rumored to feed on our sorcery, Parū!

She chuckled inside. *Have you e'er asked your little friend, Misha, about that rumor?*

Smugly, I ignored my Ryū-conscience. Thalaj had also told me the rumors were false. But to the rest, my conclusions were simple and logical, evidence that'd been seen with my father's eyes and that Mother had imparted to Nadia. Magic eaters or not, this Small King had much to atone for.

We came at last to a thicket where Tomei ducked through some shrubbery. Misha also had no trouble. But being a head and shoulders taller than my guides, I crouched, painfully contorting to move through the low opening, and avoided a majority of the thorny branches forming the low arch. It presented a nice, natural defense as the thorned shrubs clamored to a height several hands above what I could reach while standing, then curved inward. Inside a clear opening, I peered upward at the vines woven in a prickly latticework. Otarr's light still shone through, but it'd protect those inside from an aerial attack.

Ingenious for defense, but there appeared to be nothing within this cavern of thorn and vine until Tomei crossed to a large stone and placed both hands upon the rock. His hands glowed along with the boulder beneath, and within the center of the clearing, a tent appeared and dozens of Small Folk milled about. Surprised gasps only then reached my ears along with unintelligible murmurs. Wary eyes looked up but darted away, and accented words topped the din on occasion.

"A Storm Sorcerer . . ."

"One of the Giant Folk . . ."

"A big one . . ."

The tent at the center stood taller than me but the entrance would also require me to stoop. Tomei moved toward the opening, waving us forward. "Father will be inside."

Under the shelter's rough-hewn fabric, wounded Small Folk lined the perimeter. Burned flesh singed my nose. My stomach turned even as my mouth watered; the latter I assumed was a sensation I owed to the predator within.

I didn't think you feasted on people, I thought to her—slightly appalled.

I do not, she answered, and in her words, I sensed indignation. She continued, chagrin lacing her thoughts, *Yet the smell of burned flesh is the same whether it be beast or mortal.*

Several Small Folk in aprons tended to the wounded resting upon bedrolls. Around each pallet, there were stones laid at the four corners, presumably bespelled with healing enchantments. At the far end, a man dressed in a simple tunic and breeches sat cross-legged near a wounded man, holding the person's hand. For his white hair and beard, he appeared spry enough, as if his body remained limber, accustomed to bending and flexing unlike many who'd aged to that point. A small woman nearer the entrance gasped at the sight of us; her eyes with lines spreading like spiders from the corners focused intently on Misha as she wiped her hands on her apron. She looked as if she dared not believe he truly stood before her, and I assumed by his hesitantly returned smile that this woman was his mother. And for all our time together, it saddened me to not have her name.

I would have asked were it not for the commotion that garnered the attention of the white-haired man. He rose from his seat at the wounded person's pallet-side, offering a final reassurance to the patient. A series of emotions twisted his face momentarily, but he seemed to harden with every step as he slowly came forward. I imagined a muscle ticking in his jaw beneath the thick and wiry white hair and stiffened my spine in response, grateful that I could stand to my full height within the shelter. However, were I to shift into Ryū form, I'd fill the space within the canvas shelter and more. Although heat suffused my body, I prayed to the Triad that I wouldn't feel the necessity. Others around whispered and lowered their heads in deference to who must be their passing king.

Isao.

The Small King held himself sternly, stopping at Tomei's side. "Son, I wondered how you and Riah fared when you didn't return after dawn's first light. Where is your mate now?"

That he didn't address Misha scratched at my nerves.

Tomei answered, "We fared well, Father, and I have brought one who wishes to assist with our troubles"—he lowered his voice to a whisper—"with the dragons."

There was little credence to his introduction. My motives were merely directed toward setting things right within Arashi and Stormskeep—removing Imrythel and, Triad forbid, my sister if she was involved, then restoring Tennō Atheryn to his throne—but I also wouldn't refute Tomei's beliefs there in front of a man who'd suffered the loss of his city and people. In the end, if that was how he viewed our mission and he could bring the others to the same opinion, our agendas might align for the greater good of Nantai.

And then, I could see to recovering Thalaj.

Small King Isao then looked over at his lost son, bitterly assessing him from head to toe.

Misha tipped his head forward, but kept his posture tall. He'd accepted the disowning before, he'd made a life for himself and his mate, and while he showed respect for societal hierarchy, he clearly wouldn't shrink before his father. My chest felt tight with pride for my dear friend.

Isao then turned his gaze upward to me, yet he still addressed Tomei. "Mayhap we should discuss this privately—me and my sons alone—before I entertain this . . . *Storm Sorcerer's* requests."

That he'd included Misha in his private council offered hope. But my blood ran hot over the distaste in his tone when he'd labeled me Storm Sorcerer. I felt the flame in my cheeks, but I didn't see white in my periphery and somehow maintained a level tone. "Very well, King Isao. But I will speak with my travel companion Misha alone before."

He lifted his chin. "You may speak outside my tent," he said to me, then to Misha, "Join us when your business with her is finished."

Outside, Misha and I moved to a clearing near the thorny perimeter. In majority, the Small Folk gave me a wide berth with askance glances from time to time. That was just as well. I crouched to my knees, looking at my companion at eye level, but it was he who spoke first.

"My kōgō," he started, clearly wishing to allay my worry, "I must assure you of my understanding and my loyalty to you and your cause. You've shown that you wish not to share your bond with the people of Brennmor at this time, and I dare say it is a wise decision."

"Thank you, Misha." I expelled a long breath. I hadn't corrected his reference to my position, and his words almost seemed an oath of fealty—a vow I treasured regardless of its rightfulness. "Your words ease my soul, but I have some concern for you too. Are you well enough to speak to your father on this matter? I understand that there has been much heartache between you and your family, and I do not wish to put you in a position that will cause you further pain."

He reached for my hand then. "Kyr and I have traveled with you for many long moons now. We didn't always believe in you so, but we trusted Hoaris who trusted

Thalaj who was loyal to you despite the turmoil he worked so hard to extinguish within his heart."

I bowed my head; the sound of his name on another's lips brought his loss and my heartache too close to the surface.

Misha continued, "We've seen you rise to many challenges . . . and watched you suffer another great loss to rectify the one you had set out to correct. You've had success too, more than I believe you know. Though you've taken on another burden, you did achieve what you set out to do. Your destiny continues to change, daily it would seem, and both Kyr and I will be at your side until the very end—whatever *end* that may be."

I coughed and swept a hand under my nose, stifling the sting of tears threatening to fall—this time, they weren't reflecting sadness, only that he'd moved me. In my heart I didn't feel I'd done anything deserving of such respect, but the words on his lips said otherwise. I shooed him away, eager to both hide the gathering emotion and be on with this business.

When he'd ducked back inside the tent, I scanned the yard, watching small people as they went about their chores and watched me with a suspicion bred from so much loss in their lives. There was naught special or different about them other than size, and in their day-to-day chores and other normalcy, I could see why my mother had wished to unite them with the remainder of Nantai. They had several small gardens planted with sprouts just peeking through the loosened soil. Though for the seeds to have sprouted this much, they must have spent many days tending the land, yet another cycle of Selene's many faces would pass before their small crops bore enough to feed even the population here, and much like Tomei and Riah, many of the others' clothing hung looser than it obviously once had. I wondered if there were similar camps hidden in the forest around the Appi River. How many crops had been burned? How many homes destroyed, tools for gardening burned, shops rendered useless?

I held myself as motionless as possible near the perimeter, not wanting to create a disturbance more than we already had, until Misha returned. In truth, not much time had passed since he'd left my side. As he strode toward me, his stature and scowl fueled more worry in my mind, and I noticed a stone within his hand.

He took a seat at my side. "King Isao has agreed to meet with you, but he bids you carry a truth stone during the meeting."

"Will he carry one as well?" I asked, my voice sharper than I'd intended.

"I can return and ask as much." The small man furrowed his brows. Misha started to stand, but I placed a hand upon his arm, holding him in place.

"No," I stated. "Truth is the easy part. If I must carry a stone bespelled to keep me honest, I would ask that he instead carry a charm that will bind him to silence with whatever he might learn from our conversation." I mused for a minute, then amended, "Better still, if he is unwilling to rally to my cause, I would prefer he forget the substance of our conversation altogether."

He took a long breath and said on a sigh, "I can cast such a binding, but it will take the night."

"I've come this far, one more night will cause no harm." I nodded, giving him leave to return with my bidding. The second time he went to stand, I didn't stop him, but as he took the first steps back toward the tent, I called, "Misha?"

He turned. "Yes?"

"Can you be certain the only spell upon that stone is regarding truth?"

"I wish I could," he said sadly and returned to the tent.

◇◇◇◇◇◇◇◇◇◇◇◇◇◇◇◇◇◇◇◇◇◇◇◇◇◇◇◇◇◇

MISHA AND I HAD removed ourselves from King Isao's camp for the night, and I'd given my form over to Parū to stand watch while Misha spun his spells upon a stone he had gathered from the shallow waters of the Appi. By the time we arrived back at the camp, Misha looked haggard, deep purple circles forming around his eyes. But he stayed alert long enough to deactivate the spell upon the stone that obfuscated the camp, something that caused another rash of whispers and murmurs throughout the camp.

One man ventured near and asked him how he knew what to do, to which he replied, "I've been casting stone spells since the time I took my first steps in Isao's long house in Brennmor, and I am many years older than I may appear." The man backed away, eyes wide, but he spoke no more.

Inside at the back of the tent, beyond the burned and wounded Brennmorians, I met Isao at a small makeshift table—a low but large-girthed stump with pillows on either side serving as chairs. Tomei, who'd stayed in camp overnight, handed me a stone reportedly carrying the truth spell, and I nodded to Misha to hand over the stone he'd worked on for long hours the night before.

Isao flipped a hand, shooing Tomei and Misha from the room.

Before leaving, Misha leaned in, whispering, "I'm going to ask Mother for a place to rest. Find her when you are done, and she'll find me."

When the brothers were gone, Isao opened bluntly, "You seek my help."

It may have been a question if he'd used different intonation, but as said, it seemed merely an observation.

I countered, "I seek to know what manner of help you may have to offer."

"You can see the state of my people with your own two eyes, *Lady Evangale*." The man barely moved, legs crossed beneath him with his elbows resting on his knees and the stone held gently in an upturned palm. It surprised me that he'd accepted the stone so readily, but he must have trusted in the magics of his people not to do him harm.

Indeed, I wished him no harm, but I also offered him no trust given history and the continued slanted remarks. "Ah, so I have no need to inform you of who I am. That will help to shorten the conversation. It is true that I can see what little you have to offer in this camp. It is small, I acknowledge. And it saddens me."

"Your family is too well known in these parts," said Isao. The intent in his words remained clear—a veritable slap across the face. *I'll not bow to your family* was the meaning hidden within.

Mirroring his calm, I pressed gently, "Will you tell me what is meant by those words. For what actions is my family so infamous?"

"The taxes you'd have levied upon us season after season *would have* caused our starvation." He left unsaid the remainder of his more than obvious thought: *had you not burned our crops.* "And what do we receive in return for offering our crops to the high and mighty Storm Sorcerers sitting in the fortress at Arashi?"

I expected his ire and replied with as much diplomacy as I could recall from Father's lessons. "If I am correct, King Isao, my mother worked tirelessly to alleviate the tax burden upon your people."

"Ah, yes. But your wicked sister has increased the grain due at harvest threefold, and when we refused, she sent her dragons to burn our crops and the small city we've called home for generations. And they terrorize us to this very day . . . even after they have burned everything we own." From the way he sat, he remained a model of serenity though his words contained venom from the most poisonous snake.

Parū sneered inside. *I do not like the little king. Why does this tiny person tie your actions to that of your family's?*

Even in responding to her, I felt the truth spell working on my mind, purposeless though it was with our bond. I replied in thought to the best of my ability, *I know very little of Isao's motivation, Parū.* And in response to the king, I felt uncertain if I should rebut directly. That he hadn't asked me a question left the stone's power dormant. So I focused elsewhere. "You say *dragons,* in the plural. Tomei hasn't been able to confirm the numbers. Can you? And can you distinguish between them?"

His eyes turned downward toward the table between us, and I needed no words to confirm what I'd suspected. Fear and uncertainty lined his accusations. I had no doubts that one of the Ryū had a claw or breath in this matter, but I couldn't be certain of more.

Isao's lip curled in a snarl, and he spat, "If you were in this area under the cover of darkness last night, you would have heard their cries. Did you not?"

I had, and the stone compelled my answer remembered through Parū's presence. "Yes, but they were in the distance. Not near enough to harm this camp or any others nestled along the Appi."

"Who else did they terrorize then?"

"That is a question for which I have no answer," I said in truth. His suggestion contained a possibility I might come to deal with later. For the serpent, I wished to move past meritless accusation and inconsequential grudges. "King Isao," I said, pausing after to allow my wariness to fill the gap. "Would you simply share with me the reasons why you harbor such a hatred for my family? I came to seek your help, and to do so I must understand the source of your reluctance."

The Small King held his tongue, but the stone in my hand—or so I imagined—pushed my case through my lips without having been asked for such information. "I am young, and I tire of trying to ferret out a history in which I had no direct influence.

King Isao, I have been apart from this land for many of Selene's, the Night-Seer's, turns in search of my father, the rightful Tennō Atheryn Evangale. And now, when I return to Nantai with him at my side, there is unfathomable destruction across my land. I truly claim ignorance for the machinations brewing in Stormskeep at the moment."

"Convenient for you, young Evangale." He sneered on one side of his mouth.

I ignored his rebuke. "The reason we are here is to seek help in making it right once more. I . . . we . . . only wish to return the tennō to the Serpentine Throne and see that the peace he and my mother worked toward is restored." Heat kindled hotter inside, and if Parū had form, she'd be circling in her current state of agitation. It felt almost to the point where I'd boil over. I blinked to keep the light from my eyes, but my speech quickened, "I need to know what people you have and what, if any help at all, you might offer. What do you wish from me so that we may discuss the urgent issue at hand?"

Isao leaned in. "I wish for you to make it clear to me how you will confront and stop these beasts. And I wish for clarity on how you will help my people after we come to your aid. The scales seem tipped in your favor, young Evangale, but surely having held the ruler's power for a short time, you'll understand my position. I have need to protect my own people at all costs."

His nostrils flared as he paused, and though there were no spells invoking truth from him, anger fueled a further rant. "I have but a few thousand remaining where Brennmor once boasted thirty thousand and more. That is my fault, my people's naïvety, that we remained in the open where we might become prey for the Ryū to see and destroy so easily. Rest assured that those of us who remain will not make that mistake again. I once called my brethren in Umbra paranoid for taking such measures, placing snares and traps that'd protect their tiny community. No more. We will ensure all our settlements are hidden from view going forward."

A few thousand, I mused.

Isao pressed on, "We have few supplies and no transport for those of us who remain, save on foot. How do you think we can help against these . . ." His lips twisted then as he searched for another slanderous word.

Inside, Parū grew more and more agitated, heating my blood to the point I wished to shed some of the few clothes I wore.

"What, say you, do you intend to do?" he demanded.

I closed my eyes, begged Parū's help. After a moment, I felt a calming presence settle over me as if we were about to shift and I'd be able to rest, but my form remained steady. My breathing leveled out but rasped more like hers when we took Ryū form.

Open your eyes, minikin, she said in my mind. *Show him,* she growled.

The world had changed, my vision now prismatic, and before me, Isao gaped. To credit his fortitude, he didn't move from his seat across the improvised table. My skin burned, my body on the precipice of becoming Ryū but stopping just before transformation. I glanced down to where I still palmed the truth stone. My hands glistened with pearlescent scales.

When I spoke, my voice boomed and grated like gravel filled my throat. In truth, though I'd gathered thought, it was Parū who spoke—my words and her own as if we were one.

"Tiny King," her voice growled through my throat. "You've snared my soulbound with this stone she holds."

I lifted my scaled hand reflecting her words. Isao trembled before us, his eyes wide, yet he remained still.

She continued. "Be you certain that the power of your small spell will not work so on me. Though you need not worry about falsehood. I've chosen Mairynne Evangale. The Fey and the Ryū called upon her, and she came to us in the realm between. I am sad that her mother, and your spokesperson within the castes, perished as a result of our schemes. But never doubt that her—*and my*—intentions are pure. She now carries a burden for all the races in Nantai, and our pursuits—yours, hers, and mine—are well aligned."

Parū, let me speak, I thought frantically.

Her will subsided, and I took over. "We, my *soulbound* as she called me, have returned from other lands to see the green dragon subdued—"

"A misguided dragon, Guin is," Parū scoffed, surfacing again without warning. "I have promised the Fey queen, Amare, that I will return her to the realm between. The Fey will hold her and see that she never harms the people of Nantai again."

FORTY-EIGHT

A Fiddle on the Wind

AGREEMENTS MADE WITH THE SMALL King, I prepared my heart for farewells as I packed my meager belongings. I intended to strike out on my own. Under this plan, there would be no need to carry rations. I would wander during Otarr's hours of light, searching for the Tsinti, and give my body over to Parū to fly during the night. She could hunt while I slept and the nourishment she took would sustain our shared energy until I could find Yankos and his caravan.

To those ends, King Isao and I had arranged for all my traveling companions to remain in camp and help the Small Folk with preparations. I stepped away from the group and wandered to the Appi's shore as they began working through details of how they'd build boats to sail toward the Evernight and gather reinforcements. I knelt and splashed some of the clear water on my face, then lifted my face to the skies where the Triad watched over my people. My eyes stung as I breathed deeply, but then a crunch of gravel sounded behind me.

My body had gone rigid as I stood and spun to face the intruder, but the tension flowed away when I looked into Father's storm-gray eyes.

"I won't allow you to travel alone." He pressed his mouth into a firm line, a set of double lines forming on his brow between whitening brows.

A spark of pain flashed behind my eyes, and I rubbed my temples to calm it. "I'm not asking for permission," I said on a sigh.

"I am not suggesting you are. Nevertheless, I will follow where you go, Daughter."

I searched his face but found naught but determination. 'Twas no wonder Mother and Aunt Nadia had commented so frequently on my willfulness; I'd inherited it from my father.

Still more obstinate than me, he moved closer, his voice stern. "I will not remain here after you have sacrificed your position, your youth, and someone you loved on my behalf. I doubt I will ever be the emperor you wish to return to power, but as long as that is your mission, I will try."

I hugged myself around the midsection, wanting to refute his demands further. His company would limit my progress, and mayhap accepting his demand revealed my weakness. But I hadn't the heart to part from him again. I carefully explained the situation to Father. "When the Fey queen, Amare, took your and Mother's soul stones, I lost my assurance that I'd be able to find the Tsinti again. I know not how long we will wander."

Ever the steadfast father, he wrapped an arm around my shoulders. "Well and so. *We* will wander together then," he said simply.

I nodded my acceptance into his shoulder. Though there was little certainty about what I'd find upon the Central Grasslands, I would wander until either I heard the notes upon the wind that Yankos had mentioned when we'd said farewells or a caravan of Tsinti found me. The choice to join me was his, and reluctantly, I honored that. With arms around one another, we returned to the others.

I hugged Misha then Kyr, and before leaving them, peered over to where Honera petted the mule, Speck. "Care for her, Kyr?"

"We will." She slid her hand into Misha's. "She's a good girl."

Smiling, I lowered my voice. "I believe she has sorcery she hasn't yet discovered."

Kyr's eyes went wide. "We'll watch for that . . . and her, lovely. Never you worry. You have a bigger duty on your shoulders than you realize. We'll see you again before you know it."

I regretted having to leave Honera after saving her from such trauma only recently. She wouldn't speak much, either about the Ryū attack upon the City by the Sea or other matters, but it'd be safer for the girl with the Small Folk than where I intended to wander. "She's had a tough life. I wish I knew more about her family or how she ended up on the streets. And how she survived the fiery Ryū breath upon Kōkai defies the reach of my imagination."

Misha nodded solemnly and placed an arm around his love's shoulders. "Kyr and I will care for her as if she were our own until we meet you at the gates of Arashi."

I left them then and went to Honera, hugging her tightly with hopes that Misha's promise of reunion became reality. I had no words for her, nothing I could promise in the moment, so I stood and went to say a few final words to Tao and Oshun. The sailors had already begun to size up trees for the timber they'd use to build vessels. They'd agreed to ferry the Small Folk down the Appi to the Gulf of Yōtei and up the Umbral Gorge into the Evernight Marshes. I had no idea how they'd fare with the traps set by the more paranoid Small Folk in that region, but King Isao bade me to leave that worry to him.

I did, trusting in the Small King and his two remaining sons, Misha and Tomei.

In our negotiations and further conversations, we'd learned that Isao's other son and Misha's brother, Davao, had perished in the Ryū attack upon Brennmor. The news reaffirmed my need to see the green dragon banished from Nantai.

As I discussed the preparations with Tao, a woman of the Small Folk jogged over with a scroll held out to me.

"Thank you, Gyna. Did you have enough time to make a passable copy?" I asked, accepting the map that Taurusyn had provided when we parted ways in Safaia. The small woman, a scribe in King Isao's service, had had the task of forging a copy of the landscape from my scroll. They'd lost all others within the Small Folks' library during the siege.

"I did. Many thanks." Gyna bowed, then scurried off.

Father and I filled what containers we had with water and fastened them to the packs across our steeds' backs—Speck the mule and Star the horse. I worried for their safety in the open and the heat, but with Father at my side, the choice between livestock and family remained clear. We'd look for springs or small streams, but if there was no water in the sea of grasses, we had none to spare. It seemed tragic that as Storm Sorcerers, we couldn't use the magic granted our caste to pull water from far distances or deep within the earth. I hadn't tested the boundaries of my sorcery's range, but if the plains were arid, I couldn't call more than a dry wind.

I asked Parū.

She considered, but eventually answered in thought, *I haven't enough knowledge of the Nantai people's magic, minikin. Had I known you'd have such questions, I'd have inquired with Amare.*

<hr>

AFTER GOODBYES, FATHER AND I struck a course northward into the grasslands. We'd be in the open under both Selene's silvery moon and Otarr's golden rays. Certain that we'd find little shade, we'd begged material to wrap about our exposed skin. Father wrapped it around his head, then over his nose, and draped it around his neck. When he'd finished, all I could see of his face were his stormy gray eyes. I wrapped my head and neck in similar fashion. Though a necessary measure, containing my body's heat any more gave me a roasting sensation at the mere thought.

Days passed wandering under Otarr's light, and Speck was the first to falter. We relieved him of his burden, said a brief prayer to the Triad, and left the carcass to the scavenger birds. Two days later, we lost Star as well. Father and I took what supplies we could and continued to wander on foot by daylight. I allowed Parū to fly at night, but she wouldn't leave to hunt. Instead, we sheltered Father, kept close by fear he'd fall prey to something much larger. Thrice, we heard a Ryū call in the distance while Selene traced her path across the starry skies, but we never met the source.

Despite the heat and the dryness, having lost our animals, and running low on our own water, we wandered on, my desperation to find the Tsinti my sole driving force. In the hot and quiet wandering, I worried over what castes Karynne and the bonded pair Imrythel and her green dragon had called or, more likely, coerced to their cause. That drove my steps further as I needed all the allies I could muster. I couldn't be certain if they knew of my quest . . . that I'd returned to Nantai or that we intended to remove Karynne from the throne. But if they did, the Tsinti represented a hope I believed they wouldn't count in our favor.

Morning arrived and Otarr's heat felt more searing than it had the day before. We walked but stopped at every rough-hundred paces. Our day-seeing god was the bringer of light and he helped all things grow, but in excess, his heat seared. Our bodies expended too much energy simply to remain cool, depleting reserves that would press us forward. Nantai people, as do all things living, need shelter and clouds and rain on occasion. In the absence of these things and more sustenance than some dried and salted meat, Father and I wasted. After Otarr reached his peak in the sky that day, Father knelt and held his hand above his eyes and let out a long sigh.

"Mairynne," he said, "you and Parū must fly. You must leave me here and see to restoring the peace in our lands."

I fell to my knees before him, tightness clenching at my throat. "Father, no. I won't." I shook my head fervently. "We will march toward water if we must, but I will not leave you. I will give Parū control, and she will carry you in her claws, but I've traveled too far and given too much of myself to lose you again. And if I carry you to safety, we'll not find the Tsinti. We must press on, or we risk the wrath of the green dragon upon our arrival in Arashi."

Father appeared too haggard to continue. "If your friends have remained true to their words, they will meet you there. I will not be necessary."

"The last is categorically untrue! You are the emperor of Nantai, and you must return." I dropped my face so he wouldn't see my fear. "It is also possible they have failed. We have no way to know."

He reached a shaky hand forward and lifted my face. "You must have faith in your people, Mairynne. The best leaders always do, and that is your destiny . . . to rule the Nantai people."

I shook my head again, refuting that destiny and all that accompanied it. Refuting that I might have to lose my father twice over to meet the demands that destiny set. Refuting that I'd lost Thalaj for naught. "No," I snapped, swallowing my tears. "We have enough water for two more days. If the Tsinti have not found us by then, I will relent, and Parū will carry you back with me."

"Daughter—"

"No, Father. If you wish me to rule, this is how *we* will do it. I won't be leaving you behind to die of thirst, heat, or starvation." I still held hope that he'd recover enough to return to the throne, but if I that was the only method I had to drive him onward, so be it.

He took a deep breath, closed his eyes, and exhaled slowly. "You remind me of Noralynne."

I chuckled, the thin cloth over my nose and mouth puffing. "Funny. I believe she'd say I remind her of you—determined and at times obstinate."

"Mayhap a little of both, then. Or perhaps neither." He slipped his hand in mine. "Help an old man up."

I smiled and stood, relief washing through me as I offered him my strength. "I despise this, but if we return to Stormskeep now, without more help, we'll certainly face defeat alone. I don't know to what extent Imrythel has corrupted Karynne. But . . . we are not ready for such a confrontation." The last weighed heavy on my soul.

Tennō Atheryn, weathered and tired, pulled himself to his feet and started walking at my side.

Just before Otarr rested for the night, we rolled out beds under the sky. A fire wasn't required or even a desire as the coolness of the night felt nice upon our skin. Even Father discarded the materials to let his neck and torso breathe before he lay on his back. I paced in the gloaming, wondering what—if anything at all—I could do to entice the Tsinti to find us. After many paths back and forth and back again, I spread my arms, threw my head backwards, and called the names of the Tsinti I remembered into the night, "Zofi, Yankos, Jorani, or Detsa, hear me!" I cared little what Father thought of my outcry. It seemed a last resort, but if it worked, we'd be better for the meager attempt. Quieter, I begged, "Find us tonight, please."

That night, I didn't shift into Parū's form. She too felt the pull of the long days and nights upon the grasslands, and if we were to take flight on the morrow and she couldn't hunt to build her energy, she needed the rest. The night was quiet, but I didn't feel tired, my mind alive with thoughts of all flavors. I sat and watched while Father started snoring softly. I waited and breathed and kept vigil until . . . I remembered nothing more.

I dreamed.

Long dreams played out vibrantly in my mind; about the castes presenting treasures at my ascension, of Tsanseri offering the cuff that I wore about my upper arm, about sneaking out of Stormskeep with Thalaj, of the blue dragon in Safaia, Hoaris, Misha and Kyr, the casteless, Filtch—better known as Alto-Trea, of my night with Sarangarel and the yisun she'd sent with me in search of Father, of the sailors, Umu-Zimi, the tribes on the island nation of Ise, and the Fey queen, Amare. Heat suffused my body at the vision of the Abatwa prince Osmar hovering above me, kissing me deeply, and sinking into me. Then, I saw again the black dragon in his pool of tears. I relived the feelings of when I found my father but had to leave Thalaj in his place. Then even in my dream, I settled back into darkness, weary from the long journey. Dream knowledge still present that tomorrow we'd fly to face whatever chaos the green dragon had rained down upon my home. And someone called.

"Mairynne?"

My body shook, pressure on my shoulders.

"Lady Mairynne?" it called again and again until I heard a fiddle on the wind.

My eyes flew open.

Forty-Nine

Inward Twice

"Z OFI?" I SCRAMBLED BACKWARD ON the ground where I'd been sleeping until my boots found traction. Stumbling, I clumsily gained my feet. The light behind her seared my sleepy eyes and cast her form in shadow. "Zofi, of the Tsinti? Of Yankos's caravan. Is that you?" I squinted and held my hand against Otarr's morning light.

"Yes, child. It is. You called for us and I came." She turned, still in shadow but clearly regarding my father. "What are two Storm Sorcerers doing this far north on the Central Grasslands alone . . . so near the Great Sands? And royalty too?"

I scanned the field for anything that might indicate the caravan had come too, but nothing. I turned in a full circle, then raised my chin, straining my ears. A small smile pulled at the corners of my mouth when I heard the distinctive draw of a bow across fiddle strings. It sounded far, far away, but the point was: I *could* hear it. My shoulders eased away from my ears, the shock of being awakened so ebbing and relief settling in. I returned to my bedroll and sat with my legs folded.

"We've been searching for you for uncountable days," I said, working my tongue against the roof of my mouth. My voice sounded as dry as my mouth and throat felt— parched, dusty, and swollen. "And the rest of the Tsinti. I need your help to help my people. Will you take us to the caravan? To Yankos?"

Zofi, appearing only the height of a youth with wiser-than-her-years eyes, head bound in the colored garb the women used while under *tsym*, took the empty space at my side. "Where is the totem we returned to you?"

I hung my head. "It was taken from me along with the stones I carried around my neck." I touched the place where they had rested for many moons.

"Aah . . ." She crossed her legs and settled in. With her hands palm-up on her knees—a picture of serenity—she sighed her regret. "You are aware of our ways. Our lives are apart." Her words suggested she wouldn't accept us under the caravan's magical protection.

Hope ebbed, but I tried again, shifting to face her and clasping her hand, pleading. "Zofi, I have stories to tell. Ones that I believe your people will relish." Then I switched tongues—a scene Father watched with ever-growing interest. With my head bowed humbly, I spoke in the Romani: "I found a home for a time with the wandering people. I practiced your ways and grew to love each and every tradition and person within your caravan. Though you live apart, I consider you my own. I have no intention to rule Nantai"—I glanced at Father as I said this, hopeful yet not certain that he had no comprehension of the language—"as I have much to accomplish in my life yet."

I closed my eyes for a moment, taking a long and cleansing breath.

Thalaj. I needed no stones around my neck to tell me he still lived somewhere in the Fey Realm.

Eyes open and refocused, I went on, "As a friend, I beg your aid. You once said to me, 'Face this day's challenges today and leave the rest for the morrow.' Wise words. And ones I have heeded time and time again over the seasons I've traveled. I've met many people . . . of many forms." I thought of each of them, such a close semblance of the dream I'd just experienced before waking. Those had been meetings I wouldn't trade despite the peril I now faced as we made our way back toward Arashi and my home, Stormskeep.

I coughed then, the dust lodging between my words. Zofi watched me intently, waiting for whatever I'd say next. Father handed me the near-empty water skein, and I drank the remaining few drops. We'd return to Nantai's jewel city today if I couldn't convince this Tsinti witch wife before me to bring me to Yankos. With a sigh and still speaking in the Romani, I continued, "When you read my cards, you foretold transformation upon seeing the card of Death. That has indeed come to pass. The cards also predicted a merging of two things . . ."

Parū stirred inside, gazing through my eyes and studying the woman so intently, I blinked several times. When I focused back upon her, her eyes were wide and her mouth formed an *O*. So much surprise twisted her features that I knew Parū's slitted eyes had overtaken my own for a moment. We shared so much with our souls bound, it had become a commonplace feeling to me—something I called upon when I needed sight beyond what a person's vision could manage. As I looked upon Zofi now, I saw her aged form. Though the witch woman possessed some magic that kept her appearance, the Ryū sight saw past such a guise. I wondered if it would also be so with the Cloud Courtiers.

Slowly, Zofi worked her lips, and her words held marvel when she spoke, a thrilled whisper. "Can it be?" She reached her hand over and rested it on the back of mine for only a moment. Her other hand hovered shakily in midair, and her eyes and voice seemed distant, like they'd drifted into the past. "With heated skin and a diamond-like gaze, they will return . . ." She blinked thrice, and said on a sigh, "Yes."

The witch woman, Zofi, then turned to Father who regarded her with ease and patience. Her stature presented a diminutive, but well-kept woman in eccentric colored attire, seemingly of little threat. I wondered if Father had ever had dealings with the Tsinti. If he had, he'd know otherwise . . . that one would never know which Tsinti were a threat and which were not, and this woman held untold powers within her tiny being. She'd changed. Resolve grasped hold of her. As she stood, she said naught but turned, raised her hands above her head, and brought them together. Steepled, she lowered them until they rested under her chin and said, *"Kai zal'o drom."*

"Here goes the road," I repeated reverently in the common tongue for Father's benefit. Also, an ode to my own memories of the wanderers.

The air shimmered and folded upon itself in Otarr's early light. Father stepped to my side, placing an arm about my shoulders, and inhaled sharply as he watched the unveiling of the Tsinti *tsym.* Covered wagons and a gathering of the Tsinti appeared before us. Father leaned close and murmured in my ear reverently, "There is magic beyond what I'd have ever believed. How well you have done in negotiating it, daughter of mine."

◇◇◇◇◇◇◇◇◇◇◇◇◇◇◇◇◇◇◇◇◇◇◇◇◇◇◇◇◇◇

JORANI AND BALDEO WERE the first to greet me, rushing forward as if they had been watching and waiting. They'd been my trainers before in the dance with swords, but now they threw their arms about me with unexpected hugs.

Jorani looked down at the weapons I'd braced around my hips and nodded with approval. She grasped my shoulders and shook slightly. "I see and feel in your strength that you've continued your training."

I gave her a warm smile. "I have, if not as regularly as I did when I traveled with your clan."

Baldeo clapped me on the back, a blow that might have sent me stumbling before and I took with ease given my increased constitution—another thing I could attribute to my bond with the Ryū, Parū. *Thank you,* I said inwardly as I stepped forward, teasing him into the dance.

"Oh no you don't, little one. I don't dance for just anyone." He winked, then held his hands out wide and looked around. "Speaking of, where is your guard, Thalaj?"

His inquiry stole the spring from my step and erased the joy of reunion I felt at seeing old companions again. "That is a story for another day, Baldeo, and should I survive what I will soon face, I shall tell you all about it as we share a tankard around a great fire."

"I will hold you to that, little one."

I backhanded him across the chest. "I think I've outgrown that name."

He laughed. "No. It is one you'll never outgrow in my mind."

"Mairynne!" called another voice I never thought to hear again. "Detsa?" I searched the crowd.

The small portly woman who'd shared her wagon with me before, popped through, ran over, and slipped her arms about my waist. She squeezed tightly, her head against my chest. Had she always been this short? Or had I grown? Either way, I happily returned her embrace.

When she pulled away, she couldn't make eye contact. Instead she tugged at me and in the Romani said, "Come-come. Come with me. We'll dress your hair, and you'll feel like a new woman."

I held my ground, and when she peered at me with confusion, answered, "Can you bring the bans to me here, Detsa?" I asked in her language as well, looking up to see Yankos approaching with a youngling toddling at his side—Janci. The babe I'd met around the fire who hadn't been walking yet had grown so much and wore a thicket of fine but wild curls, and he clearly resembled his father. To Detsa, I added, "I have much to discuss with Yankos but haven't the days to pass in normal tradition."

She looked puzzled, but after a second nodded and scurried back through the crowd on her errand. I looked to Father then, considering the tradition Thalaj had had to undertake with the Tsinti.

As if reading my worry, Zofi looped her arm through his and said, "I'll see your father fed, given some ale, and well tended." She arched a brow suggestively as she looked up to him. He nodded tightly, bittersweetly. On his mind must have been Mother, as I harbored thoughts of her too. But she had passed on to be reborn, her soul released from the funeral fields with the nymphs. Should another offer to attend his needs, what place would I have in stopping him in finding a small bit of comfort?

Yankos handed Janci over to his wife, then he and a couple of others pulled the tsym back into place over the caravan. I felt my storm's magic diminish, but the cloaking magic had no effect on Parū's fey nature. That eased my worry of being trapped with the wandering folk for another long period of time—as Thalaj and I had been before. Although we had purpose for staying then as we had yet to understand the small prophecy Zofi had shared on our last night with the caravan. Now, under the tsym's protection at least, Father wouldn't face the fate that had awaited us outside. Mayhap, Parū and I should fly under the cover of darkness when Selene took her place in the night's sky. If I found that need, I wouldn't consult with Father again before leaving.

I went to Yankos when the gathered Tsinti began to disperse. "Your son has grown."

"You've been away for more than twelve of the moon's cycles. Four seasons, Mairynne. Babes grow," he said, diminishing my small attempt at connection.

With a hand on his arm, I pulled at his tunic. "Yankos, I'm not good at small talk, and as I told Detsa, I'm short on time. I must ask. What have your wanderers seen across Nantai? I've been back only a short time, and it seems so much has been laid to waste."

"Come, have an ale with me," he said and led me to his wagon.

Outside his rolling home, his wife had a table set with a carafe and two glasses—apparently expecting we'd return behind her. Some thumping and giggles from within the wagon indicated she wrestled with their son. We took our seats at the table upon makeshift stools, no more than upended buckets and the same seating arrangements the rest of the Tsinti brought to their nightly fires. Yankos grabbed the carafe and filled two tankards with ale. I sipped, sighing with relief as the cool, frothy beverage slid over my tongue. I'd had naught but tepid water since we'd left the Small Folk along the Appi River, and while the ale wasn't cold, it had flavor and felt cooler on the tongue given the stoneware in which they transported the liquid within their wagons.

After Yankos had taken a long gulp, he wiped his mouth with his bloused sleeve and said, "Aye, we have seen or heard of the destruction happening across Nantai. We head north now from the Copper Coast, a small town called Aomori. It's been overrun with traders who escaped the City by the Sea when it burned to the ground. We'd traveled there to purchase the copper our men use to cast the wares we sell at market. The natural resource was more scarce than we'd ever seen, hard to find someone who dealt in the raw metal that hadn't been cut with a less pure ore, and the authentic stuff carried a far greater price."

I followed Yankos's gaze over to where two men worked at a small forge. One tended the melted copper while the other polished a vase made of the tawny-colored metal. Less than a dozen other shaped vessels sat nearby in the setting sun with the gleaming greenish swirls apparent in their luster.

I swallowed another drink and prompted, "What else?"

"We encountered the Small Folk after Brennmor had been decimated." Yankos shifted, propping a boot across one knee.

The casual way he mentioned this scrubbed at my nerves. "And you wouldn't offer them your help?"

Yankos glared at me, disbelief that I'd ask such a thing apparent in his stare. "We offered the survivors a place within the caravan. Yet they are a prejudiced people and chose to remain."

That struck me as odd since Misha had once mentioned he had searched out the Tsinti to become one of the wanderers, yet they had reportedly turned him away too. It shed light on the contrast between the two groups. Seemingly they simply couldn't communicate with one another in a way that'd move them past their prejudices. The notion would aid me in future dealings with the people of Nantai, assuming I at some point accepted the duty to the people and country.

"Is there more," I asked, my heart sinking with every new story.

Thankfully, he shook his head. "Nothing we are aware of, but we are not an all-knowing people. As you well know, we try to keep to ourselves. We travel now toward Biei at the southern tip of the cold lake, Kōdaina Kori, in hopes that the destruction hasn't found the northerly reaches of the land. I've begun to fear we'll need to make our way east across the Great Sands and form a new life in Engaru, Saroma, or even the far east reaches of Seria."

A leader's need to protect his people, ensure they are provided for adequately, and maintain their way of life—this much of leadership I understood. Yet heat flared in my chest at the thought they might desert my beloved country. Nantai. I wanted the Tsinti to be my people too. They were a part of the whole, and their absence, even if not seen, would leave a hole in the fabric of our culture. They deserved to feel at home on Nantai soil . . . and safe. I stood abruptly, feeling myself giving over to the blood boiling inside, feeling heat upon my skin, and seeing white at the edges of my vision. One hand on a hip, I paced.

Somewhere near, I heard a sharp intake of breath and whirled on the culprit.

Jorani stared at me with a hand covering her mouth. "Your skin, Mairynne, it gleams. Are those—"

"Yes," I snapped. An octave lower than normal, my voice growled and broke between my own and the guttural sounds Parū makes, which don't resemble words of any language the Nantai would speak. I moved about, trying to cool myself until Zofi shuffled over to Yankos's wagon with a tray of tea.

"Hmmm," she said, "Sit, young kōgō." She poured from the pot. "What is your Ryū's name?"

"Ryū?!" cried Jorani, despite the fact that she'd just seen evidence of the matter.

Others had gathered and murmurs began to crawl through the loose crowd, but Jorani's voice continued to break through. Her words, calmer then, felt reverent as she asked, "The legends are coming to pass? A bonded sorcerer has come to speak with the wanderer who bested the devil . . . here? Within our small caravan on the grasses." She looked down to the golden grasses around her boots, working out a puzzle or mayhap some foretelling I had no knowledge about.

My brow furrowed as I watched this.

Zofi nodded at Jorani. "Yes, dear. It means the green dragon who has wrought destruction across our land is the same one who refused to depart Nantai after her mate had left during the Ryū Wars. The one who turned her back on her own kind and hid, burrowing deep within Nantai's earth until she could rise again."

Awed, Jorani said, "I never thought I'd see such legends come to pass."

Her surprise did little to quell my growing irritation, but I fought to remain in my human form. The mention of the green Ryū didn't help. Parū wanted to erupt and seek vengeance on the people's foe, and apparently the Ryū's alike. I took my seat at long last. And with a shaking hand, I accepted a cup of tea from Zofi. The drink, hot though it was, soothed.

Gaining full control over myself and my bonded Ryū, I answered the question the witch wife had asked before. "Parū," I growled. "Parūdragon is my Ryū's name. A great pearlescent dragon," I clarified with pride, then turned to Yankos. "This is your caravan of wanderers. Your people. Certainly they will follow where you lead, whether 'tis your will to be leader or not. I beg of you to stay upon your land—*our* land. Nantai is your home, as well as it is mine. I plead with you to help me, fight alongside me—us—to retake our home. I have sent others to gather the Nantai of both the north and the south. I have stirred the Small Folk to my cause as well. We need your help too."

Yankos folded his arms across his chest and laughed, singularly and without humor. The red mark under his one eye stretched as he raised a brow. "You think the Frost Fighters and the Fire Forgers will work together? Otarr must have impaired your mental ability."

I took a deep breath through my nose and exhaled slowly. "It is a risk, I will grant you that, but I must reserve some hope that the diverse peoples will come together to protect what they hold dear. Were Thalaj here, he'd go to the Frost Fighters, but I've sent another in his stead. They will also visit Gnoble Brimr of the Underhill Dwellers on their path inland toward the North Woods."

The Tsinti leader still appeared skeptical. "You speak of something that hasn't transpired since the Ryū Wars themselves. Five ages past."

With my chin tucked, I acknowledged his fears. "I do. And I fear we may face a second one before our mandalas are drawn in sand and the nymphs are set free in honor of our lives."

"Insanity!" he scoffed.

"Yankos, hear her out," Zofi said patiently. "She carries her own companion, so this news tears her soul in half." She held a hand out to me in a proceed gesture.

I started again, "I've traveled far with two Frost Fighters and five yisun soldiers of the Stone Singers. I've lost Thalaj, though hopefully not forever. The yisun who traveled at my side have gone in search of their caste, wherever they may have scattered after Kōkai fell. As far as I am concerned, castes and casteless can be damned. Uniting in this is our only hope." I drank the tea again, waiting for another to reply. In the silence, I sent a small prayer to the Triad in their heavenly home that my traveling party would have their favor in this mission. "The Ryū—aside from one—do not wish another battle with the Nantai either."

All remained silent for many long moments following. Feeling an uncomfortable need to press my case, I mused, "I cannot speak for how well recruitment of the Fire Forgers will go, but I trust that Hoaris of the Frost Fighters and a member like Thalaj of the Unseen Guild will find creative ways to coax their leaders to support our cause. The only ones I cannot easily reach are the illusionists who roam the skies. We had a beacon at the citadel in Arashi, but I'll have to pass within the city's streets to reach it."

Softly, Zofi laughed and as she did, it crescendoed in both sound and hilarity until she held her side and her eyes watered. All about turned to look at the witch wife while her humor waned, as unable as I to understand what she found so amusing. When she exhausted herself at length, she asked, "Have you still the cuff from Cirro-Tsan? The one you wore when you traveled with us before?"

I peered at her, my brow heavy with confusion as I worked through her words, then placed the name, and my eyes grew wide. "Tsanseri?" My hand drifted to the cuff still wrapped around my upper arm. Of all the things I'd lost in this journey, the pretty bauble hadn't been one of them. I'd kept it close always—silly sentimentality, I'd believed. Could that really be the key to connecting with an ally in the Cloud Courts?

"What of it, Zofi?" I asked carefully, scarcely daring to believe.

She looked at me as if I were indeed a youngling, ignorant of older and wiser ways. "Mayhap Storm Sorcerers are not so aware of common Courtier sayings." A knowing smile played on her lips as she said in sing-song, "Inward twice, Selene pass thrice, and love's court . . . you shall entice."

FIFTY

Storm at the Edge of the North Woods

THE TSINTI GATHERED AROUND A fire that evening as per their daily tradition. Sitting on upturned buckets, some thumped on drums upon their laps or between their legs while others, Yankos included, drew bows across fiddle strings. Father watched as everyone filtered in, amusement apparent within his keen gaze and small smile. When we'd all taken seats and the music had begun in earnest, he leaned over to me. "You've done what you can, Mairynne. I encourage you to relax and enjoy the reprieve."

I offered no response but took the advice to heart and blushed in the darkness, thankful for the firelight upon my face to hide my chagrin. Breathing slowly helped still my tendency to fidget with my hands and bouncing leg. Father and Zofi sat to my side, close but not touching, and I wondered about the viability of their immediate connection when—or if—we restored the empire to the way it'd been before. Only time would tell, but I reminded myself in that moment of my father's wise words, *Truth to thine self first.*

A few of the younger women moved nearer the fire and danced as the fiddlers picked up the *Csárdás.* The tempo began slowly, and as it started to quicken, men joined in the dance the women had started. Before long, they were whirling around the fire in their colorful garb, and others were clapping and cheering to the beat. When the dance had finished, Yankos handed his fiddle to his wife—Kezia, I'd learned earlier in the day—and found a blanket upon the ground. Janci straddled one of Kezia's hips with his head sleepily lolling on her shoulder. Darkness descended as she cradled their son in one arm and Yankos's fiddle in the other and left the fire.

I peered at the leader of the Tsinti across the fire; he seemed deep in thought, worries creasing his normally smooth brow. Just as I was considering joining him,

Jorani left Baldeo's side and went to Yankos who sat with his knees up, arms resting upon them, and hands clasped. She knelt beside him, not quite making herself comfortable enough for the conversation to endure. They spoke intently for long moments, more seriously than I recalled having seen between the two of them before. When the conversation had run its course, Jorani placed a hand on his shoulder, then stood in one lithe movement. Baldeo joined her with an arm about her waist and they, too, left the circle of light. To see the coupling that'd developed between the fighters over the seasons since Thalaj and I had taken our leave warmed my heart yet made me yearn for something I couldn't have. At least for the time. Others followed and the fire died down to small flames and flickering embers. Through the remainder of the music and gaiety, Yankos hadn't moved, and he didn't then either. He appeared mesmerized by the flame, but I imagined his mind worked silently on the problem I'd presented to him earlier. When we were the only two people remaining, I stood and went to him, considering how many nights it'd been since Parū had hunted.

Thank you, minikin, she said inside me.

"May I," I asked when I reached Yankos, to which he held out a hand toward the blanket. Sitting, I made more small conversation. " 'Tis a beautiful night."

He looked up to the half of Selene that shone amidst the stars in the black sky. "Oy, yes. That it is."

"How far north are we upon the Central Grasslands?" I asked. "It proved difficult to keep track as we wandered in search of your caravan."

Yankos sighed. "We're northeast of Arashi, nearing the grassy gap between the North Woods and the Great Sands."

Farther than I had imagined. Surprising, how desperation had driven Father and me many leagues with so little. "You will forgive my directness, Yankos, but in the course of traveling, I've lost many people and things—" I tried not to choke on the words as I added, "chiefly among them is Thalaj. But I've also been robbed of the totem that allows me to enter the tsym."

"I assumed as much given how long you searched for us. It's good you finally called for Zofi and that she heard."

"It seems my Ryū can see beyond the tsym from the inside, and it does not quell her magic as it does mine. But I fear that she will not find the caravan from afield." I paused for his comment then, but none came. I continued, "That is good, because it hides you from Imrythel's sight too. She is the companion of the green dragon we believe has been causing the destruction across the land."

Yankos made no reaction to the news, but if I were him, I would be committing the name to memory.

I sighed. "I need to allow Parū to hunt too."

Tight-lipped, he nodded. "How long will you be away on this hunt?"

Relief loosened the tension in my shoulders. By his question alone, I knew he'd understood my plea. He pulled a totem from his pocket and held it before him. The fire lit the small stone.

Staring at the shadowy statue, I answered, "She can manage within the course of a night." Then I cast my gaze back to the fire, contemplating.

Yankos palmed the totem and wrapped his fingers around it. "But?" he asked, reading me well and turning to face me. The dying embers set the side of his face with the red mark aglow.

I shook my head. "It's of no matter."

Minikin, I can carry your attire to meet your kin in the Sands, Parū answered my unspoken, even partly-formed thoughts.

Warmth suffused my spirit. *Thank you, Parū. I will need clothes to visit others away from here.*

"Mayhap though"—I placed a hand on Yankos's arm—"mayhap it will matter. The Sandsgales live within the Great Sands. They are unlike the rest of the Storm Sorcerers who prefer the mountains and the cliffs on the western coast of Nantai overlooking the Syrensea. Yet Imrythel claimed Sandsgale as her surname. If she is not there now, Parū and I can approach my people of the desert. I'd need a full day, but mayhap—"

"Mairynne," Yankos stopped me. "Since our conversation earlier, I've been approached by several wanderers, Jorani and Baldeo among them. They agree that we should rally to your aid and protect you as one of our own. I'd be remiss to let you wander into such peril alone." His face twisted with a sense of something I'd rarely seen upon one of the Tsinti—a distaste for the outside world, mayhap, but also a foreboding.

Yet the sentiment of the wandering folk brought me a promise I had believed I'd lost after the midday conversation at Yankos's wagon.

He held the totem in his fingertips between us. "I will only give you this if you swear to me that you will return by dawn."

"But, Yankos," I began, needing to be certain that agreement among his people extended to aiding me if the situation should call for combat. "You hinted that you won't stand with us in a fight. If I can assume that still holds truth, I still have much to arrange and sitting idle for two more days while I wait for a court in the clouds to find me will do little for my cause. Since Father is safe here under the tsym for now, and we are waiting for Tsanseri's court to arrive three mornings hence, it is the perfect opportunity for me to use my Ryū's flight and seek more allies."

When I reached for the totem, he retracted it back into his fist. "I did not say I wouldn't help. I merely pointed out the persistent conflict between the two northern castes. Fire Forgers and Frost Fighters are natural enemies." He huffed. "I hope what you say is true, that your friend—what was his name?"

"Hoaris."

"Yes, Hoaris—a Frost Fighter, true?"

"He is, though very different from Thalaj."

"Well, I hope that Hoaris can convince his people, as well as somehow entice the Fire Forgers. However, one of my caravan has connections within the ranks of the Fire Forgers too."

My breathing stopped on the precipice of hope, but I held it back tightly.

"As you ascended to the Serpentine Throne, you will have encountered the gnobles from every caste. At the legendary Nantai ceremonies in the High Cloud Court, I believe. Yes?"

My eyes flitted away momentarily as memories returned. The thoughts I'd harbored before urged me to have members of *all* of Nantai's peoples present for such an event. Exclusion and prejudice, if they'd seemed undignified then, now felt abhorrent since I'd come to know these people. I'd truly become one of them in the time I spent learning the dance of swords with Jorani, Baldeo, and Yankos. I considered how my soul relaxed when I'd met the Tsinti for a second time and now felt easy among this caravan. More at peace than I'd ever felt in Stormskeep within Nantai's jewel city, Arashi.

"Mairynne?" Yankos brought me forward from the past.

Finally, I let out a breath. "I'm sorry. Yes, I met with the gnobles of every *named* caste. It had been an overwhelming time after having mourned my mother's death and father's disappearance."

"Do you recall the names of the caste leaders?"

I searched my memory, running through the various castes. I recalled Strato-Ymar of the Cloud Courtiers and Aljir Tenkara of the Frost Fighters. But at the thought of the Stone Singers, my heart ached. Kōkai had burned, so had Sarangarel—

"Does the name Yuos Atith strike a chord with you?" Yankos interrupted my efforts.

My eyes widened. "Yes, I made acquaintance with the Fire Forger gnoble at my ascension ceremony. How do you know of him?"

Yankos shifted, crossing his legs and curling his spine forward. "You may know this of the Tsinti after you've traveled with us, we do not lay claim to an ethnic identity. There is rarely a blood tie that makes one Tsinti. Our lives are of our own choosing, and we remake ourselves in the present by relation to others significant in our lives.

"Jorani's mother, Sinfi, once mated with Yuos Chakara, brother to Atith. Jorani's full name is Yuos Jorani, and she . . . though she was raised by her mother in the caravan and follows the Tsinti ways, she is niece to the caste leader, Atith." Yankos paused to take a long breath, the weight of this all clearly weighing on him heavily. "Jorani and Baldeo have requested leave to take a small scouting team to the Fire Forgers in Biei, upon the southern tip of the Kōdaina Kori. She believes she can help push from another angle. Sinfi will travel with the team as she is still able-bodied, and between them both, Jorani hopes it will aid in whatever incentive your friend Hoaris contrives."

My jaw hung in sheer awe. These people—the Tsinti I'd lived amongst for a time and wandered alongside—had always been a peaceful people, a group attentive to only their own choices and unbothered with the politics of the castes throughout Nantai.

If he noted how I stiffened to quell my anxious hope, Yankos said naught of it, instead he continued, "You and I will meet with the scouting party at daybreak—another reason you may not venture far from the caravan." He peered sideways at me, his mouth drawing into a rueful smile. "I never thought to be discussing tactics for war among leaders of the Nantai, but here we are. Your campaign against Stormskeep will require strategy and likely deception. Strategy may not be our forte, because we seek to live peacefully under tsym. The latter, however, may be where we can help."

Raw emotion constricted my throat, so I nodded my agreement. How incredibly humbling that they'd rise to my support as if I were one of their own . . . someone they believed *significant* in their lives for whom they'd risk all they knew. I couldn't find words to adequately thank their reluctant leader. Yankos, a small but strong fighter, showed me aspects of leadership that'd been beyond Father's teachings. Sitting casually before me now, he spoke for his people in a way he clearly wouldn't have imagined either.

"As for the remainder of the caravan," he continued, "we will make our way to the southern edges of the North Woods. My older folk will set up a more permanent camp under tsym there, the children will remain in their care, and those of us who are more able-bodied will embark upon this strange sky island at your side. That is, assuming it is of sufficient size and strength to transport my people. We haven't much experience with such transportation, but we will try."

I launched at Yankos, nearly bowling him over as I hugged him tight. He chuckled, a sound rarely heard upon his lips. When we parted, he opened his fingers and offered the totem with a smile. His eyes glistened in the dim light. "Fly only this night, my kōgō."

◇◇◇

WE FLEW AND PARŪ hunted that night. Detsa had offered me the same small bed I'd used before, but I had little need of a bed during this visit. Instead, I allowed Parū to fly in the night; my mind and soul rested deep within as she controlled both body and consciousness. When back in human form, she took her rest. For three evenings straight, when the fire had died, all had retired to their covered wagons, and Selene shone brightly in the skies, I surrendered myself to the Ryū within. On the third day after we'd joined the caravan, we entered the edges of the North Woods, where the wanderers began to build a more permanent camp.

On the third morning following my conversation with Yankos, Parū landed near the tree line where we'd left the Tsinti. After shifting back into human form, I padded toward the clothes I'd hung on a low branch. The gloaming that signaled the break of day had arrived grayer than normal. A damp smell forecasted rain, and the hairs on my arms rose under a current also charging the air. As I dressed, lightning split the sky and thunder rolled across the grassland like a herd of wilderbeasts in full stampede—a sight I'd only read about in the libraries at Stormskeep.

The plains to the east from where the storm approached appeared empty. Inside the forest's edge, still under the cover of tsym, the Tsinti camped. I performed the movements to release the cloak, intoning, "*Kai zafo drom.*" The air shimmered and revealed the cluster of covered wagons scattered amidst the trees. Where naught but underbrush had been only a day before, leaves and sticks had been swept away, tables had been set, and the camp seemed as if it had been in place for many days.

I turned back to peer at the storm rolling across the plain, a curtain of gray rain pouring from even grayer clouds, and I held close to my heart that within those thunderheads, Tsanseri approached. The Tsinti had started to rise to greet Otarr, some shaking off the effects of the ale drunk around the prior night's fire, others already preparing the morning meals. I rushed through camp to find Yankos and have him wake the others to begin their packing or other preparations.

When I had delivered news of Tsanseri's approach, I ran to Zofi's wagon and rapped on the wooden walls. "Father, the Cloud Courtier comes." Though I needed no room to sleep, Detsa had reserved her spare bed for me. And so, Zofi had taken Father into her home. If they shared more than sleep, I wouldn't ask.

He stepped out the back, fully dressed as if he'd been awake for hours. "Tsanseri," he mused, combing his fingers through his white beard, now trimmed neatly whereas it'd been wild before joining the wanderers.

It hadn't been a question, but I felt compelled to answer. "It must be. We haven't seen a cloud for days, and now—*a storm*!" I said with delight, then peered into the opening at the back of the witch wife's wagon. "Where's Zofi?"

Father's carefully blank look said enough.

I hugged him tightly, happy to see his health returning in measures. "Gather your things and come to the plains. I'm going to enjoy the storm." It'd been a long while since I'd danced in the rain, and I relished the thought as the first drops began to fall. Barefoot still, I ran across the soft grasses until the clouds above opened up. I spread my arms and whirled with abandon in the deluge. My hair dripped with rainwater, but I cared little. I let my focus turn inward, feeling the pool of my storm sorcery. I opened my palms and called the winds, felt the charges gathering in the air, and pushed harder to spark the lightning. I pulled my palms close to one another and watched it flicker within my grasp. I delighted in the rumble I felt throughout my body as a bright flash struck again. The thick clouds descended in slow measures. How long I danced, I couldn't say, but it lasted until the cloud had fully settled onto the plain at the edge of the North Woods and the rain had ceased.

Gasps went up within the Tsinti who had gathered around slowly, watching. Mist danced all around and crawled about the feet of the onlookers. I turned to a vision of stairs solidifying and extending toward the ground from the clouds. The gray resolved to whites and blues as I'd recalled from my time at the High Cloud Court. Dressed conservatively for the illusionist who presided over Love's Court, Tsanseri wore a simple blue dress with a high waist and material that caught the light as she moved. Her hair auburn and flowing in waves over one shoulder, she took measured, deliberate steps down the stairs, never taking her eyes from me. Her brow furrowed. She'd pinpointed the source of the call drawing her to the edge of the North Woods, but it seemed she couldn't fathom who had called or why.

I stilled while facing the Cloud Courtier, my breathing still labored from the dance. My heart beat still with exhilaration and lingering sorcery flowing through my veins.

"Why—or perhaps a better question—how have you called for me?" She scanned me from wet hair, over soaked tunic and breeches, and down to the tips of my feet in the doused grasses.

I'd grown confused by the time she lifted her gaze back to my own and asked, "Tsanseri, do you not recognize me?"

"I'm afraid I do not." She stood taller, holding her position several cloud steps from the grass, clearly not wishing to place her feet within the wetness her storm had left behind.

I moved forward and she backed up the stairs. There wasn't another Cloud Courtier in sight, but I doubted that she traveled alone. A guard could materialize from the mists in the time it took to blink. I swiped my hands over my hair, pulling it to the side and wringing the water from the ends, speaking as I did. "I visited your court at the time of my ascension."

A smattering of interest twisted her face, but she recovered all too quickly. I couldn't tell if it held any recognition.

I continued, "Within your court, I sat with my first guard, Thalaj."

Still, she didn't relent.

Very well, I thought, *I must remind her of the session and hope she'd recall.* I regretted having to share news of my sister's betrothal with my father so. Why I hadn't considered sharing it before escaped me. I had no excuse aside from the other losses that weighed on my soul and the journey I'd faced immediately upon my bonding with Parū. I took a deep breath, then said, "I vouched for my sister Yasmynne Evangale and her betrothed, Nestrin." In my periphery, I searched for Father but didn't see him. Surely, he'd be here somewhere watching, listening.

Something flashed across her eyes then, and she turned her head as to peer at me askance, mayhap with fear and disbelief. When I lifted the right sleeve of my tunic to show the bauble she'd given, her mouth opened in gaping surprise.

I smiled, "Yes, Cirro-Tsan, it's me. Mairynne Evangale."

She paused for only an instant more, then hurried down the three steps, suddenly heedless of the dress wetting at her feet or the silken material of her skirt. The cloud mists swirled as she rushed over and grasped onto both my shoulders. "It cannot be." She searched my face, hers contorting this way and that as if she recognized me, but didn't. "You're alive? You look so different, harder. And you're very"—she shook her hands, sending water droplets off the fingertips—"very wet," she finished.

I laughed at her annoyance, a bit of energy still tingling in my fingertips after the rain dance. "It surely *can* be. I imagine that months at sea, many hard travels, and weapons training amongst other things have changed me from the girl who left Arashi so many months ago."

"Left?" She scoffed. "The castes were told you were kidnapped. Killed. Your body was even presented for the rites of mourning."

I shrank back from this thought, sharply inhaling. "But surely you can see that is not possible as I stand here before you."

"I'd claim you a specter had I not just felt your body so solidly under my grip," she countered.

Shaken to the core, I turned to search out my father's stare but I still couldn't find him. So many troubles rumbled around inside me. A body? If there was a body, who'd perished for Imrythel's scheme? Back to Tsanseri, I asked, "I have heard rumors of Karynne ascending to the throne, and I believe—no, I know beyond doubt—that the dragon who has been terrorizing the land is companion to the woman my sister had chosen as her first adviser, Imrythel." I took the opportunity to ask after those I loved and left behind. "What of Aunt Nadia? Of my sister, Yasmynne?"

The Cloud Courtier, comtesse of Love's Court, gathered my hand, cupping it in both of hers. Her brows furrowed and she looked upon me with patience and kindness that spoke of another side of love than what I'd witnessed with her manner toward my sister's petition. "We have much to discuss. Won't you join me for tea?"

A clatter, the sound of a wooden crate falling, drew everyone's attention. The Tsinti front line parted and Zofi stepped around the crate, holding her hand out to Father. Together they moved forward and Zofi said, "Her father, Tennō Atheryn Evangale, and I will join you, Cirro-Tsan."

Tsanseri turned, hissing breath through her teeth. "Tennō?" she said in awe as she released my hands, bowed, and waited for Father to release her.

Ever the leader whether he carried the title or not, he placed one hand on her shoulder, lifted her chin with the other, and nodded for her to stand. "At the moment, I do not believe that salutation mine." Father smiled gently, his eyes crinkling at the corners. He didn't say to her that it may never be again, but I heard it on the wind, and I hardened my resolve. Tennō Atheryn Evangale *would* be emperor of the Nantai people again, one day soon. They loved him as was apparent by the comtesse's immediate deference.

Tsanseri rounded on Zofi, her eyes widening to what surely must have been their limits. She hissed another breath. "Cirro-Zofia?" she breathed.

The Tsinti witch wife held up a hand, eyes closing in a wince at the naming. "No. Just Zofi," she corrected. "As you said, there is much to discuss." She raised a brow to me, then to Father, then she turned and searched out her son, Yankos, in the line of Tsinti waiting to embark on an unfamiliar adventure. Her shoulders lifted and lowered as she addressed the courtier again. "But before we retreat for tea, will you have room upon your vessel to transport those gathered here? I'm certain you are not the only person upon this cloud isle. Have you attendants to show them where they can load our things while we discuss the matters at hand?"

FIFTY-ONE

A Reunion, of Sorts

AS WE APPROACHED THE CLOUD island and climbed the misty stairs to the open area before a smaller version of the High Cloud Court, the skies cleared. Under Otarr's gaze, they seemed more azure than even the long and cloudless days before when Father and I had wandered. Though scaled to perhaps half the size of the High Cloud Courts, Tsanseri's castle within the cloud appeared very similar in structure to the only other island in the skies I'd visited. With Yankos leading, the Tsinti followed me into the open area before the white buildings capped with spires the same color as the vast skies above. Father and Zofi stepped to my side as the caravan came to a rest in a semicircle.

Three courtiers greeted us. One—clearly naught more than a servant guised as a young woman in a simple gray dress that hugged her delicate curves—offered me a thin blanket that'd absorb the water left in my hair and clothes. Accepting it, I toweled the dripping ends and wrapped the blanket around my shoulders.

"Strato-Elea," began Tsanseri to the girl, "have the wanderers shown to the guest quarters."

The young woman made eye contact with the two courtiers at her flanks; each nodded and moved to attend to their duties. As it had been when I ascended to the Serpentine Throne, I watched them pass, curious about their uniform appearance.

At my side, Yankos turned to me with a questioning look.

I touched his arm gently, trying to reassure him in the midst of my own uncertainty. "Settle in. I'll find you once I've spoken more with Tsanseri."

We parted. Tsanseri looped her hand through my arm and motioned to her servant. Strato-Elea led us inside the castle, down a hall, and out into a courtyard, never uttering a word.

When we approached another simple and airy structure within the enclosed garden, the comtesse flourished a hand. "This room is where I take tea daily. We can discuss our *many things* here." Waggling her brows, she entered before us. She sat upon a traditional tatami at the far end of a low table, indicating we should take our seats.

More servants filtered in—identical in appearance—proffering trays of pastries, steaming teapots, and small earthenware cups, one for each of the people present. Father and Zofi made no show of surprise. Father, I presumed, had more experience in the ways of the Cloud Courtiers, and Zofi wasn't often fazed by oddities. The spread seemed extravagant, far more than the four of us could possibly consume, but the excess from Tsanseri shouldn't have been a shock.

"Many thanks, Strato-Elea," the comtesse said to the one who served her. "Will you pull the screens on your way out."

With only one, her name had been clear, but other servants had joined the bustle. It baffled me how Tsanseri or anyone knew to call one person Strato-Elea and the next by another name. None wore a symbol upon their shoulders. As such, I had no means by which to discern the differences, and they all had taken on a curvaceous form. So strange they so ill-resembled the thin, angular androgyny I'd witnessed at the High Cloud Court. For the first time in what seemed an age, I wished for my replica of Atun's mirror, the one gifted to me during my ascension. It would allow me to see beyond the guises and find individuality within the group.

Tsanseri, by contrast, always remained a form unto herself. She turned back to us, her guests, as the others exited. "I am fortunate they all choose to be here and serve me so."

"Choose?" I scrunched my forehead.

"Is that so hard to believe, dear? That people of my own caste would *choose* to serve me?" Tsanseri sat back and lifted the tea to her lips with her brows arched toward her hairline.

I had no answer, but the corner of my heart still owned by my friend Jessa ached. She and Mother Feathergale and others served my family as a matter of choice. Why should this be different?

One of the servants filled each of our cups from the same pot and left the others for refills. As the courtier had served my father, Zofi, myself, and Tsanseri alike, I worried little about the possibility of poison. However, along with the blessed mirror, I missed having the small golem created for me by the spellcaster in Arashi, Zafrynne. Regardless of the belief the tea seemed safe, both Father and I waited for Tsanseri to take the first sip. The warm and herby liquid on my tongue soothed my soul with familiarity of something I'd partaken of daily as a youngling. Barley tea. But the liquid soured on my tongue. The evil that overshadowed my home as I took this pleasure clouded the fleeting nostalgia. I placed the cup back onto the low table and turned my focus to the reason I'd called Comtesse Tsaneri to my aid.

"You'll forgive my direct approach," I started, "but I am unable to measure what time I have remaining. I've called you here, because I, along with the Tsinti who have agreed to help, need faster transport than their caravan will allow. I fear returning to Stormskeep and whatever evil has come to the castle, but there is also little choice."

Tsanseri cast her eyes downward into the cup she held cradled between both hands. "Stormskeep and Arashi are dark places indeed these days, and my island is far from one equipped to fly into what might escalate to a battle in the skies." She set the cup on the table. "You'll understand, Lady Evangale. I deal in love . . . patience and kindness . . . in nurturing satisfaction and enduring bonds between a couple. My currency lies in making good matches, not enabling hostility."

Zofi scoffed and hissed. "Ignus fatuus! You—self-appointed *Comtesse* Tsanseri, Cirro-Tsan by birth—deal in naught save deception and idolism."

For my part, I shrank from her vehemence, but if Tsanseri was cut by Zofi's words, she made no show of the matter. "Were you not born of the same blood, *Cirro-Zofia*?"

The Tsinti witch wife bristled, seemingly growing taller in her seat as she stated, "I have remade myself."

An echo of Yankos's words from three nights past: *We remake ourselves in the present by relation to others significant in our lives.* An illusionist by birth, Zofi had chosen, and consistently endeavored, to leave their ways behind. I grasped that which I hadn't before . . . all the small differences in her appearance since I'd first encountered her within Detsa's wagon had been attributable to more than attire or any magic I thought inherent to the Tsinti.

"You, Cirro-Zofia"—the distaste between the two finally infiltrated Tsanseri's calm—"have *un*made yourself."

I held out my arms, the blanket forming makeshift wings as I called a stop to their quarrel. "I do not claim knowledge of the history between the two of you, but it is not my concern at the moment." To Zofi alone, I added, "You have been a guide upon my journey. Though you have not traveled at my side, you advised me, accepted me, and have spoken for me. For those things, I will be forever grateful. However, if you cannot put aside your animosity in this room, I'll ask you to wait elsewhere."

Zofi's nostrils flared as she breathed through her hostility. If the witch wife held a Ryū within her, she might have expelled smoke with the breath, her eyes might have shifted, and her skin might have glittered with erupting scales. But that was not the case. She composed herself well. "You are right, Kōgō."

"Let us set matters straight . . . I am not a kōgō or empress. Only Mairynne or, if you must, I will accept *Lady* Mairynne. My interest here is beyond rulers, it is about the people who call Nantai home, and I am merely one of you all."

Father reached his hand across the table, asking for mine. When I accepted, he said, "That is all anyone asks of a leader, Daughter."

Though his words suggested more than I wished to accept, I squeezed my thanks and turned to Tsanseri. "Comtesse, I do not ask you to fight. Every person who calls thyself Nantai has resources, individual strengths, and value to offer." I paused to give emphasis to my next ask. "I only ask that we use them together. Share what we know and help one another so that we may return peace to our empire."

I waited for her to respond, but she merely regarded me in silence, her eyes wide.

I continued, "I will admit, the ways of the Cloud Courtiers befuddles me. I fail to understand the value of maintaining appearances so alike to one another that people sacrifice individuality. Yet . . . though I do not understand such things, I shall not cast judgment on those who do." I glanced at Zofi, who seethed in her own judgment, but I hoped my words were clear enough to emphasize my expectation to both her and the comtesse.

Tsanseri issued a singular laugh. "Certainly, with the company you keep passing such castigation, how can you claim to be different?"

I smiled then at the Comtesse of Love's Court. "I do not come here to petition you for what others ask within your courts. As you see, Zofi of the Tsinti understands what I ask of the people, and she now holds her acerbic tongue. I ask the same tolerance of you and two more favors. First, I wish you to provide the usage of your vessel to carry us across the skies to Stormskeep, and secondly, to share what news you have about the state of other cities and towns . . . what you may have seen over the last months where you have traveled—any knowledge you may have. I demand naught more and naught less."

Tsanseri lifted another teapot and refilled her cup, a mild, nearly unnoticeable tremor wavering the liquid as it flowed. She may be shaken but seemed hardly convinced.

Father released my hand and leaned forward, his elbows upon the table. "My daughter speaks with wisdom beyond her years, Comtesse Tsanseri."

As he prepared himself to deliver a speech, heaviness gathered in his shoulders and upon his brow. His throat worked and his storm-gray eyes bored into the Cloud Courtier. The emotion carried in his very presence portrayed the Tennō Atheryn I'd known when he and Mother were happy, yet the timbre of his voice carried a foreboding I couldn't fathom. "It would be easy to vilify those who captured me . . . or to say I was captured by ill fates. I dare say many who see me returned now will do just that, and so I have remained silent since my daughter came to find me."

Tsanseri blinked. "Would you claim they are wrong? They stole peace from the castes and our land, and they robbed us of our ascended emperor, the one who dined with Atun, Otarr, and Selene. You were blessed by our Triad. You represented the people of Nantai. So why are we to believe they do not harbor ill will against us?"

"I was the one who'd seen things wrongly," Father answered. "We relied too heavily upon our caste system, on the value we placed on the type of sorcery a person possessed, and on the senseless hierarchy we placed on Nantai people. Yet I also believe that decreeing it dismantled would have caused chaos within the cities, countryside, and cultures who call Nantai home. Noralynne, may she be reborn and one day find her way to the side of Atun, understood this and worked to mend the divides between all cultures across our lands." He bowed his head, slain by the loss of my mother, his beloved. "I only have come to the same understanding after a period of stasis in the Fey Realm . . . held there by those who truly exist between our world and the worlds beyond."

"They murdered your partner, and you would still not call them the enemies of Love itself?" Tsanseri demanded.

With a glance toward me, one that showed she meant no ill, Zofi spoke then, "Cousin, please. Hear him further." She'd foreseen this—how I knew, I could not say, but the Tsinti witch wife simply tried to allay the tension with her words.

I nodded my thanks to her as Father said, "The Fey who took me were not responsible for Noralynne's death. *That* can be attributed to another. They saved me from the same fate and isolated me within their realm as a manner of protection. They left behind two stones from the Fey Realm. Stones that were tied to our souls and our daughter's." Father turned tear-filled, storm-gray eyes upon me. "In doing so, they may well have done our people the greatest favor of all time."

The inside of my nose burned and my eyes flooded, a hot tear overflowing.

But Tsanseri interrupted, disbelief scratching in her voice, "And you will tell me of this *favor* now, Tennō?"

Father smiled then. I did as well, wiping the tear from my cheek and feeling pleased that she still deferred to him as emperor of the Nantai people through the honor-bound title. It would make seeing him back upon the throne an easier feat.

He continued, "I have held this knowledge throughout our travels so far, allowing Mairynne here to deepen her bond with the pearl dragon, Parū."

The Comtesse gasped, and she nearly spilled the tea. As she lowered it carefully to the table, her violet eyes cut toward me with a flash and a thousand questions.

But, stealing any reaction she intended to voice, Father pressed on, "Nantai has been on this path since Tennō Makenyn forcibly severed the Ryū named Kuroi from his soul. He sent the dragon into deep mourning, and Kuroi returned to the realm between, the place all fey creatures call home. Some call it Fey, but there are many names. You may know the stories, but after the Ryū Wars, the Serpentine Throne was built from the bones, scales, and hide of the last Ryū. Such a tragic and senseless war."

He took a deep breath then continued, "The people of Nantai loved Tennō Makenyn while he and his companion were bonded, but once he violated that bond and declared war against the dragons, he began forcing the same ritual of separation upon other bonded Nantai. It drove the division that led to the war, and the green dragon who still thrives on our shores was at the helm." Father shook his head. "That is a story for another time. As for Makenyn, his soul was so accustomed to the bond, he fell into true madness without it in place."

She'd been listening intently, engrossed in his story, but Tsanseri gathered herself. She scoffed. "With due respect Tennō, you would call the emperor our people have come to call the Father of the Nantai a traitor?"

Father took a deep breath. "On the contrary, I call him a victim of his own machinations. What I learned from the fey creatures in the months that have passed since I left Nantai is that the Ryū bond requires one of exceptionally strong constitution to withstand and nurture the union. The dragons choose their companions carefully.

Whether it be that I was too advanced in years or that I was at such an emotionally challenging time in my life, I wouldn't have been strong enough to endure the process. "The Fey—or the Abatwa as you met them, Mairynne—left behind a calling for someone to follow. The Fey cast spells upon the stones, much like the Small Folk spell stones. My daughter heard the call, Tsanseri, and she followed. It warms my heart and reinforces how right I had been to name the youngest of my three daughters as my heir."

I lowered my gaze, my face heating under Father's praise, as well as Tsanseri's scrutiny. Her violet eyes regarded me piercingly, as if they were trying to see the Ryū within—something that was only possible if Parū and I allowed such a thing.

"You do seem much changed, Lady of Evangale." She turned back to Father. "But she bears no resemblance to any of the Ryū paintings or anything other than a Nantai Storm Sorcerer for that matter."

My blood heated inside. Parū growled, albeit silently. As Father held a hand toward me, his eyes pleading, we both stifled the anger.

"You call yourself Comtesse Tsanseri, Comtesse of Love's Court, intoning that you are the partner or widow of Love itself, and you decree that you hold court in matters of the heart. I know not what authority grants you that right, but I will offer you this, *Comtesse*. The matters of our Evangale hearts lie with the Nantai people, and I, my daughter, and her bonded Ryū, Parū, only wish to save that which we love from darkness."

She lifted her earthenware cup and said, "Very well. Continue, Tennō Atheryn," as if she were the one still in control of this conversation.

Father ignored her manner and returned to his story. "Guin, the green Ryū and her partner have plotted and schemed since the days of Makenyn to overthrow our culture for naught more than hate and revenge and misunderstanding. The green dragon is not like Mairynne's Parūdragon. She holds too much rage within her heart over the events of long, long ago, and she has forsaken the natural ways of the bond between Ryū and person. She has maintained a bond long beyond the natural lifetime of any Nantai person, and the Fey believe Guin's soulbound companion has also fallen into insanity as a result."

Within my heart, I worried how much of my sister's will Imrythel had bent in the process.

Silence grew thick in the room until more quietly, and as if speaking my own fears, Father added, "The great green Ryū's name is Guin, and she is bonded to Imrythel, who was or mayhap still is my eldest daughter's first adviser. Guin and Kuroi were mated. Kuroi, the blackest dragon, was also Tennō Makenyn's Ryū companion."

The understanding erupted and overflowed throughout me, making the entire world seem brighter for the knowledge. However, my dragon felt an immense weight from the truth revealed. As such, my soul was divided though still one.

Parū said to me, and me alone, though the others would have benefited from the message as well, *And so you come to understand the nature of our bonded history, minikin.*

The soberness in the tearoom spread between the five of us present—Parū included—for long moments. It was my father who broke it once again. "So, I'll ask you again the same questions as my daughter, Comtesse. Though I'd pose them as a call to action instead. Tell us of what destruction you may have witnessed across our lands since Mairynne's ascension. And when you have answered, take the necessary measures to deliver us unto Stormskeep at the center of Arashi."

"Your chronicle depicts an ominous future for Nantai." Tsanseri pursed her lips and twisted her mouth sideways. Following a deep inhale, she added, "But it sounds like you believe this is the true-hearted course of action."

Zofi opened her mouth to speak, but Tsanseri pushed a hand forward, forestalling her words. The Cloud Courtier then lifted a bell from beneath the table and jingled the delicate thing. The sound rose in high tinkling notes, but nothing happened immediately.

Tsanseri said, "This story of yours is terrible and fascinating. But there is now more to be understood." She lifted her chin when a servant appeared. "Ah yes, Strato-Elea, please send word to my navigator that I'd like him to join me here in the tearoom. Verify with the Tsinti leader, aah . . ." She snapped her fingers.

"Yankos," I offered.

Tsanseri nodded in my direction and repeated, "Yankos. Verify with him that his people have all boarded. Then bring another service. The tea grows cold." She waved to the table.

Strato-Elea bowed to Tsanseri and closed the screen upon leaving.

"As you have revealed more to me than it seems you had even told your beloved daughter, I will provide transport upon this cloud island in the direction of Arashi. I can promise little more than that at the moment. And as you have shared so much, I will begin with what I know . . . though the island's navigator will have better information as it is his duty to follow the winds and tend to our course over Nantai."

I breathed a heavy sigh of relief. "Comtesse Tsanseri, if I may?"

She held out a hand, urging me on.

Questions flowed without restriction whether she would answer or not. "How many Courtiers are upon this island? How many other islands are there? And would you be able to reach any of your caste?"

The door screen behind me slid noisily aside, I turned, and my breath seized within my lungs.

In the door, framed by light, stood a form unlike the servants. Straight lines as opposed to curvaceous forms. Hair kept close to the scalp. Simple gray clothes from neck to boot. A form I recognized yet never thought to see again.

Filtch.

Fifty-Two

The Night-Blooming Gardens

THE VERY PERSON WHO'D ONCE attempted my abduction in the City by the Sea . . . the very same person who'd clearly aligned himself with Karynne's plot to become empress of Nantai . . . stood in the back-lit doorway. He had taken the same form as he had in Kōkai, and though his face appeared in shadow, there wasn't a shred of doubt in my mind as to this Cloud Courtier's identity. Mayhap this image of a simple young man was his natural form, or perhaps he remained in disguise as Filtch and hid some other natural form. With the caste's penchant for illusion, and my mirror long gone, I had no way to uncover that truth. He regarded me with as little expression as he had so many moons before when he had stood beside a cold fire on the night he drugged me. Yes, there existed a small possibility that he'd acted solely out of a misplaced sense of duty to the empire, no matter the empress's intent. Yet as he'd placed emphasis on the reward upon my head and that of my first guard's, I had believed he'd done so for little more than personal profit. Faced with him again, it remained hard to believe otherwise.

Despite her choice in navigator, I held Comtesse Tsanseri in high regard. By the way her expression had opened upon his arrival, welcoming him, I presumed her trust for this person far exceeded my own.

"Mairynne Evangale." Filtch inclined his head, then shifted his gaze to my father. At the sight of Nantai's lost emperor, he sucked in a breath, sank swiftly to one knee, and bowed his head. "Tennō Atheryn Evangale? You live?"

An objection had been ripe on the tip of my tongue. The surprise and deference within Filtch's voice, combined with a reticent glance back to me, encouraged me to hold my tongue.

When he had encircled the table and sat, Tsanseri smiled. "Welcome, Alto-Trea."

Aah, yes. She wouldn't refer to him by the name intoning his leadership of the casteless in Kōkai, rather she would use his Cloud Courtier name—Alto-Trea.

The Swan.

My eyes shifted to his shoulder where, indeed, a black swan emblem proudly peered back at me.

Beneath the table, I fisted and released my hands as a long conversation ensued. By the time Tsanseri had brought Alto-Trea current with our requests, I had been sitting so long I'd grown stiff. Furthermore, I'd consumed enough tea to require other necessities, so I welcomed the opportunity to move when it arrived. To some small relief, the comtesse hadn't spoken a word regarding our situation with the Ryū, my companionship, or aught of the dire circumstances Father had laid out before the Swan had arrived. It endeared her to me more that she showed inherent understanding of my need for discretion where Parū and my companionship were concerned. She merely asked that her navigator chart a course for Arashi and review his plan with us later in the day.

If the request surprised Alto-Trea, he kept the reaction hidden under a solemn façade.

Tsanseri moved from her cross-legged position to her knees, finishing the instruction, "Upon our next meeting, you will also share all you know of the settlements across Nantai that have been touched by the tyrant empress's dragon." She then stood in a single lithe motion and addressed Father and me. "I'll have Strato-Elea show you to rooms you may call your own while you're guests upon my island."

We gathered in the garden outside the tearoom. Elea motioned to another servant who approached. She smiled at the Tsinti witch wife. "Alto-Tash will take you to the rest of the wanderers."

With a fond touch and a look shared with Father, Zofi left us then to find the Tsinti.

The rooms Elea led us into were much like those in which I'd slept at the High Cloud Court, mayhap smaller, but similar in airy decor and furnishing. Father and I shared a common area with bed chambers to either side. I commented dryly to Father under my breath, " 'Tis pristine and white. So little warmth." I thought for the first time in many, many months of my chambers in Stormskeep within Nantai's jewel city, Arashi. Home. Shades of amber, red, and gold were woven into the tapestries, cushions, and linens, and though the walls were naught but stone, the rich hues decorating my private space kept things warm and inviting. The fashion here, by contrast, chilled my very bones.

The servant, Elea, extended a hand before Father and said, "You may sleep there," then turned to the closer of the two rooms. I followed, eager to change from the clothes that remained damp after my impromptu rain dance. Several gowns lay on the bed, all in a high fashion that served little practicality. Some had multiple pieces that would barely cover my middle section, and there were some with sashes and flowing fabric that would certainly interfere if I had to fight, while others boasted heavy beadwork and lace. My traveling pack rested in a chair at the far side of the room.

"Thank you, Elea," I said.

The Cloud Courtier tipped her head and left without another word.

In the end, I forewent the fancy garments and changed into the clothes from my pack. As Father and I had little upon finding Yankos's caravan, the Tsinti had provided some durable travel clothes—fabrics meant for rougher conditions and far more comfortable than the formality Tsanseri had had delivered. After hanging my wet clothes to dry, I returned to the common room. Father too had remained in his rough-spun breeches, tunic, and vest, and that brought a thin smile to my lips. Apparently, we'd been of the same mind. These times didn't call for regalia or pomp. What awaited us felt more like a maelstrom brewing between the Nantai peoples and an ancient dragon bent on power and revenge . . . an event that'd require sweat, tears, battle, and blood in the place of parade. These thoughts chilled my soul and erased any evidence of a smile in my heart or upon my lips.

While I'd gathered some support to my cause—if in sentiment alone—I had so little knowledge in the way of strategies and tactics likely required for whatever we faced. The only Nantai castes I'd trust to have developed those skills were the Fire Forgers and Frost Fighters. I missed Thalaj; of anyone, he would have had a solid grasp on our next moves. Without him, I had little but questions on my mind. Hoaris might help, too, as he'd also been part of the Unseen Guild, but he wasn't at my side for the moment either. If he'd reached his people and Gnoble Tenkara, would he have swayed the leader of the Frost Fighters to come to our aid by now? Likewise, I felt uncertain how Jorani and Baldeo would bring Gnoble Yuos Atith and the Fire Forgers to Arashi for our defense. Then, should both casts agree and ally together for the first time in history, their movement from the northern regions around the great lake toward the southern tip of the Rausu Mountains would be slow. The fastest travel in Nantai was via ship along the coast, barge by river, or cloud island over land. Even upon a cloud, the documented speed was only thrice that of a person upon a steed, and the clouds often required detours to account for the currents in the skies. The absolute fastest and truest transport would be by wing—a dragon's flight.

If only we could fly everyone to the outer gates of Arashi, I mused to Parū.

Such a feat is not possible, Parū grumbled inside. *I can carry only a few people at once. We would need a Ryū army, and I believe that would undermine your purpose, minikin.*

"I know," I whispered, casting my eyes toward the floor.

With plans in place to discuss the cloud island's route later, I tried hard to put it out of my mind for the time. I expelled a long breath and went to Father, outstretching my arms. Travels had been hard until Zofi found us, but since that time, a slower pace with the caravan and a good number of hearty meals had treated him well. He felt solid and larger, more like the person I believed him to be when I'd been a youngling in the keep at Arashi.

"What worries you, Mairynne?" he asked, holding me as he'd done many times before.

Shaking my head into his shoulder, I answered, "Too many things, but none that we can solve in this moment. It is comforting to have you back." My throat tightened then. "You knew about . . ." I left the thought hanging.

But Father had my meaning. "Everything. Yes, I knew," he said, hugging me tighter.

We separated, further words over the matter not necessary, but a knot released within me, the worry I'd carried about his judgment flowing from me. For the first time, a glimmer of hope entered my heart—something entirely new and unexpected. After all this and once Nantai was peaceful again, perhaps I'd be able to show such understanding to a youngling of my own.

I cleared my throat. "Shall we walk? See how Yankos and his people are settling in? I haven't been with the wandering folk a single day in which they didn't gather around a fire under Selene's watch. This travel on a cloud with little fuel for a fire will be different for them."

Father and I meandered about the grounds surrounding Tsanseri's cloud castle. I had noticed the castle and the landscape before but observed finer details as we walked. We crossed the path leading to the front entry and I commented to Father, "This island is the same but smaller than the High Cloud Court. Yet there are comforts here that I could only attribute to the Comtesse of Love's court." I inclined my head toward the embellishments around the front doors.

He clasped his hands low behind his back and peered over, then nodded toward some gardens. "It's similar, true, but see there . . ." Within gardens, there were several smaller cottage-like structures, their roofs peeking above the greenery. A labyrinth of walking paths spread through the garden, all shrubbery and some taller than a person and what appeared to be flowering plants. Yet none bloomed. "There are many outbuildings that are not present upon the island where the Nantai caste leaders hold court. Likely those are docked and can separate into smaller islands when necessary."

I narrowed my eyes against Otarr's light, brighter on the cloud's topside than upon Nantai's soil. "That is where Elea said the Tsinti were staying, yes?"

Father nodded his assent.

There were no Tsinti visible in the gardens or near the small houses, so we followed what appeared to be the shortest trail toward a cottage to the left. Several other small footpaths forked from the main, but we walked slowly and stuck to the wider, more trodden path. The flowers weren't in bloom at the height of Otarr's intensity, yet the air still carried a floral scent that I hadn't smelled since visiting Nadia's gardens around her small cottage on the grounds at Stormskeep. Father reached out to one of the bushes and lifted a closed bud with hints of pink. "The oshiroi," he mused. "She only opens each day in time for Selene to look upon her petals." He scanned the greenery. "They're all night-blooming."

We continued and I felt another small smile pulling at the corners of my mouth. The moment—such normalcy against a chaotic backdrop—struck me. "I had no idea you knew so much of flowers, Father."

He held his silence but a small knowing smile spread across his face. Several steps later, a familiar, nasally voice stopped me in my tracks. I placed a hand on Father's arm, pulling us both to a halt. With a finger across my lips, I moved closer to the nearest tall bush and strained to hear the voices on the other side.

An air of familiar superiority laced the words. "When I attend to Lady Tsanseri this evening, you will take the outermost skiff and send word through the messenger network," said the Swan.

I covered my mouth and pressed my lips tighter. My instincts had been true in not trusting him. What message did he plan to send through the network? So far, we'd had the advantage of anonymity, but if he sent messengers to alert Stormskeep or others throughout Nantai before we arrived, it would ruin any opportunity for surprise we possessed. I lurched, intent on pushing my way through the bushes and confronting Filtch directly, but a hand clasped about my elbow. Strong and sure, it halted my progress. I cut my eyes over to Father; he shook his head in a slow warning.

"Be gone now and keep silent about this until you are away," Filtch hissed. Scurrying footsteps pattered away upon the path, fading into the distance. Filtch's slower and heavier gait followed as he moved away from where Father and I eavesdropped.

Quietly, I whispered, "Who is he sending? And why wouldn't you let me go after him? He clearly is working against our cause. We can't allow him to expose us."

"You're assuming much, Daughter. What makes you so wary of his intentions?"

I regarded him sharply with surprise. Of course he wouldn't know about my last interaction with Alto-Trea, and it wasn't a story that seemed right for the moment.

"Ah, yes," he continued. "I did take note of how you glared at the courtier in Tsanseri's tearoom. But he has made no obvious move against you. You do not know that this meeting is anything more than sanctioned by Tsanseri. Whatever history you have fuels your assumption that his message is about you."

Chagrined, I watched my fingers as they brushed over one of the leaves near my knee.

Father stood. "Let us continue." He led me back onto the path and in the opposite direction of where Filtch had gone. "Furthermore, if he does plan aught against you, you assume he works alone in the matter. It would be wiser to assume that everyone on this cloud island is of the same mindset."

I inhaled sharply to object, but before I spewed the words, Thalaj's advice also replayed in my mind. I repeated it aloud, musingly, distantly, "Remain open and calm. Observe and listen. Trust slowly. You never know where you might find an ally... or an adversary." My chest ached as I imagined the richness of his voice in the place of my own. "You're right, Father. He has given me cause for mistrust in the past, but I react too soon."

Father wrapped an arm around my shoulder. "Thalaj is a wise warrior," he said, obviously knowing the words.

I had no reply. Speaking of him hurt too much.

After several more steps, I asked, "Should we speak of the matter with Tsanseri?"

Father pursed his lips. "I'm uncertain, but we do have an advantage of our own in this game." He raised a brow and peered at me sideways, a twinkle in his eye.

My eyes went wide. "*Cirro*-Zofia! Father, you're brilliant."

I moved along at his side, a little lilt in my step, but other concerns still rolled around in the back of my mind. Before we went to the front door of the first cottage, I stopped. "Let's assume we make it to Arashi upon this cloud island. If Karynne and Imrythel have gained the support of the Storm Sorcerers, guards, and the casteless within the city, we could be walking into something bigger than we can handle."

My father nodded sagely. "You have rallied many to your cause, Mairynne. Should the third and fourth castes arrive, and the Small Folk, you can match their numbers. And if the yisun find and bring the Stone Singers, well . . ." He spread his hands.

"There are still too many ifs for my taste, Father. Did you not just warn me to assume everyone is on the opposite side?"

Tennō Atheryn Evangale chuckled and pushed a lock of my dark hair over my shoulder. "I suppose I'm an old man who is merely being hopeful now. And I stand here looking at a daughter who, though young and sometimes quick to react, is wise beyond her years." He sniffed, rubbed a hand under his nose, and turned away.

Latching onto him and turning him to face me, I wanted naught more than to offer comfort. Yet mayhap I held this hope close to my heart as well. "Possibly, we can slip in and speak with Karynne privately without stirring the guards about Arashi. But if that is not possible, we'll survive this thing, Father, and then . . ." I lowered my gaze for a moment. He had to survive, to take back his position as emperor, while I returned to Ise to free Thalaj. " . . . at least for a time, we will restore *you* to the position you had to leave."

He started shaking his head, his mouth opening and poised for objection.

But I refused his objection. Sternly, I said, "This has been my entire reason for being, and I will not stop until I see you restored."

He took my hands and held them both gently. "As I said before, I am an old man. I have some time and energy left, but—"

"You have much time left." I wouldn't tolerate his self-doubt. "You grow stronger every day, and had the Fey not taken you, you would still sit upon the Serpentine Throne today. You, Father, are the rightful emperor of Nantai."

Father pressed his lips together and nodded. "Should we find the Tsinti?"

I doubted I'd swayed his mind, but I was as certain of this as I had been in leaving Arashi in search of him. He grew heartier by the day. He only needed more time to see his path as I did.

"Soon," I said, then thought to Parū, *Do you think we can find the others? Those who have gone north on my behalf.*

My Ryū stretched inside, a yawn rippling through her soul. *Yes, minikin. The question is how long it will take.*

For the moment, I needed my father to tend to the Tsinti and this cloud island while I resolved other concerns. I said, "We've sent Hoaris, Jorani, and the yisun on certain errands. I think it would be good if we could speak with them before our arrival in Arashi." I didn't look at him as I finished, fretting over his possible rebuke. "I imagine we have several days before we reach the jewel city. Once we learn from Tsanseri and Alto-Trea the plan for travel, I will give Parū leave to fly to them by night."

FIFTY-THREE

The Journey North

WE WERE TO RECONVENE IN the tearoom as Selene took to the skies, and when Father and I entered, Tsanseri and Alto-Trea were already seated and awaiting our arrival. That they'd gathered in advance of our arrival heightened my suspicion of them both.

A new pot of hot tea and earthenware cups sat to one side of the table on a tray awaiting our attendance. Comtesse Tsanseri appeared much as she had earlier in the day but wore a flowing and translucent gown that resembled one of the outfits I'd left untouched on the bed within my chambers.

"Were you not happy with the clothing I had delivered to your chambers?" she asked, a small pout upon her lips.

I bowed my head. "I mean you no disrespect, but we are not here for ceremony, Comtesse."

Alto-Trea had guised himself in a similar manner to when I'd attended Love's Court on behalf of my sister. His face appeared more heart-shaped, and he wore a golden gown that hugged curves and accentuated the auburn tone he'd chosen for his hair, which was longer and coiffed into curls that fell over one shoulder. But upon the shoulder, he wore his Cloud Courtier emblem.

A swan.

The deceit I felt in his ever-changing appearance left me with a sour taste, but the thought of the last time I'd seen that personage so guised pressed hard onto my heart.

Yasmynne.

I'd fretted for so long now about Karynne and Imrythel that I hadn't thought of her much. How would my sweet sister be handling all of this? If Arashi and Stormskeep had already been seized, how would she fare in a game of power? Nadia too. I hoped Corwyn and his sister Solarynne were seeing to their well-being in my absence.

Tsanseri bowed gracefully and said, "Be welcome, Tennō Atheryn and Kōgō Mairynne."

In an imitation of Father, I inclined my head. Although it bothered me that she referred to us both by the honorary royal title.

With a hand out to the Swan, she continued, "My navigator and team have prepared a travel plan for Arashi. Will you sit?"

Alto-Trea moved to the corner, returning with scrolls and laying them on the side of the table while he knelt. He spread one, and I gazed upon a detailed map of my beloved Nantai. Overlaying the image of the land, there were curved lines and arrows I had never seen on a map of the country.

He pointed with fingers that seemed an illusion as well—dainty, with red-lacquered nails.

I must have worn my distaste upon my face because he pulled back, shifting his weight backwards onto his heels. Clasping both hands in his lap, he said, "Lady Mairynne, it appears we have gotten off to a poor start in our reunion."

Truer words couldn't have been spoken, but for my part, we'd gotten off to a poor start from the first time I stepped upon the High Cloud Court and this Courtier had insulted my first guard. Indignant after he abducted me, I'd grown even more so in the gardens earlier today when I believed he'd instructed someone to send word through the messenger network. I had no proof that this secretive errand involved me or my quest other than a heavy feeling in my stomach, and now he sat here playing court as if he were my grandest supporter. Recalling Thalaj's guidance as well as Father's, I took a long cleansing breath, schooling myself toward tolerance. "Let us simply tend to the business at hand. I am most interested in our path back to Arashi at this moment, so I am willing to allow the past to remain in the past if you will do the same."

With a lascivious smile that sent a chill down my back, Alto-Trea nodded once and leaned forward over the maps once again. "We have rooms full of scrolls, you see, but the aerologist who works on my team says that these maps show the current wind patterns." The Swan ran a manicured finger over the curved lines in an easterly direction toward Yōtei, then south, covering the coast near the Mannaka Sea, crossing the Gulf of Yōtei and over Aomori before finally moving north toward the Rausu Mountains and Arashi. "And within a twelve-day, they will change to these." He spread a second scroll across the table. "Unfortunately, the time it will take us to travel these channels puts us at risk of meeting this cross current."

I studied the two as did Father, but he was the one to ask. "So, what your team predicts is that our travels will last another twelve to fourteen days?"

"Regretfully, for our fastest course of travel, it looks like fourteen, mayhap sixteen days." Alto-Trea slid the top scroll away. "But if we drop from the current here, before we enter Yōtei, my team believes they can steer the island southwest to meet up with where the stream runs north. Unfortunately, traveling outside of the currents slows progress, and we will only shave a day or two from the journey. However, it should be enough to miss the cross wind and that would certainly push the island well off course."

Tsanseri poured tea, appearing satisfied with her navigation team's work. "I have one of our most talented and accurate aerologists among the Cloud Courtiers upon my island. You can absolutely trust in her predictions."

Father's brow furrowed, and he breathed through his nose. "We'd hoped to arrive sooner."

True, we had, but . . . My mind spun in all directions but mostly northward. "That may be perfect, Father." I placed a hand on his forearm, silently begging him to accept the time frame. As long as the Tsinti could be kept busy, it would work well. I'd dreamed up an idea to use the enmity between the Frost Fighters and Fire Forgers to my advantage when we arrived at Arashi. This offered the time necessary to find Hoaris and Jorani and organize the people. I inclined my head to Alto-Trea and Tsanseri. "Is there more we should discuss? It has been a long day and I'd like to rest."

"Lady Mairynne," Tsanseri started. "You haven't touched your tea."

"Your hospitality is kind, Comtesse, but I fear I took my fill earlier." I gave her a rueful smile.

Alto-Trea glared at me with smug satisfaction, and I wondered if this plan was to merely buy time for whatever missive he'd issued. As he rolled the maps, he said, "It would be my pleasure to meet you here nightly to update you both on the island's progress."

"Very well." I stood and paced the tatami. "Nightly updates will be good. I will appoint one of the Tsinti to receive the news."

Both Cloud Courtiers' eyes went wide, but the Swan was quicker to object. "Lady Mairynne, these are matters between the first and second castes. You dare suggest that we should provide updates to those who so actively choose to reject our ways?"

My blood heating, I rounded on him. "As you may or may not be aware, Alto-Trea, Filtch, or whichever name you wish, my mother's life's work was to unite the people. To erase caste lines. Had it not been for the Cloud Courtier Cirro-Zofia turned Tsinti witch wife, I never would have found Father, and we wouldn't be standing here today. Zofi made a choice with which I agree in whole heart. I trust the caravan implicitly, and I will not have you counter my commands." I glanced at my father then who appraised me with approval enough that I felt emboldened and continued. "You will provide your reports to whomever I deem fit to receive them."

I turned on a heel and exited the tearoom.

Behind me, Father said, "You have our instruction. Goodnight now."

◇◇◇◇◇◇◇◇◇◇◇◇◇◇◇◇◇◇◇◇◇◇◇◇◇◇◇◇◇◇

I'D HAD FAR TOO many goodbyes for the relatively few seasons I'd seen in my lifetime, and I didn't relish experiencing more. So, upon the farthest edge of Tsanseri's cloud island, I hugged my father tightly and said, "This is only temporary. I'll see you soon, and we can see this to the end." I had no words to adequately state my trepidation, but I'd use whatever vague sentiment I could to avoid the finality of that accursed word.

I hugged Zofi and Yankos too, whispering in the Tsinti leader's ear. "Please watch after Father. I've been through too much to lose him again."

"We will," assured Zofi, overhearing.

Yankos nodded when we parted from the hug, and his brown eyes lowered for a moment, but he said nothing. I'd entrusted him to the evening meetings regarding navigation. He'd led many scouting parties, and though they had always been overland, he understood the basics. And he was one of the few I believed would stand up to the Swan when necessary.

To Zofi, I asked, "You saw the messenger away?"

"Better than that, young Mairynne." A devious spark danced in her gaze. "We have stowed someone upon the small vessel to follow him. I don't know if you'll recall Maladros, but he's—"

"I do." My eyes stretched wide with the vision of when the larger Tsinti had clubbed Thalaj as my first guard had tried to rescue me from sparring with Yankos. Maladros had also been one of the scouts who'd captured us in the Yubar Forest so long ago. "I hadn't realized Maladros had joined us on this journey. If we see him again, I will have to find a way to express my gratitude for his efforts."

Yankos chuckled. "That man has left the caravan so many times, and he always finds his way back. You'll see him again. I assume in Arashi when this campaign of yours comes to a head. 'Tis too bad you won't be able to carry your weapons on your travels."

Inside, Parū scoffed.

"Yes, I will miss the scimitynes, but I carry blades with me now, bound to my soul. I appreciate your worry though, dear friend."

He sniffed. "Well then . . . you should go now. You're wasting the darkness. I do look forward to seeing your Ryū fly from this vantage. I'm certain Selene paints her pearlescent scales in a heavenly light."

My pack resting on the stones at my feet, I turned from the trio and ran, diving from the island's edge. Free falling, I relished in the sensations. The wind lifted my hair and whipped against my skin as my blood heated inside. I'd become accustomed to the crackling when my body began the transformation, and I effortlessly shifted into Parū in midflight. She dove for a time before spreading her wings and allowing the wind to lift her upward again—back toward the cloud.

Swooping down, she retrieved my pack with her claws and lowered her snout to the three people watching us in awe. As we took flight once again, Parū roared into the night.

And we were gone.

A new search began for old friends who carried messages to the people in northern Nantai.

They were castes—though I began to despise that word—I hoped and prayed would come to our aid in the name of all we believed and all we could be with the truth of the Ryū bond restored. Mayhap the term caste could be erased from the Nantai tongue once this was done.

You know where to begin? I thought to my bonded dragon.

Parū answered, *Nantai has changed since I left its shores, but I remember where the Frost Fighters dwell. Sleep now, minikin. I'll awaken you when we're near.*

In temporary peace, I retreated, curled my soul inside the great pearlescent dragon, and trusted my fate and the fate of Nantai to her.

My companion.

Parūdragon.

Part Five
Call of the Maelstrom

FIFTY-FOUR

On Dragon Wing

MY BONDED RYŪ DRAGON, PARŪ, and I traveled north upon dragon wing, taking leave from Tsanseri's cloud island. I prayed this errand away from Father would be short, and I only had a ten-day span before the comtesse's court arrived near Arashi. Had Yankos and the Tsinti not been present, I never would have considered being away for so many days as my heart was reticent still. I trusted in my bonded Ryū dragon to find our way to Biei along the southern shore of the great frozen lake in the north, Kōdaina Kōri. So, freed of my body's constraints, I tucked my soul into a corner of our Ryū-bonded consciousness and allowed my mind to recall all we had experienced since that day Thalaj and I had escaped from Arashi.

In what most would consider a short lifetime, I had traveled farther and encountered more foreign people than most who call Nantai home. My journey had come about unexpectedly after so many summers sequestered in Stormskeep. As the youngling decreed to inherit the Serpentine Throne, I had no course in life other than becoming empress of Nantai. The first time I'd left the jewel city of Arashi and met many of the castes who also called my country home had been the day I embarked upon the High Cloud Court, a castle upon an island floating through the sky over our land. This roving place in the sky was where I ascended to the Serpentine Throne, though many then had still considered me a youngling.

After Mother's body was discovered and Father disappeared, rumors in the streets had grown wings larger than the grandest dragon's. In the markets, people had whispered, "Poor girl, it seems only yesterday was she suckling at her slain mother's breast." Others asked, "How will such an inexperienced girl lead the Storm Sorcerers and Nantai? How will she keep order amidst the castes?"

On a day before the High Cloud Court arrived to whisk me away for my ascension ceremonies, I'd been in the citadel offering loaves of bread at Selene's altar. As I paid homage to the moon goddess, a particularly wrinkled lady came to me. She took my hand in a shaky grip with blue lines showing through speckled skin on the backs of her hands and asked, "I do not wish to insult my future empress, but have you ever met an Underhill Dweller or a Fire Forger, my dear?"

Her meaning had been clear enough. At the time, I hadn't enough worldly experience to lead a people I barely even knew. I'd harbored the same fears and turmoil as I dealt with my childhood friend's death and the council's demands that I follow Father's decree. But something beyond had called to me through small stones I'd worn about my neck. Soul stones, I'd named them, believing that they contained my parents' souls. To every one of my counselors' surprise, save for Solarynne Dawnsgale, when I took my oath, it had a provision allowing me to follow the calling. And so I abdicated my position as head of Nantai's first caste with confidence I would find Father and return him to the throne.

My travels beside Gensui Thalaj Northerngale, my first guard, afforded me friendships with many of the lower castes, the Tsinti wanderers, and even the casteless who dwelled within my beloved land. I met many people, both friend and foe, upon the Nantai shores, the Vesterisles, and the land of Ise beyond the Syrensea before I found Father.

Though I thought my quest had been fulfilled when I found him, there'd been a cost steeper than I'd wished to pay. In return for allowing me to take the emperor of Nantai from the Fey Realm, the Fey queen, Amare, demanded I leave behind the man I'd loved since I could recall having interest in such things—Thalaj. But for the fact that he refused me and instructed me to leave him, perhaps I would have chosen otherwise. In the wilderness of Ise, apart from my people of Nantai, the loss might have shattered my soul if he hadn't sacrificed himself willingly. I would have unleashed whatever power I could muster upon the mystical people. And had it not been for the duty I owed my people across the Syrensea, I'd have raged unto my own death against the Fey who'd kidnapped my father solely to gain my attention, the ones responsible for calling me from my home.

Had it only been my interests at stake, I may never have seen Nantai again.

Alas, service to my people and country had prevailed. Chambui of the yisun helped me cope with the loss of Thalaj and the new presence of my bonded companion. Then, alongside Hoaris, the yisun, and Misha and Kyr, I returned to the *Swell Mistress*. The land and sea voyage eastward had been easier than the journey west, but before reaching Nantai, the desolation of Kōkai became apparent. The City by the Sea had burned.

The blackened buildings and rising smoke shattered my soul. I had once believed my quest would be simple and filled with excitement. But over the seasons of travel, I learned. I grew, loved, and lost. Now, my home, my birthland, and my people begged with silent voices for salvation.

Near the charred City by the Sea, my companions and I had parted ways. Most of the sailors returned to the Vesterisles, save for two who traveled inland with Father, Misha, Kyr, and me. Hoaris and the yisun had gone north, intent on approaching

Gnoble Tenkara and the Frost Fighters to beg their assistance. Would they stand against my sister—who'd stolen the throne for herself for reasons I'd yet to discover?

As we had moved inland, rumors had spread like a plague, horrid tales of other cities and towns across my country falling to the same fate. Nantai lives erased. Marks I'd bear on my soul for all time. When we stopped in Safaia, the traders told us tales of the green dragon—Guindragon, as I came to know through Parū—and how she'd torched cities without regard for human life or preyed upon farm animals across the land. We encountered another decimated city's aftermath near Brennmor, the seat of King Isao and the Small Folk.

After leaving Brennmor and finding the Tsinti, we embarked upon Tsanseri's sky island and charted our course for Arashi and Stormskeep. For all we had seen, and as far as we could judge, word of our presence upon Nantai soil had not yet reached the empress. Though frustrating when I wished to speak with those I'd sent north on my behalf, the slowness with which news traveled in Nantai had been to my good fortune. Yet what we faced upon our return to Arashi left dread knotted in the center of my gut. I hadn't the training for strategy like my first guard.

Thalaj.

My heart sighed.

Trusting my father to Yankos's protection and Zofi's care upon Tsanseri's island in the clouds, Parū and I now approached the northern frostline near the Fire Forger city of Biei. Two Tsinti friends, Jorani and Baldeo, had gone ahead of us to find Gnoble Yuos Atith of the Fire Forgers, and Hoaris had gone in search of Gnoble Aljir Tenkara of the Frost Fighters. Our mission now, within a short ten days' time, was to find them, come together with a renewed cause, and develop a strategy. Little time remained before Tsanseri's sky island approached Arashi and Stormskeep, so, as there was no travel faster than on the wings of my dragon, Parū and I flew.

I rested well until Parū woke me from slumber, a foreboding sense of heaviness upon her soul.

Minikin, I am sorry. Her words surfaced in my mind only seconds before the odor— something yet again had been marked by flame. Mayhap it still burned.

Looking out through her eyes, trails of black smoke climbed from blackened rubble dotting the shore of the great frozen lake, and I knew. Beyond doubt, my heart plummeted with understanding of the terror the green dragon, Guin, had brought upon another of my cities. I grasped onto the only hope that seemed possible: more had survived here than we'd found in Kōkai.

Fifty-Five

The Fire Forgers and the Ruined City of Biei

PARŪ LANDED ALONG THE SHORE, at the mouth of the river Koya, northeast of Biei. Otarr was high in the sky. There were a few women and children washing household items in the clear, babbling waters running from beneath the ice of the frozen lake. Parū dropped the bundle with my clothing and touched down some distance from the people, careful of how they'd react to the presence of a fire-breathing beast after the damage done by one of her kind.

Sun-kissed younglings played in the cold water, squealing and splashing while the women washed soot from items they'd clearly salvaged from the fire's tongue. Who would have believed those born of fire would have suffered from it so? Before Parū had the opportunity to settle and allow the shift back to my person's form, a small girl with matted hair pointed and released a scale-shattering scream. Everyone at the mouth of the Koya stood and turned to face us. Regardless, we diminished, my naked form emerging from the dragon's. The mother of the youngling who'd called attention to me whispered to her son, and he splashed across the stream toward Biei's remains. He wove up a winding path toward the remnants of buildings—sets of metal spikes pointing toward the sky, the wooden walls reduced to ash and embers. For Nantai's people who could manipulate the flame, this destruction seemed the most ironic.

With my spine straight and chin lifted, I padded across the stony shoreline to the bundle of my supplies and dressed. The onlookers whispered and hissed and watched, and I struggled to hold my composure, to resist running to them and offering to help in whatever way I could. As I pulled a tunic over my head, someone called my name.

Water splashed, and I turned toward the familiar voice. On a sharp inhale, I asked, "Jorani?"

She barreled toward me, a grin on her face. She wore oiled leathers and tall boots to protect her from the cold while standing in the water. Those around her murmured and shot us wary looks, but I focused on the Tsinti swordswoman. "Where's Baldeo?"

"He's in the forest, felling trees with the others to help with the rebuild," she answered, slightly breathless.

I reached for her arm. "I haven't much time, and I need the help of the Fire Forgers. How long have you been here?"

She lowered her head. "We arrived on the eve the green dragon torched the city. We witnessed the entire thing from a half-day's ride away and arrived as Otarr retired for the day."

Sensing her dismay, I softened my voice. "Jorani, there was naught you could have done if you had been closer."

"That, I know," she replied. "But, Mairynne, there are so many dead."

Looking around, I said, "There are more alive here than there were in Kōkai when we happened upon the City by the Sea. And I believe the largest of Nantai's port cities had far greater numbers at the time of its destruction."

Jorani pursed her lips and nodded, my words clearly of little solace.

Well and so, one tragedy does not erase the weight of another. She had connections among these people, had been born in one of their villages. Would that I could spend time comforting her as my friend, but I had to return to Tsanseri's sky island before it reached Arashi. "I understand the comparison is of no consolation, and I wish I could offer more. Unfortunately, time is of import." My eyes flitted away with regret, and I swallowed as I took in the scene at the river and the ruins beyond. "Did your father survive? What of your uncle, Gnoble Yuos Atith?"

A commotion from the direction of Biei's ruins interrupted our conversation. Fire Forger guards charged forward, swords of all shapes and sizes in their hands.

"Jorani?" I asked urgently, "Did you find the Fire Forger gnoble? Did he survive?"

She kept her eyes on the guards, a regretful note in her voice as she answered, "Aye, and I suspect you'll see him shortly." Facing me, she grasped my hand. "There was naught I could do but try to reach you before the guards once the boy came with news of your arrival."

The guards crossed the river atop stones peeking above the water. In a single file, they leaped from the last stone onto the shore and approached me, each with their swords at the ready. I raised my hands into the air in a sign of surrender. As I intended them no harm, I meant to comply. "You'll go with me?" I whispered out of the corner of my mouth.

"I will," she answered.

Lifting my voice as the guards continued to surround me, I said, "There is no need for force; I will join you willingly. I wish to speak with your gnoble, and I mean the Fire Forgers no ill will. In truth, I only wish to help."

The woman who'd sent the boy to retrieve the guards spat into the water and sneered, "You wish us to buy your dung. You are naught but a beast in your heart. You carry the same evil as the green monster who took my husband."

The pain in her voice etched a new scar upon my soul, and I turned to her. I took a small step, but on the second, a sword snaked its way under my chin.

I raised my head away from the blade. "I am so deeply sorry for your loss, Lady . . ." I waited for her to provide her name, but she refused. I continued, "But truly, I mean the people here only prosperity. Many have lost their lives to Guin's foul breath, and though I have the power to breath fires as hot as she, I will not."

We will not, corrected Parū.

I know. Though I believe it best to leave the dragon intentions aside for now, I answered my Ryū.

The Fire Forger woman let out a grunt that said more so than words how little faith she put in what I had to say. "Take her to Phy Sovann," she barked, dismissing the scene and returning to her work. Others washing in the river followed her lead.

I began to ponder the differences between Mother's and Father's approaches to the world outside Arashi, and I wondered how much fear had driven my father's stance on sheltering his daughters from the rest of Nantai. Father had been a veritably great emperor, but how shortsighted had he been? He'd always been larger than life to me in my youngling naïvety. But as I faced the Forgers now, I mulled over how he may have better prepared me to rule Nantai. Knowing these people and their language would have been of great use as I faced this woman's ire. I had no idea who or what *brathan* was. By the bend in her sounds, the word hailed was from the language used in the north. Tasmynne had often referenced the *old tongue* when younglings gathered at her feet for the tales that came with the storyboards, namely the stories of the predatory nekodai that roamed the Iced Plains and the frozen waters of Kōdaina Kōri. Sadly, I'd never thought to pursue learning more of the words. I turned my head to the side to address the guard. "Are you Phy Sovann?"

His dark eyes held mine and a muscle ticked in his jaw.

I took his silence for assent. "I come to speak with your gnoble. Will you and your guards escort me to Yuos Atith?"

When he finally spoke, his words sounded merely dutiful. "It seems you and Chanthavy are in agreement." He tilted his head, indicating the widow in the stream, then lifted his gaze to another of the guards. "Din Arun, take the lead. Ny Chanthavy, you will come to provide your account of her arrival to the gnoble."

The guard, Din Arun, leaped into action, deftly crossing atop the stones. The woman huffed but handed her wares to another in the stream and joined us. A sword at my back urged me to follow the appointed guard across the stones.

Jorani assured me, "Directly behind you, my kōgō."

Chanthavy snorted at the use of the title, and Jorani reached for her weapons belt.

I extended an arm between the two women, keeping my focus on the widow rather than Jorani. "We have no need for swords. Ny Chanthavy only responds from fear. I'll not create more where none should exist." Turning, I followed the guards.

Others wore boots to protect their feet, but to mine, the stones felt smooth and cold, like walking on ice. Before my Ryū bond, shivers would have racked through my bones, but it bothered me little with my now elevated body heat.

Between six of the Fire Forger soldiers, Chanthavy, Jorani, and I climbed the winding path, then marched the streets of Biei. Our path snaked between decimated structures that'd once been part of a thriving culture. *How many had been homes?* I mused, mourning the losses. Given the Fire Forgers' magical affinity—how they could call fire forth and manipulate it much like I could call the wind—their core construction used forged metal as the bones of their buildings. Within the other cities of Nantai, structures favored solid wood or stone. In Biei, large spikes outlined the perimeters of each building at somewhat broad intervals. In truth, it surprised me that they used the talent so sparingly. Perhaps ore was simply less available than the wood they used to span the spaces in between the spikes. Further into the maze of streets, some Forgers cleaned the ash from stone floors while others repaired spikes that'd been damaged in the city's fall.

I stumbled when I became engrossed in one scene—an older Forger crouched beside his youngling, instructing him on how to call to his magic. Together, they pulled flames from a small forge nearby and blasted them upward along a corner pillar. Calling to the flame would be easy enough for the young one but manipulating it would require practice and precision. I yearned to watch for longer, this father passing on the skills.

Jorani chuckled and reached to steady me; we shared a laugh at my distraction. Deeper into Biei, we climbed constantly. The slope was steep enough that my breathing grew heavier, but I resisted calling upon magical aid. My body had grown stronger over the seasons I'd traveled, but the people here were heartier still . . . thicker with muscle than my longer and thinner limbs. They weren't as stout as the Stone Singers or the Underhill Dwellers, but within their leathers, the Fire Forgers' thighs and calves each had more significant curves than the Storm Sorcerers who inhabited Arashi.

Our guards led us near another group forging smaller metal brackets in quantity. The harmony struck me, the people working in concert to restore all they'd known before the devastation. They flashed glances as we neared and passed, but no matter what thoughts crossed their minds, they returned quickly to the task. These, too, were people I wanted to call my own—not as their empress, ruler, or one from a superior caste, but as Nantai and kindred folk. Clearly, they each held similar hopes and desires to my own and worked now for happier times. I sensed an inexplicable absence in the streets and felt certain they'd once been boisterous, more like the Tsinti, who danced and made merry around the fire at night, than those of my caste. It would surely be rare to find the Forgers sitting indoors after evening meal sipping fire-flower wine. Though this was the first time I had trodden the cobbled streets of Biei, it seemed a place for simplicity, jocularity, and an endless display of Forger skill. It felt, in a word, warm. I hoped to return one day within those happier times.

Did Karynne know the extent of the green dragon's deeds and the sorrow she had cast upon our homeland? And if so, did my sister support her first advisor in bringing this destruction? Heat swelled within my breast, and I sighed.

"What troubles you, Kōgō?" Jorani whispered.

"Do you sense the missing laughter here? That weighs heavy, along with the people who perished. Do your people's spirits seem to have burned to ash in the dragon's fire?" I asked. I hadn't tried to keep my voice quiet. If Chanthavy or the guards wondered where my heart lay, they should hear my words too. There, spread throughout the ruins, was yet another reason to see Guindragon and her companion, Imrythel, banished from Nantai.

And we will return Guin to Amare in the lands between, minikin, Parū said in response to my trailing thoughts.

Yes, Parū, but what of Imrythel? She is one of my people too.

Amare will see her reunited with your gods.

Is it not possible to return her to Nantai? Mayhap—

She has lived too many lives for a mortal being, Mairynne. Her return will not be possible.

Though reticent, I trusted Parū's wisdom in this. I dared not ask how her death would come to pass as it wasn't a person's place to meddle in the affairs of deities or even the Fey who seemed to exist somewhere between person and Gods. We continued to climb. Step after step, I wondered about the connection between Fey and the Triad, what foot they had in the heavens or the hells, and how Thalaj fared in this space between. I hoped against all hope that when I returned to Ise, they would welcome me again and allow me into the Fey Realm. If they would not, mayhap I'd become lost in the effort. Mayhap I'd become like Z, who had guided us through the jungles of Ise to the banks of the Seleucid River.

Bringing me back to the world outside my heart and soul, Jorani answered, "Aye. I do feel their loss. Have you been to Biei before this, Mairynne?"

I shook my head.

"It is colder here than I recall," Jorani said. Her observation struck an odd note, but before I could ask, she continued, "Despite the climate, it has always felt hotter in these streets given they work with fire upon the cobblestone. Notice there, how there is a channel built into the street stones?" She pointed. "And how distant the channel is from the fronts of the building frames?"

I lifted my gaze, measuring.

"Twenty long strides," Jorani offered, "and it is the same on both sides of each street. My people do not bring carts or steeds into the city. They forge and practice arts by wielding the flame between the culverts. And there, do you see that three-legged structure?"

I hadn't taken notice of them until she pointed, but at regular intervals, there were tripods with metal platforms atop. All were too narrow to be a building of any use, though they towered above the people's heads.

"Those are turrets for water storage and release in case one of the forgers loses control." She went on, pointing as she explained. "The Forgers released them all when the dragon breathed her fire, but the efforts mattered little."

I clung to every word, resting a hand on my friend's shoulder when she choked on the last.

Phy Sovann picked up the explanation where Jorani had abandoned it. "Pipes run from siphons at the great lake, as well as from the Koya and Shiabi rivers on either side of Biei."

"Fascinating," I breathed, then flashed him a smile. "There are so many other uses for the water system your people have devised. If only . . ." I trailed away as thoughts spun. What benefits this invention would bring to other cities throughout Nantai! And how would it pair with the force and power of the Sundai Falls in Arashi? Our people would be—no, could be—so much stronger together if only they shared their talents.

We passed more of the same as we continued our journey. People worked in groups. Some structures stood empty while clusters worked together, smaller communities within the whole. If time would only afford the opportunity, I craved time to spend learning the Fire Forger ways; but I'd come for a purpose and that seemed near as we approached what had been a circular building. A stack of fresh wooden planks lay to one side of the circle.

Within the ring, a group of Fire Forgers clustered around a makeshift table, several large timbers spanning across rough trestles. Upon the surface, they had sketched a map on the wood and used rocks to mark positions. This appeared the heart of the rebuilding efforts, where the leaders in Biei planned the work and dispatched their people to tackle various tasks. We climbed the steps.

Phy Sovann and Chanthavy moved ahead of Jorani, me, and the others and dropped to one knee.

The guard laid his sword gently on the ground and said, "Gnoble Yuos Atith, we have need of your direction."

The dark-haired Fire Forger I recalled from my ascension ceremony in the castle upon the High Cloud Court parted from the group and walked forward, his attention upon the people bowed before him. "Stand Sovann and Chanthavy," he said easily, holding both hands forward as if to help them up. Then his eyes lifted toward me. His face, the black of his irises, and his entire posture hardened. His subservient people forgotten, and his voice now as cold as the ice upon the frozen Kōdaina Kōri, he said, "Why have you come, Mairynne Evangale?"

I hesitated, wished I'd thought before this moment to ask Jorani how to best address the gnoble of the Fire Forger caste. I kept my eyes locked on Yuos Atith though the people who'd been working with him at the table moved closer. Amidst them, I believed Baldeo took a position to my right, but I fought the urge to look.

"Gnoble Atith," I began.

He bristled, nostrils flaring.

Jorani leaned closer and whispered, "Too familiar. Use his full name."

"My apologies, Gnoble *Yuos* Atith. I am still learning the ways of all of Nantai's children."

"I will ask you again, *youngling*, what are you doing in my city?" He spread his hands. "Your sister's *mercy* is evident enough, is it not? And the messenger boy told of how you bring another serpentine beast to our shores." His lip curled as if he might growl.

My blood heated, and in my anger over his sarcasm, Parū came close to the surface. My shoulders expanded; I glanced at my arm where scales began to shimmer; and my breath felt hot in my throat. The guards, as well as the men who'd been hovering over the table, drew swords and aimed them at me. All save one. I swallowed several times, still refusing to turn toward Baldeo.

Instead, I focused inward. *No, Parū,* I thought to her. *This is not the time.*

Chanthavy stammered, "Y-you see, Gnoble Atith, how she threatens to change now? She arrived as one of the Ryū, near the helpless people cleaning in the Koya. They wish to end us, these accursed Storm Sorcerers." As she spoke, her words had grown more confident, and when she finished, she spat on the stones at my feet.

I ignored the act and answered the gnoble, "As I said to your people along the river, I mean the Fire Forgers of Biei no ill will."

Yuos Atith threw his head back and scoffed disbelievingly. If possible, his eyes were even harder and colder and more coal-like when he returned his gaze to mine. "The actions of the Storm Sorcerers have proven contrary to your words."

I forced my knees to unlock and lowered into a crouch in the same manner as Phy Sovann and Chanthavy. Words from Karynne's mouth echoed in my mind: *Never forget, you are their empress, receiving your subjects. If you slip, they will take advantage.* I had to disagree. As their empress, I would be naught but their servant. They—Yuos Atith especially— needed to see me put their interests before my own.

This gave the gnoble pause, but he recovered himself with haste. "It is clear that the Evangales of Stormskeep do not wish my people the same prosperity as I once lifted up to you when you ascended to the Serpentine Throne. First, your sister and her dragon burn our town and our fields and leave us with nothing but standing spikes and the land, and then you come on her heels threatening to shift into a dragon yourself? Have the Evangales not scorned us enough?"

"Gnoble Yuos Atith," I began again, "you will have seen Selene's face wax and wane many, many times since I left the Nantai shores in search of my father, Tennō Atheryn Evangale."

The gnoble laughed and came closer. "That, youngling, is of little concern." His nostrils flared, then he ranted, "What that says to me is that you have brought home more of the hateful first caste. It tells me you are building your numbers and wish to demand more of my people than they can offer and still survive. No, that is not help. That is you strengthening your numbers. And that you have bonded with one of the Ryū yourself, you clearly intend to force your will on us no matter our concerns."

Chanthavy rolled her shoulders back, smirking.

Paying her no heed, I continued, "I wish nothing more than to help you and your people. To learn of your ways and change whatever harm my family has caused. That is why I came. Not to force more heartache upon you."

His charred eyes bore down into mine. "Your family has forsaken all we have stood for in Nantai since the Ryū Wars and the forging of the Throne. Why am I to believe any differently of you? Words are empty, *youngling*."

I hung my head, trying not to let his accusation and belittlement sear a hole within my soul. If a sword came down upon the back of my neck while I humbled myself before him, so be it. My eyes burned as I answered, "The only thing I ever wished was to continue the work my mother, Kōgō Noralynne Evangale, started. I want everyone to have a voice in Nantai—the casteless, the Tsinti, the Small Folk, and every caste. What my sister has done breaks me."

"I believed in you once, Mairynne Evangale. I won't make that mistake again." He turned and walked back to the table, waving a hand in the air behind him. How could he infuse so much loss, disappointment, and fury into those few words?

On a sharp inhale, he then commanded, "Chain her to the guardhouse near the shores of Kōdaina Kōri. Let the cold take her."

"Wait!" Jorani wailed.

In my periphery, Baldeo came to her side.

Remaining upon my knee, I held out a hand, motioning for the Tsinti to hold. Then I raised my voice to the gnoble's back. "What can I do to prove otherwise to you?"

Yuos Atith turned and paused. After long, silent, and tense moments, his lips pursed and twisted pensively until a small smile split his lips. "Use that dragon of yours to help us rebuild. We'll keep her chained and tethered close to the ground. I'll have chains of iron fashioned so that we can bind her snout and prevent the fiery breath. She can speed the process of felling trees to remake our homes." He raised a brow. "Rumor tells that iron prevents the companions from shifting between forms. Mayhap it will give us an equal defense to have the Ryū at our command."

Parū's soul twisted inside.

I bit down, held my breath, and willed her to remain calm. *We need their assistance.*

Chanthavy faced me, her darkling eyes satisfied with how her gnoble had turned the tide. "Your wisdom is as abundant as always, Gnoble Atith."

The leader paid her no attention as he continued, "In the evenings, when we rest from a long day's work, I can have your bonds removed and allow you to serve me personally. If I recall, I once vowed the service of the Fire Forgers to you as our empress. Yes . . . mayhap returning that very sentiment is what I need to trust in an Evangale once more."

Sensing naught but acerbic venom within his words, I snapped, "What of banishing the dragon who did this thing to your city?"

Atith laughed. "And you think you can do this?"

"You judge me—no, us—wrongly, Yuos Atith," I hissed.

He flourished a hand. "Have you faced it? Have you seen the terror of a people under attack by that beast? You are but a youngling yourself, and you believe you have enough power to banish that hateful green dragon?"

"You forget that I have sorcery of my own, that I can call upon the storm's magic. And how quickly you dismiss the fact that I, too, have a companion. Both of these—I will add—are tools I have *not* used when approaching your people. Yet still, you make assumptions about my character and wrongly place judgment upon me because of my blood relation to Karynne and the dragon you seem to believe is hers." Even as I said the words, I hoped my sister wasn't capable of such things. The motivation originated with Imrythel, and that is where I'd judge the guilt until facts proved otherwise. I had to believe Karynne's advisor had coerced her through some unknown means.

He turned from me then, clearly preparing to dismiss me to an unsavory fate at the hands of his guards. "I have little else to base judgment upon, but in the end, the protection of my people is my charge. You own something deadly within your body and poisonous to your soul. I only err on the side of caution."

"You err on the side of *fear*!" I wailed. "My companion's name is Parūdragon, and she has returned from the lands between to see Guin, the green dragon, removed from Nantai. She only wishes peace for our people, Fire Forgers included."

The gnoble turned so that he faced to my right, his eyes cutting sideways toward me.

I continued, "If my aid is what would prove my intentions to you and your people, I would choose to stay here. To serve you and your people for as long as you wished. You would have no need to hold us in bonds. But what we face now is larger than your people alone, and while you fear the dragon's fire breath, I fear what will happen across Nantai if I remain."

Atith leaned his head back and gazed into the sky.

I hoped that indicated he listened.

On I went, "As I kneel before you here, there are others gathering and crossing Nantai and marching toward Stormskeep. Within less than a fortnight, I must also visit the Frost Fighters before I can return to the people who have already sworn me their support. You may not believe in my strength, but my dragon possesses as much power as the other. And know this, *Gnoble*. I must be there when my allies arrive in Arashi as I am the only one equipped to fight the green dragon who terrorizes Nantai." I took a breath and shot him a challenging stare. "I came to beg your help."

FIFTY-SIX

The Fire Gnoble's Judgment

GNOBLE YUOS ATITH LOOKED UP then, beyond me to the guards, and nodded.

The *schling* of swords brushing against their scabbards sounded behind me, and I fought an urge to close my eyes. My father had always said, *Closing your eyes, Daughter, will not change the truth before you*. Metal clanged and two sets of strong hands hoisted me to my feet. Heeding the wisdom in Father's words, I locked my gaze on Yuos Atith.

The gnoble said, "A hint, young one, mention of the Frost Fighters in Biei will help your cause little. You'll understand that I must consider the matter." He waved a hand to the guards in a proceed motion.

Chanthavy moved closer to Atith, still wearing a grin. I grimaced. Mayhap she'd won this match, but the game was far from complete.

My captors turned me from the gnoble, and Din Arun approached. Regret furrowed his brow as he spread a chain between his hands, a metal cuff on either end. My heart began to pound in the hollow at the base of my neck. I searched the faces of all who had gathered. I'd believed I'd made a small connection with Phy Sovann. Despite that he'd joined in with Jorani's description of Fire Forger ways on the path from the river, he bowed his head now, dutifully deferring to his leader.

Give me control, minikin! The manacles that person holds will not fit about my limbs.

I couldn't. Giving over to the dragon they feared so much seemed the least sagacious of my options. *Atith begged our help, Parū. I have no wish to battle him or his people. If I give over to anger and wrath now, that will only prove his point. We have a day or two. I'll give him that to think.*

The Tsinti Baldeo held his position, portraying no thought or emotion across his now-bearded face. In truth, it reminded me of when the scouting party had captured Thalaj and me in the southern reaches of the Yubar Forest. Given the wandering folk had held Thalaj and me hostage within their caravan for the passing of several moons, I couldn't expect more or less of the man. He would only show loyalty to whomever Jorani decided deserved the allegiance. And Atith's actions seemed perfectly in line with any customs he'd learned as a wanderer.

Resigned though I was becoming to my captivity, it shocked me when Jorani rushed past. "Uncle, do not do this. Baldeo and I have come here on behalf of Mairynne. Please hear us out."

As much as possible, I glanced over my shoulder, trying to witness their exchange. Alas, there was little I could view.

"You and your Tsinti friend remain here. As a favor to my brother, Yuos Chakara, I will hear your plea," answered Yuos Atith. "Take her from my sight."

My captors pushed my arms forward and Din Arun deftly fastened the manacles around each wrist.

Within my chest, my heart sank, a fire diminishing inside. Suddenly, for the first time since I'd ventured into the jungles in Ise and before I'd leaped into the fey pool, I felt a chill. My companion's fey magic had faded.

Parū said, *There is naught I can do to help you now.*

I know, I answered, lowering my head. *All we can do now, my Ryū, is hope.*

Two guards held me at the elbows as we moved down the hill toward the great frozen lake. More frequently than when we'd climbed to the highest point in Biei, Fire Forgers along the streets stopped their work and turned to watch, whispering to one another. None approached or spoke at a volume I could understand. In our trail, the whir of flame resumed repeatedly once we had passed.

Upon the shores of Kōdaina Kōri, there stood the remnants of a building I assumed had been the prison. I had no name for the guard who fastened my chain to one of the spikes sticking from the ground. This all passed in silence, and when they had me secured, all guards dispersed save for Phy Sovann. He pulled a whetstone from the purse at his waist, sat on a large rock, and began honing his blade.

I watched him in silence for a long time before I asked, "Do you believe I mean to harm anyone here?"

"It matters little what I believe," he answered as he lifted the blade and eyed the edge.

My voice wavered as cold crept further into my bones. "W-what *everyone* believes matters to me," I countered.

Phy Sovann placed his sword and the stone beside the boulder and stood. He moved behind me, then returned with an armful of wood, which he arranged in a small tripod nearby. He then retrieved a stone from his purse and walked to the nearest metal spike. He struck the stone against the metal once. Sparks flew. He cupped his free hand and struck the stone again. This time, when the clash ignited, he made a pulling motion with his arm between where he'd created the spark and the small tripod of wood. Flames leaped and arced, following the path he directed toward the fire's fuel, and in the next moments, the wood ignited.

"Incredible," I breathed, moving a smidgen closer to the flames.

Returning to his sword and stone, he chuckled. "Not so much. That is normal. It is what my people do . . . the essence of our magic lives in the spark."

"Much like mine lives in the wind," I mused. "I always thought Fire Forgers created fire."

"No," he said with a shake of his head. "As far as I know, there is no magic in this world that creates, only that which manipulates."

It made sense as I needed the connection to the skies to call the wind and a water source to cause it to rain. I'd never considered asking as much of Thalaj. "What of the Frost Fighters? They create cold, right?" No longer certain of the statement, my brow furrowed.

Phy Sovann grimaced, and his voice sounded dead when he answered, "I know little of the frost magic the cold people wield."

I winced at the hollow tone of his words. Recalling Gnoble Yuos Atith's advice, I offered, "My apologies, Sovann. I meant no offense. May I call you Sovann?" The last, I asked in afterthought.

"Aye. You may." He nodded, seeming to accept my amends easily. "It is an old rivalry, and I shouldn't react so. But it is hard when you've been raised to believe they are your enemy." He swiped the blade against the whetstone again. "Regardless, my answer is the same. Theirs is a magic I do not understand, though I imagine it works in an opposite manner to mine. In some way, it must remove heat to leave only the cold."

An image of blue lightning dancing along Thalaj's scimitynes surfaced in my mind. Lightning and cold. Though I couldn't recall a time when he'd called lightning from the skies or frozen anything in abundance. Questions twisted and turned within, but they were a matter to learn of in more peaceful times.

"Can I ask you again," I started, "if you truly feel I seek destruction upon the Fire Forgers?"

Sovann sighed, his attention remaining on the blade's edge. "I do not, but it only matters what Yuos Atith finds. I do not wish to own the burdens he bears, so I will follow what orders I am given and go about my life."

"Sovann?" I called and waited for him to look up. "If you believe Atith's burden is great, imagine the burden I bear for all people of Nantai. I believe any word you could offer to your leader may help."

"Mayhap, but there is no way to know as I am now assigned as your guard, away from whatever court they hold." He pointed uphill with the blade.

I shivered then against the cold. With the iron about my wrists dampening Parū's inner heat, I could no longer withstand the cold of the north. My toes felt numb and shivers ran over my body in waves. The fire Sovann had constructed helped some. Yet my fingertips and the end of my nose now felt ice hardened as well. I watched the Fire Forger work, trying not to focus on how my exposed skin began to ache. At length, I ventured, "I have made no attempts to escape. If I vow to go nowhere, to remain with you here and await your leader's decrees—whatever those may be—will you consider removing the iron from my wrists?"

Regret shown in his eyes as he peered over from the blade.

Needing no voiced answer, I asked, "Could you build the fire larger then? Or mayhap find a blanket?"

He sloughed his outer coat and wrapped it about my shoulders. Then, before returning to his chore, he lifted a hand. Answering his call, the fire flared. I relented, waiting with him in silence and relishing the increased warmth. At regular intervals, he added wood and stirred the flames higher, inquiring how I fared.

Otarr crossed overhead while he continued the routine. When he set aside the sword and unsheathed the knife at his hip, I asked if he played dice—anything to pass the time.

But Sovann shook his head. "I would not have the first idea where to find the marked bones after everything burned."

I pinched my lips and gave a single nod. "Do you have family, Sovann?"

"Aye." The corner of his mouth lifted in a half grin. "A wife and three younglings."

His smile was infectious as he spoke, and my own bloomed in response. "And they all survived?"

"They did. My Phy Boupha is caring for our youngest, Piseth, near the cold spring." His smile faded then, replaced by worried lines between his brows. "He suffered many burns when we lost our home."

I lifted my chin and said a prayer to Atun, thanking him for preserving Sovann's family and asking that the All-Seer watch over Phy Piseth as he healed. Sovann's gaze flitted to mine in silent thanks, and he returned to his sword.

And so, I waited. The sun reached the apex in the sky, and I finally, blessedly, felt warm and allowed the coat to sag from my shoulders. The woman, Chanthavy, brought food. She passed a plate with a leg of some beast, a crust of bread, and some greens as a side to Sovann, then handed me a bowl that contained little more than warmed oats. Regardless, I devoured what was offered.

When Otarr neared the horizon, I pulled Sovann's coat tighter and crept closer to the flames. As gloaming started to steal the light from the day, a hopeful signal finally arrived.

Mayhap my fate had been decided.

Jorani ran down the hill, smiling.

STILL MANACLED, BUT CONTINUING to make my compliance evident, I climbed the hill again between Jorani and my warder, Sovann. My feet, unshod as I'd favored since forging the bond of companionship, had numbed since we'd left the side of the small fire. Within the circular foundation overlooking the city of Biei, the gnoble, Baldeo, and several unfamiliar faces awaited my return. Jorani went to the large Tsinti's side.

Baldeo placed an arm around her shoulder and looked at me.

He smiled.

Tension fled from my shoulders and my heart soared. In that simple and rare smile, his message couldn't have been more clear. Whatever Gnoble Yuos Atith would announce would be in my favor. Though it seemed tiny and so much remained before me, this moved us one step closer. I wanted to thank him before I'd even heard his decree, but I held my tongue and waited.

The gnoble held out a hand to a man at his side who resembled him in many ways. "Yuos Chakara, my brother, believes his daughter returns to her people on an honorable mission. She and her man, Baldeo, have told us of your first encounter with the wandering folk alongside your mixed-blooded gensui."

Though it was hard to discern if his animosity was because of the intermingled castes or that Thalaj had been half Frost Fighter, I bit down on my tongue to squelch my objection to the slight. What difference did it make that his mother was Storm Sorcerer while his sire was Frost Fighter? For all I cared, Thalaj could be casteless and he'd mean the same to me.

Clearly I hadn't hidden my reaction enough, because Atith raised his brows momentarily before he continued, "Yuos Jorani shared a near unbelievable tale of your journey across the Syrensea where you lost your man and returned with a dragon." He placed his hands on his hips and quirked a brow. "It is too fantastic to believe, if you ask me to speak plainly."

A protest to the fantastic nature lodged in my throat. After all, the story held naught but truth. Yet the tales were indeed much like the ones told to younglings for the mere sake of excitement and adventure. Sensing more wisdom in silence, I nodded my understanding.

Atith continued, "If we survive, and mayhap if we do not, the bards will have much to sing of, young Mairynne Evangale."

My teeth chattered as I inhaled, and I began haltingly, "Gn-Gnoble Yuos A-Atith"—thankfully, my voice strengthened with use—"as I have remained with your guard Sovann throughout this day and have not called upon my sorcery to refute my status as your captive, is it evident enough that I do not wish to slip from your grasp? I wish to work with you and your people, and I have need of you as well. Will you release my hands from these bonds so that we may speak as people with shared interest rather than as captor and captive?"

He looked to the man who'd held me captive for the day with a question, and it renewed my faith in these people when Sovann answered, "There is little risk in allowing her freedom from the cuffs and chain."

Atith considered. "She has made no move toward manipulation or escape?"

Sovann lifted his chin. "She has not. She has shown interest in my family and our people. She asked the same question of me you ask now . . . if I believe she brings harm to the Fire Forgers." Sovann looked over at me, then back to his leader. The knot in his throat bobbed before he straightened and answered, "I do not. And I do not wish to go into any battle resembling the dragon wars of the bards' songs. I believe she may offer hope where we might otherwise suffer."

"What convinces you of such things, Issō Phy Sovann?"

This question held a charge to him in his official capacity as a leader within Gnoble Atith's guard, and I sensed his answer would be a testament to his duty. If his answer proved falsely here, Yuos Atith wouldn't hesitate to evict him from his station among the Forgers and send him into the wild.

"Sovann," I whispered, "I do not expe—"

"I know," he hissed. Then he held his head high and said to the gnoble, "I stand by my words. She has concern for us, and we would do well to listen to her requests. While she flew north on dragon's wing, she did not alert us to her presence with destruction. No. It was only that we had people from Biei working within the cool waters of the Koya River at the moment that we knew a dragon had landed near our city. The other . . . the green one . . . never spoke to our people and never landed upon our soil. It only loosed fiery breath and rendered Forgers like the woman Ny Chanthavy widows. Her husband, Ny Boran, did not deserve his fate, nor did my son Phy Piseth deserve the burns that he will wear all his days. And Mairynne Evangale does not uphold those losses as honorable. She believes none of our people should suffer so. She offered thanks to the Triad when we spoke of how my family survived even though the smallest of my younglings will wear burn marks upon one side for the remainder of his days.

"If she brings justice on our behalf, I will risk my family, my home, and—yes—my position as second in command to the Fire Forger gensui to help in that cause."

At some point during his words, I'd turned to him. Tears came to my eyes at hearing his sentiment. I touched my forehead, chin, and heart and mouthed, "Thank you."

A number of torches encircled the gnoble as the others gathered, shining light upon the city plan still laid across the makeshift table. Yuos Atith cleared his throat and said, "Very well, release her."

When Sovann released the iron cuffs from my wrists, a surge of heat rushed through my limbs as if I'd been transported in the span of a heartbeat to the Vesterisles or the Copper Coast. The searing heat of companionship heated my cheeks. My feet and fingers tingled as I wriggled and curled them to rid the awakening sensation of pins and needles. Then, there was Parū. I hadn't felt so far distanced from her since before the bonding, and to have her consciousness surge back to life within me relieved me in a manner for which I had no description. The only satisfaction I could fathom as comparable would be to have Thalaj back at my side. That remained yet another journey to be had.

One day. Not soon enough, but one day . . .

Yuos Atith, without turning in my direction, commanded. "Come and let us discuss what brings you north, Lady Evangale."

It wasn't kōgō, but it sufficed. I stepped lightly over the ash-covered earth toward the table, relishing the twitch of each muscle as it pumped hot blood through my body. I walked carefully to the other side of the table and appraised the map in detail. The group watched as my finger traced the path I'd walked through the streets from the Koya River to where I now stood. "Please know, Gnoble Yuos Atith, that if I were not necessary to stop the bleeding at the heart of Nantai that I would stay here and help you until every last building appeared as if the dragon's breath had never touched your city."

Baldeo came to my side, placing a strong hand on my shoulder. Then, to the gnoble, he offered his reassurance, "She would." Simple and gruff, but no more seemed necessary.

Atith harrumphed. "Words are voiced cheaply. They cost you nothing."

"Well and true," I replied. "Though I have nothing to offer at the present aside from my word and my honor behind it. To you now, I vow that other castes, including my own, will help you rebuild. When this is done, you will have more than the numbers remaining among your people to recover your city. I promise that you and I together will see Biei returned to her glory."

He folded his arms over his chest and gave a single nod. "Well and so. About the other . . . help me understand what strategy you propose."

FIFTY-SEVEN

Claws of the Nekodai

SOMETIME LATER, DARKNESS HOVERED IN the skies above. The torches encircling our gathering created a dome in the darkness, the sky beyond blacker than most nights. In the legends, the stars always shone brighter in the north and cast a bright glow upon the snow on the Iced Plains of Nantai, but I couldn't see those now. I couldn't see aught beyond the circle of people cloistered in the one-time seat of the Fire Forger gnoble. Ny Chanthavy had left us after Phy Sovann freed me from the shackles and Gnoble Yuos Atith made his decree. The woman's eyes had been full of loss and regret, and at the bottom of the grand steps, she had locked eyes with me one final time and spat in the dust before striding into the darkness.

Sovann had offered a regretful smile and said, "She's a good woman. Hurting, but a good woman nonetheless."

Din Arun brought a map forward and spread it on the table, this one larger than the plan for Biei's rebuild and showing the length of Nantai from the Iced Plains in the north to the Narrows in the South just before the neighboring country, Baiu. It also depicted the breadth of Nantai from Yōtei to the Syrensea and the Isle of Himitsu in the northeastern sea where the Unseen were rumored to train.

Those remaining moved closer, and Sovann produced a string from his pocket. He measured the distance from the city of Biei to Arashi in several different directions. At length, he pointed and said, "This time of year, our best option is to follow the Mu River to the Grasslands, then west to the mountain pass in the north. From there, we can follow the western edge of the Rausu Mountains where they meet the Yubar all the way to Arashi."

Atith issued a grunt, seemingly in agreement with his guard's assessment. "How many people can we spare? What rations will we need? And what of those who remain behind?"

Jorani, Baldeo, and I watched and listened as the discussion went well into the night. When it had run its course, Jorani and Baldeo accompanied me upon my return to the mouth of the Koya where we said farewells. The moon goddess, Selene, had averted her eyes completely and would slowly turn to watch over Nantai over the next several nights, but I hadn't the time to wait. By the time her light could glimmer upon Parū's pearlescent scales, I hoped to have found the Frost Fighters and be well on my way back to Tsanseri's island in the sky. We only spoke a few words in parting, then I shifted to dragon form and Parū took to the skies.

She hunted before we began the journey further into the Iced Plains. In preparation for the cold and possibly long flight, she needed to restore the strength the iron had leeched from her essence. Afterward, we followed the cliffs along the coast of the great lake deeper into the frozen landscape. I had little hopes of finding a city like we had with the Fire Forgers. The annals maintained in Stormskeep told how the people who lived this far north maintained distance from one another, choosing instead to live in small nomadic clans that could easily thrive in smaller caverns within the ice cliffs. They didn't live solely underground, so they hadn't developed features for navigating in darkness such as the Underhill Dwellers' incandescent eyes. Instead, they roamed the Plains by day, camping in different caverns each night, trading furs with other clans, and sharing any news or stories within their caste. After Father had read to us the stories of how the Frost Fighters lived, my sisters and I had built caves within our bedchambers and pretended to be from a lower caste. It had seemed naught more than pretend then, but the thought of them being *lower* now turned my stomach.

Not lower, only different, I thought. Mayhap I can rewrite the stories to say as much.

Parū grumbled and purred. *Your way of thinking is kind, minikin, but consider how that may erase all you've learned about the caste hierarchy.*

What do you mean, Parū?

All knowledge is well worthwhile. Even that which seems hurtful may teach your younglings valued lessons. But also, with such knowledge, you must teach them to think on the flaws within the tales.

My thoughts twisted, the urge to defend my stance ripe. But her words held a spark of truth and gave me pause. Regardless, as we traveled, I hoped there would be a hint of the clans, fires mayhap, or simply movement of color upon the vast vision of white that lay before us.

I feared, however, the Frost people would hold as much animosity toward my dragon as had the Fire Forgers, so I thanked Atun for the clouds that rolled in and blanketed the skies during our first night of northward travel. Grayness lingered the following day and allowed us to fly within the haze with little risk of someone upon the ground taking notice. Our search continued without pause, and to our ill fortune, the land remained barren for as far as could be seen. Eventually, darkness fell again. I began to worry over our most scarce resource—time. I needed to find Hoaris if not Gnoble Lady Aljir Tenkara to secure their support and send them south to Arashi.

Parū and I continued our path well into the second night. Toward dawn, the clouds broke, revealing bright stars and blue-green lights dancing above. Certainly, if any gazed upward, the lights would outline our form. Hoping for more complete darkness later, after Otarr made another daily pass, we found a wall of ice that jutted out slightly, creating a small shelter. I needed the dragon's warmth, so we remained in Parū's form and curled into a ball beneath the overhang. The white of snow, the ice wall to one side, and the similar coloring of Parū's scales should obfuscate our presence. I released the anxiety that had riddled my mind as Parū had flown. Hidden in the small alcove in relative safety, we both found sleep.

A sound, somewhere between a purr and a roar, stirred me from sleep.

Be still, minikin, Parū said.

Remaining in place isn't under my will, I answered, *you have command of our physical form.*

I clamored to peer through her eyes, to find the source of the rumble, and when I saw, the world stopped. If possible, I would have gasped or hissed breath through my teeth, mayhap scrambled backward. Thankfully, in current form, Parū had a calmer state of mind.

She remained utterly still. She hadn't lifted her head, only watched as a cat the size of her prowled toward us. The silver-white fur was thicker around its neck, and it probably outweighed my dragon by half her weight. A nekodai. Drawings from the story boards in the citadel—the ones designed to warn younglings of the dangers in our world—flashed in my mind. Of crimson blood dripping from white fur and splattered across the snow.

Of the three Hallowgales, the clergy of the Triad, Tasmynne had been the most bard-like. Younglings, myself included, had gathered in the citadel about the boards, listening to her bring the stories to life. The nekodai—large white cats with venomous claws that roamed the north—had been the most terrifying of the stories. They'd featured in my nightmares each time the priestess told the tale of the young couple who wandered onto the ice and fell victim to one of the beasts.

Whatever you do, beware of the claws! I thought urgently to Parū as I transformed into a terrified babe, cowering within and watching for the horror I expected to follow.

Parū waited, still and hopeful she'd blend in with the shades of gray and purple in the ice. But the cat held its massive head low, muscles in the shoulders shifting and bunching with each placement of a mammoth white paw. My soul trembled. I feared the cat didn't need to sight its prey to sniff out the opportunity for a meal that'd keep it well-sated for days to come.

The rumbling stopped. In its place, silence deafened the air. The only sound remaining . . . a whoosh-whoosh of blood pumping faster and faster. Parū's. Mine. The nekodai took another step forward. Parū tensed, readying herself. Through the window of her eyes, I searched for an escape. But it seemed the giant cat had us trapped.

What will you do? I thought to my Ryū. *Fire breath?*

Only if necessary, minikin. I do not wish the creatures of Nantai harm other than what I must eat for sustenance. For that I give many thanks. But if the predator attacks, I may have no choice.

Golden eyes with dark slits, rimmed in black, fixated upon us. Its nose twitched, scenting us. Another white paw lifted, flipped, and pressed hard into the snow under the nekodai's weight.

Parū moved, positioning her weight on her feet and grasping the ground with the claws at the bend of her wings. Her arrow-tipped tail reared back with scales raised along the spine like barbs—at the ready.

The nekodai lifted its head, opened massive jaws, and let out a roar that shook our bones. Top and bottom fangs opened like claws ready to grapple. Saliva dripped from the tips of the upper fangs and drooled from the cat's jowls. Hot breath rushed over Parū's scales like a summer's gale.

Parū held her head low, muscles bunched. Still. Watching. Waiting.

The nekodai crouched. Weight shifted to its back paws.

Parū lifted and reared back with her tail, crouching on her back claws.

The cat pounced. Parū leaped sideways, swinging her tail. Her scales slashed across the nekodai's face. With the overhang, she couldn't fly and walking for a dragon was too slow. She couldn't make it far and turned back to keep the cat in her line of vision. Blood dripped from the gash under one eye, the red almost appearing black as it soaked into the white fur. But as it dripped from the chin, it turned bright against the snow.

The cat circled to our right, moving Parū back toward the wall. It lunged again. Parū feinted to the other side, but the cat's body wrapped over the spot above her wing. She twisted onto her back and writhed under the nekodai's weight until she slithered free. Clamoring to her feet, heat started to rise in her chest and throat.

For all its bulk, the cat twisted in midair. Impossible agility bent its spine until it landed upright again, facing us with a snarl. In a breath's span, it had us cornered against the ice wall once more.

I was helpless. Any thoughts or words to my dragon now would distract her. I wanted to call a storm. But I had no form. If I could use my sorcery from within Parū, it was a skill I had yet to learn. I needed to help. But there was naught I could do save watch, as if glass separated me from the action.

The nekodai swiped a paw larger than a person's head with claws extended and reminiscent of Thalaj's scimitynes. Upon her feet, Parū slid right. Her wings flailed as she pulled back and away, balance faltering. The cat roared and jabbed with the other paw toward her underside, venomous claws spread wide. The dragon snaked away for a third time, and a clang echoed off the ice wall at our backs. A claw against scale. Within, Parū fretted more with every slash, bite, and push. I frantically sent my consciousness over her body where the cat connected, relaxing only a bit when I'd assured myself it hadn't penetrated—safe from the poison for the moment.

Parū expanded her chest, pulling in air, kindling the fiery breath. The giant cat backed away and prowled to and fro before us, always keeping our form in view of one yellow hungry eye. Parū fell forward, the claws at the bend of her wings stabilizing her body upon the ground. The temperature climbed in my dragon's chest.

When the nekodai lunged again, Parū opened her mouth. Sizzling and hissing sounded as she pushed fiery breath between her jaws. The first exhale only sent a lick of flame, but it was enough to put the cat into a retreat. At a safer distance, it crouched, shoulders bunching together and eyes turning amber-hard . . . apparently measuring what would happen the next time it attacked. Within those eyes, I read calculation more than I would have thought possible for the feral predator. It seemed more than simply hungry. There was determination there that spoke of something more vital than food. My soul trembled.

Parū inhaled again.

The cat roared.

My dragon aimed, narrowing her eyes and opening her lower jaw. Smoke trailed from her nostrils. A sound like the striking of flint with steel echoed from her throat.

The nekodai pounced.

Parū breathed, pushed from the depths of her chest. A wave of orange and blue flame billowed from between her jaws, and for the tiniest of moments, I imagined the space between my ears burning as flames seared my throat. The cat bounced right, around the fire cloud. The flames passed without contact, but I smelled singed hair as the nekodai crashed into Parū.

Everything spun.

White. Gray. Ice Blue.

Freezing cold hit upon Parū's back, her wings.

She rolled, and I tried to make sense of the scene before Parū. As she faltered and fumbled in a wild attempt to stand, the landscape shifted and jerked. The cat circled. But there was something behind the nekodai. Men, perhaps? Parū grasped onto the ground with one back claw and righted herself. Her vision winked in and out of blackness, but yes, through the window of her eyes, there were blurry people-like forms beyond the giant cat. Between Parū's heavy-lidded blinking, the image formed. They held spears at the ready. And then the image vanished as Parū snaked her head around to peer at her side.

Crimson liquid flowed over white, pearlescent scales. Her life's blood dripped onto the fresh snow below.

Every sight and sound faded.

The darkness became absolute, but I held on to consciousness. Parū had fallen, and our form was shifting. Ever so slowly, I felt her diminishing and the snow upon my side chilling my body more and more. I shivered, tried to breathe, to scream. Numbness flowed over my limbs. Cold? Poison? The nekodai had connected with her side when it'd plowed into her. I—we—hadn't felt the searing pain under her wing until . . . Again and again, I blinked, tried to regain vision.

Shouts sounded somewhere near.

A growl.

Grunts.

A roar.

More grunting.

I blinked. Light finally started to appear. A blur of white, darkening and brightening.

"Mairynne!" someone called.

Or mayhap I imagined it, wished in vain for someone to save us.

I gathered breath as the light darkened again and whispered, "Hoaris?"

Fifty-Eight

The Wiser Path

BELLOWING, I FOLDED AT THE waist and sprang from the cold, flat bed. A nostril-searing stench had ejected me from sleep. The burn strangled my voice so that it sounded foreign to my ears. I raised a hand to my throat, the raspy outcry more from the memory of the nekodai attack than from pain. Yes, a zing pulled at my right side, tight and numb, but it didn't hurt. My eyes remained bleary, watering as I waved away the healer's hand and coughed. "What is that?"

Once I'd swiped away the tears, the distancing form of the healer became clearer. Slender with dark hair trimmed neatly at the gray collar, he moved to the table on the far side of the sterile room. "Spirits of hartshorn." Even his voice held no warmth. "Once the antidote took effect, your wounds sealed over almost immediately." He turned, an eyebrow raised, questioning. Dressed in gray almost the color of the barren white walls and with both hands on the table at his back, he waited.

I narrowed my eyes. In the three heavens, what could he expect me to say? Whoever rescued me had clearly seen my transformation from Ryū into my human form, and certainly they had said as much to this healer when delivering me. What answers did this smug healer believe I held? I swiped the sheet from my waist and lifted my tunic—one cleaner than any I still owned. Peering at my side, four silvery white lines crossed my otherwise unmarred skin from rib to hip. I carefully replaced the cloth over my midriff and snapped my head back to the healer. "How long have I been here? And unconscious? How did I get here? And who are you?"

If possible, the man's quirked brow crept even higher and the other dropped in scrutiny, all of this ire dancing above eyes slanting in a way that reminded me of Thalaj—my protector and heart's companion. I swallowed before allowing his name to echo through my mind, but the half-thought silenced me on the spot.

"I am Sentei Besso Ken'ichi." He lowered his eyes, resigning himself to a kindness necessary to care for others. "The hunters tracking the nekodai who attacked you brought you here, but you've only been recovering for a single day. Quite miraculous by any healing standards I've ever known. Though your elevated body heat would still suggest some malady remains."

My heat. Of course. I focused inward, searching. *Parū? Are you there?*

I waited.

Parū? Please, you cannot leave me now.

I waited, my heartbeat rising into my throat. My eyes stung.

Parū! I veritably screamed inside.

Mmmmmrrrmm, she finally replied.

I breathed a long sigh of relief and began calculating time. We had three days remaining which would give us only enough time to speak with the Frost Fighter gnoble and spend two days in rapid flight back to intercept Tsanseri's Cloud Court before they reached Arashi. That was assuming . . .

"Have I reached the seat of Gnoble Tenkara?" I asked.

Ken'ichi remained where he was, silent and contemplative.

I reached down, untangled my feet from the sheet, and stood. The room spun, then righted itself. The sentei merely observed, making no move to steady me, but when I took one step forward, he grabbed a board with papers attached from nearby and scribbled some observation near the bottom.

I moved in measured steps around the bed toward him. "Do you know who I am, Sentei Ken'ichi?"

"Aye, I do. And as you seem to be steady on your feet, I believe it is time for you to leave this place. Go back to southern Nantai and leave my people to roam peacefully over the Iced Plains."

"Are those the words of your gnoble, Sentei Ken'ichi?"

With a huff, he dropped the board haphazardly back onto the table. "I do not need the word of Gnoble Tenkara to know how my people feel about such fearsome beasts . . . especially those emerging from the Fey Realm."

"If that be truth in your words, was it not a simple solution to allow me to die by the nekodai's poison? It would have been a natural death between beasts, and you would have been a hero among your superstitious people." I took one step closer.

His eyes darted, seeking escape. His knuckles whitened where he gripped the table, and I smelled something sour but sweet upon the air.

Nostrils flared, I sucked air through my nose and deeply into my lungs, all the while peering confusedly at the man. Yet I couldn't recognize the odor. *Parū? Do you . . .*

Yes, minikin, our bond deepens. 'Tis why you recognize the scent of fear upon the healer.

I closed my eyes and expanded my chest, drawing in more of the delicious sensation. Surprisingly, Ken'ichi didn't move as the smell imprinted itself upon my brain. "I am smaller than you, Sentei, and I have no weapons. Why do you fear me?"

His jaw worked. Was that an attempt to sort through his stupefied thoughts? I smiled, feeling something sinister pull at the corners of my mouth.

Parū grumbled inside, *It is well that he does not flee in the face of his fear. Such strength shows steel within his soul. Heed that strength, minikin, and resist this temptation.* Her words were measured, disapproving.

I believed her with my heart and soul, but I also needed to know if Guindragon had reached this far north. The lure of his fear held power over me, and I used it to my advantage. Taking another step forward, I dropped the smile and pressed for a reply. "I have asked two questions that have gone unanswered. Must I resort to other measures?"

"No, no," he shook his head. "No. Please. I just want—"

"It matters little to me in this moment what *you* want," I declared, stepping once more toward Ken'ichi.

Be careful, minikin. Do not let his fear intoxicate you. I chose you because I believed you had the strength to resist the darker temptations. Take a step away.

Gritting my teeth, I thought to my dragon, *Not until he provides an answer.*

His voice trembled. "Healers take an oath to become sentei. We are bound to do no harm and provide every effort to heal any person requiring attention." He straightened, gaining strength when he found his voice. Clearly, his words acted as a reminder to himself of his purpose, and I respected the faith he held in his life's chosen path. A faith for which he would sacrifice his very well-being. The sweetly sour smell ebbed ever so slightly.

With my next step, I put more distance between us. But I would give him no room to avoid my questions. "And Gnoble Aljir Tenkara?"

"I'm afraid her caravan departed last night after your wounds began knitting themselves back together. While her attendants packed up, she argued for hours with the man who carried you here."

She'd gone? I made for the door.

"Wait. Where are you going?" Ken'ichi said.

"She has only a day on me by foot. I haven't much time." I stopped and scanned the room. Where were my clothes—no, my pack and my boots? I could deal with the soft tunic and pants, but Parū's claws were large and it would be troublesome to hold the loose garments. "Where are my things? I need to find Tenkara before it's too late." A cabinet stood near the door. I crossed the room and flung the door open to find naught but glass phials clinking and canisters rattling with labels resembling Sentei Rivergale's assortment at the healing house in Arashi.

Then, finally, the thought struck me. Tenkara had been arguing with a man. Why? I whirled to face Ken'ichi. "Who brought me here?"

"Hoaris Nishikara and his Stone Singer yisu." Ken'ichi veritably spat the epithet.

"Hoaris," I breathed. "And Chambui?" My brows pinched. What had they been doing in the wilds of the Iced Plains? But there had been more men . . . had to have been more to fight off a nekodai. Even Parū couldn't match the wildcat's feral and predatory strength. Fearsome as they were, Hoaris and Chambui alone wouldn't have been able to fight it off without help. "But there were others too?"

Ken'ichi stepped forward, his face turning as solid as the blue ice upon Kōdaina Kōri. "Yes. Our best hunt leader, Su Almazaj suffered the same injury as you." His shoulders fell, and he clasped both hands. Eyes downcast, he watched as the palms and fingers rubbed over one another as if he slathered them with balm. "You are well enough in comparison." He hesitated, then made for the exit—a mere opening with a heavy fur hung between the convalescent room and whatever lay beyond. "I'll retrieve Hoaris."

The name of the hunt leader struck a familiar note, and I placed a hand on the healer's arm before he reached the door. "The hunter, Su. *Yamakara* Su Almazaj, I presume? How does he fare?" I held no affection for the man who'd been Thalaj's tormentor in youth. Nor did I want him to perish at the venomous claws. For all intents, he remained a stranger to me, and I had no rights to own a grudge over how he'd treated Thalaj as they passed through their awkward adolescent years. People grow and change, and clearly the clan here depended upon Su Almazaj to provide them with food.

Ken'ichi peered down at my hand, then lifted his dark, glistening eyes to mine. Pain and torment warred in their depths. "He rests in the room adjacent. In a . . . shall we say . . . *tenuous* state." By the strangle in the healer's voice, Su clearly meant a great deal to him on a more personal level.

"I am truly sorry, Sentei. It was never my intent to endanger any of the Frost Fighters as *you* are my people too." I lifted my hand from his arm, freeing him.

He pressed his lips together, nodded once, and slid between the fur and the wall.

Sentei Besso Ken'ichi did not return. When the fur peeled away from the doorway, Hoaris filled the empty arch, a grin splitting his red beard. He held back the brown-gray furs, and Chambui, smaller but stout in her own right, peered beneath his massive arm. Hoaris wore a simple, lightweight tunic, as he always had, but he'd traded his rough-spun traveling pants for garments similar to the ones Sentei Ken'ichi wore. A large band secured wide-legged pants about his waist—a *hakama*, if I recalled correctly from Tasmynne Hallowgale's teachings. My eyes drifted downward to the simple slippers adorning his feet.

"They're far more comfortable," he said with a smirk.

Chambui, by contrast, had bundled herself in mostly white fur with silvery flecks, the color offsetting her dark skin. "I'm surprised you're well so soon, Mairynne." She scooted past Hoaris and opened her arms along with the fur wrap.

I entered her embrace as if I had left this life and her simple affection would save my soul from walking the land—lost and unable to find my place alongside the Holy Triad within the night's sky.

"You're so warm, young one." She squeezed tighter. "I presume that's your Ryū since you wear so few clothes."

Nodding, I swallowed hard into her shoulder, fighting the urge to cry from exhaustion and peril. I enjoyed having Chambui at my side. She'd been a solid friend when we traveled over the Syrensea to Ise and back. Her calm strength allowed me to be weak and more open than I could with most people, and I loved my friend for that grace. Though I desired naught more than to melt into her at the moment, I pushed away quickly and wiped my nose, recovering as I glanced up at Hoaris. "You saved me from the nekodai. I suppose I owe you my life. Thank you."

Hoaris gave me a stalwart one-armed hug. "None of that life-death talk, Mairynne."

With the quick and awkward affection out of the way, he stepped back. Chambui then went to his side, and he draped his arm casually around her shoulders. Their comfort with each other warmed my cold soul. I'd witnessed how Jorani and Baldeo had deepened their relationship, but that'd been after a long time apart. When I'd left them, they'd been merely sparring partners. With Hoaris and Chambui, I'd been present when the spark developed. My heart swelled to see them growing even closer now, but it distracted me and piqued my curiosity.

I tilted my head and asked, "Do you not worry about inter-caste relations?"

True to form, he bellowed with laughter, then dropped a kiss on the top of Chambui's head. He answered, "Not in the least, little one. That nonsense didn't enter my mind when I was a youngling and stood up for Thalaj. Joining the Unseen only expanded my horizons. Why would coming back to the area where I gained my majority sway my views?"

I pursed my lips, remembering. "Su. He came with you to my rescue and suffers now because of that."

Hoaris opened his mouth to speak again, but I held up a hand and shook my head.

"Don't mind that," I rushed. "There's not time to worry over his condition now or how he may have changed. Where are we now, Hoaris? Are we near where Parū fell to the nekodai? Have you spoken with Tenkara? Why did she leave?"

"Hold up there with the blizzard of questions, Mairy." Hoaris chuckled, but then his brows knitted together. "We are near the ice shelf where you fell, at Hokutō Clanhold on the northeastern shores of Kōdaina Kōri."

Chambui chimed in. "We'd been awaiting Tenkara's decision as to whether or not she would ask the Frost Fighters to travel to Arashi on your behalf."

Hoaris added, "The waiting had grown tiresome, so Chambui and I had gone out with Su's hunting party to track the nekodai that'd been hovering around this clanhold. Perhaps he scented we were near and hunted us as well. I suspect your dragon distracted him from our scent."

They both fell silent then, exchanging a look that bespoke of more answers they wished not to share.

"And?" I prompted.

Chambui turned soft eyes toward me. "Gnoble Tenkara did not know you were bonded with Parū. When she learned this, her decision came quickly. 'I'll not help anyone possessed by one of those fey demons,' she told us."

I dropped my gaze. "So there was a possibility before I arrived," I said, allowing the dejection to enter my voice.

"Aye," Hoaris agreed, "I had almost convinced her to gather the clans, but your arrival in dragon form did my case no favors."

In a blink, anger pulsed hot through my blood. "So she simply ran without deigning to speak with me? What kind of leader is so gods-forsaken shortsighted?"

Chambui reached forward and grasped my hand. "She's afraid, Mairynne. Every clansman here fears the omen you bring."

"Aye," echoed Hoaris. "I'm not familiar with what histories they teach to Storm Sorcerers in Arashi, or in the stone-masoned Stormskeep, but our priests work exceedingly hard to ensure we understand what the Ryū Wars meant for the people of the north. That time caused more Frost Fighters to perish than perhaps any of the other Nantai people. We were once more advanced than other castes, having built great cities from ice over the course of many, many seasons." His eyes dropped momentarily, then returned to mine. "Understand, Mairynne, there is no rebuilding an ice city over the course of a few moons."

I threw my hands in the air and began pacing. "But I'm trying to protect the ways of life of *all* Nantai's people." I whirled around. "Can she not see that? Can she not take an hour to simply hear my request?"

The burly man before me took a deep breath, then continued, "Aljir Tenkara believes that if her people participate in your quest, it will draw attention to the north. They've heard rumors of how several of the cities south of the frost line have been burned to ruins. The Ryū Wars changed the Frost Fighters' entire way of life. We have rebuilt our dwellings to be invisible from above, but now that we—no, *I*—have invited a Ryū-bonded Storm Sorcerer into one of our clanholds, she believes it's the beginning of the end." Hoaris, in an uncharacteristic show of defeat, dropped his head and shoulders.

I stared at the man before me, someone I considered a dear friend. Strong and typically the person watching in the wings, he appeared sadder than I'd ever noticed. Granted, I hadn't given others much heed after I lost Thalaj in the Fey Realm. But for him to explain so much to me must have been an exhausting feat in its own right. "I regret that I have caused so much strife between you and your people, but please, tell me you understand that this fight is for more than any one person or any one caste."

Hoaris nodded.

Chambui rubbed a hand up and down his arm, comforting him while keeping her stare fixated on me. "Tenkara has given command to the first of her guard to send you south and to destroy this clanhold once Su Almazaj can be transported."

◇◇◇◇◇◇◇◇◇◇◇◇◇◇◇◇◇◇◇◇◇◇◇◇◇◇◇◇◇◇◇◇◇

AS IF BECKONED, SOMEONE, a severe-looking woman wearing the same gray uniform with wide-legged hakama as Hoaris, threw back the curtain barring the exit. Her lips pinched, and her eyes narrowed into angled slits. She wore her clearly ample black hair in a tight knot on the top of her head. As she stepped inside, she held a short, curved sword in one hand and a blue flickering orb in her free palm.

"Leave!" she barked.

"Saqie—"

She glared. "Don't, Hoaris. Just don't." Then she turned her attention back to me. "This is a battle you will not win, demon-bonded sorcerer."

I flinched; blinked my eyes at her several times. Yes, people who knew of my dragon often feared me at first, but none had accused me of accepting such a dark pact. Slowly, I said, "If you refer to my bonded Ryū, she is no demon."

Saqie stiffened. "Call it what you will, but you will leave this place now."

With a sigh, I asked, "You are Tenkara's gensui?"

With the blizzard's energy pulsing in her palm, she gripped her sword tighter and pushed it in my direction as she circled behind me. In this clanhold, I had no connection to the skies and thus had no magical defense.

I held up my hands, resigning myself to having missed the opportunity to persuade the Frost Fighters to stand with other castes and the casteless across Nantai. I hated relenting so easily. However, at the moment, time was not my friend; I'd lost a day already. "Well and so." I glanced at Hoaris and Chambui. "Show me the way out of this clanhold."

Hoaris stepped to my side, toward the woman soldier. "Saqie," he pleaded, "such venom isn't needed. *Cousin*—"

"Cousin?" Saqie pushed the orb closer to him. "How dare you call me kin . . . *Cousin*?" Spittle flew from her lips. Heedless, she continued, "You know Tenkara's decision will not waver. You can leave with her—on foot or in the talons of her *demon*, for all I care—if you cannot respect our gnoble's decisions."

Hoaris pressed closer to her with his hands raised, the same cautious posture I held. I made little move but watched intently, wondering why Gnoble Tenkara would have chosen a guard who seemed so nervous and vehement, and mayhap insecure.

"She was dear to Thalaj," Hoaris said, his voice more soothing.

The tone failed in its attempt as Saqie retorted, "Then any fondness I held for him once was also in vain—especially if he can care so for a Ryū."

"Mairynne wasn't bonded when Thalaj cared for her, and he now walks a foreign land alone. For all we shared as younglings, please, I beg you to hear her out."

I remained silent.

Saqie hesitated, but then resolved herself to her original cause, though there was more behind her agitation. "When you and Thalaj left me alone with . . . *him*"—she swallowed—"that broke any bonds the three of us had shared. Now, out. Su's fever has broken and we'll be leaving soon. I have my orders." She motioned with her sword but it seemed less fervent and more dutiful.

My heart sagged, but I held a regal posture. Efforts with Saqie seemed a waste. "Hoaris, show me out of the clanhold. But Saqie, I'd like a word with my friends before I leave."

Her brows knitted. "I need to see you fly south, so I cannot leave you entirely. But I'll stand nearby and give you a moment." She tilted her head toward the door.

We walked in silence through the ice halls, my feet still bare and melting spots upon the floor as I moved. Having Parū's heat back was a blessing of the Fey and the Holy Triad in this regard, else I would have shivered under furs like Chambui. Behind us, Saqie sheathed her sword as we walked, an action I couldn't see but which issued the distinct sound of metal sliding into its home.

Outside, she stepped away but held both hands at the ready, prepared to channel a blizzard if necessary.

We huddled together, and I said in low tones, "Go north with the clan if you can. Try again, but I need you in Arashi soon. The Fire Forgers are coming too, and my plan was to stage a diversion beyond Arashi's gates while I found my way inside by other means. We have a half-moon mayhap, but not much longer. By the time Selene reaches her fullest, I'll need all the support I can muster."

Chambui hugged me. "Be safe, Mairynne."

"I'm afraid there's little safe in these days, but I will do my best." I gave her a weak smile.

Hoaris nudged my shoulder. "We can find mutts and a sled to get us to the southern end of Kōdaina Kōri and the Nansei Clanhold, but we'll need steeds to make it to Arashi in that time. Or maybe . . ."

I raised a brow, questioning.

He stroked his red beard, lost in thought and staring off into Otarr's skies.

"Maybe . . . ?" I prompted, tilting my ear closer as if I could hear his thoughts.

He shook his head then, waving a hand in the air as if the thought made little sense.

Chambui backhanded him. "You can't do that and not tell us."

"I was considering how close Nansei is to the Northerly Barrows. Mayhap we could find a terrawyrm and travel below ground."

The yisu laughed. "Those are myth."

"Oh, but *are* they truly?" he quipped.

Saqie exaggerated a cough and narrowed her eyes again.

"Well and so." I waved to her and began to undress.

Hoaris turned away, and I handed the bundle of clothes to Chambui and stepped back.

Parū, I called.

Ready, minikin.

With a last smile and wave, we transformed into the great pearlescent dragon. Parū glanced down at her side where the nekodai's claws had slashed through her more delicate scales. There were four unprotected lines—scars she'd wear forever. I shared in her pride at having faced one of the venomous cats and that she'd lived to tell.

When we meet them again, you will thank the one named for hoarfrost on my behalf, minikin?

It wasn't quite a question, but I answered regardless, *Of course I will.*

◇◇◇◇◇◇◇◇◇◇◇◇◇◇◇◇◇◇◇◇◇◇◇◇◇◇◇

HOARIS AND CHAMBUI DWINDLED as Parū spread her wings and caught an updraft, lifting us higher and higher. Saqie, now awestruck, stepped to Hoaris's side. Would that I could have heard the words exchanged as they watched us soar away.

Hours passed, and though my soul felt deep exhaustion, I couldn't rest.

As Parū soared through the sky, my heart felt heavy after the desolation in Biei and the Frost Fighter rejection. The Ryū Guin had charred the seat of the Fire Forger gnoble, Yuos Atith, but at least Atith had rallied and would join me to reclaim the Nantai ways of life. The clanholds carved within the ice cliffs on the northeastern shore of the great Kōdaina Kōri hadn't yet been touched. My heart felt heavy over the notion that the northerners would destroy an entire clanhold simply because I, and by extension Parū, now knew the location. They had escaped the real terror and threat. I feared it was only a matter of time before Guin found the other clanholds scattered throughout the Iced Plains. Although, if the ways the Frost Fighters had adapted after the wars proved the wiser path, they might be the only ones to survive the downfall of Nantai.

Fifty-Nine

Return to Love's Court

HAZE DIFFUSED OTARR'S MORNING RAYS, so it surprised me when Parū so easily found Tsanseri's cloud island within the mist.

A dragon's sense of direction is far superior in the skies, minikin, she said, landing with one clawed foot. She dropped my bundle of clothing, then placed her other talon onto the solid surface beneath the mists floating across the isle. She then glided forward until the claws at the bends in her wings dug into the soft ground near the stone. *'Tis time I find my rest,* she added, and she withdrew. Her body diminished and shifted into mine, my consciousness coming to the forefront and hers fading into the depths of my soul.

Mist tingled on my skin, and it hissed as it evaporated immediately from the warmth. The transformation completed, I sighed and opened my eyes.

"Mairynne," Father gasped from behind.

I turned more slowly than I might have several days before, but it felt good to hear his voice and see his face materialize through the fog. He held something white—a sheet mayhap—over one arm. Only when he averted his eyes out of a clear sense of propriety did I realize I stood before my father entirely naked. The state had ceased to bother me, but clearly it edged beyond his boundaries of comfort. He spread a robe reminding me of the cloud itself while keeping his gaze pointed intently in the direction of the castle's blue spires peeking above the fog.

I slid one arm inside, then the other. After I had secured the tie at my waist, he turned his storm-gray eyes back to me and smiled. His kind eyes wrinkled at the corners as he ran his hands over both my upper arms. He looked well, no, radiant and healthier than he had only ten days before when I'd left. The knowledge did my heart well. Yet darkness in his look intoned worry, said he wished he could alleviate my pain or help in another manner. Mayhap he wished to relieve my burden, but I no longer believed that possible.

"I'm warm enough, Father." I looked bleakly into his eyes.

He flinched, a minute move, but he couldn't recover quick enough for me to miss it. "What troubles your eyes then?" he asked. "You're pale and"—he lifted a hand to my cheek—"there are dark circles here like I've never seen on you before. You don't look well."

I tucked my chin and smiled at the turn. It hadn't been so long when I fretted so over him. "It's only exhaustion. A meal would do wonders. Walk me to Tsanseri's tearoom and then gather the others. I'd like to recount the story only once." I laced my arm through his and we walked. Reluctantly, I added, "Father, I'm scared. You'll understand why soon enough, but my last desire is to see a war pass over Nantai or our jewel city. I fear Arashi will never be the same after this."

He released my hand from his arm and drew me into a tight hug. Not only did he appear stronger, he felt stronger too. " 'Tis also the last scenario I'd wish, my daughter. I've held too many happy memories in Stormskeep with your mother, you, Karynne, and Yasmynne. And even longer before, I spent so much time exploring the streets during my youngling years. To see any of that erased . . ." He looked up musingly, then added, "Mayhap there is hope that it will not come to a battle or a war. If there is aught you or I can do, I'm certain we will find the solution."

My stomach issued a dreadful rumble. Lips tight over the impending events, I swallowed the lump in my throat and urged us forward to address my more basic and immediate needs.

The tearoom where we'd supped, planned, and plotted before was abandoned. The smells of barley tea still lingered. Therefore clearly, it'd only been vacant for a matter of hours. Yet the emptiness reflected the feeling in the pit of my stomach. A small bowl gong rested on a cushion at the center of the table with a mallet alongside the pillow. I lifted the pair and struck the instrument once. A bell-like chime, higher in pitch than the larger gong at the rear of the room, announced our presence. In short order, Strato-Elea entered. Surprise took her and she stammered, "Oh, y-you're not the comtesse."

I circled the table with bare feet upon the tatami and took a pillow that offered me the best views of the main entrance and the servants' doors at the other end of the room—the end behind Tsanseri's red velveteen pillow. "Do you have aught with which I might break my fast?"

The servant nodded, wrung her hands, and turned on a heel.

"Wait, Strato-Elea?"

"Yes, Kōgō Mairynne?" She tipped her head forward in supplication.

I averted my eyes but pinched my lips to refrain from any objection to the title. It came with duty I felt ill-prepared to accept, and it weighed on my soul. Regardless of my position amidst the Nantai and despite all the efforts I had put forth, would there still be a way to prevent the looming strife? How many would perish? I lifted my eyes as if to ask Father how to avoid the terror I felt enclosing about me . . . us. Mayhap had I not followed the soul stones, I would have avoided this fate with Guin. I pressed my palms against my browbones and pressed to relieve the building tension. "Will you send someone to fetch Tsanseri and her navigator?"

"Mairynne, you should eat," Father objected. "Then rest, then we can worry over these matters. We have days before we arrive yet. There's time for—"

"Not enough time, Father." I nodded and waved Elea onto her task. When she'd gone, I sighed. To Father, I added, "Will you gather Zofi and Yankos, or shall I ring for a servant to do that bidding?"

Resigned, he asked, "Are you certain you are well enough to remain alone?"

Even as he spoke, I reached for the gong. But he stopped me with a squeeze around both hands. I relished how his still rough skin felt on the backs of my hands. Royalty, true, but Father had never shied away from labor with his hands. It comforted me that he still wore the signs.

Father lifted my hands to his lips and placed a soft kiss on the backs of each. "I can go, Mairynne. The Tsinti will do better to have me bring your message than one of the Courtiers."

"Thank you, Father." I watched him leave, grateful for a few moments alone while I awaited food.

Parū chose that time to offer reassurance. *You doubt yourself too much, minikin. Do not allow those questions to consume your mind.*

Ah, alone, but not, I thought in return.

I will leave you to your thoughts, she added, her voice sounding cut after the sardonic suggestion in my words. *But do work to keep the inner workings of your mind in the light.*

Her presence retreated then—there, but not there. Close enough to call if I should have the need, but not intermingled in every thought. That felt well enough. There had been a time in those early days after the Ryū bonding when her presence had been all-consuming. It had almost seemed our connection had grown strong enough to push those boundaries, and I couldn't chase away a small proud smile blooming at the corners of my mouth.

Strato-Elea delivered a carafe of steaming barley tea, a small dish of honey, and a platter full of meats, cheeses, and sweet rolls. I had finished the tea and devoured my first serving before anyone returned.

My father and Zofi entered first, Zofi lifting her skirts and scurrying over to sit at my side. "Are you well, child?"

"Better now that I've eaten," I answered and truly felt a surge of energy rushing through my veins.

Father took a seat at the corner of the table next to Zofi, trailing one hand over her back. "The dark swaths under Mairynne's eyes are lighter than even an hour ago. I do believe the food helped." He smiled at me.

"Hai, all is as I said. I needed food," I said, reaching for another serving of rolls and meat. "Tell me, what has happened since I've been gone," I demanded as I folded the piece of meat and took a bite.

Zofi started, "There has been very little on this sky island to keep the Tsinti entertained. Yankos has spent much time with my cousin, pouring over our route."

"Someone rang?" Yankos stepped inside wearing a half-cocked grin; Tsanseri followed.

Despite my current worry, I forced a smile. The small, dark-haired man with the red mark under one eye gave me a sense that things would work out in their own time. Strange, as I'd once believed him more deadly than Baldeo or even the hulking Maladros—the man he'd sent to follow Filtch's messenger. The thought struck a chord. "Where is Alto-Trea?" I stared at Tsanseri.

Everyone's face darkened.

"Kōgō, Mairynne." The leader of the cloud island bowed her head to me.

Eyes wide, I demanded again, "Where is your navigator?"

Her face twisted as if she tasted the bitterness of a too-young Aomori apple. "Alto-Trea was found sabotaging our plans to drop from the sky currents and travel south. His second in command, Alto-Nior, came to me with the news. Had she not, we would have ended up north of Yōtei with little hope of maintaining the schedule he'd promised."

I tossed the bread back onto the plate in front of me and pushed it away, my appetite suddenly diminished. "And where is *Filtch* now?" I wasn't sure if she'd known him by the name, but she read my meaning.

"I've banished him from my island, Kōgō."

I gritted my teeth. Alto-Trea . . . the Swan . . . *Filtch* . . . had been a nettle hair in my paw since the day I met him at the High Cloud Courts. We'd met again in the Yubar, and then he'd intercepted me when I'd been searching for transport in the City by the Sea. Kōkai, where I'd met Sarangarel and began my journey across the Syrensea. Filtch had been there, too, to sabotage my search. Banishing him from this island left too much uncertainty. Where had he sent that messenger? Where had he gone now? When would he turn up again? I stood, searching Tsanseri's face.

"I presume you did not merely toss him to his death over your walls and that you have no clue where he has gone?" I asked, already suspecting the answer.

"I would commit no such acts of violence against another person." With a jeweled hand hovering at her throat, she straightened, resolving herself. "He has betrayed you and thereby has betrayed my wishes. He is ill-welcome at Love's Court, so I granted him a servant's transport vessel to leave and never return."

"And how will you be certain he will not don a new mask and find his way back to your isle?" I snapped, then took several long breaths. Narrowing my eyes to a pointed glare, I lowered my voice. Dry, it sounded, and more deadly than I believed myself capable when I added, "You would have done better to shackle the traitor."

Heavy silence blanketed the room for long, trickling moments. The Comtesse of Masks, being well-accustomed in games of the court, faced the accusation with aplomb, raising her chin higher and higher by small measures. Steadfast, I held Tsanseri's glare while the others moved minutely in my periphery. Father looked from me to the comtesse and back, his gaze slicing the air. Zofi smoothed the skirts covering her knees, and Yankos fidgeted.

"We, ah, do have good news, little one." Yankos moved into my line of vision and winked. "We believe we can cast tsym over the cloud island as we arrive at Stormskeep. It should allow us to move in without being noticed."

My tension unraveled with that bit of hope. "That is wonderful news. How much time before we arrive?"

"Alto-Nior estimates three days, four at most," Yankos answered.

I breathed my relief. I'd returned with plenty of time remaining. I'd be with the Tsinti and Father when we arrived at Arashi, but I feared we would still arrive before any reinforcements could journey to the southwestern slopes of the Rausu Mountains and surround Arashi. Mayhap the tsym would allow us to lie in wait until some strategy finally grew into an executable reality. And with hope, perhaps Hoaris would be able to convince the Frost Fighter gnoble to join us. After all, I had only requested they act as a diversion alongside the Fire Forgers.

I wondered though . . .

Good thoughts, Parū grumbled. *We don't need any reinforcements for me to face Guindragon. Go ahead and ask your wandering friend.*

"Yankos," I began, "do you think it would be possible to cast tsym over only one or two people? In closer proximity?"

The Tsinti leader rubbed his hand over the bit of stubble sprouting from his chin. "Tsym is a broad spell. It creates a fold in time itself. It needs to be bound to something, but it spreads. Besides reading the herbs and Zofi's abilities that are blended with illusionary magic of the Cloud Courtiers, it is our one talent, and it has been honed to cover broad spaces."

My hopes flickered between life and death like a candle's flame under the siege of a strong gale.

Yankos raised one finger. "But . . . we can try."

Zofi added, "You may need help from a spellcaster—a shaman, mayhap?"

Father mused, " 'Tis a shame Small Folk no longer travel with us."

Tsanseri's face lit. "You traveled with Small Folk? Amazing," she breathed, then shook her head, her expression turning contemplative. "But we do have a Courtier aboard who has studied with a shaman. Granted, she only endeavored to learn spells and charms to sway the heart."

Zofi groaned and moved for the gong at the center of the table. "Are we waiting for her to hear our need on the sky currents?"

Dong . . .

The bell's ring lingered in the air, a backdrop to the simmering enmity between Zofi and her cousin, Tsanseri.

◇◇◇◇◇◇◇◇◇◇◇◇◇◇◇◇◇◇◇◇◇◇◇◇◇◇◇

OUTSIDE, WE GATHERED NEAR the night-blooming gardens and waited for Strato-Elea to return with the shaman's student—Cirro-Bree. When the two arrived, it was clear that Bree was still a youngling, not only because she appeared small to have gained her majority, but also because she hadn't quite grasped the intricacies of the illusions the others around her had perfected. Hers shifted. Once when I looked at her, her body appeared to have ample curves with waist-length hair, but the next time I glimpsed her, her hair barely swept her frail-looking shoulders. The shape of her face wavered in appearance too. In one instant, it appeared like the round, pink flesh of an Aomori apple, but in the next, it'd taken on a heart shape with a severely pointed chin.

If she couldn't maintain the illusionary magic intrinsic to the Cloud Courtier caste, how on the Nantai soil or in the clouds above would she have the experience to bind the Tsinti's most advanced spell to anyone or anything?

I turned questioningly to Tsanseri who scanned all our faces in turn. Clearly, Father, Zofi, and Yankos displayed the same skepticism as I.

The comtesse stood taller—indignantly—and adjusted the informal but still vibrant sash about her waist. "You wished for someone with spellcasting or binding ability. Bree is who I have to offer. Use her." She shrugged. "Or don't." She pushed her chin higher, turned on a heel and marched away.

Strato-Elea reached into a pouch at her waist, fished out a handful of gems, and offered them to me in cupped hands. "Here are some jewels that might be used in the binding." She pushed them forward, inviting us to take them.

"Elea!" Tsanseri yelled.

Elea's eyes darted between us and the comtesse until I held my palm open. Offering my thanks, I accepted the faceted stones. With a final regretful look, she followed her mistress. In unison, those of us remaining behind turned to Bree. The youth twisted her fingers together before her, the illusions she'd been trying to maintain flickering in and out of existence.

Zofi sighed, stepped forward, and placed an arm around Bree's shoulders. "You have no need to mask yourself with us, youngling. We have better use for your magical energy."

The Tsinti witch wife was short, but Bree only reached her brow at full height. Zofi urged Bree into the gardens toward a small alcove amidst the cascading Bells of Selene. Golden-tipped buds by the hundreds would open under Selene's light and turn the air sweet, but for Otarr, they held their faces and scents inside closed petals. Zofi strolled casually, her long skirts flowing over the white marbled path. We followed, trusting that she understood best how to urge the youth toward aiding our need. As she stepped to the nook's center, she pulled Bree to face her and kept her voice soft in the same manner she had when I'd first met her seasons before in Detsa's covered wagon.

"Once, child," she began, "I stood in your shoes, trying to disguise myself and blend in with the older Courtiers."

Bree widened her eyes at Zofi's announcement.

Zofi continued, " 'Tis true, I am Cloud Courtier by birth, pure of the second caste's blood. Like you, I spent seasons upon seasons trying and failing and then honing that natural ability to bend reality about myself. It now comes to me as easily as breathing."

Zofi's image shifted then, and she resembled Tsanseri more than I would have liked to admit. As soon as she'd made the transformation, her face returned to the softer visage with fine lines around her eyes that showed how much she'd smiled in her lifetime. This was the face I'd come to know. Father stood nearby, his arms folded over his chest. He wore a small smile as he watched Zofi with the young Cloud Courtier.

"I've separated myself from the perceived need to maintain certain *appearances*," Zofi added with a meaningful look. A wise woman in truth, her manner worked on Bree as it once had on me.

The girl nodded, eased her stance visibly, and solidified into a wispy form with a heart-shaped face and honey-colored waves framing her face. Her hands, clasped before her, stilled. A youngling indeed, albeit one more at ease.

"So," Zofi smiled and urged, "you agree to help us?"

"I do," she replied and looked up at me.

In light of all I'd experienced, I couldn't find the same patience as Zofi. I marched forward, handed Bree the jewels, and blurted, "I'd ask after your mother and father and why you've chosen to serve the Comtesse of Masks, but we haven't the time for such bonding." Even to me, my voice sounded clipped, cold, but it held a truth and desire that resonated in my bones. I'd grown overly tired of illusion and machination and simply wished for this endeavor to end. I wished to return to the peace I'd once believed existed in Nantai. Whether I believed now that peace had ever thrived—after having seen the desolation of my cities and the attitudes of the Frost Fighters—I no longer knew. Yet that desire for peace or a semblance thereof fueled my every action in the present days.

"All right, child," Zofi started. The way she folded her hands in front of her, long fingers intertwining gracefully and lightly falling to rest, kindled another memory of the day I first met the Tsinti witch wife, the tenuous moments after Jorani had wrapped my hair in the Tsinti bans. The remembrance prompted notice of her now unwrapped hair. Not one white strand marked the otherwise black thicket of waves. In contrast to Father, who stood next to her, Zofi's face also showed no lines, yet she clearly had lived as many seasons as Father.

Mayhap the inevitable wisdom accompanying those seasons showed differently for Cloud Courtiers . . . Though she didn't work to draw the same illusions as those of her birth caste, her Triad-gifted nature seemed to innately smooth the more visible signs. Tsanseri had had the same look when I caught her in a moment of vulnerability but it had seemed so much less subtle.

Cirro-Bree hung on Zofi's every word, her eyes wide and brows raised in anticipation of whatever instruction came next. I felt a likeness to the youngling, as if I could naïvely take her place and cling to answers only her newfound teacher would have.

Zofi said, "Can you show us what you know of the shaman's binding?"

Bree's mouth gaped like the fish the sailors aboard the *Swell Mistress* had pulled from the Syrensea. "I-I . . . What kind of spell should I bind to the stone?"

Yankos, clearly leaving the spells to those who knew better than him, walked over to a table with two benches and straddled the closest. There, he leaned an arm casually on the stone tabletop, watching and waiting. He fidgeted idly with something in his hand. I followed him, taking the mirroring seat.

Zofi answered Bree, "Whatever spell you feel comfortable with will work. The nature of it matters little; I'm merely curious about your ability. The Tsinti tsym isn't a simple spell, it's more of a ritual. And I'm uncertain that you'll be able to capture its essence in any of these stones, but we must try." She waved a long-fingered hand in the air. "Just do what you've learned and walk me through how you infuse them with magic."

I lowered my voice, asking Yankos, "Do you think this will work?"

He raised a brow and the red mark jumped on the cheek beneath his right eye. His sigh sounded doubtful. "I cannot say. All we can do is hope. May I ask what you are planning that would call for tsym to be cast upon an individual?"

"In all truth, I do not yet know. The answer will lie in how I need to get into Arashi. Mayhap we won't need it at all, but I'd rather be prepared."

You will, minikin. Or you will need something, Parū said with the rasp of exhaustion and a note that said she possessed more knowledge about this than me.

I ground my teeth. *What have you seen, Parū, that I have not?*

We flew over Arashi on the return from the north. The city's gates were closed and guards stood upon the walls in large numbers. Perhaps this has always been the case in your time. I cannot say, for I have not visited Arashi or Stormskeep in ages.

My eyelids dropped, pinched tightly. *No, my dragon. In my years at Arashi and living in Stormskeep, the city's gates always stood open, inviting others inside. That they are closed now does not bode well. I'd hoped to slip in wearing a disguise or, in a worse case, under tsym.*

"Mairynne?" Yankos called. When I looked over, he asked, "Where'd you go?"

Returning to the world outside, I answered with a small chuckle, "I'm here. Parū distracted me. I'd hoped I could use the cover of tsym to pass through the Arashi gates unseen. Although, perhaps, given what Parū witnessed while we flew south from the Iced Plains, the gates will no longer allow anyone to pass." I focused sadly on the bench between my legs, then the white marble pebbles on the ground beyond.

Several long moments passed in silence. Father stood beside Zofi as she and Bree worked quietly over one of the stones. Bree bowed her head at times, whispering words over a bright red gemstone. Yankos and I watched from the table until the stone Bree was working blossomed into a faceted flower. Zofi and Father smiled with approval.

Yankos clapped. "Oja, oja! Yes! Little Janci would adore such tricks."

Bree's cheeks turned bright pink. "It is of little use though, only a pretty bauble that can be gifted to a loved one. 'Twill whisper reassurance when they doubt the gifter's love."

"Well and so," Zofi said, accepting the flower from the youngling and holding it to the light. Red and orange flecks filtered through onto her cheeks; a smile bloomed as she turned and handed the flower to Father.

Embarrassment kindled hot patches on my cheeks as I watched the exchange, both happy for Father and Zofi, but missing Mother.

My mother, Kōgō Noralynne, and his partner in the life she lived, would certainly wish him this happiness even though she could no longer walk at his side.

Parū had been right before; I tried to simply be happy for what they'd found.

After the exchange, Zofi looked back at Bree with a nod. "Meet us back here on the morrow with the stones in hand. We'll try to cast tsym upon one or more of these stones then."

◇◇◇◇◇◇◇◇◇◇◇◇◇◇◇◇◇◇◇◇◇◇◇◇◇◇◇◇◇◇◇◇◇

THE FIRST DAY WITH Cirro-Bree had been unsuccessful, but Zofi learned a good deal about Bree's talents, or so she said. The second day, Zofi brought Buharro, another of the Tsinti who'd joined us upon the cloud island, to help in the efforts.

"No. Stop!" yelled Zofi in the midst of another failing attempt.

I took a deep breath, trying to hold onto hope that the efforts would eventually come to fruition. We'd all returned to the small alcove framed by Bells of Selene. Father and I sat at the table watching as Zofi, Buharro, and Yankos said the words to cast tsym over and over again. I rolled a small marble pebble between my fingers as they said the incantation so many times, I was beginning to believe I could cast it. Although that belief remained unlikely, because I only understood one in five of the nuanced words used in the ritual. Mayhap Bree had the same challenge.

"Again," barked Buharro.

Bree jumped.

His voice booming, Buharro incanted again, "*ame garadjoram . . .*"

We hide, I translated as he continued chanting. I'd gained knowledge of the Romani language before, but it was so nuanced, I found it hard to do more than pick out a word or two despite the fact that I could mimic the sounds. The inflections and variations of words they used for this spell weren't common in the dialog I'd learned when I'd worked with the women outside Detsa's cart.

Zofi motioned a hand to Bree who began murmuring. She never said the words of binding loud enough that anyone other than herself could comprehend. I thumped my heel as I watched the scene play out again. The air shimmered, but none of those working the magic vanished entirely from sight.

When they slumped again in defeat, I huffed and flung the pebble.

As it skipped into the flowers, Zofi snapped her eyes up from the ground, alight with a new idea. "Mayhap the incantation must change to be so narrowly focused," she mused. "Mayhap it must be assigned to one soul. Mairynne?" She waved me over. Standing, I crossed over the loose marble as Zofi continued to Buharro, "Instead of *ame garadjoram*, try *tu garadjoran*, and so on." When I arrived at her side, she grabbed my hand and flipped it palm up without ceremony. She thrust a yellow gem the size of my palm inside. "Continue, Buharro, Bree."

Buharro grumbled the guttural words again, and at some point, the yellow facets began glowing with an amber hue. The surface of the stone grew hotter in my hand.

"Now, Bree," Zofi said, her brown eyes intent on the stone.

A buzzing sensation filled the air around me. My hair lifted from the top of my head and from where it had lain flat over my shoulders. Buharro's voice seemingly grew deeper and deeper, rumbling, rumbling, until . . .

The ground beneath my feet shook, trembled.

Bree stumbled into Zofi. Buharro staggered backward. The stone slipped through my fingers, clattering to the ground—a yellow light amidst the white marble.

I whipped my head around to Father who gripped the table as if it'd save him from whatever had stirred.

"What was that?" I asked, searching Yankos's wide eyes.

Bree recovered. "It's only a storm."

We all turned to her, and she pinkened under our stares.

With a shrug, she added, "It's what a rolling thunderstorm feels like from up here—like an earthshake below, but worse. We're likely hitting a cross current."

I hissed in air through my teeth and searched the skies. In the distance, a wall of black clouds gathered. Electric bolts hopped between them as they billowed higher. Father and I should be able to hold off the storm, but I didn't want to knock us off course by doing so blindly. "Zofi, can you, Buharro, and Yankos continue working with Bree? Father, ready?" I waited for him to nod his understanding, then set my focus. "Well and so. Let us find the comtesse and her navigator."

Sixty

Navigating the Storm

RUUUMMMBLE . . . BOOM!

The ground shook again as we arrived at the door to Tsanseri's tearoom. I grasped the frame for balance and reached to steady Father too. Inside, Tsanseri sat alone. Her dark eyes were rounded with fright while her hands splayed upon the table as if she could hold everything in place.

Over the commotion, I shouted, "Is this the cross current we were trying to avoid?"

The comtesse didn't answer but stared at me with glazed and shifting eyes.

"It is, my kōgō," a voice behind me said, calm in the midst of the quake.

Turning to find Alto-Nior, I braced myself again against the shifting ground. She stood still, sure-footed before me, waiting for me to allow her inside. *Her?* I questioned in my own thought. *The navigator's preference or Tsanseri's?* I blinked and shook it off as I stepped aside. My jaw clenched with my anger over the errant musing. What did it matter? Naught. It mattered naught, but the constant question twisted my instincts in strange ways. I cared little about their guises, but in a way, it made me question myself, feel like I couldn't be as precise as I wished when addressing the Courtiers. *My* mental blockade, not theirs. And it seemed something I needed to put aside. *Her* persona was feminine; therefore, I'd remain with *she* and *her* until corrected.

Tsanseri had asked something of the navigator while I wrestled with myself, but I hadn't heard the question.

I set my lips in a tight line as Alto-Nior replied to Tsanseri, "No, my lady. Will you join us below on the navigation deck?" A flit of disgust scurried across Tsanseri's face. She clearly felt her position above such menial work.

But Nior pressed, "It's the best place to drive through this storm."

Stepping forward, I asked the navigator, "Where is your navigation deck? Father and I will join you and do anything within our power as Storm Sorcerers to help."

She stared at me, cut her eyes to Tsanseri, pursed her lips, then said, "Follow me."

I made for the door, and in my periphery, Tsanseri stood. Nior rushed outside, then made a sharp right, turning down a corridor alongside the tearoom. The ground shivered again and I stumbled while rounding the corner. With my hand gripping Father's, I growled deep in my chest, called the wind, and we rode it the rest of the distance to where Nior had entered a tiny building—something that appeared no bigger than a small wardrobe. The door slammed closed behind her before we could see aught inside. I dropped the wind suddenly and let our feet connect again with the marble below. I peered over my shoulder before entering.

Another boom, crack, sizzle . . .

Tsanseri flew off her feet and landed in a tangle of limbs.

I hadn't seen her follow, but Strato-Elea cried out, a peal rivaling the thunder and calling the deep booms into submission if only for an instant. She ran to her mistress. I'd covered my ears as the sound Elea emitted sent chills up and down my spine, but in the quiet moment after, I understood. As Elea fell over the twisted body, I jolted toward where Tsanseri had fallen, but Father wrapped a strong hand around my wrist and pulled. My eyes burning, I searched his face for . . . what? Permission? Compassion?

"You do not have time, Mairynne. *We* don't," he emphasized. "Her servants will see to her and find her a healer if she is not beyond that." His eyes reflected the storm, gray and heavy but determined. "For now, we must see how we might help with the squall."

"But . . ." I started but couldn't complete the thoughts. Had the Comtesse of the Masque been killed by the strike? Who would preside over Love's Court if she'd perished? And on my behalf. Had I caused another death? I grasped my chest with my free hand, and my voice wavered. "I don't think my soul can handle another life lost." A tear brimmed and streamed along my cheek until it dripped from my chin.

Sternly, Father pushed me toward the door. When he opened it, he went first down the stairs, and I followed, although it felt as if I ran through knee-deep mud, my heart drawn back to see if Tsanseri could be saved.

Your father is right, minikin, Parū encouraged. *The servant will see to her, and if she has love's good fortune, she will survive. You must focus now.*

My feet slowed. *Can I give you control? You deal with this new horror, get us to Arashi. Give me time to recover?* The comtesse's tangle of arms, legs, and colorful cloth flashed again in my mind.

Here, minikin? In the tiny staircase? I will not have room, and you would be trying in vain to escape a duty laid upon your shoulders.

"Mairynne?!"

My vision snapped back to the present, the stairwell. Father stood at the bottom, motioning for me. If this descent were inside Stormskeep, it would be dark, near blackness. Here, the walls glowed with Otarr's light like all places in a cloud court. Seemingly though, as I descended toward Father and the door, it grayed, as if we moved toward where the clouds prepared to shower the land below.

Crack! Boom!

The foundation shifted again and I fell from the final step into Father's arms. He helped me to my feet, concern writ upon his brow.

I pushed him back, steeling myself. "I am well enough."

You are, minikin. You are strong enough to host one of the Ryū. That makes you strong enough for this too.

Inside the room and along the walls, there were stations with controls and contraptions of which I'd never seen the like. A Courtier tended each station. Closer to center, there were tables spaced around the perimeter, all laden with maps. In the center, the floor was open to the land below. Nantai. No, not open, but shielded by something akin to glass. It looked down over the Yubar Forest near the edge of the vale. I recognized the river Thalaj and I had followed seasons before—the Sundai. Upriver lay Arashi. Unwittingly, I moved closer until a hand pulled me back.

Alto-Nior gripped my elbow. "This way, Kōgō Mairynne."

But I had no time to react before another Courtier—Alto-Tash, I recognized the other of Tsanseri's servants—rushed forward, reared back, and swung her arm forward, connecting.

My head whipped sideways a split second before I felt the sear on my cheek.

"You had Trea banished," she verily sobbed. "What right do you have to come to a Cloud Court and divide our caste so?"

Alto-Nior hissed in a sharp breath through her teeth and turned. "Kann, Pith, take Tash from my navigation chamber!"

Trea? As in Alto-Trea?

Tash turned toward the now-lead navigator. "You . . . So you'll work with a traitor to your people? To your own caste. How many others will you see die before you see the treachery before you, Alto-Nior? We should send the Storm Sorcerers to the surface on a transport cloud, turn around, and forget about all of this!"

The two Courtiers Nior had called seized Tash by her upper arms. Tossing accusations all the while, she pulled and railed against them as they carried her from the room.

Alto-Nior raised a hand to my cheek. "My regrets, Kōgō Mairynne," she started. "I'll—"

"No," I snapped. "I understand the frustration, but for now, let us tend to this storm. You can deliver the Tsinti, Father, and me to a location near Arashi, then be on your way if that's the will of . . ." I guarded the thoughts of how Tsanseri may not survive. "Well, of those aboard Love's Court."

Nior nodded and started barking questions and orders to those on the deck, order after order, so fast I couldn't keep up as the other Courtiers flew into motion. The room tilted and I grabbed onto a table to hold myself upright.

Father shouted, "Where is the cross current coming from?"

"Over here." Nior motioned us to the largest table.

Slowly, Father and I both made our way to where she leaned over a map. Then, while pointing between the map and the glass below, Nior said, "We are here. See the curve of the Sundai? This sky current crosses here. We are on the lower edge. Things will only get worse from here if we continue the course toward Arashi."

As if prophesied, the room vibrated again violently at the clash of the winds; papers from all tables went flying about the room. A jumble of voices called out positions. "Level on port rear quarter," "Level on starboard front quarter," "Level at aft." It reminded me of the commands I'd heard Asahi's sailors use upon the *Swell Mistress*, but we'd never encountered such fierce commotion upon the rolling waves. It amazed me that my stomach didn't roil as it had on the voyage toward Ise, but Parū had quelled the sickness of the seas upon our return. I assumed she did so now.

Nior held on tightly to the map she'd been using for reference.

Father and I could help, but not when barred from the elements. Across the table, I looked the Cloud Courtier square in the eye. "Is there access to the open air from this room?"

She shook her head. "No. We push our magic through the control stations to keep the cloud aloft and guide it gently on the layers of air in the skies."

"Well and so." I hesitated, scrubbing a hand over my lower lip. I cut my eyes over to one of the stations. Could Father and I channel our storm sorcery through that contraption? Unlikely. "Guiding us will be harder above, where we can't see the ground, but we need the connection to the air and skies to work the storm's magic. Father?" I said, tipping my head toward the door.

I ran, Father at my heels. Flinging the door wide, I took the stairs two at a time. The wind howled, and a faint click, click, click of frozen rain sounded outside the door. The handle was cold when I grasped onto it and pulled. With the change in the weather outside, the door now felt as if it were made from solid stone. I yanked harder until it broke free, and the gale sucked me from inside. Sleet pelted my face. On the surface of the cloud island, I crouched, blocking the wind and called to the age-old sorcery that lived deep within me. Father stood in the doorway still, bracing himself and squinting against the squall. As I stood, I opened my arms and pushed with all the energy I could muster. It felt as if I lifted a boulder upon my shoulders, so much heavier than the storms upon the ground.

Use my strength, minikin, Parū said, and I sensed her presence closer to the surface.

My skin heated as I delved deeper into the well of magic and pushed harder against the storm. I'd been out of practice with controlling storms, but the skill grew stronger as I continued to pull from that place in my center where I felt Nantai's magic pulsing and feeding from my dragon's fey fortitude. Parū didn't create more magic, but she gave me the stamina to access my own more freely. My hair whipped in the wind, and the sleet gnashed and slashed at my cheeks. And I reached deeper, pulled harder. Then, a dome of calm blossomed about me.

Father rushed forward, expanding the dome. I could see strain on his face from exerting himself so, but at the same time, I admired his will. If my muscles for accessing our sorcery were starved, his must have been weaker still after his long sleep in the Fey Realm. The dome stretched to engulf the door by the time Alto-Nior appeared, two unknown Cloud Courtiers in her trail. Under her arm, she held the rolled map tightly to her torso.

The navigator pointed. "Over there, we should be able to view the ground over the wall. Can you move with the eye you've created?"

"Yes," I panted. "But make sure all who need to move are inside." I groaned again, reinforcing the invisible shield around us. "You—" I narrowed my eyes at one of the new people who'd joined us. "In the garden near the Bells of Selene"—I strained, drawing more power from within—"the Tsinti leader . . . Yankos . . . find him . . . bring him."

The Courtier wrung her hands and looked to Nior, seemingly for approval.

Through gritted teeth and laced with Parū's beastly timbre, I growled, "Go. Now."

She cowered, fidgeted, ran. I could only imagine what she and the others saw in that moment. My skin likely shimmered with the hint of pearlescent scales, and perhaps my eyes flashed diamond like. But I hadn't the time to tarry over how I may have scared the timid thing.

I shifted the winds to our aid and commanded, "Walk!" even as I moved.

Sleet pebbled and scratched on any surface it could find. The wind bellowed around the shelter, roaring and shrieking as it battered against my magic. But I withstood and even felt the power swell within.

"We need to drive the island that way," Nior hollered above the noise, pointing in the direction we ran. "Arashi is there."

"Father, I have the shelter." I angled my head so I could see his face. "Can you circle the winds to push us in that direction?"

He gave a single nod and pushed both hands toward his rear as if sending an invisible force behind him. The gales hearkened to the call of some of the most powerful storm sorcery in our caste. In all the chaos and determination to return and try to reason with my sister Karynne, I'd forgotten how strongly I could feel this sorcery within every fiber of my body. It seemed as if lightning awakened and crawled from my spine outward until it verily crackled upon my skin. I breathed it in, relishing the power.

✧✧✧✧✧✧✧✧✧✧✧✧✧✧✧✧✧✧✧✧✧✧✧✧✧✧✧✧

AT THE WALL, THE edge of Tsanseri's sky island, the sight countered my exhilaration, halted me, haunted my soul. Peering over the wall, I had a clear view of the empty vale spread before Arashi's gates, the city, and my home. A hollow grew in the pit of my stomach as I traced a path from the storm's edge across the Otarr-lit, empty fields—the very fields where I'd hoped to find allies gathering. My eyes prickled over their absence, but I continued following the path through the city streets and into the shadows surrounding Sundai Falls and the keep herself. Higher, my gaze traveled until I sighted another court. 'Twas hard to fathom how a cloud court appeared as naught but billowing mist in the skies when observed from below given the marble and structures within. Yet from this altitude at the edge of the storm's swell, the shadow's source clarified. Silhouettes of buildings gleamed atop the much grander High Cloud Court hovering above the spires of Stormskeep.

Arashi, the once bustling jewel city, lay too quiet below as light glinted off the scales of a circling green Ryū dragon.

Guindragon, hissed Parū, echoing my own thought.

Fortunately, Nior's awe-laced words grounded me. "What should we do, my kōgō?"

It was Yankos's voice who answered, "We need more time. Can you pull us back into the storm while we raise the tsym?" The Tsinti leader grasped onto the necklace that hung inside his tunic, pulled out the totem, fell to all fours, and began the incantation.

Noir nodded swiftly and ran for the door. "I'll have the navigators shift their magic," she yelled in parting, the wind whipping her hair as she escaped the calm bubble I'd created. She'd left the other, useless Courtier, and I strove to ignore her. Father released the winds at our backs, and the island folded backward into the gray clouds and storm. Yankos continued chanting, and Buharro burst into the calm and joined him in his efforts, each of their combined words growing louder with repetition.

"ame garadjoram . . . ame garadjoram . . . ame garadjoram . . ."

Yes, I thought furiously. *We must hide and figure a way inside without everyone knowing we are here.* Then I recalled the clearing above the Sundai Falls at the same time I caught sight of the inept Courtier. Mayhap she had use after all. "You. Are you a navigator?"

"A-an apprentice, Kōgō."

Well, at least she knew who I was. I turned to face where I'd last seen Arashi and pointed. "If Arashi is there"—I held one hand forward to point out the landmarks while I maintained the safety of the dome with the other—"Stormskeep is there, and the citadel, there." I waited for her to nod her understanding as she peered over my shoulder before continuing. "Sundai Falls lies between them and originates higher in the mountain than the keep. Beyond the cliff, before where the river spills, there is an open grove. Go tell Alto-Nior to get us to that grove."

She curtsied, said, "Yes, Kōgō," and darted away.

I settled my gaze on the gray thicket where I'd last seen the jewel city of Nantai and sighed. In the back of my consciousness, in my mind's eye, I saw Guin circling. Terror for my beautiful home scratched at the walls of my heart. I couldn't handle the vision of the cozy, cobbled streets lined with naught but coal and ash as Biei had been. But the green Ryū held a sacred and ancient bond with Imrythel, and my sister's advisor had been present in Arashi since long before Mother's death, Father's disappearance, and my fateful dance with the Serpentine Throne. Maybe, perhaps, she didn't intend to see Arashi in ruin. Perchance she wished for something more within that city? And, if the Triad was willing, Jorani, Baldeo, and the Fire Forgers would find us before her plans could be realized. Then I held onto the minimal hope that the kind Selene would guide the Frost Fighters to my aid.

"Oh, Hoaris," I whispered for no one other than myself, or perhaps with a prayer that the Triad would carry my message north into the Iced Plains, "I do hope you've gained Tenkara's support."

Through my extra sense, the sorcery woven into my being, I felt a surge before it hit. An upward wind swelling, driving higher to one side of the cloud island. I spread my stance and tightened every muscle in my body. Thunder, Atun's legendary rage, clapped as the updraft slammed into the current holding us aloft, and it reverberated, rolled, shook, and drove cracks within the solid foundation at my feet.

'Twas a blessing that Yankos and Buharro still crouched and worked the Tsinti ritual. Father though . . . I locked stares with him and bellowed, "Brace yourselves!" as the island jilted and became a slave to the storm.

Sixty-One

A Small Surprise

SCIMITYNES CROSSED ABOVE MY HEAD, I blocked Yankos's longsword from cleaving into my shoulder. With his legs and feet unclad, he crouched in the wet morning grass, smiling and pulling his sword to the ready again. Otarr's dawn light, the freshest after-the-storm kind of rays, streamed into the clearing beside the Sundai upriver and up-mountain from the falls and Arashi. We'd cleared the squall overnight, and Yankos and Buharro had been successful in their ritual to cloak Tsanseri's island in tsym.

I spun away, bare toes gripping the dewy blades beneath my feet. As I settled into the ready position, I flashed back to Tsanseri's broken body upon the marble. Her servant, Strato-Elea had taken control of the island and they had soared away under the final hours of Selene's watch in search of a healer. Returning Yankos's sadistic grin, I coiled down, sending energy into my thighs and calves before launching forward into the spinning attack I'd learned from my first guard, my gensui. I poured every heartache I'd suffered over the recent seasons into that attack, blindly slashing and thrashing at my opponent, yet still my friend. Still, I couldn't see him for the white-hot rage built up inside me.

Strike . . . Mother.

Reverse . . . Father.

Counter . . . Corwyn, Aunt Nadia.

Tilt, turn, retreat . . . Sarangarel, Tenkara, Tsanseri, how many more?

With every slash, turn, and jab, another person battered at my heart and soul while the brook babbled on at our sides. Of the people I'd sparred with and aside from

Thalaj, Yankos had always been the most capable, so I poured my fury into the match and cast aside any worry of hurting the lithe Tsinti leader.

Clang.

Halt . . . Thalaj.

I crumpled.

"Mairynne," Yankos said, soft concern lacing my name. He crouched, moving his sword and my scimitynes aside, then pulled me into a friendly, comforting embrace. "You're crying."

I pushed at his chest, looking over into the shadows where Buharro and Bree were already working on casting and binding a smaller version of the Tsinti cloaking ritual—a personal tsym I intended to use to sneak into Stormskeep and find my sister. They'd begun while others slept in makeshift tents nearby, even before Yankos and I had arrived to spar. I swiped at the tears dampening my cheeks. The mere thought of crying, of showing such weakness stung as much as any blow I'd taken.

"You realize," I started with a half-smile at Yankos, "this very place is where the legend of Sosano and Inara takes place." I peered upstream to where the river was wide but shallow, toward another waterfall. This one was smaller and calmer, flowing over a ridge naught more than two peoples' height. "This grove is considered a holy place amidst the castes, and only bears such beauty because priests and priestesses of the Holy Triad have traveled here to pay homage to Atun, Otarr, and Selene." I looked down at my bare toes and slid them forward in the thick-bladed grass toward the rocky shore. "I suppose it's not considered a safe journey in these dark times."

"But you've never been here?" Yankos took a seat beside me, nearer the gravel, and searched through the pebbles.

"Until now?" I answered. "No. I've only heard tales of this place from Tasmynne Hallowgale."

Yankos peered over at me with a brow quirked. Clearly, he needed further explanation.

"She's the priestess of Selene in Arashi," I began, "mother of the citadel's sanctuary. Or she was when I left in search of Father. Younglings, myself included, always gathered in her sanctuary where she would recount Nantai traditions through parable." It ached in my chest to recall those times, my youngling seasons when all seemed so peaceful. The days when I had no cares aside from running with my sisters, listening to Father's stories, and exploring Stormskeep to discover all her age-old secrets. To this day, I didn't believe I'd learned all she held within her stone walls.

"Ah, the enduring innocence of the babes." Yankos threw a small stone and watched it skip across the water. "And I believe this grove appears very much like the scene where my namesake, the *Wanderer*, bested the devil and reclaimed his fiddle. Perhaps these places are merely makings for peoples' comfort," he speculated, standing again. "The Nantai people, casted and casteless alike, live and die by their traditions. We may hold different traditions sacred, but in the end, we are all the same in how we find comfort."

Silence fell as crepuscular creatures settled for the day's sleep. The only sounds remaining were gently rustling leaves, babbling water, and whispers punctuating Buharro and Bree's efforts.

Traditions, I mused, considering how alike and different we all were as another wonder struck. *Parū?*

Minikin? she replied, slow to come around from her slumber.

Are there similar Ryū traditions?

I do not follow your meaning, for I was sleeping after the flight in the night. Similar to what, you ask? She groaned and stretched her consciousness, filling the edges of my mind with mild annoyance.

Yankos and I were speaking about legends and traditions, and I wondered about any traditions held by your kind.

Parū sifted through my recent thoughts, replaying the conversation. *Aahhh, no, minikin. Traditions imply social connection within a group. The Ryū are solitary creatures, save for our bond with you. The only other traditions we boast are mating rituals.* She shared a vision of her with a silver-scaled dragon atop a mountain in the white-skied Fey Realm.

I shied away with a head shake, feeling I'd intruded on something more private than necessary.

Her amusement rumbled again as she settled back into her slumber, and I returned to the conversation with the Tsinti leader.

"Yankos," I said suddenly, followed by a burst of laughter spattered with a hysterical tone. I'd flashed on the more recent past, when Thalaj and I had just set out on this adventure. I stood and crossed to him. "All those seasons ago when we met in the Yubar, who would have believed you and I would be standing here now? And conversing about how our people are so alike."

He echoed my wry chortle and added, "Or that Jorani would have returned to the Fire Forgers on your behalf. You may not have been aware, but *she* demanded I leave you and your protector in the forest. Apparently, she and Baldeo had an encounter with Gensui Thalaj and his friend in Safaia a season before." He skipped another pebble. "She surprised me more than anyone when she helped you adapt to the wandering life so readily. It only happened after she and Zofi nigh came to blows over it."

I angled my head, drawing my brows together as I'd failed to consider his reasons then. "Why did you take us into your caravan?"

A trill drew his attention to the forest behind us.

Only a bird, I thought.

No, Parū, suddenly alert within, corrected.

"Buharro," Yankos hissed, gesturing for silence with one hand while he lifted his longsword with the other.

Subconsciously, I readied my scimitynes. *What evil lurks out there, Parū?*

In my bones, I felt her relax, then chuckle as the sound became a full-on whistle, a person's whistle. One I recognized, and it quickly devolved into a song the sailors aboard the *Swell Mistress* seemed overly fond of.

Roll again, roll again

Make your bets, no regrets

And when you fall

Tip your gin and roll again

"Hoaris?!" I cried, lunging toward his voice.

He stepped from the darkness between two trees, arms spread wide and an open grin splitting his red beard. "You called?"

Chambui appeared heartbeats later, and I left my scimitynes where they lay in the grass and ran across the small field into their shared embrace.

"Tenkara?" I asked after squeezing them both with all the relief and appreciation I could muster. As I asked after the Frost Fighter gnoble's decision, I pulled back, hopeful, but the grim looks on both their faces trampled the spark.

Chambui shook her head grimly. "She said she'd build a barrier to separate the Plains from Nantai. She rallied a group of Frost Fighters and gave quite the incendiary speech. 'We'll forge our own country!' she said."

Hoaris added, "Amidst a ton of other things: 'The Frost Fighters are strong in our new clans! The clanholds are invisible to them. Kōgō Mairynne Evangale only found us because of the great cat's attack. We can use the nekodai in our quest against the Nantai,' she told the crowd. Later, we heard others commenting that because you and your Ryū fell to the great cat's claws, they now have the power to stand against the caste structure. They can be free. At least that's what they're beginning to believe."

I lowered my head. How could they believe they could escape the wrath of the green Ryū, Guin? Heat suffusing my skin, I snapped my gaze back up to the burly man's. "If a dragon intended harm upon our northern Nantai brethren, their ice halls in the clanholds would be no barrier. They would melt under the Ryū breath and all drown within."

Chambui ran a hand down my arm, soothing. "Mairynne, we all know this but they have not seen the cities laid to waste."

Kōkai, then Biei simmered in my mind. And Brennmor, though I had only seen the camp of those who'd fled the burned city where the Small Folk had thrived.

The yisu warrior continued, "If we have one hope amidst the Frost Fighters, it will come from Saqie Kitikara, Tenkara's second, and Su Almazaj." She peered over to Hoaris who nodded. "They escorted us from the Hoppō Clanhold, but as we parted, Saqie bore a strange look. Su, still recovering from his own nekodai attack, stood solemnly nearby. He portrayed no emotion, but that he was there, it seemed odd. I do not understand their intentions, but it seemed . . . odd."

"Su is a hunter, an explorer among the clans. I wonder if he witnessed aught of the destruction in Biei before he fell to the nekodai," said Hoaris.

Tightly, I nodded, turning my thoughts to another seed I'd cast into the winds. "I have Tsinti friends, Jorani and Baldeo"—I touched Yankos's arm—"who went to speak with Gnoble Yuos Atith. Did you perchance encounter the Fire Forgers on your way south?"

They hadn't, and in discussing their routes, it was unclear if they had even had the possibility of crossing paths. Hoaris and Chambui had moved at speeds a meandering army couldn't have hoped to attain, and the routes traveled would likely have paralleled one another toward Arashi. Hoaris mentioned they'd tried the northern pass but found it blocked with stone rubble, so they'd followed the curve of the Rausu Mountains ridge. I suspected the Fire Forgers would have taken a more direct route through the North Woods and over the Central Grasslands. It may have been well enough that we couldn't sway the Frost Fighters to our cause. Given all I'd learned in my short time with the Fire Forgers, the resulting battle may have been more real than staged, and that would have weighed heavier on my soul than the lives of the Nantai people who'd already been lost to this senseless strife. Likewise, I felt keen pain over those who might yet perish before we found peace again. Guilt riddled my soul over using the animosity between the two castes to my advantage, but the more dire this situation, the greater the necessary measures. If it were still a possibility, I'd use it and pay the consequences sometime down the road.

Hoaris brightened suddenly, distracting me from the worry. "But I do have someone else who might lighten your morn."

Rustling sounded beyond the tree line. The bushes and undergrowth swayed. Dry leaves crackled, and I heard one of the sweetest voices I knew . . .

"Just you wait, we're coming, lovely!"

SIXTY-TWO

Allies Gather

STUNNED, I WATCHED SLACK-JAWED AS Misha and Kyr climbed over a fallen log. I hadn't hoped to see them here and now, and the delight, confusion, and familiarity stole not only my breath, but my words too. As they made it out of the woods and both spread their arms wide with a what are you waiting for look, I glanced back and forth between them and where Bree and Buharro had halted their efforts to watch the commotion.

I gasped, covering my mouth. Though I relished having them back at my side, another idea rattled through my mind. "Spelled stones," I mumbled into my hands, my eyes widening as I balled my hands into fists and verily cheered, "Invisibility! Yankos, we no longer need to bind the tsym to a smaller area!"

Hoaris strode over and placed a heavy hand on Misha's shoulder. "I found them in the Yubar. We had to take the southern pass because the Underhills have blocked off the northern one."

Kyr looked up and scoffed. "You mean *we* found *you*, Red Bear. There's a reason I call you that, and it's not only that strange red hair that grows on your face. You sound like a bear rummaging through the brush. How could we have miss it?" Folding her arms, she rolled her eyes and crossed over to me. "C'mere, lovely. Give me a hug. I've missed you."

Sinking to my knees onto the grass, I hugged the small woman. The bittersweet reunion tasted metallic on my tongue. "This would be so much sweeter," I said, "if we weren't facing such a dark and confusing foe." I looked in the direction of Arashi.

A motherly gesture, Kyr grasped my chin with both her hands and focused my attention back on her. "What do we know of the future, lovely? You've come this far, and you've grown stronger with every one of your Otarr's watches. You've restored yourself with each of your goddess Selene's nights. You will find your way through this." She released me, nodded. "And we will help."

She was right. I'd endured for this long, and we could find a way through the rest of this journey. Hopes were important, and I needed to maintain mine now.

"You draw the eclectic group, Mairy," Misha observed, pointing to each person in the clearing in turn. "A Tsinti leader and one of his wanderers." He moved past Buharro to Bree, narrowing his eyes. "A young Cloud Courtier? Interesting, if I do say . . ." Looking up and to the side where Hoaris stood with an arm around Chambui, he added, "A deserted Frost Fighter and a lone yisu of the Stone Singers. And then you have us, two of the Small Folk, outcast and invited back into King Isao's good graces. We've traveled afar with you and still return to watch over your path. You couldn't ask for much more, dear."

Kyr curled into him. "Don't forget her Ryū, Meesh."

I smiled, humbled to have my blessings narrated so. Right again, I simply needed the reminder. Their appearance alone brought hope. My initial plans to stage a diversion before Arashi's gates between the ever-bickering Frost Fighters and Fire Forgers were failing fast. I needed to face that now and correct the course. Perhaps sneaking into Arashi with the help of invisibility would allow me to gather inside supporters before confronting Karynne and Imrythel and taking back my city.

Yes, minikin, these are good and loyal people to remember, Parū echoed my thoughts. *You will give Misha the time to spell new stones, and meanwhile, I can show you something new of our bond that will help when it is time to confront Guin.*

I hesitated, turned, and paced, rubbing my temples as positions of people, castes, casteless, friends, enemies—so much and more—swam around in my mind. "Did King Isao's Small Folk make the journey from the south at your side? What of those from the Evernight? Did you find them in your travels?" I asked Misha and Kyr, my eyes widening as I remembered even more. "Honera? And what of the sailors, Tao and Oshun?"

Kyr chuckled. "Easy there, lovely."

"They're following," Misha answered, "but they'll head for Arashi's gates rather than here."

"That may be well enough," I said and kept moving, ideas forming with every step. I had to get inside but worried over someone finding me before I could confront Karynne. The battle of frost and fire would have been the perfect diversion, but . . . "Do you think a confrontation between the Small Folk and the Fire Forgers would be believable?" I turned to the group; they'd huddled together, further demonstrating my eclectic support network.

Misha, folding his arms across his chest, twisted his lips, then answered, "There's been a long history of unrest between the castes of Nantai, but the Small Folk have never engaged in open battle. I think it would be reason for suspicion."

"You'll need another plan, Mairynne," Yankos offered.

Chambui watched in silence, waiting.

To her, I asked, "Where did you leave the rest of the yisun?"

She shook her head. "They are sworn to the gnoble of the Stone Singers and had no cause to follow me. As you well know, Mairy, our people follow heart above all else. I had good cause to travel with Hoaris"—she moved closer to his side—"but they went in search of Lady Sarangarel."

I pursed my lips and continued pacing. My fingers found and worried at my lower lip while I thought more. Ideas formed, flickered, reformed, but what remained certain was that I needed to gain support from within. Mayhap Gaelynne could help gather support among the guards. And I'd always been close to Tasmynne, priestess of Selene. Or . . . Aunt Nadia and Corwyn, assuming he wasn't still weak from the poisoning. But he's a Dawnsgale. *Yes!* The Dawnsgales in their keep in the cliffs, even higher than Stormskeep. Solarynne would certainly help. She had to!

I hoped.

And . . . *Parū, can you fly me there if we can hide your form?*

'Tis a large form, minikin, she answered wearily.

I turned back to the Small Folk. "Misha, how big of a stone can you spell?"

His brow furrowed. "Not larger than my person, why?"

"And how long will it take you to spell more stones?"

"Several hours," he began, "but it drains energy. Three, perhaps four in a day's ti—"

"Three," Kyr insisted, ever the protector of those she loved.

"As she says," he agreed. "But for a large one, only one in a day's span. How many do you need? And when?"

What I have to show you, minikin, may take several days' time.

"Well and so," I said. "One large one first, then three a day will have to suffice. Do you have the stones you and your mate use on your person?"

Misha lifted his shirt sleeve. "We've mounted them into these." A silver band encased his upper arm with a smooth, near transparent, sparkling stone.

"Bree? Come closer." I waited while the young Cloud Courtier came to my side.

"Yes, Kōgō?" She bowed, pending my command.

"See this stone? Find others along the river that seem similar, and if you can find a very large one, all the better. Then you and Buharro bring them back to camp when you have a good number."

<hr>

MUCH LATER IN THE afternoon, I went alone from the Tsinti camp into the forest, far enough away that I would no longer be hidden under the tsym the Tsinti had cast to hide my small band of wandering support. I stood on the rock ledge overlooking Arashi. In the distance beside the Sundai Falls, Stormskeep stared back at me, the High Cloud Court encircling her spires. Higher up would be the face of the Dawnsgale stronghold, though I couldn't see it from this distance, even with the enhanced Ryū sight.

My blood boiled after I learned what Parū intended in order to confront the green dragon. "I cannot believe you have held this information from me for all these seasons!" I shouted at Parū, not that the voice was necessary, but it felt right to release my frustration into the skies.

She still rested inside me as I allowed the anger to simmer across our bond, then at length, Parū calmly said, *Were our circumstances any different, this isn't something I'd share with you at such an early stage of our bond.*

I balled my fists. "But you let me believe I'd never be alone with myself again. That I'd never share an intimate moment in my own mind without you there to bear witness. I accepted that, and now you tell me it's possible?"

'Tis dangerous, minikin. Kuroi shared too much with your first emperor, Makenyn. Betimes, such knowledge results in madness. Yet, to our ill fortune, I fear we haven't the time, and I bear little hope . . . I am certain that Guin and her bonded Nantai developed the ability to part many, many seasons ago. Mayhap even ages.

My jaw agape, I craved more of this story, more about the black dragon and my ancestor Makenyn. The reasons Makenyn had excised the bond had been a mystery to the Nantai people and my fellow Storm Sorcerers for ages. And now, there seemed more to this story. Releasing my tension on a long breath, I thought to my Ryū, *What do you know of how Makenyn banished Kuroi, Parū?*

Only what the great black dragon recanted to me in the Fey Realm, but 'tis a dire story to tell.

Nevertheless, and despite that time was of the essence, that we needed to hone this skill to become two beings while remaining one, I wanted to hear this story here and now.

You can have both, minikin. Kuroi's story may help to distract you from the magic I work. I will tell you what the blackest dragon once told me.

My brow heavy with confusion, I asked, *What do you mean by "you work"? Do I not participate in the parting?* A shudder racked my spine as I recalled the initial process of joining, the fire searing my very soul as two became one. How foreign it had felt then, but that was no longer the truth. The sensation of having her inside—having her thoughts, feelings, and even the unconscious mannerisms exposed to me—had become so ingrained, it seemed unreal to have it suddenly gone.

Banished.

She chuckled, not a sound, but another familiar sensation rumbling through my core. *Do not think of it as banished, minikin. I will not be gone. The Ryū bond will remain whole while our bodies part. This is only afforded through fey magic, exercised and woven by a fey creature.*

You?

Hai, minikin. Me. She ran a mental scan over my body and being. *You have calmed, so we should begin. Find somewhere to sit where you will be comfortable.*

As she instructed, I found a large, flat rock from where I could keep watch over Arashi while she prepared to pull threads of magic from the fey realm. I still fretted and worried over how her absence would feel. What would I do with the space in my mind she occupied while her consciousness was absent?

You will still feel me. It will be similar to when you fly with me, but I must caution you also. You cannot lose yourself in what I see or feel. You will need to hone your thoughts to focus on that which is in front of you at all times. You must push the feelings of whatever I experience to the back of your mind. She paused for a long moment, in which I keenly felt her hesitation. *Else, it can result in both our deaths. The parting leaves a part of my soul with you while I take part of yours with me.*

An errant notion, that a Nantai person's lifespan flickered in comparison to a dragon's near immortality, had me asking aloud, "But if the Ryū are ancient and leave their persons at the ends of their natural lives, how is it possible that you do not die at the time?"

Her manner grew stern, a demeanor I once would have associated with Mother when her tolerance with my sisters and me went threadbare. Now there were times when Kyr wore the same tender but hard outer shell. Breath, not mine but Parū's, huffed in the back of my throat as her words sparked, *You are too easily distracted by such thoughts. If I so choose, minikin, I can pull away from a person's soul entirely. There are cruder ways to forcibly separate the two as well, as your first emperor banished Kuroi. Although the ritual Makenyn performed was unnatural and ill-recommended. Kuroi told your first emperor the same. Are you ready?*

Sufficiently chided, I ran sweaty palms over the rough-spun fabric of my breeches, took a deep breath, and straightened my spine, affirming.

I shall begin, she said.

I had no adequate description for the sensations following those simple three words. The best explanation I could offer hearkened to sitting within a closed room, air stale and stagnant, while something nearby opened. Perhaps a door or a space between some invisible barrier parted and a storm churned on the other side. Yet my body remained in a calm center with only a light breeze tickling the small hairs upon my arms. Parū's thoughts divided, and I couldn't stretch my mind beyond the part of her speaking to me, beginning to recount the story Kuroi had told her.

In Kuroi's time, there were many Ryū roaming the lands of Nantai and beyond. Of many sizes and shapes. The giant wyrms burrowed beneath the northeastern hills in the lands you call the Barrows now. Wingless drakes roamed over Nantai, Yōtei, and the Engaru sand dunes. Tiny hummingdragons, not larger than my last knuckle but quick with their fire breath, populated the tree-covered and marshy regions. And then was about the time when our six-limbed brethren, the dragons, departed into the west.

Before the Erasure, the people of Nantai and Ryū kind lived in harmony here on your lands, often forging the most sacred Ryū bond.

"The Erasure?" I asked, slowly putting together the pieces and whispering, "The Ryū Wars."

Hai, yes, minikin. That is how the Ryū refer to the war following Makenyn's ritual separation from Kuroi. Though perhaps you can understand why we, as Ryū kind, do not refer to that event by the same name as you. It weighs heavily in my heart how your people's traditions and legends have twisted something sacred.

Upon this sadness, there was a tug starting at the tips of my fingers and toes, fey magic coming alive between us as if two threads once wound tight slowly uncoiled. It tickled and sent twinges through all the tiny bones in my hands and feet.

Parū grumbled, *Breathe, Mairynne,* until which time I hadn't realized I held my breath in suspension, waiting, and anticipation. Rolling my shoulders, I followed her instruction.

As you have seen when you were in the Fey Realm, there is never an absence of light. When Kuroi offered his story to me, in some manner, it felt like night. I remained by his pool of tears as Kuroidragon recounted his story in the Ryū tongue. I will translate for you to the best of my ability.

"I chose him, Parūdragon," Kuroi had said, stopped, and started again, "Too young myself, but I was the blackest Ryū —proud, fierce, and foolish."

Mind, minikin, that the blackest Ryū is the most revered among dragonkind, Parū interjected. *As he went on, I could feel the depths of his sadness within the words he growled: "I knew better than those who mentored me against such actions, or such was my belief. I shared with my Nantai person, Makenyn, all I knew about our connection, openly, readily, believing for every scale upon my spine that the openness would make us both stronger. It would enable a trusting bond that would have exceeded in strength every sacred Ryū bond that had ever gone before. But such was not so . . ."*

Parū maintained focus on her split tasks more easily than I, and while I tried to listen, I couldn't entirely ignore the hum in my legs and arms. The threads that'd begun unwinding within me moved upward along one leg, then the other, one arm, and the last. A hum-hum-hum sliding through my limbs. I breathed.

Heedless of my strained focus, Parū continued her recount, *"Makenyn craved more,"* *Kuroi said. "Always, he needed to know something else, and when I had exhausted my own well of information, he changed. He began trying new ways to pry the non-existent secrets from my mind."*

My hips stretched, pulled, thrummed, and the unraveling sensation crept up my spine. I closed my eyes to block out anything else that threatened to steal my attention.

Over the course of the next several seasons, Makenyn turned against Kuroi and developed the idea of banishing him and all other Ryū from Nantai.

I turned my neck, and it cracked. Suddenly, everything seemed quieter. Had the birds stopped singing? The Sundai stopped flowing? Quiet, solitude, foreign and so loud it echoed through my mind.

Open your eyes, minikin, Parū said, her voice soft and coaxing.

But also, she sounded distant as I realized what the lack of thrumming within my body meant. I inhaled sharply, but no breath followed as I opened my eyes to the gloaming. Beside me, on the cliff overlooking Arashi, next to my Ryū, I sat.

Alone.

Quiet inside—*too* quiet.

And . . . *cold.*

◇◇◇◇◇◇◇◇◇◇◇◇◇◇◇◇◇◇◇◇◇◇◇◇◇◇◇◇◇◇◇◇◇

UPON THAT RIDGE, WE peered out over Arashi. Deep into the night, torches lit the streets between dwellings and fires upon hearths painted many small arched windows with an orange glow. More firelight punctuated the columns upon the wall surrounding the city. Torches of the men standing guard, no doubt. A cloud supporting the High Cloud Court hung persistently about the upper spires of Stormskeep itself, the very spires to where I'd banished the old man in gray who'd poisoned my oldest friend and the daughter of my attendant Mother Feathergale.

Jessa.

My heart twisted; the once searing pain now merely ached. It seemed an age had passed since her murder before I'd left my home on this journey, and the sorrow still lingered. I doubted I'd ever be free of it. Mayhap I should have sentenced her murderer to death. Given all I'd learned over my travels, I no longer believed I'd hesitate in making that decree. Alas, I hadn't the courage at the time, and I wondered now if the man with the fleck in his eye, who took Jessamynne Feathergale's life and also poisoned Aunt Nadia's consort, Corwyn, still lived in the uppermost reaches of the castle.

On occasion, the shadow of a dragon blocked out the city's lights. With effort, I put the thoughts of the past out of my mind and hardened myself for the fight that lay before me.

How long we sat on the ridge, apart but together and watching the scene, I couldn't say. Selene peeked through and climbed partway above the trees across the vale by the time either of us stirred. Behind us, within the swath of the Yubar, the Tsinti had built a fire. Still within the sphere of the tsym, I could hear their voices rising in nightly celebration. Yet upon my skin and in my heart hung a thick feeling, charged with deadly serenity as if the land, Nantai herself, had paused to show reverence in the wake of a cataclysm.

Until Parū broke the stillness. *We will remain free of one another for the night while I hunt. I fear the days to come will be trying so I need to build strength. But do not fret; I will be there, minikin, in your mind. All you have to do is focus your thoughts on me, and I will answer.*

Her words in my tongue were as clear in my mind as the Syrensea upon the coast of Ise. The notion occurred that I'd never held a conversation with her in another form. Or truly aloud.

She peered down at me from thrice my height and merely issued a low rumble in her chest. *Ryū mouths are not shaped such that we can speak your language,* she answered my wandering thoughts.

"Do you hear what I think while we are apart?" I asked.

I do not unless you intend as much, but you wear the question in the mask you wear, upon the fold on your brow, and the squint in your eye. And alas, 'tis a logical question, and our bond helps me infer your meaning. Though, you do not need vocalize the words you wish me to hear. The bond is forged from fey magic and allows thought to travel between us though we do not inhabit the same being.

Shivering, I stood and moved closer to my Ryū. She remained utterly still with her snout pointed toward the triple jewel view within Arashi—the Sundai Falls flanked by Stormskeep and the citadel of the Triad. I followed her gaze to what could be seen of these pillars of my youth in the dying light and under the heavy mist of the High

Cloud Court.

"You sense me come closer? Sense my movement?" I asked, simultaneously and instinctively knowing the answer. I placed both hands on her silvery-white scales, my palms heating as I made contact. Relief flooded through my palms and arms.

Return to the Tsinti camp, minikin. You have not worn shoes or warm clothing in many seasons . . . the kind suitable to keep a person warm in these falling temperatures.

We were not heavy on supplies, but . . . "Mayhap there is a cloak or blanket I might use," I agreed. "You go. Soar, hunt, and then return to me. I've grown accustomed to your warmth and do not enjoy the crisp mountain air." I patted her twice and turned for the forest.

She waited for me to reach the edge of the trees and then spread her wings. A hot sense of her worry over how I'd fare for the night bloomed within, so I turned, spread my arms, and in a gesture that I'd be well enough for the night, I called the wind. *Return to me,* I thought, sending the gale toward her and upward.

I'll be waiting here at Otarr's first light, she affirmed, her pearlescent scales catching Selene's silver light as she rose higher into the sky.

The Tsinti camp rested in a small copse of trees, sunken between the ridge overlooking Arashi and the knoll near the upper Sundai. As soon as I'd turned away from the view of the city, I could see the glow hovering in the center. I started for the fire, descending over leaf-covered ground with sticks crackling beneath my bare and chilled feet until I felt the flames' warmth reach my skin. I moved closer to the bonfire than I'd been since my days roaming the Central Grasslands amidst the caravan. Still trembling, I held my hands forward to the fire, watching as the Tsinti, happy to have their feet upon the soil once more, milled about. When I'd warmed my hands, arms, and face enough, I closed my eyes and turned to heat my back.

Mentally, I reached for Parū, and she sent an image of what she saw: the buildings of the High Cloud Court hovering in mist above Arashi—the city I'd vacated long ago. Even now, I remained uncertain as to if I wished to live there again. So much would be different once we'd vanquished Guindragon back to the Fey Realm for Amare to handle. The entire image seemed brushed in silver and blue strokes, eerie in the night. Yet Parū assured me, *All seems quiet, minikin. Now, rest among your people.*

The image faded. When I opened my eyes, focusing into the darkness, Father stood before me with a blanket spread wide. His expression held a gentle question and true concern. "What differs, Daughter?"

"Parū flies away to hunt tonight," I answered, accepting his warm, blanket-laden embrace. "I have the remaining dark to rest alone."

Without ado, without words, and with only a parent's acceptance, he turned me toward the small camp he'd made with Zofi. The Tsinti witch wife had built a small fire of mostly peat so that it burned warm and smoky in the night but remained dull.

"Rest here with us and be comfortable this night, Mairynne." Zofi urged me to sit beside the fire. "The morrow will be a new day with new promises."

She and Father sat near one another on the other side.

As I willed my body to calm and yawned, I hoped her words held truth. I fought the urge to search for Parū's mind, instead focusing on the ground beneath me, the sounds of the night, and simply being me. Selene rose higher, her rays broken by the treetops. Creatures chirped nocturnal songs. And the peat and sticks crackled before me. I sank to one side, curling deeper into the fur-lined blanket in which Father had swaddled me. The darkness spread but my bones warmed. Slowly, ever so slowly. Languor encircled my limbs, drawing me into oblivion.

The sounds lulled my soul, chirp, chirp, crackle, until . . .

SNAP!

In the woods. I jerked upright, threw away the fur, and lurched to my feet, spreading my palms to call lightning from the skies above. What intruder would find us here? And hidden by tsym?

All sounds save the singe of the peat moss fire at my back ceased. I listened closer, probing the night, to hear . . .

Murmurs?

Sixty-Three

Return to Stormskeep

ZOFI AND FATHER STOOD, AND I glanced over a shoulder. Questions flickered on their faces like the dim and dancing firelight, but I brushed a finger over my lips asking for quiet. I tilted my head toward the snap and possible voices. They rounded the peat fire and stood at my back, waiting.

Ki-ki-koo, a bird called.

Zofi's hand grasped my wrist. "Shh." She looked at Father. "The call of the Black Grassland thrush. 'Tis a wanderer's call."

"Who's there?" I demanded of the shadows.

Ki-ki-koo ki-ki- ki-ki-koo.

After the song, footsteps rustled in the dry leaves. With no answer, I pooled my sorcery inside me, searching externally for dry air and readying to arc the lightning to my will. Naught but darkness stared back but the rustling continued.

"Ye're jumpy, little one," a man drawled, and Baldeo stepped into the dim light.

Tension gushed from my body and I slumped with relief.

"Where's your blades, Mairynne?" Jorani asked.

I closed my eyes and reopened them slowly several times as if I could clarify the image before me. Jorani and Baldeo had been the last two people I'd expected to see in the Tsinti camp. They were to bring the Fire Forgers to the gates of Arashi for the diversion, but here they were before me, looking expectant—Jorani with her brows raised and Baldeo with his thumbs tucked into a belt.

I hadn't moved, and my thoughts were dull and muddled as I stood motionless, struck dumb. Several heartbeats passed as I sensed Father and Zofi easing at my side. My arms still faced upward, and I still held the storm's magic ready. So, unwittingly, I called the wind and ran, launching into Baldeo's arms for a tight hug, then Jorani's, while the wind swept around us. Even here in the night, the feeling of solitude and loss had changed. With every person who arrived to fight at my behest, I felt stronger if not better about our position. Even the separation from Parū for the night seemed, in many ways, right.

◇◇◇◇◇◇◇◇◇◇◇◇◇◇◇◇◇◇◇◇◇◇◇◇◇◇◇◇◇◇

THE FOLLOWING MORNING IN the grayness of dawn, I arose before the others and crept through camp back to the overlook where Parū had promised to return at first light. I'd wrung my hands, nervous anticipation guiding every step, but the merge back into one surprised me with its simplicity.

It will only be easier for us from this point forward, minikin, Parū intoned from within.

I sighed, hot relief suffusing every fiber of my being after the bond of companionship had been restored. I asked, *Did you see aught that would raise need for alarm during the night?*

Guin circled Arashi most of the night, keeping close to Stormskeep and above the High Cloud Court. Yet I didn't fly near enough to make my presence known. It didn't seem that her flight meant more than merely keeping guard over Arashi.

Regardless, I wondered about the terror she kept alive within the people of our jewel city by circling above. Of what I could see from this far away, the empty streets and greenways told how the city's people huddled within shelters to avoid the terror they sensed above. And could anyone lay blame upon their doorsteps? They sensed danger, but if they had seen the destruction and waste within the other areas of Nantai, how much worse would it be?

Morning fog misted over dew-covered grasses within camp, and Otarr's light cast it in a quiet haze. Barefoot and warm once more, I trod back to where I'd left Jorani and Baldeo with Father and Zofi, all four still asleep at the time I'd gone. They'd woken in my absence and welcomed me back with a bowl of steaming stew.

After breaking our nightly fast and the others rising from their rest under the tsym began to stir, I gathered with the trusted people who'd once accompanied me across the Syrensea—Hoaris and Chambui, Misha and Kyr. I also welcomed Jorani and Baldeo, and at my side in the clearing near the upper Sundai stood my father, Zofi, several of the Tsinti leaders, Buharro, and the young Cloud Courtier Bree. Owed to the fact that Yankos and Jorani bestowed trust upon the Tsinti, I too placed my faith in their abilities, and considered how I might add one or more of them to a council of advisors who would support Nantai's leader into a new age. I watched Father observe their actions too, and when we locked gazes, I sensed we shared in our speculations.

Hoaris and Baldeo each measured the other from opposite sides of the circle. I hid a smile at the two, both so similar in many ways yet differing in their wandering habits. A protective streak also ran through the core of both men. I suspected they'd become hearty friends given the chance.

Scanning the mismatched castes and Small Folk, I began, "Misha, how fare you with the stones?"

Perhaps the restoration of the fey creature within me afforded me enhanced sight, for I believed a light glowed within Misha's eyes as he extended both arms, opened his hands, palms up, and smiled. In the nest of each hand, resembling a small bird's egg, two smooth bluish stones with metallic flecks shone in Otarr's light.

Kyr took one between two fingers, lifting it up to me. "Do you recall the word, lovely?"

"Mmm . . ." I considered. "Yes, *mekoifieu.*"

Others in the clearing inhaled, stammered, and oohed, echoing sounds that betrayed any surprise they may have otherwise hidden. Speaking from my first personal encounter with the charms of invisibility, I understood their reactions. Breathing the magic word once more, I lifted the spell and bent to thank the small man. "And you will complete more today?"

Kyr pulled at his arm, eying me with warning. "Only after he's been well fed, lovely."

"Well and so," I assented, touching the small woman lightly upon the shoulder. I raised my gaze to the others before standing, and as I straightened, I addressed the newest comers in our party. "Baldeo, are the Fire Forgers hidden somewhere here in the Yubar?"

Hoaris grumbled. "If the fires on the facing slope under Selene's watch last night were any indication, hai, they have arrived." He turned his red head and spat, raised a lip in a sneer, then added, "Giving away our approach if you ask me. They've never been too subtle."

Jorani's chest expanded as she reached for her weapon.

Baldeo stepped between her and Hoaris, eyes narrowed. "Do you mean to do battle here in this garden?"

Jorani pulled out her short sword and examined the blade, then looked beyond her partner at Hoaris. "And how do you know it's not the accursed Frost Fighters over there betraying our position?" She'd grasped the reins on her immediate reaction, squelching her inner Fire Forger, and returned to the nonchalant yet forthright Tsinti wandering woman. She jutted a hip and ran the pad of her thumb over the honed blade.

The air thickened, felt heavier. Chambui smirked, crossing her arms over her chest. Baldeo slid a hand to his weapons belt. Yankos leaned one shoulder on a small white-barked tree about five paces from everyone else, quietly listening to the banter and looking up on occasion to make whatever silent observation. His head snapped up when Hoaris threw back his head and bellowed laughter into the skies.

Latching onto Misha's arm, Kyr giggled and said to Jorani, "Now you've poked the Red Bear, Miss Firefly." Kyr's new moniker seemed fitting for the young woman who fled the Fire Forgers for a wanderer's life.

Hoaris Nishikara—Frost Fighter by birth—moved his hands before him and summoned a sphere with glowing blue lightning dancing between the edges. In my presence, he hadn't shone his powers often, but in his palms, he held all the energy of a northern blizzard encapsulated within what seemed a harmless orb. A gust of cold wind surrounded us, further emphasizing the nature of his magic. Hoaris answered, "We're attuned to cold, draining the air of all heat. You will never see a Frost Fighter carry a torch with a dancing yellow light or set a fire that'll cast an orange glow. Aside from that, on the rare occasion when Frost Fighters wander this far south, they swelter, having little need for a campfire's heat. Fire Forgers burn what's in sight." He extinguished the orb, clasping his large palms together.

Yankos's face contorted, and he pushed away from the trees. The Tsinti caravan had never ventured into the lands touched by frost, and his quizzical look proved he lacked familiarity with the northern people. "What of cooking?" he asked. "If you don't build fires, how do your people prepare meals? Or how do you give thanks for the day and ward off the evil within the darkness each night?"

The red-bearded man tipped his head toward the Tsinti leader, malice dissipating, and returned to his jovial nature in the face of true curiosity. "We only consume cured or deeply frozen meats, fresh fish, root vegetables grown in the warmer season when the ground can be worked on the southern end of the Iced Plains. There are many caves near the great frozen lake where we gather mushrooms, and in the warming season, we gather snow berries that break through—"

Splashing broke Hoaris's explanation and startled the group into silence. In unison, we turned toward the sound. From under the waterfall in the small branch of the Sundai River where we had gathered, two figures appeared, feeling their way along the wet rocks to the bed of grass along the bank. When they reached it upon all fours, they shook the water off, their tentacle mustaches wafting in the air.

Misha latched onto my hand and hissed, "W-what is that?"

"Easy . . . recall we are hidden under tsym," I whispered as I lay a hand over his. Tension left my shoulders too, as I reconciled who stood so near us now. "They're Underhill Dwellers," I added, then turned to Hoaris with a questioning gaze. Had he spoken with them on his travels?

Understanding my unspoken question, he raised his brows and shook his head.

Two more surfaced from the water—one I recognized as the gnoble, Brimr.

The first two brandished swords that had been hidden somewhere on their bodies amidst the feelers. They all wore dark-lensed spectacles like the ones I recalled Brimr and Svarta wearing during my ascension at the High Cloud Courts. But behind the shadow of the lenses, if one studied them closely, a soft moonlike light dimly glowed. On the closest one, the tentacle-like mustache moved freely in the air. "I smell the fire. Show yourselves," he grumbled.

Everyone in my party had become like the trees watching the sacred grove. They remained rooted in place, turning questioning gazes toward me, awaiting my command. Yet I had no way of knowing if the Underhill people were traveling to this place on my behalf or for another's purpose. Which was the case, I couldn't be certain, so I waited.

Brimr and his wife, Svarta, moved in front of the others, tentacles sniffing the air.

Svarta leaned closer to her mate, murmuring. Behind the lenses, Brimr's brows lifted with new understanding. They both knelt.

The Underhill gnoble said, "Kōgō Mairynne Evangale," lowered his head, then waited in silence.

Long moments passed in which I scarcely breathed before I finally motioned Yankos to my side. Their deference and patience spoke of their loyalty and hinted at the reasons they'd traveled southward from the Northerly Barrows.

The Underhill guards crouched at either side of the gnoble and his wife, readied for attack as Yankos moved toward me. The Tsinti leader's feet traveled over the wet grasses silent enough that I perceived no sound. His eyes never left the guards, and their feelers followed where he moved. As he drew close enough to whisper, I could see a double line formed between his brows. "Do they . . . *see* us?" he asked.

"No," I said, still without concern for them hearing my voice. "They exist in the dark, having adapted to the caverns beneath the Barrows and within the Rausu Mountains. Without the lenses, their eyes resemble Selene in the night sky. They've adapted other senses accordingly. For lack of a better description, they most likely *smell* us. Is there a way to allow them inside without lifting the tsym?"

"Hai," he still whispered even though I spoke in normal tones. "Anyone currently within the veil only needs to touch them, and the tsym will welcome them inside."

With a nod, I stepped toward the gnoble and his wife, straightening my spine and expanding my chest. "Gnoble Brimr, why have you come?" I asked with as much force behind the words as I could gather.

Brimr answered with his head still bowed. "We heard through the messenger network that you planned to unseat the beast from Stormskeep. Having sworn our allegiance to you, we were bound to offer what help we could."

I stood straighter still, though he couldn't witness my posture. "Did you not swear the same to my sister Karynne when she ascended?"

In my periphery, Father winced. Zofi crept closer to him, offering solace, but I hadn't the time nor the space to worry over the matter. I also needed to be assured this was no hoax to draw me forth. I hoped to return Karynne from the demon that held sway over her, but if it came to a choice between my sister and my land . . . I pressed my lips tightly together, wishing to swallow the knowledge of the onerous decision I might still face.

Her chin held high in the air, Svarta answered my question, "Against our caste's wishes, my kōgō."

"And why, gods tell," I began, "did your people block the northern pass through the Rausu Mountains? The efforts would not halt one of the Ryū in her tracks."

Brimr snuffled. "We knew not at the time what sides would form between the peoples of Nantai. Our purpose was twofold. Aside from it being a gateway to the Rausu trails, there is a well-known entrance there into our underground network. The destruction was in defense of both."

I searched each face within the circle, each of my supporters bound to my cause by blood or shared experience. Most offered little in the way of guidance, but Yankos, Hoaris, and Father each nodded in succession. Moving over the grasses, I approached the Underhill Dwellers. "Welcome, then," I said as I lay a hand on the nearest Underhill guard, the second, then Gnoble Brimr and Svarta. "I am more than pleased to have you at my side. My prior plan to enter Stormskeep would not work. Mayhap you can help us arrive at a new strategy."

Those gathered passed introductions, Father and Gnoble Brimr speaking in brevity about Tennō Atheryn Evangale's ascension to the Serpentine Throne. In their words and distant, memory-ridden looks, the time had been something sweet to them. They threw their heads back, howling laughter to the Day-Seer at the mention of another gnoble who'd been in attendance. The moment passed too fleetingly, the fond remembrance of those days before my sisters and I had been a thought to Father. I allowed the conversation to spin its natural cycle, hiding a small smile on occasion, until the tone faded.

"Those were the times," Brimr mused, his laughter dwindling as he dug gnarled knuckles into his flank.

As we had accepted the Underhills into the circle, more appeared from the cave beneath the falls. I hadn't known the entrance existed until that morn, yet it stood to reason. If so many people recited legends about this place, naturally, all peoples would find a road to return. A morning's worth of speculation, conversation, and questionable strategies babbled forth under the trees. People moved about, some sitting in the grass or leaning against trees. I reclined on a large boulder and listened absently to the conversation. A majority of talk, though, I either didn't hear or couldn't fathom as helpful information. I played in my palm with the two smooth stones Misha had offered. The shimmery blue stones weren't the same, but they brought memories of two other stones to the surface—Mother's and Father's soul stones. They'd called me away from Arashi, and I'd been so certain on that course. And so certain about the course at Thalaj's side.

I sighed as someone said, "It's a day's march into Arashi from here, should we move camp closer?"

Grasping the stones, I pinched the bridge of my nose. "No. I want to get us inside more than most of you. My family still lives inside. But we need support and more knowledge before moving closer to the city." Otarr hadn't reached the apex in the sky for the day, leaving plenty of time. "I will go alone and return in time for the evening fire."

"Mairynne," started Father, "I cannot allow you to go alone."

"Is there another way?" I challenged.

He ran both hands down his sides, rolling his shoulders back. "There are two stones there for invisibility. You and I can ride the winds into Stormskeep or into the Dawnsgale stronghold."

Gnoble Brimr lumbered back and forth near the water, his tentacles worrying in the air as he clearly contemplated. At length, he peered over from behind his dark lenses. "We have skirted about the details, and I understand your family is inside. But can you be assured of their loyalty to you or to this cause?"

I couldn't answer because I could *not* be assured of such things. I'd been away for too long. There had been rumors about my death. Others didn't know about Father's return. Brimr spoke truth, and though the thoughts stung, I needed to acknowledge such things. Any Storm Sorcerer I'd trusted before and who still lived within Arashi may have come to support Karynne and, by extension, Imrythel.

"What would you have me do, Gnoble Brimr? I can ill-handle this waiting for much longer. And the longer we wait, the more lives we risk."

"Hai, Kōgō Mairynne, well and so. Well and so . . ." He crossed to his partner's side and exchanged an embrace with the portly Underhill woman. Turning while still within her arms to face me again, he said, "I do not believe any should wait here while you and your father risk your lives on everyone's behalf. I propose we all travel closer. Together."

Lips tight, I shook my head. "I cannot risk such movement. Or so many lives."

Yankos moved closer. "But we will maintain the cloak of tsym, Mairynne. Gnoble Brimr speaks wisely."

I shook my head harder. Something I couldn't name clenched around my chest, having me believe it a terrible plan.

"No," barked Brimr. "That is not what I suggest. We have another way. There are tunnels through the prime mountain. They lead into the caverns far below Stormskeep. They are the ones that were sealed after Emperor Makenyn's separation from the black dragon. People, Underhills included, haven't traveled them for ages, but they are there. 'Tis a route any enemy will never expect."

Covering my mouth with both hands, I considered the possibilities. Rumors of that place had held much mystery when I'd been a youngling, but as I'd grown, they became no more than rumor, or so I'd believed. Jessa and I had searched for them long and hard as younglings. I blinked several times as memories washed over me—the pretend games we played where we'd each bonded with a Ryū dragon from Father's stories. The flash of Jessamynne's sweet face pressed hard at my mind, heart, and soul. Breathless, speechless, I had to turn away, remembering the young woman—my friend—who'd lost her life far too soon.

Had she not been my friend, I thought, perhaps . . .

I kicked myself to a stand, gripping the stones in my palm. "Well and so." I held each and every person's gaze for a heartbeat. Though this was no little matter and certainly was not only my fight, in the views of these people, it had become mine to lead. I couldn't guarantee safety or assure we'd prevail, but Father had never shown ill-decisiveness, and I wouldn't now. Settling my gaze on the Underhill gnoble, I said, "Brimr, Svarta, and Underhill Dwellers, I will trust your suggestion. And as such, I see no further reason to delay."

SIXTY-FOUR

Betrayal

DAMP AND DANK AND DARK, the tunnels beneath the falls were everything I expected from a cave. The Underhills each removed their spectacles as we entered. Despite their moonlike eyes offering a soft glow, I couldn't see much while my eyes adjusted from Otarr's bright daylight. After we crouched behind the water curtain under solid earth, my dragon stirred nervously beneath my skin, and I found it nigh impossible to remain still. As a youngling and even as I'd gained my majority inside of Stormskeep, I'd traveled often enough through the hidden passages. As such, I tried to ease her into the idea.

But minikin, she replied. *I cannot even be here in Ryū dragon form. There is not space sufficient to be here with wings folded.*

We must travel thus. Will you be able to abide this until we find our way into the keep? I scrubbed at my arms to fight the sensation of aari bugs swarming over my skin. My dragon didn't reply but I sensed her assent as I scratched. The feeling wasn't reality as aari bugs only thrived in arid spaces. Rather the itchy crawling beneath my clothing was how Parū's nervous energy manifested. For her to be in such a state disconcerted me more than I would have admitted. *It is temporary,* I thought to her, assuring her and taking long, deep breaths in an effort to sate her nerves.

In the near dark, a blue light flickered to life and formed into an orb over my head. Hoaris, holding the winter's magic, grinned—an expression made more eerie by the gray shadows than the feral nekodai I'd faced in the north. Frost Fighters spent plenty of time inside ice-formed caverns, so Hoaris seemed as if he had returned home. And though creepy, his smile was naught less than jovial. Contrary to his demeanor, Yankos and his wanderers had no experience with tight places. They were accustomed to the expansive grasslands, with not more than a tree or covered wagon above their heads. And our young Courtier at Buharro's side had only known the Cloud Courts. Bree's and each of the Tsinti's eyes stretched to the size of small saucers as they tried to gather what little light they could. Jorani ran a hand over the end of a torch she'd carried inside. I pressed my lips tight to hide a small smile. 'Twas the first time I'd seen her embrace the Fire Forger sorcery within, and it heartened my soul. Yet another barrier crumbling before my eyes. Mayhap she, too, began to see that caste abilities didn't make us so different.

Svarta's tentacle mustache twitched in the air. 'Twas a manner singularly belonging to the Underhill Dwellers and an unconscious reaction resembling annoyance. Her words reinforced that semblance.

The Underhill woman sneered. "Fire is not a necessity, *Forger*. It will make it harder to breathe. And see." She narrowed her eyes to glowing slits.

Jorani squinted back. "If it's all the same, Baldeo and I will travel at the group's rear. In that case, I will have need of the flame. Our eyes do not alight the paths like yours."

Svarta snorted and moved deeper within the cave, beyond the party, where none of her form except her eyes remained visible in the shadows.

Owed to the time Misha and Kyr had spent making a home in the cave beneath Safaia along the Betsu River, they seemed more at ease than many of the others as they each whispered over a stone. Soft amber lights flared to life, countering Hoaris's cold and harsh blue orb.

Chambui leaned down to Kyr. "Do you have an extra one of those, little one? Mayhap several?" Chambui, being a Stone Singer, had spent plenty of time in smaller spaces as her people mined for gems. Her approach was merely practical and logical, the solid Chambui I had known since the morning after my time with Sarangarel in Kōkai. She had been, and I prayed to the Triad would always be, a stable figure in my fluid life.

Gnoble Brimr waited nearby while Misha and Kyr handed out what stones they had from satchels slung across their bodies and while the rest of our party adjusted to the darkness. When adaptation had run its course, Brimr lay a hand on one of his guards' shoulders. "Hjalmarr, lead us to the keep." In his voice, a note of resignation sounded, the arrival of the ominous, unspoken weight between us all. To me, he lowered his voice and explained, "Hjalmarr is our best guide. He has the most experience here in the southern Rausu *cavernal network*. Not much should interfere with our course, so now, we travel."

Hoaris grumbled and asked, "What of the terrawyrm?"

Hjalmarr stretched to a height I wouldn't have imagined possible and clapped Hoaris on the shoulder. Eyes softening as he regarded me, he said, "Tragedy, but the terrawyrms dove deeper into the crust below Nantai after the Ryū dragons were banished in the Great Wars." The Underhill guide then slumped back into his more common crouched form and loafed in the direction Svarta had gone.

Travel, as Brimr said, we did. After Hjalmarr, the gnoble and his lady followed. Then, I walked between Hoaris and Chambui while possible until the narrowing cave forced us into single file, and when the rock walls opened again, we resumed the original formation. At times, the cavern shrank in height, forcing us to crawl on all fours. This seemed natural for the Underhill Dwellers as they'd spent ages adapting and navigating their underground cavernal networks. For those of us who rarely found such cause, the travel went slower. But the Underhills waited patiently as the *overlanders*—as I heard Svarta mutter—found our footings as best we could.

We passed by tunnels that jutted off to the right or left, some traveled downward from our path while others appeared to be uneven stairs worn into the stone over many seasons. The cavernal network apparently spread in all directions, leading to higher or lower altitudes within the mountains.

How fascinating, I mused at one point, but Parū still refused an answer. It seemed she hovered within the corner of our consciousness like a frightened youngling. I'd allow as much until the air about us felt less stagnant and I could feel the wind again.

Time seemed nigh impossible to factor without the aid of the Day-Seer or the Night-Seer, but we must have traveled several hours into Selene's watch before Hjalmarr, who had scouted ahead, returned.

"A window in the cliff lies ahead and to the right," he said to his leader, "with a level-floored cave to the left. We can rest there for the remainder of the dark hours." Hesitatingly, he lowered his head to me and added, "Your dragon may fly from there if you wish, Kōgō Mairynne."

I conveyed her thanks and we continued climbing onward in silence. When we arrived at our camp for the night, I breathed in the fresh air. Calling a draft up the side of the mountain, I stepped to the edge, peered out the window Hjalmarr had mentioned, and gasped. From the distance and using Parū's dragon-enhanced vision, the sight held color that wouldn't otherwise be visible in the night as well as unexpected promise. It seemed as if a great flood of troops from either end of the vale flowed toward the open fields outside Arashi's gates. From one direction, torches glowed orange and red in the night, and from the other . . . the blue of ice and white of a northern blizzard.

I looked at Hoaris, mouth agape, but as he approached, I recovered. "They came," were the only words I could muster.

Chambui hopped over a chasm in the stone and came to a stop at my side, resting a hand on my shoulder. "It looks like your ruse might work after all, young kōgō. We'll have to offer our gratitude to Saqie and Su." 'Twas ill-likely she could see much detail, but the clouds of opposing colors painted the scene well enough for the person's naked eye.

"And to Gnoble Aljir Tenkara," Hoaris added. "Even if they encouraged it, she made the decision."

On the walls of Arashi, Storm Sorcerers of the guard—*my* guard—gathered, each of their arms held wide. They called with their sorcery and clouds darkened the vale as a great green dragon descended from the High Cloud Court. Cauldrons with flames burned at evenly spaced intervals, and above their heads, Guin flew. A screech pealed through the night, the same screech I'd heard in those days of mourning before I'd entrusted the Serpentine Throne to Aunt Nadia. Were it not for Parū's presence within, the sound might have curdled my blood in the same manner it had when I heard it from the terrace outside my rooms before my ascension. The same sound *we* had heard.

Thalaj.

But then . . .

Another screech joined the first, and my eyes found the second dragon's form, smaller than Guin but equally as deadly. I pulled my hands over my mouth. The second Ryū soared through the night sky, not green but blue, and added its voice to the cacophony. No, not its—*her* voice. I'd met that dragon before. I'd *helped* the Ryū dragon retrieve her egg. My heart fell from my chest and splintered.

What happened to that egg? I wondered.

A violent knock pounded at my spine, then my chest, made me stumble, and Chambui reached to steady me.

Let me fly, minikin! my Ryū dragon demanded. The angst she'd built up over the confined space fueled her desire to fly after Guin. It grew from a simmering flame into a wildfire, only held in control by our bond and my human form.

Gritting my teeth, I tightened my muscles to retain my form. Upon my hands, pearlescent scales dappled my skin. I replied aloud, "It is not time, Parū. We . . . agreed." I held my breath, hoping beyond hope I had the wherewithal to hold her inside. If she didn't allow it, I doubted my strength, but I had to try. Silently, I begged, *Please, Parū, I need to try to reason with my sister first. Then I promise to give you the freedom to follow Amare's command. Do not be so impatient; you will return Guin to the Fey Realm, I promise you that.*

How, minikin, can you make such promises? she growled, her outrage simmering through my arms and legs.

I took a breath and clenched the muscles in my shoulders, back, and thighs. *Have we failed one another yet?*

Her breath came hotly through my nostrils, clouding the air. *No,* she answered with as much strain as I felt. But it lessened ever so slightly. Parū eased and closed herself off to me so I no longer had the ability to use her senses. My vision dimmed as she said, *I will wait as you ask, minikin.*

Settling back to myself, I opened my eyes to find Hoaris and Chambui both standing too near. They each wore a weary look in their eyes, although neither spoke.

Will you be well? Chambui's gaze inquired.

Are you turning Ryū? Hoaris's asked.

Sighing, I answered their unspoken questions, "All is well enough. For now." We moved back to the ledge where trees surrounded the mouth of the cave, roots were embedded between the rocks, and trunks grew parallel to the cliff's face.

As the others in our party approached, they lingered near the opening, clearly craving the fresh air. Eventually, Yankos said, " 'Tis a good place to rest. The air is cleaner here than it has been for hours." He turned toward the cave and said to

Buharro and Baldeo, "Gnoble Brimr and Hjalmarr have taken the Underhill Dwellers to a place deeper than the one here. If anyone has kindling, they've given us the space to build a small fire."

"But the wood here lives," objected Hoaris.

Wanderers filtered toward the cave where we were to take our evening's rest.

Yankos smirked at Hoaris. "There are shriveled roots within the cave, my friend. I just hope they're not too damp, else the fire may smoke us out." He followed his wanderers inside, leaving me there with Hoaris, Chambui, and Jorani.

Chambui ran a slender, jeweled hand down Hoaris's arm. "I'll join the others. Whistle if you have need of me."

Jorani remained, leaning backward against the cave's mouth with one foot propped on the rocks behind her. She'd put away the torch and rested both hands on the weapon hilts at her belt. I presumed the others had joined the Tsinti inside and returned my attention to Arashi. Silence permeated the space between the three of us . . . Storm Sorcerer, Fire Forger, and Frost Fighter by birth, but all having chosen paths differing from our respective castes.

Parū remained hidden deep within me, and I held my breath as the opposing forces of fire and ice neared one another in the distance. The Fire Forgers sent the first ball of fire into the air, and Jorani nodded once. Hoaris scowled. Before the fire could land, the Frost Fighters raised a shield of blue ice, protecting the entire army.

Hoaris hooted, cutting a sideways glance at Jorani.

With magical life of its own, the fire burned against the shield, and the ice melted. But the fire wasn't strong enough. The flames dissipated as ice turned to water, and the skies went clear once again. Upon Arashi's walls, the Storm Sorcerers appeared to only watch, not making a move to interfere. I squinted, hoping to see better. Was the diversion I'd all but given up on now working?

Parū, please? I begged.

I am sorry, minikin. I cannot.

The Ryū circled above the city, not moving out over the fields. With the Storm Sorcerers and the Ryū frozen, seemingly suspended, I had to assume the battle before them caused the questions and confusion I'd intended. My shoulders, spine, and even the bones in my legs felt heavy. I needed rest, although it worried me to take such a pause when events had just turned in my favor. I could send my dragon onward, but what of her consuming need to bring Guin back at all costs? What of the others who traveled with me in a show of solidarity? That the northern castes had turned up was good, yet I despised the fact that I'd used long-nurtured caste rivalries to my advantage. To the two standing with me, I asked, "Do you think the battle will last well into the morn?"

"Hai," answered Hoaris, eying Jorani sideways.

She nodded, expounding on his simple answer, "The grudges run deeper than hoarfrost. All we can do now is hope they remember the battle is for show alone."

She kicked away from the wall, returned Hoaris's friendly but challenging stare, and added, "Else we'll wake to red fields and the Frost and Fire peoples near extinction." She folded her arms across her chest and passed into the cavern now aglow with the fire the wanderers had kindled.

✧✧✧✧✧✧✧✧✧✧✧✧✧✧✧✧✧✧✧✧

OTARR'S LIGHT SHONE INTO the cavern the following morning, awakening us as soon as he'd lifted his gaze above the horizon. When the Day-Seer's rays stung my eyes, I gained my feet. The evening fire had been small and burned out in the hours while we'd slept. Others followed my lead, stowing away any small blankets they'd used in the night.

I stepped out and onto the ledge, reaching inwardly toward Parū. *Are you well this morn?*

Several long heartbeats passed as I lifted an arm to shield Otarr's radiance and peered out over the vale. I blinked several times. Still, I waited for my dragon to stir within. In the expanse before Arashi, the vale had emptied. Several scorch marks marred the greenery, but the armies of Frost and Fire were no longer in battle. I searched the tree lines. They could not have simply vanished.

"*O d'ives* to you, little one."

Despite my confusion, I smiled at the sound of the familiar voice and answered, "*O d'ives*, Yankos." I'd replied politely, but so much was wrapped up in the Tsinti morning greeting. *How goes the day? Good day. What are your worries this day?* The Tsinti language had a knack for brevity, and this appeared no exception as Yankos stared at me with one brow quirked.

"Ah." I nodded, understanding. Still, I waited.

Well enough, minikin, Parū finally grumbled. Her thoughts felt resigned, but more at ease than the prior evening.

One worry allayed, I finally answered, "The battle?" I flung my hand toward where the action had been fully alive in the dark hours.

Yankos rubbed the eye above the red mark on his cheek, seeming nonplussed if still fighting the pull of sleep. "They retreated into the trees there and there." He yawned.

"Retreated?" Hoaris boomed into the conversation, Chambui and Jorani in tow.

Jorani halted, feet apart, hands on the hilts of her short swords, and head cocked. "The Fire Forgers wouldn't consider such a thing."

Hoaris rasped his hand over his red beard and shrugged with the other shoulder. "Maybe they simply took a break."

"A break?" challenged Jorani. Her chest inflated and eyes narrowed. "Who takes a break in the midst of battle?"

"Stop," I demanded. "It's not war, and the battle was staged. The castes are not in true battle and such things should not be uttered. Jorani, you've been one of my best allies, but I fear you've allowed Forgers' bias into your thoughts." I went to her, latching onto both her wrists. "I like that you've begun to use your powers, but I beg you not to let go of the reasons for why you wander."

She simmered, nostrils flaring as she took several deep breaths. Hoaris ignored her frustration and pursed his lips thoughtfully as he peered out over the vale. Further tempering the situation, Hjalmarr loped into the area on all fours.

"Are all ready to continue?" he asked. "We finished the climbing part yesterday, so 'tis all a descent from this point forward."

I sent Yankos and Jorani to gather the others, and when they had left us, I turned to Hjalmarr. "Is there a path down from here outside the cavernal network?"

"Hai, Kōgō. 'Tis that way," he replied, his mustache drifting in the direction from where he'd appeared.

"Fascinating," Hoaris said, eyes narrowed at Hjalmarr and hand still stroking his beard.

"Will you go in search of Saqie and Su?" I asked tentatively of him and Chambui.

His heavy brows dipped into a *V*.

Touching him on the back, Chambui answered, "We will, my kōgō. Whatever it is you need to see the green dragon defeated."

I nodded tightly, holding the urge to correct her wording. I no longer objected to the address by my imperial title, but I wished defeat on no one. Although, it seemed the reasonable word in most everyone's mind. War. Defeat. Against my own people and against the Ryū, who I now considered my people too. When I fled Arashi before, I'd never imagined I'd be facing such times. "Thank you, Chambui. Shall we find the exit?"

We followed Hjalmar to another, smaller crevice in the rock face, this one opening to a path that hugged the mountainside.

The guide returned to the larger cave, reportedly to gather everyone else, but I sensed it was an excuse to allow me to speak with those I had sent on a new errand.

"What are we to do out there?" Hoaris shook his head. "Thalaj would use his scimitynes to open my neck from ear to ear if he knew I was leaving you to enter that castle alone."

"I'm not alone, Hoaris. I'll never be alone." I looked down, then back up to meet his gaze. "I do not know what we face beyond the gates of Arashi or inside Stormskeep. Inside, I am more familiar. I need people I trust to see to the scene without. You"—I circled my hand into Chambui's and squeezed—"and you are my most trusted and capable companions. See to this for me so I can focus on my sister?"

By the time Hjalmarr returned, I was watching Hoaris and Chambui navigate the narrow path downward.

"Are you ready, Kōgō Mairynne?" the guide asked.

"I am." I held out a hand for him to lead the way, and I followed.

In a smaller cave, we retrieved Brimr, Svarta, and the half-dozen Underhill guards at their stations. The wanderers and Small Folk lit their stones. I trod behind the three leaders but before the other Underhill Dwellers. While I'd had Hoaris's light to guide me the prior day, today, I navigated by the Selene-like light given off by the Underhills' luminescent eyes. And we walked. At times, we had to crouch and near-slide down steeper slopes, but we pressed on. Time, again, became a void, unreadable in the dimness but creating space for me to worry over what transpired outside. My feet, calves, and knees ached more and more as the hours passed, ever descending, until Hjalmarr stopped.

"These are the tunnels we take into the keep," he said, waiting as if to silently ask if I was ready for the journey's next leg.

I held out a hand, gesturing for him to lead the way. The ground leveled off but the tunnel remained narrow enough that we marched one by one toward Stormskeep, closer to Karynne with every step. After a hundred paces, a keening wail reached my ears.

"What is that?" I asked to no one specific, and no one had an answer to share.

Onward, we moved.

The keening grew louder, then softer, then louder again. It echoed the army of aari bugs itching over my skin once again.

Alas, we came to a sharp turn where the corridor seemed to double back on itself. I followed Svarta around the corner and halted abruptly at a wall, no, a door. Scratching sounded softly from inside but this wasn't the source of the mourning.

"This is?" I whispered, brows heavy.

Hjalmarr, Brimr, and Svarta shrugged. The scratching grew louder. With us stopped, the party behind us backed up.

"Why've we stopped?" Yankos's voice called from within the darkness behind me.

I turned to one of the guards at my rear. I maintained the whisper and bade, "Slide through and bring the Tsinti leader to me."

He dipped his head and obeyed.

The scratching intensified.

"Hai, who's there?" a raspy, ill-used voice croaked from behind the door. Though it held a familiar tone.

I leaned closer.

"Free us, please, help . . . us . . ." *She* trailed off. Scratches sounded again from the door's far side.

Jaliqai? I thought, sliding my hands over the door and the old latch. Locked or merely stuck. *Could it truly be?* "Yisu Jaliqai?"

No answer came from within.

Hai, minikin, Parū answered. *I believe it is your other Stone Singer friend.*

Yankos arrived at my side, eyes widening as he took in the door.

"Have you ways to open a barred door?" I asked, then searched the faces nearest me. "Has anyone?"

The Tsinti leader answered, "I do not, but I'll ask the others," and disappeared around the corner.

After pulling, pushing, and trying once again to turn the ring-shaped handle, I splayed my hands onto the heavy, age-blackened, and rusted door. "Jaliqai," I started gently. "Hold fast, we're looking for a way."

Scratch . . . scratch . . .

In some manner, the noise sounded . . . sad.

Scratch . . .

FOR ALL THE TALENT I had at my command, I hadn't one person with the skillset for thievery. The Tsinti wanderers spent their days out of doors. Locks and ancient barred doors within the dark underground weren't things they encountered upon the grasslands. Bree, the Cloud Courtier who'd joined us from Tsanseri's island, hadn't aged enough to develop such interests. When we met, she'd been trying to simply learn to control the illusionary magic native to her caste. Under Zofi's guidance over the last few days, she had opened up and now appeared more confident in her own skills. Zofi still encouraged her sorcery, but on the girl's own terms rather than the stricter ways of the Courtiers.

The Underhills seemed our best bet for the job. Although every person in that caste had the knowledge and practice in tunneling, all who'd come with Gnoble Brimr were guards. Hjalmarr mentioned digging through the wall instead of toiling over the door, but that could take as long as spelling stones and might bar our path in other ways.

Shaking my head, I said, "Let us try everything with the door first."

Jorani and Baldeo appeared around the corner. Svarta hissed in a sharp breath when the torch entered the small space, then recoiled from the group, moving further up the tunnel.

Shorter than both but broad through the shoulders, Yankos stepped between the two Tsinti. "I wasn't able to find anyone, but perhaps we can use force and fire?" He looked up at Jorani.

Behind closed lips, she gnashed her teeth, made more apparent by the muscle tick in both jaws and her widening stare. Her eyes shifted like she looked for an answer she couldn't find. Her knuckles around the torch's base had turned white from her grip.

Sensing a fear I shared, one of being trapped in the expectations of my own youth and caste, I moved closer. "Jorani, if there wasn't a life possibly at stake behind this door, I wouldn't ask you to use the fire's magic. Yet it may be our only option." I flicked my eyes up to her torch. "You use it for utility. Why not this? It doesn't make you any less a wanderer or more a Forger that you use an ability you were born to wield."

It took several minutes and several deep, grappling breaths, but she relented.

I turned over one shoulder. "Brimr, can you and the other Underhills move further away? I do not wish to further offend, but as I said to Jorani, I have no other method of entry."

Hjalmarr passed us and rounded the sharp corner, mumbling, "I'll move the others back."

Brimr joined Svarta further up the tunnel, and they continued walking until I could no longer discern the luminescent glow from their eyes. I remained alone with three of the scouting party who'd captured Thalaj and me within the Yubar, seasons before. Yet, now, they supported my cause. I leaned onto the cold metal, speaking to the yisu within, "Stand far away from the door."

Taking three backward steps, I flourished my hand palm up and tipped my head toward the door. Baldeo pulled a dagger from his boot as Jorani handed the torch to Yankos. "Hold that close," she said as she ran her hands over the door and down to the latch, a large ring mounted toward the left side.

"No keyhole. Hrmmm. Have you tried turning it? There may . . . be . . ." Her fingers traced the plate behind the ring, then she reached for the flame with one hand and drew a trail of orange heat toward her other hand that lay flush over the ring. Dim, but brightening, a glow outlined her hand upon the door. She inhaled sharply, closed her eyes, and tilted her head toward the door as if she could hear it speak. Her face seemed drawn, like using the Forger's sorcery pained her.

Both Baldeo and Yankos shrugged when I looked to them in question.

Silence thrummed in my ears as we waited.

Eventually, Jorani turned the handle left, back to the home position, left again, then in a full circle to the right, and . . .

Snick!

The door popped slightly outward with a whine, yet not enough to see within.

I gasped. "Jorani, how did you?"

She smiled ruefully. "The Forgers call it Fire Listening." Taking the torch from Yankos, she latched onto Baldeo's arm and they rounded the corner, out of sight. From spelled stones and the Underhill Dwellers' luminescent eyes, a soft glow still lit the corridor enough to make out shapes.

I blinked hard several times after Jorani, both to adjust my eyes and shocked at my latest discovery. There was so much—too much—about my people I failed to understand. This fell among my ill-qualifications for empress, ruler over all of Nantai. It reaffirmed the need to have Father rule for some time more. Mayhap one day, after I'd had the opportunity to spend time with each of the castes, I'd be better suited. However, I also doubted Karynne had much more knowledge or experience with the castes and casteless than me.

That singular thought reaffirmed my quest.

For now, Jaliqai waited behind that door, a prisoner for some mysterious reason. But who held her captive?

Zofi's voice, though she remained somewhere behind in the caverns with Father, reached me then with advice she'd provided long, long ago. *Face this day's challenges today and leave the rest for the morrow.*

Yes, I would free her now and worry over the jailer later. I pulled the heavy ring, throwing my weight into the move as a counterbalance. The squeal emitted by the hinges echoed to my right and left, stirring a series of moans from around the corner. Yankos squinted one eye and rubbed his ear with a finger. I stopped when it stood wide enough open to allow a person to pass into the darkness beyond. I had to stifle a gag when I stuck my head inside. The stench of a person's stagnating waste made my eyes water, so I halted my breathing. How long had she been here unattended? *Parū?* I beckoned my bonded dragon, unable to see aught given the absolute darkness within.

"Jaliqai?" I then whispered aloud.

Yes, minikin? Parū answered first.

"Mairynne?" the yisu answered from my right side and downward, toward the ground. The word, my name, seemed uncertain if not outright disbelieving.

I focused on Parū and a way to see inside. *May I use your sight? Will it work in the darkness?*

Ryū sight will not help in the dark. It does not alter the need for light to see within the darkness. It is only useful for seeing afar. I could allow you the flaming breath if you wished?

No. There are no windows. "Yankos, do you have one of the stones?" I turned to him.

"Let me find the Small Folk."

"Grab the first light you see. If 'tis an Underhill, so be it," I ordered, returning to where I'd heard Jaliqai, crouching and reaching toward where I thought the voice originated. "Take my hand. Are you well enough to stand?"

Her hand landed on my bare forearm first and felt like ice from Kōdaina Kōri. I grasped onto it with my other hand and held her trembling fingers tightly between my palms while I waited for only heartbeats. Yankos returned, one of the Underhill guards at his side. Without bothering to ask his name, I motioned him forward and scanned the room in the moonlit eeriness. Jaliqai's cheeks, normally round with impish delight, were sunken, but her eyes still held her spirit within.

As I narrowed my eyes, three more people came into view, each sitting with their backs against the wall and legs splayed. One slept, or I hoped that was the case. The source of the offensive smell became quite clear; a chamber pot overflowed in one corner. Near it, discarded bones and trays lay in a pile. If they did not intend to empty the waste, why would the captor feed them? *Why not just leave them to starve?*

To extend the torture they must endure, minikin.

I gnashed my teeth at that, refocusing. Making out faces was difficult, but once I placed the first, the rest could be assumed. "Timur?" I asked, my heart leaping into action. "Baidu? Nachin?"

The others moved, and Jaliqai pushed back against the wall. "It's really you, my kōgō?" Her other hand found mine and squeezed with more strength than I would have anticipated she had remaining. "We'd given up."

Baidu, Nachin, and Timur all pushed to their feet, their boots slipping on the wet stone floor beneath their boots. At least they still wore boots.

Timur said, "We figured we'd get some two-day-old food and one of *her* guards would push us back into our hole at spearpoint. I can't reckon time, but it's been days since we've had anything to eat."

They moved closer as I helped Jaliqai to her feet.

"*Her*?" I asked, mimicking Timur's inflection. Soul-shattering shock rankled. I swallowed the bile rising in my throat and added, "Did my sister put you here? Why would she do such a thing? Or her advisor, Imrythel?"

Guin? Parū growled inside.

"Nay," Baidu answered, "not your sister or any other from your caste." His voice no longer sounded like the jovial Stone Singer I'd known upon the *Swell Mistress*. Rather he'd turned brusque and bitter, spitting the words, "The Stone Lady."

Sixty-Five

A Youngling

AH, SO HE WAS NOT bitter, but he and the others had been betrayed by their leader. The news seared a path through my chest, and I snapped my gaze to him. "Sarangarel? What? Why?" I searched their faces for an answer they clearly did not have, each hanging their head after I'd met their gaze. I squeezed my eyes, centering myself. This day's challenges today, Mairynne, I reminded myself and shook my head. "There seems little we can control over that in the moment. Let us get out of this hole, as you named it."

Yankos, who had covered his nose and mouth in the crook of his arm, mumbled, "Pit's a better word. Cesspool maybe."

After we'd all moved into the hallway, the Tsinti leader shouldered the iron door closed, the lock clicking back into place. No sooner had he sealed off the stink than the Underhills—Brimr, Svarta, and Hjalmarr—loped up to us in the narrow space.

Svarta panted. "Listen," she said, looking urgently over her shoulder as some evil stalked her from behind.

Everyone fell silent, and the hall remained quiet as Hjalmarr's tentacles lifted into the air; his nose twitched. Clearly puzzled, his eyes shifted between the four yisun. Then he straightened from all fours to peer at me. "You're calm? They're familiar? There's but one conclusion. You know these Stone Singers, hai?"

"Hai," I answered, lifting my chin. "They are trusted companions who, along with Chambui, traveled with me over the Syrensea. And back."

Despite that Hjalmarr lived beneath Nantai's surface, surely he knew of the tales, of how few who ventured westward ever returned. Yet if he knew the legends spun by the coastal people, he made no show, and my quest into the unknown seemed of little interest to the Underhill guide. Instead, he turned both his lighted eyes and tentacles toward the door. "That was the room where your Makenyn sequestered himself before—"

As if to belabor the age-old heartache and hopelessness the chamber contained, a keening moan echoed from further up the corridor.

She moved closer to Brimr. "Wait. Keep listening."

After a beat, muffled but there, mayhap outside the cavernal network, a shriek trumpeted. Realization rocked my balance.

A Ryū's cry, Parū grumbled, her agitation starting to thrum through my limbs again. *But that is a different sound than the moans ahead. Yet those moans are . . . I do not know . . . unfamiliar yet in some manner, kin.*

Her hesitation and thoughts gave me pause. I dropped my brow and focused on the Underhill gnoble. "How close are we to Stormskeep?"

Protectively, Brimr hugged his mate closer. "We *are*, by a technicality, inside. That corner marks the entrance."

I hadn't pegged Svarta as a skittish type, and something had Parū off balance. What did we face further down, or up as it may be, this hallway? I bit down on the inside of my lip. We had too many people to be subtle if danger lay ahead. Were Hoaris and Chambui here, I'd seek their advice on my next moves within this pawn game.

Parū offered, *Discover what causes the moaning beneath your castle, minikin. I must know also. Then find your supporters in Arashi. Then, and only then, you may worry why this Stone Lady Sarangarel sequestered her very own yisun soldiers here. From your memories, it seems far beyond her constitution to treat her own thusly.*

"Hjalmarr, is there more than one way out and into Arashi from here?" I asked.

The guide considered. "It has been an age since I've navigated these caverns, but hai, there is a *T* ahead and to the right. It leads behind the Sundai Falls toward your citadel. The straightaway continues into Stormskeep itself."

With that, I decided and shared my plan with Yankos and Brimr. We would do as Parū suggested and find what person or beast wailed ahead. Then I would go into Stormskeep with only a few at my side, those I trusted to protect me and themselves. Although I trusted Yankos, Baldeo, and Jorani, I also needed someone to protect the others as they went into the citadel. Father could lead the way, and the Tsinti trio could ensure their safety. I'd join them when I'd learned more of our position, perhaps after I'd found my aunt Nadia, Corwyn, and others. Surely, if Hoaris and Chambui had reached the Forgers, another diversion would have begun in the vale beyond Arashi's gates, granting me time. I needed what space I could create. With luck, my caste would have eyes turned away from the keep, assuming it lay safe against Mount Sundai, protected as it had always been from such attacks.

As we climbed in the dim light, Parū's agitation crawled inside my skin until her shock drew me up short.

"What is it, Mairynne," Jaliqai asked, but all I could do was shake my head.

'Tis not a moan but a cry. A babe's cry, my dragon said.

A babe? That is no youngling's cry, I countered, eyes growing wider. *You mean a Ryū babe? A youngling dragon?*

Hai, a Ryūling.

I pushed past Brimr and Svarta to Hjalmarr's side and ahead still. Their eyes cast enough light from my rear for me to navigate. The keening grew louder until I finally rounded the corner to hear it echo from the deep cavern walls, a window to outside in the distance. It allowed enough light that I could now see without the glow of the Underhill's eyes. They, on the other hand, stayed back, pulled their hoods, and donned their spectacles to shield their eyes.

At the center of the expansive cavern, a heavy chain was anchored into the midpoint of a large stone slab. In the shadows, the chain rattled, and a pained wail rolled around the room. Bound by the chain, the youngling hung its head low, grandiose even for a Ryū who hadn't thrived for ages. It held utterly still. Slowly, I approached the mouth of the cavern, edging my way around the Ryū youngling. He—yes, I sensed 'twas a male Ryū babe—bore the color of the frozen glaciers within the great lake, Kōdaina Kōri, with scales somewhere between blue and green.

When he sighted me, the babe pulled on the chains. Crying, keening, whining bleated off the cave's rock walls. Glittering tears poured from his eyes as the chains rattled. I made shushing sounds and tried to move closer, hopeful he'd sense the Ryū within. Kin called to kindred. But he railed harder, cried louder, until I backed into the shadows.

"Parū," I whispered. "It would be good to change now. There is room." I scanned the cave. "Surely, it would calm this youngling."

Does everyone here know of our bond? If you transform, you will be unable to speak with the others.

"Perhaps we should try the separation then. We have reason, motivation." I watched the baby dragon, my heart cracking with each of his cries and melting with each tear.

She hesitated. *Well and so. Are you certain you do not wish to speak with the others first? Whenever you are ready.*

I turned to the yisun who were lined up at my side, jaws gaping at the sight. To Jaliqai, I asked, "Do you know aught of the bond I forged in Ise? Of the companion I hold within me?"

Her brows dipped to a *V* and she peered at me blankly. It seemed Chambui had not spoken of my secret. I had asked as much in the jungles of Ise, and she had honored her word until now. Though I'd shown Misha and Kyr as well as the sailors, Tao and Oshun, I'd parted with the yisun before I felt comfortable enough to share. I appreciated the promise Chambui made, but it would have been easier had she told her fellow soldiers.

"I appreciate Chambui's discretion, but . . ." I tried to move closer to the baby dragon, but he railed against the chains again. "While in Ise, I visited the Fey Realm."

Baidu chuckled. "Myth," he accused.

I glared at him. "Before I jumped into that pool, I would have said the same, but the creature before you is a creature from beyond the veil."

He went silent then, and I motioned them nearer to me. "I have no more time to keep secrets. In exchange for Father's life, I bonded my soul to one of the Ryū. But harder still, I left my gensui behind as part of the price." I swallowed hard, then choked out his name. "Thalaj. So, if you ever wondered what happened, 'tis my doing that he no longer walks in this realm. Regardless, my Ryū dragon's name is Parū, and I believe I will need her to get close to the youngling." Looking at each of the yisun in turn, I asked, "Will you all retreat to the entrance of this cavern? And I beg you not to be terribly shocked by what you are about to witness. I promise you she will mean no harm to any of you."

Eyes wide with shock or mayhap fear, they turned on their heels and followed my request.

I reached out and clasped a hand on Jaliqai's arm before she could leave, intent on asking her to allay the fears of the Underhills also, but then I recalled the positioning between the castes. I doubted Jaliqai or any of the others felt such animosity toward another caste, but I couldn't be certain about Brimr, Svarta, or any of the others who'd come along. Instead, I went to speak in person with Brimr as the yisun took up their stations.

"Your people, do they fear the dragons?" I asked.

The Underhill leader made several deep-throated sounds. "My people have never suffered their fiery breath directly, but the great green dragon has imprinted fear upon the hearts of every Nantai person. The Underhills are not immune to such dread. And given that dragons are prone to creating flares of light through breath alone, they aren't terribly compatible with my people." He paused for a long moment with a meaningful look toward his mate. Then he added, "But in the old times, caves like this were home to the Ryū in Nantai, and the Underhills lived in close proximity with the dragons. Once, some of our kind cared for the dragons' cavernal homes. I daresay we are more compatible than it would seem."

Parū offered, *The relationship he mentions was once symbiotic, and by instinct a Ryū will hold his or her fiery breath for the dark-dwellers.*

Tight-lipped, I nodded as another puzzle piece about my people fell in place. "I bear a secret I must share with you, Brimr, Chief among the Underhills. I hold within myself a companion. She is a great pearlescent dragon from the Ryū of old."

To his credit, Brimr gave naught away through the positioning of his features, but the tendrils extending south from his chin twitched, betraying some small anxiety.

I continued, "The Ryū believe the severing of the Kuroidragon from Makenyn's soul was devastating. It started what the Ryū now call the Erasure and the people in Nantai call the Ryū Wars. That one act laid waste to the beauty of the bond both races once nurtured." I took a deep, centering breath. "I met the Kuroidragon. In the Fey

Realm. Since the Erasure, he has existed for five ages in a deep sorrow over the matter. Look there." I pointed. "See the tears this youngling cries? Imagine a majestic dragon who would fill this cavern and more with black scales that shone blue when lit. And then imagine that dragon resting in a mirrored pool of his own tears."

The tentacles of Brimr's mustache drooped, and I felt the very sadness he expressed within my own heart. I continued, "I went to find my father, but I returned to new challenges. Righting that wrong is a charge I accepted when I took on the bond of companionship with Parū. Yes, it is true that I received my father as compensation for the sacrifice, but I lost a man I loved dearly in the process." *And one I hope to find again,* I added in thought.

Brimr turned his bright eyes to me, then bowed his head. He grasped my arm about my wrist and turned the palm face up, then placed a kiss onto the soft skin. His deference, respect, and a promise to his empress laced that kiss.

"Thank you, Brimr," I said. "Now, I am going to release the pearl dragon into this cavern."

I'd expected him to flinch or show concern, mayhap even fear, but he did none of those things. He merely regarded me in anticipation of what I'd say next.

I continued, "I'd ask that your people wait in the hall."

He turned, intent on serving my wishes, but then stopped and faced me again. With head bowed, he said, "I will send the others away, but may I stay, Kōgō Mairynne Evangale? If for no other reason than to offer testament to my people afterward."

I lay a hand on his shoulder and smiled. "You may, Gnoble Brimr." The man truly fit with his title, a serene humbleness and strength shelled in one person's soul, and I respected him more than most for that alone.

"Jaliqai," I turned to the yisu, concerned for the Singers' states of mind. "Are the yisun prepared? Or should you wait with the Underhills outside?"

She bowed her head. "We will remain with you, my kōgō."

Baidu lifted his chin. "The oath we swore to the Stone Lady is forsaken. Not by us, but by the Lady herself. Our next oath is to you, Kōgō Mairynne Evangale, and we will not be forsworn to that."

"Hai," Timur and Nachin echoed as one.

"May the Triad bless you all," I said, warmed by their allegiance.

Before returning to the babe, I ran a hand down Jaliqai's arm and gave her a grateful smile. She and the others seemed hale enough despite Sarangarel's betrayal and their dark imprisonment. Slowly, I went to the area near the dragon youngling; chained, he keened still. He watched me warily as I crouched onto one knee and focused inwardly. *All is ready, my Ryū,* I thought.

So it is, minikin.

Before, when Parū had pulled away from me, she'd also distracted me from the fey magic flowing through our shared being. Now in silence, I kept both eyes on the youngling. She watched the small dragon, too, as the strange sensation began—painless, but flesh peeling away from my bones. When the lines of magic converged at my center, I lost my breath and stumbled backward, my eyes closing by reflex. And when I breathed easily again, I opened them to the final image of Parū taking the form of her majestic pearlescent self, her wings settling. She lowered herself to the cavern's floor and swung her head snout-first toward the babe.

Chains jangled. A whine beat the stone walls. The metallic taste of fear twanged in my mouth. The scales shimmered with iced teal and blue colors, reflecting light from the cave's opening to the air beyond as he backed away.

Deep within Parū's chest, a grumble began—a low sound I'd heard once before, in the Fey Realm when she'd spoken with Kuroi. Then I'd been too preoccupied with Father and Thalaj to realize I'd heard *their* language.

Yes, the Ryū tongue, minikin. I merely tell the babe to be calm, that we are here to help, that we wish to free him from the bonds.

"Does he believe you?" I blurted, unable as of yet to put faith in the silent communication over the bond we shared though our bodies were apart.

Not yet. She rumbled again.

The babe pulled back with another pained screech, different from the ones I'd heard before from Guin over Arashi and from Barū over Safaia. I peered closer at the manacles around his feet and the claws at the bend in his wing. Rusty brown and angry red encircled the scales beneath each bond. "What are those marks?" I asked Parū.

The chains and fetters are made from iron ore. She paused, and her eye flashed back to me momentarily. *The metal is poison to fey creatures.*

Another fissure formed between my breasts. *Who would do such a thing to this youngling? Surely neither Guin nor the blue dragon would inflict such pain upon one of their own. Could it be Sarangarel?* I glanced at the yisun. If she had the capacity to imprison her very own elite guard, perhaps she had it within herself to be so cold. Or mayhap Karynne or Imrythel had devised such a plan? Could they be working against the green Ryū Imrythel held within herself?

Save your wonder, minikin. Your thoughts are distracting me. She began grumbling again and continued until the youngling lowered to the ground, the chains slackening. *He has relented. Can you and the yisun release the fetters? There should be no locks. He is only bound by the position in which they hold him.*

At least that had been easier than expected. "Jaliqai, Baidu, Timur, Nachin, help us free him," I called even as I moved toward his back claw.

Unhesitatingly, Jaliqai joined me there and held as I pulled on the latch. We both winced when another sizzle burned the youngling before we could free his foot. The other yisun moved slowly toward the other three manacles. Each latch took two of us to pry apart, and when the deed was done, he tried and failed to fly within the cave. Parū caught him, grumbled, wrapped him up in her wings, tucked his head inside the leathery cocoon, and rumbled softly. Though I could not understand, I could sense the calming nature of her words and sounds. She'd make a fine mother dragon.

Minikin, she said after several long, tense moments. *As your friend Brimr implied before, the Underhill Dwellers once cared for the needs of the Ryū who made Nantai their home. Can you ask him if there are guards among his party who will remain with the babe?* All of this she asked of me as she released the babe and settled herself with all four limbs onto the cave floor. Parū craned her neck toward a dark corner. Her snout disappeared in the darkness, then pulled something across the floor. A carcass. A lamb, I discerned as I looked closer. She dragged it to the cave's exit. *Advise Gnoble Brimr to shield his eyes.*

I advised the gnoble as she asked, then she breathed her Ryū breath upon the carcass and pushed it over to the youngling. *He is hungry and is too young to have developed his breath. We prefer cooked flesh.*

The babe crept toward Parū's offering and timidly began to eat.

It took all my will to turn away from the dragons and approach Brimr. The yisun followed in a manner that indicated they were leery of remaining near the Ryū dragons without me.

"The dragon youngling will remain in this cave," I told the yisun and the gnoble. "Brimr, do you think any of your guards will watch over him while we see to what havoc my sister has brought to Arashi?"

"Kōgō Mairynne"—the gnoble coughed—"should a fight come to us, we are happy to take up arms for your cause. But alas, the Underhill Dwellers will only travel at your side as far as the network will allow. We are ill-suited for fighting above ground. So, where the tunnels meet the Stormskeep halls, we would have taken our leave regardless.

"The charge you offer honors us and allows us to serve you in another manner." He tucked his chin. "We will be happy to care for the dragon while you and the others mind the treason within Arashi. And as there has been no sign of treachery within the cavernal network, Hjalmarr, myself, and half my guard can lead you the remainder of the way through the tunnels. Svarta can remain here with the others to care for the Ryūling. Excuse me momentarily, and I will seek volunteers for each post."

◇◇◇◇◇◇◇◇◇◇◇◇◇◇◇◇◇◇◇◇◇◇◇◇

BEFORE WE CONTINUED ON the march to Stormskeep, I followed Brimr back into the caves and lifted my voice. "Yankos?" I called.

The caverns answered, "Yankos, Yankos, Yankos . . ."

Given the echo, I could have simply called out to Father, but the Tsinti leader pushed through the Underhill guards positioned around the door into the larger cave. I asked my friend to find Father and Zofi and bring them forward. I hadn't understood Father's reasoning, but he traveled with the other Tsinti rather than at my side. I'd had Hoaris and Chambui at the time, then the yisun. And he had Zofi. But after all that'd transpired in this, I craved, if not needed, his counsel.

While I awaited their return, I reached out to Parū, asking if all would be well enough. I grew anxious to resume our bond and the path we'd been on since our initial joining in Ise.

Her voice in my mind seemed urgent too. *Yes, minikin, he will thrive, and we should tend to Guindragon with haste. Did the prime Underhill agree to watch over the babe until we might return?*

Hai, Parū, he did. Half will see us onward and the others will remain. Have you learned aught of the youngling's origin?

I have not. He is too young to make meaningful responses. Where have you gone?

She opened her senses to me then, emphasizing more than mere curiosity. I sensed her worry over the youngling's condition, both the signs that he'd been starved and the iron burns about his ankles and wing claws, as she searched the cavern for my presence.

I watched for movement among the Underhill guards, for Father to weave his way forward. *I am not far, my Ryū, just beyond the door into the cave. I need to speak with Father and then I will return to you. I am sorry for this discovery, Parū, but we will see that the youngling is well cared for, and if necessary, we can return him to the Fey Realm once we have restored peace to Nantai. At least he eats when he is fed properly,* I offered.

Father appeared then with Zofi and Yankos at his back, worry creasing his brows.

I squeezed him hard when he wrapped his strong arms around me, then I pulled them aside and told them of the babe and the plans to split once we reached the place in the tunnels where we could only turn right or left. "The yisun and I will take the left into Stormskeep, and you will travel right toward the citadel with the Tsinti. Find Selene's priestess, Tasmynne Hallowgale. She will certainly shelter you while Parū and I attend to the dragon matters. And Karynne."

Father made no objections, only nodded tightly and pulled me into another embrace. "You make an old man proud, my daughter," he whispered into my hair. "And though she's caused you strife, please be kind to your sister."

I fought a sudden urge to cry at his words and replied, "All I am, I learned from you and Mother. I still hold hope in my heart for Kahry."

The two Tsinti and Father followed me back into the cave, all three sucking in a breath when they sighted Parū and the shimmering ice-blue young dragon near the cave's exit. I introduced Father and Zofi to the yisun. Each one of the Stone Singers reverently bowed to Tennō Atheryn Evangale, laying a customary kiss within his palm. Afterward, I asked for a quiet moment and moved to my dragon's side. The Ryūling had finished the roasted lamb and was sucking the marrow from a cracked leg bone.

With a hand upon Parū's neck, I thought, *'Tis time.*

Reunited with my companion, I breathed easier as I crossed behind what appeared to be a large stone altar and approached Jaliqai. "Will you retrieve Svarta and the Underhill guards who would remain there with the babe?"

The yisu disappeared briefly and returned with Svarta after a half-dozen guards had entered on all fours. Brimr reached for his mate, bringing her into an embrace involving their arms and tentacles. I blushed and looked away, sensing I'd intruded on a moment more intimate than a simple hug. Yet they didn't seem shy or chagrined for showing such emotion. Mayhap it was more common in their caste to embrace so openly. It brought my sister Yasmynne to mind. She would be delighted over the openness they showed, so much so I could imagine her bubbling with joy like she had after we'd visited Love's Court. I smiled, then ran both hands over my face.

Treachery awaited my arrival, and I hadn't the luxury of basking in such reminiscence. "Onward," I commanded and turned on my heel, bound for the tunnels and for Stormskeep. With a desperation I couldn't deny, I wanted this quest complete. For my people, I wanted to restore a sense of security within their own homes. And once that had been established, I needed to return to Ise to retrieve a piece of my heart.

Deeper in the tunnel, darkness closed in on me and I had to wait for Hjalmarr and Brimr to catch up so I could see. When they reached my side, they took the lead. I followed at some distance in silence until shining worried eyes turned back to me.

"What is it?" I asked.

Hjalmarr had removed the heavy hammer he wore across his back and was using it as a walking stick. His gnarled fingers gripped tightly around the handle. "The way is blocked, my kōgō. The cave has fallen in ahead."

<h1 style="text-align:center">SIXTY-SIX</h1>

Homecoming

"THIS IS RECENT." MY VOICE sounded as ghostly as I felt. The rubble meant the yisun and the babe had been locked away and perhaps left for dead. Unless the captor was indeed . . .

Guindragon, Parū offered.

Hai, I answered without voice, knowing that only one who could fly or traverse the cavernal network would find those sequestered within.

Hjalmarr moved past me toward the other guards and barked some unfamiliar words. Over the last days, I'd spent enough time with them to understand they favored moving upon all fours. But now, the others pulled their hammers from the straps across their backpacks and joined Hjalmarr, using their tools to aide in their two-legged movement.

Brimr came to my side. "Wait here, Kōgō Mairynne. My guards and I will clear the way." He slipped out of his pack and hefted a hammer of his own. His was smaller than Hjalmarr's but gleamed with inlaid gold. As he pulled on the hammer, it snagged on a strap and a scabbard slipped from the handle, revealing a broadsword beneath. I widened my eyes at the complexity of the multipurpose instrument, both tool and weapon with uncounted uses—a flat hammer on one end opposing an enormous claw, tall enough from hammerhead to end to be used as a walking staff, and a sheath hiding a heavy bladed weapon. It showed the Underhills were fearsome warriors by their own rights, and I thanked the Triad that they'd chosen my cause over my sister Karynne's.

No—not Karynne's, I reminded myself. She was Imrythel's victim too, like every other Nantai person who'd succumbed to the green dragon's destruction. She fell to this fate like those who perished in Kōkai and all who had suffered the same fate in

Brennmor and Biei. But *she,* like those who survived the Ryū breath, would also suffer the trauma that would follow. And I feared hers would be worse as this was not the first time she'd fallen victim to another's ill will.

The Underhills made short work of the rocks blocking the tunnels into the castle, swinging the pointed side of their hammers. Once they'd cleared enough, a couple of the guards slipped beyond the boulders.

I waited as patiently as possible with Father, the Tsinti, Misha, and Kyr. Misha pulled at my hand and placed several stones inside.

"For light," Misha said.

Then all remained quiet until the Underhills who'd gone beyond the rubble returned and had spoken with their gnoble. Afterward, Brimr loped over and replaced his hammer within the straps on his pack.

"Kōgō Mairynne," he began, "this is where my people leave you. Beyond the boulders, the hall to the right will circle behind the Falls. To the left, you will find the passageways that ascend into Stormskeep."

Tightening my mouth, I nodded and extended my hand to the Underhill gnoble. "You said as much before, but your people will watch over the Ryūling until I return?" I confirmed.

"With everything we have, Kōgō Mairynne," Gnoble Brimr replied and tried to pull my palm forward to offer the kiss due an empress.

I resisted. "That honor is not truly mine, Brimr." I clasped his hand in both of mine, his skin cool over gnarled knuckles. "I thank you for everything you have done and will do to protect the Ryū. And though I appreciate your allegiance, do you recall the oath I made at my ascension?"

"Morwyn's oath," he mused.

"Hai. And as such, the measure of deference you offered belongs to my father still."

His moonlike eyes shifted to Father then returned to me. "Mayhap. For the time," he said, took the three steps to Tennō Atheryn Evangale, turned my father's palms upward, and placed a kiss in both.

On all fours, Hjalmarr, Brimr, and the Underhill guards retreated.

Without the Underhills' eyes to light the way, darkness closed around me. "*Mekoilieu,*" I intoned to activate the stones I held and handed one to each of the yisun.

Jaliqai placed her hand on my shoulder and gave a nod indicating they were ready. The others did the same. We all moved beyond the boulders to where the tunnel teed off. The yisun stood in the mouth of the left passage, waiting.

I whispered to Yankos, "I'm trusting the emperor's well-being to your people. Watch over him?"

He tucked his chin and closed his eyes, then stepped back.

Hugging my father once more, I followed the yisun into the way ahead as Brimr had suggested. Before long, the tunnel met up with the secret passageway I'd traveled from my chambers so many seasons before and so frequently as a youngling myself. It opened near the base of the Sundai Falls, just above the small forest and green park beside the pool where the people of Arashi gathered on warm days to be near the centerpieces of Arashi—Stormskeep, the citadel, and Sundai Falls. Strange, I thought, how I'd never considered the set of three before and how mayhap they depicted the Triad itself. Though nostalgia called to my heart, I turned and climbed, leading the yisun upward.

Familiar steps.

Memories flooded back with every step, crushing my heart and soul even more. The last time I'd traveled these stairs, Thalaj had guided me from the park below all the way to my chambers. But on this trip, I didn't take the small passage to the right that'd lead to my private rooms. I followed the main path toward the antechamber behind the throne room. Everything seemed eerily quiet, save for the turmoil within my heart, where explosions and clashes rang within my imagination as loudly as if I were standing in the thick of battle.

I halted before entering the antechamber. I'd forgotten the dimness, and Jaliqai bumped into my back.

"Oh, pardon," she murmured.

"Shhh," I hissed, listening from behind the tapestry that covered the opening.

If possible, the room beyond the woven decor was quieter than the tunnels behind the keep. Pulling it back, I slid inside. Empty indeed, and free of furnishings as it had always been. The chamber had never been used for luxury, only the occasional meeting that required a modicum of privacy. Now that we'd come closer to the outside and the stone walls weren't so thick to insulate us, the faintest sounds of distant commotion rumbled in the air.

A diversion of Frost and Fire.

I crossed to the door leading to the backside of the council chambers and into the short hallway, listening again. There were no immediate sounds, only the distant thunder of battle and the ever-running waters of Sundai Falls. One caused my soul to quake and the other soothed it like a balm. I turned to find Baidu had taken Jaliqai's place at my rear.

I searched his face, then the others', silently asking if they were ready.

Timur, who had been at the rear of our single file, swung one of the Underhills' weapons, then planted the butt end of the scabbard at his left boot toe. I hadn't seen him carry it, and who he'd conned out of that, I didn't ask. It held little importance now.

"Longer, but not so different from the hammers we use when mining for stones," he said with a nod. "We'll need weapons for the others though."

Jaliqai and Nachin agreed with choreographed nods. Baidu grunted.

"We've never kept weapons near this room. 'Twas considered a danger to the Nantai regent," I mused. "But outside, the balcony overlooks a courtyard. Near the entrance, there is a guardhouse. If there are weapons nearby, they would be stored there." I left out the other possibility—the holy weapons stored in the citadel across the bridge. "Let's go. It sounds like this area of the keep has emptied thanks to the Fire Forgers and Frost Fighters outside Arashi's walls."

Jaliqai blinked disbelievingly.

Chagrin pulled my eyes to the floor. "I am using their mutual dislike for one another to my advantage."

With the small explanation, the yisu pursed her lips, understanding. "If battle awaits, let us find these weapons and be ready."

I rushed into the council chamber toward the doors on the other side, ignoring the scene I 'd known by heart. The throne sitting at the end of a long, low table with cushions lined upon the tatami along either side. The meeting room where the small council chosen by the Storm Sorcerer regent gathered. The seat of the emperor or empress, the *Serpentine Throne*, at the room's head. Of a sudden, an icy-hot skewer pierced my heart. My dragon verily wailed inside and I lost my breath, turning to face the abomination of a chair.

His name was Moya, Parū said, bringing a tear to my eye. *And that the Nantai have compared our kinds to snakes thus insults us, as well as our companions.*

Moyadragon, I thought to her with all the reverence I could infuse into the formal name. My words fumbled in my mind as I viewed the steely-gray throne with a sour taste in my mouth. *I am sorry, my Ryū. I never considered . . .*

Mmm, she grumbled. *One day, minikin, I will tell you his story. But please, for now, can we abandon the name Serpentine?*

Though I craved knowledge of Moya, it would wait. I turned from the throne, vowing to Parū and myself that I'd remove the anathema soon. Very soon.

Outside, the courtyard had emptied. The guards who trained there and any other people were markedly absent. To the yisun, I pointed and said, "There," indicating the stairs that led down. Rather than following, I took a moment to look out over the city and the fields beyond. The streets lay quiet. Guards in numbers I hadn't fathomed lined Arashi's exterior walls. Braziers burned in their midst, awaiting the opportunity to light their arrows. Beyond, the Forgers launched fireballs into the sky from one side, while the Frost Fighters sent ice shards to counter each attack. Shields of fire and ice arced occasionally above each cast at regular intervals, yet neither side seemed to gain a solid stdvantage. Dipping out of and rising back into the clouds, the green dragon hovered above. But where was the blue one?

The Storm Sorcerers did naught but watch and wait.

In a state of stasis, it seemed.

I lifted my arms and called the wind, thankful again to have the connection to the skies.

On the gust, I lowered myself into the yard, bowed, and kissed the ground that'd been the pyre field for my mother's funeral. An expanse where mandalas of sand and ash had been painstakingly painted by the priests, priestesses, and acolytes of our Holy Triad. Grateful for the moment, I remained bowed in supplication as I lifted a prayer to Atun, then to Otarr even though the clouds in the sky blocked his light, and finally to Selene wherever she rested for the day.

Metal clanged in the guardhouse, the yisun sorting through weapons to make their choice.

A throat cleared.

I rose from my supplication.

Smirking before me only steps inside the gates, Filtch stood proudly in his nondescript gray, his hands folded over his chest. A hoard of casteless filtered through the gates at his back.

◇◇◇◇◇◇◇◇◇◇◇◇◇◇◇◇◇◇◇◇◇◇◇◇◇◇◇◇◇◇◇◇◇◇

"WELL, WELL, WELL, HERE we meet again, Storm Sorcerer." The Cloud Courtier walked the perimeter, shifting forms until he was hunched, aged, and wearing gray. At the far corner, he lifted a fist and lowered it to his mouth, opening his palm to the sky. The now old man blew and rose petals flew into the air, landing on the grass.

I gasped at the familiar scene before me. Guised as an elderly Storm Sorcerer with a fleck in his eye, he'd done the same when we'd gifted my mother's ashes to our people. And he was the one I'd sentenced to the towers in the wake of Jessamyne Feathergale's death. Was this simply an illusion? Had he learned of this somehow? Or was he one and the same? Had he been trailing me since before I'd even decided to leave in search of Father?

The casteless continued to filter into the yard.

Metal clanked again in the guardhouse. Where were the yisun? Would they hurry, or would I have to deal with this alone?

Filtch walked the next length of the field, shifting again. This time, he took on the form of the first Cloud Courtier who'd insulted my guard at the High Cloud Court. Alto-Trea.

The Swan.

He lifted his voice and called, "Or is this a better vision?"

Slowly, I gained my feet, seething with every shift of muscle within my body. My skin grew hotter and hotter. My eyes burned, and surely, they flashed with my companion's presence.

Should I char this traitor? Parū, sensing my thoughts and temper, asked.

No! I snapped. *This one is mine,* I answered, resolving myself to the task that'd been inevitable since the day he breathed the rose petals over the sacred fields. I refused to use my companion's power to take care of this foe.

After the next few steps, he shifted into the black-robed narrator from the Cloud

Courtier rendition of the legend Sosano and the Inara. "How about this visage, young empress?" he crooned in the same theatrical voice.

I clenched my fists, willing myself to wait. Bearing down on my teeth, I gritted out, "I should have allowed my guards to put you to death after you murdered Jessa."

He tsked. "But that wouldn't have made for a good reputation for the newly ascended empress, now would it? Putting an old man to his death would not have shown a young, benevolent leader—the image you so desired to portray. True, *Lady Mairynne?*" He turned into the woman servant from Tsanseri's court, Alto-Tash, and stepped onto the grass, moving toward me.

My mind reeled. That was impossible; I'd seen them together. And Tash had been present after Alto-Trea was banished. Or did Tsanseri plot against her too? I began filtering through memories from within the tearoom and in the gardens. Surely—

"Three hells, what does it matter the form you take. You've been after me since long before. How long, exactly?" I asked, my voice sounding calmer than I felt inside.

He didn't answer. Instead, he asked, "Which version of me do you like best, my dear?" His words purred as he rolled his hips in the seductive new form.

I took a deep breath. "I am no longer the youngling I was when I left Arashi. I am also not the naïve girl you met in Kōkai. I am not one so easily abducted." I spread my arms, palms to the sky.

"Oh, but you are not ready to be empress of Nantai either. You have said as much yourself," Alto-Trea, now in his favored Cloud Courtier form, taunted. "Your sister knew as much and took the Serpentine Throne for herself under the wise guidance of her first advisor." He maintained his distance, but strode around me, circling and tapping a forefinger on his lips. "The green dragon, Guin, is something to behold, is she not?"

Imrythel. He'd been working at her behest the entire time?

I wouldn't give him the satisfaction of more useless words. Inhaling, I reached for the sorcery within, moved the air to create enough friction to pull the lightning from the sky, then pushed both hands forward. It wasn't terribly exerting as the skies were already primed for the storm. Thunder clapped when the current sailed from the dark clouds above, through my palms, and wrapped the deceitful Cloud Courtier in a crackling, fiery net. He shifted through all the forms I'd seen since the Giving of the Sands. For the first time, the Nantai person before me meant no more than a bird's excrement upon my shoe as I raged against him. When it was done and he lay charred before me, no longer a threat, I sagged with relief.

Parū spoke up inside. *You see, minikin, you have always held a dragon's soul within yourself.*

◇◇◇◇◇◇◇◇◇◇◇◇◇◇◇◇◇◇◇◇◇◇◇◇◇◇◇◇◇◇◇◇

I TOOK A DEEP breath and lifted my gaze to the hoard of casteless who had filtered in. Standing at their head was the woman I recalled taking me from the rundown building in the City by the Sea to Filtch.

"Wren," I said to her. "The look of the warrior is better on you than the pious thing you pretended to be in Kōkai."

She took a step forward, a sneer on her face, and gripped a short sword tighter.

I pressed a hand forward, the same hand that'd just taken her leader's life. She stopped mid-stride, fear striking her before my lightning could.

Raising my brows, I said, "I suggest you reconsider your alliances. If you have followed Filtch and thereby Imrythel and my sister Karynne, you have chosen a side that believes the casteless are naught but tools, and you have been badly used." I stepped forward, one careful step at a time.

Wren turned her head and shouted, "Hold your ground. Imrythel has promised us we will no longer be overshadowed by the castes. The ancient one has sworn she will do away with such constructs. Only she has such power over the accursed Storm Sorcerers!"

A rumble went through the casteless, some cheered and some murmured to one another.

A laugh at the absurdity of those empty promises bubbled up in my throat. "If you truly think that holds true, you are sorely mistaken. My sister's first advisor plays politics more subtly, slyly, and *evilly* than any one person I've ever encountered. If you believe Imrythel is not manipulating you now as pawns in her game of revenge, you are a greater fool than I would have judged."

I breathed in deeply and stepped toward her again. "I have sailed across the Syrensea and returned to tell the tale. I gained a companion of old, and I hold her within myself now." I allowed the heat to flash in my eyes and glimmer upon my skin. "Mine, the great pearlescent Ryū, Parūdragon, is older than Imrythel's by an age, and she means to rid Nantai of one such as Guindragon. There is no place in our land for one who would see our cities burned to ash. Our cities are not only where the castes thrive, but they are where all people live, love, and make their lives. Casteless included."

Focusing on my mother, I tried to recover her purpose, her desire for Nantai to consist of one people united, without the division of castes. Holding my palms out, I lifted my face to the skies and allowed a small amount of my magic to pour into my palms. Lightning crackled there, keeping the casteless at a distance. When I focused back on them, they verily trembled and looked between one another. Yet for some unfathomable reason, they held their ground. I released the lightning and raised my voice. "Kōgō Noralynne, my mother, worked endlessly for the lesser represented people of Nantai, and once I take my place as empress, I vow to you that I will do the same. There is much to be done before that time, but for now, I will leave you here to reconsider who you will support in this war."

The yisun reappeared then, weapons readied.

To Parū, I asked, *If you separate from me, can you carry the five of us and their weapons in your claws?*

How far, minikin?

I looked up to the rooftop, showing her my intention. But as I did, the blue dragon I'd met in Safaia peered over, eyes boring into us, into me. She roared. Blue flames licked out from her jaws and nostrils, but either she remained too far above or didn't truly wish to cause harm.

I can, insisted Parū, *and it will give me freedom to speak to the blue dragon.*

I turned to the yisun and lowered my head. "Stand back and ready yourselves to fly."

In my periphery, Wren stepped forward.

Pushing my palm toward her, I glared. "The last thing I desire is to harm any one of you, for you are my people too. You are Nantai's children, the same as I. But I will not hesitate if you stand in my way of removing this terror from our lands."

When she had backed away, I bent and focused on clearing my mind, allowing Parū to call upon the fey magic and divide us bodily from one another. Quicker this time, Parū broke from me, our souls still joined, and I looked upon the great pearlescent dragon as she stood at my side, her tail coiling around me on the field. She bellowed toward the dragon on the roof, and the blue dragon replied. An angered conversation ensued that I couldn't hope to comprehend.

The casteless scrambled away and poured out of the gates and back into the streets of Arashi. Satisfied, I waved the yisun over and lifted my eyes to my bonded Ryū. *Now, Parū.*

The Ryū conversation ceasing, she spread her wings. I called the wind to help her into flight. There, she hovered, curling her talons around us. I stepped into the hook of one claw and held on. With worried eyes, the yisun did the same, but they hugged onto her for everything they had as she lifted higher into the sky.

Above us, the blue dragon disappeared.

Without looking, I shouted to the terrified foursome, "Just a little farther. We're only flying to the top of Stormskeep."

None seemed to have the breath to reply, save for Baidu, the quietest and quickest to anger. He captured my attention again and nodded. *We will be fine,* the motion said, reassuring me.

When we landed on the top of the roof in the haze of the High Cloud Court, my sister Karynne stood in the center, wearing a long blue robe, an extravagant crown with inlaid blue gems, and an expression of pure superiority. Mother Feathergale stood at her side, gazing up to her with pride. At the edge of the roof, a form lay crumpled, the white in his hair peeking out from beneath the robes.

Father?

SIXTY-SEVEN

Clash of the Evangales

"**K**ARYNNE?!" I RAN TO FATHER, placing a hand on his cheek, then feeling for his breath beneath his nose. Thankfully, it tickled my finger. "What have you done?" I demanded, standing slowly and searching for the blue dragon.

She moved around the roof, the clouds wisping and misting around her. "Is it not clear, Mairynne?" As she fixed me with her gaze, a blue light flashed in her eyes. She seemed to ignore Parū entirely.

Careful, minikin. She is bonded, Parū spoke into my mind, though the words of caution were no longer necessary.

Father stirred, and I helped him to his feet. Karynne lifted her arms, palms up to the sky, and laughed. For a moment, I feared she'd call upon her sorcery and put an end to my quest there upon the roof at Stormskeep. But she didn't.

Our father whispered to me, "I am okay, Mairynne. See to your sister."

Karynne's head whipped around to face him. She sneered, "And why, dear father, can you not *see to me*? Because you are weak?" she spat. "Because you never saw me as a daughter worthy of the throne? Because you allowed me to be captured by that tiny, evil king of the Small Folk and allowed him to feed upon my sorcery?" Anger twisted her face for several long moments, then more quietly, she added, "Because you thought me weak yourself." She turned away, resuming her circuit around the rooftop.

Father started, "Karynne, you misunderstand my—"

She whirled, cloak flaring upon the air. "No, Father! There is no misunderstanding. You chose. Between your three daughters, you favored the youngest. Against what had always been done in the way of lineage, you chose Mairynne over me. It is as simple as that." She took a deep breath and shot him a venomous grin. "But I am no longer weak, Father."

Karynne crossed back to the stairs—the steps I'd once climbed in preparation for my ascension to the Serpentine Throne.

"Come," she said to people unseen above her. Then she turned to stand before us once more.

At her one-word command, a host of Cloud Courtiers and casteless poured down the misty steps. I recognized Flea and Gnat. They'd both grown and filled out and regarded me with utter disgust. Imrythel's poison had turned so many of my people, it cracked my heart. The uniform Cloud Courtiers filed out and lined up with their heads held high. I wondered how they could support this, but in my heart, I knew they desired power and perfection more than almost anything. I thought of Zofi and what she'd fled. Then young Bree's face entered my mind's eye. The illusionists' views saddened me too, and I hadn't an inkling of how to change their ages-ingrained ways. From this distance, I couldn't make out any emblems upon their shoulders to discern if I'd once considered any of them friend or foe. How long had they been against me? Had they once wished I wouldn't ascend?

There wasn't a way to know these answers, and my worry over it wouldn't help anything at the moment. I searched the faces for Tsanseri, hoping I wouldn't see her amidst the others. Hoping beyond hope that she hadn't been part of Filtch's betrayal too. But I didn't find her, and I felt certain she'd stand out as she always had.

I counted their numbers in comparison to my own. We both had one dragon, though Karynne would have to shift to free hers. Imrythel was nowhere to be seen. The hundred Courtiers plus another few dozen casteless armed with short swords severely outnumbered my four yisun, though I felt certain each of the Stone Singers could handle a dozen casteless with one hand tied behind their backs. The notion terrified me as I truly hoped to lose none of my people in swaying Karynne from this path. The Fire Forgers and Frost Fighters, who'd come to act as a diversion, would be of no help to me now. And the Underhills wouldn't fight above ground.

Looking at Parū, and willing her to hear with everything I had, I thought, *Do you think she can part from her bonded dragon as we can?* If she couldn't, it would give us a slight advantage if the situation came to blows, here and now.

I prayed it wouldn't.

Karynne reached up and removed the crown from her head. After handing it to Mother—*No!* I'd no longer call her *mother*, but *Idalynne* Feathergale—my sister reached for the clasp at the neck of her cloak.

"Mairynne," a voice crackled on the air. It strained as if under a great pressure, but the tenor resonated so very familiarly.

'Twas the voice of a man I only held in the corner of my heart with meager hope. The tone and seemingly impossible caress upon my name sprung tears in my eyes. Could it be? I froze afraid to turn. A tear sprang to my eye and rolled down my face. Afraid to see if I was wrong, I couldn't breathe. Equally, I was afraid to see if I was right. Something constricted my chest. *Force yourself, Mairynne. If it is not him, you'll still return to find him . . . one day.* After what seemed minutes of not breathing, I turned.

◇◇◇◇◇◇◇◇◇◇◇◇◇◇◇◇◇◇◇◇

PRAISE TO ATUN, OTARR, and Selene and any gods who may have had a hand in such things, Thalaj stood at the top of the long stairs. But for as much praise as I could offer to any deity, I drew up short once again, realizing who had him captive. Imrythel held him from behind, one arm across his chest. How? In human form, Thalaj should be able to easily subdue her. But she had partially shifted into dragon form, her other hand a green dragon's claw, and she had it poised at my first guard's throat along the very line where his lifeblood flowed. His hands were bound behind him, and I wanted to scream, to fight, to call out. To send Parū to save Thalaj. But my feet had grown roots. A gust of wind rippled at my back, and I heard Father inhale sharply through his teeth.

I turned to find Karynne restraining Father in the same position Imrythel held Thalaj, a blue finger with gleaming claw ready to rip out his throat.

What is this thing, Parū? How do they partially change? I cannot make this choice again. Tears streamed from my eyes, and were I less stunned, I believed I'd sob.

That is something we can do as well, minikin. I just hadn't thought to show you, she answered, a hint of regret in her voice.

I counted as I breathed, grounding myself. *There is naught to regret, Parū. An oversight. But help me now; what are we to do?*

You keep with Karynne. I'll handle Guin.

Please be careful not to harm Thalaj. With a glance back to my gensui and fighting the draw in his direction, I moved toward my sister. With caution, I held my hands forward in hopes that we could find some common ground. We once had on the cloud island at the High Cloud Court. She whispered something in Father's ear that twisted his face into a fearful and hollow vision, then she roared—a person's voice blended with a dragon's. I lurched toward Father, but she held a hand forward, lightning crackling between her fingers, even as she pulled him away. I took another step. She smiled. A smile that told me she knew my weakness well. Then she turned her crackling hand toward Father.

"No!" I screamed.

The currents at her fingers gathered and danced around her wrist and upward into the loose sleeve of the cloak. As her gaze settled back onto me, her normally dark brown eyes flashed blue, the same color as the Frost Fighter's winter sorcery. And it resembled the very lightning Thalaj had used to guide me through the hidden passages in Stormskeep. As Storm Sorcerers, we were tied to the wind, so this power stemmed from her dragon, her *blue* dragon.

Yes, minikin, said my dragon. *'Tis Barū.*

Barū, the sad blue dragon I'd helped retrieve her egg at Safaia.

A mother who had only wanted her child.

A baby dragon . . . in chains.

How could she bind her own youngling? I asked my dragon, outraged. Aloud, I begged, "Karynne, don't! It doesn't have to be like this." Tears had dried on my face, and my voice cracked. "The Ryū are not what the stories have told." I tried hard to keep my focus with my family and not on the scene Parū had walked into, but our hearts and souls were joined. I no longer existed singularly within my body. I experienced her battle too, as she did mine.

Imrythel never flinched from where she held Thalaj, but a growl laced her voice as she narrowed her uncovered eye at Parū and said, "You should not have returned. Nantai is my land now. Mine, my young's, and her youngling's. We will raise Barū's Ryūling to be the strongest, most fierce dragon either the Ryū or Nantai has ever known."

I couldn't breathe as everything fell into place, one piece at a time.

Barū, daughter of Guin and Kuroi.

The babe below Stormskeep, their next generation.

I pulled in breath so deeply, my entire body straightened, and focused on the companions before me—my sister and her bonded dragon.

Karynne released the clasp at her throat and the blue robe fell into a pool at her feet, leaving her naked. "Oh, Mairynne, I tried to connect with you once before, but you still betrayed me." As she began, her skin took on a bluish tinge and the outline of scales began to form. "Why couldn't you simply stay away and allow me to rule as Empress over Nantai?"

My hands still held forward, I tried to soothe her, to prevent her transformation. If she changed, it'd come down to my sorcery versus her claws, fire breath, and fierce fangs. I feared we'd be ill-matched. "Kahry, please, this is not what was intended for companionship."

"What do you know of companionship?"

I sucked in a breath as a new awareness settled over me. She didn't know companions could separate. Imrythel hadn't shared this ability with her protégé. And the knowledge gave me an advantage. I looked over my shoulder to Parū, asking, *Will Imrythel know we are bonded? My sister doesn't.*

Not immediately, her voice rumbled in my mind, but her focus remained on her foe.

I turned my attention to Parū and focused, the conversation between them becoming clear again. Audibly, Parū's voice sounded as a low rumble to my ears. But because I was her companion, and she thought the words for me in Nantai even while she made her plea to Imrythel in the dragon's tongue.

You, old one, have desecrated the beliefs of the Ryū and the Fey. You have extended this person's life beyond what is natural. Amare bids that you release her soul and return to the realm between. Call an end to this assault.

"It is flattery that you address me as *old one* as you exceed my years by many," Imrythel sneered and snatched the lace from her face, revealing two claw marks across a disfigured eye. Yet from the malformation, the pupil still shone with an intense green. Her voice rumbled, clearly echoing Guin's words rather than Imrythel's, and the words were almost indiscernible as she answered, "You, the one who left my companion with this very mark, would dare confront me in this manner?"

Parū lowered her head. *That has been ages, Guin. I have learned to control the rage within, and I am sorry for that which your bonded person has suffered. But my past actions do not give you cause to harm this land and its people as you have done.*

"I shall not heed your words, Parūdragon. This is my due. The people of Nantai—these *Storm Sorcerers*—owe me this much. They belittle our kind, reducing Moya to a snakelike figure by so naming their throne. Given their crimes against the most ancient Ryū, it is my right as Kuroi's mate to reclaim this land as I see fit."

My eldest sister cackled, drawing my attention back to my immediate foe. Her body now covered in shining blue scales, Karynne's voice sounded a half-snarl as she said, "You see, dear sister, you should not have favored Aunt Nadia when I was here and capable. I would have been your greatest ally had you not forsaken me." She sauntered away, discarding Father like a dirty piece of laundry.

He crumpled at the foot of the column.

I scanned the rooftop. Idalynne Feathergale had disappeared with Karynne's cloak and crown, never having given me a second glance. What had Karynne done to convince her I posed the empire any danger? Or had she simply feared losing another person in her care since she'd lost Jessa, then me? I couldn't toil over the matter. The Cloud Courtiers stood poised, statuesque on the second line behind the casteless. Clearly, they would let those without magic find their deaths first with little remorse—sickening.

The four yisun who'd arrived with me protected Parū's back, weapons at the ready. Father lay helpless, but I could see his shoulders rising with breath. He lived for the moment. The casteless people of Nantai shifted, gripping and regripping their swords, awaiting orders from someone more organized than any one of them, and occasionally swiping a palm over their breeches to remove the sweat. They would serve as little more than a feint if things came to a brawl, and likewise, I had little concern over the illusionists. They craved power, but also beauty. For them to mar themselves would be beyond comprehension.

Without a backward glance at Father or me, Karynne tilted her chin toward the sky and bellowed, "I have become powerful by my own making. I chose my first advisor with wisdom, and she bestowed this gift upon me, and I will not lose the Serpentine Throne now to one as weak as you. It's something you don't have the strength or power within yourself, *little sister,* to experience."

Though beholding the sight of her transformation was both fearsome and beautiful—something I'd experienced but hadn't witnessed—her words cut to my very core. Imrythel or Guin had just cursed the throne's title, but Karynne used it freely.

After everything, every loss I'd endured and feat I'd accomplished, I knew to the root of my companionship and my soul that *weak* wasn't a word that could or would ever describe me. In place of sadness, rage pulsated throughout my body, a maelstrom gathering as my sorcery twisted and turned. The last thing I desired was to fight my sister in her dragon form. I tried to reason with her one last time. "Karynne, please. We can work this out as sisters. That bond is strong too. I understand what it is you feel in the connection to the Ryū. We can have that too and do this together."

"Oh, little Mairynne . . ." She teetered on the edge of transforming, her voice growing deeper with every word. "*Baby* sister . . ." She walked slowly toward the misty stairs in front of the ragged army of casteless who stood for her. "You may not have intended to twist the blade already protruding from between my ribs. Nevertheless, you did so when you echoed Father's disapproval of me. In choosing Aunt Nadia as your successor, you proved that you are truly forged from the same metal as he."

When she reached the foot of the stairs, she looked over to me with a smirk, her teeth elongating into the fangs of her Ryū. "I have another surprise for you. Lady?" she called up the stairs.

The Stone Lady, Sarangarel, stepped into view at the top, clad in leather armor and brandishing an axe with a honed stone head.

◇◇◇◇◇◇◇◇◇◇◇◇◇◇◇◇◇◇◇◇◇◇◇◇◇◇◇◇◇◇◇◇

I WOULD HAVE NEVER imagined footsteps on the misty floors of the cloud islands could echo, but as the rest of Lady Sarangarel's warriors joined her on the steps, my pulse pounded to the sound of their footsteps moving closer, then down the stairs and onto the roof. A dozen Stone Singers with their own battle-axes in hand stood behind their leader.

Words wouldn't come, though my mouth hung open.

Sarangarel scoffed. "Oh, Mairynne, love, why do you seem so surprised? Kōgō Karynne offered our caste an elevation."

Jaliqai wailed, a warrior's cry of disbelief as she turned from Parū's side and launched toward Sarangarel. I held out a hand, casting a bolt of lightning into her path yet far enough that it wouldn't strike her.

The yisu came to a stop, wailing, "How could you? You assigned us to this empress and now you follow another? Do your vows mean nothing?"

With her chin held high and hand outstretched, Sarangarel said diplomatically, "Join me, soldier. Kōgō Karynne has elevated the Stone Singers to the third caste— ahead of the Fire Forgers and Frost Fighters. Something that imposter would never consider."

To my surprise, Jaliqai turned her head and spat on the ground. "From this moment forward, I am no longer Stone Singer. You may call me casteless, but I'll not join them either. My empress is Mairynne, and I will fight for her until my very last breath."

Timur pounded the hilt of the Underhill's axe on the stone under his feet thrice, flashing a satisfied grin when Sarangarel's eyes widened at the display of his weapon. Nachin swung dual short swords and squared off toward Sarangarel.

Baidu took a readied stance and spoke more words than I believed I'd heard from him since our initial meeting. "The four of us are united in this, Sarangarel. And I am certain your most favored soldier, Yisu Chambui, will feel the same. Mairynne is a leader who cares naught for castes. In her vision of Nantai, people are merely people, and that is the Nantai I, too, envision."

His words remained calm, odd for Baidu, but the omission of any title for the Stone Lady spoke volumes. And that he recognized my intent without me having ever said as much, comforted my soul. Things had come so far, and I cherished these Stone Singers as my own people, much like Misha and Kyr, and the Tsinti I'd become so close with as well. But given our situation here and now, facing off with two dragons to my one, a hoard of casteless, and now Stone Singers who Karynne had promised unspeakable things to, doubt crept into my mind. Hoaris, Jorani, Baldeo, Misha, Kyr, the Small Folk and Tsinti who'd followed us this far, the Fire Forgers and Frost Fighters . . . all were out of my reach at the moment. With my father already fallen, Thalaj in the arms of Guin, how would only Parū, the four now forsworn yisun, and I survive this?

Behind my yisun, Parū coiled and readied herself to strike the moment Imrythel gave her cause.

Imrythel, or mayhap it was Guin, still held Thalaj by the throat. A droplet of his life's blood dripped down her claw and one ran into the hollow at the base of his throat. I locked eyes with him for a long moment, trying with desperation to read what he thought. His eyes had always been dark, but they seemed harder now, like onyx. What had he endured in the realm between after I'd left him in Amare's care?

Vaguely answering my rhetorical question, Parū said, *He is changed, minikin.*

The simple words held an ominous note, and as I narrowed my eyes, his gleamed. It wasn't a bright light, but the way black stone shines when polished or a sword of the darkest iron catches the light. *Can it truly be?*

Yes, minikin, answered my dragon. *Amare saved them both.*

My hand trembled as I covered my mouth. Parū lowered her head, and more rumbling ensued. My focus held solely on the man I'd most desired, the one I'd thought lost in the Fey Realm, the one I believed I needed to save. He pulled from Imrythel's grip and transformed before my eyes into the blackest of the Ryū. I'd met Kuroidragon once before, but he'd been mourning. Now, he caused the very air about me to shiver. I couldn't rip my eyes from the majesty of the ancient black dragon, the majesty of the bond Thalaj had formed. But in my periphery, the casteless backed away. The marching sounds of Sarangarel's yisun silenced. Even Imrythel peered up at the black dragon in awe.

The transformation held everything in abeyance. I daresay not a soul on the roof of Stormskeep took a breath.

The moment separated itself from reality . . . a pause before the tempest truly arrived.

SIXTY-EIGHT

A Cyclone—Magnificent and Tragic

KUROI TURNED, SWIPING HIS GREAT barbed tail toward Imrythel. She leaped into the air. Time for talk had passed and only action remained. Karynne's partial transformation completed, and Barūdragon slithered between the casteless, Courtiers, and yisun soldiers.

Still allowing for my understanding, Parū grumbled to Kuroi, *You can handle Guin?*

My ears heard only a growl, but through my companion, I understood Kuroi's words. *It is my duty to handle the green Ryū. You watch over your companion.* The black dragon lowered his snout to peer at me, and my heart ached with the knowledge Thalaj peered out from behind the dark eyes.

Parū came to my side then, facing the blue dragon.

The green and black dragons roared to the sky, a gush of wind from their wings blasting all who remained. The sound of their howls reverberated over Stormskeep, down into Arashi, and rolled like thunder through the valley outside the gates. Parū kept her attention on Barūdragon, but I turned to see what transpired upon the fields beyond the city's gates. The fireballs and ice shards paused in reverence as every Forger and Fighter upon the field lifted their faces to the sky.

The blue dragon moved toward Parū.

Though I kept my eyes upon the fields, I projected my thoughts toward my companion, *Please, have care. She is the mother of the babe below, and my sister lives within. Bring her to our side if you can.*

Barū lowered her head, roared, and breathed a lick of blue flame at Parū. My dragon sheltered the yisun from the blast, then shooed them toward where I stood.

Movement below caught my eye, and I squinted downward to better see. People climbed the outer stairs toward the roof. At the front—Hoaris. They were almost to the landing before the final stairway to the roof.

I turned holding my hands out to the side and calling down the lightning. As it struck the roof, I cried, "Enough!"

Momentarily, all motion halted and every head on the roof turned to me.

Sarangarel said, "It is not enough. Yisun, capture the traitors." She pointed with her axe toward *my* yisun soldiers.

Baidu, Timur, Jaliqai, and Nachin might no longer be Stone Singers, but I'd adopted them as my own. They would retain the title of yisun as long as they lived. They crouched defensively, bravely, as they faced off with the men and women who had once been their comrades in arms.

"Stop!" I yelled again. "If this is what you are and what you choose to do, we will always be a people divided. Listen to me! My sister and the green dragon have used your prejudices against you. What we need now as a people is acceptance of one another. Tolerance and patience. The companionship with the Ryū can make our people whole again. It served a purpose once, and our first emperor broke the sanctity of that purpose. What followed divided us as a people too. It created these gods-forsaken castes."

The blue dragon swung her head toward me, and through my bond, I felt Parū coil to attack. I projected, *Wait, my Ryū.* To my sister's companion, I said, "Listen to me, Barū."

The blue dragon snarled her upper lip. Smoke licked from her nostrils. One eye fixed on me as hard as a blue gemstone, or as the blue stone that had once graced the center of Safaia. The egg on display for all to see.

I persisted. "Listen past the words Karynne has spoken to you and beyond whatever evil your own mother Guin has laid upon your soul. I helped you retrieve your babe in Safaia, and I met your youngling in the caves below Stormskeep. Please, hear me now!" If she burned me here upon this roof, at least I would have said my piece, but I held hope within like a spark of the storm. I'd met her before she'd known Karynne. I'd defended her then, and I now hoped I'd left an impression worth honoring. Somewhere inside, I worried that this, too, would twist within Karynne's mind and she'd view my words as yet another betrayal. But for everyone on this rooftop, for those who climbed to my aide now, for the northerners who'd shown up to capture the Storm Sorcerer's attention, and for all the people across Nantai, I had no choice but to try to reason with this dragon. Mayhap I could appeal to the things she cared the most about within the fiber of her being.

Barū moved her snout so close I could reach out and touch it if I so wished, but also so close that she could burn me alive before anyone could stop her, Parū included. If she were a person, her brow would have furrowed as she made a few grumbles ending with a long mewl.

Instinctively, I flitted a questioning glance to my companion. Blood thrummed in my ears, echoing the sound of the Sundai Falls nearby.

Your sister, the dragon's companion, Parū started, keenly narrowing her eyes at the Ryū. *Barū says she's livid inside her. But Barū is listening to you, minikin. I have always known you possessed the heart worthy of the Ryū and the soul needed to be Kōgō of Nantai, but to gain this attention from a dragon despite her companion's protests . . . In the ages I have existed, I have never witnessed such an oddity as what I witness now.*

MY HEART SWELLED UNDER Parū's praise and the sheer awe in her voice. It bolstered the courage I was working so hard to muster. In the pause, Parū's long body created a barrier between the opposing sides of the yisun, and from where I stood, I could easily protect Father or call a squall to take us from this rooftop. And, if necessary, Parū could also carry the four yisun to safety.

The supporters I'd gathered over longer than four seasons would crest the roof in a matter of seconds. That last climb from the landing was steep and narrow, and they'd appear one at a time, but they were coming. This swayed me toward hope too.

And I had finally learned who controlled the casteless. Sarangarel grunted and motioned toward them, urging them forward. I called the storm's magic from the depths of my soul and pressed outward, creating a wall of wind and slowing their advance. Hoaris stormed onto the roof, sword in one hand and a flickering blue orb of winter's wrath in his other.

I pointed, commanding him. "Hold them back!"

Flooding onto the roof at his back came other friends I'd won. Chambui joined the other yisun. Yankos, Jorani, Baldeo, Zofi, and the remainder of the Tsinti, each brandishing a different weapon. Saqie Kitikara followed, leading a dozen more Frost Fighters. Most of the Frost Fighters didn't carry weapons, but I'd seen the winter shields they'd cast over the fields and I'd been raised around a half Frost Fighter. I knew how deadly their cold sorcery could be, and I said a quick thanks to Selene that they'd answered my call.

Finally, Misha and Kyr appeared, followed by Misha's family—his father, the Small King Isao, and his brother Tomei. Another dozen, mayhap two, scurried onto the roof. Misha came to my side.

"Are there more?" I asked.

"No. The rest tend the battle on the fields," he answered.

I still held the wind, but the constant flow began to drain my powers. "Join Yankos and the Tsinti. Hoaris?!"

He turned his head and shot me a grin and a wink. Everything about his visage said this battle was what he'd been awaiting for a long, long time.

I had to fight the smile pulling at the corners of my mouth despite the desperate situation before me. "Focus the Frost Fighters on the yisun and Sarangarel."

The Stone Lady bellowed at my command, laughing as if they held no power against her elite warriors. But the Frost Fighters were already building a shield of ice.

Yankos and his wanderers were a scrappy folk, more so than the casteless could imagine. They wouldn't fight with any organization, but that made them a good match for those who certainly had no training in combat or even self-defense. At least the Tsinti sparred regularly within their camps. The casteless were only proficient in carrying messages through the messenger network, thievery, and simple survival skills. I'd never seen the Small Folk fight, but if what Karynne said about them feeding on magic was true, they would do best to handle the Courtiers who currently used the casteless as a shield.

Certain that I had the situation covered on all fronts, I released the wind and sagged. For someone who had never seen the world before my mother's death and father's abduction, I'd done well enough in navigating. Mayhap I'd been lucky but I wanted to believe that I'd forged connections with these people and that was what afforded me success in this dire moment.

The blue dragon hadn't moved in the few seconds it'd taken me to orchestrate everything—another something that glimmered with hope. It seemed she watched me to see what I might command next; whether it was interest, suspicion, or vigilance on her part, I couldn't tell. I had need to speak with her but hadn't the ability to communicate in the Ryū tongue. In truth, the low growling sounds didn't seem possible for a person to replicate given the dragons produced the sounds in their long throats. So I relied on my connection to Parū for translation. Comprehension didn't come as quickly as when hearing my native tongue; she had to understand and process the thoughts in Nantai before I could respond, but that worked faster than if she needed to voice the words in my tongue as well.

Barū asked, *"You are bonded?"* her eyes drifting to my dragon.

Parū replied, *"Yes. Amare sent the Small Folk to find Mairynne Evangale and set her on the path to find me."*

"Wait, what?" I asked, shifting a confused look toward Parū.

She ignored me. *"The tiny ones didn't use methods the Fey wished to employ, but the result was the same. Amare regrets the loss of the former Nantai empress Noralynne Evangale to the cause, but the ends were worth the sacrifice."*

I couldn't discern if her words were directed at Barū or me, but it answered so very many questions. It confirmed the Small Folk within the Evernight had sacrificed Mother. It confirmed the Fey had set them onto the task. It confirmed they had orchestrated everything. All of this simply to remove one Ryū dragon.

No, minikin. All of this to restore peace and equality to your lands, and all of this to restore the sacred bond of companionship. I mourn your mother's soul, but I hope you will forgive these things one day.

I hadn't the opportunity to think, feel, or respond as in the distance, roars echoed up and down the valley. They shook the very stone walls upon which we stood atop Stormskeep. I gave the dragons roiling in the clouds and the awestruck armies below only a fleeting glance as a sour taste rose in the back of my throat. My stomach flopped. Coldness and heat chased each other through my body much like the slender green and black bodies twisting in the sky. I began to sweat. I swallowed hard, time and time again, and drew in long, cleansing breaths until I could focus again. Putting those details away for later, I rolled my shoulders back.

"Barū," I choked out, my voice low and resonant, a tone I poured all my strength and will into. Then, after some soft growls from both dragons, I softened my voice and added, "And Karynne, I speak to you both now. I do not know what evil Guin and Imrythel have put in your minds, but I do not wish to lose my sister."

I paused while grumbles transpired between the dragons. At the end of my sentiments to Barū, Parū added her own color to my plea. *Guindragon is broken and has need of our Fey mother for soul-deep healing.*

"Yes," I echoed, "the green dragon has harbored her revenge for five ages. She carries burdens we shall never fully understand." I peered at my father, considering the connection he'd found recently with Zofi. "If she will release the vengeance she holds so closely, she may find peace once again. One thing is certain though, as long as she chooses anger, her soul will not rest. What my ancestor, Makenyn—" I looked to the skies, to the tangle of green and black that held Thalaj somewhere inside.

Following my gaze and heart, Parū spoke gently, *Sometimes, that is how the Ryū talk, minikin. Do not worry over much.*

I blinked slowly, feeling Barū's warm breath encircling me still, sensing her waiting and holding my sister within so that I may finish. So much had transpired, yet we hadn't moved. To the notion of how dragons might communicate, I answered, "I know, but I wish I could know more of what they say to one another than I can see from this distance. It matters little to this moment though." To Barū and Karynne, I continued, "*Our* ancestor, Makenyn Evangale, created this by his choice to sever his companionship with Kuroi. And for the sins of my forefather, I hold the deepest regret." I swallowed. It seemed so many regrets were culminating in this moment and what would follow.

Rumbling between my sister's blue dragon and my pearlescent dragon ensued as Barū answered, *It is the first apology I have heard from the people of Nantai. I dare to guess Mother Guin has not heard such words spoken either.*

Her words drove me onward. "Would that she wanted to hear such words from my lips; I would say them over and over again. Barū, whatever torment you have seen or experienced through Guin's pain, I am sorry for that also. Karynne, please, I beg you to hear this now. There is no cause to hold fast to such a vicious divide in our family." Tears clouded my vision yet again, and one streamed down my face. I'd cried enough tears throughout this that I hoped to never shed another, but this wasn't done yet.

Upon the roof, everyone had fallen silent and watched our exchange. Sensing the blue dragon ease, I moved forward around Barū's snout so that I could look deeper into her sapphire-colored eye. I placed a hand on the bridge of her nose—cool to the touch though she could breathe fire through her nostrils. Barū allowed it with a vertical, then horizontal blink of her double lids.

I searched inside the dragon's eye, seeking my sister. "Karynne, I know it is unfair that you cannot reply, but I know you can hear me from within. Father and I only wish to have you at our sides, to see you heal like the Fey want to see for Guin. And Barū, we . . . Parū and I . . . want to see you reunited with your youngling. You should watch him grow into a strong and fantastic dragon. We released him from his chains, and there are people tending his wounds as we speak. It would be a shame for him to lose his mother."

Barū lifted her snout and long neck and bellowed into the sky, knocking me off my feet.

Parū growled but I held out a hand. "I am well. She mourns." I stood.

The blue dragon sucked in a breath when the first wail had run its course and released a stream of flames into the clouds. The Cloud Courtiers, casteless, Small Folk, Stone Singers, and Frost Fighters watched the sky in awe. Weapons had fallen to their sides, forgotten. When Barū had settled her head back beside me, she grumbled to Parū, but my dragon didn't allow me inside this time.

Barū focused one eye upon me. Tears with a hint of the color of her scales leaked from the corner of her eye, then she leaped into the sky.

"Wait, no!" I cried as she wove her blue body into the clouds and disappeared.

I sank to my knees, allowing tears to fall freely.

Lost.

She needs time, minikin. Your sister may need time also. Focus on your people now while I go. Parū lifted her snout toward the dragon battle over the valley.

I jerked my head up. "No, you cannot fly into that. Please."

She swung her great head back to me. *Guin is the reason I have returned to Nantai, and I'm certain she is the reason Amare graced your gensui with Kuroi's companionship, as well as the reason the blackest dragon agreed. I must go, minikin.*

Balling my fists, I gained my feet. "Then join back with me. Allow me to fly with you. I cannot lose you to that fray!"

Parū closed her eyes and reopened them slowly. She motioned to the audience we had upon the rooftop. Her voice in my mind felt severe, forlorn. *Your people have need of their empress. We will remain connected, but we have separate duties for now.*

"But we are one. How can we be so far apart?" I lifted my chin to the clouds again.

We are two sides of the same, and I will return to you when this is done. Search your heart, dear one. You will find you already know this is our path.

Ignoring the audience around, I lurched forward, hugging her about the snout. "Swear you will return," I sobbed.

As long as it is within my power, I will return to you and remain with you for all your days.

I pulled away, wiping the tears from my face, again. Finding my command, I said, "Go. Fly." I called to my sorcery, lifting my arms to the skies, and offered a wind to begin her ascent. As she flew away, I looked at Chambui and my yisun. "Take the Stone Lady into custody."

They moved without hesitation. Chambui grasped her free arm while Timur took her weapon. When her right arm was free of the axe, Baidu seized her as well. Sarangarel hung her head when she finally accepted defeat. But she had thought wrongly about positioning herself within our hierarchies, caste structure was not the way of our future. I would see to that.

My father stirred beside me, and I helped him to a sitting position. He had blood running from a cut above his eye but he grasped me with strength, nodded, and rasped, "I will be well, Daughter. Tend to them." He indicated the people watching.

Standing, I addressed everyone present, letting a stream of sorcery lift my words on the wind so they echoed into everyone's ears. "As we move into a new age, the castes will come to an end. In this new age, Nantai will have no caste lines between our peoples. It doesn't matter if you are an illusionist. It makes little difference if you conjure fire, wield winter's magic, or call upon the storm's sorcery. I care not if you practice alchemy or shamanism, cast fey spells, see into the future with augury, or travel while cloaking yourself with a fold in time. And if you hold no magic at all—be you one who lives beneath the ground and can light the night with your gaze or one who has been referred to as casteless—that does not make you less Nantai than those of us who are born with certain gifts. *All* people are *my* people. I have work yet to do. *We*, as people of Nantai, have a nation to rebuild."

Falling silent to allow the message time to penetrate, I turned, waving a hand to the sky where Parū approached the aerial melee. "The Ryū bond is natural. I have reclaimed it on behalf of our people. Makenyn, the Scarred was wrong to have severed his sacred bond with Kuroidragon. And Guindragon was wrong to have burned our cities—*your* cities. My companion is the great pearlescent Ryū, Parūdragon, and we mean to bring peace and safety to your land. My bonded dragon assures me the Fey from the realm beyond yet in between all others, the keepers of the magic and the dragons, will support us in this endeavor.

"I beg that you all stand with me here and now, but it is neither for power nor for revenge that I ask this of you. I ask this because Nantai is my home, and I have come to know so many of her people, and . . ." I looked at Sarangarel, sadness weighing on my heart. "I have loved so many of them until now. I hope to love more in the age to come.

"It is for that love I pray to our Holy Triad that you will accept me now as your leader"—I couldn't believe the words that bubbled in my throat—"as Empress of Nantai." Yet I'd never been more certain of a path. This was the position my journey and now my companionship with Parū had enabled. This was the duty my father had seen me fit to ascend to. My ignorance be damned. I could learn. The ceremony around ascension be damned. I had those who loved me, those I considered friend and family, for support.

This was my purpose.

◇◇◇◇◇◇◇◇◇◇◇◇◇◇◇◇◇◇◇◇◇◇◇◇◇◇◇◇◇◇◇◇◇

HOARIS WAS THE FIRST to bend to one knee and shout, "Hear! Hear! Kōgō Mairynne!" and wink again.

The Frost Fighters followed his lead. Yankos pounded his heart twice, his dagger still in hand, and bowed his head. As the Tsinti followed their leader's sign of deference, they seemed unified in this, much like the only other regular tradition of theirs—gathering around the fires at night under tsym. My yisun bent to one knee save Chambui and Baidu who held Sarangarel. Instead, they bowed their heads. The yisun who'd sworn allegiance to the Stone Lady fell to their knees one by one.

Twisting in Chambui and Baidu's grip, Sarangarel shouted at her soldiers, "Sniveling cowards. You were named yisun, an honor reserved for steadfast loyalty and strength! Who trained you to relent to matters so soft?"

Chambui, the woman warrior who'd proven herself steadfast at my side and had been so devoted throughout my journey I'd never had cause to question her, raised both brows, showing clear annoyance. It was Sarangarel, I judged, who'd become a turncoat in reality. I steeled myself, preparing a response to Sarangarel, when Chambui balled a fist, shot me a half-smile, and sailed a stone-hardened punch into the gnoble's gut. The Stone Lady coughed and doubled over but she remained silent thereafter.

With every person on the rooftop who lowered themselves before me, something inside my heart swelled. At one point, I believed my sorcery would erupt and shower a joyous rainstorm upon the roof. If that'd been the case, it wouldn't have been a rain of sorrow as it'd once been. No, it would have been a rain that would have washed away the treachery brought upon Stormskeep by the sins of my ancestors and the revenge of a wronged dragon.

King Isao took a knee. The Small Folk—the ones I now understood were part fey or helpers of the Fey at least—fell in beside him. I pondered, eying the Small King, were they like the Abatwa in Ise? Misha and Kyr were the last to bow, but they did so happily, pride swelling with their smiles.

The casteless fumbled as they tried to bow, something none of them had ever done before. A haggard bunch wearing ill-fitting and battered armor, but their enthusiasm caused happy tears to well in my eyes. As a group of people, they were the meek, the ones who'd been most wronged by the layers and layers within Nantai's society. No longer.

As for the Cloud Courtiers, they held out the longest. I faced off with the one who seemed their leader, though I could make out none of their identifying shoulder symbols. Still, I held my position and waited. Curiosity about the forward Courtier circled in my thoughts—mayhap it was Strato-Ymar, the gnoble of the caste, but possibly not. Thick moments passed, and I waited. If they wouldn't relent, I'd have them taken into holding as well. They were illusionists, unable to call a wind to transport them past the others toward the misty stairs. Their paths back into the High Cloud Courts were blocked by others who'd joined my cause, physically stronger Nantai than they. At this juncture, there were enough of my supporters upon this roof, I could easily subdue them.

Hands spread wide, the forward illusion vanished before my eyes and in its place, Lady Tsanseri appeared. She lifted and lowered her arms, and the likenesses of the Courtiers changed to individuality. She smiled at me across the roof and nodded once. Approval.

With her chin high, she called to me, "If it is *love* you wish, Kōgō Mairynne Evangale, you have our everlasting adoration."

Cirro-Vior—Viordyn, as I'd known him as a child—stepped to her side and wrapped an arm around her waist. To her other side, an elderly gent flourished a hand above his head and the image of a lily that grows in the vale outside Arashi's walls danced above his head. Gnoble Strato-Ymar.

I tipped my head forward, closing my eyes and touching my fingers to my forehead, thanking them from afar. A smile spread on my lips as I looked around at the diversity among my people—a people who now held my heart in the palms of their hands.

Father stood at my side and lay a hand on my shoulder. "I am proud of you, youngest daughter."

I turned and looped my arms around him and squeezed for a long beat before returning to the business that still needed attention. I took a half-dozen long steps to Hoaris and motioned for him to stand. "Take them to the fields. We need to see to any wounded there and work to bring the two sides together."

Beyond him, I found the Tsinti—Yankos, Baldeo, then . . .

"Jorani?" I asked.

She perked and trotted obediently to my side.

"Once on the fields, find Gnoble Yuos Atith," I commanded.

She answered with a curtsy. An oddly fitting move for her, I thought.

"Yes, Kōgō Mairynne," she answered.

Seeing angst in her mimicry of courtly customs, I laid a hand on her shoulder. "I am the same person you knew before. The one who traveled with your caravan under tsym, whom you taught the ways of the Tsinti, and whom you trained in the dance of swords. You chose the wanderers who live apart over the caste-life. I respect that choice, and though the movement becomes your more graceful side, I do not hold you to customs with which you are unfamiliar."

Her eyes glittered, searching my face. Apparently, she found the sincerity she desired because the smile on her lips grew as she looked to the Tsinti and back to me. "As you will, Mairynne."

"Thank you," I said, then added to Hoaris, "You find Gnoble Tenkara. I need you both to get the gnobles into the center of the battlefield while everyone below remains stunned by the dragon fight above." Wearily, I glanced back at the thundering roars and tangle of green, black, and now white in the sky.

"Yes, Kōgō M," Hoaris replied and moved the Frost Fighters into action, then the Small Folk.

The Tsinti needed little guidance. They followed Jorani, Yankos, and Baldeo naturally.

Misha lingered, wandering over.

Folding my arms over my chest, I scowled at the small man. "You never told me of the Small Folk's connection to the Fey."

He shrugged and chattered something to Kyr who'd came to his side, the place she always belonged.

She peered up, her eyes sparkling as she curved herself into Misha. "Lovely, you never asked."

I groaned. "Fair enough, but once this is all done, I'll need to hear all of it. Meanwhile, tell me one thing . . ."

Kyr turned and stared at me sideways, suspiciously.

"Was there a way into the Fey Realm here? In Nantai?"

The small woman's brows shot toward her hairline and she winked. "Of course there is, lovely, but it was not ours to offer."

Misha chuckled knowingly. "We'll share with you all we have knowledge of. We aren't the Fey, more like the Abatwa."

"As I've just begun to suspect." I said, feeling a bit smug. "Had I known, it would have saved a trip across the Syrensea, it would have been well worth the knowledge." I tilted my head, indicating for them to follow the rest.

Misha took my hand, turned it upward, and laid a kiss in the palm. Then they trailed the others.

When many had gone save for the yisun and Cloud Courtiers, Tsanseri approached, Viordyn at her side.

"Why did you not reveal yourself sooner?" I asked.

"Timing is everything, young empress. The Cloud Courtiers have been second caste for these five ages because of our patience alone. We never would have made a good ruling caste, but as we have had the power to hold the courts and travel the skies, we haven't been subject to the battles between the others." She looked meaningfully toward the fields. "We will take our leave now and spread word of your wishes throughout Nantai. Our bards will record and practice the reenactments of the events that have transpired today in this cyclone over Arashi. Hmm." She folded her arms and placed an index finger over her lips. "Mayhap that will be a fine title for the performance. *A Cyclone—Magnificent and Tragic*." She smiled with satisfaction.

As she turned, I grasped her at the elbow. "Tsanseri, what do you know of Filtch?"

Her brows puckered. "I haven't seen him since he left my island. He supported your sister whole-heartedly and was instrumental in bringing the casteless to Arashi and her aid. He wished to prevent your arrival, and thus the reason I sent him away. I . . . no"—shaking her head, she peered at Viordyn—"*my love* and I wished to see if you could change the course Karynne Evangale and Imrythel Sandsgale had set us upon. As you have. Alto-Trea never made it to the High Cloud Court where I went after leaving you atop Mount Sundai. That is the extent of my knowledge."

Viordyn hugged Tsanseri about the shoulders, rubbing her upper arm. "As we see what you can do, we do hope he is not about causing further heartache."

Though my actions had been just, I lowered my head, regret flooding throughout my body and soul. "I have taken his life. His body lies in the courtyard below. It is not a matter I intended, and 'tis something that will always weigh heavily upon my soul."

Viordyn reached forward and lifted my chin. His eyes were gentle as he soothed, "Even when I knew you as a child, Kōgō Mairynne, you cared more about people than anyone I've met. Certainly, your heart will mourn the act, but it is also certain that the Triad will see to your healing. If I read you correctly, Alto-Trea suffered a death of his own making. You merely held the weapon that finished the job."

Remembering all the heartache he'd wrought, on my childhood friend Jessamyne, and his appearance at the time I most needed to find Father, I nodded tightly. "Before I left Stormskeep, I banished him to the prison in the spire for the murder of a dear friend." I swallowed. The point of the tallest spire upon Stormskeep loomed over us now, slightly misted but still watching. "As I have now learned, that is no prison for one who has allies in the clouds." I laughed without humor.

Roars cut through the sky, rumbling the roof beneath my feet once more.

Tsanseri clasped both hands on my shoulders. "We must go now, Mairynne. You have much to attend." She nodded toward the dragon battle in the sky. "But I shall return to see you in your place upon the throne."

I winced. Parū's reaction to the Serpentine Throne in the council chambers had showed me that something aught was necessary as we entered into the next age. "I'll need a new throne. Or perhaps I don't need a symbol of such vanity at all."

Tsanseri quirked a brow in question, and I envisioned her once again sitting upon her pillows in Love's Court. The image I had of when she'd presided over Yasmynne's plea for her blessing.

Yasmynne. My sister's whereabouts along with the others I cared so much about in Stormskeep threatened to distract from the matter at hand. I shook my head, heeding the comtesse's advice to focus. "Given the restored companionship, that reminder of the Ryū Wars shall be destroyed. Perhaps the Serpentine Throne can be burned in a funeral pyre, spread across the fields in colorful mandalas, and offered to our people as a measure of remembrance. And Moyadragon may fly with the Gods at long last."

Father wrapped an arm around my shoulders. "A generous decree," he said with a small, sad smile.

"Tennō Atheryn Evangale," Tsanseri offered her hand. "My sister is upon the High Cloud Court. She can tend that head wound and see you recovered before we return to Arashi."

Father looked at me with question in his storm-gray eyes.

I nodded. "Join Zofi." At long last, I felt confident enough in my abilities with the people of Nantai that he'd better serve me in a place I could be assured of his safety and healing. I bade the Courtiers and my father farewell. They moved toward the misty stairs, forming two lines as they climbed.

Chambui and Baidu descended the final hazy steps and came to me. Sarangarel still writhed between them, and I marveled at the stubbornness to which she clung. When I'd allowed her to take me as her lover, I'd been naïve, thinking her attention flattery. Facing her now, I saw her actions then for what they truly had been—her pride. She'd bedded the imperial ruler. As she stood there before me, she raised her chin defiantly.

Before she could speak again, I held up a hand. "The gentleness you once showed me is something for which I will forever be grateful, though your motives for our lovemaking diminish the beauty of that shared night."

Her voice cool and controlled, she answered, "I achieved what I wanted, as has always been my way."

"I believed you cared for me," I countered.

"I did, and do still. But you will understand that my heart has always been with the Stone Singers. Everything I've ever done has been to earn my people the respect we deserve."

Under such an accusation, I bristled. "Did I ever offer you aught but respect, Gnoble Sarangarel? That I lay with you under Selene's watchful eye should show that I held you in high regard."

"Kōgō Mairynne, let us not be coy," she demurred. "You used me as much as I used you that night. You needed a ship, and I needed prestige. I'd say the deal was fairly made."

I sank my teeth into the inside of my lip, hurt and unable to fathom how she cheapened the experience by making it sound so businesslike. My virginity bartered for a ship.

"Well and so," I answered, nodding to Baidu then Chambui.

"What shall we do with her?" Yisu Chambu asked.

"There are guest chambers on the main level. As she is accustomed to certain comforts, I'll allow her those as a prison. Be certain to place her in the rooms away from the windows and stand guard. I will go to the gates and send guards to relieve you from the post and to watch over her until we have settled the rest of this matter and I can return. As for the remainder of the yisun"—I lifted my voice to be certain Sarangarel understood the price I extracted in exchange for her betrayal—"I now claim your allegiance."

They lifted their axes and pounded them thrice upon the roof, accepting. Their silent oath was well-made for I would not have hesitated to offer them similar accommodations to what I offered Sarangarel.

"Follow the others toward Arashi's gates," I commanded. "I'll meet you there."

As the yisun soldiers obeyed my order and before I turned toward the edge of the rooftop, I ran a hand down my once lover's cheek. "Farewell, my lady Sarangarel."

SIXTY-NINE

A Shower After the Squall

ALONE AT THE EDGE OF Stormskeep's roof, I climbed onto the stone wall and closed my eyes. High above training fields, the regent's chambers, and the keep's courtyard, I waited. Higher than the bridge that crossed the Sundai Falls and connected Stormskeep to the Citadel, I searched within myself for my connection to Parū. Distance silenced the bond but I found her and focused on the dragon's battle that raged in the clouds.

I opened my eyes to watch from afar what I felt through her more closely. In the fray, heat surrounded her; flames brushed her scales as Guin breathed her anger at Kuroi, then at Parū. Kuroi sometimes dodged and sometimes responded with flames of his own. I wished I could speak with Thalaj, learn how he was adapting to the bond. Parū was too focused, too intent on her attempt to subdue the black and green dragons for me to seek any answers. From the top of the keep, the fire breath appeared like lightning gathering within the summer's storm—not striking the ground but setting the accumulating clouds aglow from time to time.

They communicated in their low grumbling language, sometimes escalating to a roar that filled the valley and caused the armies of Frost Fighters and Fire Forgers to tremble and move closer to one another. However, the Ryū communication was passing too quickly for me to eavesdrop effectively. Understanding both dragon's voices and which belonged to whom I found even more difficult until I felt Parū form a reply.

He chose you, Guin. Ages ago, he chose you! Parū dove into Guin's chest, knocking her body backward from the coil of Ryū bodies.

Her reply came full of venom as she pointed and darted back toward my dragon. Parū only shared snippets of her words—*matters little . . . the people . . . the curse . . . tearing him . . . mourning . . .*

I gasped, but Parū darted to the side.

As I breathed out some of the tension, Kuroi's voice boomed, *Makenyn forced . . . didn't ask for this . . . torn companion . . .*

Though I strained, my ability to follow their words remained inept. Instead, I watched through Parū's eyes. Kuroi turned in midair, lashing his tail toward Guin, but she dodged and dove for him, claws piercing into the softer area near his arms. I couldn't move, as if my remaining still would call a halt to the battle.

Minikin, your people, Parū's voice came back to me, in my tongue.

I made a choked sound as, through her eyes, I saw a green tail whip toward her head and coil about her throat.

You worry about what is in front of you, Parū! I screamed to her in thought. *Free yourself and return to me.* She couldn't breathe and neither could I as the tail squeezed. She clamored to gain purchase on Guin but couldn't.

"No!" I screamed, strangled at the end.

Darkness twinkled in her vision. She shouldn't have worried over me, should have focused on the battle. I clutched at my chest, feeling the air that brought life to her waning as the green dragon squeezed tighter. Then . . . she was freed and sucked in hot air. I inhaled and focused again. The black dragon had Guin in his claws. Both he and Parū were larger than her, older.

Kuroi stretched her so far, the spines along her back seemed to separate. Shocked, I began to understand without translation as he grumbled, *Guin, please!* He pleaded over and over, the growl in his chest growing louder as he begged her to stop.

Parū grabbed onto Guin's tail to prevent it from lashing either her or Kuroi.

My teeth sank painfully into my lip as this played out.

Parū said, *Guin, please let me return you to Amare. She will see your soul healed.*

The green dragon fought, twisted, pulled, shook her head, lifted it, and bellowed fire into the sky so high, it shone above the clouds. Then, she sagged in Kuroi's clutches.

The scene slowed and Parū let me deeper into her mind as Guin spoke, *I have spent five ages seeking revenge upon the Nantai for what they did to you, Kuroidragon. Now, you return to tell me that is not our path. Mourning has softened you.*

No, Guindragon, Kuroi replied, *mourning was necessary. Leaving our bonded people places a scar upon us when it is natural, but when it is forced, you cannot know the pain it causes. It is worse than losing a mate. You allowed this to turn you bitter, but what I felt was a loss of part of myself, something from which I shall never recover. I pray no Ryū must endure such a thing again. But what has offered me healing is my new minikin.*

The black dragon released Guin slowly, and Parū followed suit. Guin curled and coiled in on herself, keeping her snout low but remaining silent. Then, she turned from them and bolted across the skies, north in the direction of Kōdaina Kōri.

Parū and Kuroi looked at one another, grumbling confusion. When Kuroi flinched as if to follow, Parū wrapped a tail about his leg. *No, Kuroi. You stay. My minikin needs her gensui. I came to retrieve Guin and return her to Amare. I will fulfill that oath.*

Go with care, Parūdragon, Kuroi replied.

"Nooo!" I bellowed, so inept from this distance, helpless to change.

But Parū took flight, calling back to me, *I promised to return, minikin, and I shall. I said before, you have a dragon's soul within. Until we are joined once more, see to your people. Reunite with Kuroi's bonded Nantai. See the empire into an age where the peace you desired reigns.*

If the span from the keep to the skies over the vale distanced our companion's bond, it was naught to the feeling of Parū's strength leaving me, slipping through my fingers as if it were a cloud carried away on the breeze and leaving me so very, very cold.

◇◇◇◇◇◇◇◇◇◇◇◇◇◇◇◇◇◇◇◇◇◇◇◇◇◇◇◇◇◇

MY CHIN AND SHOULDERS fell under the temptation to weep for Parū's absence when movement within the streets reminded me of the situation still churning within Arashi and beyond her walls. I couldn't discern the people but the small crowd moving toward the gates was surely the party I'd sent ahead. Alone then upon the roof, the thundering of the dragon's battle quelled and none of the three dragons visible beneath the clouds, I steeled myself, held my arms wide, and called an updraft. This time, I had no need to close my eyes. Loss, determination, and my destination—Arashi's gates to confront the city's guard—fueled my sorcery. I stepped into the current and directed the power over the city toward the vale.

Traveling up or down in bursts or calling the wind to aid in moving faster or carrying heavy objects had always been the extent of strength I'd known with Storm Sorcerer's powers. It drained our energy to pour too much into the air. In my lifetime, I couldn't recall a Storm Sorcerer traveling on a gale from the castle to the gates. Yet I felt the storm's magic flow through me stronger than ever. Mayhap it was reckless and I'd collapse once my feet hit the ground. Mayhap it was power lingering from my companionship with Parū. But as the wind's current carried me, I felt hale still. I held my head high as I approached, and Arashi's guards turned to me, readying bows and swords, some holding out their hands as if they were ready to call on the storm themselves.

Many squinted against the gale as it lifted and whipped their hair.

"Be at ease," I spoke softly, but the sound traveled with the wind to each of them. "The dragon battle in the sky is done. My sister and Imrythel have also fled Stormskeep and Arashi. This battle—no, by the three heavens, this *war*—is over."

I may have imagined it, but it seemed the guards gathered released a collective sigh, their weapons easing slightly toward the ground. With one bare foot then the other, I landed on the soil just behind the gates and lowered my arms. Roryn and Gaelynne stepped through the line of soldiers.

Gaelynne's brows knitted together as if she refused to believe I stood before her. "Mairynne?" she breathed, leaning forward ever so slightly.

Issō Roryn held up his fist, signaling the guards to stand down. He now wore the emblem of the first guard, a gensui rather than an issō, a thin braid of gold around his left arm. The emblem Thalaj had worn more than twelve of Selene's cycles before.

"Yes, I have returned with my father, Tennō Atheryn Evangale." I raised my voice so that all might hear. "He lives and is well. Once we have settled all here, he will return to Arashi."

"Will he ascend to the Serpentine Throne once more?" one of the guards to my left called.

I answered, "I'll leave that concern for another day. Today, I beg of you to help me call an end to this nonsense among our people."

"We believed you dead," Gaelynne said, her voice still disbelieving. Her stare fixated on me, brows drawn together in confusion.

"That"—I softened my voice for her—"may be partly ruse and partly my sister's doing. Or mayhap her first advisor's, I cannot be certain."

Hearing the veritable stampede behind me, I looked over my shoulder as Hoaris ran from between two buildings. Rushing forward at his side, the Small Folk, yisun, Tsinti, and small company of Frost Fighters made for a strange yet beautiful scene. My heart rejoiced as they came to a stop with weapons at the ready, their chests rising and falling with exerted breaths.

Mimicking Roryn, I held up a fist to put them at ease, nodded to Hoaris—who cocked a half-smile—and turned back to Roryn and Gaelynne. "Time now is of the essence," I started. "The armies outside of these gates are stunned. We will not face them with weapons drawn but open our doors to them and welcome them into Arashi. I will go forward with you, Roryn, and one from each of the castes and casteless behind me."

I flared an arm toward Hoaris, who stepped forward and bowed to one knee.

"Yes, Kōgō," he said. "Saqie Kitikara will join us as she has been an advisor to Gnoble Aljir Tenkara for many seasons now."

"Stand. Both of you." I inclined my chin to the woman. "Welcome, Saqie." When she stood, I offered her a hand and a warm smile.

She remained silent but took my hand and placed a kiss in the palm.

To the others, I called, "Yankos of the Tsinti, King Isao of the Small Folk, Timur of the Stone Singers, will you stand with us as one?" I wished Brimr of the Underhill Dwellers or Strato-Ymar of the Cloud Courtiers were here to present a united front, but alas, I was working with those available. Hoaris and Saqie would have to represent our plea to the Frost Fighters, but that left us without a Fire Forger representative. I hoped Gnoble Yuos Atith would welcome us.

Yankos stepped forward and, as if reading my mind, suggested, "Take Jorani in my stead. She is both Fire Forger and Tsinti and holds my trust."

I tipped my head forward. "Thank you, dear friend, but I believe you both should walk at my side. You will represent the Tsinti and Jorani will serve as emissary for the Fire Forgers." As she had backed my plea to the leader of their caste once thus far, Yankos was right in suggesting she accompany us onto the battle field. When Jorani stepped forward, Baldeo folded his arms over his expanding chest, smiled, and gave a single, satisfied nod.

Turning to Roryn and Gaelyne, I commanded, "Have the guards open the gate and clear a path. Then I welcome you both to walk with us."

Without command, the soldiers parted behind their issō and second guards. Two moved quickly to open the heavy gates, and Roryn stood sideways allowing me the lead. As I passed, he and Gaelynne fell into step behind me.

Roryn leaned closer, his voice lowered such that only I could hear his question. "What of Gensui Thalaj Northerngale?"

WE CROSSED UNDER THE large archway onto the fields where a din of befuddled Fire Forger and Frost Fighter voices lifted on a crescendo and waited with upturned eyes for more action to emerge from the clouds. On the heels of Roryn's question, I also looked up to the clouds, wishing I could connect with Kuroi the way I could with Parū. I had no bond with the blackest dragon, and as I could no longer feel my own bonded Ryū, I had no idea if Kuroidragon lingered in the clouds above. I hoped he did, and I hoped he'd return with Thalaj so that I might learn of my first guard's adventure.

I lay a hand on Roryn's shoulder. "He may be near, but I cannot say at the present."

We walked between the two armies, my feet squishing into the mud where fire had melted ice in the battle between the castes. Whispers started on both sides and rolled through the people gathered. They flowed around us like water, standing upon the field in strained peace. I said nothing as I passed but made purposeful eye contact with as many people as I could. For the few who seemed desperate for connection, I reached out a hand, took theirs in mine, and squeezed.

"May Atun guide you," I said to one Fire Forger. "May Otarr's light shine upon you," I added to a Frost Fighter, and I bestowed Selene's blessing on yet another, uncaring about her caste. I wanted them all to sense my intention—that I was but a person too, that I wanted the things my mother had worked for, that I held no one caste above another.

We worked our way to the center of the field, and slowly, all the attention turned from the skies to us.

Gnoble Yuos Atith pushed through his Fire Forgers on one side, a curved blade in one hand. "What is this?" he demanded.

The Frost Fighters on the other side parted and Gnoble Tenkara stepped forward, her hands clasped serenely behind her back. Mayhap she hid a weapon but she seemed peaceful enough. "For once, the Forger gnoble and I are in agreement. What transpires here?"

Jorani went to stand near her uncle and Saqie went to Tenkara.

Wanting to see more of my people, I tapped on Hoaris's shoulder. He grasped me around my waist and hoisted me onto one of his broad shoulders. He looped his broad arm over my thighs to secure me in place, and I felt surprisingly stable.

I stretched my arms and called a soft breeze to carry my words. "People of Nantai," I started, careful not to label any present. "This battle is ended, and today, we—as one common people of Nantai—begin a new age."

On the north side of those gathered in the vale, within the Frost Fighter ranks, gasps and voices sounded; hands pointed into the air.

"Thalaj," I said on a sigh as the black dragon snaked from the clouds.

Hoaris peered up to me, his lips poised to ask but words not finding voice.

Vigorously, I nodded, tears pooling in my eyes. My voice cracked as I told him, "Yes, he returned with Kuroi moments before you arrived on the roof of Stormskeep."

Hoaris's eyes glistened, too, as he asked, "Kuroi? The first emperor's companion?"

I pressed my lips together, nodding once more.

The blackest dragon's great wings flapped, directing his body toward me in the center of the field. Murmurs grew within the crowd, fear running its course.

"Be still. Remain calm!" I called, sending the words sailing. With hands in the air, I sent the breeze and my message outward from where I sat upon Hoaris's shoulder. "The black dragon means no harm to the people of Nantai! Fire Forgers, he is not the same one who brought destruction to Biei. That was Guin, the green dragon, and she is no longer among us."

"How do you know these things?" one of Yuos Atith's men shouted. Looking closer, I recognized him as the man who'd guarded me when I had been shackled near the great lake.

"Because, Phy Sovann, I bore witness to the battle. I watched the Ryū's green scales slithering off through the clouds. I watched this through my own companion, Parūdragon." I paused, waiting for attention to turn to me. "Yes!" I answered to the more stunned Frost Fighters. "I possess the bond with one of the Ryū dragons, and it is a beautiful thing. Something that our first emperor, Makenyn, defiled. A bond that the green dragon, Guin, has manipulated because she harbored resentment. But hear this now! That is not the way of the Ryū," I bellowed as Kuroi hovered.

The crowd parted behind me and he landed. He rose up on his claws, lifted his snout to the clouds, and roared black fire into the sky. Then, before everyone's eyes, he began to diminish, the air around him shimmering. He shrank back into the form of a man, crouched naked in the mud.

I searched my people and found a Fire Forger wearing a cloak. "You." I pointed. "Give him your cloak."

The Fire Forger obeyed, scurrying over and wrapping Thalaj in the rough brown woolen cloak.

My guard rasped, "Thank you," and turned his gaze upward toward me.

I lost myself in the familiar almond shape of his eyes, blacker than the nights when Selene slept over the grasslands. I slid down from Hoaris's shoulder until my feet touched the cool mud once more. Thalaj pulled the cloak tighter, covering his nakedness, and seemed worried or confused but also like he longed for me as much as I'd yearned for him. My guilt over leaving him melted away because his time in the Fey Realm had given him something no one could ever take from him, the gift of companionship. Without even asking, I understood how special that was. I took one step, two. A mist started falling from the clouds, weeping over my people and me. The cool droplets on my skin made me shiver, and at once, my mind conjured the times when Thalaj had walked into the room and it cooled around me. I recalled how warm his cool touch had made me feel inside. My lips tingled at the memory of our kiss, the one and only time our lips had danced, in the hull of Captain Asahi's *Swell Mistress*.

Fifty paces parted us, but our eyes held a conversation of their own. My body was drawn to his, his to mine. My heart beat the rhythm of hooves in stampede within my chest. Under a soft shower, spring's mist, joyous tears leaked down my cheeks. These, I couldn't regret. My breathing hitched and quickened as the corners of Thalaj's lips turned upward and he moved ever so slightly, opening his arms to me.

I called the wind and rushed into his arms.

Home.

We clung to one another for an eternity, alone at the center of so many people. And when we parted, his hands found my face and mine found his. There were no words, none that could describe the feelings surrounding us in that moment. Castes finally forgotten, he searched my face and ran his thumb over my bottom lip. At last, after so long, he crushed his lips to mine.

Cheers resounded throughout the valley, echoed in my heart and soul.

And when the shower after the squall had passed, only newness, hope, and love remained.

EPILOGUE

A Spring Affair

THE DAY AFTER THE BATTLE, I visited the citadel to make offerings to the Holy Triad. I lit incense upon Atun's alter, lay a branch upon Otarr's, and brought bread to Selene's. I had little choice but to trust that Parū would return to me in her own time. For now, to feel whole required faith I wasn't sure I possessed. Yet the constant sounds of Sundai Falls, my home within Stormskeep, and the familiar serenity of this holy place lent me whatever solace could be had.

After my offerings were made, I stood at the railing in the open-air sanctuary, eyes closed, hands extended, and breathed in the smells of Arashi.

"Mairynne?" a hesitant voice uttered, a sweet and familiar sound.

An image of my mother and her sister materialized in my mind. Twins and similar in so many things, but Nadia's voice carried a distinctive smoky sound that had been absent from Mother's. I breathed deeply, squeezing my eyes tighter as if I could embrace the image of the sisters together once more. As with all memories, it fluttered away. I answered, "Aunt Nadialynne," on a bittersweet sigh, a smile tugging at the corners of my mouth.

When I finally turned, my lungs and heart stopped as my eyes prickled with joy. At not twenty paces away, Nadia stood between her partner Corwyn Dawnsgale and his sister Solarynne. All three grinned, warm and welcoming smiles that went further in soothing my soul. My sister Yasmynne also stood awaiting my notice arm in arm with her betrothed, Nestryn. She wore a smile as large as the one she'd worn on the day we visited Love's Court. And when my eyes drifted downward, they rested upon the hand she held protectively over her swollen belly. No longer betrothed, I presumed.

Every one of them appeared happy to see me, save for a small pull of sorrow in the corners of their eyes. I felt it too, as we'd possibly lost Karynne to whatever despair she'd grasped onto within her heart for so very long. Mayhap returning to Stormskeep without losing another had been far too much to ask of the Gods who cared for this world, the next, and even the Fey Realm between. We hadn't any ideas as to where my sister may have retreated, but I protected a seed of hope in my heart that the blue dragon, Barū, would bring her back to us one day.

Only time would tell.

I reached a trembling hand toward my family, and we came together, sharing hugs and the comfort of kin.

"Where were you during the mayhem?" I asked.

"We've all been sequestered at Solarynne's home. We watched all that transpired from the mountain above."

"I assumed you'd retreated to the Dawnsgale keep. My intent was to find you there before I confronted Karynne, but fate had other plans," I said before a lump lodged in my throat and I couldn't bring myself to say more. I swallowed, then added quietly, "When I didn't see you, I worried that Imrythel or Karynne had done something truly regrettable. I'm happy to see you all are well."

Nadia cupped my cheek. "Your sister is in there still, and though she banished us from Stormskeep, I do not believe she had the capacity to do us true harm."

"Banished you?" I asked, then closed my eyes and leaned into her touch with a shake of the head. "It doesn't matter. You're all here now. Yasmynne, you are well? And expecting?"

My sister grasped my hand, as enthusiastic as she had always been. "Aside from becoming a mother myself, I'm no different than when you left." She pouted a moment. "Sad, like everyone, about Kary, but I'm desperate to hear of your journey. Did you find Father?"

"Aahhh," I breathed, forgetting that they hadn't received word of what'd transpired. "Yes, but he is recovering at the High Cloud Court presently. Strato-Ymar, Tsanseri, and Cirro-Vior are carrying word to the other islands in the skies and beyond, I am sure. Tsanseri will return him to us when all has settled."

"But how is he, Mairynne? I cannot wait to see him. What did he endure? Where did you find him? *How* did you find him? When ar—"

"Yasmynne." I stopped her with a touch and gentle smile. "I have many, many stories to answer your questions. Far too many to share in one morning."

She smiled sweetly and innocently, as she always had . . . my beautiful, eager, and curious sister. "But you *will* tell them, yes? Like Father once told us stories?"

"I will." I squeezed her hand. "And your youngling too. Unfortunately, I have other matters to deal with today." I dropped my gaze.

Sarangarel.

MY FAMILY ACCOMPANIED ME on my return to the castle to deal with the Stone Lady. Nadia walked at my side, the others trailing. I had toiled over how best to handle Sarangarel's betrayal, but I hadn't come to any conclusions in the hours between yesterday's battle and now. For the moment, I intended to keep her apart from others as I took the time to decide the best course of action, yet I would allow her the continued comfort of the suite. Guards would rotate in shifts at her door and food would be provided at the regular times. I'd also consult with those who were once on my small advisory council for guidance before making a final decree.

As we crossed the bridge high over Sundai Falls, I inclined my head to Nadia and asked, "What of the rest of Father's small council—Lukos and the others?"

"They have also retreated to their familial homes upon Karynne's orders. As kōgō, she kept only Imrythel and Idalynne Feathergale near her as advisors." Nadia tucked her chin and frowned. "I'm sorry I couldn't maintain the duty you bestowed upon me when you left. I fear I'm more suited for the gardens and tending a home. And I am truly sorry about your former nursemaid."

I had no answer or reply for these apologies, so I remained silent. At another dozen silent steps, we turned and descended a set of stone stairs. I wanted to soothe Nadia's worry and forgive, but I had no knowledge of what had truly transpired. With the little information I held, I'd be just in assuming her actions as treasonous as Idalynne Feathergale's. I wanted to exercise an empathetic ear and offer my aunt the grace of understanding before I passed judgment. A feeling, mayhap hope, told me there was little she could have done to prevent my sister's actions that wouldn't have resulted in her own death. And such a fate would have been far worse in the name of remaining loyal to what I had written in the annals. Torn, I replied, "The presence of a scorned Ryū so close to one of us wasn't something any could have predicted, Nadia. I've seen Imrythel and her companion, Guin, in full force. I cannot hold you to blame for their actions. Though, when it is done, I would ask that you tell me all the details of how she usurped the throne."

My aunt nodded briskly.

The soldiers standing guard at Sarangarel's door pulled their feet together, rolled their shoulders back, and held their eyes forward. Stiff formality, as established custom commanded.

I raised a hand and said, "Be at ease."

In unison, they moved their feet back to the width of their shoulders and tucked their hands behind their backs, peering down at me.

"Has she broken her fast?" I asked.

"Yes," the guard nearest answered. "An hour has passed since the attendant retreated with the remnants of her morning meal."

"Well and so," I answered, then gently commanded, "You'll unlock the door and allow me inside?"

The second guard pulled a key from his pocket and unlocked the door. When I stepped forward, Corwyn moved too.

Placing a hand on his chest, I said, "I'll see her alone."

Solarynne objected, "That is not advisable. You should have at least one other with you at all times."

"I am well aware of protocols for dealing with captives, but I have a history with the Stone Lady, and I wish to discuss matters with her in private. She may be more amicable to an agreement this way." At the very least, I hoped this would be true.

Nadia ran a hand down my arm, slipping it into mine, then squeezing. "Corwyn, Solarynne, and I will wait for you here." She motioned to a bench across the hall from Sarangarel's door.

I nodded my thanks.

Unexpectedly, Yasmynne threw her arms around me and kissed me on the cheek, then looped her arm through Nestryn's. "I'd like to revisit my rooms. We will find you later. Mayhap for midday meal?" She quirked a brow.

"Of course," I answered.

Save for two voluptuous sofas and an intricately carved table separating them, the first room was empty. The guards pulled the door closed behind me as I strode across to the hallway leading toward other areas within the suite. "Sarangarel," I called.

No answer.

The hallway passed a small kitchenette, which was also unoccupied, then opened up into a large chamber that served as a sitting room at one end and a bed chamber at the other. There was no movement inside. I turned to the bed, the only place the Stone Lady could be. Though it seemed strange, mayhap boredom called for dozing at midmorning to pass the time. The curtains around the bed were drawn and no rustling sounded from within to indicate anyone's presence. I reached a hand forward, latching onto the fabric. Heavy velvet was soft in my palm as I pulled away the veil.

A form lay curled under stuffed, pillow-like blankets, unmoving.

I reached for the form, touched the shoulder lightly, and budged her. Indeed, she felt as solid as I remembered under the covers, but I hadn't recalled Sarangarel sleeping so solidly from our night together. My heart picked up its pace as the slumber seemed something other . . . something *not* characteristic.

"Lady Sarangarel," I whispered.

Only a soft snore replied. Alive, thank the Triad.

I reached for the blanket and slowly pulled it back.

When revealed, I hissed in a breath through my teeth and yanked the blanket away.

The form—*not* the Stone Lady, but an attendant I recognized from my years as a youngling in Stormskeep—turned over, working her mouth and falling promptly back to sleep. In the bed beside her lay a folded card and a necklace bearing inlaid gemstones surrounding a large blood-red ruby.

Snatching the card and the necklace from the sheets, I bolted for the door. Outside, I held the jewelry in one palm and commanded to one of the guards, "Find Thalaj!" and to the other, "Bring me Yisu Chambui and my other yisun. They should be in the guest chambers on the third level."

The guards bowed, turned on their heels, and fled in opposite directions. Nadia, Corwyn, and Solarynne gaped at me.

Answering their unspoken question, I said, "She traded places with the attendant." I crossed to the bench, sank to the cushion between Nadia and Corwyn, handed Nadia the necklace, and read:

My dearest Mairynne,

Watch over the jewels of the Stone Singer gnoble until we meet once more.

My love, my adoration,

Sara—

WHEN THE YISUN ARRIVED, fully armored and brandishing weapons, I showed Chambui the necklace. She knew without explanation and simply asked, "How long?"

"One, mayhap two tolls of the bell," I answered.

Chambui bowed at my feet. "We will find her, Kōgō Mairynne."

Baidu grunted his agreement.

Jaliqai cocked a half-smile and winked at Nachin. "Looks like we're off on another adventure!"

I stifled a smile over the return of Jaliqai's joviality.

Nachin, the ever-silent and somber yisun, cracked a toothy grin and his cheeks flushed red under Jaliqai's affection. Tipping his head in a single nod, he too indicated his readiness.

Aside from Chambui, I'd always judged Timur the practical one, and he proved that true as he tackled the situation. "She can't be out of Arashi yet."

Hoaris had come to stand behind Chambui with a hand on her shoulder. "I'll go too."

I hadn't expected any less from the red-bearded man who'd fallen completely for Chambui. "May the Triad watch over you all," I said and hugged each of them in turn.

With less than a day's rest, my yisun had a new mission and skipped away eagerly, a new purpose in their strides.

THE FROST FIGHTERS RETURNED to their homes within the ice cliffs along

Lake Kōdaina Kōri with the assurance that the Cloud Court would send them word when we had decided on plans for the future of Nantai's leadership. At the time I bade Aljir Tenkara and Saqie Kitikara farewell, I'd been uncertain of the form the next regime would take. Though Thalaj had returned, I had little desire to remain sequestered in Stormskeep. I'd traveled too far with the Tsinti wanderers, with the sailors from Lu Galen, and even with Umu-Zimi into the jungles of Ise. My experiences told me that travel meant meeting new people, seeing new landscapes, learning about the unknown, and discovering new ways of life. Yet I had promised Nantai a new age and that duty burned within me too. I needed time to consider a balance of the two.

After very little ado, Yuos Atith and his Fire Forgers also took leave of Arashi, eager to rebuild their own capital city of Biei after much of it had burned. A retinue of Storm Sorcerers who welcomed the intermingling of castes traveled with the caravan to assist in the effort. Jorani had sworn her aid to her uncle, promising Yankos and the Tsinti she'd search out the caravan once the city had been reforged. Since the time I first joined Yankos's caravan so long ago, I'd watched Baldeo—the brawny Tsinti man who'd elbowed Thalaj in the gut upon our capture—grow closer and closer to Jorani. For all his surliness, Baldeo smiled then and threw an arm over Jorani's shoulder as they left. Knowing he would follow her wherever she wandered gave me chills as I watched them leave.

The Tsinti retinue also accompanied the Fire Forgers on their journey northward, but Yankos had duties to the wanderers he'd left behind when he joined my cause. He'd said to Jorani, "We'll travel with you to the edge of the North Woods. Then we must take news of the new age to the others who wait for us under tsym. We will resume our migration over the grasslands, and you can join us once Biei is rebuilt." He placed a necklace in her palm with a small statue pendant.

When we exchanged goodbyes, I hugged the small leader of the wandering people tightly, then brushed a finger over the mark under his right eye. I thought to ask, but felt the mark was better left to mystery. It was merely part of him. Yankos, the man who'd bested the devil with his fiddle, or so said the folklore. Mayhap that was only legend, but he certainly had played a vital role in overcoming the demons in my battle. There was little more to be said, so I pushed him away.

Yankos chuckled. "*Kai zal o drom*, Mairynne."

"Here goes the road," I answered and watched him saunter toward the others. To his back, I called, "Watch for the Cloud Court when the time comes."

He didn't look back but lifted a hand in the air.

I hoped they'd answer when the Cloud Courtiers called, but the wanderers were a people who lost themselves in time. They lived apart. Whether he'd hear, see, or take notice remained anyone's guess.

But I would see him again . . . one way or another.

Along his way to joining the parting procession, Yankos waved for Misha and Kyr to join his group. Kyr wouldn't make eye contact, but I glimpsed redness upon her face and tears streaming as she left. In the days following the battle, I'd had long conversations with Misha and learned more of how the Small Folk were connected to the Fey. Their bond resembled followers of a deity, almost as the Nantai people were connected to our Holy Triad. They were at liberty to part the veil between the planes only when allowed to do so by Amare. I marveled that their deities had played such a vital role in Nantai's coming age and felt honored beyond words that I'd had the opportunity to commune with veritable gods. Mayhap, one day we would meet again. I couldn't find a way to express my gratitude to Amare, so I offered to have a space within Arashi constructed as an homage to the Fey queen.

Misha laughed at the suggestion. " 'Tis not the way of the Fey. They call for no temples or monuments, only a natural and peaceful place. The veil between our worlds can only exist in a place touched by no person, only the mother of the land herself."

Before he fell in with his mate, the Tsinti, and the Fire Forgers, Misha touched his forehead, chin, and heart, then bowed to me.

After so long on their own, the wandering Small Folk had finally been accepted as Tsinti. Misha had reconciled with his father as they had my cause to unite them, but in the end, he chose not to return to the Small Folks' cities. Well and true, I thought. When King Isao had banished Misha, my two traveling companions had chosen a wandering way of life despite being shunned by the true wanderers. Now, no longer dismissed, they chose it once more.

All for them seemed well and right, as it was meant to be.

Many of King Isao's Small Folk left Arashi under the cover of night, the Small King among them, never affording me the opportunity to offer farewells.

The casteless disbanded, some assuredly returning to carrying messages throughout Nantai, others likely finding new towns where they could make new lives. But Flea and Honera remained in Arashi. Flea joined the soldiers and began training with scimitynes under Thalaj's instruction. Honera, when cleaned and dressed in properly fitted clothes, became a beauty to behold—porcelain skin, golden hair, and clear blue eyes. Most of Arashi's people called her Selene's daughter reborn, and when things had settled within the city, she joined the acolytes in service to our moon goddess. To me, that seemed a fine offering to the lady of the night skies I'd prayed to so many times during my travels.

◇◇◇◇◇◇◇◇◇◇◇◇◇◇◇◇◇◇◇◇◇◇◇◇◇◇◇◇◇◇

MOONS PASSED, A SEASON changed, and I could scarcely separate myself from Nantai's affairs. Yet a sense of gaiety hung in the air. Warm days oversaw flowers into full bloom throughout Arashi's gardens and the valley beyond where her gates once stood. Along with my message to the people of Nantai that there was to be no division among our people, I'd ordered the heavy wooden gates removed and pared down to wooden timbers I would one day use as the funeral pyre upon which the Serpentine Throne would burn.

That event, however, would not pass until Parū had returned to bear witness.

I went to the roof one morning just as Selene tucked herself into the western horizon and waited for Otarr to dawn in the eastern skies. I'd never discussed with Parū when or how she would return to me, but I believed with all my heart it would be at this time of day—the time between darkness and light. But this day, as Otarr took to the skies, a cloud descended over the roof between Stormskeep's spires. When the stairs had unfolded, Father descended, looking as fit as he had before his journey into the realm beyond ours, the realm between all others. The Fey Realm. His hair had turned solid white save for a lingering dark streak that reminded me of the color it had been when he told me stories at his feet. Zofi walked at his side, wearing a gown I would never have expected of the Tsinti witch wife. The silver embroidery upon the midnight blue fabric matched the highlights in her hair. Together, it seemed they'd found happiness.

"How have things been, Daughter?" Father asked.

"We've been well and recovering." I smiled into his shoulder as I welcomed him home with a tight hug.

From behind him, a voice called us apart. "I understand, Kōgō Mairynne, that you and your first guard may have need to attend Love's Court?"

Parting, we both turned to Tsanseri.

"Mayhap after the new regime is established. Or mayhap we do not require a judgment at all," I answered, taking the cuff from my upper arm. I offered it back to her.

She came forward, placed her hand on mine, and folded my fingers back around the bauble. "No, dear. A gift given cannot be returned. You may call upon me at any time. And mayhap it is not a judgment you need, but a blessing. Regardless, I am here."

"Many, many thanks, Tsanseri. Do my friends travel with you?"

"See for yourself." The comtesse flourished a hand and many of the Courtiers I'd met and more flooded down the misty steps onto Stormskeep's roof.

It wasn't Parū's return, but it was Father's and our people's, and I'd revel in that for the time.

I welcomed them each in turn—the people of Nantai rather than the castes—and we descended the stairs toward the room where the Serpentine Throne once stood. There, around a low table upon the tatami, we'd attend to the business of deciding the future governance over Nantai. Ascension implied something old. My intentions for the new age involved an emperor or empress in title alone—a measure to ease the transition to a land ruled by people rather than *a person* or one ruling caste, a place where all people had choice, and a nation that'd welcome diversity in all things. I'd pen the decrees to make our decisions official. Mayhap it would take dozens of Selene's cycles to work through the details, but these people who'd come to the cause would certainly see it done at my side.

◇◇◇◇◇◇◇◇◇◇◇◇◇◇◇◇◇◇◇◇◇◇◇◇◇◇◇◇◇◇◇◇◇◇◇◇◇◇

THAT NIGHT, SELENE SHOWED her full face and I slept restlessly. Only half the night had passed when I heard a faint call. I thought it a dream—one of those that comes between the depths of sleep and the rise to wakefulness.

Mairynne, it called . . . softly as if on the wind.

I turned over in the bed, pulling the covers under my chin.

Unrelenting, it echoed, *Mairynne*, like chimes blowing in a summer's breeze.

I tossed myself onto my back, frustrated that I couldn't find the rest I needed for the following day's meeting with the people who'd arrived to represent Nantai's people.

The voice quieted for a while, and my eyelids fell heavily once more. I was finding the edge of sleep when . . .

Mairynne . . .

I started. Could it be?

Yes. Come to me, minikin.

I shot upright in bed, the covers flying, and asked to the empty room, "Where?"

Come to me at the grove that reminded you of Sosano and Inara.

I dressed hastily in clothes I'd use to travel rather than meet with the people to conduct business, but it mattered little. If my Ryū had returned to me, I could travel naked and bask in warmth. There was time to reform the country, but I needed this now. I stopped to consider finding Thalaj or Father or anyone to let them know where I went but reconsidered. Rather, I stepped onto the balcony outside my rooms and called a current with my sorcery. The mere connection to my soul's twin even over a distance further fueled my powers and gave me strength.

The wind carried me to the side of Mount Sundai near the falls where I'd have a path still to climb, but I feared using the power to travel the full distance through the air would drain too much of my energy. Still, with my feet upon the ground, I allowed some of the old magic to flow and speed my ascent. When I arrived at the top and entered the clearing near the smaller waterfall, the area stood empty.

Despair pulled at my shoulders, and I sank to my knees in the damp grass.

Do not fret; I am almost there, minikin.

Her words in my mind were stronger, and I turned to look out over the cloud island positioned atop Stormskeep and the sleeping city beyond. Our companionship bond drew me in that direction. Parūdragon would return to me from somewhere in the skies over Nantai's jewel city.

I waited.

Blood pounded in my ears, and I listened to my breathing and the sounds beyond. Small jittering noises came from the tree cover nearby, and one of the night birds cooed in low tones.

Still, I waited.

Running water and the babbling stream provided a backdrop to the silence. Selene's face cast the clearing in deep silvery and gray hues.

My eyes fixated on the clouds over the vale, I waited. Until . . .

Something glimmered in Selene's light.

I squinted for long moments and then she appeared. Snaking through the sky, her wings stroking the wind, then gliding, Parū moved toward me. Tears flowed down my face.

I yearned to touch her, to resume our Ryū bond, but I had to settle for words. *Finally! My heart has ached since you left.* Although the sentiment wasn't enough to express how much I missed my companion.

We need each other, minikin. She sounded as pained as I'd felt. *Soon.*

What of Guin? I asked, an attempt to distract us both until she landed and we could join as one.

Warm feelings from Parū flooded my chest. *She is with Amare.*

And the blue dragon? I hoped she'd have news of Karynne too.

But the glow subsided then.

As Parū landed in the grasses near me and lay her head beside where I knelt, she said, *We will find her again, minikin. We will not rest until we do. Her babe needs her to return, and you need to mend relations with your sister.*

Trusting and gathering my faith—things Parū reinforced within my heart—I bowed my head.

Parū's voice then brought a most welcome offer. *Would you join with me again, minikin, and fly?*

◇◇◇◇◇◇◇◇◇◇◇◇◇◇◇◇◇◇◇◇◇◇◇◇◇◇◇◇◇◇◇◇◇◇

WE FLEW TO THE cavern that sheltered the Ryūling, and when we landed, he stirred. Parū dropped my clothing from her claws in a recess shadowed in darkness and grumbled shushing noises to the babe. With each rumble, his restlessness ebbed. From the darkness, Kuroi stirred and moved his snout into a sliver of Selene's light. For a moment, his warm breath enfolded and warmed Parū's scales. Then, the blackest dragon retreated.

Parū wrapped her neck around the babe's, attempting to ease the longing for his mother. My heart cracked at the understanding and empathy I felt as his loss reminded me of my own mother—Kōgō Noralynne. At least hope remained that he'd one day reunite with his.

Minikin, Parū said, *I have traveled long distances. It is time I rest.* She moved into the darkness near my clothes and gave over to the change. As we shifted into my person's form, the cool air brushed my skin. Chilled bumps erupted over my naked skin. I swiped my hands over my arms to warm myself as I grabbed my clothes and dressed.

Fully clothed, I whispered, "Rest now, my dragon," and slowly padded over to the youngling.

In a sliver of Selene's light, he rested. I stood near, marveling over his immature scales—ice blue with hints of green, but several were turning into a sanguine red on the very edges. He seemed to know me now and no longer feared I'd torture him with the iron chains. With sleepy eyes, he coiled back into himself, lowered his head onto a long section of his body, and let out a grumble as he settled back into slumber.

"Mairynne," Thalaj's soft tenor called my attention.

My heart kicked in my chest as I gained my feet and faced him. Since his return, the battle, and our tentativeness to approach one another, we hadn't had much time alone to discuss all that felt necessary. Yet in that moment within the cavern near the young dragon, as we looked at one another, there weren't many words that seemed prudent. We had time aplenty for talk of all we'd endured. I reached for him, touching his face gently.

He closed his eyes and pressed into my hand as if it were a touch that'd bring him new life.

"Where are the Underhills?" I breathed.

Thalaj took my hand and held it between us. "They have made rooms within the tunnels and are resting there now."

Alone. Our bonded dragons always with us, we were as near alone as we would ever be.

I moved closer, telling him with my body that I wished for us to be together. Where our hands were clasped, I pulled his around my waist, then wrapped my arms around his broad shoulders. They seemed even broader now that we were so close together in the darkness.

He pushed his other hand into the hair at the base of my neck. His eyes searching mine for long moments as our breathing mingled in the narrow distance between us. He'd denied this connection before. As we held one another already so intimately, I wanted to give him the opportunity to decide again now, either the same or differently. And so I waited and hoped.

At long last, his lips touched mine. Ever so softly, they caressed me. It felt like silk. He whispered, "Mairynne," against my mouth, infusing so much longing into the way he breathed my name. Then, he pulled me even closer, pressing our bodies and lips tighter together. Soft kisses grew stronger, deeper, more desperate. My eyes burned with joy, and my sense of emptiness vanished, replaced with long awaited passion as our mouths danced and tangled. This was more satisfying, so full of love and care, so much better than the urgent kiss we'd shared below deck on the *Swell Mistress*. This kiss carried intention and far more than desire alone. And it continued until I pulled back, breathless, to look into Thalaj's dark eyes.

He pressed his forehead to mine.

Our eyes locked.

Noses touched.

And he held me in the best way I could imagine.

He had always been mine.

And I his.

The End

THANK YOU FOR READING

The Serpentine Throne!

For more by Susan Stradiotto, Visit her website at: https://susanstradiotto.com/susansportfolio

THE SERPENTINE THRONE GLOSSARY

Aari bugs: small bugs similar to ants

Aomori apple: the most favored apple in Nantai, from the orchards in Aomori.

Aardwolf: Small animal native to Ise

Bells of Selene: plants; Golden-tipped buds by the hundreds would open under Selene's light and turn the air sweet, but for Otarr, they held their faces and scents inside closed petals. Bottomside district

Cavernal network: Where the Underhill Dwellers live. Caves beneath hills and mountains connected by tunnels.

Casteless: the people of Nantai who do not have magical abilities

Citadel: the place of worship in Arashi

Clanhold: underground (under-ice) caverns where the Frost Fighter clans hold up for a while when they stop.

Csárdás: name of a song played on the fiddle with an accompanying dance

Daijō-sai: part of ascension process

Daisai: medicine, to relieve menstrual cramping

Dea: Goddess of fertility of the Rundi tribespeople

Deep Demon: Asahi's [sailor's] curse word

Djecmas: Tsinti term for Mairynne's people

Dragon flight

Dragonkind: similar to humankind

Dragonsight: similar to eyesight

Serpentine Throne

Eeyoza: Rundi word for soap or bath

Erasure: the term the Ryu use for the Ryu Wars

Eight-Span Mirror of Truth: a holy artifact; part of the ascension ceremony

Gensui: term for first leader of a guard in Nantai

Giant Folk: the name the Small Folk call the Nantai

Gnoble: the head of each caste. A leader, similar to a noble family, but of an entire race. Also used as an address/a title as in "Gnoble name" or "Gnoble Lady Svarta"

Golem: an artificial human being endowed with life to test for poison

Great Market: Southern Fork Market; at southernmost fork of the Betsu River

Hai: yes

Heavenly Sword of Gathering Clouds: Holy artifact; Sword Otarr gave to Atun; Pending: whether 'heavenly' is an adjective or part of name as affects capitalization

High Cloud Court: place in the clouds where court of all castes is held on a regular basis. Place where new emperors and empresses ascend to the throne. Consists of a series of castles in the clouds, which move around over Nantai.

High Tower: place where prisoners are kept.

Holy Triad (formal) / Triad (casual): the core gods in Nantai

Hyrax: a bird in Ise

Islandgale: a people from the Vesterisles of Nantai (a clan of Storm Sorcerers)

Issō: term for Captain, used in *Into the Evernight* for Jun and *Call of the Maelstrom* for Phy Sovann.

Ketill pants: loose, bloused pants

Kōgō / kōgō: honorific for an empress

Mekoilieu: word to activate the spells on stones.

Minikin: term of endearment used by dragons for their companion.

Mon: coin in denominations of (from least to most valuable) iron, copper, bronze, strung iron, strung copper, and strung bronze.

Mon strings: 96 mon strung together to equal 100 pieces worth of each

Mynthe: An herb used by the Tsinti

Nantai:

i. Country: Nantai

ii. People: a/the Nantai, and "Nantai" if "a/the" doesn't fit in, e.g., "other bonded Nantai" or "a Nantai Storm Sorcerer"

iii. Language: Nantai

iv. Adjective: Nantai (similar to Thailand/a Thai person / the Thai people / Thai / Thai (adj)The language.

Nekodai: giant winter cats that live in the Iced Plains of Nantai, plural and singular = nekodai

O d'ives: Tsinti greeting, means several things: *How goes the day? Good day. What are your worries this day?*

O drom: Tsinti term meaning *the road*; has a lot of meaning for the Tsinti: "embodies one's life and very existence. It encompasses everyone you have met and everyone you will ever meet."

Obi: robe or belt

Ōdachi: great sword

Orb-light: light source

The Order: secret society where assassins are trained

Overlanders: a word used by the Underhill Dwellers for anyone who lives above ground, outside of the cavernal networks

Phial: vial, container

Primlock: grows on the Lower Peninsula of Yōtei. If consumed will cause vomiting, diarrhea, tremors, sores in the mouth, difficulty breathing, and convulsions often resulting in death

Reiki healer: Tsinti healer

Ringo: tree fruit, grows in Nadia's gardens

Rundi Tribes: Khirundi, Zhorundi, Mhorundi

Ryū: the Fey race of dragons; typically in wyvern form.

> *Other types of dragons:*
>
> *giant wyrms created the Northerly Barrows,*
>
> *Wingless drakes roamed over the Nantai, Yotei, and Engaru sand dunes,*
>
> *Tiny hummingdragons, not larger than my last knuckle but quick with their fire breath, populated the tree-covered and marshy regions,*
>
> *Doragons, Six-limbed cousins (4 legs and 2 wings), departed into the west*

Ryū bond: bond between a person and the bonded dragon;

Ryū breath

Ryū call: sound the dragon makes when calling out/screaming

Ryūling: a young Ryū dragon

Scimitynes: small curved swords. A mini version of a Scimitar

Seleucid: a place on Ise

Small Folk: Nantai's name of the race of small people

Soulbonded, soulbound: Dragon term for person bound to a dragon

Soul stone: the stones Mairynne held that were representative of her father and mother

Southern Fork Market: Great Market; at southernmost fork of the Betsu River

Speck: mule in Book 4, female

Star: horse in Book 4, female, has a white four-pointed marking between her eyes

Storm sorcery: Noun used in general sense of ability to perform certain magic

Syren: mythical creature rumored to apprehend ships on the sea. (a.k.a. Siren)

Tennō / tennō: honorific for an emperor.

Tsym: a curtain in time. Hides the Tsinti caravan from view.

Umeboshi: medicine, calms a turning stomach

Wilderbeasts: a herd animal that roams the plains in Nantai

Yarikhgüi yarikh: Stone Singer term, translates to "speak no speak" or in Nantai "talking stone"

Yisun (m. & pl.)/Yisu (f.): Ancient Nantai term, means *nine* which is a lucky number for the Stone Singer people.

Yubar: type of tree for which the Yubar Forest is named